STORIES

STORIES

CONTEMPORARY SOUTHERN SHORT FICTION

Edited by Donald Hays

The University of Arkansas Press
Fayetteville London 1989

Manufactured in the United States of America
99 98 97 96 95 5 4

Designed by Chiquita Babb

♾ The paper used in this publication meets the minimum requirements of the American National Standard for Permanence of Paper for Printed Library Materials Z39.48-1984.

LIBRARY OF CONGRESS CATALOGING-IN-PUBLICATION DATA

Stories: contemporary Southern short fiction / edited by
Donald Hays. p. cm.
ISBN 1-55728-038-X (alk. paper).
ISBN 1-55728-039-8 (pbk. : alk. paper)
1. Short stories, American—Southern States. 2. Southern
States—Fiction. 3. American Fiction—20th
century. I. Hays. Donald.
PS551.S73 1988 88-20585
813'.01'08975—DC19 CIP

Acknowledgments

Spirits and Other Stories, "All the Way in Flagstaff, Arizona," Copyright © 1979, 1983, 1985, 1986, 1987 by Richard Bausch. Reprinted by permission of Linden Books, a division of Simon & Schuster, Inc., and of Harriet Wasserman Literary Agency, Inc., for British Commonwealth rights.

Beasts of the Southern Wild and Other Stories, "The Ugliest Pilgrim." Reprinted by permission of Russell & Volkening as agents for the author. Copyright © 1973 by Doris Betts.

"Let Him Live" from *Tongues of Flame* by Mary Ward Brown. Copyright © 1986 by Mary Ward Brown. Reprinted by permission of the publisher, E. P. Dutton/Seymour Lawrence, a division of NAL Penguin, Inc.

"If They Knew Yvonne" from *Separate Flights* by Andre Dubus. Copyright © 1975 by Andre Dubus. Reprinted by permission of David R. Godine, Publisher.

"Rock Springs" reprinted from *Rock Springs* by Richard Ford. Copyright © 1987 by Richard Ford. By permission of the Atlantic Monthly Press.

"Just Like a Tree" by Ernest J. Gaines. Copyright © 1963 by Ernest J. Gaines from *Bloodline.* Reprinted by permission of Doubleday, a division of Bantam, Doubleday, Dell Publishing Group, Inc.

"Just Like a Tree" from *Bloodline* by Ernest J. Gaines. Reprinted by permission of JCA Literary Agency, copyright © 1963 by Ernest J. Gaines.

"A Wreath for Garibaldi" from *An Evening Performance* by George Garrett. Copyright © 1985 by George Garrett. Reprinted by permission by Doubleday, a division of Bantam, Doubleday, Dell Publishing Group, Inc., and of John Farquharson, Ltd., for British Commonwealth rights.

"The Lower Garden District Free Gravity Mule Blight or Rhoda, a Fable" from *Victory over Japan* by Ellen Gilchrist. Reprinted by permission of Don Congdon Associates, Inc. Copyright © 1984 by Ellen Gilchrist.

"The Lower Garden District Free Gravity Mule Blight or Rhoda, a Fable" from *Victory over Japan* by Ellen Gilchrist. By permission of Little, Brown and Company.

Contents

Preface

To have been considered for inclusion in this anthology, a writer must be Southern, contemporary, and the author of at least one full-length collection of short fiction. I consider the Southern writer to be one who was either born and raised in the South or has lived in the South for many years. By the *South* I mean the eleven states of the old Confederacy plus Kentucky and West Virginia. (Oklahoma and New Mexico are western; Kansas and Missouri are midwestern; Maryland is close, but not close enough.) By *contemporary* I mean the last thirty years. (All of the stories in this anthology were first published since 1960 except for "The Bride of the Innisfallen." Eudora Welty has not published a collection of new stories in the past thirty years, but she has published *Losing Battles, The Optimist's Daughter,* and *The Collected Stories.* It would be absurd not to consider her our contemporary.) By *short fiction* I mean just that. Neither novellas nor excerpts from novels were considered. Cormac McCarthy and William Styron are first-rate novelists, but since neither of them has published a book of stories, neither of them appears in this anthology. There are, of course, several very good novelists who *have* published collections of stories but who, nevertheless, are not included here. That is because their stories are not, in my opinion, as good as the ones that are included. I tried not to let the reputation of the novelist (or the poet or the playwright) influence my judgment of his or her stories.

You will find no typical Southern story here. These stories are too distinctive to be typical of anything. What you will find is a great variety. Each writer has a personal style and particular concerns. And even though this is a book of stories by Southerners, there is a wide range of settings, from Italy to Ireland to Montreal to Barbados to Rock Springs, Wyoming. Even stories happening in roughly the same area have strikingly different settings. Steve Stern's Pinch, right there in the heart of Memphis, is a world away from anything in Peter Taylor's Tennessee. Barry Hannah's Mississippi is not Lewis Nordan's nor, for that matter, William Faulkner's. That is as it should be: place is always both particular and various. And if I were to venture one generality about Southern short story writers it would be that they still know that better than most others do.

There are, of course, those who disagree with all that, those who believe that in late-Twentieth-Century America place has become homogenous, that living in a condominium in Tupelo is pretty much like living in a condominium in Butte or Southampton. They tend to believe, too, that no one any of us knows is capable of real thought or genuine emotion, that, anyway, politics and philosophy are banal, and that, therefore, the prose of fiction should be systematically denatured.

Well, you and I know they're wrong. Besides, they have their own anthologies, in which, appropriately, one story is much like the next. None of that here. As you go from story to story in this anthology, you will, I hope, be surprised and pleased by the differences.

But, enough of that. These are strong stories, and they will speak for themselves. Contemporary Southern short fiction is doing quite well, thank you.

STORIES

RICHARD BAUSCH

Richard Bausch was born in Fort Benning, Georgia, and lives in Fairfax, Virginia. He is the author of three novels: *Real Presence, Take Me Back,* and *The Last Good Time.* His first collection of stories, *Spirits and Other Stories,* was published in 1987.

All the Way in Flagstaff, Arizona

SITTING in the shaded cool quiet of St. Paul's Church in Flagstaff, Walter remembers a family picnic. This memory is two years old, but nothing ever fades from it. It takes place in a small park called Hathaway Forest, on Long Island, one Sunday afternoon in early summer. He and his wife, Irene, spread blankets on the grass next to a picnic table and a brick barbecue pit; it is a warm, clear-blue day, with a breeze. Irene has insisted that they all go, as a family, and so soccer games, trips to the movies and to the houses of friends, have been put aside. Because Walter is hung over, he tries to beg off, but she will not hear of it; she will not cater to his hangovers anymore, she tells him. So they all go. He and Irene sit quietly on the blankets as, in the grass field before them, the children run—William, the oldest, hanging back a little, making a sacrifice of pretending to have a good time: he is planning for the priesthood these days, wants to be Gregory Peck in *The Keys of the Kingdom.* He saw the movie on television a year ago and now his room is full of books on China, on the lives of the saints, the missionaries, the martyrs. Every morning he goes to Mass and Communion. Walter feels embarrassed in his company, especially when William shows this saintly, willing face to the world.

"I wonder if it would help William to discover masturbation," Walter says. "He's at that age, isn't he? Don't boys start at fourteen? When did I start? I guess I should remember."

"I forgot the baked beans," Irene says. "I left them sitting in the middle of the kitchen counter." She has this way of not hearing him when she wants to avoid a subject; she will not talk about William. "You want some lemonade?"

"No, thanks." He makes a face; she smiles. He can always make her laugh.

The children form a ring, and begin to move in a circle. Susan, the second child, orchestrates this, calling in a kind of singing cadence as they contract and expand the ring by raising and lowering their arms. They are playing well together, cooperating; even William seems to have forgotten about heaven and hell for the moment, moving a little too fast for the youngest, the baby, Carol, to keep up with him. There is something mischievous about the way he causes the girl to falter and lose her hold on him.

"You should light the charcoal, honey," Irene says.

"Certainly," he says. He is anxious to please. He knows she will again have to ask her father for money, and she will again use the word *borrow*. There is always the hope that something will change. He stands over the brick barbecue pit and pours charcoal, while she pours more lemonade, not bothering to ask him this time if he wants any. In the car, in the space under the spare tire, hidden by a half-used roll of paper towels, is a fifth of Jim Beam. He thinks of it with something bordering on erotic anticipation, though his head feels as if it were webbed with burning wires. As he sprinkles lighter fluid on the coals, he begins to plan how he will get to the bottle without the others knowing he has done so.

"Dad."

It is William, standing a little apart from Susan and the younger children. He holds up a Nerf football, wanting to pass it.

Walter smiles. "I'm cooking. I'm the chef of the day."

William wants to get a game up, boys against the girls; he wants Irene to play. She refuses, cheerfully, and so does Susan, and the younger boys begin a desultory game of keep away from Carol, who begins to take it seriously, crying and demanding that she be given a chance to throw and catch the ball. William and Susan walk off toward the far edge of the woods, talking, William pausing now and then to pick up and throw a stone or a piece of wood. Irene sits reading a magazine, with a pad and pencil on her lap. She likes to write down the recipes she finds, and keeps the pad for this purpose. In fact, she doesn't read these magazines as much as she ransacks them, looking for things to save. She's a frugal woman; she's had to be. She controls the money now, what there is of it. Since the last hitch in the Army, Walter has worked seven different jobs; now, at forty-six, he's night clerk in a 7-Eleven store.

"That's enough," Irene calls to the two younger boys, Brad and James, who have tormented Carol to the point of a tantrum. Carol is lying on her stomach, beating her fists into the grass, while they toss the ball above her head, keeping it just out of reach. "Brad! Bra-a-a-a-d! James!"

The two boys stop, finally, walk away scuffing the ground. In a moment they are running across the field, and Carol has come crying to her mother. Because she is the youngest and the smallest, she has learned to be feisty and short-tempered; she seems somehow always dogged, face into the wind, dauntless. "Don't pay any attention to them," Irene is saying.

Walter lights the fire, stands watching it.

"You go on, now, and play," Irene says, and Carol whines that she doesn't want to, she wants to stay here. "No—now, go on. Go have fun. I don't want you hanging back all afternoon. Go on—go."

Carol wanders over to a little play area near the car; it is, in fact, too near: it will be hard for Walter to get anything out of the trunk if she stays where she is, riding a sea dragon on a corkscrew-like metal spring.

"I don't like her being over there by herself," Walter says.

"She's fine," says Irene. "Let her alone."

He sits down, rubs his hands; he wants a drink.

"You want to put the hot dogs on sticks?" Irene asks.

"That tire's low," he says.

"No, it's not."

"It is—look. Look at it. It's low. I better change it."

"You're in no shape to change a tire."

He gets up. "I think it's low."

"Walter."

"I'm just going to look at it."

"Hi, Daddy," Carol says as he approaches.

"Go see your mother."

"I'm riding the dragon."

"Your mother wants you."

"I don't wanna."

"Come on," he says, "I have to look at this tire." He lifts her from the dragon, puts her down on her feet, or tries to: she raises her legs, so that he comes close to falling forward; he lifts again, tries again to set her down, and it's as if they dance. "Stop it," he says, "stand up." She laughs, and he sets her suddenly, with a bump, down on her rear end. "Now you can sit there," he says. She begins to cry. He walks over to the car and stands gazing at the right rear tire, which is not low enough. Even so, he opens the trunk, glances back at Irene, who is lying on the blanket like a sunbather now, her arms straight at her sides, her eyes closed. Carol still whines and cries, sitting in the dust in the foreground.

"Go on," Walter says, "you're not hurt."

"Carol," Irene calls without moving, "come here."

Walter is already reaching into the little well beneath the spare. The Beam is wrapped in a paper bag, and carefully he removes it, leaning into the hot space. In almost the same motion, he has broken the seal on the bottle and held the lip of it to his mouth, swallowing. He caps it, peers out at Irene and Carol, who are frozen for him in a sort of tableau: Carol beginning to move toward her mother, and Irene lying face up to the sun. He leans in, takes another swallow, caps the bottle again and sets it down, rattles the jack, stands back slowly and puts his hands on his hips.

"Walter."

"It's okay," he calls. "I guess it'll have to do—the spare's no better." He looks at Irene, sees that Carol has reached her, that she is involved with Carol, who wants her to fix and bow her hair. So he leans into the trunk again, swallows more of the whiskey. Then he recaps the bottle one more time, puts it back in its place, retrieves it almost immediately, and takes still another swallow. He closes the trunk hard, walks steadily across to the blanket, where Irene and Carol are busy trying to get Carol's hair braided and bowed. He sits down, looks at the flames licking low along the whitening coals. When Carol asks him to look at how pretty her hair is, he tells her she is the most beautiful little girl he ever saw. He reaches for her, pulls her to him, and hugs her. "You are my sweet sweet sweet sweet thing," he says. "You are my sweetie-pie. My little baby love darling boost-a-booter."

"I love you, Daddy."

She removes herself from him, dances, for his benefit, in a circle around the blanket. Then she runs off to meet William and Susan, who are coming across the crest of the field.

"It could be like this all the time," Irene says.

He says, "Yeah." He gets up, stands over the fire. "The coals are almost ready."

"What's the mat—" she begins.

He has swayed only slightly; he pretends to have simply lost his balance on an unevenness in the ground, looks at his feet, lifts one leg, puts it down. It is a beautiful blurred world, and he believes he can do anything.

"It's brave of you to come out today," she says.

"I wanted to."

"You know, Walter, I am going to leave you."

"Right now?"

She ignores this. "I don't want to. I love you. But I really am. You don't believe me, Walter, because you've never believed me. But this time you're wrong. In a while, very soon, I'm going to take the children and go."

"But don't you see?" he says. "I'm going to quit. I'm never touching the stuff again."

"No," she says.

"Come on, kid," he says.

"Let me tell you, dear, what you were thinking all the way here, and what you finally got your hands on a few minutes ago. You were thinking all the time, weren't you, about the bottle of booze you had stashed in the trunk of the car."

"What bottle of booze?"

"I believe it was Jim Beam?" She looks at him.

He wonders if she can see the color changing in his face and neck, the blood rushing there. "Jim Beam," he says. "Jim Beam."

"It won't work, Walter."

"You think that's it? You think I've been—you think that's what I've been doing, huh." He is nodding, looking away from her, trying to control his voice. "You think—on a beautiful day like this, when I'm with my family—some—a bottle of booze in the trunk—"

"Forget it," she says.

"I didn't know—I didn't even know if there was a bottle of booze in the goddamn spare-tire well."

"Please," she says.

"You think I've been thinking about a goddamn bottle of booze in the trunk of the car."

"All right, then."

"That's what you think of me. I mean—we've come that far—that you'd think I could be standing here on this nice day thinking about sneaking drinks like there's some—like there's a problem or something—"

"Walter," she says.

"I mean like it wasn't just—you know, a drink in the afternoon or something—"

"Don't say any more," she tells him.

"Just something I found and—you think I haven't been sick at heart for what I've done, Irene." He has never meant anything more. "I didn't even think anything about it, honey—you think I'd do anything to hurt you or the kids—something—some bottle or something that's supposed to be hidden or something. Like I planned it or something. I swear I just remembered it was there—I didn't—didn't want to worry you, Irene—Irene—"

"The sad thing," Irene says, "is that I could've stopped you today—just now. I knew what you were doing—after all, Walter, you've become a bit sloppy in your various deceptions and ruses. They've become pretty transparent. I could've stopped you, only I just—I just didn't have the energy."

"I don't know what you're talking about," he says. He looks at his children, all of them coming now from the crest; they seem somehow not together, though they come in a group, no more than five feet apart.

"I wish I could feel anything but this exhaustion," Irene says.

"It's not anything like I'm drunk or anything," Walter says. "I just need to get calmed down, honey."

"No," she says.

"You know me, Irene. I always—haven't I always come through?"

She looks at him. "I think—now—that you think you have."

"I just need a little time," he says.

"Walter."

"That's all, honey. Just let me get straight a little." He doesn't want to talk anymore. He drops down at her side. "I'm nervous, kid. I get real bad nervous—and—and I'm not going to drink anymore. I'm simply—absolutely done with it. Forever, Renie. Okay? I'm going to pull it together this time." As he gazes out at the field, at his children returning, he is full of resolve, and courage. Irene sighs, pats his shoulder, and then takes his hand into her own. "Poor Walter," she says, "so sick."

"I'll be all right," he says. "I just need to be calm."

The children are there now, and the picnic is made ready: William puts hot dogs on the grill, and Susan dishes out potato salad, Jell-O, bread, pickles. there is a lot of vying for attention, a lot of energy and noise. It all rises around Walter and his wife, who do not look at each other.

Anyone walking into St. Paul's at this hour will see a man sitting in the last pew, hands folded neatly in his lap. He sits very straight, with dignity, though his clothes are soiled and disheveled. In his mind are the voices of two years ago, the quality of light on that day, and how the breezes blew, fragrant and warm. He can hear the voices.

"Oh," William says, shortly before they start to eat. "We forgot to say grace."

"It's too late now," Susan says.

"It's not too late. It can't ever be too late."

"It's too late."

"It's not too late—that's just silly, Susan."

"Daddy, isn't it too late?"

"It's not too late," Irene says. "William, go ahead."

"Bless us, O Lord, and these Thy gifts which we are about to receive from Thy bounty, through Christ our Lord, amen."

"I still say it was too late," Susan says.

Irene says, "Susan."

"I've decided I'm going to be a nun," Susan says.

"Susan—that's nothing to joke about."

"It's not a joke. I'm going to be a nun and wear icky black clothes and have my hair cut off at the roots and sit in church with my hands open in my lap and sing off tune like Sister Marie does."

"That's a sacrilege," William says.

"What's a sacrilege?" Brad asks.

"It's when you talk like Susan," says William.

"A sacrilege," says Susan, "is when you take Holy Communion with a mortal sin on your soul."

"And when you say you're going to be a nun when you're not," William says.

"Come on now, kids," Walter says, "let's get off each other a little. Let's talk about something nice."

"I know," says Brad, "let's talk about Pac-Man."

"Who wants to talk about *that,*" says Carol.

"All I said was I was going to be a nun," Susan says, "and everybody gets crazy. Mostly Saint William. You should've heard Saint William a little while ago, planning his martyrdom in China—shot by the Commies. Right, William?"

"That's enough," Walter says. "Let him alone. Let's everybody let everybody else alone. Jesus."

"Have mercy on us," William mutters.

"Oh, look," Walter says, "don't do that. Don't pray when I talk."

Irene says, "Let's just eat quietly, all right?"

"Well, he keeps praying around me. Jesus, I *hate* that."

"Have mercy on us," says William.

"When're you leaving for China, son?"

"You don't have to make fun of me."

"Okay, look—let's all start over. Jesus." Walter spins around, to catch William moving his lips. "Jesus Jesus Jesus Jesus Jesus," he says.

William crosses himself.

"Amazing. The kid's amazing."

"Let's all please just stop it and eat. Can we please just do that?"

Susan says, "I've changed my mind about being a nun. I'm going to be a priest."

"Oh," William says, "that *is* a sacrilege."

"William," says Walter, "will you please pronounce the excommunications so we can all go to hell in peace?"

"I don't even like this family," the boy mutters.

"Perhaps you should've asked your Father in heaven to have chosen another family for you to be raised in on your trek to the cross."

"Have mercy."

"I don't believe I used any profanity that last time."

"Have mercy on us," William mutters.

"All right!" Irene shouts. "We're going to eat and stop all this arguing and bickering. Please, Walter."

"You might address your displeasure to the Christ, here. Or is it the Vicar of Christ?"

"Have mercy on us."

"I'll be the first lady priest in the Catholic Church, " Susan says, "and then I'll get married."

Walter says, "Don't pay any attention to her, William. Think of her as a cross to bear."

"Walter," Irene says.

He stands. "Okay. Truce. No more teasing and no more bickering. We are a family, right? We have to stick together and tolerate each other sometimes."

They are looking at him. He touches his own face, where his mouth, his lips are numb. His eyes feel swollen.

"And then," Susan says, "after I'm married, I'll become Pope."

Walter bursts into laughter as William turns to Susan and says, "You are committing a mortal sin."

"Susan!" Irene says.

Walter says, "Judge not, lest ye be judged, William, my boy."

"I know what a mortal sin is," Brad says.

"Everybody knows that," says James.

"Look for the mote, William. When you see the gleam, look for the mote," Walter is saying.

William mutters, "I don't even know what that means."

"Walter, sit down," Irene says. "Let him alone. All of you let him alone."

"Let's all leave each other alone, that's right," Walter says. He sits down. They eat quietly for a while, and he watches them. Irene wipes mustard from Carol's mouth, from the front of her dress. William's eyes are glazed, and he eats furiously, not looking at anyone. He has been caught out in his pride, Walter thinks, has been shown to himself as less perfect than the glorious dream of a movie he wants to live. It dawns on Walter that his son probably prays for him, since he does not go to church. He wonders, now, what they all think of that, of the fact that he is, by every tenet of their religion, bound for hell. This makes him laugh.

"What?" Irene says. "Tell me."

"Nothing. I was—" He thinks for a moment. "I was thinking about this one," pointing to Susan, "planning to be a married lady priest."

Susan beams under his gaze.

And then he looks at William, feels sorry. "It's okay, William," he says, "it's all in fun."

The boy continues to eat.

"William."

Irene touches Walter's wrist.

"No," Walter says, "the kid can accept somebody's—a gesture—can't he? My God."

William crosses himself again.

Walter stands. "That's the last time."

"Father Boyer, at church," William says almost defiantly, "he told us to do it whenever someone used the Lord's name—"

Walter interrupts him. "I don't care what Father Boyer said. I'm bigger than Father Boyer. I can beat the *shit* out of Father Boyer."

"Not another word from anyone!" Irene shouts.

For a moment no one says anything.

"Well," Walter says, "aren't we a happy bunch?"

James says, "What do you expect?"

"Why don't you explain that one, James?"

The boy shrugs. He is always saying these mysteriously adult things that seem to refer slyly to other things, and then shrugging them off as if he is too tired to bother explaining them. Last year, at the age of eight, he announced to Irene that he did not believe in God. It was a crisis; Irene feared that something serious was wrong. James has since revised himself: he will grant the existence. Those are the words he used. Walter looks upon him with more than a little trepidation, because James is the one who most resembles him. More even than William, who, now, with his heart in the lap of God, is hard to place. Even Irene, for all her devoutness, finds William irritating at times.

"I am going to be a priest," Susan says now. "All I have to do is get them to change the rules."

"You," says Walter, "are the saint of persistence. You know what a wolverine is?"

"Some kind of wolf?"

"The wolverine kills its prey by sheer persistence. I mean, if it decided it wanted you for dinner, you could take a plane to Seattle, the wolverine would meet you at the airport, bib on, knife and fork ready, licking his chops. Salt and pepper by the plate, oregano, parsley, a beer . . ."

Susan laughs.

"Daddy's funny," Carol says.

"When I'm the first lady priest and married Pope, I'll buy a wolverine and keep it as a pet," Susan says.

"Have mercy on us," says William.

"All right," Walter says, "let's drop it, please, William. No more prayers, please. We're all right. God will forgive us, I'm sure, if we all just shut the fuck up for a while."

"Walter!"

"I'm sorry, I'm sorry," he says.

They are quiet, then, for a long time. The youngest ones, Brad and James and Carol, look at him with something like amazement. He makes two more trips to the trunk of the car, not even hiding it now, and in the end he gets Carol and James to laugh at him by making faces, miming someone sliding off a bench, pretending to be terrified of his food. Susan and William laugh too, now, as he does a man unable to get a hot dog into his mouth.

"You clown," Irene says, but she smiles.

They all laugh and talk now; the afternoon wanes that way: Walter tosses the football with William, and Brad and James chase a Frisbee with Susan and Carol. Irene sits on the picnic table, sipping her lemonade. It grows cooler, and others come to the field, and finally it's time to leave. They all work together, gathering the debris of the afternoon, and Walter packs the trunk. He's bold enough to take the bottle of Beam out of its place and drink from it—small sips, he tells Irene, offering her some. She refuses as she has always refused, but she does so with, he is sure, a smile. It strikes him that there is nothing to worry about, not a thing in the world, and he clowns with his children, makes them laugh, all the way home, Irene driving. He calls to people out the window of the car, funny things, and they are all almost hysterical with laughter. They arrive; there is the slow unwinding, getting out of the car and stretching legs and arms, and Walter begins to wrestle with Carol, bending over her, tickling her upper legs, swinging her through his own as she wriggles and laughs. Brad jumps on his back, then, and he pretends to be pulled down, rolls in the grass with the boy, and then chases him, bent over, arms dangling, like an ape's. He is hearing the delightful keening sound of his children's laughter in the shadows. It is getting dark. He chases Brad and James around to the backyard, and they are hiding there, just beyond the square lighter shape of Irene's garden. He crouches in the shadow of the house and makes an ape sound, *whooo-hooo, whooo-hooo hah-hah-hah-hah.* He can hear them talking low and he thinks, Why this is easy, this is fun. Carefully he works his way closer, seeing William and Susan running along the back fence, their silhouettes in the dusky light. *Whoo-hoo, whoo-hoo.* And now he makes his run at them, changes direction, follows Brad, while the others scatter. When he catches Brad, he carries him under his arm, kicking and struggling, to the house, the screened-in back porch, where the others have gathered and are huddling, laughing in the dark. He comes stumbling up onto the porch and he has them, they are trapped with him. He puts Brad down in the mass of struggling arms and legs; he engulfs them, kneeling; he has them all in the wide embrace of his arms; he's tickling a leg here, pinching or squeezing an arm there, roaring, gorilla-like. He catches one of them trying to get away, then turns and grabs another. He's got them all again, and they are yelling and laughing, there is light on them now, a swath of yellow light, and he looks up to see Irene's shape in the doorway, everything speeding up again, until there is a long shout, a scream.

And he stops. He stands, sees that they are cringing against the base of the porch wall, to the left of the door, cringing there and shaking, their eyes enormous, filled with tears.

"Kids?" he says.

They are sobbing, and he steps back, nearly tumbles backward out the screen door and down the stairs. "Kids?" he says.

Nobody moves.

"H-hey. Kids?"

Irene steps down, bends to help William rise. They all get up slowly, looking at him with the tremendous wariness of animals at bay.

"H-hey—it's me," he says, holding out one hand. "Kids?"

"Come on," Irene is saying," don't be silly. Your daddy would never hurt you." She makes each of them kiss him, then ushers them inside. "Susan, will you start the bath water?" The door closes on them. Walter looks at his hands and says "God. Oh my God." He doesn't really hear himself. And in a moment Irene opens the door and steps out lightly, closing it behind her. All around, now, the insects are starting up. Irene's voice begins softly: "We've been through so much, Walter, so much together—and I simply can't do it anymore. I don't know what to say or do anymore. I love you, but I can't make it be enough anymore." She kisses him on the side of the face, turns, and is gone.

Yet it takes more than a year for her finally to leave him. She gives him every chance. She waits for him to put it together as he keeps saying he will. He tries for a while, in fact: he goes to a doctor, a psychologist specializing in family counseling, who tells him he has not broken with his father, and instructs him to find some ritual way of making the break. So he goes back to Alabama to stand over his father's grave. At first, nothing happens. He feels anger, but it is only what he expected to feel. And then there is a kind of sorrow, almost sweet, welling up in him. It makes him wince, actually take a step back from the grave as if something had moved there. When he was seven years old his father took him outside of the house in Montgomery and made him urinate on his mother's roses. He tells himself, standing over the grave in Montgomery, that children have been through worse; indeed, he himself has. Yet it takes all the moisture from his mouth, remembering it. Perhaps it is the fact that it was done to him not for himself but to get at his mother—there is something so terrifying about being used that way, merely as an instrument of wounding. In any case, it has haunted him, and now at the gravesite he spits, he rages, he tears the grass. It all seems simply ordained. It is a role he plays, watching himself play it. It exorcises nothing.

He returns from Alabama with a sense of doom riding him like a spirit, a weight on his neck, the back of his shoulders. He visits the psychologist, who seems slightly alarmed at the effect of the journey on him. He is determined, vibrant with will, and hopelessly afraid. The psychologist wants to know what his exact thought was the first time he ever picked up a drink. Walter can't remember that. His father never drank. He believes he wanted at first to show his freedom, like other boys. He says finally he wanted it to relax and be kind, to relieve some of the tensions that build in him. And so the psychologist begins to try to explore, with him, those tensions. They are many, but they all have the same root, and there is no use talking about childhood trauma and dreams: Walter is versed in the canon; his hopes are for something else. He can tell the psychologist the whole thing in a single sentence: he has always been paralyzed by the fear that he will repeat, with his own children, the pattern of his father's brutality. What he wants is for the psychologist to guarantee him that this won't happen, tell him categorically that there will be no such repetition, and of course this can't be done. Life must be lived in the uncertainty of freedom of choice, the psychologist says. The problem is that Walter is afraid to take responsibility for himself. It is all talk, and it is all true. Walter's father had a thing he liked to call "night dances," in which, for the benefit of Walter, for his correction and edification, Walter's father became a sort of dark gibbet that Walter danced beneath, held by the wrist within the small circumference, the range, of a singing swung belt whose large buckle was embossed with the head of a longhorn steer. This all took place in the basement of the house in Montgomery, before Walter was ten years old. There was no light at all in the basement, and so it was necessary for the boy to dodge blindly, and to keep from crying too loudly, so he could hear the *whoosh-whoosh* of the belt. Walter trembles to think of that. He tells the psychologist how his father would swing the belt calmly, without passion, like a machine, quiet in the dark. He shakes, telling it. He talks about the ancient story: the man who, in the act of trying to avoid some evil in himself, embraces, it, creates it.

The visits end. He is dry for about two weeks, but falters, and Irene finally does leave him.

This is what happened to him. He is in Flagstaff, Arizona. He sits gazing at the small stained-glass windows on either side of the church, where in a few minutes he will probably be talking to a priest. God, he thinks, Flagstaff, Arizona. There is no reason for it. Perhaps he will go somewhere else, too. There is no telling where he might wind up. Irene and the children are all the way in Atlanta, Georgia, with Irene's parents. He has not had anything to drink today, and his hands shake, so he looks at them. He wonders if he should wait to talk to a priest, if he should tell a priest anything, or just ask for food, maybe. He wonders if maybe he shouldn't tell the priest about the day of the picnic that he has been remembering so vividly, when Irene came out on the porch and told him she couldn't make it be enough anymore. He wonders if he should talk about it: how he walked out to the very edge of the lawn and turned to look upon the lighted windows of the house, thinking of the people inside, whom he had named and loved and called sons, daughters, wife. How he had stood there trembling, shaking as from a terrific chill, while the dark, the night, came.

DORIS BETTS

Doris Betts is a native North Carolinian. Since 1966, she has taught at the University of North Carolina at Chapel Hill. She is the author of four novels, including *The River to Pickle Beach* and *Heading West.* Her three collections of stories are *The Gentle Insurrection* (1954), *The Astronomer and Other Stories* (1966), and *Beasts of the Southern Wild* (1973).

The Ugliest Pilgrim

I SIT in the bus station, nipping chocolate peel off a Mounds candy bar with my teeth, then pasting the coconut filling to the roof of my mouth. The lump will dissolve there slowly and seep into me the way dew seeps into flowers.

I like to separate flavors that way. Always I lick the salt off cracker tops before taking my first bite.

Somebody sees me with my suitcase, paper sack, and a ticket in my lap. "You going someplace, Violet?"

Stupid. People in Spruce Pine are dumb and, since I look dumb, say dumb things to me. I turn up my face as if to count those dead flies piled under the light bulb. He walks away—a fat man, could be anybody. I stick out my tongue at his back; the candy oozes down. If I could stop swallowing, it would drip into my lung and I could breathe vanilla.

Whoever it was, he won't glance back. People in Spruce Pine don't like to look at me, full face.

A Greyhound bus pulls in, blows air; the driver stands by the door. He's black-headed, maybe part Cherokee, with heavy shoulders but a weak chest. He thinks well of himself—I can tell that. I open my notebook and copy his name off the metal plate so I can call him by it when he drives me home again. And next week, won't Mr. Wallace Weatherman be surprised to see how well I'm looking!

I choose the front seat behind Mr. Weatherman, settle my bag with the hat in it, then open the lined composition book again. Maybe it's half full of writing. Even the empty pages toward the back have one repeated entry, high, printed off Mama's torn catechism: GLORIFY GOD AND ENJOY HIM FOREVER.

I finish Mr. Weatherman off in my book while he's running his motor and getting us onto the highway. His nose is too broad, his dark eyes too skimpy—nothing in his face I want—but the hair is nice. I write that down, "Black hair?" I'd want it to curl, though, and be soft as a baby's.

Two others are on the bus, a nigger soldier and an old woman whose jaw sticks out like a shelf. There grow, on the backs of her hands, more veins than skin. One fat blue vessel, curling from wrist to knuckle, would be good; so on one page I draw a sample hand and let blood wind across it like a river. I write at the bottom: "Praise God, it is started. May 29, 1969," and turn to a new sheet. The paper's lumpy and I flip back to the thick envelope stuck there with adhesive tape. I can't lose that.

We're driving now at the best speed Mr. Weatherman can make on these winding roads. On my side there is nothing out the bus window but granite rock, jagged and wet in patches. The old lady and the nigger can see red rhododendron on the slope of Roan Mountain. I'd like to own a tight dress that flower color, and breasts to go under it. I write in my notebook, very small, the word "breasts," and turn quickly to another page. AND ENJOY HIM FOREVER.

The soldier bends as if to tie his shoes, but instead zips open a canvas bag and sticks both hands inside. When finally he sits back, one hand is clenched around something hard. He catches me watching. He yawns and scratches his ribs, but the right fist sets very lightly on his knee, and when I turn he drinks something out of its cup and throws his head quickly back like a bird or a chicken. You'd think I could smell it, big as my nose is.

Across the aisle the old lady says, "You going far?" She shows me a set of tan, artificial teeth.

"Oklahoma."

"I never been there. I hear the trees give out." She pauses so I can ask politely where she's headed. "I'm going to Nashville," she finally says. "The country-music capital of the world. My son lives there and works in the cellophane plant."

I draw in my notebook a box and two arrows. I crisscross the box.

"He's got three children not old enough to be in school yet."

I sit very still, adding new boxes, drawing baseballs in some, looking busy for fear she might bring out their pictures from her big straw pocketbook. The funny thing is she's looking past my head, though there's nothing out that window but rock wall sliding by. I mumble, "It's hot in here."

Angrily she says, "I had eight children myself."

My pencil flies to get the boxes stacked, eight-deep, in a pyramid. "Hope you have a nice visit."

"It's not a visit. I maybe will move." She is hypnotized by the stone and the furry moss in its cracks. Her eyes used to be green. Maybe, when young, she was red-haired and Irish. If she'll stop talking, I want to think about trying green eyes with that Cherokee hair. Her lids droop; she looks drowsy. "I am right tired of children," she says and lays her head back on the white rag they button on these seats.

Now that her eyes are covered, I can study that face—china white, and worn thin as tissue so light comes between her bones and shines through her whole head. I picture the light going around and around her skull, like water spinning in a jar. If I could wait to be eighty, even my face might grind down and look softer. But I'm ready, in case the Preacher mentions that. Did Elisha make Naaman bear into old age his leprosy? Didn't Jesus heal the withered hand, even on Sunday, without waiting for the work week to start? And put back the ear of Malchus with a touch? As soon as Job had learned enough, did his boils fall away?

Lord, I have learned enough.

The old lady sleeps while we roll downhill and up again; then we turn so my side of the bus looks over the valley and its thickety woods where, as a girl, I pulled armloads of galax, fern, laurel, and hemlock to have some spending money. I spent it for magazines full of women with permanent waves. Behind us, the nigger shuffles a deck of cards and deals to himself by fives. Draw poker—I could beat him. My papa showed me, long winter days and nights snowed in on the mountain. He said poker would teach me arithmetic. It taught me there are four ways to make a royal flush and, with two players, it's an even chance one of them holds a pair on the deal. And when you try to draw from a pair to four of a kind, discard the kicker; it helps your odds.

The soldier deals smoothly, using his left hand only with his thumb on top. Papa was good at that. He looks up and sees my whole face with its scar, but he keeps his eyes level as if he has seen worse things; and his left hand drops cards evenly and in rhythm. Like a turtle, laying eggs.

I close my eyes and the riffle of his deck rests me to the next main stop where I write in my notebook: "Praise God for Johnson City, Tennessee, and all the state to come. I am on my way."

At Kingsport, Mr. Weatherman calls rest stop and I go straight through the terminal to the ladies' toilet and look hard at my face in the mirror. I must remember to start the Preacher on the scar first of all—the only thing about me that's even on both sides.

Lord! I am so ugly!

Maybe the Preacher will claim he can't heal ugliness. And I'm going to spread my palms by my ears and show him—this is a crippled face! An infirmity! Would he do for a kidney or liver what he withholds from a face? The Preacher once stuttered, I read someplace, and God bothered with that. Why not me? When the Preacher labors to heal the sick in his Tulsa auditorium, he asks us at home to lay our fingers on the television screen and pray for God's healing. He puts forth his own ten fingers and we match them, pad to pad, on that glass. I have tried that, Lord, and the Power was too filtered and thinned down for me.

I touch my hand now to this cold mirror glass, and cover all but my pimpled chin, or wide nose, or a single red-brown eye. And nothing's too bad by itself. But when they're put together?

I've seen the Preacher wrap his hot, blessed hands on a club foot and cry out "HEAL!" in his funny way that sounds like the world "Hell" broken into two pieces. Will he not cry out, too, when he sees this poor, clubbed face? I will be to him as Goliath was to David, a need so giant it will drive God to action.

I comb out my pine-needle hair. I think I would like blond curls and Irish eyes, and I want my mouth so large it will never be done with kissing.

The old lady comes in the toilet and catches me pinching my bent face. She jerks back once, looks sad, then pets me with her twiggy hand. "Listen, honey," she says, "I had looks once. It don't amount to much."

I push right past. Good people have nearly turned me against you, Lord. They open their mouths for the milk of human kindness and boiling oil spews out.

So I'm half running through the terminal and into the café, and I take the first stool and call down the counter, "Tuna-fish sandwich," quick. Living in the mountains, I eat fish every chance I get and wonder what the sea is like. Then I see I've sat down by the nigger soldier. I do not want to meet his gaze, since he's a wonder to me, too. We don't have many black men in the mountains. Mostly they live east in Carolina, on the flatland, and pick cotton and tobacco instead of apples. They seem to me like foreigners. He's absently shuffling cards the way some men twiddle thumbs. On the stool beyond him is a paratrooper, white, and they're talking about what a bitch the army is. Being sent to the same camp has made them friends already.

I roll a dill-pickle slice through my mouth—a wheel, a bitter wheel. Then I start on the sandwich and it's chicken by mistake when I've got chickens all over my backyard.

"Don't bother with the beer," says the black one. "I've got better on the bus." They come to some agreement and deal out cards on the counter.

It's just too much for me. I lean over behind the nigger's back and say to the paratrooper, "I wouldn't play with him." Neither one moves. "He's a mechanic." They look at each other, not at me. "It's a way to cheat on the deal."

The paratrooper sways backward on his stool and stares around out of eyes so blue that I want them, right away, and maybe his pale blond hair. I swallow a crusty half-chewed bite. "One-handed grip; the mechanic's grip. It's the middle finger. He can second-deal and bottom-deal. He can buckle the top card with his thumb and peep."

"I be damn," says the paratrooper.

The nigger spins around and bares his teeth at me, but it's half a grin. "Lady, you want to play?"

I slide my dishes back. "I get mad if I'm cheated."

"And mean when you're mad." He laughs a laugh so deep it makes me retaste that bittersweet chocolate off the candy bar. He offers the deck to cut, so I pull out the center and restack it three ways. A little air blows through his upper teeth. "I'm Grady Fliggins and they call me Flick."

The paratrooper reaches a hand down the counter to shake mine. "Monty Harrill. From near to Raleigh."

"And I'm Violet Karl. Spruce Pine. I'd rather play five-card stud."

By the time the bus rolls on, we've moved to its wider back seat playing serious cards with a fifty-cent ante. My money's sparse, but I'm good and the deck is clean. The old lady settles into my front seat, stiffer than plaster. Sometimes she throws back a hurt look.

Monty, the paratrooper, plays soft. But Flick's so good he doesn't even need to cheat, though I watch him close. He drops out quick when his cards are bad; he makes me bid high to see what he's got; and the few times he bluffs, I'm fooled. He's no talker. Monty, on the other hand, says often, "Whose play is it?" till I know that's his clue phrase for a pair. He lifts his cards close to his nose and gets quiet when planning to bluff. And he'd rather use wild cards but we won't. Ah, but he's pretty, though!

After we've swapped a little money, mostly the paratrooper's, Flick pours us a drink in some cups he stole in Kingsport and asks, "Where'd you learn to play?"

I tell him about growing up on a mountain, high, with Mama dead, and shuffling cards by a kerosene lamp with my papa. When I passed fifteen, we'd drink together, too. Applejack or a beer he made from potato peel.

"And where you headed now?" Monty's windburned in a funny pattern, with pale goggle circles that start high on his cheeks. Maybe it's something paratroopers wear.

"It's a pilgrimage." They lean back with their drinks. "I'm going to see this preacher in Tulsa, the one that heals, and I'm coming home pretty. Isn't that healing?" Their still faces make me nervous. "I'll even trade if he says . . . I'll take somebody else's weak eyes or deaf ears. I could stand limping a little."

The nigger shakes his black head, snickering.

"I tried to get to Charlotte when he was down there with his eight-pole canvas cathedral tent that seats nearly fifteen thousand people, but I didn't have money then. Now what's so funny?" I think for a minute I am going to have to take out my notebook, and unglue the envelope and read them all the Scripture I have looked up on why I should be healed. Monty looks sad for me, though, and that's worse. "Let the Lord twist loose my foot or give me a cough, so long as I'm healed of my looks while I'm still young enough—" I stop and tip up my plastic cup. Young enough for you, blue-eyed boy, and your brothers.

"Listen," says Flick in a high voice. "Let me go with you and be there for that swapping." He winks one speckled eye.

"I'll not take black skin, no offense." He's offended, though, and lurches across the moving bus and falls into a far seat. "Well, you as much as said you'd swap it off!" I call. "What's wrong if I don't want it any more than you?"

Monty slides closer. "You're not much to look at," he grants, sweeping me up and down till I nearly glow blue from his eyes. Shaking his head, "And what now? Thirty?"

"Twenty-eight. His drink and his cards, and I hurt Flick's feelings. I didn't mean that." I'm scared, too. Maybe, unlike Job, I haven't learned enough. Who ought to be expert in hurt feelings? Me, that's who.

"And you live by yourself?"

I start to say "No, there's men falling all over each other going in and out my door." He sees my face, don't he? It makes me call, "Flick? I'm sorry." Not one movement. "Yes. By myself." Five years now, since Papa had heart failure and fell off the high back porch and rolled downhill in the gravel till the hobblebushes stopped him. I found him past sunset, cut from the rocks but not much blood showing. And what there was, dark, and already jellied.

Monty looks at me carefully before making up his mind to say, "That preacher's a fake. You ever see a doctor agree to what he's done?"

"Might be." I'm smiling. I tongue out the last liquor in my cup. I've thought of all that, but it may be what I believe is stronger than him faking. That he'll be electrified by my trust, the way a magnet can get charged against its will. He might be a lunatic or a dope fiend, and it still not matter.

Monty says, "Flick, you plan to give us another drink?"

"No." He acts like he's going to sleep.

"I just wouldn't count on that preacher too much." Monty cleans his nails with a matchbook corner and sometimes gives me an uneasy look. "Things are mean and ugly in this world—I mean *act* ugly, do ugly, be ugly."

He's wrong. When I leave my house, I can walk for miles and everything's beautiful. Even the rattlesnakes have grace. I don't mind his worried looks, since I'm writing in my notebook how we met and my winnings—a good sign, to earn money on a trip. I like the way army barbers trim his hair. I wish I could touch it.

"Took one furlough in your mountains. Pretty country. Maybe hard to live in? Makes you feel little." He looks toward Flick and says softer, "Makes you feel like the night sky does. So many stars."

"Some of them big as daisies." It's easy to live in, though. Some mornings a deer and I scare up each other in the brush, and his heart stops, and mine stops. Everything stops till he plunges away. The next pulsebeat nearly knocks you down. "Monty, doesn't your hair get lighter in the summers? That might be a good color to ask for in Tulsa. Then I could turn colors like the leaves. Spell your last name for me."

He does, and says I sure am funny. Then he spells Grady Fliggins and I write that, too. He's curious about my book, so I flip through and offer to read him parts. Even with his eyes shut, Flick is listening. I read them about my papa's face, a chunky block face, not much different from the Preacher's square one. After Papa died, I wrote that to slow down how fast I was forgetting him. I tell Monty parts of my lists: that you can get yellow dye out of gopherwood and Noah built his ark from that, and maybe it stained the water. That a cow eating snakeroot might give poison milk. I pass him a pressed maypop flower I'm carrying to Tulsa, because the crown of thorns and the crucifixion nails grow in its center, and each piece of the bloom stands for one of the apostles.

"It's mollypop vine," says Flick out of one corner of his mouth. "And it makes a green ball that pops when you step on it." He stretches. "Deal you some blackjack?"

For no reason, Monty says, "We oughtn't to let her go."

We play blackjack till supper stop and I write in my book, "Praise God for Knoxville and two new friends." I've not had many friends. At school in the valley, I sat in the back rows, reading, a hand spread on my face. I was smart, too; but if you let that show, you had to stand for the class and present different things.

When the driver cuts out the lights, the soldiers give me a whole seat, and a duffel bag for a pillow. I hear them whispering, first about women, then about me; but after a while I don't hear that anymore.

By the time we hit Nashville, the old lady makes the bus wait while she begs me to stop with her. "Harvey won't mind. He's a good boy." She will not even look at Monty and Flick. "You can wash and change clothes and catch a new bus tomorrow."

"I'm in a hurry. Thank you." I have picked a lot of galax to pay for this trip.

"A girl alone. A girl that maybe feels she's got to prove something?" The skin on her neck shivers. "Some people might take advantage."

Maybe when I ride home under my new face, that will be some risk. I shake my head, and as she gets off she whispers something to Mr. Weatherman about looking after me. It's wasted, though, because a new driver takes his place and he looks nearly as bad as I do—oily-faced and toad-shaped, with eyeballs a dingy color and streaked with blood. He's the flatlands driver, I guess, because he leans back and drops one warty hand on the wheel and we go so fast and steady you can hardly tell it.

Since Flick is the tops in cards and we're tired of that, it's Monty's turn to brag on his motorcycle. He talks all across Tennessee till I think I could ride one by hearsay alone, that my wrist knows by itself how far to roll the throttle in. It's a Norton and he rides it in Scrambles and Enduro events, in his leathers, with spare parts and tools glued all over him with black electrician's tape.

"So this bastard tells me, 'Zip up your jacket because when I run over you I want some traction.'"

Flick is playing solitaire. "You couldn't get me on one of them killing things."

"One day I'm coming through Spruce Pine, flat out, throw Violet up behind me! We're going to lean all the way through them mountains. Sliding the right foot and then sliding the left." Monty lays his head back on the seat beside me, rolls it, watches. "How you like that? Take you through creeks and ditches like you was on a skateboard. You can just holler and hang on."

Lots of women have, I bet.

"The Norton's got the best front forks of anybody. It'll nearly roll up a tree trunk and ride down the other side." He demonstrates on the seat back. I keep writing. These are new things, two-stroke and four-stroke, picking your line on a curve, Milwaukee iron. It will all come back to me in the winters, when I reread these pages.

Flick says he rode on a Harley once. "Turned over and got drug. No more."

They argue about what he should have done instead of turning over. Finally Monty drifts off to sleep, his head leaning at me slowly, so I look down on his crisp, light hair. I pat it as easy as a cat would, and it tickles my palm. I'd almost ask them in Tulsa to make me a man if I could have hair like his, and a beard, and feel so different in so many places.

He slides closer in his sleep. One eyebrow wrinkles against my shoulder. Looking our way, Flick smokes a cigarette, then reads some magazine he keeps rolled in his belt. Monty makes a deep noise against my arm as if, while he slept, his throat had cleared itself. I shift and his whole head is on my shoulder now. Its weight makes me breathe shallow.

I rest my eyes. If I should turn, his hair would barely touch my cheek, the scarred one, like a shoebrush. I do turn and it does. For miles he sleeps that way and I almost sleep. Once, when we take a long curve, he rolls against me, and one of his hands drifts up and then drops in my lap. Just there, where the creases are.

I would not want God's Power to turn me, after all, into a man. His breath is so warm. Everywhere, my skin is singing. Praise God for that.

When I get my first look at the Mississippi River, the pencil goes straight into my pocketbook. How much praise would that take?

"Is the sea like this?"

"Not except they're both water," Flick says. He's not mad anymore. "Tell you what, Vi-oh-LETTE. When Monty picks you up on his cycle" ("sickle," he calls it), "you ride down to the beaches—Cherry Grove, O.D., around there. Where they work the big nets in the fall and drag them up on the sand with trucks at each end, and men to their necks in the surf."

"You do that?"

"I know people that do. And afterward they strip and dress by this big fire on the beach."

And they make chowder while this cold wind is blowing! I know that much, without asking. In a big black pot that sits on that whipping fire. I think they might let me sit with them and stir the pot. It's funny how much, right now, I feel like praising all the good things I've never seen, in places I haven't been.

Everybody has to get off the bus and change in Memphis, and most of them wait a long time. I've taken the long way, coming here; but some of Mama's cousins live in Memphis and might rest me overnight. Monty says they plan to stay the night, too, and break the long trip.

"They know you're coming Violet?" It's Flick says my name that way, in pieces, carefully: Vi-oh-LETTE. Monty is lazier: Viii-lut. They make me feel like more than one.

"I've never even met these cousins. But soon as I call up and tell them who I am and that I'm here . . ."

"We'll stay some hotel tonight and then ride on. Why don't you come with us?" Monty is carrying my scuffed bag. Flick swings the paper sack. "You know us better than them."

"Kin people," grunts Flick, "can be a bad surprise."

Monty is nodding his head. "Only cousin I had got drunk and drove this tractor over his baby brother. Did it on purpose, too." I see by his face that Monty made this up, for my sake.

"Your cousins might not even live here anymore. I bet it's been years since you heard from a one."

"We're picking a cheap hotel, in case that's a worry."

I never thought they might have moved. "How cheap?"

When Flick says "Under five," I nod; and my things go right up on their shoulders as I follow them into a Memphis cab. The driver takes for granted I'm Monty's afflicted sister and names a hotel right off. He treats me with pity and good manners.

And the hotel he chooses is cheap, all right, where ratty salesmen with bad territories spend half the night drinking in their rooms. Plastic palm bushes and a worn rug the color of wet cigars. I get Room 210 and they're down the hall in the teens. They stand in my doorway and watch me drop both shoes and walk the bed in bare feet. When Monty opens my window, we can hear some kitchen underneath—a fan, clattering noise, a man's crackly voice singing about the California earthquake.

It scares me, suddenly, to know I can't remember how home sounds. Not one bird call, nor the water over rocks. There's so much you can't save by writing down.

"Smell that grease," says Flick, and shakes his head till his lips flutter. "I'm finding an ice machine. You, Vi-oh-LETTE, come on down in a while."

Monty's got a grin I'll remember if I never write a word. He waves. "Flick and me going to get drunker than my old cousin and put wild things in your book. Going to draw dirty pictures. You come on down and get drunk enough to laugh."

But after a shower, damp in my clean slip, even this bed like a roll of fence wire feels good, and I fall asleep wondering if that rushing noise is a river wind, and how long I can keep it in my mind.

Monty and Flick edge into my dream. Just their voices first, from way downhill. Somewhere in a Shonny Haw thicket. "Just different," Monty is saying. "That's all. Different. Don't make some big thing out of it." He doesn't sound happy. "Nobody else," he says.

Is that Flick singing? No, because the song goes on while his voice says, "Just so . . ." and then some words I don't catch. "It don't hurt"? Or maybe, "You don't hurt"? I hear them climbing my tangled hill, breaking sticks and knocking the little stones loose. I'm trying to call to them which way the path is, but I can't make noise because the Preacher took my voice and put it in a black bag and carried it to a sick little boy in Iowa.

They find the path, anyway. And now they can see my house and me standing little by the steps. I know how it looks from where they are: the wood rained on till the siding's almost silver; and behind the house a wet-weather waterfall that's cut a stream bed downhill and grown pin cherry and bee balm on both sides. The high rock walls by the waterfall are mossy and slick, but I've scraped one place and hammered a mean-looking gray head that leans out of the hillside and stares down the path at whoever comes. I've been here so long by myself that I talk to it sometimes. Right now I'd say, "Look yonder. We've got company at last!" if my voice wasn't gone.

"You can't go by looks," Flick is saying as they climb. He ought to know. Ahead of them, warblers separate and fly out on two sides. Everything moves out of their path if I could just see it—tree frogs and mosquitoes. Maybe the worms drop deeper just before a footstep falls.

"Without the clothes, it's not a hell of a lot improved," says Monty, and I know suddenly they are inside the house with me, inside my very room, and my room today's in Memphis. "There's one thing, though," Monty says, standing over my bed. "Good looks in a woman is almost like a wall. She can use it to shut you outside. You never know what she's like, that's all." He's wearing a T-shirt and his dog tags jingle. "Most of the time I don't even miss knowing that."

And Flick says, disgusted, "I knew that much in grammar school. You sure are slow. It's not the face you screw." If I opened my eyes, I could see him now, behind Monty. He says, "After a while, you don't even notice faces. I always thought, in a crowd, my mother might not pick Daddy out."

"My mother could," says Monty. "He was always the one *started* the fight."

I stretch and open my eyes. It's a plain slip, cotton, that I sewed myself and makes me look too white and skinny as a sapling.

"She's waking up."

When I point, Monty hands me the blouse off the doorknob. Flick says they've carried me a soda pop, plus something to spruce it up. They sit stiffly on two hard chairs till I've buttoned on my skirt. I sip the drink, cold but peppery, and prop on the bed pillows. "I dreamed you both came where my house is, on the mountain, and it had rained so the waterfall was working. I felt real proud of that."

After two drinks we go down to the noisy restaurant with that smelly grease. And after that, to a picture show. Monty grins widely when the star comes on the screen. The spit on his teeth shines, even in the dark. Seeing what kind of woman he really likes, black-haired as a gypsy and with a juicy mouth, I change all my plans. My eyes, too, must turn up on the ends and when I bend down my breasts must fall forward and push at each other. When the star does that in the picture, the cowboy rubs his mustache low in the front of her neck.

In the darkness, Monty takes my hand and holds it in his swelling lap. To me it seems funny that my hand, brown and crusty from hoeing and chopping, is harder than his. I guess you don't get calluses rolling a motorcycle throttle. He rubs his thumb up and down my middle finger. Oh, I would like to ride fast behind him, spraddle-legged, with my arms wrapped on his belt, and I would lay my face between his sharp shoulder blades.

That night, when I've slept awhile, I hear something brushing the rug in the hall. I slip to my door. It's very dark. I press myself, face first, to the wood. There's breathing on the other side. I feel I get fatter, standing there, that even my own small breasts might now be made to touch. I round both shoulders to see. The movement jars the door and it trembles slightly in its frame.

From the far side, by the hinges, somebody whispers, "Vi-oh-LETTE?"

Now I stand very still. The wood feels cooler on my skin, or else I have grown very warm. Oh, I could love anybody! There is so much of me now, they could line up strangers in the hall and let me hold each one better than he had ever been held before!

Slowly I turn the knob, but Flick's breathing is gone. The corridor's empty. I leave the latch off.

Late in the night, when the noise from the kitchen is over, he comes into my room. I wake when he bumps on a chair, swears, then scrabbles at the footboard.

"Viii-lut?"

I slide up in bed. I'm not ready, not now, but he's here. I spread both arms wide. In the dark he can't tell.

He feels his way onto the bed and he touches my knee and it changes. Stops being just my old knee, under his fingers. I feel the joint heat up and bubble. I push the sheet down.

He comes onto me, whispering something. I reach up to claim him.

One time he stops. He's surprised, I guess, finding he isn't the first. How can I tell him how bad that was? How long ago? The night when the twelfth grade was over and one of them climbed with me all the way home? And he asked. And I thought, *I'm entitled.* Won him a five-dollar bet. Didn't do nothing for me.

But this time I sing out and Monty says, "Shh," in my ear. And he starts over, slow, and makes me whimper one other time. Then he turns sideways to sleep and I try my face there, laid in the nest on his damp back. I reach out my tongue. He is salty and good.

Now there are two things too big for my notebook but praise God! And for the Mississippi, too!

There is no good reason for me to ride with them all the way to Fort Smith, but since Tulsa is not expecting me, we change my ticket. Monty pays the extra. We ride through the fertile plains. The last of May becomes June and the Arkansas sun is blazing. I am stunned by this heat. At home, night means blankets and even on hot afternoons it may rain and start the waterfall. I lie against my seat for miles without a word.

"What's wrong?" Monty keeps asking; but, under the heat, I am happy. Sleepy with happiness, a lizard on a rock. At every stop Monty's off the bus, bringing me more than I can eat or drink, buying me magazines and gum. I tell him and Flick to play two-handed cards, but mostly Flick lectures him in a low voice about something.

I try to stop thinking of Memphis and think back to Tulsa. I went to the Spruce Pine library to look up Tulsa in their encyclopedia. I thought sure it would tell about the Preacher, and on what street he'd built his Hope and Glory Building for his soul crusades. Tulsa was listed in the *Americana,* Volume 27, Trance to Venial Sin. I got so tickled with that I forgot to write down the rest.

Now, in the hot sun, clogged up with trances and venial sins, I dream under the drone of their voices. For some reason I remember that old lady back in Nashville, moved in with Harvey and his wife and their three children. I hope she's happy. I picture her on Harvey's back porch, baked in the sun like me, in a rocker. Snapping beans.

I've left my pencil in the hotel and must borrow one from Flick to write in my book. I put in, slowly, "This is the day which the Lord hath made." But, before Monty, what kind of days was He sending me? I cross out the line. I have this wish to praise, instead of Him, the littlest things. Honeybees, and the wet slugs under their rocks. A gnat in some farmer's eye.

I give up and hand Flick his pencil. He slides toward the aisle and whispers, "You wish you'd stayed in your mountains?"

I shake my head and a piece of my no-color hair falls into the sunlight. Maybe it even shines.

He spits on the pencil point and prints something inside a gum wrapper. "Here's my address. You keep it. Never can tell."

So I tear the paper in half and give him back mine. He reads it a long time before tucking it away, but he won't send a letter till I do—I can tell that. Through all this, Monty stares out the window. Arkansas rolls out ahead of us like a rug.

Monty has not asked for my address, nor how far uphill I live from Spruce Pine, though he could ride his motorcycle up to me, strong as its engine is. For a long time he has been sitting quietly, lighting one cigarette off another. This winter, I've got to learn smoking. How to lift my hand up so every eye will follow it to my smooth cheek.

I put Flick's paper in my pocketbook and there, inside, on a round mirror, my face is waiting in ambush for me. I see the curved scar, neat as ever, swoop from the edge of one nostril in rainbow shape across my cheek, then down toward the ear. For the first time in years, pain boils across my face as it did that day. I close my eyes under that red drowning, and see again Papa's ax head rise off its locust handle and come floating through the air, sideways, like a gliding crow. And it drops down into my face almost daintily, the edge turned just enough to slash loose a flap of skin the way you might slice straight down on the curve of a melon. My papa is yelling, but I am under a red rain and it bears me down. I am lifted and run with through the woodyard and into the barn. Now I am slumped on his chest and the whipped horse is throwing us down the mountainside, and my head is wrapped in something big as a wet quilt. The doctor groans when he winds it off and I faint while he lifts up my flesh like the flap of a pulpy envelope, and sews the white bone out of sight.

Dizzy from the movement of the bus, I snap shut my pocketbook.

Whenever I cry, the first drop quivers there, in the curving scar, and then runs crooked on that track to the ear. I cry straight-down on the other side.

I am glad this bus has a toilet. I go there to cool my eyes with wet paper, and spit up Monty's chocolate and cola.

When I come out, he's standing at the door with his fist up. "You all right, Viii-lut? You worried or something?"

I see he pities me. In my seat again, I plan the speech I will make at Fort

Smith and the laugh I will give. "Honey, you're good," I'll say, laughing, "but the others were better." That ought to do it. I am quieter now than Monty is, practicing it in my mind.

It's dark when we hit Fort Smith. Everybody's face looks shadowed and different. Mine better. Monty's strange. We're saying goodbyes very fast. I start my speech twice and he misses it twice.

Then he bends over me and offers his own practiced line that I see he's worked up all across Arkansas, "I plan to be right here, Violet, in this bus station. On Monday. All day. You get off your bus when it comes through. Hear me, Viii-lut? I'll watch for you?"

No. He won't watch. Nor I come. "My schedule won't take me this road going back. Bye, Flick. Lots of good luck to you both."

"Promise me. Like I'm promising."

"Good luck to you, Vi-oh-LETTE." Flick lets his hand fall on my head and it feels as good as anybody's hand.

Monty shoves money at me and I shove it back. "Promise," he says, his voice furious. He tries to kiss me in the hair and I jerk so hard my nose cracks his chin. We stare, blurry-eyed and hurting. He follows Flick down the aisle, calls back, "I'm coming here Monday. See you then, hear? And you get off this bus!"

"No! I won't!"

He yells it twice more. People are staring. He's out of the bus pounding the steel wall by my seat. I'm not going to look. The seats fill up with strangers and we ride away, nobody talking to anyone else. My nose where I hit it is going to swell—the Preacher will have to throw that in for free. I look back, but he's gone.

The lights in the bus go out again. Outside they bloom thick by the streets, then thinner, then mostly gone as we pass into the countryside. Even in the dark, I can see Oklahoma's mountains are uglier than mine. Knobs and hills, mostly. The bus drives into rain which covers up everything. At home I like that washing sound. We go deeper into the downpour. Perhaps we are under the Arkansas River, after all. It seems I can feel its great weight move over me.

Before daylight, the rain tapers off and here the ground looks dry, even barren. Cattle graze across long fields. In the wind, wheat fields shiver. I can't eat anything all the way to Tulsa. It makes me homesick to see the land grow brighter and flatter and balder. That old lady was right—the trees do give out—and oil towers grow in their place. The glare's in my eyes. I write in my notebook, "Praise God for Tulsa; I am nearly there," but it takes a long time to get the words down.

One day my papa told me how time got slow for him when Mama died. How one week he waded through the creek and it was water, and the next week cold molasses. How he'd lay awake a year between sundown and sunup, and in the morning I'd be a day older and he'd be three hundred and sixty-five.

It works the other way, too. In no time at all, we're into Tulsa without me knowing what we've passed. So many tall buildings. Everybody's running. They rush into taxis before I can get one to wait for me long enough to ask the driver questions. But still I'm speeded to a hotel, and the elevator yanks me to a room quicker than Elijah rode to Heaven. The room's not bad. A Gideon Bible. Inside are lots of dirty words somebody wrote. He must have been feeling bad.

I bathe and dress, trembling from my own speed, and pin on the hat which has traveled all the way from Spruce Pine for this. I feel tired. I go out into the loud streets full of fast cars. Hot metal everywhere. A taxi roars me across town to the Preacher's church.

It looks like a big insurance office, though I can tell where the chapel is by colored glass in the pointed windows. Carved in an arch over the door are the words "HOPE OF GLORY BUILDING." Right away, something in me sinks. All this time I've been hearing it on TV as the Hope *and* Glory Building. You wouldn't think one word could make that much difference.

Inside the door, there's a list of offices and room numbers. I don't see the Preacher's name. Clerks send me down long, tiled halls, past empty air-conditioned offices. One tells me to go up two flights and ask the fat woman, and the fat woman sends me down again. I'm carrying my notebook in a dry hand, feeling as brittle as the maypop flower.

At last I wait an hour to see some assistant—very close to the Preacher, I'm told. His waiting room is chilly, the leatherette chairs worn down to the mesh. I try to remember how much TB and cancer have passed through this very room and been jerked out of people the way Jesus tore out a demon and flung him into a herd of swine. I wonder what he felt like to the swine.

After a long time, the young man calls me into his plain office—wood desk, wood chairs, shelves of booklets and colored folders. On one wall, a colored picture of Jesus with that fairy ring of light around His head. Across from that, one of His praying hands—rougher than Monty's, smoother than mine.

The young man wears glasses with no rims. In this glare, I am reflected on each lens, Vi-oh-LETTE and Viii-lut. On his desk is a box of postcards of the Hope and Glory Building. *Of* Glory. *Of* Glory.

I am afraid.

I feel behind me for the chair.

The man explains that he is presently in charge. The Preacher's speaking in Tallahassee, his show taped weeks ahead. I never thought of it as a show before. He waits.

I reach inside my notebook where, taped shut, is the thick envelope with everything written down. I knew I could never explain things right. When have I ever been able to tell what I really felt? But it's all in there—my name, my need. The words from the Bible which must argue for me. I did not sit there nights since Papa died, counting my money and studying God's Book, for nothing. Playing solitaire, then going back to search the next page and the next. Stepping outside to rest my eyes on His limitless sky, then back to the Book and the paper, building my case.

He starts to read, turns up his glitter-glass to me once to check how I look, then reads again. His chair must be hard, for he squirms in it, crosses his legs. When he has read every page, he lays the stack down, slowly takes off his glasses, folds them shining into a case. He leaves it open on his desk. Mica shines like that, in the rocks.

Then he looks at me, fully. Oh. He is plain. Almost homely. I nearly expected it. Maybe Samuel was born ugly, so who else would take him but God?

"My child," the man begins, though I'm older than he is, "I understand how you feel. And we will most certainly pray for your spirit . . ."

I shut my eyes against those two flashing faces on his spectacles. "Never mind my spirit." I see he doesn't really understand. I see he will live a long life, and not marry.

"Our Heavenly Father has purpose in all things."

Stubbornly, "Ask Him to set it aside."

"We must all trust His will."

After all these years, isn't it God's turn to trust mine? Could He not risk a little beauty on me? Just when I'm ready to ask, the sober assistant recites, "'Favor is deceitful and beauty is vain.' That's in Proverbs."

And I cry, "'The crooked shall be made straight!' Isaiah said that!" He draws back, as if I had brought the Gideon Bible and struck him with its most disfigured pages. "Jesus healed an impediment in speech. See my impediment! Mud on a blind man's eyes was all He needed! Don't you remember?" But he's read all that. Everything I know on my side lies, written out, under his sweaty hand. Lord, don't let me whine. But I whine, "He healed the ten lepers and only one thanked. Well, I'll thank. I promise. All my life."

He clears his long knotty throat and drones like a bee, "By the sadness of the countenance the heart is made better.' Ecclesiastes. Seven. Three."

Oh, that's not fair! I skipped those parts, looking for verses that suited me! And it's wrong, besides.

I get up to leave and he asks will I kneel with him? "Let us pray together for that inner beauty."

No, I will not. I go down that hollow hall and past the echoing rooms. Without his help I find the great auditorium, lit through colored glass, with its cross of white plastic and a pinker Jesus molded onto it. I go straight to the pulpit where the Preacher stands. There is nobody else to plead. I ask Jesus not to listen to everything He hears, but to me only.

Then I tell Him how it feels to be ugly, with nothing to look back at you but a deer or an owl. I read Him my paper, out loud, full of His own words.

"I have been praising you, Lord, but it gets harder every year." Maybe that sounds too strong. I try to ease up my tone before the Amens. Then the chapel is very quiet. For one minute I hear the whir of many wings, but it's only a fan inside an air vent.

I go into the streets of Tulsa, where even the shade from a building is hot. And as I walk to the hotel I'm repeating, over and over, "Praise God for Tulsa in spite of everything."

Maybe I say this aloud, since people are staring. But maybe that's only because they've never seen a girl cry crooked in their streets before.

Monday morning. I have not looked at my face since the pulpit prayer. Who can predict how He might act—with a lightning bolt? Or a melting so slow and tender it could not even be felt?

Now, on the bus, I can touch in my pocketbook the cold mirror glass. Though I cover its surface with prints, I never look down. We ride through the dust and I'm nervous. My pencil is flying: "Be ye therefore perfect as your Heavenly Father is perfect. Praise God for Oklahoma. For Wagoner and Sapulpa and Broken Arrow and every other name on these signs by the road."

Was that the wrong thing to tell Him? My threat that even praise can be withheld? Maybe He's angry. "Praise God for oil towers whether I like them or not." When we pass churches, I copy their names. Praise them all. I want to write, "Bless," but that's *His* job.

We cross the cool Arkansas River. As its damp rises into the bus and touches my face, something wavers there, in the very bottom of each pore; and I clap my rough hands to each cheek. Maybe He's started? How much can He do between here and Fort Smith? If He will?

For I know what will happen. Monty won't come. And I won't stop. That's an end to it.

No, Monty is there. Waiting right now. And I'll go into the bus station on tiptoe and stand behind him. He'll turn with his blue eyes like lamps. *And he won't know me!* If I'm changed. So I will explain myself to him: how this gypsy hair and this juicy mouth is still Violet Karl. He'll say, "Won't old Flick be surprised?" He'll say, "Where is that place you live? Can I come there?"

But if, while I wait and he turns, he should know me by my old face. . . . If he should say my name or show by recognition that my name's rising up now in his eyes like something through water . . . I'll be running by then. To the bus. Straight out that door to the Tennessee bus, saying, "Driver, don't let that man on!" It's a very short stop. We'll be pulling out quick. I don't think he'll follow, anyhow.

I don't even think he will come.

One hundred and thirty-one miles to Fort Smith. I wish I could eat.

I try to think up things to look forward to at home. Maybe the sourwoods are blooming early, and the bees have been laying-by my honey. If it's rained enough, my corn might be in tassel. Wouldn't it be something if God took His own sweet time, and I lived on that slope for years and years, getting prettier all the time? And nobody to know?

It takes nearly years and years to get to Fort Smith. My papa knew things about time. I comb out my hair, not looking once to see what color sheddings are caught in the teeth. There's no need feeling my cheek, since my finger expects that scar. I can feel it on me almost anywhere, by memory. I straighten my skirt and lick my lips till the spit runs out.

And they're waiting. Monty at one door of the terminal and Flick at another.

"Ten minutes," the driver says when the bus is parked, but I wait in my seat till Flick gets restless and walks to the cigarette machine. Then I slip through his entrance door and inside the station. Mirrors shine everywhere. On the vending machines and the weight machines and a full-length one by the phone booth. It's all I can do not to look. I pass the ticket window and there's Monty's back at the other door. My face remembers the shape of it. Seeing him there, how he's made, and the parts of him fitted, makes me forget how I look. And before I can stop, I call out his name.

Right away, turning, he yells to me "*Viii*-lut!"

So I know. I can look, then, in the wide mirror over a jukebox. Tired as I am and unfed, I look worse than I did when I started from home.

He's laughing and talking. "I been waiting here since daylight scared you wouldn't . . ." but by then I've run past the ugly girl in the glass and I race for the bus, for the road, for the mountain.

Behind me, he calls loudly, "Flick!"

I see that one step in my path like a floating dark blade, but I'm faster this time. I twist by him, into the flaming sun and the parking lot. How my breath hurts!

Monty's between me and my bus, but there's time. I circle the cabstand, running hard over the asphalt field, with a pain ticking in my side. He calls me. I plunge through the crowd like a deer through fetterbush. But he's running as hard as he can and he's faster than me, And, oh!

Praise God!

He's catching me!

MARY WARD BROWN

Mary Ward Brown lives on a farm near Marion, Alabama. She is a graduate of Judson College and studied writing at the University of North Carolina and at the University of Alabama at Birmingham. Her book of stories, *Tongues of Flame* (1986), won the Ernest Hemingway Foundation Award for Best First Fiction.

Let Him Live

ALL he had to do was wake up. The surgeon said the tumor was encapsulated and nonmalignant. They had taken it out without bothering his brain at all, so everything would be fine when he came to. He had already moved the foot and leg that were paralyzed, and sometimes a tear rolled out of his eye as if he knew things. But still he didn't wake up, and now something had gone wrong, some bleeding, swelling, something. His condition was so bad his family, including his eighty-year-old mother, had gone up to the hospital in Birmingham.

In Wakefield, where he'd been probate judge for three terms without opposition, the first thing anyone said was, "What's the news from Carter?" Only the very young, or the old and formal, called him Judge Reese. Everyone liked and respected him, both black and white.

"I sho hope the Lord don't take him," an old black woman said, sitting on the cement curbing in front of the courthouse, eating a cinnamon roll. "Do, it won't be nobody to keep them folks straight. Everybody know Amzi and them can't run no cotehouse." Two black girls in jeans, sitting farther down, turned to look at her coldly.

Members of the churches were all praying for him. In the chapel of his own church, on the corner of Jeff Davis and Green, an around-the-clock prayer vigil was in progress. Every half hour people went in and out, taking part in an unbroken chain of petition for his life.

Down the street, Saint Thomas's Episcopal Church was without a priest and had been for months. Its members were so few, so hard to please, and so set in their ways that the bishop had trouble finding a priest to take them on, even temporarily. Among the communicants were a state legislator whose opinion had to be heard on every parish matter, a retired admiral accustomed to command, a conservative banker, and a woman liberal. Several young couples dutifully brought their children while their middle-aged counterparts, duty done, came or not as they pleased.

Of the remaining members, most were widows with gray hair and good incomes, but there was one who had to do sewing and alterations to support herself and her handicapped son, Arthur. There was a busy doctor who never came, and one dedicated Christian, a sixty-year-old woman. Between priests, two lay readers kept things going; and once a year in November, the women put on the best bazaar in town.

When Carter grew worse, Sally Wingate, president of the churchwomen, called Rich Callaway, the senior warden.

"Carter's got to live, Rich," she said. "If he dies, they'll take over the town and county both. What do you think of our having a prayer vigil too?"

"Well." Rich was the conservative banker. He stood for tradition, even in what he wore, long-sleeved shirts and ties the year round. "I never heard of us doing anything like that, but like you say. . . . Who will you get to pray?"

"Oh, we'll all have to help. Everybody. And for more than just thirty minutes."

"Sounds all right to me," he said. "Where will you have it?"

"In the church. We can kneel at the altar rail, or use that prayer desk on the left. And Carter's in trouble *now.* Why don't you go on down, light the candles, and start it off? I'll have somebody relieve you as soon as I can."

Sally sat with the phone in her lap, in an upstairs bedroom of Wingate Hall. Her husband, Johnny Wingate, had died two years ago, leaving her the legacy once left to him, a house built by his ancestors' slaves. Sally was only fifty-three. In a sundress, her shoulders tanned by the country-club sun, she looked younger; and with her features, she would be good-looking twenty years from now. But there was no one in Wakefield to marry her or even take her out now and then. She was on the shelf here already, and she knew it.

She spent hours of the night worrying about her future, but at present she was more concerned about the future of the town than she was about her own. Blacks had outnumbered whites in Wakefield for years, but by 1985 more blacks than whites voted. Led by Amzi Nettles, preaching Black Power, most blacks voted for black candidates. Already, the majority of county officials were black. Public schools were mostly black. Except for Carter, the courthouse was black. Leading businesses such as City Electric, Skinner Brothers, and Pope's Hardware had recently sold out and closed their doors, with rumors of closings to come. Whites had begun moving away from Wakefield.

Sally's dream that her son Bobby would come home to live and work had faded, but her goal was the same. She must hang on to Wingate Hall no matter what, and see that it stayed in the family if she could. Besides Bobby, she had Jane and Sarah, and there were other Wingates who could afford the house and might want it. But not if the whole town died.

After Rich, she dialed Honey Lamar, the new bazaar chairman. Short, plump, usually in high heels, Honey said she'd just served refreshments to her bridge club. She was enthusiastic about a vigil. "Why, of course I'll help. Do we have enough people?"

"If some double up, we do. I will, and I know Ann Louise will." Ann Louise was the Christian. "I'll take some of the worst time, like from one to three, or three to five in the morning."

"Two hours? Lawsy."

"Well, I'm willing. Carter's the only thing left between us and them."

"You can say that again. Something has finally dawned on me, Sally. We should have picked our own cotton." Honey waited while Sally laughed. "All right, give me the list," she said, "and I'll start calling. I'll get somebody here to help me."

Ann Louise answered the phone in bed. She had a middle-ear problem, she told Sally, and couldn't walk without holding on to something. Couldn't drive the car at all. "Why can't I take my turn here at home? I've been praying for Carter off and on all day, anyway."

"Well, somebody has to keep vigil in the church. Who else could we get?"

"Let me think." Sally could see Ann Louise in an old nightgown that ought to go to the Goodwill. She spent nothing on herself anymore but gave all her money away, and paid an accountant to help her. "What about Arthur?" she asked. "He's young. He could lose a whole night's sleep and not miss it."

"But he's not all there, is he?"

"He's innocent, like a child, but he can pray. Better than we can, maybe."

Arthur was at church every Sunday, prayer book in hand, left foot dragging. He'd been injured at birth, people said. One arm was shorter than the other and his coordination was off, but he'd been the church sexton for years. Except for Ann Louise, who invited him to meals, kept him in junior books to read, and remembered his birthday, nobody paid much attention to him. Sally thought he'd rather not be noticed when she ran into him dusting the church or mopping the parish house kitchen.

Honey called to say people were lined up until midnight already. Everyone wanted to help, and the "old" widows would take all day tomorrow. She, Honey, would take from twelve to one tonight. "That only leaves three hours after you."

"Ann Louise suggested Arthur."

"Arthur?" Honey paused. "Well, okay by me. We need to wrap this up and take a nap before we go. We won't be able to pray half asleep."

Arthur answered the phone out of breath. His mother, already scheduled for tomorrow, had called him in from mowing the lawn. "Yes, ma'am?" he gasped into the receiver.

"I wonder if you'd help with the prayer vigil, Arthur," Sally said. "We need someone for a bad time, three to five or six in the morning. You'd come after me."

"Oh, yes, ma'am. I'll come any time. Judge Reese is one of my best friends. I was praying for him anyway." He stopped to catch his breath. "He bought me my lawn mower."

At twelve-thirty Sally's alarm clock went off. She was in bed, lights out, still awake after two hours of trying to fall asleep. Glad to get up, she slipped on a skirt and blouse, combed her hair, and put on lipstick. In the kitchen she drank a cup of strong black coffee and, just before one, parked her car beside Honey's in the churchyard. The front of the church was lighted each night, but tonight someone had turned on lights in the back as well. Sally went in the back.

Honey half knelt and half sat like a wilted plant, her forehead on the altar rail. She looked up at Sally with eyes not quite back from where they'd been the past hour.

"My turn," Sally whispered, kneeling beside her on the red velvet cushion. "Good night, love."

Saint Thomas's simple stained-glass windows were blacked out by the night, but candles burned on the altar and lights were on in the nave. Plain wooden walls, varnished when the church was built, subtly reflected the light. The altar itself, of carved walnut with a memorial plaque in front, was backed by a reredos given much later. Darker in color and slightly too wide, the reredos had caused violent objections at the time it was added, had been a source of contention for years after. Now it was considered a part of the altar. The prescribed "fair linen cloth," its embroidered IHS lined up with the cross, hung halfway to the floor on each side. The fringed brocade hangings were green.

As the sound of Honey's car died away, silence in the church became alive and tense, waiting. Sally took a deep breath and made her petition. Let him live. With everything else blocked out of mind, she began to say the words silently over and over like the Jesus prayer. Let him live, let him live.

In Wakefield, Carter walked a tightrope on which no one else could balance. Everything was now black or white, and you sided with your race or else. Carter alone could rise above it. When Amzi's mother died, before anyone knew how sick he was, Carter had gone to the funeral. And not only funeral but burial afterward, way out in the country in a black graveyard, where he stood with his hat off through the whole thing, someone said. He was the only white person there and had been criticized at the time, but not for long. Amzi's mother had been a good woman who tried to hold her wild son down, and soon everyone knew that Carter had stood there with a tumor on his brain, seeing double.

Sally thought of the Old Testament city where, if they could find one good man, the city would be spared. That's us, she thought, and Carter. She was asking for his life on behalf of the town.

"And not just for us," she added quickly. "For them, too."

As repeating words became automatic, she began to see scenes—cooks and maids from the past, polishing silver, ironing sheets, serving biscuits so hot they burned your fingers when you took one from the napkin. Everything was "Yes, ma'am," "No, ma'am," and "Ain't that nice." When she was bad, her nurses never told. "Chile, chile," they said, never unkind. "You ought to be shame." They could crack pecans with their teeth.

Now daughters and granddaughters of the cooks, maids, and nurses stood on Saturday streets with signs around their necks. SHUT DOWN THE TOWN, one sign said, IF IT DON'T DO TO SUIT YOU. Black children ran wild in stores, darted into streets as if daring someone to hit them. Their eyes despised you, not because you were you but because you were white.

Amzi and his followers would take over Wakefield unless something stopped them. What would it be like then?

"People are up to here with this," the white men were saying. "Some redneck will shoot one, and that will be it."

Sally tightened her discipline. Make a mental picture, an expert on prayer had said. Visualize the person well and happy, then frame the picture in your mind. Hold it up to God. She pictured Carter at Market Day on the courthouse square, speaking to people, shaking hands; but the expression on his face was a problem. On the street, in the office, at banquets and rallies, he looked as if he'd been awake all night, worrying while everyone slept. Sally put a smile on his face, made him look happy, then held up the picture to what she thought of as the great ruling psyche of the universe. She held it up until her whole body ached.

For relief she opened a prayer book and turned to the back where a prayer for the sick used to be. It was no longer there, but in the new Ministration to the Sick there were several. "Mercifully accept our prayers," one read, "and grant to your servant the help of your power, that his sickness may be turned into health, and our sorrow into joy." Repeatedly, as in a trance, she read the prayers one after the other, trying to concentrate on the words.

She wanted to look at her watch and see how long she had prayed, but thought it would show lack of dedication. Instead, she brought back the frame, framed the town, and changed the town as she'd changed Carter's face. No picketers with hostile stares. No empty stores. On the contrary, people moving back and forth as busy and harmonious as ants or bees. Faces with pleasant expressions. Sunshine on newly painted houses, little gardens in back with vegetables or flowers.

Up from her subconscious suddenly popped a new scene, just down the hill at the black church, Bethel—Bethel, famous from the sixties when black leaders spoke from its pulpit, shook hands on its porch, stood on its steps while cameras flashed. Now, inside the church, black people were praying for Carter too. Not one at a time as here, but all together, praying and singing in the old way. On the pews elderly black men sat bent over, holding their heads in their hands. Little black girls with freshly plaited pigtails swung their feet above the bare floor and looked around with eyes surprised by nothing. When the choir sang, the others hummed, murmured "Lord, Lord," or joined in at will. It was music that, if you heard it as a child, you never got over, because it went with the nurses who wouldn't tell, with bare black feet, steaming corn bread and vegetables cooked with salt pork, with a way of life now gone forever. It went with people you had loved.

Sally knew the scene for what it was, a daydream of her own. She wiped it out, framed a healthy new picture of Carter behind his desk, and held it up as before.

Now and then the frame threatened to get away like a kite with all the string let out; but she brought it back each time, back to the center of a clear blue sky where the eyes of God couldn't miss it. Meanwhile, down below, she moved into a quiet semidarkness without time, thought, or feeling. All discomfort gone, she slumped against the altar rail and sank down on the cushion, one cheek pillowed on the rail.

Arthur woke her with a touch on the shoulder. "Miss Sally?" His face, looking down, was shocked.

"Oh, God." She came to all at once. "What have I done?"

"You went to sleep," he said, his eyes wide.

Sally straightened up. She had huddled against the altar rail so long one foot was numb. Her mouth tasted of dissipation. The church had a close waxy smell, as in the hour following weddings and funerals.

"I'm sorry, Arthur," she said. "I didn't mean to go to sleep. I'll stay on and make it up."

"But you can't make it up, Miss Sally," he said. "You broke the chain."

Foot dragging, he went to the prayer desk and lowered himself onto one knee, then the other. He crossed himself, closed his eyes, and shut Sally out.

She stared at her watch as if the watch were to blame. Three o'clock. Three minutes after. How long had she slept? she wondered. Maybe not as long as she feared. Maybe only minutes before Arthur came. It couldn't be as bad as he thought. Arthur was naïve. There was nothing that couldn't be made up, put back together, replaced, forgiven, or sometimes erased altogether.

She began to pray harder than ever. Let him live, let him live. She was saying the Lord's Prayer, concentrating on "thy will be done," when the back door opened and someone came in. Someone to relieve Arthur, she thought, without looking up. It had nothing to do with her, for she would go on. Like a jogger into running, she felt she could go on all night.

But the person who came in cleared his throat for attention, and she turned to see Rich standing beside Arthur. Rich had on pants over a pajama top, bedroom shoes on his feet. A quick comb had missed the back of his hair. With one hand on Arthur's shoulder, he looked at Sally.

"I hate to tell you, but Carter didn't make it," he said, and cleared his throat again. "His preacher just called."

Sally gripped the altar rail so hard her rings hurt. Arthur lowered his head and covered his face with his hands.

"They said he wouldn't be the same if he lived," Rich went on. "So maybe it's a blessing."

In the silence that followed Sally got up and tiptoed past Arthur—still on his knees with his head down—to where Rich stood waiting. Her feet seemed remote from her body, almost beyond her control. Her hands were icy.

"I went to sleep, Rich," she said. "Was it my fault?"

He puts his arm around her. "He was doomed from the start," he said. "Nothing we did could have saved him."

When the town clock began to strike, she didn't count the strokes. Whatever the hour, she thought, it was too late. She watched Rich go to the front, bow to the cross, and take a snuffer from its holder. Carefully, an acolyte since boyhood, he began putting out candles one by one.

ANDRE DUBUS

Andre Dubus was born in Lake Charles, Louisiana, and lives in Haverhill, Massachusetts. He is the author of a novel, *The Lieutenant,* a novella, *Voices from the Moon,* and five collections of stories: *Separate Flights* (1975), *Adultery and Other Choices* (1978), *Finding a Girl in America* (1980), *The Times Are Never So Bad* (1983), and *The Last Worthless Evening* (1986).

If They Knew Yvonne

to Andre and Jeb

I GREW up in Louisiana, and for twelve years I went to a boys' school taught by Christian Brothers, a Catholic religious order. In the eighth grade our teacher was Brother Thomas. I still have a picture he gave to each boy in the class at the end of that year; it's a picture of Thomas Aquinas, two angels, and a woman. In the left foreground Aquinas is seated, leaning back against one angel whose hands grip his shoulders; he looks very much like a tired boxer between rounds, and his upturned face looks imploringly at the angel. The second angel is kneeling at his feet and, with both hands, is tightening a sash around Aquinas's waist. In the left background of the picture, the woman is escaping up a flight of stone stairs; her face is turned backward for a final look before she bolts from the room. According to Brother Thomas, some of Aquinas's family were against his becoming a priest, so they sent a woman to his room. He drove her out, then angels descended, encircled his waist with a cord, and squeezed all concupiscence from his body so he would never be tempted again. On the back of the picture, under the title *Angelic Warfare,* is a prayer for purity.

Brother Thomas was the first teacher who named for us the sins included in the Sixth and Ninth Commandments which, in the Catholic recording of the Decalogue, forbid adultery and coveting your neighbor's wife. In an introductory way, he simply listed the various sins. Then he focused on what apparently was the most significant: he called it self-abuse and, quickly sweeping our faces, he saw that we understood. It was a mortal sin, he said, because first of all it wasted the precious seed which God had given us for marriage. Also, sexual pleasure was reserved for married people alone, to have children by performing the marriage act. Self-abuse was not even a natural act; it was unnatural, and if a boy did it he was no better than a monkey. It was a desecration of our bodies, which were temples of the Holy Ghost, a mortal sin that resulted in the loss of sanctifying grace and therefore could send us to hell. He walked a few paces from his desk, his legs hidden by the long black robe, then he went back and stood behind the desk again and pulled down on his white collar: the front of it hung straight down from his throat like two white and faceless playing cards.

"Avoid being alone," he said. "When you go home from school, don't just sit around the house—go out and play ball, or cut the grass, or wash your dad's car. Do *any*thing, but use up your energy. And pray to the Blessed Mother: take your rosary to bed at night and say it while you're going to sleep. If you fall asleep before you finish, the Blessed Mother won't mind—that's what she *wants* you to do."

Then he urged us to receive the Holy Eucharist often. He told us of the benefits gained through the Eucharist: sanctifying grace, which helped us fight temptation; release from the temporal punishment of purgatory; and therefore, until we committed another mortal or venial sin, a guarantee of immediate entrance into heaven. He hoped and prayed, he said, that he would die with the Holy Eucharist on his tongue.

He had been talking with the excited voice yet wandering eyes of a man repeating by rote what he truly believes. But now his eyes focused on something out the window, as though a new truth had actually appeared to him on the dusty school ground of that hot spring day. One hand rose to scratch his jaw.

"In a way," he said softly, "you'd actually be doing someone a favor if you killed him when he had just received the Eucharist."

I made it until midsummer, about two weeks short of my fourteenth birthday. I actually believed I would make it forever. Then one hot summer night when my parents were out playing bridge, Janet was on a date, and I was alone in the house, looking at *Holiday* magazine—girls in advertisements drinking rum or lighting cigarettes, girls in bulky sweaters at ski resorts, girls at beaches, girls on horseback—I went to the bathroom, telling myself I was only going to piss, lingering there, thinking it was pain I felt but then I knew it wasn't, that for the first wakeful time in my life it was about to happen, then it did, and I stood weak and trembling and, shutting my eyes, saw the faces of the Virgin Mary and Christ and Brother Thomas, then above them, descending to join them, the awful diaphanous bulk of God.

That was a Tuesday. I set the alarm clock and woke next morning at six-thirty, feeling that everyone on earth and in heaven had watched my sin, and had been watching me as I slept. I dressed quickly and crept past Janet's bedroom; she slept on her side, one sun-dark arm on top of the sheet; then past the closed door of my parents' room and out of the house. Riding my bicycle down the driveway I thought of being struck by a car, so I rode on the sidewalk to church and I got there in time for confession before Mass. When I got home Janet was sitting on the front steps, drinking orange juice. I rode across the lawn and stopped in front of her and looked at her smooth brown legs.

"Where'd you go?"

"To Mass."

"Special day today?"

"I woke up," I said. "So I went."

A fly buzzed at my ear and I remembered Brother Thomas quoting some saint who had said if you couldn't stand an insect buzzing at your ear while you were trying to sleep, how could you stand the eternal punishment of hell?

"You set the alarm," she said. "I heard it."

Then Mother called us in to breakfast. She asked where I had been, then said: "Well, that's nice. Maybe you'll be a priest."

"Ha," Daddy said.

"Don't worry, Daddy," Janet said. "We don't hate Episcopalians anymore."

I got through two more days, until Friday, then Saturday afternoon I had to go to confession again. Through the veil over the latticed window Father Broussard told me to pray often to the Virgin Mary, to avoid those people and places and things that were occasions of sin, to go to confession and receive Communion at least once a week. The tone of his whispering voice was kind, and the confessional itself was constructed to offer some comfort, for it enclosed me with my secret, and its interior was dark as my soul was, and Christ crucified stared back at me, inches from my face. Father Broussard told me to say ten Our Fathers and ten Hail Marys for my penance. I said them kneeling in a pew at the rear, then I went outside and walked around the church to the cemetery. In hot sun I moved among old graves and took out my rosary and began to pray.

Sunday we went to eleven o'clock Mass. Janet and I received Communion, but Mother had eaten toast and coffee, breaking her fast, so she didn't receive. Most Sundays she broke her fast because we went to late Mass, and in those days you had to fast from midnight until you received Communion; around ten in the morning she would feel faint and have to eat something. After Mass, Janet started the car and lit a cigarette and waited for our line in the parking lot to move. I envied her nerve. She was only sixteen, but when she started smoking my parents couldn't stop her.

"I just can't keep the fast," Mother said. "I must need vitamins."

She was sitting in the front seat, opening and closing her black fan.

"Maybe you do," Janet said.

"Maybe so. If you have to smoke, I wish you'd do it at home."

Janet smiled and drove in first gear out of the parking lot. Her window was down and on the way home I watched her dark hair blowing in the breeze.

That was how my fourteenth summer passed: baseball in the mornings, and friends and movies and some days of peace, of hope—then back to the confessional where the smell of sweat hung in the air like spewed-out sin. Once I saw the student body president walking down the main street; he recognized my face and told me hello, and I blushed not with timidity but shame, for he walked with a confident stride, he was strong and good while I was weak. A high school girl down the street gave me a ride one day, less than an hour after I had done it, and I sat against the door at my side and could not look at her; I answered her in a low voice and said nothing on my own and I knew she thought I was shy, but that was better than the truth, for I believed if she knew what sat next to her she would recoil in disgust. When fall came I was glad, for I hoped the school days would break the pattern of my sins. But I was also afraid the Brothers could see the summer in my eyes; then it wasn't just summer, but fall and winter too, for the pattern wasn't broken and I could not stop.

In the confessional the hardest priest was an old Dutchman who scolded and talked about manliness and will power and once told me to stick my finger in the flame of a candle, then imagine the eternal fire of hell. I didn't do it. Father Broussard was firm, sometimes impatient, but easy compared to the Dutchman. The easiest was a young Italian, Father Grassi, who said very little: I doubt if he ever spoke to me for over thirty seconds, and he gave such light penances—three or four Hail Marys—that I began to think he couldn't understand English well enough to know what I told him.

Then it was fall again, I was fifteen, and Janet was a freshman at the college in town. She was dating Bob Mitchell, a Yankee from Michigan. He was an airman from the SAC Base, so she had to argue with Mother for the first week or so. He was a high school graduate, intelligent, and he planned to go to the University of Michigan when he got out. That's what she told Mother, who believed a man in uniform was less trustworthy than a local civilian. One weekend in October Mother and Daddy went to Baton Rouge to see L.S.U. play Ole Miss. It was a night game and they were going to spend Saturday night with friends in Baton Rouge. They left after lunch Saturday and as soon as they drove off, Janet called Bob and broke their date, then went to bed. She had the flu, she said, but she hadn't told them because Mother would have felt it was her duty to stay home.

"Would you bring me a beer?" she said. "I'll just lie in bed and drink beer and you won't have to bother with me at all."

I sat in the living room and listened to Bill Stern broadcast Notre Dame and S.M.U. I kept checking on Janet to see if she wanted another beer; she'd smile at me over her book—*The Idiot*—then shake her beer can and say yes. When the game was over I told her I was going to confession and she gave me some money for cigarettes. I had enough to be ashamed of without people thinking I smoked too. When I got home I told her I had forgotten.

"Would you see if Daddy left any?"

I went into their room. On the wall above the double bed was a small black crucifix with a silver Christ (Daddy called it a graven image, but he smiled when he said it); stuck behind the crucifix was a blade from a palm frond, dried brown and crisp since Palm Sunday. I opened the top drawer of Daddy's bureau and took out the carton of Luckies. Then something else red-and-white caught my eye: the corner of a small box under his rolled-up socks. For a moment I didn't take it out. I stood looking at that corner of cardboard, knowing immediately what it was and also knowing that I wasn't learning anything new, that I had known for some indefinite and secret time, maybe a few months or a year or even two years. I stood there in the history of my knowledge, then I put down the cigarette carton and took the box of condoms from the drawer. I had slid the cover off the box and was looking at the vertically arranged rolled condoms when I heard the bedsprings, but it was too late, her bare feet were already crossing the floor, and all I could do was raise my eyes to her as she said: "Can't you find—" then stopped.

At first she blushed, but only for a second or two. She came into the room, gently took the box from me, put the cover on, and looked at it for a moment. Then she put it in the drawer, covered it with socks, got a pack of cigarettes, and started back to her room.

"Why don't you bring me a beer," she said over her shoulder. "And we'll have a little talk."

When I brought the beer she was propped up in bed, and *The Idiot* was closed on the bedside table.

"Are you really surprised?" she said.

I shook my head.

"Does it bother you?"

"Yes."

"You're probably scrupulous. You confess enough for Eichmann, you know."

I blushed and looked away.

"Do you know that some people—theologians—believe a mortal sin is as rare as a capital crime? That most things we do aren't really that evil?"

"They must not be Catholics."

"Some of them are. Listen: Mother's only mistake is she thinks it's a sin, so she doesn't receive Communion. And I guess that's why she doesn't get a diaphragm—that would be too committed."

This sort of talk scared me, and I was relieved when she stopped. She told me not to worry about Mother and especially not to blame Daddy, not to think of him as a Protestant who had led Mother away from the Church. She said the Church was wrong. Several times she used the word love, and that night in bed I thought: love? love? For all I could think of was semen and I remembered long ago a condom lying in the dust of a country road; a line of black ants was crawling into it. I got out of bed, turned on a lamp, and read the *Angelic Warfare* prayer, which ends like this: *O God, Who has vouchsafed to defend with the blessed cord of St. Thomas those who are engaged in the terrible conflict of chastity! grant to us Thy suppliants, by his help, happily to overcome in this warfare the terrible enemy of our body and souls, that being crowned with the lily of perpetual purity, we may deserve to receive from Thee, amongst the chaste bands of the angels, the palm of bliss. . . .*

Janet didn't do so well in the war. That January she and Bob Mitchell drove to Port Arthur, Texas, and got married by a justice of the peace. Then they went to Father Broussard for a Catholic marriage, but when he found out Janet was pregnant he refused. He said he didn't think this marriage would last, and he would not make it permanent in the eyes of God. My parents and I knew nothing of this until a couple of weeks later, when Bob was discharged from the Air Force. One night they told us, and two days later Janet was gone, up to Michigan; she wrote that although Bob wasn't a Catholic, he had agreed to try again, and this time a priest had married them. Seven months after the Texas wedding she had twin sons and Mother went up there on the bus and stayed two weeks and sent us postcards from Ann Arbor.

You get over your sister's troubles, even images of her getting pregnant in a parked car, just as after a while you stop worrying about whether or not your mother is living in sin. I had my own troubles and one summer afternoon when I was sixteen, alone in the house, having done it again after receiving Communion that very morning, I lay across my bed, crying and striking my head with my fist. It was a weekday, so the priests weren't hearing confessions until next morning before Mass. I could have gone to the rectory and confessed to a priest in his office, but I could not do that, I had to have the veiled window between our faces. Finally I got up and went to the phone in the hall. I dialed the rectory and when Father Broussard answered I told him I couldn't get to church but I had to confess and I wanted to do it right now, on the phone. I barely heard the suspicious turn in his voice when he told me to come to the rectory.

"I can't," I said.

"What about tomorrow? Could you come tomorrow before Mass, or during the day?"

"I can't, Father. I can't wait that long."

"Who is this?"

For a moment we were both quiet. Then I said: "That's all right."

It was an expression we boys used, and it usually meant none of your business. I had said it in a near-whisper, not sure if I could speak another word without crying.

"All right," he said, "let me hear your confession."

I kneeled on the floor, my eyes closed, the telephone cord stretched tautly to its full length:

"Bless me Father, for I have sinned; my last confession was yesterday—" now I was crying silent tears, those I hadn't spent on the bed; I could still talk but my voice was in shards "—my sins are: I committed self-abuse one time—" the word *time* trailing off, whispered into the phone and the empty hall which grew emptier still, for Father Broussard said nothing and I kneeled with eyes shut tight and the receiver hurting my hot ear until finally he said:

"All right, but I can't give you absolution over the phone. Will you come to the rectory at about three?"

"Yes, Father."

"And ask for Father Broussard."

"Yes, Father, thank you, Father—" still holding the receiver after he hung up, my eyes shut on black and red shame; then I stood weakly and returned to the bed—I would not go to the rectory—and lay there feeling I was the only person alive on this humid summer day. I could not stop crying, and I began striking my head again. I spoke aloud to God, begging him to forgive me, then kill me and spare me the further price of being a boy. Then something occurred to me: an image tossed up for my consideration, looked at, repudiated—all in an instant while my fist was poised. I saw myself sitting on the bed, trousers dropped to the floor, my sharp-edged hunting knife in my right hand, then with one quick determined slash cutting off that autonomous penis and casting it on the floor to shrivel and die. But before my fist struck again I threw that image away. No voices told me why. I had no warning vision of pain, of bleeding to death, of being an impotent freak. I simply knew; it is there between your legs and you do not cut it off.

Yvonne Millet finally put it to good use. We were both nineteen, both virgins; we started dating the summer after our freshman year at the college in town. She was slender, with black hair cut short in what they called an Italian Boy. She was a Catholic, and had been taught by nuns for twelve years, but she wasn't bothered as much as I was. In the parked car we soaked our clothes with sweat, and sometimes I went home with spotted trousers which I rolled into a bundle and dropped in the basket for dry cleaning. I confessed this and petting too, and tried on our dates to keep dry, so that many nights I crawled aching and nauseated into my bed at home. I lay very still in my pain, feeling quasi-victorious: I believed Yvonne and I were committing mortal sins by merely touching each other, but at least for another night we had resisted the graver sin of orgasm. On other nights she took me with her hand or we rubbed against each other in a clothed pantomime of lovemaking until we came. This happened often enough so that for the first time in nearly seven years I stopped masturbating. And Saturday after Saturday I went proudly to confession and told of my sins with Yvonne. I confessed to Father Grassi, who still didn't talk much, but one Saturday afternoon he said: "How old are you, my friend?"

"Nineteen, Father."

"Yes. And the young girl?"

I told him she was nineteen. Now I was worried: I had avoided confessing to Father Broussard or the Dutchman because I was afraid one of them would ask about the frequency of our sins, then tell me either to be pure or break up with her and, if I did neither of these, I could not be absolved again. I had thought Father Grassi would not ask questions.

"Do you love her?"

"Yes, Father."

"At your age I think it is very hard to know if you really love someone. So I recommend that you and your girl think about getting married in two or three years' time and then, my friend, until you are ready for a short engagement and then marriage, I think each of you should go out with other people. Mostly with each other, of course, but with other people too. That may not help you to stay pure, but at least it will help you know if you love each other."

"Yes, Father."

"Because this other thing that's going on now, that's not love, you see. So you should test it in other ways."

I told him I understood and I would talk to my girl about it. I never did, though. Once in a while Yvonne confessed but I have no idea what she told the priest, for she did not see things the way I saw them. One night, when I tried to stop us short, she pulled my hand back to its proper place and held it there until she was ready for it to leave. Then she reached to the dashboard for a cigarette, tapped it, and paused as though remembering to offer me one.

"Don't you want me to do it for you?" she said.

"No, I'm all right."

She smoked for a while, her head on my shoulder.

"Do you really think it's a worse sin when it happens to you?" she said.

"Yes."

"Why?"

I told her what the Brothers had taught me.

"You believe that?" she said. "That God gave you this seed just to have babies with, and if you waste it He'll send you to hell?"

"I guess so."

"You have wet dreams, don't you?"

"That's different. There's no will involved."

"What about me? It just happened to me, and I didn't use up any eggs or anything, so where's my sin?"

"I don't know. Maybe sins are different for girls."

"Then it wouldn't be a sin for me to masturbate either. Right? I don't, but isn't that true?"

"I never thought of that."

"Well, don't. You think too much already."

"Maybe you don't think enough."

"You're right: I don't."

"I'll tell you why it's a sin," I said. "Because it's reserved for married people."

"Climax?"

"Yes."

"But you're supposed to be married to touch each other too," she said. "So why draw the line at climax? I mean, why get all worked up and then stop and think that's good?"

"You're right. We shouldn't do any of it."

"Oh, I'm not sure it's as bad as all that."

"You're not? You don't think it's a sin, what we do?"

"Maybe a little, but it's not as bad as a lot of other things."

"It's a mortal sin."

"I don't think so. I believe it's a sin to talk about a girl, but I don't think what you do with her is so bad."

"All right: if that's what you think, why don't we just go all the way?"

She sat up to throw her cigarette out the window, then she nestled her face on my chest.

"Because I'm scared," she said.

"Of getting pregnant?"

"I don't think so. I'm just scared of not being a virgin, that's all."

Then she finished our argument, won it, soaked her small handkerchief in my casuistry. Next morning at breakfast I was tired.

"You're going to ruin your health," Mother said. "It was after one when you got home."

I flexed my bicep and said I was fine. But now Daddy was watching me from his end of the table.

"I don't care about your health," he said. "I just hope you know more than Janet did."

"*Honey,*" Mother said.

"She got it reversed. She started babies before she was married, then quit."

That was true. Her twin boys were four now, and there were no other children. Bob had finished his undergraduate work and was going to start work on a Ph.D. in political science. Early in the summer Mother had gone up there and stayed two weeks. When she got back and talked about her visit she looked nervous, as though she were telling a lie, and a couple of times I walked into the kitchen where Mother and Daddy were talking and they stopped until I had got what I wanted and left.

"I won't get pregnant," I said.

"Neither will Yvonne," Daddy said. "As long as you keep your pants on."

Then finally one night in early fall we drove away from her house, where we had parked for some time, and I knew she would not stop me, because by leaving her house she was risking questions from her parents, and by accepting that she was accepting the other risk too. I drove out to a country road, over a vibrating wooden bridge, the bayou beneath us dark as earth on that moonless night, on through black trees until I found a dirt road into the woods, keeping my hand on her small breast as I turned and cut off the ignition and headlights. In a moment she was naked on the car seat, then I was out of my clothes, even the socks, and seeing her trusting face and shockingly white body I almost dressed and took her home but then she said: Love me, Harry, love me—

The Brothers hadn't prepared me for this. If my first time had been with a whore, their training probably would have worked, for that was the sort of lust they focused on. But they were no match for Yvonne, and next morning I woke happier than I had ever been. At school that day we drank coffee and held hands and whispered. That night on the way to her house I stopped at a service station and bought a package of condoms from a machine in the men's room. That was the only time I felt guilty. But I was at least perceptive enough to know why: condoms, like masturbation and whores, were something the Brothers knew about. I left that piss-smelling room, walked into the clear autumn night, and drove to Yvonne's, where they had never been.

For the rest of the fall and a few weeks of winter, we were hot and happy lovers. I marveled at my own joy, my lack of remorse. Once, after a few weeks, I asked her if she ever felt bad. It was late at night and we were sitting at a bar, eating oysters on the half shell. For a moment she didn't know what I meant, then she smiled.

"I feel wonderful," she said.

She dipped her last oyster in the sauce, and leaned over the tray to eat it.

"Do we have enough money for more?" she said.

"Sure."

They were ninety cents a dozen. We watched the Negro open them, and I felt fine, eating oysters and drinking beer at one in the morning, having made love an hour ago to this pretty girl beside me. I looked at her hair and wondered if she ought to let it grow.

"Sometimes I worry though," she said.

"Getting pregnant?"

"Nope, I never said you had to use those things. I worry about you."

"Why me?"

"Because you used to think about sins so much, and now you don't."

"That's because I love you."

She licked the red sauce from her fingers, then took my hand, squeezed it, and drank some beer.

"I'm afraid someday you'll start feeling bad again, then you'll hate me."

She was right to look for defeat in that direction, to expect me to move along clichéd routes. But, as it turned out, it wasn't guilt that finally soured us. After a couple of months I simply began noticing things.

I saw that she didn't really like football. She only enjoyed the games because they gave her a chance to dress up, and there was a band, and a crowd of students, and it was fun to keep a flask hidden while you poured bourbon into a paper cup. She cheered with the rest of us, but she wasn't cheering for the same thing. She cheered because we were there, and a young man had run very fast with a football. Once we stood up to watch an end chasing a long pass: when he dived for it, caught it, and skidded on the ground, she turned happily to me and brushed her candied apple against my sleeve. Watch out, I said. She spit on her handkerchief and rubbed the sticky wool. She loved sweets, always asked me to buy her Mounds or Hersheys at the movies, and once in a while she'd get a pimple which she tried to conceal with powder. I felt loose flesh at her waist when we danced, and walking beside her on the campus one afternoon I looked down and saw her belly pushing against her tight skirt; I lightly backhanded it and told her to suck her gut in. She stood at attention, saluted, then gave me the finger. I'm about to start my period, she said. Except for the soft flesh at her waist she was rather thin, and when she lay on her back her naked breasts spread and flattened, as though they were melting.

Around the end of November her parents spent a weekend with relatives in Houston, leaving Yvonne to take care of her sister and brother, who were fourteen and eleven. They left Saturday morning, and that night Yvonne cooked for me. She was dressed up, black cocktail dress, even heels, and she was disappointed when she saw I hadn't worn a coat. But she didn't say anything. She had already fed her brother and sister, and they were in the den at the back of the house, watching television. Yvonne had a good fire in the living room fireplace, and on the coffee table she had bourbon, a pitcher of water, a bucket of ice, and a sugar bowl.

"Like they do in Faulkner," she said, and we sat on the couch and drank a couple of toddies before dinner. Then she left me for a while and I looked into the fire, hungry and horny, and wondered what time the brother and sister would go to bed and if Yvonne would do it while they were sleeping. She came back to the living room, smiled, blushed, and said: "If you're brave enough, I am. Want to try it?"

We ate by candlelight: oyster cocktails, then a roast with rice and thick dark gravy, garlic-tinged. We had lemon ice-box pie and went back to the fireplace with second cups of coffee.

"I love to cook," she said from the record player. She put on about five albums, and I saw that we were supposed to sit at the fire and talk for the rest of the evening. The first album was Jackie Gleason, *Music, Martinis, and*

Memories, and she sat beside me, took my hand and sipped her coffee. She rested her head on the back of the couch, but I didn't like to handle a coffee cup leaning back that way, so I withdrew my hand from hers and hunched forward over the coffee table.

"I think I started cooking when I was seven," she said to my back. "No, let's see, I was eight—" I looked down at her crossed legs, the black dress just covering her knees, then looked at the fire. "When we lived in Baton Rouge. I had a children's cookbook and I made something called Chili Concoction. Everybody was nice about it, and Daddy ate two helpings for supper and told me to save the rest for breakfast and he'd eat it with eggs. He did, too. Then I made something called a strawberry minute pie, and I think it was pretty good. I'll make it for you some time."

"Okay."

I was still hunched over drinking coffee, so I wasn't looking at her. I finished the coffee and she asked if I wanted more, and that irritated me, so I didn't know whether to say yes or no. I said I guess so. Then watching her leave with my cup, I disliked myself and her too. For if I wasn't worthy of the evening, then wasn't she stupid and annoyingly vulnerable to give it to me? The next album was Sinatra; I finished my coffee, then leaned back so our shoulders touched, our hands together in her lap, and we listened. Once she took a drag from my cigarette and I said keep it, and lit another. The third album was Brubeck. She put some more ice in the bucket, I made toddies, and she asked if I understood *The Bear.* I shrugged and said probably not. She had finished it the day before, and she started talking about it.

"Hey," I said. "When are they going to sleep?"

She was surprised, and again I disliked myself and her too. Then she was hurt, and she looked at her lap and said she didn't know, but she couldn't make love anyway, not here in the house, even if they were sleeping.

"We can leave for a while," I said. "We won't go far."

She kept looking at her lap, at our clasped hands.

"They'll be all right," I said.

Then she looked into my eyes and I looked away and she said: "Okay, I'll tell them."

When she came back with a coat over her arm I was waiting at the door, my jacket zipped, the car key in my hand.

We broke up in January, about a week after New Year's. I don't recall whether we fought, or kissed goodbye, or sat in a car staring mutely out the windows. But I do remember when the end started; or, rather, when Yvonne decided to recognize it.

On New Year's Eve a friend of ours gave a party. His parents were out of town, so everyone got drunk. It was an opportunity you felt obliged not to pass up. Two or three girls got sick and had to have their faces washed and be walked outside in the cold air. When Yvonne got drunk it was a pleasant drunk, and I took her upstairs. I think no one noticed: it was past midnight, and people were hard to account for. We lay on the bed in the master bedroom, Yvonne with her skirt pulled up, her pants off, while I performed in shirt, sweater, and socks. She was quiet as we stood in the dark room, taking our pants off, and she didn't answer my whispered Happy New Year as we began to make love, for the first time, on a bed. Then, moving beneath me, she said in a voice so incongruous with her body that I almost softened but quickly got it back, shutting my ears to what I had heard: This is all we ever do, Harry—this is all we ever do.

The other thing I remember about that night is a time around three in the morning. A girl was cooking hamburgers, I was standing in the kitchen doorway talking to some boys, and Yvonne was sitting alone at the kitchen table. There were other people talking in the kitchen, but she wasn't listening; she moved only to tap ashes and draw on her cigarette, then exhaled into the space that held her gaze. She looked older than twenty, quite lonely and sad, and I pitied her. But there was something else: I knew she would never make love to me again. Maybe that is why, as a last form of possession, I told. It could not have been more than an hour later, I was drunker, and in the bathroom I one-upped three friends who were bragging about feeling tits of drunken girls. I told them I had taken Yvonne upstairs and screwed her. To add history to it, I even told them what she had said.

Waiting in line for my first confession in five months I felt some guilt but I wasn't at all afraid. I only had to confess sexual intercourse, and there was nothing shameful about that, nothing unnatural. It was a man's sin. Father Broussard warned me never to see this girl again (that's what he called her: this girl), for a man is weak and he needs much grace to turn away from a girl who will give him her body. He said I must understand it was a serious sin because sexual intercourse was given by God to married couples for the procreation of children and we had stolen it and used it wrongfully, for physical pleasure, which was its secondary purpose. I knew that in some way I had sinned, but Father Broussard's definition of that sin fell short and did not sound at all like what I had done with Yvonne. So when I left the confessional I still felt unforgiven.

The campus was not a very large one, but it was large enough so you could avoid seeing someone. I stopped going to the student center for coffee, and we had no classes together; we only saw each other once in a while, usually from a distance, walking between buildings. We exchanged waves and the sort of smile you cut into your face at times like that. The town was small too, so occasionally I saw her driving around, looking for a parking place or something. Then after a while I wanted to see her, and I started going to the student center again, but she didn't drink coffee there anymore. In a week or so I realized that I didn't really want to see her: I wanted her to be happy, and if I saw her there was nothing I could say to help that.

Soon I was back to the old private vice, though now it didn't seem a vice but an indulgence, not as serious as smoking or even drinking, closer to eating an ice cream sundae before bed every night. That was how I felt about it, like I had eaten two scoops of ice cream with thick hot fudge on it, and after a couple of bites it wasn't good anymore but I finished it anyway, thinking of calories. It was a boring little performance and it didn't seem worth thinking about, one way or the other. But I told it in the confessional, so I could still receive the Eucharist. Then one day in spring I told the number of my sins as though I were telling the date of my birth, my height, and weight, and Father Broussard said quickly and sternly: "Are you sorry for these sins?"

"Yes, Father," I said, but then I knew it was a lie. He was asking me if I had a firm resolve to avoid this sin in the future when I said: "No, Father."

"No what? You can't avoid it?"

"I mean no, Father, I'm not really sorry. I don't even think it's a sin."

"Oh, I see. You don't have the discipline to stop, so you've decided it's not a sin. Just like that, you've countermanded God's law. Do you want absolution?"

"Yes, Father. I want to receive Communion."

"You can't. You're living in mortal sin, and I cannot absolve you while you keep this attitude. I want you to think very seriously—"

But I wasn't listening. I was looking at the crucifix and waiting for his voice to stop so I could leave politely and try to figure out what to do next. Then he stopped talking, and I said: "Yes, Father."

"*What?*" he said. "*What?*"

I went quickly through the curtains, out of the confessional, out of the church.

On Sundays I went to Mass but did not receive the Eucharist. I thought I could but I was afraid that as soon as the Host touched my tongue I would suddenly realize I had been wrong, and then I'd be receiving Christ with mortal sin on my soul. Mother didn't receive either. I prayed for her and hoped she'd soon have peace, even if it meant early menopause. By now I agreed with Janet, and I wished she'd write Mother a letter and convince her that she wasn't evil. I thought Mother was probably praying for Janet, who had gone five years without bearing a child.

It was June, school was out, and I did not see Yvonne at all. I was working with a surveying crew, running a hundred-foot chain through my fingers, cutting trails with a machete, eating big lunches from paper bags, and waiting for something to happen. There were two alternatives, and I wasn't phony enough for the first or brave enough for the second: I could start confessing again, the way I used to, or I could ignore the confessional and simply receive Communion. But nothing happened and each Sunday I stayed with Mother in the pew while the others went up to the altar rail.

Then Janet came home. She wrote that Bob had left her, had moved in with his girlfriend—a graduate student—and she and the boys were coming home on the bus. That was the news waiting for me when I got home from work, Mother handing me the letter as I came through the front door, both of them watching me as I read it. Then Daddy cursed, Mother started crying again, and I took a beer out to the front porch. After a while Daddy came out too and we sat without talking and drank beer until Mother called us to supper. Daddy said, "That son of a bitch," and we went inside.

By the time Janet and the boys rode the bus home from Ann Arbor, Mother was worried about something else: the Church, because now Janet was twenty-three years old and getting a divorce and if she ever married again she was out of the Church. Unless Bob died, and Daddy said he didn't care what the Church thought about divorce, but it seemed a good enough reason for him to go up to Ann Arbor, Michigan, and shoot Bob Mitchell between the eyes. So while Janet and Paul and Lee were riding south on the Greyhound, Mother was going to daily Mass and praying for some answer to Janet's future.

But Janet had already taken care of that too. When she got off the bus I knew she'd be getting married again some day: she had gained about ten pounds, probably from all that cheap food while Bob went to school, but she had always been on the lean side anyway and now she looked better than I remembered. Her hair was long, about halfway down her back. The boys were five years old now, and I was glad she hadn't had any more, because they seemed to be good little boys and not enough to scare off a man. We took them home—it was a Friday night—and Daddy gave Janet a tall drink of bourbon and everybody talked as though nothing had happened. Then we ate shrimp *étouffée* and after supper, when the boys were in bed and the rest of us were in the living room, Janet said by God it was the best meal she had had in five years, and next time she was going to marry a man who liked Louisiana cooking. When she saw the quick look in Mother's eyes, she said: "We didn't get married in the Church, Mama. I just told you we did so you wouldn't worry."

"You *didn't?*"

"Bob was so mad at Father Broussard he wouldn't try again. He's not a Catholic, you know."

"There's more wrong with him than that," Daddy said.

"So I can still get married in the Church," Janet said. "To somebody else."

"But Janet—"

"Wait," Daddy said. "Wait. You've been praying for days so Janet could stop living with that son of a bitch and still save her soul. Now you got it—right?"

"But—"

"Right?"

"Well," Mother said, "I guess so."

They went to bed about an hour past their usual time, but Janet and I stayed up drinking gin and tonic in the kitchen, with the door closed so we wouldn't keep anybody awake. At first she just talked about how glad she was to be home, even if the first sign of it was the Negroes going to the back of the bus. She loved this hot old sticky night, she said, and the June bugs thumping against the screen and she had forgotten how cigarettes get soft down here in the humid air. Finally she talked about Bob; she didn't think he had ever loved her, he had started playing around their first year up there, and it had gone on for five years more or less; near the end she had even done it too, had a boyfriend, but it didn't help her survive at all, it only made things worse, and now at least she felt clean and tough and she thought that was the first step toward hope.

The stupid thing was she still loved the philandering son of a bitch. That was the only time she cried, when she said that, but she didn't even cry long enough for me to get up and go to her side of the table and hold her: when I was half out of my chair she was already waving me back in it, shaking her head and wiping her eyes, and the tears that had filled them for a moment were gone. Then she cheered up and asked if I'd drive her around tomorrow, down the main street and everything, and I said sure and asked her if she was still a Catholic.

"Don't tell Mother this," she said. "She's confused enough already. I went to Communion every Sunday, except when I was having that stupid affair, and I only felt sinful then because he loved me and I was using him. But before that and after that, I received."

"You can't," I said. "Not while you're married out of the Church."

"Maybe I'm wrong, but I don't think the Church is so smart about sex. Bob wouldn't get the marriage blessed, so a priest would have told me to leave him. I loved him, though, and for a long time I thought he loved me, needed me—so I stayed with him and tried to keep peace and bring up my sons. And the Eucharist is the sacrament of love and I needed it very badly those five years and nobody can keep me away."

I got up and took our glasses and made drinks. When I turned from the sink she was watching me.

"Do you still go to confession so much?" she said.

I sat down, avoiding her eyes, then I thought, what the hell, if you can't tell Janet you can't tell anybody. So looking at the screen door and the bugs thumping from the dark outside, I told her how it was in high school and about Yvonne, though I didn't tell her name, and my aborted confession to Father Broussard. She was kind to me, busying herself with cigarettes and her drink while I talked. Then she said: "You're right, Harry. You're absolutely right."

"You really think so?"

"I know this much: too many of those celibates teach sex the way it is for them. They make it introverted, so you come out of their schools believing sex is something between you and yourself, or between you and God. Instead of between you and other people. Like my affair. It wasn't wrong because I was married. Hell, Bob didn't care, in fact he was glad because it gave him more freedom. It was wrong because I hurt the guy." A Yankee word on her tongue, *guy,* and she said it with that accent from up there among snow and lakes. "If Bob had stayed home and taken a *Playboy* to the bathroom once in a while I might still have a husband. So if that's sin, I don't understand sin."

"Well," I said. Then looking at her, I grinned and it kept spreading and turned into a laugh. "You're something, all right," I said. "Old Janet, you're something."

But I still wasn't the renegade Janet was, I wanted absolution from a priest, and next morning while Mother and Daddy were happily teasing us about our hangovers, I decided to get it done. That afternoon I called Father Grassi, then told Janet where I was going, and that I would drive her around town when I got back. Father Grassi answered the door at the rectory; he was wearing a white shirt with his black trousers, a small man with a ruddy face and dark whiskers. I asked if I could speak to him in his office.

"I think so," he said. "Do you come from the Pope?"

"No, Father. I just want to confess."

"So it's you who will be the saint today, not me. Yes, come in."

He led me to his office, put his stole around his neck, and sat in the swivel chair behind his desk; I kneeled beside him on the carpet, and he shielded his face with his hand, as though we were in the confessional and he could not see me. I whispered, "Bless me Father, for I have sinned," my hands clasped at my waist, my head bowed. "My last confession was six weeks ago, but I was refused absolution. By Father Broussard."

"Is that so? You don't look like a very bad young man to me. Are you some kind of criminal?"

"I confessed masturbation, Father."

"Yes? Then what?"

"I told him I didn't think it was a sin."

"I see. Well, poor Father Broussard: I'd be confused too, if you confessed something as a sin and then said you didn't think it was a sin. You should take better care of your priests, my friend."

I opened my eyes: his hand was still in place on his cheek, and he was looking straight ahead, over his desk at the bookshelf against the wall.

"I guess so," I said. "And now I'm bothering you."

"Oh no: you're no trouble. The only disappointment is you weren't sent by the Pope. But since that's the way it is, then we may just as well talk about sins. We had in the seminary a book of moral theology and in that book, my friend, it was written that masturbation was worse than rape, because at least rape was the carrying out of a natural instinct. What about that?"

"Do you believe that, Father?"

"Do you?"

"No, Father."

"Neither do I. I burned the book when I left the seminary, but not only for that reason. The book also said, among other things, let the buyer beware. So you tell me about sin and we'll educate each other."

"I went to the Brothers' school."

"Ah, yes. Nice fellows, those Brothers."

"Yes, Father. But I think they concentrated too much on the body. One's own body, I mean. And back then I believed it all, and one day I even wanted to mutilate myself. Then last fall I had a girl."

"What does that mean, you had a girl? You mean you were lovers?"

"Yes, Father. But I shouldn't have had a girl, because I believed my semen was the most important part of sex, so the first time I made love with her I was waiting for it, like my soul was listening for it—you see? Because I wouldn't know how I felt about her until I knew how I felt about ejaculating with her."

"And how did you feel? Did you want to mutilate yourself with a can opener, or maybe something worse?"

"I was happy, Father."

"Yes."

"So after that we were lovers. Or she was, but I wasn't. I was just happy because I could ejaculate without hating myself, so I was still masturbating, you see, but with her—does that make sense?"

"Oh yes, my friend. I've known that since I left the seminary. Always there is too much talk of self-abuse. You see, even the term is a bad one. Have you finished your confession?"

"I want to confess about the girl again, because when I confessed it before it wasn't right. I made love to her without loving her and the last time I made love to her I told some boys about it."

"Yes. Anything else?"

"No, Father."

"Good. There is a line in St. John that I like very much. It is Christ praying to the Father and He says: 'I do not pray that You take them out of the world, but that You keep them from evil.' Do you understand that?"

"I think so, Father."

"Then for your penance, say alleluia three times."

Next afternoon Janet and I took her boys crabbing. We had an ice chest of beer and we set it under the small pavilion at the center of the wharf, then I put out six crab lines, tying them to the guard rail. I remembered the summer before she got married Janet and I had gone crabbing, then cooked them for the family: we had a large pot of water on the stove and when the water was boiling I held the gunny sack of live crabs over it and they came falling out, splashing into the water; they worked their claws, moved sluggishly, then died. And Janet had said: *I keep waiting for them to scream.*

It was a hot day, up in the nineties. Someone was waterskiing on the lake, which was saltwater and connected by canal to the Gulf, but we had the wharf to ourselves, and we drank beer in the shade while Paul and Lee did the crabbing. They lost the first couple, so I left the pavilion and squatted at the next line. The boys flanked me, lying on their bellies and looking down where the line went into the dark water; they had their shirts off, and their hot tan shoulders and arms brushed my legs. I gently pulled the line up until we saw a crab just below the surface, swimming and nibbling at the chunk of ham.

"Okay, Lee. Put the net down in the water, then bring it up under him so you don't knock him away."

He lowered the pole and scooped the net slowly under the crab.

"I got him!"

"That's it. You just have to go slow, that's all."

He stood and lifted the net and laid it on the wharf.

"Look how big," Paul said.

"He's a good one," I said. "Put him in the sack."

But they crouched over the net, watching the crab push his claws through.

"Poor little crab," Lee said. "You're going to die."

"Does it hurt 'em, Harry?" Paul said.

"I don't know."

"It'd hurt me," he said.

"I guess it does, for a second or two."

"How long's a second?" Lee said.

I pinched his arm.

"About like that."

"That's not too long," he said.

"No. Put him in the sack now, and catch some more."

I went back to my beer on the bench. Paul was still crouching over the crab, poking a finger at its back. Then Lee held open the gunny sack and Paul turned the net over and shook it and the crab fell in.

"Goodbye, big crab," he said.

"Goodbye, poor crab," Lee said.

They went to another line. For a couple of hours, talking to Janet, I watched them and listened to their bare feet on the wharf and their voices as they told each crab goodbye. Sometimes one of them would stop and look across the water and pull at his pecker, and I remembered that day hot as this one when I was sixteen and I wanted to cut mine off. I reached deep under the ice and got a cold beer for Janet and I thought of Yvonne sitting at that kitchen table at three in the morning, tired, her lipstick worn off, her eyes fixed on a space between the people in the room. Then I looked at the boys lying on their bellies and reaching down for another crab, and I hoped they would grow well, those strong little bodies, those kind hearts.

RICHARD FORD

Richard Ford was born in Jackson, Mississippi. He attended public schools there and also spent a considerable amount of time in his youth in Little Rock, Arkansas. He attended college at Michigan State University, as well as the University of California, and Washington University Law School in St. Louis. He is married to Kristina Ford and lives in western Montana and in Mississippi. He is the author of three novels, *A Piece of My Heart*, *The Ultimate Good Luck*, and *The Sportswriter*, and one volume of stories, *Rock Springs* (1987).

Rock Springs

EDNA and I had started down from Kalispell, heading for Tampa-St. Pete where I still had some friends from the old glory days who wouldn't turn me in to the police. I had managed to scrape with the law in Kalispell over several bad checks—which is a prison crime in Montana. And I knew Edna was already looking at her cards and thinking about a move, since it wasn't the first time I'd been in law scrapes in my life. She herself had already had her own troubles, losing her kids and keeping her ex-husband, Danny, from breaking in her house and stealing her things while she was at work, which was really why I had moved in in the first place, that and needing to give my little daughter, Cheryl, a better shake in things.

I don't know what was between Edna and me, just beached by the same tides when you got down to it. Though love has been built on frailer ground than that, as I well know. And when I came in the house that afternoon, I just asked her if she wanted to go to Florida with me, leave things where they sat, and she said, "Why not? My datebook's not that full."

Edna and I had been a pair eight months, more or less man and wife, some of which time I had been out of work, and some when I'd worked at the dog track as a lead-out and could help with the rent and talk sense to Danny when he came around. Danny was afraid of me because Edna had told him I'd been in prison in Florida for killing a man, though that wasn't true. I had once been in jail in Tallahassee for stealing tires and had gotten into a fight on the country farm where a man had lost his eye. But I hadn't done the hurting, and Edna just wanted the story worse than it was so Danny wouldn't act crazy and make her have to take her kids back, since she had made a good adjustment to not having them, and I already had Cheryl with me. I'm not a violent person and would never put a man's eye out, much less kill someone. My former wife, Helen, would come all the way from Waikiki Beach to testify to that. We never had violence, and I believe in crossing the street to stay out of trouble's way. Though Danny didn't know that.

But we were half down through Wyoming, going toward I-80 and feeling good about things, when the oil light flashed on in the car I'd stolen, a sign I knew to be a bad one.

I'd gotten us a good car, a cranberry Mercedes I'd stolen out of an ophthalmologist's lot in Whitefish, Montana. I stole it because I thought it would be comfortable over a long haul, because I thought it got good mileage, which it didn't, and because I'd never had a good car in my life, just old Chevy junkers and used trucks back from when I was a kid swamping citrus with Cubans.

The car made us all high that day. I ran the windows up and down, and Edna told us some jokes and made faces. She could be lively. Her features would light up like a beacon and you could see her beauty, which wasn't ordinary. It all made me giddy, and I drove clear down to Bozeman, then straight on through the park to Jackson Hole. I rented us the bridal suite in the Quality Court in Jackson and left Cheryl and her little dog, Duke, sleeping while Edna and I drove to a rib barn and drank beer and laughed till after midnight.

It felt like a whole new beginning for us, bad memories left behind and a new horizon to build on. I got so worked up, I had a tattoo done on my arm that said FAMOUS TIMES, and Edna bought a Bailey hat with an Indian feather band and a little turquoise-and-silver bracelet for Cheryl, and we made love on the seat of the car in the Quality Court parking lot just as the sun was burning up on the Snake River, and everything seemed then like the end of the rainbow.

It was that very enthusiasm, in fact, that made me keep the car one day longer instead of driving it into the river and stealing another one, like I should've done and *had* done before.

Where the car went bad there wasn't a town in sight or even a house, just some low mountains maybe fifty miles away or maybe a hundred, a barbed-wire fence in both directions, hardpan prairie, and some hawks riding the evening air seizing insects.

I got out to look at the motor, and Edna got out with Cheryl and the dog to let them have a pee by the car. I checked the water and checked the oil stick, and both of them said perfect.

"What's that light mean, Earl?" Edna said. She had come and stood by the car with her hat on. She was just sizing things up for herself.

"We shouldn't run it," I said. "Something's not right in the oil."

She looked around at Cheryl and Little Duke, who were peeing on the hardtop side-by-side like two little dolls, then out at the mountains, which were becoming black and lost in the distance. "What're we doing?" she said. She wasn't worried yet, but she wanted to know what I was thinking about.

"Let me try it again."

"That's a good idea," she said, and we all got back in the car.

When I turned the motor over, it started right away and the red light stayed off and there weren't any noises to make you think something was wrong. I let it idle a minute, then pushed the accelerator down and watched the red bulb. But there wasn't any light on, and I started wondering if maybe I hadn't dreamed I saw it, or that it had been the sun catching an angle off the window chrome, or maybe I was scared of something and didn't know it.

"What's the matter with it, Daddy?" Cheryl said from the backseat. I looked back at her, and she had on her turquoise bracelet and Edna's hat set back on the back of her head and that little black-and-white Heinz dog on her lap. She looked like a little cowgirl in the movies.

"Nothing, honey, everything's fine now," I said.

"Little Duke tinkled where I tinkled," Cheryl said, and laughed.

"You're two of a kind," Edna said, not looking back. Edna was usually good with Cheryl, but I knew she was tired now. We hadn't had much sleep, and she had a tendency to get cranky when she didn't sleep. "We oughta ditch this damn car first chance we get," she said.

"What's the first chance we got?" I asked, because I knew she'd been at the map.

"Rock Springs, Wyoming," Edna said with conviction. "Thirty miles down this road." She pointed out ahead.

I had wanted all along to drive the car into Florida like a big success story. But I knew Edna was right about it, that we shouldn't take crazy chances. I had kept thinking of it as my car and not the ophthalmologist's, and that was how you got caught in these things.

"Then my belief is we ought to go to Rock Springs and negotiate ourselves a new car," I said. I wanted to stay upbeat, like everything was panning out right.

"That's a great idea," Edna said, and she leaned over and kissed me hard on the mouth.

"That's a great idea," Cheryl said. "Let's pull on out of here right now."

The sunset that day I remember as being the prettiest I'd ever seen. Just as it touched the rim of the horizon, it all at once fired the air into jewels and red sequins the precise likes of which I had never seen before and haven't seen since. The West has it all over everywhere for sunsets, even Florida, where it's supposedly flat but where half the time trees block your view.

"It's cocktail hour," Edna said after we'd driven awhile. "We ought to have a drink and celebrate something." She felt better thinking we were going to get rid of the car. It certainly had dark troubles and was something you'd want to put behind you.

Edna had out a whiskey bottle and some plastic cups and was measuring levels on the glove-box lid. She liked drinking, and she liked drinking in the car, which was something you got used to in Montana, where it wasn't against the law, but where, strangely enough, a bad check would land you in Deer Lodge Prison for a year.

"Did I ever tell you I once had a monkey?" Edna said, setting my drink on the dashboard where I could reach it when I was ready. Her spirits were already picked up. She was like that, up one minute and down the next.

"I don't think you ever did tell me that," I said. "Where were you then?"

"Missoula," she said. She put her bare feet on the dash and rested the cup on her breasts. "I was waitressing at the AmVets. This was before I met you. Some guy came in one day with a monkey. A spider monkey. And I said, just to be joking, 'I'll roll you for that monkey.' And the guy said, 'Just one roll?' And I said, 'Sure.' He put the monkey down on the bar, picked up the cup, and rolled out boxcars. I picked it up and rolled out three fives. And I just stood there looking at the guy. He was just some guy passing through, I guess a vet. He got a strange look on his face—I'm sure not as strange as the one I had—but he looked kind of sad and surprised and satisfied all at once. I said, 'We can roll again.' But he said, 'No, I never roll twice for anything.' And he sat and drank a beer and talked about one thing and another for a while, about nuclear war and building a stronghold somewhere up in the Bitterroot, whatever it was, while I just watched the monkey, wondering what I was going to do with it when the guy left. And pretty soon he got up and said, 'Well, good-bye, Chipper'—that was the monkey's name, of course. And then he left before I could say anything. And the monkey just sat on the bar all that night. I don't know what made me think of that, Earl. Just something weird. I'm letting my mind wander."

"That's perfectly fine," I said. I took a drink of my drink. "I'd never own a monkey," I said after a minute. "They're too nasty. I'm sure Cheryl would like a monkey, though, wouldn't you, honey?" Cheryl was down on the seat playing with Little Duke. She used to talk about monkeys all the time then. "What'd you ever do with that monkey?" I said, watching the speedometer. We were having to go slower now because the red light kept fluttering on. And all I could do to keep if off was go slower. We were going maybe thirty-five and it was an hour before dark, and I was hoping Rock Springs wasn't far away.

"You really want to know?" Edna said. She gave me a quick glance, then looked back at the empty desert as if she was brooding over it.

"Sure," I said. I was still upbeat. I figured I could worry about breaking down and let other people be happy for a change.

"I kept it a week." And she seemed gloomy all of a sudden, as if she saw some aspect of the story she had never seen before. "I took it home and back and forth to the AmVets on my shifts. And it didn't cause any trouble. I fixed a chair up for it to sit on, back of the bar, and people liked it. It made a nice little clicking noise. We changed its name to Mary because the bartender figured out it was a girl. Though I was never really comfortable with it at home. I felt like it watched me too much. Then one day a guy came in, some guy who'd been in Vietnam, still wore a fatigue coat. And he said to me, 'Don't you know that a monkey'll kill you? It's got more strength in its fingers than you got in your whole body.' He said people had been killed in Vietnam by monkeys, bunches of them marauding while you were asleep, killing you and covering you with leaves. I didn't believe a word of it, except that when I got home and got undressed I started looking over across the room at Mary on her chair in the dark watching me. And I got the creeps. And after a while I got up and went out to the car, got a length of clothesline wire, and came back in and wired her to the doorknob through her little silver collar, then went back and tried to sleep. And I guess I must've slept the sleep of the dead—though I don't remember it—because when I got up I found Mary had tipped off her chair-back and hanged herself on the wire line. I'd made it too short."

Edna seemed badly affected by that story and slid low in the seat so she couldn't see out over the dash. "Isn't that a shameful story, Earl, what happened to that poor little monkey?"

"I see a town! I see a town!" Cheryl started yelling from the back seat, and right up Little Duke started yapping and the whole car fell into a racket. And sure enough she had seen something I hadn't, which was Rock Springs, Wyoming, at the bottom of a long hill, a little glowing jewel in the desert with I-80 running on the north side and the black desert spread out behind.

"That's it, honey," I said. "That's where we're going. You saw it first."

"We're hungry," Cheryl said. "Little Duke wants some fish, and I want spaghetti." She put her arms around my neck and hugged me.

"Then you'll just get it," I said. "You can have anything you want. And so can Edna and so can Little Duke." I looked over at Edna, smiling, but she was staring at me with eyes that were fierce with anger. "What's wrong?" I said.

"Don't you care anything about that awful thing that happened to me?" Her mouth was drawn tight, and her eyes kept cutting back at Cheryl and Little Duke, as if they had been tormenting her.

"Of course I do," I said. "I thought that was an awful thing." I didn't want her to be unhappy. We were almost there, and pretty soon we could sit down and have a real meal without thinking somebody might be hurting us.

"You want to know what I did with that monkey?" Edna said.

"Sure I do," I said.

"I put her in a green garbage bag, put it in the trunk of my car, drove to the dump, and threw her in the trash." She was staring at me darkly, as if the story meant something to her that was real important but that only she could see and that the rest of the world was a fool for.

"Well, that's horrible," I said. "But I don't see what else you could do. You didn't mean to kill it. You'd have done it differently if you had. And then you had to get rid of it, and I don't know what else you could have done. Throwing it away might seem unsympathetic to somebody, probably, but not to me. Sometimes that's all you can do, and you can't worry about what somebody else thinks." I tried to smile at her, but the red light was staying on if I pushed the accelerator at all, and I was trying to gauge if we could coast to Rock Springs before the car gave out completely. I looked at Edna again. "What else can I say?" I said.

"Nothing," she said, and stared back at the dark highway. "I should've known that's what you'd think. You've got a character that leaves something out, Earl. I've known that a long time."

"And yet here you are," I said. "And you're not doing so bad. Things could be a lot worse. At least we're all together here."

"Things could always be worse," Edna said. "You could go to the electric chair tomorrow."

"That's right," I said. "And somewhere somebody probably will. Only it won't be you."

"I'm hungry," said Cheryl. "When're we gonna eat? Let's find a motel. I'm tired of this. Little Duke's tired of it too."

Where the car stopped rolling was some distance from the town, though you could see the clear outline of the interstate in the dark with Rock Springs lighting up the sky behind. You could hear the big tractors hitting the spacers in the overpass, revving up for the climb to the mountains.

I shut off the lights.

"What're we going to do now?" Edna said irritably, giving me a bitter look.

"I'm figuring it," I said. "It won't be hard, whatever it is. You won't have to do anything."

"I'd hope not," she said and looked the other way.

Across the road and across a dry wash a hundred yards was what looked like a huge mobile-home town, with a factory or refinery of some kind lit up behind it and in full swing. There were lights on in a lot of the mobile homes, and there were cars moving along an access road that ended near the freeway overpass a mile the other way. The lights in the mobile homes seemed friendly to me, and I knew right then what I should do.

"Get out," I said, opening my door.

"Are we walking?" Edna said.

"We're pushing."

"I'm not pushing." Edna reached up and locked her door.

"All right," I said. "Then you just steer."

"You're pushing us to Rock Springs, are you, Earl? It doesn't look like it's more than about three miles."

"I'll push," Cheryl said from the back.

"No, hon. Daddy'll push. You just get out with Little Duke and move out of the way."

Edna gave me a threatening look, just as if I'd tried to hit her. But when I got out she slid into my seat and took the wheel, staring angrily ahead straight into the cottonwood scrub.

"Edna can't drive that car," Cheryl said from out in the dark. "She'll run it in the ditch."

"Yes, she can, hon. Edna can drive it as good as I can. Probably better."

"No she can't," Cheryl said. "No she can't either." And I thought she was about to cry, but she didn't.

I told Edna to keep the ignition on so it wouldn't lock up and to steer into the cottonwoods with the parking lights on so she could see. And when I started, she steered it straight off into the trees, and I kept pushing until we were twenty yards into the cover and the tires sank in the soft sand and nothing at all could be seen from the road.

"Now where are we?" she said, sitting at the wheel. Her voice was tired and hard, and I knew she could have put a good meal to use. She had a sweet nature, and I recognized that this wasn't her fault but mine. Only I wished she could be more hopeful.

"You stay right here, and I'll go over to that trailer park and call us a cab," I said.

"What cab?" Edna said, her mouth wrinkled as if she'd never heard anything like that in her life.

"There'll be cabs," I said, and tried to smile at her. "There's cabs everywhere."

"What're you going to tell him when he gets here? Our stolen car broke down and we need a ride to where we can steal another one? That'll be a big hit, Earl."

"I'll talk," I said. "You just listen to the radio for ten minutes and then walk on out to the shoulder like nothing was suspicious. And you and Cheryl act nice. She doesn't need to know about this car."

"Like we're not suspicious enough already, right?" Edna looked up at me out of the lighted car. "You don't think right, did you know that, Earl? You think the world's stupid and you're smart. But that's not how it is. I feel sorry for you. You might've *been* something, but things just went crazy someplace."

I had a thought about poor Danny. He was a vet and crazy as a shit-house mouse, and I was glad he wasn't in for all this. "Just get the baby in the car," I said, trying to be patient. "I'm hungry like you are."

"I'm tired of this," Edna said. "I wish I'd stayed in Montana."

"Then you can go back in the morning," I said. "I'll buy the ticket and put you on the bus. But not till then."

"Just get on with it, Earl." She slumped down in the seat, turning off the parking lights with one foot and the radio on with the other.

The mobile-home community was as big as any I'd ever seen. It was attached in some way to the plant that was lighted up behind it, because I could see a car once in a while leave one of the trailer streets, turn in the direction of the plant, then go slowly into it. Everything in the plant was white, and you could see that all the trailers were painted white and looked exactly alike. A deep hum came out of the plant, and I thought as I got closer that it wouldn't be a location I'd ever want to work in.

I went right to the first trailer where there was a light, and knocked on the metal door. Kids' toys were lying in the gravel around the little wood steps, and I could hear talking on TV that suddenly went off. I heard a woman's voice talking, and then the door opened wide.

A large Negro woman with a wide, friendly face stood in the doorway. She smiled at me and moved forward as if she was going to come out, but she stopped at the top step. There was a little Negro boy behind her peeping out from behind her legs, watching me with his eyes half closed. The trailer had that feeling that no one else was inside, which was a feeling I knew something about.

"I'm sorry to intrude," I said. "But I've run up on a little bad luck tonight. My name's Earl Middleton."

The woman looked at me, then out into the night toward the freeway as if what I had said was something she was going to be able to see. "What kind of bad luck?" she said, looking down at me again.

"My car broke down out on the highway," I said. "I can't fix it myself, and I wondered if I could use your phone to call for help."

The woman smiled down at me knowingly. "We can't live without cars, can we?"

"That's the honest truth," I said.

"They're like our hearts," she said, her face shining in the little bulb light that burned beside the door. "Where's your car situated?"

I turned and looked over into the dark, but I couldn't see anything because of where we'd put it. "It's over there," I said. "You can't see it in the dark."

"Who all's with you now?" the woman said. "Have you got your wife with you?"

"She's with my little girl and our dog in the car," I said. "My daughter's asleep or I would have brought them."

"They shouldn't be left in the dark by themselves," the woman said and frowned. "There's too much unsavoriness out there."

"The best I can do is hurry back." I tried to look sincere, since everything except Cheryl being asleep and Edna being my wife was the truth. The truth is meant to serve you if you'll let it, and I wanted it to serve me. "I'll pay for the phone call," I said. "If you'll bring the phone to the door I'll call from right here."

The woman looked at me again as if she was searching for a truth of her own, then back out into the night. She was maybe in her sixties, but I couldn't say for sure. "You're not going to rob me, are you, Mr. Middleton?" She smiled like it was a joke between us.

"Not tonight," I said, and smiled a genuine smile. "I'm not up to it tonight. Maybe another time."

"Then I guess Terrel and I can let you use our phone with Daddy not here, can't we, Terrel? This my grandson, Terrel Junior, Mr. Middleton." She put her hand on the boy's head and looked down at him. "Terrel won't talk. Though if he did he'd tell you to use our phone. He's a sweet boy." She opened the screen for me to come in.

The trailer was a big one with a new rug and a new couch and a living room that expanded to give the space of a real house. Something good and sweet was cooking in the kitchen, and the trailer felt like it was somebody's comfortable new home instead of just temporary. I've lived in trailers, but they were just snailbacks with one room and no toilet, and they always felt cramped and unhappy—though I've thought maybe it might've been me that was unhappy in them.

There was a big Sony TV and a lot of kids' toys scattered on the floor. I recognized a Greyhound bus I'd gotten for Cheryl. The phone was beside a new leather recliner, and the Negro woman pointed for me to sit down and call and gave me the phone book. Terrel began fingering his toys and the woman sat on the couch while I called, watching me and smiling.

There were three listings for cab companies, all with one number different. I called the numbers in order and didn't get an answer until the last one, which answered with the name of the second company. I said I was on the highway beyond the interstate and that my wife and family needed to be taken to town and I would arrange for a tow later. While I was giving the location, I looked up the name of a tow service to tell the driver in case he asked.

When I hung up, the Negro woman was sitting looking at me with the same look she had been staring with into the dark, a look that seemed to want truth. She was smiling, though. Something pleased her and I reminded her of it.

"This is a very nice home," I said, resting in the recliner, which felt like the driver's seat of the Mercedes, and where I'd have been happy to stay.

"This isn't *our* house, Mr. Middleton," the Negro woman said. "The company owns these. They give them to us for nothing. We have our own home in Rockford, Illinois."

"That's wonderful," I said.

"It's never wonderful when you have to be away from home, Mr. Middleton, though we're only here three months, and it'll be easier when Terrel Junior begins his special school. You see, our son was killed in the war, and his wife ran off without Terrel Junior. Though you shouldn't worry. He can't understand us. His little feelings can't be hurt." The woman folded her hands in her lap and smiled in a satisfied way. She was an attractive woman, and had on a blue-and-pink floral dress that made her seem bigger than she could've been, just the right woman to sit on the couch she was sitting on. She was good nature's picture, and I was glad she could be, with her little brain-damaged boy, living in a place where no one in his right mind would want to live a minute. "Where do *you* live, Mr. Middleton?" she said politely, smiling in the same sympathetic way.

"My family and I are in transit," I said. "I'm an ophthalmologist, and we're moving back to Florida, where I'm from. I'm setting up practice in some little town where it's warm year-round. I haven't decided where."

"Florida's a wonderful place," the woman said. "I think Terrel would like it there."

"Could I ask you something?" I said.

"You certainly may," the woman said. Terrel had begun pushing his Greyhound across the front of the TV screen, making a scratch that no one watching the set could miss. "Stop that, Terrel Junior," the woman said quietly. But Terrel kept pushing his bus on the glass, and she smiled at me again as if we both understood something sad. Except I knew Cheryl would never damage a television set. She had respect for nice things, and I was sorry for the lady that Terrel didn't. "What did you want to ask?" the woman said.

"What goes on in the plant or whatever it is back there beyond these trailers, where all the lights are on?"

"Gold," the woman said and smiled.

"It's what?" I said.

"Gold," the Negro woman said, smiling as she had for almost all the time I'd been there. "It's a gold mine."

"They're mining gold back there?" I said, pointing.

"Every night and every day." She smiled in a pleased way.

"Does your husband work there?" I said.

"He's the assayer," she said. "He controls the quality. He works three months a year, and we live the rest of the time at home in Rockford. We've waited a long time for this. We've been happy to have our grandson, but I won't say I'll be sorry to have him go. We're ready to start our lives over." She smiled broadly at me and then at Terrel, who was giving her a spiteful look from the floor. "You said you had a daughter," the Negro woman said. "And what's her name?"

"Irma Cheryl," I said. "She's named for my mother."

"That's nice. And she's healthy, too. I can see it in your face." She looked at Terrel Junior with pity.

"I guess I'm lucky," I said.

"So far you are. But children bring you grief, the same way they bring you joy. We were unhappy for a long time before my husband got his job in the gold mine. Now, when Terrel starts to school, we'll be kids again." She stood up. "You might miss your cab, Mr. Middleton," she said, walking toward the door, though not to be forcing me out. She was too polite. "If *we* can't see your car, the cab surely won't be able to."

"That's true." I got up off the recliner, where I'd been so comfortable. "None of us have eaten yet, and your food makes me know how hungry we probably all are."

"There are fine restaurants in town, and you'll find them," the Negro woman said. "I'm sorry you didn't meet my husband. He's a wonderful man. He's everything to me."

"Tell him I appreciate the phone," I said. "You saved me."

"You weren't hard to save," the woman said. "Saving people is what we were all put on earth to do. I just passed you on to whatever's coming to you."

"Let's hope it's good," I said, stepping back into the dark.

"I'll be hoping, Mr. Middleton. Terrel and I will both be hoping."

I waved to her as I walked out into the darkness toward the car where it was hidden in the night.

The cab had already arrived when I got there. I could see its little red-and-green roof lights all the way across the dry wash, and it made me worry that Edna was already saying something to get us in trouble, something about the car or where we'd come from, something that would cast suspicion on us. I thought, then, how I never planned things well enough. There was always a gap between my plan and what happened, and I only responded to things as they came along and hoped I wouldn't get in trouble. I was an offender in the law's eyes. But I always *thought* differently, as if I weren't an offender and had no intention of being one, which was the truth. But as I read on a napkin once, between the idea and the act a whole kingdom lies. And I had a hard time with my acts, which were oftentimes offender's acts, and my ideas, which were as good as the gold they mined there where the bright lights were blazing.

"We're waiting for you, Daddy," Cheryl said when I crossed the road. "The taxicab's already here."

"I see, hon," I said, and gave Cheryl a big hug. The cabdriver was sitting in the driver's seat having a smoke with the lights on inside. Edna was leaning against the back of the cab between the taillights, wearing her Bailey hat. "What'd you tell him?" I said when I got close.

"Nothing," she said. "What's there to tell?"

"Did he see the car?"

She glanced over in the direction of the trees where we had hid the Mercedes. Nothing was visible in the darkness, though I could hear Little Duke combing around in the underbrush tracking something, his little collar tinkling. "Where're we going?" she said. "I'm so hungry I could pass out."

"Edna's in a terrible mood," Cheryl said. "She already snapped at me."

"We're tired, honey," I said. "So try to be nicer."

"She's never nice," Cheryl said.

"Run go get Little Duke," I said. "And hurry back."

"I guess *my* questions come last here, right?" Edna said.

I put my arm around her. "That's not true."

"Did you find somebody over there in the trailers you'd rather stay with? You were gone long enough."

"That's not a thing to say," I said. "I was just trying to make things look right, so we don't get put in jail."

"So *you* don't, you mean." Edna laughed a little laugh I didn't like hearing.

"That's right. So I don't," I said. "I'd be the one in Dutch." I stared out at the big, lighted assemblage of white buildings and white lights beyond the trailer community, plumes of white smoke escaping up into the heartless Wyoming sky, the whole company of buildings looking like some unbelievable castle, humming away in a distorted dream. "You know what all those buildings are there?" I said to Edna, who hadn't moved and who didn't really seem to care if she ever moved anymore ever.

"No. But I can't say it matters, because it isn't a motel and it isn't a restaurant."

"It's a gold mine," I said, staring at the gold mine, which, I knew now, was a greater distance from us than it seemed, though it seemed huge and near, up against the cold sky. I thought there should've been a wall around it with guards instead of just the lights and no fence. It seemed as if anyone could go in and take what they wanted, just the way I had gone up to that woman's trailer and used the telephone, though that obviously wasn't true.

Edna began to laugh then. Not the mean laugh I didn't like, but a laugh that had something caring behind it, a full laugh that enjoyed a joke, a laugh she was laughing the first time I laid eyes on her, in Missoula in the East Gate Bar in 1979, a laugh we used to laugh together when Cheryl was still with her mother and I was working steady at the track and not stealing cars or passing bogus checks to merchants. A better time all around. And for some reason it made me laugh just hearing her, and we both stood there behind the cab in the dark, laughing at the gold mine in the desert, me with my arm around her and Cheryl out rustling up Little Duke and the cabdriver smoking in the cab and our stolen Mercedes-Benz, which I'd had such hopes for in Florida, stuck up to its axle in sand, where I'd never get to see it again.

"I always wondered what a gold mine would look like when I saw it," Edna said, still laughing, wiping a tear from her eye.

"Me too," I said. "I was always curious about it."

"We're a couple of fools, aren't we, Earl?" she said, unable to quit laughing completely. "We're two of a kind."

"It might be a good sign, though," I said.

"How could it be? It's not our gold mine. There aren't any drive-up windows." She was still laughing.

"We've seen it," I said, pointing. "That's it right there. It may mean we're getting closer. Some people never see it at all."

"In a pig's eye, Earl," she said. "You and me see it in a pig's eye."

And she turned and got in the cab to go.

The cabdriver didn't ask anything about our car or where it was, to mean he'd noticed something queer. All of which made me feel like we had made a clean break from the car and couldn't be connected with it until it was too late, if ever. The driver told us a lot about Rock Springs while he drove, that because of the gold mine a lot of people had moved there in just six months, people from all over, including New York, and that most of them lived out in the trailers. Prostitutes from New York City, whom he called "B-girls," had come into town, he said, on the prosperity tide, and Cadillacs with New York plates cruised the little streets every night, full of Negroes with big hats who ran the women. He told us that everybody who got in his cab now wanted to know where the women were, and when he got our call he almost didn't come because some of the trailers were brothels operated by the mine for engineers and computer people away from home. He said he got tired of running back and forth out there just for vile business. He said that "60 Minutes" had even done a program about Rock Springs and that a blow-up had resulted in Cheyenne, though nothing could be done unless the boom left town. "It's prosperity's fruit," the driver said. "I'd rather be poor, which is lucky for me."

He said all the motels were sky-high, but since we were a family he could show us a nice one that was affordable. But I told him we wanted a first-rate place where they took animals, and the money didn't matter because we had had a hard day and wanted to finish on a high note. I also knew that it was in the little nowhere places that the police look for you and find you. People I'd known were always being arrested in cheap hotels and tourist courts with names you'd never heard of before. Never in Holiday Inns or TraveLodges.

I asked him to drive us to the middle of town and back out again so Cheryl could see the train station, and while we were there I saw a pink Cadillac with New York plates and a TV aerial being driven slowly by a Negro in a big hat down a narrow street where there were just bars and a Chinese restaurant. It was an odd sight, nothing you could ever expect.

"There's your pure criminal element," the cabdriver said and seemed sad. "I'm sorry for people like you to see a thing like that. We've got a nice town here, but there're some that want to ruin it for everybody. There used to be a way to deal with trash and criminals, but those days are gone forever."

"You said it," Edna said.

"You shouldn't let it get *you* down," I said to him. "There's more of you than them. And there always will be. You're the best advertisement this town has. I know Cheryl will remember you and not *that* man, won't you honey?" But Cheryl was asleep by then, holding Little Duke in her arms on the taxi seat.

The driver took us to the Ramada Inn on the interstate, not far from where we'd broken down. I had a small pain of regret as we drove under the Ramada awning that we hadn't driven up in a cranberry-colored Mercedes but instead in a beat-up old Chrysler taxi driven by an old man full of complaints. Though I knew it was for the best. We were better off without that car; better, really, in any other car but that one, where the signs had turned bad.

I registered under another name and paid for the room in cash so there wouldn't be any questions. On the line where it said "Representing" I wrote "Ophthalmologist" and put "M.D." after the name. It had a nice look to it, even though it wasn't my name.

When we got to the room, which was in the back where I'd asked for it, I put Cheryl on one of the beds and Little Duke beside her so they'd sleep. She'd missed dinner, but it only meant she'd be hungry in the morning, when she could have anything she wanted. A few missed meals don't make a kid bad. I'd missed a lot of them myself and haven't turned out completely bad.

"Let's have some fried chicken," I said to Edna when she came out of the bathroom. "They have good fried chicken at Ramadas, and I noticed the buffet was still up. Cheryl can stay right here, where it's safe, till we're back."

"I guess I'm not hungry anymore," Edna said. She stood at the window staring out into the dark. I could see out the window past her some yellowish foggy glow in the sky. For a moment I thought it was the gold mine out in the distance lighting the night, though it was only the interstate.

"We could order up," I said. "Whatever you want. There's a menu on the phone book. You could just have a salad."

"You go ahead," she said. "I've lost my hungry spirit." She sat on the bed beside Cheryl and Little Duke and looked at them in a sweet way and put her hand on Cheryl's cheek just as if she'd had a fever. "Sweet little girl," she said. "Everybody loves you."

"What do you want to do?" I said. "I'd like to eat. Maybe *I'll* order up some chicken."

"Why don't you do that?" she said. "It's your favorite." And she smiled at me from the bed.

I sat on the other bed and dialed room service. I asked for chicken, garden salad, potato and a roll, plus a piece of hot apple pie and iced tea. I realized I hadn't eaten all day. When I put down the phone I saw that Edna was watching me, not in a hateful way or a loving way, just in a way that seemed to say she didn't understand something and was going to ask me about it.

"When did watching me get so entertaining?" I said and smiled at her. I was trying to be friendly. I knew how tired she must be. It was after nine o'clock.

"I was just thinking how much I hated being in a motel without a car that was mine to drive. Isn't that funny? I started feeling like that last night when that purple car wasn't mine. That purple car just gave me the willies, I guess, Earl."

"One of those cars *outside* is yours," I said. "Just stand right there and pick it out."

"I know," she said. "But that's different, isn't it?" She reached and got her blue Bailey hat, put it on her head, and set it way back like Dale Evans. She looked sweet. "I used to like to go to motels, you know," she said. "There's something secret about them and free—I was never paying, of course. But you felt safe from everything and free to do what you wanted because you'd made the decision to be there and paid that price, and all the rest was the good part. Fucking and everything, you know." She smiled at me in a good-natured way.

"Isn't that the way this is?" I was sitting on the bed, watching her, not knowing what to expect her to say next.

"I don't guess it is, Earl," she said and stared out the window. "I'm thirty-two and I'm going to have to give up on motels. I can't keep that fantasy going anymore."

"Don't you like this place?" I said and looked around at the room. I appreciated the modern paintings and the lowboy bureau and the big TV. It seemed like a plenty nice enough place to me, considering where we'd been.

"No, I don't," Edna said with real conviction. "There's no use in my getting mad at you about it. It isn't your fault. You do the best you can for everybody. But every trip teaches you something. And I've learned I need to give up on motels before some bad thing happens to me. I'm sorry."

"What does that mean?" I said, because I really didn't know what she had in mind to do, though I should've guessed.

"I guess I'll take that ticket you mentioned," she said, and got up and faced the window. "Tomorrow's soon enough. We haven't got a car to take me anyhow."

"Well, that's a fine thing," I said, sitting on the bed, feeling like I was in shock. I wanted to say something to her, to argue with her, but I couldn't think what to say that seemed right. I didn't want to be mad at her, but it made me mad.

"You've got a right to be mad at me, Earl," she said, "but I don't think you can really blame me." She turned around and faced me and sat on the windowsill, her hands on her knees. Someone knocked on the door, and I just yelled for them to set the tray down and put it on the bill.

"I guess I *do* blame you," I said, and I was angry. I thought about how I could've disappeared into that trailer community and hadn't, had come back to keep things going, had tried to take control of things for everybody when they looked bad.

"Don't. I wish you wouldn't," Edna said and smiled at me like she wanted me to hug her. "Anybody ought to have their choice in things if they can. Don't you believe that, Earl? Here I am out here in the desert where I don't know anything, in a stolen car, in a motel room under an assumed name, with no money of my own, a kid that's not mine, and the law after me. And I have a choice to get out of all of it by getting on a bus. What would you do? I know exactly what you'd do."

"You think you do," I said. But I didn't want to get into an argument about it and tell her all I could've done and didn't do. Because it wouldn't have done any good. When you get to the point of arguing, you're past the point of changing anybody's mind, even though it's supposed to be the other way, and maybe for some classes of people it is, just never mine.

Edna smiled at me and came across the room and put her arms around me where I was sitting on the bed. Cheryl rolled over and looked at us and smiled, then closed her eyes, and the room was quiet. I was beginning to think of Rock Springs in a way I knew I would always think of it, a lowdown city full of crimes and whores and disappointments, a place where a woman left me, instead of a place where I got things on the straight track once and for all, a place I saw a gold mine.

"Eat your chicken, Earl," Edna said. "Then we can go to bed. I'm tired, but I'd like to make love to you anyway. None of this is a matter of not loving you, you know that."

Sometime late in the night, after Edna was asleep, I got up and walked outside into the parking lot. It could've been anytime because there was still the light from the interstate frosting the low sky and the big red Ramada sign humming motionlessly in the night and no light at all in the east to indicate it might be morning. The lot was full of cars all nosed in, a couple of them with suitcases strapped to their roofs and their trunks weighed down with belongings the people were taking someplace, to a new home or a vacation resort in the mountains. I had laid in bed a long time after Edna was asleep, watching the Atlanta Braves on television, trying to get my mind off how I'd feel when I saw that bus pull away the next day, and how I'd feel when I turned around and there stood Cheryl and Little Duke and no one to see about them but me alone, and that the first thing I had to do was get hold of some automobile and get the plates switched, then get them some breakfast and get us all on the road to Florida, all in the space of probably two hours, since that Mercedes would certainly look less hid in the daytime than the night, and word travels fast. I've always taken care of Cheryl myself as long as I've had her with me. None of the women ever did. Most of them didn't even seem to like her, though they took care of me in a way so that I could take care of her. And I knew that once Edna left, all that was going to get harder. Though what I wanted most to do was not think about it just for a little while, try to let my mind go limp so it could be strong for the rest of what there was. I thought that the difference between a successful life and an unsuccessful one, between me at that moment and all the people who owned the cars that were nosed into their proper places in the lot, maybe between me and that woman out in the trailers by the gold mine, was how well you were able to put things like this out of your mind and not be bothered by them, and maybe, too, by how many troubles like this one you had to face in a lifetime. Through luck or design they had all faced fewer troubles, and by their own characters, they forgot them faster. And that's what I wanted for me. Fewer troubles, fewer memories of trouble.

I walked over to a car, a Pontiac with Ohio tags, one of the ones with bundles and suitcases strapped to the top and a lot more in the trunk, by the way it was riding. I looked inside the driver's window. There were maps and paperback books and sunglasses and the little plastic holders for cans that hang on the window wells. And in the back there were kids' toys and some pillows and a cat box with a cat sitting in it staring up at me like I was the face of the moon. It all looked familiar to me, the very same things I would have in my car if I had a car. Nothing seemed surprising, nothing different. Though I had a funny sensation at that moment and turned and looked up at the windows along the back of the motel. All were dark except two. Mine and another one. And I wondered, because it seemed funny, what would you think a man was doing if you saw him in the middle of the night looking in the windows of cars in the parking lot of the Ramada Inn? Would you think he was trying to get his head cleared? Would you think he was trying to get ready for a day when trouble would come down on him? Would you think his girlfriend was leaving him? Would you think he had a daughter? Would you think he was anybody like you?

ERNEST GAINES

Ernest Gaines was born in Oscar, Louisiana. He attended San Francisco State College and Stanford University. He has written five novels: *Catherine Carmier, Of Love and Dust, The Autobiography of Miss Jane Pittman, In My Father's House,* and *A Gathering of Old Men.* He published a collection of stories, *Bloodline,* in 1968. Mr. Gaines teaches creative writing at the University of Southern Louisiana in Lafayette.

Just Like a Tree

I shall not;
    I shall not be moved.
I shall not;
    I shall not be moved.
Just like a tree that's
planted 'side the water.
    Oh, I shall not be moved.

I made my home in glory;
    I shall not be moved.
Made my home in glory;
    I shall not be moved.
Just like a tree that's
planted 'side the water.
    Oh, I shall not be moved.
        from an old Negro spiritual

CHUCKKIE

PA hit him on the back and he jeck in them chains like he pulling, but ever'body in the wagon know he ain't, and Pa hit him on the back again. He jeck again like he pulling, but even Big Red know he ain't doing a thing.

"That's why I'm go'n get a horse," Pa say. "He'll kill that other mule. Get up there, Mr. Bascom."

"Oh, let him alone," Gran'mon say. "How would you like it if you was pulling a wagon in all that mud?"

Pa don't answer Gran'mon; he just hit Mr. Bascom on the back again.

"That's right, kill him," Gran'mon say. "See where you get mo' money to buy another one."

"Get up there, Mr. Bascom," Pa say.

"You hear me talking to you, Emile?" Gran'mon say. "You want me hit you with something?"

"Ma, he ain't pulling," Pa say.

"Leave him alone," Gran'mon say.

Pa shake the lines little bit, but Mr. Bascom don't even feel it, and you can see he letting Big Red do all the pulling again. Pa say something kind o' low to hisself, and I can't make out what it is.

I low' my head little bit, 'cause that wind and fine rain was hitting me in the face, and I can feel Mama pressing close to me to keep me warm. She sitting on one side o' me and Pa sitting on the other side o' me, and Gran'mon in the back o' me in her setting chair. Pa didn't want bring the setting chair, telling Gran'mon there was two boards in that wagon already and she could sit on one of 'em all by herself if she wanted to, but Gran'mon say she was taking her setting chair with her if Pa liked it or not. She say she didn't ride in no wagon on nobody board, and if Pa liked it or not, that setting chair was going.

"Let her take her setting chair," Mama say. "What's wrong with taking her setting chair."

"Ehhh, Lord," Pa say, and picked up the setting chair and took it out to the wagon. "I guess I'll have to bring it back in the house, too, when we come back from there."

Gran'mon went and clambed in the wagon and moved her setting chair back little bit and sat down and folded her arms, waiting for us to get in, too. I got in and knelt down 'side her, but Mama told me to come up there and sit on the board 'side her and Pa so I could stay warm. Soon 's I sat down, Pa hit Mr. Bascom on the back, saying what a trifling thing Mr. Bascom was, and soon 's he got some mo' money he was getting rid o' Mr. Bascom and getting him a horse.

I raise my head to look see how far we is.

"That's it, yonder," I say.

"Stop pointing," Mama say, "and keep you hand in your pocket."

"Where?" Gran'mon say, back there in her setting chair.

"'Cross the ditch, yonder," I say.

"Can't see a thing for this rain," Gran'mon say.

"Can't hardly see it," I say. "But you can see the light little bit. That chinaball tree standing in the way."

"Poor soul," Gran'mon say. "Poor soul."

I know Gran'mon was go'n say "poor soul, poor soul," 'cause she had been saying "poor soul, poor soul," ever since she heard Aunt Fe was go'n leave from back there.

Darn cane crop to finish getting in and only a mule and a half to do it. If I had my way I'd take that shotgun and a load o' buckshots and—but what's the use.

"Get up, Mr. Bascom—please," I say to that little dried-up, long-eared, tobacco-color thing. "Please, come up. Do your share for God sake—if you don't mind. I know it's hard pulling in all that mud, but if you don't do your share, then Big Red'll have to do his and yours, too. So, please, if it ain't asking you too much to—"

"Oh, Emile, shut up," Leola say.

"I can't hit him," I say, "or Mama back there'll hit me. So I have to talk to him. Please, Mr. Bascom, if you don't mind it. For my sake. No, not for mine; for God sake. No, not even for His'n; for Big Red sake. A fellow mule just like yourself is. Please, come up."

"Now, you hear that boy blaspheming God right in front o' me there," Mama say. "Ehhh, Lord—just keep it up. All this bad weather there like this whole world coming apart—a clap o' thunder come there and knock the fool out you. Just keep it up."

Maybe she right, and I stop. I look at Mr. Bascom there doing nothing, and I just give up. That mule know long 's Mama's alive he go'n do just what he want to do. He know when Papa was dying he told Mama to look after him, and he know no matter what he do, no matter what he don't do, Mama ain't go'n never let me do him anything. Sometimes I even feel Mama care mo' for Mr. Bascom 'an she care for me her own son.

We come up to the gate and I pull back on the lines.

"Whoa up, Big Red," I say. "You don't have to stop, Mr. Bascom. You never started."

I can feel Mama looking at me back there in that setting chair, but she don't say nothing.

"Here," I say to Chuckkie.

He take the lines and I jump down on the ground to open the old beat-up gate. I see Etienne's horse in the yard, and I see Chris new red tractor 'side the house, shining in the rain. When Mama die, I say to myself, Mr. Bascom, you going. Ever'body getting tractors and horses and I'm still stuck with you. You going, brother.

"Can you make it through?" I ask Chuckkie. "That gate ain't too wide."

"I can do it," he say.

"Be sure to make Mr. Bascom pull," I say.

"Emile, you better get back up here and drive 'em through," Leola say. "Chuckkie might break up that wagon."

"No, let him stay down there and give orders," Mama say, back there in that setting chair.

"He can do it," I say. "Come on, Chuckkie boy."

"Come up, here, mule," Chuckkie say.

And soon 's he say that, Big Red make a lunge for the yard, and Mr. Bascom don't even move, and 'fore I can bat my eyes I hear *pow-wow; sagg-sagg; pow-wow.* But above all that noise, Leola up there screaming her head off. And Mama—not a word; just sitting in that chair, looking at me with her arms still folded.

"Pull Big Red," I say. "Pull Big Red, Chuckkie."

Poor little Chuckkie up there pulling so hard till one of his little arms straight out in back; and Big Red throwing his shoulders and ever'thing else in it, and Mr. Bascom just walking there just 's loose and free, like he's suppose to be there just for his good looks. I move out the way just in time to let the wagon go by me, pulling half o' the fence in the yard behind it. I glance up again, and there's Leola still hollering and trying to jump out, but Mama not saying a word—just sitting there in that setting chair with her arms still folded.

"Whoa," I hear little Chuckkie saying. "Whoa up, now."

Somebody open the door and a bunch o' people come out on the gallery.

"What the world—?" Etienne say. "Thought the whole place was coming to pieces there."

"Chuckkie had a little trouble coming in the yard," I say.

"Goodness," Etienne say. "Anybody hurt?"

Mama just sit there about ten seconds, then she say something to herself and start clambing out the wagon.

"Let me help you there, Aunt Lou," Etienne say, coming down the steps.

"I can make it," Mama say. When she get on the ground she look up at Chuckkie. "Hand me my chair there, boy."

Poor little Chuckkie, up there with the lines in one hand, get the chair and hold it to the side, and Etienne catch it just 'fore it hit the ground. Mama start looking at me again, and it look like for at least a' hour she stand there looking at nobody but me. Then she say, "Ehhh, Lord," like that again, and go inside with Leola and the rest o' the people.

I look back at half o' the fence laying there in the yard, and I jump back on the wagon and guide the mules to the side o' the house. After unhitching 'em and tying 'em to the wheels, I look at Chris pretty red tractor again, and me and Chuckkie go inside: I make sure he kick all that mud off his shoes 'fore he go in the house.

Sitting over there by that fireplace, trying to look joyful when ever'body there know she ain't. But she trying, you know; smiling and bowing when people say something to her. How can she be joyful, I ask you; how can she be? Poor thing, she been here all her life—or the most of it, let's say. 'Fore they moved in this house, they lived in one back in the woods 'bout a mile from here. But for the past twenty-five or thirty years, she been right in this one house. I know ever since I been big enough to know people I been seeing her right here.

Aunt Fe, Aunt Fe, Aunt Fe, Aunt Fe; the name's been 'mongst us just like us own family name. Just like the name o' God. Like the name of town—the city. Aunt Fe, Aunt Fe, Aunt Fe, Aunt Fe.

Poor old thing; how many times I done come here and washed clothes for her when she couldn't do it herself. How many times I done hoed in that garden, ironed her clothes, wrung a chicken neck for her. You count the days in the year and you'll be pretty close. And I didn't mind it a bit. No, I didn't mind it a bit. She there trying to pay me. Proud—Lord, talking 'bout pride. "Here." "No, Aunt Fe; no." "Here, here; you got a child there, you can use it." "No, Aunt Fe. No. No. What would Mama think if she knowed I took money from you? Aunt Fe, Mama would never forgive me. No. I love doing these thing for you. I just wish I could do more."

And there, now, trying to make 'tend she don't mind leaving. Ehhh, Lord.

I hear a bunch o' rattling round in the kitchen and I go back there. I see Louise stirring this big pot o' eggnog.

"Louise," I say.

"Leola," she say.

We look at each other and she stir the eggnog again. She know what I'm go'n say next, and she can't even look in my face.

"Louise, I wish there was some other way."

"There's no other way," she say.

"Louise, moving her from here's like moving a tree you been used to in your front yard all your life."

"What else can I do?"

"Oh, Louise, Louise."

"Nothing else but that."

"Louise, what people go'n do without her here?"

She stir the eggnog and don't answer.

"Louise, us'll take her in with us."

"You all no kin to Auntie. She go with me."

"And us'll never see her again."

She stir the eggnog. Her husband come back in the kitchen and kiss her on the back o' the neck and then look at me and grin. Right from the start I can see I ain't go'n like that nigger.

"Almost ready, honey?" he say.

"Almost."

He go to the safe and get one o' them bottles of whiskey he got in there and come back to the stove.

"No," Louise say. "Everybody don't like whiskey in it. Add the whiskey after you've poured it up."

"Okay, hon."

He kiss her on the back o' the neck again. Still don't like that nigger. Something 'bout him ain't right.

"You one o' the family?" he say.

"Same as one," I say. "And you?"

He don't like the way I say it, and I don't care if he like it or not. He look at me there a second, and then he kiss her on the ear.

"Un-unnn," she say, stirring the pot.

"I love your ear, baby," he say.

"Go in the front room and talk with the people," she say.

He kiss her on the other ear. A nigger do all that front o' public got something to hide. He leave the kitchen. I look at Louise.

"Ain't nothing else I can do," she say.

"You sure, Louise? You positive?"

"I'm positive," she say.

The front door open and Emile and Chuckkie come in. A minute later Washington and Adrieu come in, too. Adrieu come back in the kitchen, and I can see she been crying. Aunt Fe is her godmother, you know.

"How you feel, Adrieu?"

"That weather out there," she say.

"Y'all walked?"

"Yes."

"Us here in the wagon. Y'all can go back with us."

"Y'all the one tore the fence down?" she ask.

"Yes, I guess so. That brother-in-law o' yours in there letting Chuckkie drive that wagon."

"Well, I don't guess it'll matter too much. Nobody go'n be here, anyhow."

And she start crying again. I take her in my arms and pat her on the shoulder, and I look at Louise stirring the eggnog.

"What I'm go'n do and my nan-nane gone? I love her so much."

"Ever'body love her."

"Since my mama died, she been like my mama."

"Shhh," I say. "Don't let her hear you. Make her grieve. You don't want her grieving, now, do you?"

She sniffs there 'gainst my dress few times.

"Oh, Lord," she say. "Lord, have mercy."

"Shhh," I say. "Shhh. That's what life's 'bout."

"That ain't what life's 'bout," she say. "It ain't fair. This been her home all her life. These the people she know. She don't know them people she going to. It ain't fair."

"Shhh, Adrieu," I say. "Now, you saying things that ain't your business."

She cry there some mo'.

"Oh, Lord, Lord," she say.

Louise turn from the stove.

"About ready now," she say, going to the middle door. "James, tell everybody to come back and get some."

JAMES

Let me go on back here and show these country niggers how to have a good time. All they know is talk, talk, talk. Talk so much they make me buggy round here. Damn this weather—wind, rain. Must be a million cracks in this old house.

I go to that old beat-up safe in that corner and get that fifth of Mr. Harper (in the South now; got to say Mister), give the seal one swipe, the stopper one jerk, and head back to that old wood stove. (Man, like, these cats are primitive—goodness. You know what I mean? I mean like wood stoves. Don't mention TV, man, these cats here never heard of that.) I start to dump Mr. Harper in the pot and Baby catches my hand again and say not all of them like it. You ever heard of anything like that? I mean a stud's going to drink eggnog, and he's not going to put whiskey in it. I mean he's going to drink it straight. I mean, you ever heard anything like that? Well, I wasn't pressing none of them on Mr. Harper. I mean, me and Mr. Harper get along too well together for me to go around there pressing.

I hold my cup there and let Baby put a few drops of this egg stuff in it; then I jerk my cup back and let Mr. Harper run a while. Couple of these cats come over (some of them aren't so lame) and set their cups, and I let Mr. Harper run for them. Then this cat says he's got 'nough. I let Mr. Harper run for this other stud, and pretty soon he says, "Hold it. Good." Country cat, you know. "Hold it. Good." Real country cat. So I raise the cup to see what Mr. Harper's doing. He's just right. I raise the cup again. Just right, Mr. Harper; just right.

I go to the door with Mr. Harper under my arm and the cup in my hand and I look into the front room where they all are. I mean, there's about ninety-nine of them in there. Old ones, young ones, little ones, big ones, yellow ones, black ones, brown ones—you name them, brother, and they were there. And what for? Brother, I'll tell you what for. Just because me and Baby are taking this old chick out of these sticks. Well, I'll tell you where I'd be at this moment if I was one of them. With that weather out there like it is, I'd be under about five blankets with some little warm belly pressing against mine. Brother, you can bet your hat I wouldn't be here. Man, listen to that thing out there. You can hear that rain beating on that old house like grains of rice; and that wind coming through them cracks like it does in those old Charlie Chaplin movies. Man, like you know—like *whooo-ee; whooo-ee.* Man, you talking about some weird cats.

I can feel Mr. Harper starting to massage my wig and I bat my eyes twice and look at the old girl over there. She's still sitting in that funny-looking little old rocking chair, and not saying a word to anybody. Just sitting there looking into the fireplace at them two pieces of wood that aren't giving out enough heat to warm a baby, let alone ninety-nine grown people. I mean, you know, like that sleet's falling out there like all get-up-and-go, and them two pieces of wood are lying there just as dead as the rest of these way-out cats.

One of the old cats—I don't know which one he is—Mose, Sam, or something like that—leans over and pokes in the fire a minute; then a little blaze shoots up, and he raises up, too, looking as satisfied as if he'd just sent a rocket into orbit. I mean, these cats are like that. They do these little bitty things, and they feel like they've really done something. Well, back in these sticks, I guess there just isn't nothing big to do.

I feel Mr. Harper touching my skull now—and I notice this little chick passing by me with these two cups of eggnog. She goes over to the fireplace and gives one to each of these old chicks. The one sitting in that setting chair she brought with her from God knows where, and the other cup to the old chick that Baby and I are going to haul from here sometime tomorrow morning. Wait, man, I mean like, you ever heard of anybody going to somebody else's house with a chair? I mean, wouldn't you call that an insult at the basest point? I mean, now, like tell me what you think of that? I mean—dig—here I am at my pad, and in you come with your own stool. I mean, now, like man, you know. I mean that's an insult at the basest point. I mean, you know . . . you know, like way out. . . .

Mr. Harper, what you trying to do, boy?—I mean, *sir.* (Got to watch myself, I'm in the South. Got to keep watching myself.)

This stud touches me on the shoulder and raise his cup and say, "How 'bout a taste?" I know what the stud's talking about, so I let Mr. Harper run for him. But soon 's I let a drop get in, the stud say, "'Nough." I mean I let about two drops get in, and already the stud's got enough. Man, I mean, like you know. I mean these studs are 'way out. I mean like 'way back there.

This stud takes a swig of his eggnog and say, "Ahhh." I mean this real down-home way of saying "Ahhhh." I mean, man, like these studs—I notice this little chick passing by me again, and this time she's crying. I mean weeping, you know. And just because this old ninety-nine-year-old chick's packing up and leaving. I mean, you ever heard of anything like that? I mean, here she is pretty as the day is long and crying because Baby and I are hauling this old chick away. Well, I'd like to make her cry. And I can assure you, brother, it wouldn't be from leaving her.

I turn and look at Baby over there by the stove, pouring eggnog in all these cups. I mean, there're about twenty of these cats lined up there. And I bet you not half of them will take Mr. Harper along. Some way-out cats, man. Some way-out cats.

I go up to Baby and kiss her on the back of the neck and give her a little pat where she likes for me to pat her when we're in the bed. She say, "Uh-uh," but I know she likes it anyhow.

BEN O

I back under the bed and touch the slop jar, and I pull back my leg and back somewhere else, and then I get me a good sight on it. I spin my aggie couple times and sight again and then I shoot. I hit it right square in the middle and it go flying over the fireplace. I crawl over there to get it and I see 'em all over there drinking they eggnog and they didn't even offer me and Chuckkie none. I find my marble on the bricks, and I go back and tell Chuckkie they over there drinking eggnog.

"You want some?" I say.

"I want shoot marble," Chuckkie say. "Yo' shot. Shoot up."

"I want some eggnog," I say.

"Shoot up, Ben O," he say. "I'm getting cold staying in one place so long. You feel that draft?"

"Coming from that crack under that bed," I say.

"Where?" Chuckkie say, looking for the crack.

"Over by that bedpost over there," I say.

"This sure's a beat-up old house," Chuckkie say.

"I want me some eggnog," I say.

"Well, you ain't getting none," Gran'mon say, from the fireplace. "It ain't good for you."

"I can drink eggnog," I say. "How come it ain't good for me? It ain't nothing but eggs and milk. I eat chicken, don't I? I eat beef, don't I?"

Gran'mon don't say nothing.

"I want me some eggnog," I say.

Gran'mon still don't say no more. Nobody else don't say nothing, neither.

"I want me some eggnog," I say.

"You go'n get a eggnog," Gran'mon say. "Just keep that noise up."

"I want me some eggnog," I say, "and I 'tend to get me some eggnog tonight."

Next thing I know, Gran'mon done picked up a chip out o' that corner and done sailed it back there where me and Chuckkie is. I duck just in time, and the chip catch old Chuckkie side the head.

"Hey, who that hitting me?" Chuckkie say.

"Move, and you won't get hit," Gran'mon say.

I laugh at old Chuckkie over there holding his head, and next thing I know here's Chuckkie done haul back there and hit me in my side. I jump up from there and give him two just to show him how it feel, and he jump up and hit me again. Then we grab each other and start tussling on the floor.

"You, Ben O," I hear Gran'mon saying. "You, Ben O, cut that out. Y'all cut that out."

But we don't stop, 'cause neither one o' us want be first. Then I feel somebody pulling us apart.

"What I ought to do is whip both o' you," Mrs. Leola say. "Is that what y'all want?"

"No'm," I say.

"Then shake hand."

Me and Chuckkie shake hand.

"Kiss," Mrs. Leola say.

"No, ma'am," I say. "I ain't kissing no boy. I ain't that crazy."

"Kiss him, Chuckkie," she say.

Old Chuckkie kiss me on the jaw.

"Now, kiss him, Ben O."

"I ain't kissing no Chuckkie," I say. "No'm. Uh-uh. You kiss girls."

And the next thing I know, Mama done tipped up back o' me and done whop me on the leg with Daddy belt.

"Kiss Chuckkie," she say.

Chuckkie turn his jaw to me and I kiss him. I almost wipe my mouth. I even feel like spitting.

"Now, come back here and get you some eggnog," Mama say.

"That's right, spoil 'em," Gran'mon say. "Next thing you know, they be drinking from bottles."

"Little eggnog won't hurt 'em, Mama," Mama say.

"That's right, never listen," Gran'mon say. "It's you go'n suffer for it. I be dead and gone, me."

Be just like wrapping a chain round a tree and jecking and jecking, and then shifting the chain little bit and jecking and jecking some in that direction, and then shifting it some mo' and jecking and jecking in that direction. Jecking and jecking till you get it loose, and then pulling with all your might. Still it might not be loose enough and you have to back the tractor up some and fix the chain round the tree again and start jecking all over. Jeck, jeck, jeck. Then you hear the roots crying, and then you keep on jecking, and then it give, and you jeck some mo', and then it falls. And not till then that you see what you done done. Not till then you see the big hole in the ground and piece of the taproot still way down in it—a piece you won't never get out no matter if you dig till doomsday. Yes, you got the tree—least got it down on the ground, but did you get the taproot? No. No, sir, you didn't get the taproot. You stand there and look down in this hole at it and you grab yo' axe and jump down in it and start chopping at the taproot, but do you get the taproot? No. You don't get the taproot, sir. You never get the taproot. But, sir, I tell you what you do get. You get a big hole in the ground, sir; and you get another big hole in the air where the lovely branches been all these years. Yes, sir, that's what you get. The holes, sir, the holes. Two holes, sir, you can't never fill no matter how hard you try.

So you wrap yo' chain round yo' tree again, sir, and you start dragging it. But the dragging ain't so easy, sir, 'cause she's a heavy old tree—been there a long time, you know—heavy. And you make yo' tractor strain, sir, and the elements work 'gainst you, too, sir, 'cause the elements, they on her side, too, 'cause she part o' the elements, and the elements, they part o' her. So the elements, they do they little share to discourage you—yes, sir, they does. But you will not let the elements stop you. No, sir, you show the elements that they just elements, and man is stronger than elements, and you jeck and jeck on the chain, and soon she start to moving with you, sir, but if you look over yo' shoulder one second you see her leaving a trail—a trail, sir, that can be seen from miles and miles away. You see her trying to hook her little fine branches in different little cracks, in between pickets, round hills o' grass, round anything they might brush 'gainst. But you is a determined man, sir, and you jeck and you jeck, and she keep on grabbing and trying to hold, but you stronger, sir—course you the strongest—and you finally get her out on the pave road. But what you don't notice, sir, is just 'fore she get on the pave road she leave couple her little branches to remind the people that it ain't her that want leave, but you, sir, that think she ought to. So you just drag her and drag her, sir, and the folks that live in the houses 'side the pave road, they come out on they gallery and look at her go by, and then they go back in they house and sit by the fire and forget her. So you just go on, sir, and you just go and you go—and for how many days? I don't know. I don't have the least idea. The North to me, sir, is like the elements. It mystify me. But never mind, you finally get there, and then you try to find a place to set her. You look in this corner and you look in that corner, but no corner is good. She kind o' stand in the way no matter where you set her. So finally, sir, you say, "I just stand her up here a little while and see, and if it don't work out, if she keep getting in the way, I guess we'll just have to take her to the dump."

CHRIS

Just like him, though, standing up there telling them lies when everybody else feeling sad. I don't know what you do without people like him. And, yet, you see him there, he sad just like the rest. But he just got to be funny. Crying on the inside, but still got to be funny.

He didn't steal it, though; didn't steal it a bit. His grandpa was just like him. Mat? Mat Jefferson? Just like that. Mat could make you die laughing. 'Member once at a wake. Who was dead? Yes—Robert Lewis. Robert Lewis laying up in his coffin dead as a door nail. Everybody sad and droopy. Mat look at that and start his lying. Soon, half o' the place laughing. Funniest wake I ever went to, and yet—

Just like now. Look at 'em. Look at 'em laughing. Ten minutes ago you would 'a' thought you was at a funeral. But look at 'em now. Look at her there in that little old chair. How long she had it? Fifty years—a hundred? It ain't a chair no mo', it's little bit o' her. Just like her arm, just like her leg.

You know, I couldn't believe it. I couldn't. Emile passed the house there the other day, right after the bombing, and I was in my yard digging a water drain to let the water run out in the ditch. Emile, he stopped the wagon there 'fore the door. Little Chuckkie, he in there with him with that little rain cap buckled up over his head. I go out to the gate and I say, 'Emile, it's the truth?"

"The truth," he say. And just like that he say it. "The truth."

I look at him there, and he looking up the road to keep from looking back at me. You know, they been pretty close to Aunt Fe ever since they was children coming up. His own mon, Aunt Lou, and Aunt Fe, they been like sisters, there, together.

Me and him, we talk there little while 'bout the cane cutting, then he say he got to get on to the back. He shake the lines and drive on.

Inside me, my heart feel like it done swole up ten times the size it ought to be. Water come in my eyes, and I got to 'mit I cried right there. Yes sir, I cried right there by that front gate.

Louise come in the room and whisper something to Leola, and they go back in the kitchen. I can hear 'em moving things round back there, still getting things together they go'n be taking along. If they offer me anything, I'd like that big iron pot out there in the back yard. Good for boiling water when you killing hog, you know.

You can feel the sadness in the room again. Louise brought it in when she come in and whispered to Leola. Only, she didn't take it out when her and Leola left. Every pan they move, every pot they unhook keep telling you she leaving, she leaving.

Etienne turn over one o' them logs to make the fire pick up some, and I see that boy, Lionel, spreading out his hands over the fire. Watch out, I think to myself, here come another lie. People, he just getting started.

ANNE-MARÍE DUVALL

"You're not going?"

"I'm not going," he says, turning over the log with the poker. "And if you were in your right mind, you wouldn't go, either."

"You just don't understand, do you?"

"Oh, I understand. She cooked for your daddy. She nursed you when your mama died."

"And I'm trying to pay her back with a seventy-nine-cents scarf. Is that too much?"

He is silent, leaning against the mantel, looking down at the fire. The fire throws strange shadows across the big, old room. Father looks down at me from against the wall. His eyes do not say go nor stay. But I know what he would do.

"Please go with me, Edward."

"You're wasting your breath."

I look at him a long time, then I get the small package from the coffee table.

"You're still going?"

"I am going."

"Don't call for me if you get bogged down anywhere back there."

I look at him and go out to the garage. The sky is black. The clouds are moving fast and low. A fine drizzle is falling, and the wind coming from the swamps blows in my face. I cannot recall a worse night in all my life.

I hurry into the car and drive out of the yard. The house stands big and black in back of me. Am I angry with Edward? No, I'm not angry with Edward. He's right. I should not go out into this kind of weather. But what he does not understand is I must. Father definitely would have gone if he were alive. Grandfather definitely would have gone, also. And, therefore, I must. Why? I cannot answer why. Only, I must go.

As soon as I turn down that old muddy road, I begin to pray. Don't let me go into that ditch, I pray. Don't let me go into that ditch. Please, don't let me go into that ditch.

The lights play on the big old trees along the road. Here and there the lights hit a sagging picket fence. But I know I haven't even started yet. She lives far back into the fields. Why? God, why does she have to live so far back? Why couldn't she have lived closer to the front? But the answer to that is as hard for me as is the answer to everything else. It was ordained before I—before father—was born—that she should live back there. So why should I try to understand it now?

The car slides towards the ditch, and I stop it dead and turn the wheel, and then come back into the road again. Thanks, father. I know you're with me. Because it was you who said that I must look after her, didn't you? No, you did not say it directly, father. You said it only with a glance. As grandfather must have said it to you, and as his father must have said it to him.

But now that she's gone, father, now what? I know. I know. Aunt Lou, Aunt Clo, and the rest.

The lights shine on the dead, wet grass along the road. There's an old pecan tree, looking dead and all alone. I wish I was a little nigger gal so I could pick pecans and eat them under the big old dead tree.

The car hits a rut, but bounces right out of it. I am frightened for a moment, but then I feel better. The windshield wipers are working well, slapping the water away as fast as it hits the glass. If I make the next half mile all right, the rest of the way will be good. It's not much over a mile now.

That was too bad about that bombing—killing that woman and her two children. That poor woman; poor children. What is the answer? What will happen? What do they want? Do they know what they want? Do they really know what they want? Are they positively sure? Have they any idea? Money to buy a car, is that it? If that is all, I pity them. Oh, how I pity them.

Not much farther. Just around that bend and—there's a water hole. Now what?

I stop the car and just stare out at the water a minute; then I get out to see how deep it is. The cold wind shoots through my body like needles. Lightning comes from towards the swamps and lights up the place. For a split second the night is as bright as day. The next second it is blacker than it has ever been.

I look at the water, and I can see that it's too deep for the car to pass through. I must turn back or I must walk the rest of the way. I stand there a while wondering what to do. Is it worth it all? Can't I simply send the gift by someone tomorrow morning? But will there be someone tomorrow morning? Suppose she leaves without getting it, then what? What then? Father would never forgive me. Neither would grandfather or great-grandfather, either. No, they wouldn't.

The lightning flashes again and I look across the field, and I can see the tree in the yard a quarter of a mile away. I have but one choice: I must walk. I get the package out of the car and stuff it in my coat and start out.

I don't make any progress at first, but then I become a little warmer and I find I like walking. The lightning flashes just in time to show up a puddle of water, and I go around it. But there's no light to show up the second puddle, and I fall flat on my face. For a moment I'm completely blind, then I get slowly to my feet and check the package. It's dry, not harmed. I wash the mud off my raincoat, wash my hands, and I start out again.

The house appears in front of me, and as I come into the yard, I can hear the people laughing and talking. Sometimes I think niggers can laugh and joke even if they see somebody beaten to death. I go up on the porch and knock and an old one opens the door for me. I swear, when he sees me he looks as if he's seen a ghost. His mouth drops open, his eyes bulge—I swear.

I go into the old crowded and smelly room, and every one of them looks at me the same way the first one did. All the joking and laughing has ceased. You would think I was the devil in person.

"Done, Lord," I hear her saying over by the fireplace. They move to the side and I can see her sitting in that little rocking chair I bet you she's had since the beginning of time. "Done, Master," she says. "Child, what you doing in weather like this? Y'all move; let her get to that fire. Y'all move. Move, now. Let her warm herself."

They start scattering everywhere.

"I'm not cold, Aunt Fe," I say. "I just brought you something—something small—because you're leaving us. I'm going right back."

"Done, Master," she says. Fussing over me just like she's done all her life. "Done, Master. Child, you ain't got no business in a place like this. Get close to this fire. Get here. Done, Master."

I move closer, and the fire does feel warm and good.

"Done, Lord," she says.

I take out the package and pass it to her. The other niggers gather around with all kinds of smiles on their faces. Just think of it—a white lady coming through all of this for one old darky. It is all right for them to come from all over the plantation, from all over the area, in all kinds of weather: this is to be expected of them. But a white lady, a white lady. They must think we white people don't have their kind of feelings.

She unwraps the package, her bony little fingers working slowly and deliberately. When she sees the scarf—the seventy-nine-cents scarf—she brings it to her mouth and kisses it.

"Y'all look," she says. "Y'all look. Ain't it the prettiest little scarf y'all ever did see? Y'all look."

They move around her and look at the scarf. Some of them touch it.

"I go'n put it on right now," she says. "I go'n put it on right now, my lady."

She unfolds it and ties it round her head and looks up at everybody and smiles.

"Thank you, my lady," she says. "Thank you, ma'am, from the bottom of my heart."

"Oh, Aunt Fe." I say, kneeling down beside her. "Oh, Aunt Fe."

But I think about the other niggers there looking down at me, and I get up. But I look into that wrinkled old face again, and I must go back down again. And I lay my head in that bony old lap, and I cry and I cry—I don't know how long. And I feel those old fingers, like death itself, passing over my hair and my neck. I don't know how long I kneel there crying, and when I stop, I get out of there as fast as I can.

ETÍENNE

The boy come in, and soon, right off, they get quiet, blaming the boy. If people could look little farther than the tip of they nose—No, they blame the boy. Not that they ain't behind the boy, what he doing, but they blame him for what she must do. What they don't know is that the boy didn't start it, and the people that bombed the house didn't start it, neither. It started a million years ago. It started when one man envied another man for having a penny mo' 'an he had, and then the man married a woman to help him work the field so he could get much 's the other man, but when the other man saw the man had married a woman to get much 's him, he, himself, he married a woman, too, so he could still have mo'. Then they start having children—not from love; but so the children could help 'em work so they could have mo'. But even with the children one man still had a penny mo' 'an the other, so the other man went and bought him a ox, and the other man did the same—to keep ahead of the other man. And soon the other man had bought him a slave to work the ox so he could get ahead of the other man. But the other man went out and bought him two slaves so he could stay ahead of the other man, and the other man went out and bought him three slaves. And soon they had a thousand slaves apiece, but they still wasn't satisfied. And one day the slaves all rose and kill the masters, but the masters (knowing slaves was men just like they was, and kind o' expected they might do this) organized theyself a good police force, and the police force, they come out and killed the two thousand slaves.

So it's not this boy you see standing here 'fore you, 'cause it happened a million years ago. And this boy here's just doing something the slaves done a million years ago. Just that this boy here ain't doing it they way. 'Stead of raising arms 'gainst the masters, he bow his head.

No, I say; don't blame the boy 'cause she must go. 'Cause when she's dead, and that won't be long after they get her up there, this boy's work will still be going on. She's not the only one that's go'n die from this boy's work. Many mo' of 'em go'n die 'fore it's over with. The whole place—everything. A big wind is rising, and when a big wind rise, the sea stirs, and the drop o' water you see laying on top the sea this day won't be there tomorrow. 'Cause that's what wind do, and that's what life is. She ain't nothing but one little drop o' water laying on top the sea, and what this boy's doing is called the wind . . . and she must be moved. No, don't blame the boy. Go out and blame the wind. No, don't blame him, 'cause tomorrow, what he's doing today, somebody go'n say he ain't done a thing. 'Cause tomorrow will he his time to be turned over just like it's hers today. And after that, be somebody else time to turn over. And it keep going like that till it ain't nothing left to turn—and nobody left to turn it.

"Sure, they bombed the house," he say; "because they want us to stop. But if we stopped today, then what good would we have done? What good? Those who have already died for the cause would have just died in vain."

"Maybe if they had bombed your house you wouldn't be so set on keeping this up."

"If they had killed my mother and my brothers and sisters, I'd press just that much harder. I can see you all point. I can see it very well. But I can't agree with you. You blame me for their being bombed. You blame me for Aunt Fe's leaving. They died for you and for your children. And I love Aunt Fe as much as anybody in here does. Nobody in here loves her more than I do. Not one of you." He looks at her. "Don't you believe me, Aunt Fe?"

She nods—that little white scarf still tied round her head.

"How many times have I eaten in your kitchen, Aunt Fe? A thousand times? How many times have I eaten tea cakes and drank milk on the back steps, Aunt Fe? A thousand times? How many times have I sat at this same fireplace with you, just the two of us, Aunt Fe? Another thousand times—two thousand times? How many times have I chopped wood for you, chopped grass for you, ran to the store for you? Five thousand times? How many times have we walked to church together, Aunt Fe? Gone fishing at the river together—how many times? I've spent as much time in this house as I've spent in my own. I know every crack in the wall. I know every corner. With my eyes shut, I can go anywhere in here without bumping into anything. How many of you can do that? Not many of you." He looks at her. "Aunt Fe?"

She looks at him.

"Do you think I love you, Aunt Fe?"

She nods.

"I love you, Aunt Fe, much as I do my own parents. I'm going to miss you much as I'd miss my own mother if she were to leave me now. I'm going to miss you, Aunt Fe, but I'm not going to stop what I've started. You told me a story once, Aunt Fe, about my great-grandpa. Remember? Remember how he died?"

She looks in the fire and nods.

"Remember how they lynched him—chopped him into pieces?"

She nods.

"Just the two of us were sitting here beside the fire when you told me that. I was so angry I felt like killing. But it was you who told me get killing out of my mind. It was you who told me I would only bring harm to myself and sadness to the others if I killed. Do you remember that, Aunt Fe?"

She nods, still looking in the fire.

"You were right. We cannot raise our arms. Because it would mean death for ourselves, as well as for the others. But we will do something else—and that's what we will do." He looks at the people standing round him. "And if they were to bomb my own mother's house tomorrow, I would still go on."

"I'm not saying for you not to go on," Louise says. "That's up to you. I'm just taking Auntie from here before hers is the next house they bomb."

The boy look at Louise, and then at Aunt Fe. He go up to the chair where she sitting.

"Goodbye, Aunt Fe," he say, picking up her hand. The hand done shriveled up to almost nothing. Look like nothing but loose skin's covering the bones. "I'll miss you," he say.

"Goodbye, Emmanuel," she say. She look at him a long time. "God be with you."

He stand there holding the hand a while longer, then he nods his head, and leaves the house. The people stir round little bit, but nobody say anything.

AUNT LOU

They tell her goodbye, and half of 'em leave the house crying, or want cry, but she just sit there 'side the fireplace like she don't mind going at all. When Leola ask me if I'm ready to go, I tell her I'm staying right there till Fe leave that house. I tell her I ain't moving one step till she go out that door. I been knowing her for the past fifty some years now, and I ain't 'bout to leave her on her last night here.

That boy, Chuckkie, want stay with me, but I make him go. He follow his mon and paw out the house and soon I hear that wagon turning round. I hear Emile saying something to Mr. Bascom even 'fore that wagon get out the yard. I tell myself, well, Mr. Bascom, you sure go'n catch it, and me not there to take up for you—and I get up from my chair and go to the door.

"Emile?" I call.

"Whoa," he say.

"You leave that mule 'lone, you hear me?"

"I ain't done Mr. Bascom a thing, Mama," he say.

"Well, you just mind you don't," I say. "I'll sure find out."

"Yes'm," he say. "Come up here, Mr. Bascom."

"Now, you hear that boy. Emile?" I say.

"I'm sorry, Mama," he say. "I didn't mean no harm."

They go out in the road, and I go back to the fireplace and sit down again. Louise stir round in the kitchen a few minutes, then she come in the front where we at. Everybody else gone. That husband o' hers, there, got drunk long 'fore midnight, and Emile and them had to put him to bed in the other room.

She come there and stand by the fire.

"I'm dead on my feet," she say.

"Why don't you go to bed," I say. "I'm go'n be here."

"You all won't need anything?"

"They got wood in that corner?"

"Plenty."

"Then we won't need a thing."

She stand there and warm, and then she say good night and go round the other side.

"Well, Fe?" I say.

"I ain't leaving here tomorrow, Lou," she say.

"'Course you is," I say. "Up there ain't that bad."

She shake her head. "No, I ain't going nowhere."

I look at her over in her chair, but I don't say nothing. The fire pops in the fireplace, and I look at the fire again. It's a good little fire—not too big, not too little. Just 'nough there to keep the place warm.

"You want sing, Lou?" she say, after a while. "I feel like singing my 'termination song."

"Sure," I say.

She starting singing in that little light voice she got there, and I join with her. We sing two choruses, and then she stop.

"My 'termination for Heaven," she say. "Now—now—"

"What's the matter, Fe?" I say.

"Nothing," she say. "I want get in my bed. My gown hanging over there."

I get the gown for her and bring it back to the firehalf. She get out of her dress slowly, like she don't even have 'nough strength to do it. I help her on with her gown, and she kneel down there 'side the bed and say her prayers. I sit in my chair and look at the fire again.

She pray there a long time—half out loud, half to herself. I look at her kneeling down there, little like a little old girl. I see her making some kind o' jecking motion there, but I feel she crying 'cause this her last night here, and 'cause she got to go and leave ever'thing behind. I look at the fire.

She pray there ever so long, and then she start to get up. But she can't make it by herself. I go to help her, and when I put my hand on her shoulder, she say, "Lou? Lou?"

I say, "What's the matter, Fe?"

"Lou?" she say. "Lou?"

I feel her shaking in my hand with all her might. Shaking, shaking, shaking—like a person with the chill. Then I hear her take a long breath, longest I ever heard anybody take before. Then she ease back on the bed—calm, calm, calm.

"Sleep on, Fe," I tell her. "When you get up there, tell 'em all I ain't far behind."

GEORGE GARRETT

George Garrett was born in Orlando, Florida, in 1929. He attended Sewanee Military Academy and took his B.A., M.A., and Ph.D. at Princeton. He has taught at many colleges and universities and is now Henry Hoyns Professor of Creative Writing at the University of Virginia. He has published poetry, short stories, novels, essays and criticism, screenplays, and plays. He is best known for his two highly praised historical novels, *Death of the Fox* (1971) and *The Succession* (1983). *The Collected Poems of George Garrett* was published in 1984. *An Evening Performance* (1985) is a volume of new and selected stories.

A Wreath for Garibaldi

A True Story

THE beginning was perfectly casual, offhand, pleasant. We were sitting on the terrazzo of a modern Roman apartment drinking coffee and thick, sweet, bile-colored Strega. It was an afternoon in late March, the air was fresh and cool, the spring sunlight rinsed and brilliant. The English lady, a poet and translator, was in the hammock and the rest of us sat around in wicker chairs—an artist, an Italian princess, another translator, an expatriate gentleman from Mobile, Alabama, who writes poems about monkeys. A usual crowd. . . .

The talk was about politics. A Pope had died, the new Pope had been elected amid rumors and fears—"*Un Straniero per Il Papa?*" all the headlines read for a while—and errors: white smoke pouring out of the chimney of the Sistine Chapel on the very first ballot because somebody had forgotten the straw to darken the smoke. The latest government had fallen. A coalition with more strength to the right (gossip had any number of known ex-Fascists among its members) had replaced it. The talk was of politics and, inevitably, the signs of the reawakening of Fascism. Mussolini was being treated with nostalgia and kid gloves in a major picture magazine. Another magazine had been publishing a series about the war, showing how they (the Italians) lost it by a series of "mistakes" and recounting moments of bravery and success wherever they could find them. There had been a television series on recent Italian history. Everybody had been waiting to see how they would manage to handle the whole big business of Fascism and the war. It was disappointing. They treated the subject like scholars from a distant land, or maybe outer space, with careful, neutral disinterest.

There had been other things too—the young Fascists making some headlines by dropping mice in tiny parachutes from the ceiling of a theater during an anti-Fascist comedy. There had been the "striptease incident" in a Trastevere trattoria when a Turkish girl took all her clothes off and did a belly dance. It was a very large private party, and most people missed that part of the show. More noticed the American movie star, one of the new sex symbols, who came with a buzz and hive of fairies (like Lady Brett?) and danced barefoot (like Ava Gardner?). In fact it never would have been an issue at all except that somebody took some photographs. The place was full of plainclothesmen who had come to protect the jewels, but they didn't go into action until the next morning when a tabloid appeared with the pictures of the belly dance. In no time the party was officially an orgy and there were lots of political implications and ramifications. It was the special kind of public prudery that interested the observer, though, the kind that had always been associated with the Fascist days. And there had been other signs and portents like the regular toppling over and defacing of the bust of Lauro di Bosis near the Villa Lante on the Gianicolo.

Something was happening all right, slowly it is true, but you could feel it. The Italians felt it. Little things. An Italian poet noticed the plainclothes policemen lounging around the area of Quirinale Palace, the first time since the war. At least they hadn't stepped up and asked to see his papers in the hated, flat, dialect mispronunciation of Mussolini's home district—*Documenti, per favore.* But—who knew?—that might be coming, too, one of these days. There were other Italians who still bore scars they had earned in police station basements, resisting. They laughed and, true to national form and manners, never talked too long or solemnly on any subject at all, but some of them worried briefly out loud about short memories and ghosts.

We saw Giuseppe Berto at a party once in a while, tall, lean, nervous, and handsome, and, in my opinion, the best novelist of them all except Pavese. And Pavese was dead. Berto's *The Sky Is Red* had been a small masterpiece and in its special way one of the best books to come out of the war. Now he was married to a young and beautiful girl, had a small son, and lived in an expensive apartment and worked for the movies. On his desk was a slowly accumulating treatment and script of *The Count of Monte Cristo.* On his bookshelves were some American novels, including Bellow's *Seize the Day,* which had been sent to him by American publishers. But he hadn't read them, and he wasn't especially interested in what the American writers were up to. He was very interested in Robert Musil's *The Man Without Qualities.* So were a lot of other people. He was interested in Italo Svevo. He was slowly thinking his way into a new novel, a big one, one that many people had been waiting for. It was going to be hard going all the way for him because he hadn't written seriously for a good while, except for a few stories, and he was tired of the old method of *realismo* he had so successfully used in *The Sky Is Red.* This one was going to be different. He had bought a little piece of property down along the coast of the hard country of Calabria that he knew so well. He was going to do one or two more films for quick cash and then chuck it all, leave Rome and its intellectual cliques and money-fed life, go back to Calabria.

Berto seemed worried, too. He knew all about it and had put it down in journal form in *War in a Black Shirt.* He knew all about the appeal of a black shirt and jackboots to a poor, southern, peasant boy. He knew all about the infection and the fever, and, too, the sudden moment of realization when he saw for himself, threw up his hands and quit, ending the war as a prisoner in Texas. Berto knew all about Fascism. So did his friend, the young novelist Rimanelli. Rimanelli is tough and square-built and adventurous, says what he thinks. He had put it down in a war novel, *The Day of the Lion.* These people were not talking much about it, but you, a foreigner, sensed their apprehension and disappointment.

So there we were talking around and about it. The English lady said she had to go to Vienna for a while. It was a pity because she had planned to lay a wreath at the foot of the Garibaldi statue, towering over Rome in spectacular benediction from the high point of the Gianicolo. Around that statue in the green park where children play and lovers walk in twos and there is a glowing view of the whole city, in that park are the rows of marble busts of Garibaldi's fallen men, the ones who one day rushed out of the Porta San Pancrazio and, under fire all the way, up the long, straight, narrow lane first to take, then later to lose, the high ground of the Villa Doria Pamphili. When they finally lost it, the French artillery moved in, and that was the end for Garibaldi, at least that time, on 30 April 1849. Once out of the gate they had charged straight up the narrow lane. We had walked it many times and shivered, figuring what a fish barrel it had been for the French. Now the park is filled with marble busts and all the streets in the immediate area have the full and proper names of the men who fell there.

We were at a party once and heard an idealistic young European call that charge glorious. Our companion was a huge, plain-spoken American sculptor who had been a sixteen-year-old rifleman all across France in 1944. He said it was stupid butchery to order men to make a charge like that, no matter who gave the order or what for.

"Oh, it would be butchery all right," the European said. "We would see it that way today. But it was glorious then. It was the last time in history anybody could do something gloriously like that."

I thought, *Who is older now? Old world or new world?*

The sculptor looked at him, bug-eyed and amazed. He had made an assault once with a hundred and eighty men. It was a picked assault company. They went up against an SS unit of comparable size, over a little rise of ground, across an open field. Object—a village crossroads. They made it and killed every last one of the Krauts, took the village on schedule. When it was over, eight of his company were still alive and all eight were wounded. The whole thing, from the moment when they climbed heavily off the trucks, spread out, and moved into position just behind the cover of that slight rise of ground and then jumped off, took maybe between twenty or thirty minutes. The sculptor looked at him, let the color drain out of his face, grinned, and looked down into his drink, a bad Martini made with raw Italian gin.

"Bullshit," he said softly.

"Excuse me," the European said. "I am not familiar with the expression."

The apartment where we were talking that afternoon in March faced onto the street Garibaldi's men had charged up and along. Across the way from the apartment building is a ruined house, shot to hell that day in 1849, and left that way as a kind of memorial. There is a bronze wreath on the wall. Like everything else in Rome, ruins and monuments alike, that house is lived in. I have seen diapers strung across the ruined roof.

The English lady really wanted to put a wreath on the Garibaldi monument on the thirtieth of April. She had her reasons for this. For one thing, there wasn't going to be any ceremony this year. There were a few reasons for that too. Garibaldi had been much taken up and exploited by the Communists nowadays. Therefore the government wanted no part of him. And then there were ecclesiastical matters, the matter of Garibaldi's anticlericalism. There was a new Pope and the Vatican was making itself heard and felt these days. As it happens the English lady is a good Catholic herself, but of a more liberal political persuasion. Nothing was going to be done this year to celebrate Garibaldi's bold and unsuccessful defense of Rome. All that the English lady wanted to do was to walk up to the monument and lay a wreath at its base. This would show that somebody, even a foreigner living in Rome, cared. And then there were other things. Some of the marble busts in the park are of young Englishmen who fought and died for Garibaldi. She also mentioned leaving a little bunch of flowers at the bust of Lauro di Bosis.

It is hard for me to know how I really feel about Lauro di Bosis. I suffer from mixed feelings. He was a well-to-do, handsome, and sensitive young poet. His bust shows an intense, mustached, fine-featured face. He flew over Rome one day during the early days of Mussolini and scattered leaflets across the city, denouncing the Fascists. He was never heard of again. He is thought either to have been killed by the Fascists as soon as he landed or to have killed himself by flying out to sea and crashing his plane. He was, thus, an early and spectacular victim. And there is something so wonderfully romantic about it all. He really didn't know how to fly. He had crashed on takeoff once before. Gossip had it (for gossip is the soul of Rome) that a celebrated American dancer of the time had paid for both the planes. It was absurd and dramatic. It is remembered and has been commemorated by a bust in a park and a square in the city which was renamed Piazzo Lauro di Bosis after the war. Most Romans, even some of the postmen, still know it by the old name.

Faced with a gesture like Di Bosis's, I find usually that my sentiments are closer to those of my sculptor friend. The things that happened in police station basements were dirty, grubby, and most often anonymous. No poetry, no airplanes, no famous dancers. That is how the real resistance goes on, and its strength is directly proportionate to the number of insignificant people who can let themselves be taken to pieces, piece by piece, without quitting too quickly. It is an ugly business and there are few, if any, wreaths for them. I keep thinking of a young woman I knew during the Occupation in Austria. She was from Prague. She had been picked up by the Russians, questioned in connection with some pamphlets, then sentenced to life imprisonment for espionage. She escaped, crawled through the usual mine fields, under the usual barbed wire, was shot at, swam a river, and we finally picked her up in Linz. She showed us what had happened to her. No airplanes, no Nathan Hale statements. Just no simple spot, not even a dime-size spot, on her whole body that wasn't bruised, bruise on top of bruise, from beatings. I understand very well about Lauro di Bosis and how his action is symbolic. The trouble is that, like many symbols, it doesn't seem to me a very realistic one.

The English lady wanted to pay tribute to Garibaldi and to Lauro di Bosis, but she wasn't going to be here to do it. Were any of us interested enough in the idea to do it for her, by proxy so to speak? There was a pretty thorough silence at that point. My spoon stirring coffee, banging against the side of the cup, sounded as loud as a bell. I thought, *What the hell? Why not?* And I said I would do it for her.

I had some reasons too. I admire the English lady. I hate embarrassing silences and have been known to make a fool out of myself just to prevent one. I also had and have feelings about Garibaldi. Like every Southerner I know of, I can't escape the romantic tradition of brave defeats, forlorn lost causes. Though Garibaldi's fight was mighty small shakes compared to Pickett's Charge—which, like all Southerners, I tend to view in Miltonic terms, fallen angels, etc.—I associated the two. And to top it all I am often sentimental on purpose, trying to prove to myself that I am not afraid of sentiment. So much for all that.

The English lady was pleased and enthusiastic. She gave me the names of some people who would surely help pay for the flowers and might even march up to the monument with me. The idea of the march pleased her. Maybe twenty, thirty, fifty . . . Maybe I could call Rimanelli at the magazine *Rottosei* where he worked. Then there would be pictures, it would be in the press. I stopped her there.

"I'll lay the wreath," I said. "But no Rimanelli, no press, no photographers. It isn't a stunt. As soon as you start mucking around with journalists, even good guys like Rimanelli, it all turns into a cheap stunt."

She was disappointed, but she could appreciate how I felt.

And that was that. The expatriate poet started telling a long, funny story about some German scholars—"really, I mean this *really* happened"—who went down to the coast of East Africa somewhere near Somalia to study the habits of a group of crab-eating monkeys, the only crab-eating monkeys left in the whole world. These monkeys swam in shallow water, caught crabs, and ate them. So down went the German scholars with a lot of gear to study them. They lived a very hard, incredibly uncomfortable life for a year or so and collected all the data they needed. Then they came back to civilization and published a monograph. The only trouble was that the ink was hardly dry on the monograph before the monkeys, perverse and inexplicable creatures, stopped swimming entirely, stopped eating crabs for good and all, and began digging for clams.

Everybody laughed and our host poured out some more Strega.

Then it was almost the end of April. The English lady was in Vienna. I had been working on a novel, one about politics in Florida of all things, one that nobody north of the Mason Dixon was to believe as probable (south of the line it was taken, erroneously too, as a *roman à clef*) and damn few people were going to buy. I hadn't seen anybody except my own family for a while. I couldn't get much interest or action out of the people who were supposed to help pay for the flowers. Some of them were getting kind of hard to get in touch with. I had a postcard from the English lady reminding me of it all and wishing she could be there to be with me. I thought a little more about Garibaldi, read about the battle in detail in the library of the American Academy. Remembered Professor Buzzer Hall at Princeton and his annual show, the passionate "Garibaldi Lecture," the same one every year, that drew enormous crowds, cheering students and half the Italians from Mercer County and Trenton. Hall could make you want to put on a red shirt and go out and die. I had some nostalgia about red shirts too. My grandfather had ridden with Wade Hampton's Redshirts in Reconstruction days in South Carolina.

I walked in the park of the Gianicolo many times. The American Academy, where I worked, was on Via Angelo Masina, and I had hunted for Masina, found his bust, and found it defaced. Somebody had painted out Angelo and painted in Giulietta.

I was going to do it all right.

Then somebody stopped in my studio for a drink. He said I ought to think about it, maybe it was against the law or something. But how would I find out whether I was breaking the law or not? By getting myself arrested? Then I remembered I had a friend down at the Embassy and I thought I'd ask him to find out for me, even at the risk that he would get very excited and patriotic. I called and we had a conversation that went about like this:

"Hello, John," I said. "Would you do me a favor?"

"What?"

"I'm going to put a wreath on the Garibaldi monument on the thirtieth of April. Would you find out if I'll be breaking any law?"

"All right," he said. "Don't call me, I'll call you."

Not even in his tone was there the suggestion of a raised eyebrow. Strictly routine. It would probably be the easiest thing in the world. Then he called back.

"Look," he said. "This may take a little time and doing. You sure you want to lay a wreath on the monument?"

"Well, I don't know . . ."

"Do you or don't you? I mean, if you do, we'll fix it up. It's a little bit complicated, but if you want to do it, we can fix it."

I shrugged to myself. "Okay, see if you can do it."

I wasn't going to be able to hide behind the long skirts of the U.S. Government. This wasn't the timorous State Department I was always hearing about. He now acted as liaison and as a buffer between me and the Italian Government. He, or his secretary, to be perfectly factual and to complicate things a little more, called me. There was a list of questions, some things they wanted to know before I got the permission. I would get the permission all right and it really didn't make much difference how I answered the questions, so long as I did not object to answering them in principle. She read the questions over the phone, completely matter-of-fact, and I dictated answers. There was quite a list, among them:

"Why are you laying a wreath on this monument?

"What special significance do you attribute to the thirtieth of April?

"Could there be any connection between the fact that the wreath is to be put there on the thirtieth of April and that the next day is the first of May—May Day?

"How many people do you anticipate will participate in this ceremony?

"Will they march? Will there be banners, flags, music, etc.?"

And so on. The last question stopped me cold. I had also mentioned the bunch of flowers.

"Who is this Lauro di Bosis?"

I answered them all, each and every one. The secretary took down my answers, said she would relay them to Them and would call me back. A day or so went by before she called.

"It's all set," she said. "Go ahead and lay your wreath. They'll have police up there to protect you in case anything goes wrong. Just one thing, though, they're letting you do this with the full understanding that it doesn't mean anything."

"What?"

"They say it's all right because we all understand that it doesn't mean anything."

"Just a typical American stunt. No implications, some kind of a joke."

"That's the idea."

"Thanks a lot."

I was left with it in my lap then. If I put the wreath on the monument and flowers beneath the bust of Lauro di Bosis, it wouldn't mean a thing. If I did it, I was agreeing with that. They didn't care much about Di Bosis anyway. "Who was he?" they had asked. I thought they were just testing or being ironic in the heavy-handed way of governments. They were not, it appeared. I had replied simply with the information that there was a bust of the poet Di Bosis in the park. The secretary told me this was news to Them. Even if I did lay the wreath, it wasn't going to come close to fulfilling the intentions of the English lady. The hell with it. I would sleep on it and figure out what to do in the morning, which happened to be the thirtieth of April.

In the morning it was clear. The day was bright and warm and sunny. I walked over from my apartment to the Academy past the Villa Pamphili and along the route, in reverse, of Garibaldi's fallen soldiers. I passed by the English lady's apartment, the ruined house, the Porta San Pancrazio. Two horse policemen, mounted *carabinieri,* were in the shade of the great gate. A balloon man walked by, headed for the park in the Villa Sciara, which is popular with children and where there is a wall fountain celebrated in one of the most beautiful poems written in our time. Americans in the area simply refer to it as Richard Wilbur's fountain. I watched the balloon man go along the wall and out of sight, followed by his improbably bright bouquet of balloons. I had a coffee and cognac at the Bar Gianicolo and made up my mind not to do it. I felt greatly relieved. I thought she would understand under the circumstances.

But, even so, it was a long, long day. The afternoon was slow. I couldn't make my work go, spent the whole time fiddling with a sentence or two. I went for a walk in the park. Children were riding in high-wheeled donkey carts. A few tourists were along the balustrade looking at the vista of Rome. And there were indeed a few extra policemen in the area. I wondered what they thought they were looking for—some lone, crazy American burdened with a huge wreath—and what they would report when nothing happened, and who among Them would read such a report and how many, if any, desks it would pass over. I looked at Garibaldi. He wasn't troubled by anything. He was imperial and maybe a little too dignified to be wholly in character. He wasn't made for bronze. The traffic squalled around him and behind him the dome of St. Peter's hovered like a huge gas balloon, so light it seemed in the clear air, tugging on a string. If you went over to that side of the piazza you saw sheep grazing on a sloping hill beneath, with that dome dominating the whole sky. Once there had been a shepherd, too, with pipes, or, anyway, some kind of wind instrument.

I went on, took a look at Anita Garibaldi, another bronze equestrian, but this one all at a full gallop, wide open, a baby in the crook of one arm and a huge, long-barreled revolver in her other hand, which she was aiming behind her.

Diagonally across from Anita is the Villa Lante and the slender, lonely white bust of Lauro di Bosis. I went over and looked at him awhile. Pale, passionate, yes glorious, and altogether of another time, the buzz of his badly flown airplane like the hum of a mosquito and of not much more importance when you think of a whole wide sky filled with the roar of great engines, the enormous bombs they dropped, thinking of my sculptor friend losing all his friends (and in war that's all that there is) as they came up over the slight rise in the ground and rushed the village across an open field. . . . He said there was a tank destroyer captain with them. He had come along to see how it would go. He had been refused permission by Battalion to detach any of his idle tank destroyers to help the company out. He came just behind the assault, stepping over the bodies and weeping because just one tank destroyer could have taken the village and they never would have lost a man. Or thinking of all the brave anonymous men, bravery being a fancy term for doing what you have to and what has to be done, who fought back and died lonely, in police station basements and back rooms, not only in Rome but in most of the cities of the civilized world. It was a forlorn, foolish, adolescent gesture. But it was a kind of beginning. If Mussolini was really a sensitive man, and history seems to indicate that he must have been (perhaps to his own dismay), then he heard death, however faintly, the flat sound of it—like a fly trapped in a room. I looked at Lauro di Bosis for a moment with some of the feelings usually attributed to young girls standing at the grave of Keats.

And that was the end of it.

Except for one thing, a curious thing. That same night I had a dream, a very simple, nonsymbolic dream. In the dream I had a modest bouquet of flowers and I set out to try to find the bust of Lauro di Bosis and leave the flowers there. I couldn't find it. I had a sense of desperation, the cold-sweat urgency of a real nightmare. And then I knew where it was and why I hadn't noticed it. There it was, covered, bank on bank, with a heaped jungle of flowers. It was buried under a mountain of flowers. In my dream I wept for shame. But I woke then and I laughed out loud and slept soundly after that.

ELLEN GILCHRIST

Ellen Gilchrist was born in Vicksburg, Mississippi. She received a B.A. in philosophy from Millsaps College and did graduate work in creative writing at the University of Arkansas. She has lived in New Orleans and in Fayetteville, Arkansas, which is now her home. She is the author of a book of poems, *The Land Surveyor's Daughter,* two novels, *The Anna Papers* and *The Annunciation,* and a volume of essays, *Falling Through Space,* as well as three collections of stories: *In the Land of Dreamy Dreams* (1981), *Victory Over Japan* (1984), which won the American Book Award, and *Drunk With Love* (1986).

The Lower Garden District Free Gravity Mule Blight or Rhoda, a Fable

RHODA woke up dreaming. In the dream she was crushing the skulls of Jody's sheepdogs. Or else she was crushing the skulls of Jody's sisters. Or else she was crushing Jody's skull. Jody was the husband she was leaving. Crunch, crunch, crunch went the skulls between her hands, beneath her heels.

As the dream ended her father was taking her to the police station so she could turn herself in. The family was all over the place, weeping and wringing their hands. Her mother's face was small and broken, peering down from the stairwell.

She woke from the dream feeling wonderful, feeling purged of evil. She pulled on Jody's old velour bathrobe and sat down at the dining room table to go over her lists. Getting a divorce was easy as pie. There was nothing to it. All you needed was money. All you needed for anything was money. Well, it was true. She went back to her lists.

Today the real estate agent was coming to see the house. Then she would sell it. Then she would get a cute little shotgun apartment in the Faubourg-Marigny. Then she would get a job. Then she would get a new boyfriend. Everything would fall into place. Jody would hang himself and the will would still be made out in her favor and she would quit her job and go live in New York. In the meantime she might have to be poorer than she was accustomed to being.

That's okay, she told herself. She took off her robe and went into the dressing room and stood in front of the mirror. Dolphins don't have anything, she told herself. A hawk possesses nothing. Albert Einstein wore tennis shoes. I am a dolphin, she decided. I am a hawk high in the Cascade Mountains. I am not a checkbook. I am not a table. I am not a chair.

She got into the bathtub and ran the water all the way to the top, pretending she was a dolphin in the summer seas somewhere off the coast of Martinique or Aruba. The morning sun was coming in the window, making long slanting lines on the walls and shutters and the water in the tub . . . now what about those tablecloths, she began thinking, imagining the contents of a closet she hadn't opened in years. What am I going to do about all those tablecloths? She saw them stacked in rows, tied with small blue ribbons, monogrammed with her initials and her mother's initials and her grandmother's initials. Oh, God, she thought, what will I do with all those goddamn tablecloths? There won't be room for them in a tiny house in the Faubourg-Marigny. She sat up in the tub and began cleaning the mortar between the tiles with a fingernail brush.

She had worked her way up to the hot water faucet when the phone rang. "Now what?" she said. She jumped out of the bathtub and padded into the bedroom and answered it. She grabbed the receiver and threw herself down on the unmade bed, letting the sheets dry her body.

"Mrs. Wells," the soft black voice said. "I hope I didn't wake you. I've been trying to get hold of you for days."

"Who is it?" she said. But she knew who it was. It was the insurance adjuster who was in charge of her claim for the diamond ring she had sold last month.

"It's Earl," he said. "Earl Treadway. Remember, we talked last week."

"Oh, Earl. I'm so glad you called. I talked to Father Ryan about getting your son into the summer arts program. He said he was sure it could be arranged. Are you still interested in that?" Five thousand dollars, she was thinking. She shivered, a wonderful shiver that went all the way from her scalp to her groin. Five thousand dollars. Easy as pie.

"I told my son about talking to you," the black voice said. "He was excited about it. But listen, before we start talking about that, I need to see you about your claim. I think we have it straightened out now."

"Oh, God," she said. "I'd almost forgotten about it. It's all so embarrassing. I can't believe I left that ring lying out when there were workmen in the house. I guess I've just always been too trusting. I just couldn't believe it would happen to me."

"It happens to everyone sooner or later," he said. "That's what I'm for. Look, would it be possible for me to come by on my way to work? I have the check. I'd like to go on and deliver it."

"A check?"

"For four thousand, six hundred and forty-three dollars. Will that settle it?"

"Oh, well, yes. I mean, a check. I didn't know they did those things that fast. But, sure, come on by. I mean, I'm up and dressed. How long will it take you to get here? I mean, sure, that'll be fine. Then this afternoon I can go out and start shopping for a new diamond, can't I?"

"I'll be by in about thirty minutes then," he said. "I'm glad you were there. I'm glad it's all worked out. I'm looking forward to meeting you after all these nice talks we've had." Earl hung up the phone and leaned back against the refrigerator. The baby's bottle had spilled milk on the counter. He reached for a rag to wipe it up, then changed his mind and left it there. He straightened his tie and took his coat off the back of the highchair and put it on. It was too hot for his corduroy suit but he was wearing it anyway. All those nice talks, he was thinking. All those nice long talks.

Rhoda rolled off the bed and started trying on clothes. She settled on a tennis skirt and a red sweater. They love red, she told herself. They love bright colors. Besides, what had she read about red? Wear red, red keeps you safe.

Well, I don't need anything to keep me safe, she thought. All I'm doing is cheating an insurance company. It's the first time I ever stole anything in my life except that one time in the fifth grade. Everybody gets to steal something sooner or later. I mean, that little Jew stole my ring, didn't he? And Jody stole five years of my life. And this black man's going to bring that check and I'm going to take it and I don't give a damn whether it's honest or not.

She sat down on a chair and pulled on her tennis shoes and tied the strings in double knots.

Cheating an insurance company hadn't been Rhoda's idea. All she had started out to do was sell her engagement ring. All she had done was get up one morning and take her engagement ring down to the French Quarter to sell it. A perfect stone, a two-carat baguette. A perfect stone for a perfect girl, Gabe Adler had said when he sold it to Jody. It was insured for five thousand dollars. Rhoda had thought all she had to do was go downtown and turn it in and collect the money.

She drove to the Quarter, parked the car in the Royal Orleans parking lot and proceeded to carry the ring from antique store to antique store. One after the other the owners held the diamond up to the light, admired it and handed it back. "There's a place down on the Avenue that's buying stones," the last dealer told her. "Near Melepomene, on the Avenue. A new place. I heard they were giving good prices. You might try there."

"Oh, I don't think I really want to sell it," she said, slipping it back on her finger. "I just wanted to see what it was worth. I'm a reporter, did you know that? It would be a real pity if all those people out there buying diamonds found out what it's like to try to sell one, wouldn't it? If they found out what a racket you guys have going? This ring's insured for seven thousand dollars. But no one will give me half of that. I ought to write an article about it. I ought to let the public in on this."

"There's no need to talk like that," the man said. He was a big, sad-looking man in baggy pants. He took the glass out of his eye; his big droopy face was the shape of one of his chandeliers. "There's no need for that." A group of tourists lifted their eyes from the cases and turned to watch.

"You antique dealers are just a bunch of robbers," Rhoda said as loudly as she could. "Selling all this goddamn junk to people. And the jewelry stores are worse. How can my ring be worth seven thousand dollars if no one will buy it when I want to sell it? You want to tell me that? You want to explain that to me?"

"Leave the store," the man said, coming around the counter. "You just go on now and leave the store." He was moving toward her, his stomach marching before him like a drum. Rhoda retreated

"Thanks for the diamond lesson," she said. "I'll be able to use that in my work."

The place at Melepomene and Saint Charles was a modern showroom in an old frame house. There were gardens in front and a shiny red enamel door. This looks more like it, Rhoda thought. She opened the door and went inside, pretending to be interested in the watches in a case. "Can I help you?" the boy behind the counter said. He was a very young boy dressed like an old man. "I don't know," she said. "I have some jewelry I'm thinking of selling. Some people I know said this was a good place. I'm thinking of selling some things I don't wear anymore and getting a Rolex instead. I see you sell them."

"What was it you wanted to sell? Did you bring it with you?"

"I might sell this," she said, taking off the ring and handing it to him. "If I could get a good enough price. I'm tired of it. I'm bored with wearing rings anyway. See what you think it's worth."

He took the ring between his chubby fingers and held it up above him. He looked at it a moment, then put a glass into his eye. "It's flawed," he said. "No one is buying diamonds now. The prime was twenty percent this morning."

"It is not flawed," she said. "It came from Adler's. It's a perfect stone. It's insured for six thousand dollars."

"I'll give you nine hundred," he said. "Take it or leave it."

"How old are you?" she said. "You don't look like you're old enough to be buying diamonds."

"I'm twenty-five," he said. "I run this place for my father. I've been running it since it opened. Do you want to sell this ring or not? That's my only offer."

"I don't know," she said. "It's insured for six thousand dollars. I only meant to sell it for a lark."

"Well, I guess it depends on how badly you need the money," he said. "Of course if you don't like the ring there's not much sense in keeping it."

"Oh, I don't need the money." She had drawn herself up so she could look at him on a slant. "My husband's a physician. I don't need money for a thing. I just wanted to get rid of some junk." She squared her shoulders. "On the other hand I might sell it just so I wouldn't have to bother with keeping it insured. There's a painting I want to buy, at the Bienville. I could sell the ring and buy that painting. It's all irrelevant anyway. I mean, it's all just junk. It's all just possessions."

"Well, make up your mind," he said. He held the ring out to her on a polishing cloth. "It's up to you."

"I'll just keep it," she said. "I wouldn't dream of selling a ring that valuable for nine hundred dollars."

It was almost a week before she went back to sell the ring. "Seven hundred and fifty," he said. "That's the best I can do."

"But you said nine hundred. You definitely said nine hundred."

"That was last week. You should have sold it then." Rhoda looked into his little myopic piggy eyes, hating him with all her clean white Anglo-Teutonic heart. "I'll take it," she said, and handed him the ring.

He left the room. She sat down in a chair beside his desk, feeling powerless and used. He came back into the room. She was trying not to look at his hands, which were holding a stack of bills.

"Here you are," he said. "We don't keep records of these things, you know. We don't give receipts."

"What do you mean?" she said.

"There isn't any record. In case you want to file a claim."

She took the money from him and stuffed it into her handbag without counting it. "My God," she said. Her power was returning. She felt it coursing up her veins. Her veins were charged with power. A thousand white horses of pure moral power pouring up and down her neck and face and legs and arms and hands. "I've never filed an insurance claim in my life," she said. "I probably wouldn't bother to file one if I actually lost something." She stood up. "You are really just the epitome of too goddamn much, are you aware of that?" Then she left, going out into the sweltering heat of the summer day, out onto the Avenue where a streetcar was chugging merrily by.

I'm going to turn them in, she thought. As soon as I get home I'll call the mayor's office and then I'll call the Better Business Bureau and then I'll write a letter to *Figaro* and the *Times-Picayune*. I'll get that little fat Jewish bastard. My God, it must be terrible to be a nice Jew and have to be responsible for people like that. That's the strangest thing, how they all get lumped together in our minds, a saint like Doctor Bernstein and a little bastard like that. No wonder they all want to move to Israel. Oh, well. She got into the car and opened her bag and counted the money. Seven hundred and fifty dollars. Well, it would pay the bills.

It was several days before she called the insurance company and filed the claim. "It was right there in the jewelry box on the dresser where I always leave it," she told the police when they came to make a report. "I can't imagine who would take it. My housekeeper is the most honest person in this city. My friends come in and out but none of them would touch it. I just don't know. . . ."

"Have you had any work done on the house?" The police officer was young. He was standing in the doorway to her bedroom getting a hard-on but he was trying to ignore it. She was very pretty. With a big ass. He liked that in a woman. It reminded him of his mother. He shifted his revolver to the front and cocked his head sideways, giving her his late night look.

"Oh," she way saying. "I forgot all about that. I had the bedrooms painted last month. I had a whole crew of painters here for three days. You don't think . . . I mean, they all work for Mr. Sanders. He's as honest as the day is long. He paints for everyone. Still, the ring is gone. It isn't here. It was here and now it isn't."

"I'd bet on the painters," the policeman said. "There's been a lot of that going on lately. This is the third claim like this I've had in a week. In this same neighborhood."

"But why would he only take the ring?" Rhoda said. "Why didn't he take anything else? There was other jewelry here. Expensive things."

"They're after diamonds. And flat silver. They don't mess with small stuff. No, I think we've got a pretty professional job here. Looks like he knew what he was looking for."

"I only want my ring back," she told Earl the first time he called. "Or one just like it to replace it. I'm so embarrassed about this. I've never filed an insurance claim of any kind. But everyone said I had to go on and report it. I didn't want to."

"There's a lot of unemployment right now," he said. "It makes things happen."

"I know," she said. "That's why I hate to report this. I don't want to get anyone in trouble, any poor person or someone that had to steal to eat or something like that."

"You sure sound like a nice lady. I'd sure like to meet you sometime."

"Well, sure," she said. "Before this is over we'll have to see about that."

That had been the beginning. He had called her several times, asking for details of the robbery, checking facts. The conversations had drifted into discussions of movies, city politics, civil rights, athletics, her divorce, his divorce, his little boy, her connections that could get his little boy into a summer painting program. Somewhere along the way she told him the rest of the robbery story and he filed the claim and the money had been sent on its way from the home office of the insurance company.

Then he was there, standing on her doorstep, all dressed up in a corduroy suit with an oxford cloth shirt and a striped tie, six feet three inches tall, soft brown eyes, kinky black hair.

"Come on in the kitchen," she said. "Come have a cup of coffee." She led him through a dining room filled with plants. Rhoda's whole house was filled with plants. There were plants of every kind in every room. Lush, cool, every color of green, overflowing their terra-cotta pots, spilling out onto the floor. It took the maid all day Tuesday to water them. Earl followed her into the kitchen and sat down on a maple captain's chair. He put his briefcase beside him and folded his hands on the breakfast room table. He smiled at her. She was trying not to look at the briefcase but her eyes kept going in that direction.

"Where are you from, Earl Treadway?" she said. "Where in the Delta did you escape from with that accent? Or is it Georgia?"

"I escaped from Rosedale," he said. He was laughing. He wasn't backing off an inch. "My daddy was a sharecropper. How about you?"

"I escaped from Issaquena County," she said. "Sixty miles away. Well, I only lived there in the summers. In the winter I lived in Indiana. I lived up north a lot when I was young."

"Are you married? Oh, no, that's right. You told me you were getting a divorce. We talked so much I forgot half the things we said." He picked up a placemat from a stack of them at the end of the table. It was a blue and yellow laminated map of the British Virgin Islands, bright blue water, yellow islands. The names of the islands were in large block letters, Tortola, Beef Island, Virgin Gorda, Peter Island, Salt Island, The Indians. All the places Rhoda had been with her husband, Jody, summer after boring summer, arguing and being miserable on the big expensive sailboat. Dinner on board or in some polite resort. Long hungover mornings with whiskey bottles and ashtrays and cigarettes and cracker crumbs all over the deck. Anchored in some hot civilized little harbor. While somewhere ashore, down one of the dirt roads where Jody never let her go, oh, there Rhoda imagined real life was going on, a dark musky, musical real life, loud jump-ups she heard at night, hot black wildness going on and on into the night while she sat on the boat with her husband and people they brought along from New Orleans, gossiping about people they knew, planning their careful little diving trips for the morning, checking the equipment, laughing good-naturedly about their escapades in the water, wild adventures thirty feet below the dinghy with a native guide.

Earl picked up one of the placemats and held it in his hand. "What is this?" he said again. He was looking right at her. His face was so big, his mouth so red and full, his voice so deep and rich and kind. It was cool in the room. So early in the morning. I wonder what he smells like, she thought. I wonder what it would be like to touch his hair.

"My husband bought those," she said. "They're maps of the British Virgin Islands, where I have a sailboat. I used to go there every summer. I know that place like the back of my hand. I've been bored to death on every island in the Sir Francis Drake Channel. I guess I still own part of the sailboat. I forgot to ask. Well, anyway, that's what it is. On the other hand, it's a placemat."

"I like maps," he said. "I remember the first one I ever saw, a map of the world. I used to stay after school to look at it. I was trying to find the way out of Rosedale." She smiled and he went on. "Later, I had a job at a filling station and I could get all the maps I wanted. I was getting one of every state. I wanted to put them on a wall and make the whole United States."

"How old are you?" she said.

"I'm thirty-four. How old are you?"

"I'm thirty-four. Think of that. Our mothers could have passed each other on the street with us in their stomachs."

"You say the funniest things of anyone I ever talked to. I was thinking that when I'd talk to you on the phone. You think real deep, don't you?"

"Oh, I don't know. I read all the time. I read Albert Einstein a lot. Oh, not the part about the physics. I read his letters and about political systems and things like that. Yeah, I guess that's true. I guess I do think deep."

"You really own a sailboat in this place?" he said. He was still holding the placemat.

"I guess I do. I forgot to put it in the divorce." She laughed. His hand had let the placemat drop. His hand was very near to hers. "It isn't nearly as much fun as it looks in the pictures," she said. "It's really pretty crowded. There are boats all over the place there now, big power boats from Puerto Rico. It's all terribly middle class really. A lot of people pretending to have adventures." She was looking at the briefcase out of the corner of her eye. It was still there. Why don't you go on and give me the check, she wanted to say, and then I'll give you a piece of ass and we'll be square. She sighed. "What did you want to talk to me about? About settling the robbery I mean."

"Just to finalize everything. To give you the check they cut this morning."

"All right," she said. "Then go on and give it to me. Just think, Earl, in my whole life I never collected any insurance. It makes me feel like a criminal. Well, you're an insurance salesman. Make me believe in insurance."

He picked up the briefcase and set it down in front of him on the table. "Will this hurt the finish on your table? It's such a pretty table. I wouldn't want to scratch it up."

"Oh, no," she said. "It's all right. It's an old table. It's got scratches all over it."

He opened the briefcase and moved papers and took out the check. He held it out very formally to her. "I'm sorry about the ring," he said. "I hope this will help you get another one."

She took it from him. Then she laid it carelessly down behind her on a counter. She laid it down a few inches away from a puddle of water that had condensed around a green watering can. Once she had put it there she would not touch it again while he was watching. "Thanks for bringing it by. You could have mailed it."

"I wanted to meet you. I wanted to get to know you."

"So did I," she said. Her eyes dug into his skin, thick black skin, real black skin. Something she had never had. It was cool in the room. Three thousand dollars' worth of brand-new air conditioning was purring away outside the window. Inside everything was white and green. White woodwork, green plants, baskets of plants in every window, ferns and philodendrons and bromeliads, gloxinia and tillansias and cordatum. Leaves and shadows of leaves and wallpaper that looked like leaves. "What are you doing tonight?" she said. "What are you doing for dinner?"

"I'll be putting napkins in your lap and cutting up your steak if you'll go out with me," he said. "We'll go someplace nice. Anywhere you want."

"What time?"

"I have to go to a meeting first. A community meeting where I live. I'm chairman of my neighborhood association. It might be eight or nine before I can get away. Is that too late?" He had closed his briefcase and was standing up.

"I'll be waiting," she said. He locked the briefcase and came out from beside the table. "Don't lose that check," he said. It was still sitting on the edge of the counter. The circle of water was closing in. "Don't get it wet. It would be a lot of trouble to get them to make another one."

When he was gone Rhoda straightened up the house and made the bed. She put all the dishes in the dishwasher and watered the plants. She cleaned off the counters one by one. She moved the watering can and wiped up the ring of water. Then she picked up the check and read the amount. Four thousand six hundred and forty-three dollars. Eight months of freedom at five hundred dollars a month. And forty-three dollars to waste. I'll waste it today, she decided. She picked up the phone and called the beauty parlor.

Six o'clock is the time of day in New Orleans when the light cools down, coming in at angles around the tombs in the cemeteries, between the branches of the live oak trees along the avenues, casting shadows across the yards, penetrating the glass of a million windows.

Rhoda always left the drapes open in the afternoons so she could watch the light travel around the house. She would turn on "The World of Jazz" and dress for dinner while the light moved around the rooms. Two hours, she thought, dropping her clothes on the floor of her bedroom. Two hours to make myself into a goddess. She shaved her legs and gave herself a manicure and rubbed perfumed lotion all over her body and started trying on clothes. Rhoda had five closets full of clothes. She had thousands of dollars' worth of skirts and jackets and blouses and dresses and shoes and scarves and handbags.

She opened a closet in the hall. She took out a white lace dress she had worn one night to have dinner with a senator. She put the soft silk-lined dress on top of her skin. Then, one by one, she buttoned up every one of the fifty-seven tiny pearl buttons of the bodice and sleeves. The dress had a blue silk belt. Rhoda dropped it on the closet floor. She opened a drawer and found a red scarf and tied it around the waist of the dress. She looked in the mirror. It was almost right. But not quite right. She took one of Jody's old ties off a tie rack and tied that around the waist. There, that was perfect. "A Brooks Brothers' tie," she said out loud. "The one true tie of power."

She went into the kitchen and took a bottle of wine out of the refrigerator and poured herself a glass and began to walk around the house. She stopped in the den and put a Scott Joplin record on the stereo and then she began to dance, waving the wineglass in the air, waiting for Earl to come. She danced into the bedroom and took the check out of a drawer where she had hidden it and held it up and kissed it lavishly all over. Jesus loves the little children, she was singing. All the children of the world. Red and yellow, black and white, all are precious, precious, precious. Four thousand, six hundred and forty-three dollars and thirty-seven cents. A day's work. At last, a real day's work.

The doorbell was ringing. She set the wineglass down on the table and walked wildly down the hall to the door. "I'm coming," she called out. "I'll be right there."

"Now what I'd really like to do with you," Earl was saying, "is to go fishing." They were at Dante's by the River, a restaurant down at the end of Carrollton Avenue. They had stuffed themselves on Crab Thibodeaux and Shrimp Mousse and Softshell Crabs Richard and were starting in on the roast quail. It was a recipe with a secret sauce perfected in Drew, Mississippi, where Earl's grandfather had been horsewhipped on the street for smarting off to a white man. But that was long ago and the sauce tasted wonderful to Rhoda and Earl.

"I'm stuffed," she said. "How can I eat all this? I won't be able to move, much less make love to you. I am going to make love to you, you know that, don't you?"

"If you say so," he said. "Now, listen, Miss Rhoda, did you hear what I said about going fishing?"

"What about it?"

"I want to take you fishing. I'm famous for my fishing. I won a fishing rodeo one time."

"We don't have to do it tonight, do we? I mean, I have other plans for tonight as I just told you."

"We'll pretend we're fishing," he said. "How about that?" He was laughing at her but she didn't care. Black people had laughed at Rhoda all her life. All her life she had been making black people laugh.

"What are you thinking of?" he said.

"I was thinking about when I was little and my mother would take me to Mississippi for the summer and if I wanted attention I would take off my underpants and the black people would all die laughing and the white people would grab me up and make me put them back on. Well, I guess that's a racist thing to say, isn't it?"

"You want to see if it makes me laugh?"

"Yeah, I do. So hurry up and finish eating. When I think of something I like to go right on and do it. In case they blow the world up while I'm waiting." Earl took a piece of French toast and buttered it and laid it on her plate. "Are you sure you aren't married, Earl? I made a vow not to mess around with married men. I've had enough of that stuff. That's why I'm getting a divorce. Because I kept having these affairs and I'd have to go home and eat dinner and there the other person would be. With no one to eat dinner with. That doesn't seem right, does it? After they'd made love to me all afternoon? So I'm getting a divorce. Now I'll have to be poor for a while but I don't care. It's better than being an adulteress, don't you think so?" She picked up the bread and put it back on his plate.

"Why don't you stop talking and finish your quail?"

"I can't stop talking when I'm nervous. It's how I protect myself." She pulled her hand back into her lap. Rhoda hated to be reminded that she talked too much.

"I'm not married," he said. "I told you that on the phone. I've got a little boy and I keep him part of the time. Remember, we talked about that before. It's all right. There isn't anything to be afraid of." He felt like he did when he coached his Little League baseball team. That's the way she made him feel. One minute she reminded him of a movie star. The next minute she reminded him of a little boy on his team who sucked his glove all the time. "We've got plenty of time to get to know each other. We don't have to hurry to do anything."

"Tell me about yourself," she said. "Tell me all the good parts first. You can work in the bad parts later."

"Well, I'm the oldest one of thirteen children. I worked my way through Mississippi Southern playing football. Then I spent three years in the Marines and now I'm in insurance. Last year I ran for office. I ran for councilman in my district and I lost but I'm going to run again. This time I'll win." He squared his shoulders. "What else? I love my family. I helped put my brothers and sisters through school. I'm proud of that." He stopped a moment and looked at her. "I've never known anyone like you. I changed shirts three times trying to get ready to come and get you."

"That's enough," she said. "Pay for this food and let's get out of here."

"My grandmother was a free woman from Natchez," he continued. They were in the car driving along the Avenue. "A light-skinned woman, what you'd call an octoroon. She lived until last year. She was so old she lost count of the years. Her father was a man who fought with Morrell's army. I have pictures of many of my ancestors. They were never slaves . . . you sure you want to hear all this?"

"Yeah, I want to know who I'm going to bed with."

"You talk some. You have a turn."

"I have two sons. They go to school in Virginia. They're real wild. Everyone in my family's wild. It's a huge family, a network over five states. I love them but they don't have any power over me anymore. Not that they ever did. I think I'm the first person in my family to ever really escape from it. It's taken me a long time to do it. Now I'm free. I might learn to fly. I might teach in a grade school. I might be a waitress. I might move to Europe. I might learn to sew and take up hems. I don't know what I'm going to do next. But right now I'm going to go home and fuck you. I'm tired of waiting to do it. I've been waiting all day."

"So have I," he said and pulled her closer to him.

"Another thing," she said. "I stole that money from you. I sold that diamond ring you paid me for. I sold it to this fat piggy little Jewish boy on Melepomene. He paid me in cash and told me I could file a claim. I'm thinking of reporting him to the Jewish temple. Well, he thought it up. But I'm the one that did it."

"Did you see that mule?" Earl said. "That mule flying by. That's the damndest thing. A gray mule with black ears."

"I stole the money from you," she said. "The money for the diamond. Don't you care? Don't you even care?" She moved his hand from around her waist and put it between her legs.

"That's the damndest thing about those mules when they get to town," he said, turning down the street to her house. "You can't keep them on the ground. They'll take off every time. Also, I am married. I guess we might as well go on and get that on the table."

"What mule," Rhoda said. "I don't see any mules. They don't allow mules on Saint Charles Avenue."

WILLIAM GOYEN

William Goyen was born in Trinity, Texas, in 1915. He was educated at Rice University, spent five years in the U.S. Navy, and lived much of his adult life in New York and Los Angeles. He wrote five novels, including *The House of Breath* and *Arcadio. The Collected Stories of William Goyen* was published in 1972. *Had I a Hundred Mouths: New and Selected Stories, 1974–1983* appeared in 1985. Mr. Goyen died in 1983.

Figure Over the Town

In the town of my beginning I saw this masked figure sitting aloft. It was never explained to me by my elders, who were thrilled and disturbed by the figure too, who it was, except that he was called Flagpole Moody. The days and nights he sat aloft were counted on calendars in the kitchens of small houses and in troubled minds, for Flagpole Moody fed the fancy of an isolated small town of practical folk whose day's work was hard and real.

Since the night he was pointed out to me from the roof of the little shed where my father sheltered grain and plowing and planting implements, his shape has never left me; in many critical experiences of my life it has suddenly appeared before me, so that I have come to see that it is a dominating emblem of my life, as often a lost lover is, or the figure of a parent, or the symbol of a faith, as the scallop shell was for so many at one time, or the Cross.

It was in the time of a war I could not understand, being so very young, that my father came to me at darkening, in the beginning wintertime, and said, "Come with me to the Patch, Son, for I want to show you something."

The Patch, which I often dream about, was a mysterious fenced-in plot of ground, about half an acre, where I never intruded. I often stood at the gate or fence and looked in through the hexagonal lenses of the chicken wire and saw how strange this little territory was, and wondered what it was for. There was the shed in it where implements and grain were stored, but nothing was ever planted nor any animal pastured here; nothing, not even grass or weed, grew here; it was just plain common ground.

This late afternoon my father took me into the Patch and led me to the shed and hoisted me up to the roof. He waited a moment while I looked around at all the world we lived in and had forgotten was so wide and housed so many in dwellings quite like ours. (Later, when my grandfather, my father's father, took me across the road and railroad tracks into a large pasture—so great I had thought it, from the window of our house, the whole world—where a little circus had been set up as if by magic the night before, and raised me to the broad back of a sleepy elephant, I saw the same sight and recalled not only the night I stood on the roof of the shed, but also what I had seen from there, that haunting image, and thought I saw it again, this time on the lightning rod of our house . . . but no, it was, as always, the crowing cock that stood there, eternally strutting out his breast and at the break of crowing.)

My father waited, and when he saw that I had steadied myself, he said, "Well, Son, what is it that you see over there, by the Methodist church?"

I was speechless and could only gaze; and then I finally said to him, not moving, "Something is sitting on the flagpole on top of a building."

"It is just a man," my father said, "and his name is Flagpole Moody. He is going to sit up there for as long as he can stand it."

When we came into the house, I heard my father say to my mother, lightly, "I showed Son Flagpole Moody and I think it scared him a little." And I heard my mother say, "It seems a foolish stunt, and I think maybe children shouldn't see it."

All that night Flagpole Moody was on my mind. When it began raining, in the very deepest night, I worried about him in the rain, and I went to my window and looked out to see if I could see him. When it lightninged, I saw that he was safe and dry under a little tent he had raised over himself. Later I had a terrible dream about him, that he was falling, falling, and when I called out in my nightmare, my parents came to me and patted me back to sleep, never knowing that I would dream of him again.

He stayed and stayed up there, the flagpole sitter, hooded (why would he not show his face?), and when we were in town and walked under him, I would not look up as they told me to; but once, when we stood across the street from the building where he was perched, I looked up and saw how high he was in the air, and he waved down at me with his cap in his hand.

Everywhere there was the talk of the war, but where it was or what it was I did not know. It seemed only some huge appetite that craved all our sugar and begged from the town its goods, so that people seemed paled and impoverished by it, and it made life gloomy—that was the word. One night we went into the town to watch them burn Old Man Gloom, a monstrous straw man with a sour, turned-down look on his face and dressed even to the point of having a hat—it was the Ku Klux Klan who lit him afire—and above, in the light of the flames, we saw Flagpole Moody waving his cap to us. He had been up eighteen days.

He kept staying up there. More and more the talk was about him, with the feeling of the war beneath all the talk. People began to get restless about Flagpole Moody and to want him to come on down. "It seems morbid," I remember my mother saying. What at first had been a thrill and an excitement—the whole town was there every other day when the provisions basket was raised up to him, and the contributions were extravagant: fresh pies and cakes, milk, little presents, and so forth—became an everyday sight; then he seemed ignored and forgotten by the town except for me, who kept a constant, secret watch on him; then, finally, the town became disturbed by him, for he seemed to be going on and on; he seemed an intruder now. Who could feel unlooked at or unhovered over in his house with this figure over everything? (It was discovered that Flagpole was spying on the town through binoculars.) There was an agitation to bring him down and the city council met to this end.

There had been some irregularity in the town which had been laid to the general lawlessness and demoralizing effect of the war: robberies; the disappearance of a beautiful young girl, Sarah Nichols (but it was said she ran away to find someone in the war); and one Negro shot in the woods, which could have been the work of the Ku Klux Klan. The question at the city-council meeting was, "Who gave Flagpole Moody permission to go up there?" No one seemed to know; the merchants said it was not for advertising, or at least no one of them had arranged it, though after he was up, many of them tried to use him to advertise their products—Egg Lay or Red Goose shoes or Have a Coke at Robbins Pharmacy—and why not? The Chamber of Commerce had not brought him, nor the Women's Club; maybe the Ku Klux had, to warn and tame the Negroes, who were especially in awe of Flagpole Moody; but the Klan was as innocent as all the others, it said. The pastor was reminded of the time a bird had built a nest on the church steeple, a huge foreign bird that had delighted all the congregation as well as given him subject matter for several sermons; he told how the congregation came out on the grounds to adore the bird, which in time became suddenly savage and swooped to pluck the feathers from women's Sunday hats and was finally brought down by the fire department, which found the nest full of rats and mice, half devoured, and no eggs at all—this last fact the subject of another series of sermons by the pastor, drawing as he did his topics from real life.

As the flagpole sitter had come to be regarded as a defacement of the landscape, an unsightly object, a tramp, it was suggested that the Ku Klux Klan build a fire in the square and ride round it on their horses and in their sheets, firing their guns into the air, as they did in their public demonstrations against immorality, to force Flagpole down. If this failed, it was suggested someone should be sent up on a firemen's ladder to reason with Flagpole. He was regarded now as a *danger* to the town, and more, as a kind of criminal. (At first he had been admired and respected for his courage, and desired, even: many women had been intoxicated by him, sending up, in the provisions basket, love notes and photographs of themselves, which Flagpole had read and then sailed down for anyone to pick up and read, to the embarrassment of this woman and that. There had been a number of local exposures.)

The town was ready for any kind of miracle or sensation, obviously. A fanatical religious group took Flagpole Moody for the Second Coming. The old man called Old Man Nay, who lived on the edge of the town in a boarded-up house and sat at the one open window with his shotgun in his lap, watching for the Devil, unnailed his door and appeared in the square to announce that he had seen a light playing around Flagpole at night and that Flagpole was some phantom representative of the Devil and should be banished by a raising of the Cross; but others explained that what Old Man Nay saw was St. Elmo's fire, a natural phenomenon. Whatever was given a fantastical meaning by some was explained away by others as of natural cause. What was right? Who was to believe what?

An evangelist who called himself "The Christian Jew" had, at the beginning, requested of Flagpole Moody, by a letter in the basket, the dropping of leaflets. A sample was pinned to the letter. The leaflet, printed in red ink, said in huge letters across the top: WARNING! YOU ARE IN GREAT DANGER! Below was a long message to sinners. If Flagpole would drop these messages upon the town, he would be aiding in the salvation of the wicked. "The Judgments of God are soon to be poured upon the Earth! Prepare to meet God before it is too late! Where will you spend Eternity? What can you do to be saved? How shall we escape if we neglect so great salvation! (Heb. 2:3)."

But there was no reply from Flagpole, which was evidence enough for the Christian Jew to know that Flagpole was on the Devil's side. He held meetings at night in the square, with his little group of followers passing out the leaflets.

"Lower Cain!" he bellowed. "You sinners standing on the street corner running a long tongue about your neighbors; you show-going, card-playing, jazz-dancing brothers—God love your soul—you are a tribe of sinners and you know it and God knows it, but He loves you and wants you to come into His tabernacle and give up your hearts that are laden with wickedness. If you look in the Bible, if you will turn to the chapter of Isaiah, you will find there about the fallen angel, Lucifer was his name, and how his clothing was sewn of emeralds and sapphires, for he was very beautiful; but friends, my sin-loving friends, that didn't make any difference. 'How art thou fallen from Heaven, O Lucifer, son of the morning!' the Bible reads. And it says there that the Devil will walk amongst us and that the Devil will sit on the rooftops; and I tell you we must unite together to drive Satan from the top of the world. Listen to me and read my message, for I was the rottenest man in this world until I heard the voice of God. I drank, I ran with women, I sought after the thrills of the flesh . . . and I admonish you that the past scenes of earth *shall be remembered in Hell.*"

The old maid, Miss Hazel Bright, who had had one lover long ago, a cowboy named Rolfe Sanderson who had gone away and never returned, told that Flagpole was Rolfe come back, and she wrote notes of poetic longing to put in the provisions basket. Everybody used Flagpole Moody for his own purpose, and so he, sitting away from it all, apparently serene in his own dream and idea of himself, became the lost lover to the lovelorn, the saint to the seekers of salvation, the scapegoat of the guilty, the damned to those who were lost.

The town went on tormenting him; they could not let him alone. They wished him to be their own dream or hope or lost illusion, or they wished him to be what destroyed hope and illusion. They wanted something they could get their hands on; they wanted someone to ease the dark misgiving in themselves, to take to their deepest bosom, into the farthest cave of themselves where they would take no other if he would come and be for them alone. They plagued him with love letters, and when he would not acknowledge these professions of love, they wrote him messages of hate. They told him their secrets, and when he would not show himself to be overwhelmed, they accused him of keeping secrets of his own. They professed to be willing to follow him, leaving everything behind, but when he would not answer "Come," they told him how they wished he would fall and knock his brains out. They could not make up their minds and they tried to destroy him because he had made up his, whatever it was he had made his mind up to.

Merchants tormented him with proposals and offers—would he wear a Stetson hat all one day, tip and wave it to the people below? Would he hold, just for fifteen minutes every hour, a streamer with words on it proclaiming the goodness of their bread, or allow balloons, spelling out the name of something that ought to be bought, to be floated from the flagpole? Would he throw down Life Savers? Many a man, and most, would have done it, would have supplied an understandable reason for his behavior, pacifying the general observer, and in the general observer's own terms (or the general observer would not have it), and so send him away undisturbed, with the feeling that all the world was really just as he was, cheating a little here, disguising a little there. (Everybody was, after all, alike, so where the pain, and why?)

But Flagpole Moody gave no answer. Apparently he had nothing to sell, wanted to make no fortune, to play no jokes or tricks; apparently he wanted just to be let alone to do his job. But because he was so different, they would not let him alone until they could, by whatever means, make him quite like themselves, or cause him, at least, to recognize them and pay *them* some attention. Was he camping up there for the fun of it? If so, why would he not let them all share in it? Maybe he was there for the pure devilment of it, like a cat calm on a chimney top. Or for some very crazy and not-to-be-tolerated reason of his own (which everyone tried to make out, hating secrets as people do who want everything in the clear, where they can attack it and feel moral dudgeon against it).

Was it Cray McCreery up there? Had somebody made him another bet?

One time Cray had walked barefooted to the next town, eighteen miles, because of a lost bet. But no, Cray McCreery was found, as usual, in the Domino Parlor. Had any crazy people escaped from the asylum? They were counted and found to be all in. The mind reader, Madame Fritzie, was importuned: There seemed, she said, to be a dark woman in the picture; that was all she contributed: "I see a dark woman. . . ." And as she had admonished so many in the town with her recurring vision of a dark woman, there was either an army of dark women tormenting the minds of men and women in the world, or only one, which was Madame Fritzie herself. She could have made a fortune out of the whole affair if she had had her wits about her. More than one Ouija board was put questions to, but the answers were either indistinguishable or not to the point.

Dogs howled and bayed at night and sometimes in the afternoons; hens crowed; the sudden death of children was laid to the evil power of Flagpole Moody over the town.

A masked buffoon came to a party dressed as Flagpole Moody and caused increasing uneasiness among the guests until three of the men at the party, deciding to take subtle action rather than force the stranger to unmask, reported to the police by telephone. The police told them to unmask him by force and they were coming. When the police arrived they found the stranger was Marcus Peters, a past president of the Lions Club and a practical joker with the biggest belly laugh in town, and everybody would have known all along who the impostor was if he had only laughed.

A new language evolved in the town: "You're crazy as Moody," "cold as a flagpole sitter's——," "go sit on a flagpole" and other phrases of that sort.

In that day and time there flourished, even in that little town, a group of sensitive and intellectual people, poets and artists and whatnot, who thought themselves quite mad and gay—and quite lost, too, though they would turn their lostness to a good thing. These advanced people needed an object upon which to hinge their loose and floating cause, and they chose Flagpole Moody to draw attention, which they so craved, to themselves. They exalted him with some high, esoteric meaning that they alone understood, and they developed a whole style of poetry, music and painting, the echoes of which are still heard, around the symbol of Flagpole Moody. They wrote, and read aloud to meetings, critical explanations of the Theory of Aloftness.

Only Mrs. T. Trevor Sanderson was bored with it all, shambling restlessly about the hospital in her Japanese kimono, her spotted hands (liver trouble, the doctors said) spread like fat lizards on the knolls of her hips. She was there again for one of her rest cures, because her oil-money worries were wearing her to death, and now the Catholic Church was pursuing her with zeal to convert her—for her money, so she said. Still, there was something to the Catholic Church; you couldn't get around that, she said, turning her spotted hands to show them yellow underneath, like a lizard's belly; and she gave a golden windowpane illustrating *The Temptation of St. Anthony* to St. Mary's Church, but would do no more than that.

There were many little felonies and even big offenses of undetermined origin in the police records of the town, and Flagpole was a stimulus to the fresh inspection of unsolved crimes. He drew suspicions up to him and absorbed them like a filter, as though he might purify the town of wickedness. If only he would send down some response to what had gone up to him. But he would not budge; and now he no longer even waved to the people below as he had during the first good days. Flagpole Moody had utterly withdrawn from everybody. What the town finally decided was to put a searchlight on him at night, to keep watch on him.

With the searchlight on the flagpole sitter, the whole thing took a turn, became an excuse for a ribald attitude. When a little wartime carnival came to the town, it was invited to install itself in the square, and a bazaar was added to it by the town. The spirit of Flagpole had to be admired, it was admitted; for after a day and night of shunning the gaiety and the mockery of it all, he showed his good nature and good sportsmanship—even his daring—by participating! He began to do what looked like acrobatic stunts, as though he were an attraction of the carnival.

And what did the people do, after a while, but turn against him again and say he was, as they had said at first, a sensationalist? Still, I loved it that he had become active; that it was not a static, fastidious, precious and Olympian show, that Flagpole did not take on a self-righteous or pompous or persecuted air, although my secret conception of him was still a tragic one. I was proud that my idea fought back—otherwise he was like Old Man Gloom, a shape of straw and sawdust in man's clothing, and let them burn him, if only gloom stood among the executioners, watching its own effigy and blowing on the flames. I know now that what I saw was the conflict of an idea with a society; and I am sure that the idea was bred by the society—raised up there, even, by the society—in short, society was in the flagpole sitter and he was in the society of the town.

There was, at the little carnival, one concession called "Ring Flagpole's Bell." It invited customers to try to strike a bell at the top of a tall pole resembling his—and with a replica of him on top—by hitting a little platform with a rubber-headed sledgehammer; this would drive a metal disk up toward the bell. There was another concession where people could throw darts at a target resembling a figure on a pole. The Ferris wheel was put so close to Flagpole that when its passengers reached the top they could almost, for a magical instant, reach over and touch his body. Going round and round, it was as if one were soaring up to him only to fall away, down, from him; to have him and to lose him; and it was all felt in a marvelous whirling sensation in the stomach that made this experience the most vaunted of the show.

This must have tantalized Flagpole, and perhaps it seemed to him that all the beautiful and desirable people in the world rose and fell around him, offering themselves to him only to withdraw untaken and ungiven, a flashing wheel of faces, eyes, lips and sometimes tongues stuck out at him and sometimes a thigh shown, offering sex, and then burning away. His sky at night was filled with voluptuous images, and often he must have imagined the faces of those he had once loved and possessed, turning round and round his head to torment him. But there were men on the wheel who made profane signs to him, and women who thumbed their noses.

Soon Flagpole raised his tent again and hid himself from his tormentors. What specifically caused his withdrawal was the attempt of a drunken young man to shoot him. This young man, named Maury, rode a motorcycle around the town at all hours and loved the meaner streets and women who gave him ease, especially the fat ones, his mania. One night he stood at the hotel window and watched the figure on the pole, who seemed to flash on and off, real and then unreal, with the light of the electric sign beneath the window. He took deep drags of his cigarette and blew the smoke out toward Flagpole; then he blew smoke rings as if to lasso Flagpole with them, or as if his figure were a pin he could hoop with the rings of smoke. "You silly bastard, do you like what you see?" he had muttered, and "Where have I seen you before?" between his half-clenched teeth, and then he had fired the pistol. Flagpole turned away then, once and for all.

But he had not turned away from me. I, the silent observer, watching from my window or from any high place I could secretly climb to, witnessed all this conflict and the tumult of the town. One night in my dreaming of Flagpole Moody—it happened every night, this dream, and in the afternoons when I took my nap, and the dreaming had gone on so long that it seemed, finally, as if he and I were friends, that he came down secretly to a rendezvous with me in the little pasture, and it was only years later that I would know what all our conversations had been about—that night in my dream the people of the town came to me and said, "Son, we have chosen you to go up the flagpole to Flagpole Moody and tell him to come down."

In my dream they led me, with cheers and honors, to the top of the building and stood below while I shinnied up the pole. A great black bird was circling over Flagpole's tent. As I went up the pole I noticed crowded avenues of ants coming and going along the pole. And when I went into the tent, I found Flagpole gone. The tent was as if a tornado had swept through the whole inside of it. There were piles of rotten food; shreds of letters torn and retorn, as small as flakes of snow; photographs pinned to the walls of the tent were marked and scrawled over so that they looked like photographs of fiends and monsters; corpses and drifts of feathers of dead birds that had flown at night into the tent and gone so wild with fright that they had beaten themselves to death against the sides. And over it all was the vicious traffic of insects that had found the remains, in the way insects sense what human beings have left, and come from miles away.

What would I tell them below, those who were now crying up to me, "What does he say, what does Flagpole Moody say?" And there were whistles and an increasingly thunderous chant of "Bring him down! Bring him down! Bring him down!" What would I tell them? I was glad he had gone; but I would not tell them that—yet. In the tent I found one little thing that had not been touched or changed by Flagpole; a piece of paper with printed words, and across the top the huge red words: WARNING! YOU ARE IN GREAT DANGER!

Then, in my dream, I went to the flap of the tent and stuck out my head. There was a searchlight upon me through which fell a delicate curtain of light rain; and through the lighted curtain of rain that made the people seem far, far below, under shimmering and jeweled veils, I shouted down to the multitude, which was dead quiet now, "He is not here! Flagpole Moody is not here!"

There was no sound from the crowd, which had not, at first, heard what I said. They waited; then one voice bellowed up, "Tell him to come down!" And others joined this voice until, again, the crowd was roaring, "Tell him that we will not harm him; only tell him he has to come down!" Then I waved down at them to be quiet, in Flagpole Moody's gesture of salute, as he had waved down at people on the sidewalks and streets. Again they hushed to hear me. Again I said, this time in a voice that was not mine, but large and round and resounding, "Flagpole Moody is not here. His place is empty."

And then, in my magnificent dream, I closed the flap of the tent and settled down to make Flagpole Moody's place my own, to drive out the insects, to erase the marks on the photographs, and to piece together, with infinite and patient care, the fragments of the letters to see what they told. It would take me a very long time, this putting together again what had been torn into pieces, but I would have a very long time to give to it, and I was at the source of the mystery, removed and secure from the chaos of the world below that could not make up its mind and tried to keep me from making up my own.

My dream ended here, or was broken, by the hand of my mother shaking me to morning; and when I went to eat breakfast I heard them saying in the kitchen that Flagpole Moody had signaled early, at dawn, around six o'clock, that he wanted to come down; that he had come down in his own time, and that he had come down very, very tired, after forty days and nights, the length of the Flood. I did not tell my dream, for I had no power of telling then, but I knew that I had a story to one day shape around the marvel and mystery that ended in a dream and began in the world that was to be mine.

TOM T. HALL

Tom T. Hall was born in Olive Hill, Kentucky—the fourth son of a brick-plant worker and ordained minister. In 1964, after serving in the U.S. Army and attending college in Roanoke, Virginia, he moved to Nashville and began writing songs full time. Among the many songs he has written and recorded are: "Old Dogs, Children, and Watermelon Wine," "The Year Clayton Delaney Died," and "The Ballad of Forty Dollars." He is a member of the Songwriter's Hall of Fame. He is the author of a novel, *The Laughing Man of Woodmont Cove,* and a volume of stories, *The Acts of Life* (1986).

Murphy Walls and the Oriental Hummer

Murphy Walls had his thumb shot off in the Korean War. He found it and put it in a jar of alcohol and brought it home to Texas. Having his thumb shot off ended the war for him.

Here's how he explained the phantom pain that started after he had been home six months. He said that even though he knew he didn't have a right thumb on the left side of his right hand, it would hurt like hell when he was hung over.

Murphy's uncle was a dentist who lived in Ft. Worth. One weekend Murphy had his girlfriend drive him from Austin down to Ft. Worth to explain his problem to his uncle, who he figured was a kind of doctor. The trip was a big success because it turned out that people had the same problem with aching teeth, even when the teeth had been pulled. Murphy's dentist uncle gave him a prescription for some Novocain and some small syringes. When the phantom pain started in the missing thumb, Murphy would take the thumb out of the jar, give it a shot of Novocain, and the pain would stop.

Murphy became an expert on what could and could not be done with the thumb. He latched on to the theory that the thumb was the sole evolutionary cause of civilization. When he had had six or seven beers he would say that losing his thumb had made him a more understanding, aware, and caring person. Before the loss of the thumb, he had loved the joke about the man who had received a watch at retirement. When the retiree was seen on the street a few days after he had gotten the watch, someone asked him how he was doing. The retiree said, "Oh, just pissing and winding my watch." Since Murphy was right-handed he often lamented that he could do neither with the ease and comfort that he once had.

Although the loss of the thumb had made Murphy Walls a more aware person, he was not aware that a man was drinking a martini and telling his colleagues at a fashionable country club a few things about a man that Murphy was soon to meet.

The man at the country club said, "My son is not interested in banking. He is a man of letters. He has just returned from France where he has been studying the European influence on American literature."

Well, the man's son was not studying anything of the sort. The boy had been in Paris for two years drinking wine, playing chess, and writing poetry. The poet, being more sensitive than Murphy Walls, believed that there were hundreds, if not thousands, of people in Austin who considered poetry the tool, if not the cause, of communism, homosexuality, and drug abuse.

Murphy Walls was a part-time student at the University of Texas where he studied the artificial insemination of cows under the G.I. Bill. As he stood with his arm implanted deep inside the rear end of a Black Angus cow, Murphy turned to his teacher and asked, "Do you think Freud would have anything to say about my childhood on the ranch and this course I'm taking?"

His instructor said, "We teach that here at the university, but not in this department."

Murphy met the Oriental Hummer at a Chinese restaurant just off the campus of the University of Texas. While he was dining on egg drop soup, rice, egg rolls, and peas, he noticed that the waiter was humming a song. He remarked to his girlfriend, who was also studying the artificial insemination of cows at the University of Texas, that he had never before heard an Oriental waiter hum. He inquired as to whether she had ever heard of such a thing. She made one of those noises that people make when they have their mouths full, a noise that did not mean a yes or a no. Murphy went on, "Now you hear girls in truck stops humming Conway Twitty songs, and you hear cocktail waitresses in Holiday Inns humming Barry Manilow songs, but you don't hear anybody humming that yeng, yang, yong kind of tune, do you?"

The girl said, "I don't know as I ever did."

Murphy was delighted with his discovery and would not let it rest. He poured sake on the notion until it became a near law.

There is a beer joint near the campus and that's where Murphy took his girlfriend and his discovery. As they walked into the beer joint they could hear the jukebox playing Billy Joe Shaver's "Ride Me Down Easy." A cloud of cigarette smoke threw the room out of focus. The walls of the place had become a bulletin board. Although hundreds of notices of one kind or another were hung or tacked up each month, none were ever torn down from the colorfully littered walls. It was in this atmosphere that Murphy and his girlfriend found a table and ordered a beer.

It is not easy to get the attention of a crowd in such places. And so it was that the proprietor kept a twelve-gauge shotgun, the shells loaded with salt, leaned against an old mattress hung behind the bar. The bartender leveled the shotgun at the ragged mattress and fired into it. In the ensuing calm and quiet, he announced that one of Texas' great poets had returned to town and would now read a few of his poems. There was polite applause.

Murphy strained his eyes and stretched his neck to get a look at the poet, who was saying, "I'm glad to be back among my fellow Texans. . . ."

Murphy said, "Is this a poet or a politician?"

The proprietor said, "Shut up, cowboy."

Murphy said, "Yes, sir."

The poet read a few of his Paris poems to the quiet group. He then apologized for being sober and sat down. The proprietor grabbed the microphone and said, "We're proud of this boy and what he's done for Texas. He's been studying in Paris-by-god-France. He says he'll be glad to answer any questions you might have for him."

Murphy stood. "Sir," he said, "now you've traveled around a lot and you'd probably be on to this. Did you ever hear an Oriental humming?"

The poet stood and stared through the smoke at the smug Murphy. "I beg your pardon, sir, I didn't understand the question."

Murphy said, "An Oriental humming, you know, humming yeng, yang, yong type music."

Strange things happen on this planet. The entire group of people in the beer joint took up the question in earnest. The poet was the leader; he seemed fascinated by the question. And so it was the twenty-six people took their beer and marched the six blocks to the Chinese restaurant to hear an Oriental hum. There was little that could dampen the enthusiasm of the crowd, even when they discovered that the Oriental hummer was a Cheyenne Indian from Jackson Hole, Wyoming.

When last heard of, Murphy Walls had become an expert at the artificial insemination of cows and was heard to remark to a cocktail waitress in Tulsa, Oklahoma, "Did you ever notice that you never hear a Cheyenne Indian humming?"

The drunk poet now walks the early morning streets of Austin, Texas, in a near delirium of happiness. He has accomplished one of his great goals in life. He has led twenty-six people from a beer joint in Texas in search for the true meaning of poetry.

BARRY HANNAH

Barry Hannah was born in Mississippi. He graduated from Mississippi College and received an M.A. and an M.F.A. from the University of Arkansas. He has written five novels: *Geronimo Rex,* which won the William Faulkner Prize, *Nightwatchman, Ray, The Tennis Handsome,* and *Hey Jack!*. His two volumes of stories are *Airships* (1978) and *Captain Maximus* (1985). He is the writer-in-residence at the University of Mississippi.

Testimony of Pilot

WHEN I was ten, eleven and twelve, I did a good bit of my play in the backyard of a three-story wooden house my father had bought and rented out, his first venture into real estate. We lived right across the street from it, but over here was the place to do your real play. Here there was a harrowed but overgrown garden, a vine-swallowed fence at the back end, and beyond the fence a cornfield which belonged to someone else. This was not the country. This was the town, Clinton, Mississippi, between Jackson on the east and Vicksburg on the west. On this lot stood a few water oaks, a few plum bushes, and much overgrowth of honeysuckle vine. At the very back end, at the fence, stood three strong nude chinaberry trees.

In Mississippi it is difficult to achieve a vista. But my friends and I had one here at the back corner of the garden. We could see across the cornfield, see the one lone tin-roofed house this side of the railroad tracks, then on across the tracks many other bleaker houses with rustier tin roofs, smoke coming out of the chimneys in the late fall. This was niggertown. We had binoculars and could see the colored children hustling about and perhaps a hopeless sow or two with her brood enclosed in a tiny boarded-up area. Through the binoculars one afternoon in October we watched some men corner and beat a large hog on the brain. They used an ax and the thing kept running around, head leaning toward the ground, for several minutes before it lay down. I thought I saw the men laughing when it finally did. One of them was staggering, plainly drunk to my sight from three hundred yards away. He had the long knife. Because of that scene I considered Negroes savage cowards for a good five more years of my life. Our maid brought some sausage to my mother and when it was put in the pan to fry, I made a point of running out of the house.

I went directly across the street and to the back end of the garden behind the apartment house we owned, without my breakfast. That was Saturday.

Eventually, Radcleve saw me. His parents had him mowing the yard that ran alongside my dad's property. He clicked off the power mower and I went over to his fence, which was storm wire. His mother maintained handsome flowery grounds at all costs; she had a leaf mold bin and St. Augustine grass as solid as a rug.

Radcleve himself was a violent experimental chemist. When Radcleve was eight, he threw a whole package of .22 shells against the sidewalk in front of his house until one of them went off, driving lead fragments into his calf, most of them still deep in there where the surgeons never dared tamper. Radcleve knew about the sulfur, potassium nitrate and charcoal mixture for gunpowder when he was ten. He bought things through the mail when he ran out of ingredients in his chemistry sets. When he was an infant, his father, a quiet man who owned the Chevrolet agency in town, bought an entire bankrupt sporting-goods store, and in the middle of their backyard he built a house, plain-painted and neat, one room and a heater, where Radcleve's redundant toys forevermore were kept—all the possible toys he would need for boyhood. There were things in there that Radcleve and I were not mature enough for and did not know the real use of. When we were eleven, we uncrated the new Dunlop golf balls and went on up on a shelf for the tennis rackets, went out in the middle of his yard, and served new golf ball after golf ball with blasts of the rackets over into the cornfield, out of sight. When the strings busted we just went in and got another racket. We were absorbed by how a good smack would set the heavy little pills on an endless flight. Then Radcleve's father came down. He simply dismissed me. He took Radcleve into the house and covered his whole body with a belt. But within the week Radcleve had invented the mortar. It was a steel pipe into which a flashlight battery fit perfectly, like a bullet into a muzzle. He had drilled a hole for the fuse of an M-80 firecracker at the base, for the charge. It was a grand cannon, set up on a stack of bricks at the back of my dad's property, which was the free place to play. When it shot, it would back up violently with thick smoke and you could hear the flashlight battery whistling off. So that morning when I ran out of the house protesting the hog sausage, I told Radcleve to bring over the mortar. His ma and dad were in Jackson for the day, and he came right over with the pipe, the batteries and the M-80 explosives. He had two gross of them.

Before, we'd shot off toward the woods to the right of niggertown. I turned the bricks to the left; I made us a very fine cannon carriage pointing toward niggertown. When Radcleve appeared, he had two pairs of binoculars around his neck, one pair a newly plundered German unit as big as a brace of whiskey bottles. I told him I wanted to shoot for that house where we saw them killing the pig. Radcleve loved the idea. We singled out the house with heavy use of the binoculars.

There were children in the yard. Then they all went in. Two men came out of the back door. I thought I recognized the drunkard from the other afternoon. I helped Radcleve fix the direction of the cannon. We estimated the altitude we needed to get down there. Radcleve put the M-80 in the breech with its fuse standing out of the hole. I dropped the flashlight battery in. I lit the fuse. We backed off. The M-80 blasted off deafeningly, smoke rose, but my concentration was on that particular house over there. I brought the binoculars. We waited six or seven seconds. I heard a great joyful wallop on tin. "We've hit him on the first try, the first try!" I yelled. Radcleve was ecstatic. "Right on his roof!" We bolstered up the brick carriage. Radcleve remembered the correct height of the cannon exactly. So we fixed it, loaded it, lit it and backed off. The battery landed on the roof, blat, again, louder. I looked to see if there wasn't a great dent or hole in the roof. I could not understand why niggers weren't pouring out distraught from that house. We shot the mortar again and again, and always our battery hit the tin roof. Sometimes there was only a dull thud, but other times there was a wild distress of tin. I was still looking through the binoculars, amazed that the niggers wouldn't even come out of their house to see what was hitting their roof. Radcleve was on to it better than me. I looked over at him and he had the huge German binocs much lower than I did. He was looking straight through the cornfield, which was all bare and open, with nothing left but rotten stalks. "What we've been hitting is the roof of that house just this side of the tracks. White people live in there," he said.

I took up my binoculars again. I looked around the yard of that white wooden house on this side of the tracks, almost next to the railroad. When I found the tin roof, I saw four significant dents in it. I saw one of our batteries lying in the middle of a sort of crater. I took the binoculars down into the yard and saw a blond middle-aged woman looking our way.

"Somebody's coming up toward us. He's from that house and he's got, I think, some sort of fancy gun with him. It might be an automatic weapon."

I ran my binoculars all over the cornfield. Then, in a line with the house, I saw him. He was coming our way but having some trouble with the rows and dead stalks of the cornfield.

"That is just a boy like us. All he's got is a saxophone with him," I told Radcleve. I had recently got in the school band, playing drums, and had seen all the weird horns that made up a band.

I watched this boy with the saxophone through the binoculars until he was ten feet from us. This was Quadberry. His name was Ard, short for Arden. His shoes were foot-square wads of mud from the cornfield. When he saw us across the fence and above him, he stuck out his arm in my direction.

"My dad says stop it!"

"We weren't doing anything," says Radcleve.

"Mother saw the smoke puff up from here. Dad has a hangover."

"A what?"

"It's a headache from indiscretion. You're lucky he does. He's picked up the poker to rap on you, but he can't move further the way his head is."

"What's your name? You're not in the band," I said, focusing on the saxophone.

"It's Ard Quadberry. Why do you keep looking at me through the binoculars?"

It was because he was odd, with his hair and its white ends, and his Arab nose, and now his name. Add to that the saxophone.

"My dad's a doctor at the college. Mother's a musician. You better quit what you're doing. . . . I was out practicing in the garage. I saw one of those flashlight batteries roll off the roof. Could I see what you shoot 'em with?"

"No," said Radcleve. Then he said: "If you'll play that horn."

Quadberry stood out there ten feet below us in the field, skinny, feet and pants booted with black mud, and at his chest the slung-on, very complex, radiant horn.

Quadberry began sucking and licking the reed. I didn't care much for this act, and there was too much desperate oralness in his face when he began playing. That was why I chose the drums. One had to engage himself like suck's revenge with a horn. But what Quadberry was playing was pleasant and intricate. I was sure it was advanced, and there was no squawking, as from the other eleven-year-olds on sax in the band room. He made the end with a clean upward riff, holding the final note high, pure and unwavering.

"Good!" I called to him.

Quadberry was trying to move out of the sunken row toward us, but his heavy shoes were impeding him.

"Sounded like a duck. Sounded like a girl duck," said Radcleve, who was kneeling down and packing a mudball around one of the M-80s. I saw and I was an accomplice, because I did nothing. Radcleve lit the fuse and heaved the mudball over the fence. An M-80 is a very serious firecracker; it is like the charge they use to shoot up those sprays six hundred feet on July Fourth at country clubs. It went off, this one, even bigger than most M-80s.

When we looked over the fence, we saw Quadberry all muck specks and fragments of stalks. He was covering the mouthpiece of his horn with both hands. Then I saw there was blood pouring out of, it seemed, his right eye. I thought he was bleeding directly out of his eye.

"Quadberry?" I called.

He turned around and never said a word to me until I was eighteen. He walked back holding his eye and staggering through the cornstalks. Radcleve had him in the binoculars. Radcleve was trembling . . . but intrigued.

"His mother just screamed. She's running out in the field to get him."

I thought we'd blinded him, but we hadn't. I thought the Quadberrys would get the police or call my father, but they didn't. The upshot of this is that Quadberry had a permanent white space next to his right eye, a spot that looked like a tiny upset crown.

I went from sixth through half of twelfth grade ignoring him and that wound. I was coming on as a drummer and a lover, but if Quadberry happened to appear within fifty feet of me and my most tender, intimate sweetheart, I would duck out. Quadberry grew up just like the rest of us. His father was still a doctor—professor of history—at the town college; his mother was still blond, and a musician. She was organist at an Episcopalian church in Jackson, the big capital city ten miles east of us.

As for Radcleve, he still had no ear for music, but he was there, my buddy. He was repentant about Quadberry, although not so much as I. He'd thrown the mud grenade over the fence only to see what would happen. He had not really wanted to maim. Quadberry had played his tune on the sax, Radcleve had played his tune on the mud grenade. It was just a shame they happened to cross talents.

Radcleve went into a long period of nearly nothing after he gave up violent explosives. Then he trained himself to copy the comic strips, *Steve Canyon* to *Major Hoople,* until he became quite a versatile cartoonist with some very provocative new faces and bodies that were gesturing intriguingly. He could never fill in the speech balloons with the smart words they needed. Sometimes he would pencil in "Err" or "What?" in the empty speech places. I saw him a great deal. Radcleve was not spooked by Quadberry. He even once asked Quadberry what his opinion was of his future as a cartoonist. Quadberry told Radcleve that if he took all his cartoons and stuffed himself with them, he would make an interesting dead man. After that, Radcleve was shy of him too.

When I was a senior we had an extraordinary band. Word was we had outplayed all the big A.A.A. division bands last April in the state contest. Then came news that a new blazing saxophone player was coming into the band as first chair. This person had spent summers in Vermont in music camps, and he was coming in with us for the concert season. Our director, a lovable aesthete named Richard Prender, announced to us in a proud silent moment that the boy was joining us tomorrow night. The effect was that everybody should push over a seat or two and make room for this boy and his talent. I was annoyed. Here I'd been with the band and had kept hold of the taste among the whole percussion section. I could play rock and jazz drum and didn't even really need to be here. I could be in Vermont too, give me a piano and a bass. I looked at the kid on first sax, who was going to be supplanted tomorrow. For two years he had thought he was the star, then suddenly enters this boy who's three times better.

The new boy was Quadberry. He came in, but he was meek, and when he tuned up he put his head almost on the floor, bending over trying to be inconspicuous. The girls in the band had wanted him to be handsome, but Quadberry refused and kept himself in such hiding among the sax section that he was neither handsome, ugly, cute or anything. What he was was pretty near invisible, except for the bell of his horn, the all-but-closed eyes, the Arabian nose, the brown hair with its halo of white ends, the desperate oralness, the giant reed punched into his face, and hazy Quadberry, loving the wound in a private dignified ecstasy.

I say dignified because of what came out of the end of his horn. He was more than what Prender had told us he would be. Because of Quadberry, we could take the band arrangement of Ravel's *Bolero* with us to the state contest. Quadberry would do the saxophone solo. He would switch to alto sax, he would do the sly Moorish ride. When he played, I heard the sweetness, I heard the horn which finally brought human *talk* into the realm of music. It could sound like the mutterings of a field nigger, and then it could get up into inhumanly careless beauty, it could get among mutinous helium bursts around Saturn. I already loved *Bolero* for the constant drum part. The percussion was always there, driving along with the subtly increasing triplets, insistent, insistent, at last outraged and trying to steal the whole show from the horns and the others. I knew a large boy with dirty blond hair, name of Wyatt, who played viola in the Jackson Symphony and sousaphone in our band—one of the rare closet transmutations of my time—who was forever claiming to have discovered the central *Bolero* one Sunday afternoon over FM radio as he had seven distinct sexual moments with a certain B., girl flutist with black bangs and skin like mayonnaise, while the drums of Ravel carried them on and on in a ceremony of Spanish sex. It was agreed by all the canny in the band that *Bolero* was exactly the piece to make the band soar—now especially as we had Quadberry, who made his walk into the piece like an actual lean Spanish bandit. This boy could blow his horn. He was, as I had suspected, a genius. His solo was not quite the same as the New York Phil's saxophonist's, but it was better. It came in and was with us. It entered my spine and, I am sure, went up the skirts of the girls. I had almost deafened myself playing drums in the most famous rock and jazz band in the state, but I could hear the voice that went through and out that horn. It sounded like a very troubled forty-year-old man, a man who had had his brow in his hands a long time.

The next time I saw Quadberry up close, in fact the first time I had seen him up close since we were eleven and he was bleeding in the cornfield, was in late February. I had only three classes this last semester, and went up to the band room often, to loaf and complain and keep up my touch on the drums. Pender let me keep my set in one of the instrument rooms, with a tarpaulin thrown over it, and I would drag it out to the practice room and whale away. Sometimes a group of sophomores would come up and I would make them marvel, whaling away as if not only deaf but blind to them, although I wasn't at all. If I saw a sophomore girl with exceptional bod or face, I would do miracles of technique I never knew were in me. I would amaze myself. I would be threatening Buddy Rich and Sam Morello. But this time when I went into the instrument room, there was Quadberry on one side, and, back in a dark corner, a small ninth-grade euphonium player whose face was all red. The little boy was weeping and grinning at the same time.

"Queerberry," the boy said softly.

Quadberry flew upon him like a demon. He grabbed the boy's collar, slapped his face, and yanked his arm behind him in a merciless wrestler's grip, the one that made them bawl on TV. Then the boy broke it and slugged Quadberry in the lips and ran across to my side of the room. He said "Queerberry" softly again and jumped for the door. Quadberry plunged across the room and tackled him on the threshold. Now that the boy was under him, Quadberry pounded the top of his head with his fist made like a mallet. The boy kept calling him "Queerberry" throughout this. He had not learned his lesson. The boy seemed to be going into concussion, so I stepped over and touched Quadberry, telling him to quit. Quadberry obeyed and stood up off the boy, who crawled on out into the band room. But once more the boy looked back with a bruised grin, saying "Queerberry." Quadberry made a move toward him, but I blocked it.

"Why are you beating up on this little guy?" I said. Quadberry was sweating and his eyes were wild with hate; he was a big fellow now, though lean. He was, at six feet tall, bigger than me.

"He kept calling me Queerberry."

"What do you care?" I asked.

"I care," Quadberry said, and left me standing there.

We were to play at Millsaps College Auditorium for the concert. It was April. We got on the buses, a few took their cars, and were a big tense crowd getting over there. To Jackson was only a twenty-minute trip. The director, Prender, followed the bus in his Volkswagen. There was a thick fog. A flashing ambulance, snaking the lanes, piled into him head on. Prender, who I would imagine was thinking of *Bolero* and hearing the young horn voices in his band—perhaps he was dwelling on Quadberry's spectacular gypsy entrance, or perhaps he was meditating on the percussion section, of which I was the king—passed into the airs of band-director heaven. We were told by the student director as we set up on the stage. The student director was a senior from the town college, very much afflicted, almost to the point of drooling, by a love and respect for Dick Prender, and now afflicted by a heartbreaking esteem for his ghost. As were we all.

I loved the tough and tender director awesomely and never knew it until I found myself bawling along with all the rest of the boys of the percussion. I told them to keep setting up, keep tuning, keep screwing the stands together, keep hauling in the kettledrums. To just quit and bawl seemed a betrayal to Prender. I caught some girl clarinetists trying to flee the stage and go have their cry. I told them to get the hell back to their section. They obeyed me. Then I found the student director. I had to have my say.

"Look. I say we just play *Bolero* and junk the rest. That's our horse. We can't play *Brighton Beach* and *Neptune's Daughter.* We'll never make it through them. And they're too happy."

"We aren't going to play anything," he said. "Man, to play is filthy. Did you ever hear Prender play piano? Do you know what a cool man he was in all things?"

"We play. He got us ready, and we play."

"Man, you can't play any more than I can direct. You're bawling your face off. Look out there at the rest of them. Man, it's a herd, it's a weeping herd."

"What's wrong? Why aren't you pulling this crowd together?" This was Quadberry, who had come up urgently. "I got those little brats in my section sitting down, but we've got people abandoning the stage, tearful little finks throwing their horns on the floor."

"I'm not directing," said the mustached college man.

"Then get out of here. You're weak, weak!"

"Man, we've got teen-agers in ruin here, we got sorrowville. Nobody can—"

"Go ahead. Do your number. Weak out on us."

"Man, I—"

Quadberry was already up on the podium, shaking his arms.

"We're right here! The band is right here! Tell your friends to get back in their seats. We're doing *Bolero.* Just put *Bolero* up and start tuning. *I'm* directing. I'll be right here in front of you. You look at *me!* Don't you dare quit on Prender. Don't you dare quit on me. You've got to be heard. *I've* got to be heard. Prender wanted me to be heard. I am the star, and I say we sit down and blow."

And so we did. We all tuned and were burning low for the advent into *Bolero,* though we couldn't believe that Quadberry was going to remain with his saxophone strapped to him and conduct us as well as play his solo. The judges, who apparently hadn't heard about Prender's death, walked down to their balcony desks.

One of them called out "Ready" and Quadberry's hand was instantly up in the air, his fingers hard as if around the stem of something like a torch. This was not Prender's way, but it had to do. We went into the number cleanly and Quadberry one-armed it in the conducting. He kept his face, this look of hostility, at the reeds and the trumpets. I was glad he did not look toward me and the percussion boys like that. But he must have known we would be constant and tasteful because I was the king there. As for the others, the soloists especially, he was scaring them into excellence. Prender had never got quite this from them. Boys became men and girls became women as Quadberry directed us through *Bolero.* I even became a bit better of a man myself, though Quadberry did not look my way. When he turned around toward the people in the auditorium to enter on his solo, I knew it was my baby. I and the drums were the metronome. That was no trouble. It was talent to keep the metronome ticking amidst any given chaos of sound.

But this keeps one's mind occupied and I have no idea what Quadberry sounded like on his sax ride. All I know is that he looked grief-stricken and pale, and small. Sweat had popped out on his forehead. He bent over extremely. He was wearing the red brass-button jacket and black pants, black bow tie at the throat, just like the rest of us. In this outfit he bent over his horn almost out of sight. For a moment, before I caught the glint of his horn through the music stands, I thought he had pitched forward off the stage. He went down so far to do his deep oral thing, his conducting arm had disappeared so quickly, I didn't know but what he was having a seizure.

When *Bolero* was over, the audience stood up and made meat out of their hands applauding. The judges themselves applauded. The band stood up, bawling again, for Prender and because we had done so well. The student director rushed out crying to embrace Quadberry, who eluded him with his dipping shoulders. The crowd was still clapping insanely. I wanted to see Quadberry myself. I waded through the red backs, through the bow ties, over the white bucks. Here was the first-chair clarinetist, who had done his bit like an angel; he sat close to the podium and could hear Quadberry.

"Was Quadberry good?" I asked him.

"Are you kidding? These tears in my eyes, they're for how good he was. He was too good. I'll never touch my clarinet again." The clarinetist slung the pieces of his horn into their case like underwear and a toothbrush.

I found Quadberry fitting the sections of his alto in the velvet holds of his case.

"Hooray," I said. "Hip damn hooray for you."

Arden was smiling too, showing a lot of teeth I had never seen. His smile was sly. He knew he had pulled off a monster unlikelihood.

"Hip hip hooray for me," he said. "Look at her. I had the bell of the horn almost smack in her face."

There was a woman of about thirty sitting in the front row of the auditorium. She wore a sundress with a drastic cleavage up front; looked like something that hung around New Orleans and kneaded your heart to death with her feet. She was still mesmerized by Quadberry. She bore on him with a stare and there was moisture in her cleavage.

"You played well."

"Well? Play well? Yes."

He was trying not to look at her directly. Look at *me,* I beckoned to her with full face: I was the *drums.* She arose and left.

"I was walking downhill in a valley, is all I was doing," said Quadberry. "Another man, a wizard, was playing my horn." He locked his sax case. "I feel nasty for not being able to cry like the rest of them. Look at them. Look at them crying."

True, the children of the band were still weeping, standing around the stage. Several moms and dads had come up among them, and they were misty-eyed too. The mixture of grief and superb music had been unbearable.

A girl in tears appeared next to Quadberry. She was a majorette in football season and played third-chair sax during the concert season. Not even her violent sorrow could take the beauty out of the face of this girl. I had watched her for a number of years—her alertness to her own beauty, the pride of her legs in the majorette outfit—and had taken out her younger sister, a second-rate version of her and a wayward overcompensating nymphomaniac whom several of us made a hobby out of pitying. Well, here was Lilian herself crying in Quadberry's face. She told him that she'd run off the stage when she heard about Prender, dropped her horn and everything, and had thrown herself into a tavern across the street and drunk two beers quickly for some kind of relief. But she had come back through the front doors of the auditorium and sat down, dizzy with beer, and seen Quadberry, the miraculous way he had gone on with *Bolero.* And now she was eaten up by feelings of guilt, weakness, cowardice.

"We didn't miss you," said Quadberry.

"Please forgive me. Tell me to do something to make up for it."

"Don't breathe my way, then. You've got beer all over your breath."

"I want to talk to you."

"Take my horn case and go out, get in my car, and wait for me. It's the ugly Plymouth in front of the school bus."

"I know," she said.

Lilian Field, this lovely teary thing, with the rather pious grace of her carriage, with the voice full of imminent swoon, picked up Quadberry's horn case and her own and walked off the stage.

I told the percussion boys to wrap up the packing. Into my suitcase I put my own gear and also managed to steal drum keys, two pairs of brushes, a twenty-inch Turkish cymbal, a Gretsch snare drum that I desired for my collection, a wood block, kettledrum mallets, a tuning harp and a score sheet of *Bolero* full of marginal notes I'd written down straight from the mouth of Dick Prender, thinking I might want to look at the score sheet sometime in the future when I was having a fit of nostalgia such as I am having right now as I write this. I had never done any serious stealing before, and I was stealing for my art. Prender was dead, the band had done its last thing of the year, I was a senior. Things were finished at the high school. I was just looting a sinking ship. I could hardly lift the suitcase. As I was pushing it across the stage, Quadberry was there again.

"You can ride back with me if you want to."

"But you've got Lilian."

"Please ride back with me . . . us. Please."

"Why?"

"To help me get rid of her. Her breath is full of beer. My father always had that breath. Every time he was friendly, he had that breath. And she looks a great deal like my mother." We were interrupted by the Tupelo band director. He put his baton against Quadberry's arm.

"You were big with *Bolero,* son, but that doesn't mean you own the stage."

Quadberry caught the end of the suitcase and helped me with it out to the steps behind the auditorium. The buses were gone. There sat his ugly ocher Plymouth; it was a failed, gay, experimental shade from the Chrysler people. Lilian was sitting in the front seat wearing her shirt and bow tie, her coat off.

"Are you going to ride back with me?" Quadberry said to me.

"I think I would spoil something. You never saw her when she was a majorette. She's not stupid, either. She likes to show off a little, but she's not stupid. She's in the History Club."

"My father has a doctorate in history. She smells of beer."

I said, "She drank two cans of beer when she heard about Prender."

"There are a lot of other things to do when you hear about death. What I did, for example. She ran away. She fell to pieces."

"She's waiting for us," I said.

"One damned thing I am never going to do is drink."

"I've never seen your mother up close, but Lilian doesn't look like your mother. She doesn't look like anybody's mother."

I rode with them silently to Clinton. Lilian made no bones about being disappointed I was in the car, though she said nothing. I knew it would be like this and I hated it. Other girls in town would not be so unhappy that I was in the car with them. I looked for flaws in Lilian's face and neck and hair, but there weren't any. Couldn't there be a mole, an enlarged pore, too much gum on a tooth, a single awkward hair around the ear? No. Memory, the whole lying opera of it, is killing me now. Lilian was faultless beauty, even sweating, even and especially in the white man's shirt and the bow tie clamping together her collar, when one knew her uncomfortable bosoms, her poor nipples. . . .

"Don't take me back to the band room. Turn off here and let me off at my house," I said to Quadberry. He didn't turn off.

"Don't tell Arden what to do. He can do what he wants to," said Lilian, ignoring me and speaking to me at the same time. I couldn't bear her hatred. I asked Quadberry to please just stop the car and let me out here, wherever he was: this front yard of the mobile home would do. I was so earnest that he stopped the car. He handed back the keys and I dragged my suitcase out of the trunk, then flung the keys back at him and kicked the car to get it going again.

My band came together in the summer. We were the Bop Fiends . . . that was our name. Two of them were from Ole Miss, our bass player was from Memphis State, but when we got together this time, I didn't call the tenor sax, who went to Mississippi Southern, because Quadberry wanted to play with us. During the school year the college boys and I fell into minor groups to pick up twenty dollars on a weekend, playing dances for the Moose Lodge, medical-student fraternities in Jackson, teen-age recreation centers in Greenwood, and such as that. But come summer we were the Bop Fiends again, and the price for us went up to $1,200 a gig. Where they wanted the best rock and bop and they had some bread, we were called. The summer after I was a senior, we played in Alabama, Louisiana, and Arkansas. Our fame was getting out there on the interstate route.

This was the summer that I made myself deaf.

Years ago Prender had invited down an old friend from a high school in Michigan. He asked me over to meet the friend, who had been a drummer with Stan Kenton at one time and was now a band director just like Prender. This fellow was almost totally deaf and he warned me very sincerely about deafing myself. He said there would come a point when you had to lean over and concentrate all your hearing on what the band was doing and that was the time to quit for a while, because if you didn't you would be irrevocably deaf like him in a month or two. I listened to him but could not take him seriously. Here was an oldish man who had his problems. My ears had ages of hearing left. No so. I played the drums so loud the summer after I graduated from high school that I made myself, eventually, stone deaf.

We were at, say, the National Guard Armory in Lake Village, Arkansas, Quadberry out in front of us on the stage they'd built. Down on the floor were hundreds of sweaty teen-agers. Four girls in sundresses, showing what they could, were leaning on the stage with broad ignorant lust on their minds. I'd play so loud for one particular chick, I'd get absolutely out of control. The guitar boys would have to turn the volume up full blast to compensate. Thus I went deaf. Anyhow, the dramatic idea was to release Quadberry on a very soft sweet ballad right in the middle of a long ear-piercing run of rock-and-roll tunes. I'd get out the brushes and we would astonish the crowd with our tenderness. By August, I was so deaf I had to watch Quadberry's fingers changing notes on the saxophone, had to use my eyes to keep time. The other members of the Bop Fiends told me I was hitting out of time. I pretended I was trying to do experimental things with rhythm when the truth was I simply could no longer hear. I was no longer a tasteful drummer, either. I had become deaf through lack of taste.

Which was—taste—exactly the quality that made Quadberry wicked on the saxophone. During the howling, during the churning, Quadberry had taste. The noise did not affect his personality; he was solid as a brick. He could blend. Oh, he could hoot through his horn when the right time came, but he could do supporting roles for an hour. Then, when we brought him out front for his solo on something like "Take Five," he would play with such light blissful technique that he even eclipsed Paul Desmond. The girls around the stage did not cause him to enter into excessive loudness or vibrato.

Quadberry had his own girl friend now, Lilian back at Clinton, who put all the sundressed things around the stage in the shade. In my mind I had congratulated him for getting up next to this beauty, but in June and July, when I was still hearing things a little, he never said a word about her. It was one night in August, when I could hear nothing and was driving him to his house, that he asked me to turn off the inside light and spoke in a retarded deliberate way. He knew I was deaf and counted on my being able to read lips.

"Don't . . . make fun . . . of her . . . or me. . . . We . . . think . . . she . . . is . . . in trouble."

I wagged my head. Never would I make fun of him or her. She detested me because I had taken out her helpless little sister for a few weeks, but I would never think there was anything funny about Lilian, for all her haughtiness. I only thought of this event as monumentally curious.

"No one except you knows," he said.

"Why did you tell me?"

"Because I'm going away and you have to take care of her. I wouldn't trust her with anybody but you."

"She hates the sight of my face. Where are you going?"

"Annapolis."

"You aren't going to any damned Annapolis."

"That was the only school that wanted me."

"You're going to play your saxophone on a boat?"

"I don't know what I'm going to do."

"How . . . how can you just leave her?"

"She wants me to. She's very excited about me at Annapolis. William [this is my name], there is no girl I could imagine who has more inner sweetness than Lilian."

I entered the town college, as did Lilian. She was in the same chemistry class I was. But she was rows away. It was difficult to learn anything, being deaf. The professor wasn't a pantomimer—but finally he went to the blackboard with the formulas and the algebra of problems, to my happiness. I hung in and made a B. At the end of the semester I was swaggering around the grade sheet he'd posted. I happened to see Lilian's grade. She'd only made a C. Beautiful Lilian got only a C while I, with my handicap, had made a B.

It had been a very difficult chemistry class. I had watched Lilian's stomach the whole way through. It was not growing. I wanted to see her look like a watermelon, make herself an amazing mother shape.

When I made the B and Lilian made the C, I got up my courage and finally went to see her. She answered the door. Her parents weren't home. I'd never wanted this office of watching over her as Quadberry wanted me to, and this is what I told her. She asked me into the house. The rooms smelled of nail polish and pipe smoke. I was hoping her little sister wasn't in the house, and my wish came true. We were alone.

"You can quit watching over me."

"Are you pregnant?"

"No." Then she started crying. "I wanted to be. But I'm not."

"What do you hear from Quadberry?"

She said something, but she had her back to me. She looked to me for an answer, but I had nothing to say. I knew she'd said something, but I hadn't heard it.

"He doesn't play the saxophone anymore," she said.

This made me angry.

"Why not?"

"Too much math and science and navigation. He wants to fly. That's what his dream is now. He wants to get into an F-something jet."

I asked her to say this over and she did. Lilian really was full of inner sweetness, as Quadberry had said. She understood that I was deaf. Perhaps Quadberry had told her.

The rest of the time in her house I simply witnessed her beauty and her mouth moving.

I went through college. To me it is interesting that I kept a B average and did it all deaf, though I know that isn't interesting to people who aren't deaf. I loved music, and never heard it. I loved poetry, and never heard a word that came out of the mouths of the visiting poets who read at the campus. I loved my mother and dad, but never heard a sound they made. One Christmas Eve, Radcleve was back from Ole Miss and threw an M-80 out in the street for old times' sake. I saw it explode, but there was only a pressure in my ears. I was at parties when lusts were raging and I went home with two girls (I am medium handsome) who lived in apartments of the old two-story 1920 vintage, and I took my shirt off and made love to them. But I have no real idea what their reaction was. They were stunned and all smiles when I got up, but I have no idea whether I gave them the last pleasure or not. I hope I did. I've always been partial to women and have always wanted to see them satisfied till their eyes popped out.

Through Lilian I got the word that Quadberry was out of Annapolis and now flying jets off the *Bonhomme Richard,* an aircraft carrier headed for Vietnam. He telegrammed her that he would set down at the Jackson airport at ten o'clock one night. So Lilian and I were out there waiting. It was a familiar place to her. She was a stewardess and her loops were mainly in the South. She wore a beige raincoat, had red sandals on her feet; I was in a black turtleneck and corduroy jacket, feeling significant, so significant I could barely stand it. I'd already made myself the lead writer at Gordon-Marx Advertising in Jackson. I hadn't seen Lilian in a year. Her eyes were strained, no longer the bright blue things they were when she was a pious beauty. We drank coffee together. I loved her. As far as I knew, she'd been faithful to Quadberry.

He came down in an F-something Navy jet right on the dot of ten. She ran out on the airport pavement to meet him. I saw her crawl up the ladder. Quadberry never got out of the plane. I could see him in his blue helmet. Lilian backed down the ladder. Then Quadberry had the cockpit cover him again. He turned the plane around so its flaming red end was at us. He took it down the runway. We saw him leap into the night at the middle of the runway going west, toward San Diego and the *Bonhomme Richard.* Lilian was crying.

"What did he say?" I asked.

"He said. 'I am a dragon. America the beautiful, like you will never know.' He wanted to give you a message. He was glad you were here."

"What was the message?"

"The same thing. 'I am a dragon. America the beautiful, like you will never know.'"

"Did he say anything else?"

"Not a thing."

"Did he express any love toward you?"

"He wasn't Ard. He was somebody with a sneer in a helmet."

"He's going to war, Lilian."

"I asked him to kiss me and he told me to get off the plane, he was firing up and it was dangerous."

"Arden is going to war. He's just on his way to Vietnam and he wanted us to know that. It wasn't just him he wanted us to see. It was him in the jet he wanted us to see. He *is* that black jet. You can't kiss an airplane."

"And what are we supposed to do?" cried sweet Lilian.

"We've just got to hang around. He didn't have to lift off and disappear straight up like that. That was to tell us how he isn't with us anymore."

Lilian asked me what she was supposed to do now. I told her she was supposed to come with me to my apartment in the old 1920 Clinton place where I was. I was supposed to take care of her. Quadberry had said so. His six-year-old directive was still working.

She slept on the fold-out bed of the sofa for a while. This was the only bed in my place. I stood in the dark in the kitchen and drank a quarter bottle of gin on ice. I would not turn on the light and spoil her sleep. The prospect of Lilian asleep in my apartment made me feel like a chaplain on a visit to the Holy Land; I stood there getting drunk, biting my tongue when dreams of lust burst on me. That black jet Quadberry wanted us to see him in, its flaming rear end, his blasting straight up into the night at mid-runway—what precisely was he wanting to say in this stunt? Was he saying remember him forever or forget him forever? But I had my own life and was neither going to mother-hen it over his memory nor his old sweetheart. What did he mean, *America the beautiful, like you will never know?* I, William Howly, knew a goddamn good bit about America the beautiful, even as a deaf man. Being deaf had brought me up closer to people. There were only about five I knew, but I knew their mouth movements, the perspiration under their noses, their tongues moving over the crowns of their teeth, their fingers on their lips. Quadberry, I said, you don't have to get up next to the stars in your black jet to see America the beautiful.

I was deciding to lie down on the kitchen floor and sleep the night, when Lilian turned on the light and appeared in her panties and bra. Her body was perfect except for a tiny bit of fat on her upper thighs. She'd sunbathed herself so her limbs were brown, and her stomach, and the instinct was to rip off the white underwear and lick, suck, say something terrific into the flesh that you discovered.

She was moving her mouth.

"Say it again slowly."

"I'm lonely. When he took off in his jet, I think it meant he wasn't ever going to see me again. I think it meant he was laughing at both of us. He's an astronaut and he spits on us."

"You want me on the bed with you?" I asked.

"I know you're an intellectual. We could keep on the lights so you'd know what I said."

"You want to say things? This isn't going to be just sex?"

"It could never be just sex."

"I agree. Go to sleep. Let me make up my mind whether to come in there. Turn out the lights."

Again the dark, and I thought I would cheat not only Quadberry but the entire Quadberry family if I did what was natural.

I fell asleep.

Quadberry escorted B-52s on bombing missions into North Vietnam. He was catapulted off the *Bonhomme Richard* in his suit at 100 degrees temperature, often at night, and put the F-8 on all it could get—the tiny cockpit, the immense long two-million-dollar fuselage, wings, tail and jet engine, Quadberry, the genius master of his dragon, going up to twenty thousand feet to be cool. He'd meet with the big B-52 turtle of the air and get in a position, his cockpit glowing with green and orange lights, and turn on his transistor radio. There was only one really good band, never mind the old American rock-and-roll from Cambodia, and that was Red Chinese opera. Quadberry loved it. He loved the nasal horde in the finale, when the peasants won over the old fat dilettante mayor. Then he'd turn the jet around when he saw the squatty abrupt little fires way down there after the B-52s had dropped their diet. It was a seven-hour trip. Sometimes he slept, but his body knew when to wake up. Another thirty minutes and there was his ship waiting for him out in the waves.

All his trips weren't this easy. He'd have to blast out in daytime and get with the B-52s, and a SAM missile would come up among them. Two of his mates were taken down by these missiles. But Quadberry, as on saxophone, had endless learned technique. He'd put his jet perpendicular in the air and make the SAMs look silly. He even shot down two of them. Then, one day in daylight, a MIG came floating up level with him and his squadron. Quadberry couldn't believe it. Others in the squadron were shy, but Quadberry knew where and how the MIG could shoot. He flew below the cannons and then came in behind it. He knew the MIG wanted one of the B-52s and not mainly him. The MIG was so concentrated on the fat B-52 that he forgot about Quadberry. It was really an amateur suicide pilot in the MIG. Quadberry got on top of him and let down a missile, rising out of the way of it. The missile blew off the tail of the MIG. But then Quadberry wanted to see if the man got safely out of the cockpit. He thought it would be pleasant if the fellow got out with his parachute working. Then Quadberry saw that the fellow wanted to collide his wreckage with the B-52, so Quadberry turned himself over and cannoned, evaporated the pilot and cockpit. It was the first man he'd killed.

The next trip out, Quadberry was hit by a ground missile. But his jet kept flying. He flew it a hundred miles and got to the sea. There was the *Bonhomme Richard,* so he ejected. His back was snapped but, by God, he landed right on the deck. His mates caught him in their arms and cut the parachute off him. His back hurt for weeks, but he was all right. He rested and recuperated in Hawaii for a month.

Then he went off the front of the ship. Just like that, his F-6 plopped in the ocean and sank like a rock. Quadberry saw the ship go over him. He knew he shouldn't eject just yet. If he ejected now he'd knock his head on the bottom and get chewed up in the motor blades. So Quadberry waited. His plane was sinking in the green and he could see the hull of the aircraft carrier getting smaller, but he had oxygen through his mask and it didn't seem that urgent a decision. Just let the big ship get over. Down what later proved to be sixty feet, he pushed the ejection button. It fired him away, bless it, and he woke up ten feet under the surface swimming against an almost overwhelming body of underwater parachute. But two of his mates were in a helicopter, one of them on the ladder to lift him out.

Now Quadberry's back was really hurt. He was out of this war and all wars for good.

Lilian, the stewardess, was killed in a crash. Her jet exploded with a hijacker's bomb, an inept bomb which wasn't supposed to go off, fifteen miles out of Havana; the poor pilot, the poor passengers, the poor stewardesses were all splattered like flesh sparklers over the water just out of Cuba. A fisherman found one seat of the airplane. Castro expressed regrets.

Quadberry came back to Clinton two weeks after Lilian and the others bound for Tampa were dead. He hadn't heard about her. So I told him Lilian was dead when I met him at the airport. Quadberry was thin and rather meek in his civvies—a gray suit and an out-of-style tie. The white ends of his hair were not there—the halo had disappeared—because his hair was cut short. The Arab nose seemed a pitiable defect in an ash-whiskered face that was beyond anemic now. He looked shorter, stooped. The truth was he was sick, his back was killing him. His breath was heavy-laden with airplane martinis and in his limp right hand he held a wet cigar. I told him about Lilian. He mumbled something sideways that I could not possibly make out.

"You've got to speak right at me, remember? Remember me, Quadberry?"

"Mom and Dad of course aren't here."

"No. Why aren't they?"

"He wrote me a letter after we bombed Hué. Said he hadn't sent me to Annapolis to bomb the architecture of Hué. He had been there once and had some important experience—French-kissed the queen of Hué or the like. Anyway, he said I'd have to do a hell of a lot of repentance for that. But he and Mom are separate people. Why isn't *she* here?"

"I don't know."

"I'm not asking you the question. The question is to God."

He shook his head. Then he sat down on the floor of the terminal. People had to walk around. I asked him to get up.

"No. How is old Clinton?"

"Horrible. Aluminum subdivisions, cigar boxes with four thin columns in front, thick as a hive. We got a turquoise water tank; got a shopping center, a monster Jitney Jungle, fifth-rate teeny-boppers covering the place like ants." Why was I being so frank just now, as Quadberry sat on the floor downcast, drooped over like a long weak candle? "It's not our town anymore, Ard. It's going to hurt to drive back into it. Hurts me every day. Please get up."

"And Lilian's not even over there now."

"No. She's a cloud over the Gulf of Mexico. You flew out of Pensacola once. You know what beauty those pink and blue clouds are. That's how I think of her."

"Was there a funeral?"

"Oh, yes. Her Methodist preacher and a big crowd over at Wright Ferguson funeral home. Your mother and father were there. Your father shouldn't have come. He could barely walk. Please get up."

"Why? What am I going to do, where am I going?"

"You've got your saxophone."

"Was there a coffin? Did you all go by and see the pink or blue cloud in it?" He was sneering now as he had done when he was eleven and fourteen and seventeen.

"Yes, they had a very ornate coffin."

"Lilian was the Unknown Stewardess. I'm not getting up."

"I said you still have your saxophone."

"No, I don't. I tried to play it on the ship after the last time I hurt my back. No go. I can't bend my neck or spine to play it. The pain kills me."

"Well, *don't* get up, then. Why am I asking you to get up? I'm just a deaf drummer, too vain to buy a hearing aid. Can't stand to write the ad copy I do. Wasn't I a good drummer?"

"Superb."

"But we can't be in this condition forever. The police are going to come and make you get up if we do it much longer."

The police didn't come. It was Quadberry's mother who came. She looked me in the face and grabbed my shoulders before she saw Ard on the floor. When she saw him she yanked him off the floor, hugging him passionately. She was shaking with sobs. Quadberry was gathered to her as if he were a rope she was trying to wrap around herself. Her mouth was all over him. Quadberry's mother was a good-looking woman of fifty. I simply held her purse. He cried out that his back was hurting. At last she let him go.

"So now we walk," I said.

"Dad's in the car trying to quit crying," said his mother.

"This is nice," Quadberry said. "I thought everything and everybody was dead around here." He put his arms around his mother. "Let's all go off and kill some time together." His mother's hair was on his lips. "You?" he asked me.

"Murder the devil out of it," I said.

I pretended to follow their car back to their house in Clinton. But when we were going through Jackson, I took the North 55 exit and disappeared from them, exhibiting a great amount of taste, I thought. I would get in their way in this reunion. I had an unimprovable apartment on Old Canton Road in a huge plaster house, Spanish style, with a terrace and ferns and yucca plants, and a green door where I went in. When I woke up I didn't have to make my coffee or fry my egg. The girl who slept in my bed did that. She was Lilian's little sister, Esther Field. Esther was pretty in a minor way and I was proud how I had tamed her to clean and cook around the place. The Field family would appreciate how I lived with her. I showed her the broom and the skillet, and she loved them. She also learned to speak very slowly when she had to say something.

Esther answered the phone when Quadberry called me seven months later. She gave me his message. He wanted to know my opinion on a decision he had to make. There was this Dr. Gordon, a surgeon at Emory Hospital in Atlanta, who said he could cure Quadberry's back problem. Quadberry's back was killing him. He was in torture even holding up the phone to say this. The surgeon said there was a seventy-five/twenty-five chance. Seventy-five that it would be successful, twenty-five that it would be fatal. Esther waited for my opinion. I told her to tell Quadberry to go over to Emory. He'd got through with luck in Vietnam, and now he should ride it out in this petty back operation.

Esther delivered the message and hung up.

"He said the surgeon's just his age; he's some genius from Johns Hopkins Hospital. He said this Gordon guy has published a lot of articles on spinal operations," said Esther.

"Fine and good. All is happy. Come to bed."

I felt her mouth and her voice on my ears, but I could hear only a sort of loud pulse from the girl. All I could do was move toward moisture and nipples and hair.

Quadberry lost his gamble at Emory Hospital in Atlanta. The brilliant surgeon his age lost him. Quadberry died. He died with his Arabian nose up in the air.

That is why I told this story and will never tell another.

WILLIAM HARRISON

William Harrison is the author of seven novels, including *Burton and Speke* and, currently, *Three Hunters*. His collection of stories, *Rollerball Murder*, appeared in 1974. He teaches at the University of Arkansas, Fayetteville.

The Arsons of Desire

One begins in familiar ways: a civil service test, a training school, and later the excitement of one's first fires and the fancy of wearing the uniform and helmet. I began this way, becoming a fireman, setting out to serve the citizens while serving myself some needed solitude, but lately I'm ambushed with dreams and visions. This sort: I'm in the company of a beautiful girl in a room filling with smoke. We exchange a love glance, her fingers brush my face, we start to embrace, then, disconcerted by the smoke, we look for a way out. She takes my hand as I lead her around the walls searching for a door; she wears a translucent gown, flowing like flame itself, and her dark hair spills over her shoulders. Then, the room stifling, we grope and panic; somewhere in the next few moments, terrified, our hands lose grip, and when I finally kick through the thin wall with my heavy rubber boot she fails to escape with me and I lose her.

Visions of a high blaze now and lovely lost women: I believe, lately, that I'm carrying disaster with me; my mind is catching fire.

This is the station house. In the old days bachelor firemen usually lived at the stations, but now I'm one of the few in all Chicago who continue. Others here have families, work in three shifts—twenty-four hours on, forty-eight off—but I stay near the alarms, I must, and attend every call. My bed in the dorm upstairs is in a homey corner: books, clock radio, my boots and britches stacked and ready. Downstairs are the big Seagrave trucks: the two quads, the ladder truck, the new snorkel, the new pump truck with its shiny deck gun, and the Cadillac rescue unit. Over here is the classroom, the kitchen, and the rec hall with Ping-Pong and television. The office and alarm systems are near the front door and in the rear are repair shops, storage rooms, and the garage where we keep the boats and drags. Sometimes our station is involved in dragging Lake Michigan or the river, but I've traded for other duties—I do considerable cleaning and mopping up around here—so that I can stay near the alarms. A dragging operation isn't a fire, after all: one gets a sore back, a head cold or sunburn, a soggy corpse, at best, and never peers into those bright and mystic flames.

Here we go: a two-alarm, the Lake Shore station and us.

Hanging on to number one truck with Captain Max, I curse the traffic as we whip into Lincoln Avenue. The siren begins to rev me up; I pull my suspenders tight, fasten my chin strap, and wonder who awaits me. In recent weeks it has been old Aunt Betty, the old family barber, a former high-school buddy of mine from up in Skokie, a girl I used to try to pick up in a bar on Gross Point Road. Strange, all strange: I can hardly wait.

Max is something: not a particularly good captain by the book and usually in trouble with the fire marshals because he's a real buster. We hit a building and he's off the truck, yelling, coupling hoses, and going in. I stomp in behind him, naturally, pulling the hose, my ax waving like his. But he's not one to stay outside and direct the proceedings, not our Max; he's a rowdy, likes his work, and leads the way. I say he's a lovely old bastard. He keeps us trained and sharp and any man on our team can handle any task, so he never has to stand around with the crowd getting us organized and looking official. The two of us usually bust right in and go to work, then, each careful to watch out for the other. He's sixty years old, fearless, and thinks I ought to be the next captain—though, of course, that's politics as even he knows and some dreamer like me who wants to live right in the fire station doesn't have much chance.

This alarm is another dilly: an empty apartment on the second floor of a new four-floor complex has smoldered for days with its occupants gone. It has finally erupted and the entire floor crawls with flame. We attack its fringes with water as I begin to bust doors looking for occupants. My eyes are wide with excitement because I expect anyone behind the very next door: some relative, a clerk from the grocery store where I trade, perhaps a forgotten acquaintance. Everyone I ever knew is burning up, I tell you, and my throat is tight with every new room and corridor. "Here! Over here, Coker, baby!" the captain booms, and we follow the smoke looking for its source. Fire is a tricky viper: it runs in the walls, gets in the conduits and vents, strikes at unexpected moments. I charge through a room, send an end table flying, jerk a closet open. Nothing. The snorkel passes the window, Charlie Wickers peering inside like an idiot. He never knows where he's going. We cross the hall and quickly batter through another door; these new apartment houses are like kindling, but the doors are easy to bust. As Max turns the hose on the ceiling of the hallway, I hear a cry. The walls all around us are hot and scorched, but we press on; somewhere behind all this smoke is a fist of fire we have to find—and probably a tenant or two, for I think I hear the cry again.

Rafferty arrives with another hose and coupling, so that Max directs him to retrace our steps and gather what we've trailed behind us. This keeps him busy and out of our way. We run through another series of rooms, smashing windows as we go, for the smoke thickens. A dead pussycat, choked and gone. Water cascades helplessly against the outside of the building now, so that Max turns to me with a smirk, once, and says, "Jesus, they need to get in here where the fun is, right?" At about this point we meet a wall of heat: a kitchen, the source. Max lays down a steady stream from the hose while I quickly circle back into the hall to look for another entrance.

An old man wanders the hallway. Coughing and gagging, he grabs my arms as I hold him and we recognize each other. In the smoke he manages to speak my name, then gasps, "My daughter, in there!" And I point him on his way, assuring him there's no trouble in that direction, while I go in further search. My mother's former pastor, I knew him well: Rooker, his name was. The steepled Congregational church in Evanston. But now a variation of the dream: she is a lanky, naked girl, screaming her head off, and I can't be sure if it's because of the fire or because her closet filled with clothes writhes with flames; I try to wrestle her to the window, but she fights me as if I wanted to throw her out. Reasoning with her, I see her try to cover her parts; she runs here, there, like a dazed antelope. "Quit it, please," I address her, trying to sound logical. "Just stop this and follow me out!" We wrestle again, fall, and her eyes open with even wider terror at my minor disfigurement. "Look, miss," I plead, "never mind your state. Take a blanket off the bed. Here, take it." But she claws at me, tussles free, and locks herself inside the bathroom before I can catch her again. By now the wallpaper is a sagging black curl. She screams and screams from behind that door and I pause, ax ready, and call to her. "Don't resist me, lady, come on! Wrap yourself in a towel because we don't have much time!" Her scream, then, alters into a baleful moan. Too late I dislodge the door with a single stroke. The room has caved in, and she is gone to the lapping heat; the intensity turns me away, so that I find myself in the hallway, Max's voice nearby. He has discovered the pastor, who took a wrong turn immediately after leaving me, burned into a crisp pudding. Left for a moment to hold the hose and direct the stream of water, I recall the brief sensation of that girl's breasts on me; my thoughts flare and my whole life dances in the smoke and surging orange before me.

At the station Max and I take each other's Polaroid snapshot. He poses beside one of the pump trucks, the words *American LaFrance* beside his jutting jaw. I pose in his office beneath the only wall decoration in the station, an engraving of one of the old rigs with six plump firehorses, the good side of my face turned toward the camera.

Max knows a bit of what goes on with me, but doesn't ask much.

"You have to keep your pleasure to yourself in this business," he tells me solemnly, so I suspect he has a glimmer of what is happening. And of course he knows my bad luck these last weeks, all those near rescues and disasters, but he considers that I'm one of the bravest firemen he has ever known, someone who will match him step by step into the center of a blaze, and figures that all the victims were doomed anyway.

Perhaps he feels something more: that all the unusual number and kinds of alarms in our district have to do with me. But he keeps this to himself, for he's a man who likes to do battle.

We've been close, a team, telling each other our lives. He attended DePaul University long ago on a voice scholarship; now he is married, has a grown son, and doesn't go home when he can stay on call. He'll get up from the breakfast table or out of bed late at night and rush to help us, and he says it's for the extra money, but I know him too well. In his heart is nothing except a fire fighter. Meanwhile, I share a few vignettes of myself with him. Not a very happy childhood, but okay now. This birthmark on my left side covers my ear, my cheek, neck, and encircles my eyes, and it looks something like a burn—even the skin wrinkles a bit on that side like an ill-fitting mask—and my dumb mother said this was God's kiss. My less theological schoolmates turned their eyes away, pretty girls of my dreams like popular Alice Durning of the ninth grade fretted when I came near, and even now those who give me a few necessary services—waitresses, the butcher—learn to do so without looking at me. Otherwise, until lately, I'm terribly normal; I like steak and potatoes, the Cubs, movies, and girlie magazines. Last year I read mostly the *Tribune* and *Newsweek.* I weigh one-eighty and have a few dental problems.

This is one of my sleepless nights again, so I go down to the refrigerator to cut a slice of my new cheddar and there is Max watching the late show. Glad to see him, I sit down and catch Brian Donlevy and Preston Foster in World War II. Then we talk. He's sleeping at the station because his wife's sister has arrived to occupy his bedroom. We discuss the woes of marriage, Leo Durocher, Ron Santo, slumps, bad seasons, hard luck, and getting tickets from mean cops in about that order. Max, pointing a finger, says, "Policemen need guys to break the goddamn laws, you see, just like teachers need stupid students, doctors need the sick and dying, and soldiers need victims. It's all the same."

We ponder this together and talk on.

"You know this Rooker girl?" he finally asks me.

"Knew her father," I sigh. "Or rather my mother knew him. Maybe I knew the daughter, too, a long time ago when she was just a little girl."

Max doesn't press further. He is in the presence of mystery, knows it, and prefers to let well enough alone; also, he's thinking that if the alarms go tonight he'll get in on the action.

"These girls," I muse. "We're having more and more contact, but I still don't get them out. I got scratches wrestling with this last one."

"I know, kid, I know," he comforts me. "Take it easy on yourself."

A routine day passes: two grass fires, a smoking trash dump, an auto blaze, a call for us to come wash gasoline off an intersection after an accident. Nervous, I stay at the station and don't attend these minor calls. I varnish a ladder, check couplings, show two kids around, and work a crossword puzzle. Max appears for regular duty in the afternoon and brings me a milk shake.

On the following noon we have another big one: the furnace at Parkside High School explodes and the old firetrap is a sudden maze of smoke and flame. We're the first there, Max leading the way, but the noise of every unit in The Loop is just behind us. I'm pulling on my jacket, barking at Rafferty to set up the rescue unit because the lawn is already strewn with kids crying with burns; some old biddy in a charred dress wanders among us giving off a descant of hysteria, and Wickers, the idiot, tries to ask directions of her; Max and I decide to hit the basement, where the flames are a steady roar. As we head down the concrete stairs with the hose, students trapped on the second floor call for us. "Hold on," Max promises. "Others coming!" And ladders and nets are unloaded from arriving engines as we head down toward the boiler room.

No secret where the blaze is centered this time: the boiler room heat is impossible. Max stations himself outside the door and shielded by a thin hot wall aims the hose around the corner at the flames; I try to assist, but I'm useless. "Check that far door!" he yells, so I dash by the flaming door and follow a narrow hall to a door, mostly wired glass, which I demolish. Inside, protected from the boiler room by a thick fire wall, I find no trouble, so decide to circle behind the fire. Dangerous—because Max is occupied and out of sight—but there may be someone trapped there. Anyway, I figure that the fire has spiraled upward through the blown-out ceiling and except for the furnace area the basement is possibly safe, so I bust another bolted door.

I run headlong into the locker room of the girl's gymnasium.

Madhouse: twenty or thirty girls running amok, shrieking, flitting near the flames on the side of the room where I enter, then retreating like moths. The broken door lets in a swish of oxygen and the flames suck toward it, cutting off the way I've come in as a possible exit, but I have my ax and don't panic. I go to the opposite wall, scramble over benches, climb a locker, and smash two paneled windows. "Here! Girls!" I shout, but all movement blurs into a strange motion now, the room igniting in a soft and frenzied dance; the girl in white panties is Midge Prinz, I remember her well, and she glides near and brushes me. Seconds, mere seconds, I tell myself, and we're all lost, but the reel of my senses rattles and slows, everything awhirl, and here are my teachers and all the darlings of my twelfth school year—ones who refused me at the prom, others who, casting down their eyes, knew me only as a voice. The typing instructor I adored: Miss Cates. A glistening nakedness now in the scorching heat of the room, her breasts rise in a high bounce as she floats by; the same silvered fingernails, the same mouth, and she hasn't aged in all these years. (She sat cross-legged on the desk beating time on her pretty white palm with a ruler: our lovely metronome.) And I'm calling, "Get out, Miss Cates, get out everyone," and my coat is off as I help one mount the locker; she slips—my gloves are gone, too—and her body wets my hands, and she grabs my neck as we fall. Midge jumps on me and rides me, her eyes rolled back, mouth agape, and pleads to hide in my arms; the far wall begins to cave in. My suspenders off my shoulders, shirt open, I toss them toward the window, but they're like dry leaves floating in the room's hot pressure; they settle against me, delirious, and a scalding kiss finds my neck. Another burns my stomach. A willowy coed circles the room with my axe, then expires; here is Miss Donelly, too, my old homeroom teacher who taught me verses I was never allowed to recite before the class, her cotton undies in her withered grip. One girl is out, perhaps two, but the window clogs with a soft and undulating mass. Reaching up, I try to pull some of them back, but their bodies are slick with perspiration and blood where they've nicked themselves on the uneven broken glass and down we go, swooning and falling, three or four of us, and I see that my coveralls are mostly burned away, black and shredded on me, though I feel no pain. "Here!" I call again, pointing the way, but Miss Cates tackles me and over we go, my head thumping against a bench.

Then I'm outside on the cool grass. Max is there, his hands burned from holding the hose around the boiler-room door too long, and we receive treatment from two attendants. "Good work, Coke, baby," he tells me. "Just great. How you ever got out of there I'll never know."

The fire marshal visits the station, commends Max and me, but mostly talks about the increased alarms in our district. He mentions possible arson and even before he's finished his speech we're out on another call—sure enough, some joker who tries to torch his own apartment.

Back at the station later I rub salve on my neck and stomach burns and read newspaper accounts of the high-school blaze; I have to find out if I dreamed it, but here it is: two janitors dead in the initial explosion, sixteen girls and two instructors in the fateful locker room, another teacher upstairs, twenty-two on the critical list in the hospital. And here: Miss Cates and Miss Donelly and Midge Prinz, the names just right. A fever of puzzlement comes over me.

The next morning Max arrives at the station for breakfast and we linger at coffee, whispering to each other.

"These girls," he says. "All the ones you say you recall."

"What about them?"

"Maybe they're after you, trying to keep you inside until you get burned up." His face is drawn and serious and he places a bandaged hand across my arm.

"I've thought of everything," I whisper. "You ever heard of poltergeists? People who make things fly through the air or who move objects with their thoughts?"

"Could be," he answers, his jaw set. Good old Max.

"I've wondered if some corner of my brain is setting fire to things. But there's more I don't understand. Miss Cates, for example. God, how could she be in that school?"

"I know this," Max adds. "We've never had such a season for alarms. And one of the nation's biggest, too, right here in our district."

"Someone could be playing a joke on me, but I know that isn't it," I muse, my coffee going cold in my hands. "And it isn't a dream either—I know that much because of the newspapers."

Max pats my arm again and gives me a look of wonder and sympathy.

"Let's not worry about it," he concludes. "We both know something big is coming, another alarm. We feel it, right?"

"You too, eh?"

"Oh, sure, Coker, god, you think I don't feel it? My knees get weak. I know something else is coming."

Waiting, now, Max keeps me at the station during all small alarms. I set all the equipment in order: the asbestos suits, the Pyrene foam, the new soap machine, the "wet water" and other smothering agents. I dream of sophisticated disasters—all sorts of mean chemical fires and special catastrophes.

I speculate, also, on my peculiar malady; is it part of what's happening in the city, I wonder, and the whole crazy world? Is it anarchy breaking loose? The overthrow of reason by dark forces? Such involved speculations annoy me. I'm a simple case, I assure myself: a regular guy, somewhat marred, but on balance; I had some rough adolescent moments, sure, but shook them off. I wish none of these victims ill will, never did; I do my duty, think baseball and hamburgers, take pride in being Max's partner.

Why, though, why?

Somewhere, I know, a match has fallen into a chair to smolder; rags are seething into combustion in some stuffy closet; a cigarette has fallen away from someone's sleeping fingers, and my answer is out there.

On the day I begin to understand, I'm busy repairing the spring on a hose reel. Max and I have exchanged glances all morning and the afternoon has worn away into twilight. The reel is a bitch to fix, but I'm grateful for the preoccupation and my tools are spread out in the office so that I can monitor the phones and the flashboard which lights when one of the sprinkler systems in our district is set off by heat.

The bell, when it finally comes, causes me to drop a wrench. Even before I finish taking information on the call, Max comes down the pole, bandages and all, and starts up number one truck.

Another explosion: this time in the lab of the big clinic over near Seward Park.

Seconds now: our rhythms are quick, practiced, and no squad in the city is better. We're halfway there in sixty seconds, and I think of the job, a lab explosion: chemical, perhaps, after all, so I strap on a portable extinguisher filled with foam.

Outside the building, a large rambling affair of only two floors, Max neatly dispatches the troops; the problem is clearly to save lives and evacuate the hospital wing. We confer in an instant with a young doctor who shouts information about the floor plan, then off we go. Always helter-skelter in spite of briefings, we move into infernos never really knowing where things are. Just another job hazard.

Most of our men head toward the wards to aid the patients, but Max, an edge on his voice, calls for me to join him down near the blaze, where someone may be trapped. So we start down another hallway toward what seems a holocaust, though there isn't much smoke because great holes have been blown in the sides of the lab; the flames boil, then, and the heat turns us inside a room.

We stand in there panting, Max saying, "That hallway is hell. Let's check out the rooms down here real quick and not get caught out there." I nod, reach back, touch my foam gun to make sure.

Then we rush out, each of us taking one side of the hallway. My first room, an office, yields no one, so I move to the second. A small examination room, nothing again, though it has a door which leads into the next. The windows are gone, I notice, and medicines and instruments are scattered: all signs of a whopping blast. And what happens next takes only seconds, another instant frozen in that old slow motion as I perceive it—for all our work is such, a science played against the clock and one's personal daring. As I pass through the door another explosion buckles the walls and I feel the hot gush of fire at my back; hurled forward into the room, everything yellow and searing, I see a woman, a nurse, as we're enveloped. Death has its hot instant, but I have some reflexes left; we're together in the far corner beside a metal table, crouched low, fire spewing through the broken walls as I open my foam gun to fight the flames head on. The heat drives the substance back around us and suddenly we are in a cocoon of foam, a soft sponge of protection, and my eyes close, and I'm away, dreamlike, letting go.

A floating bed of airy whiteness: in its liquid folds her limbs entwine me and her body opens. We heave and settle together in the old slow dance, cushioned in rapture, and the flames are distant things, painless, as she receives me. The gun empties, my finger relaxes on the trigger, and I'm gone, my senses incandescent. Lips and legs and a glowing thrust of skin: she bakes with me, melts, while the foam holds and caresses us. Then we lie still as the room subsides.

It is Rafferty, brave soul, who comes and plucks me out.

Strange, how suddenly doom and deliverance occur; we rush in, spurt water and bust doors in what seems a comic dream, take our consequences. Fate is a moment, a mere puff.

I insist, later, on leaving the rescue unit where they've bedded me down; stepping down from the van into the street, my legs wobbly, I view the carnage. Half the building is collapsed, thousands of gallons of water are still being pumped, and the pavement is lined with stretchers. I stroll among them, doped slightly from something they've given me, checking myself; I'm a mess—second-degree burns on my back and forehead. Shouts and sirens punctuate the scene, but I don't pay attention.

They show me poor Max, who really isn't there anymore. Then I go over and look at the nurse; the attendant pulls back the sheet and there she is, calm, the little black nameplate intact on her white uniform: ALICE DURNING. I lift my eyes back to the tower of smoke which moves across the early night.

What's happening to me, what?

I wander for another hour before someone leads me back to shelter.

On the way to the hospital, I have a curious surge of elation; I think, well, I'm alive, I made it again and I'll be patched up soon enough and back listening for alarms. It's going to be exciting—and they might give me a chance at captain, so I'll always go in first. I'll be a lot like Max in that way. Then, moments later, depression sets in; my obsession waylays me again, and I think, what's wrong with me? I'm kissed by a strange and awful God; my dread and my desire are one.

MARY HOOD

Mary Hood was born in Brunswick, on the Georgia coast, and now lives in Woodstock, in the north Georgia hills. Her first collection of stories, *How Far She Went* (1984), won the Flannery O'Connor Award for Short Fiction and the *Southern Review* Prize as the best first collection of short fiction published that year in the United States. Her second collection, *And Venus Is Blue,* was published in 1986.

Solomon's Seal

WHEN they were courting her people warned her, but she knew better. Who had kept them in meat through the Hoover years? With his rabbit boxes and early mornings, he was a man already, guarding a man's politics and notions, and like a mountain, wearing his own moody climate, one she prospered in. He brought the rabbits to her mother's kitchen window and held them up by the hind legs, swinging them like bells. When he skinned them and dressed them, she watched his quick knife as though learning. But she never did.

How they started out, that was how they wound up: on the same half-acre, in the same patched cabin. He was no farmer. Anything that grew on that red clay was *her* doing. After a few years she had cleared the stones from the sunny higher ground, piling them in a terrace, backfilling with woods dirt she gathered in flour sacks on her walks. She planted strawberries there. In the red clay of the garden she grew beans in the corn, peas, tomatoes, and bunching onions an uncle had given her as a wedding present. Some years, when the rains favored, she grew squash and mushmelons, the sweet little ones like baby heads.

They never had children. They never lacked dogs. He kept a pen full of coon dogs and spent the nights with them in the moonlight, running them, drinking with his friends, unmending the darns she had applied to his overalls. He was a careless man. He had a way of waiting out her angers, a way of postponing things by doing something else just as necessary. So she postponed a few things too. She didn't even unpack her trunk filled with linens and good dishes her mama and aunts had assembled for her. They had practically blinded themselves sewing white on white, making that coverlet, but it was yellowed now, in its original folds, deep in the napthaed heart of her hope chest. What was the use of being house-proud in a house like that? She decided it was good enough for him to eat off oilcloth. She decided he didn't care if his cup matched his saucer, and if he didn't care, why should she? She decided after a time to give as good as she got, which wasn't much. The scarcity of it, and her continuous mental bookkeeping, set her face in a mask and left her lips narrowed. She used to sing to him, before they could afford a radio. Now he had the TV on, to any program, it didn't matter which, and watched it like a baby watches the rustling leaves of a tree, to kill a little time between feedings. She didn't sing to him anymore. She didn't sing at all. But she talked to her plants like they were people.

Sometimes he thought maybe there was company in the yard, and he'd move to the window to see if a man had come to buy one of his dogs. But it was only her. He'd give the wall a knock with the side of his fist, just to let her know he was listening.

"I'm praying," she'd say, without looking up from where she was pouring well water from a lard pail onto the newest seedlings.

"Witch," he'd mutter, and go back to his TV.

She had the whole place covered by now; she was always bringing in new plants, little bothersome herbs she warned him against stepping on in his splayed boots as he stumbled along the trails she had outlined in fieldstones. The paths narrowed as she took more and more room for her pretties. It was like a child's game, where he could or could not step. And what were they anyway but weeds? Not real flowers, like his mama had grown. He told her that often enough. He'd been all over that lot and had never seen one rose. Sometimes he stopped at the hardware store and lifted a flat of petunias to his nose, but they weren't like the ones he remembered, they didn't smell like anything. He asked her about it, asked if she reckoned it was the rockets and satellites. She knew better. She blamed it on the dogs.

She blamed his dogs for stinking so you couldn't smell cabbage cooking. The health department ought to run him in, she said. He said if she called them she'd wind up in hell faster than corn popping. She said if he cut across the lower terrace one more time he'd be eating through a vein in his arm till his jaw healed, if ever. When he asked what she was so mad about, she couldn't for the life of her remember, it was a rage so old.

The madder she got, the greener everything grew, helped along, in the later years, by the rabbit manure. He was too old now to run rabbits in the field. And the land had changed, built up all around, not like it used to be. So he rigged up cages at home and raised rabbits right there. Then it was rabbits and dogs and TV and his meals and that was his whole life. That and not stepping on her plants.

He removed the spare tire from the trunk of the Dodge and fastened it to the roof of the car. In the extra space, and after taking off the trunk lid, he built a dog box. He started carrying his better hounds to the field trials and she went along too, for the ride. Everywhere they went she managed to find a new plant or two. She kept a shovel in the back seat, and potato-chip bags or cut-off milk jugs to bring the loot home in. They'd ride along, not speaking, or speaking both at once, her about the trees, him about the dogs, not hearing the one thing they were each listening their whole life for.

Sometimes she drank too. Sometimes, bottle-mellowed, they turned to each other in that shored-up bed, but afterward things were worse somehow, and he'd go off the whole next day to visit with other cooners, and she'd walk for miles in the woods, seeking wake-robin or Solomon's seal. She always dug at the wrong time, or too shallow, or something. For a few hours it would stand tall as it had grown, but the color would slowly fade, and with it her hopes. She'd be out there beside it, kneeling, talking to it softly, when he'd drive in, red-faced, beery. He'd see her turned back and head on up to the kennel to stand a few minutes, dangling his hands over the fence at the leaping dogs.

Forty years like that. It surprised her very much when he told her he wanted a divorce. He had been in the hospital a week and was home again. While he was in the hospital they told her not to upset him, so she held back the news. When he got home he found out that three of his whelps were sick and two more had already died. It was Parvo virus, locally epidemic, but the vet couldn't persuade him it wasn't somehow *her* fault. He spent the nights, sick as he still was, sitting up with the dogs, feeding them chicken soup from one of her saucepans. That was how the final argument started, her resenting that. If she really wanted to help him, he said, she'd just leave him alone. We'll see how you like that, she said, and took some clothes and went to her sister's. While she was there, a man came and served her with papers. He's crazy, is what he is, she said to the ferns; consider the source, she said to the laurel. He didn't want her? She knew better.

She used the rabbit's foot to rouge her cheeks, to add a little color. It surprised her, tying on her scarf to go to court, how much her face looked like his. The likeness was so sudden it startled her into a shiver. "Rabbit running over your grave," she said, thinking she was saying it to him.

There wasn't anything to the divorce. Uncontested, it was all over with very soon. But there was some heat over the division of property. He wound up with the house and she got the lot. He had custody of the dogs. He had six months to remove them and anything he wanted from the property, and after that he must stay away forever. He had the house moved in one piece. He hired a mover to come and load it onto a truck and haul it away. He set it up on a lot north of the river, among the pines, and in a few months he had pens for the dogs built alongside so he didn't have to walk far.

She bought a secondhand mobile home and moved it onto her lot when his six months were up. He had left things pretty well torn up; the housemovers had crushed and toppled her trellises and walls. She had weeks of work to right that. Even though it was all final, she was still afraid. She painted pieces of board with KEEP OUT and DO NOT DIG and nailed them to the trees. She tied scraps of rag to wires she ran from tree to tree, setting apart the not-to-be-trod-upon areas. She listened sharp, kept her radio tuned low, in case he was out there, coming back, like he used to, knocking over trash cans, beating on the door, crying, "It's me . . . Carl . . . let me in?"

But he didn't come back. She had no word of him at all, though she knew well enough where he was living, like some wild thing, deep in the woods with his hounds. Sometimes she saw his car going down the main road, it couldn't be missed, with that funny dog crate nailed in the trunk and the spare tire on the roof. She could watch the road from the hilltop as she stood at her clothesline. He drove as slow as always. It maddened her to see him go by so slow, as though he were waiting for her to fling herself down the hill headlong, to run after him crying, "Carl! Come back!" She wouldn't. She went on with her laundry. The old towel she picked up from the basket next was so bleach-burned it split in two when she snapped it. She hung the pieces on the line between her and the road, turned her back, picked up her basket, and headed for her trailer, down the hill, where he couldn't see her, though she knew how he drove, never looking left or right, even when she rode along with him, not turning his head one inch in her direction as he went on and on about the dogs. No more neck than a whale.

She was at the post office buying a money order when she heard he had remarried. She knew that couldn't be true. It wasn't a reliable source. She asked around. Nobody knew. She let it get to her, she couldn't rest just thinking of it. She didn't care; if she just knew *for sure,* that was it. "He's seventy-two years old," she said. Meaning: who could stand him but his dogs? She was out raking leaves from the main path when she decided to go see for herself. She finished up in her garden and changed to a clean shirt. She walked out to the store and phoned Yubo to come take her. Yubo was planting Miss Hamilton's garden, always did plant beans on Good Friday, and he wouldn't be there right away. She said as soon as possible, and stood at the store waiting. It gave her time to think over what she was going to say when she got there. She knew where it was; she'd been by there once, just to see how it looked, had held her pocketbook up to shield her face in case he happened to be there and noticing anybody going by. Not that he was a noticer. She drank Coca-Cola while she waited, and when Yubo came she almost said take me home, because the long wait and the walk in the sun and the whole project was making her dizzy. But she had come this far, and so had Yubo.

The house looked about the same as when it had been hers, except it stood on concrete blocks now instead of those shimmed-up rocks from the river. She told Yubo to wait. She walked down the drive to the door, which was open, unscreened, and she called, before she could think better, "I'm home," but of course she meant, "I'm here." Confused, she didn't say anything when the woman came out to see who it was. An old woman as big and solid as Carl, bare-armed, bright-eyed. One of the dogs was out of the pen, two of the dogs, and they were following right at her heels. They had the run of the house! The old woman sat on the steps and the dogs lay beside her, close enough so she could pet them as they panted against her bare feet. "Carl's not here," the old woman said.

"I was just passing by," she said, and turned to go to Yubo, who had the taxi backed around and waiting. It wasn't a real taxi, not a proper taxi, and it was considerably run down. Still, she slammed the door harder than necessary. The wind of its closing made the just-set-out petunias in the circle around the mailbox post shiver and nod.

At home, among her borders and beds, she worked all afternoon carrying buckets of water up the hill to slop onto her tomato seedlings, her pepper sets, her potato slips. She worked till she was so weary she whimpered, on her sofa, unable to rest. She fell asleep and had a bad dream. Someone had come and taken things. She woke herself up to go check. She locked the door and moved the piled papers and canned goods off her hope chest and raised the lid. Everything she had held out against him all those years was there. She took the coverlet out and looked it over, as though someone might have stolen the French knots off it. Then she unwrapped the dishes, fine gold-rimmed plates. They weren't china, but they were good. She thought she heard someone. Startled, she turned quickly, knocking the plate against the trunk. The disk broke in two, exactly in two. She took up a piece in each hand and knelt there a long time, but the tears never came. Finally she said, "That's one he won't get," and the thought gave her peace. She broke all the others, one by one, and laid them back in the trunk. She kept the coverlet out. It would do to spread over her tomato plants; the almanac said there would be no more frost, but she knew better. There was always one last frost.

After staking the coverlet above her young plants, weighting it at the corners with rocks, she stooped to see how the Solomon's seal was doing. She had located it by its first furled shoots, like green straws, sticking up through the oakleaf duff on one of her walks; had marked the place, going home for a bucket and pail, digging deep, replanting so it faced the same way to the sun. It had not dried out. It had good soil. But already it was dying. There was some little trick to it. "You'd think I could learn," she said. But she never did.

WILLIAM HUMPHREY

William Humphrey was born in Clarksville, Texas, in 1924. He attended SMU and the University of Texas without graduating. He has taught at Bard College, Washington and Lee, MIT, Smith, and Princeton. His books are *The Last Husband and Other Stories, Home from the Hill, The Ordways, A Time and a Place, The Spawning Run, Proud Flesh, Ah, Wilderness!: The Frontier in American Literature, Farther Off From Heaven, My Moby Dick, Hostages to Fortune, The Collected Stories,* and *Open Season.* He is currently at work on a novel entitled *No Resting Place.*

The Pump

For weeks Jordan Terry had been down on his knees promising God to drink the first barrelful if only they would go on drilling and not give up; but they were about ready to haul out the rig and call it another dry hole, when at fifty-nine hundred feet they brought in a gusher. Jordan was digging turnips in a field that he was being paid by the government not to grow anything on when he got the news, and though he went out and drank a barrelful all right, it wasn't oil.

A day or so later old Jordan was rocking on his front porch and smoking a White Owl when he saw a couple of men of the drilling crew up on top of his derrick with hammers and crowbars taking it apart. Barefoot as he was he jumped out of his rocker and tore down to see what the hell was going on. They told him they were fixing to cap his well.

"Cap it?" cried Jordan with a white face. "Put ere a cap on it? Why? For God's sake, Misters, let her come! Don't go a-putting ere a cap on it!"

They explained that the derrick was just for the drilling. Like a pile driver. There was no further need of it now. They were fixing to install a pump.

"Pump? What do we need ere a pump for?" asked Jordan, remembering how it had shot up in the air, like Old Faithful. "The way it spurted out?"

"It's like opening a bottle of beer, ol' hoss," said the chief engineer. "That first little bit that foams over comes by itself. The rest you have to work for."

Work! Hah! Set on your ass in a rocking chair and knock down two bits on every barrelful! That kind of work suited old Jordan to a tee.

So the derrick was dismantled and taken away and in its stead the pump was set up. It was like an off-balance seesaw, a beam the size of a crosstie set off-center in the notch of an upright post. To either end of the beam was attached a rod which disappeared into the ground. Up and down it went, up and down, bowing in frenzied, untiring obeisance. Yes, sir, it said to Jordan, you're the boss! Yes, sir, you're the boss! Yes, sir! Listening with your ear to the ground you could hear, or could fancy that you did, a sound like a seashell makes, of endless vast waves lapping the shores of a vast underground sea. And in the pipe you could hear the mightly surge, like the pulse of a great artery drawing up a steady stream of rich, black blood. Day and night the pump went, night and day, working for him: rocket-a-bump, rocket-a-bump, rocket-a-bump. . . . In the daytime it went at about the same trot that Jordan went at in his rocking chair, at night as he lay awake grinning in the dark each stroke of the cycle matched a beat of his heart: rocket-a-bump, rocket-a-bump, rocket-a-bump. . . .

"How much you reckon she draws every time she goes up and down?" he asked the engineers.

They told him how many barrels it pumped per day. Jordan worked it out from there. He wanted to know just how much he was worth by the minute, how much richer he had grown with each rock of his rocker, each beat of his heart. He got twenty-five cents a barrel. A barrel held fifty-five gallons. It averaged twenty-five strokes a minute. Call it half a cent a stroke. Rocket-a-bump: half a cent. Rocket-a-bump: that makes a penny. Rocket-a-bump, rocket-a-bump—the last thing he heard at night, the first thing he heard in the morning. Sixty times twenty-five was fifteen hundred. Twenty-four times fifteen hundred times three hundred and sixty-five. . . .

Jordan—though he was far from being its first owner—had for some years been driving a 1921 Durant. Driving it, that is to say, whenever it felt like going. And only now did he possess somewhere about the amount of oil it demanded. Naturally a man in his position couldn't be seen around in that old flivver anymore. As even the hungriest car dealer was not going to allow him anything for it on a trade-in, it occurred to Jordan that he would be doing a mighty fine deed by making a present of it to his next-door neighbor, Clarence Bywaters. Poor son of a bitch. It must be hard on a man to have oil struck right next door to you. Like a canary bird in a cage hung out of a window, and having to watch a fat sassy old blue jay hopping about in the trees and plucking juicy worms out of the ground. They had begun drilling on poor old Clarence's land even before Jordan's, and they were still at it, but only because they had poured so much money down that dry hole that they just hated to call it quits. They were talking about pulling out any day now. Jordan remembered what he had gone through. He didn't think Bywaters would take exception to his offer. Poor son of a bitch, with all that raft of kids he wasn't in any position to despise a little charity.

Delivery on a new Duesenberg, especially one with as many custom accessories as Jordan had put in for, took some time. Meanwhile he still went about in the old Durant. He hadn't gotten around to giving it to Clarence Bywaters when the news broke one morning that they had brought in a gusher on his neighbor's holdings.

Jordan Terry was not the sort to begrudge another his good fortune. Christ, he had his! He went over and took Clarence Bywaters by the hand and congratulated him. He could not help mentioning his intention to have given him the Durant; but, rather to his irritation, Bywaters thought it was an even better joke than he did. He got fifty dollars' allowance on it (not that he needed the damned fifty dollars, but them that had it never got it by throwing any away) by threatening to cancel the order on his new Duesenberg.

It looked like a Pullman car. And it turned out to use a bit more gas and oil than the Durant. But what the hell! If there was one thing he had plenty of that was it. While he was out burning it up in those twelve big-bore cylinders, back home that little old pump, going steady as the heart in his breast, was bringing up more. And at night while the car rested, and after he himself had been lulled to sleep by that sweet cradlelike rhythm, the pump worked on, rocket-a-bump, rocket-a-bump, rocket-a-bump. . . .

One day the man who maintained the pump, on one of his periodical visits, happened to let drop something which suggested that both Jordan's and his neighbor's wells were drawing upon the same subterranean pool.

"You mean," cried Jordan with a white face, "you mean that son of a bitch is tapping onto my oil?"

What could he do about it? Nothing! Couldn't he go to law? He had got there first. Didn't a man have no rights? Couldn't they do something? Install a second pump? Replace this one with a bigger, stronger, faster one? Sink a thicker pipe? Christ, wasn't there nothing could be done to stop him, keep ahead of him, get it before he took it all?

But they didn't care, the oilmen. The same company (a Yankee outfit) had drilled both wells, his and his neighbor's. They were getting theirs on both sides of the fence, the sons of bitches. What the hell did they care which of them got more on his royalty check? It was all one and the same to them.

Jordan tried to visualize the lake of oil deep underground. It seemed to have shrunk. It had seemed bigger before, when he had thought of it as lying just under his own thirty acres, than it did now that he must think of it as extending also under his neighbor's forty-odd. Twelve acres more of it that damned Bywaters had than he had! To think there was a time when he could have bought him out at fifteen dollars an acre! A piddling six hundred dollars! Christalmighty, he spent more than that a week now. To be sure, at the time he didn't have six dollars cash money, much less six hundred, and wouldn't have spent it on Clarence Bywaters's forty acres of dust and erosion if he had had. It was enough to bring on heart failure when Jordan recalled that he had countered Bywaters's price by offering to sell out to him at ten an acre.

They had had to drill deeper on his neighbor's land. Did that mean that it was shallower on his side, that his oil was draining downhill into Bywaters's deeper pool? Was he just on the edge of it and Bywaters sitting in the middle? Since they had had to drill deeper that meant that his neighbor had a longer pipe. Jordan pictured the two of them underground, both sucking away, and the level of the pool dropping lower and lower, and suddenly his pipe made a sound like a soda straw makes at the bottom of the glass when the ice-cream soda is all gone. But his neighbor's pipe went on sucking greedily away.

The sound of his neighbor's pump, now that he knew it was pumping *his* oil, was like the steady drip of a leaky faucet: Jordan couldn't not hear it. Rocket-a-bump, rocket-a-bump, rocket-a-bump, all day long and into the night, growing louder and louder, drowning out nearer sounds, including that of his own pump.

Once Jordan's pump stopped. He was lying in bed one night, sweating, tossing, the pounding of his neighbor's pump like a migraine headache, hating his wife for her deep untroubled sleep at his side, when suddenly his pump stopped. That was his owned damned heart he heard, his pump had stopped. He leaped out of bed, ignoring his wife's sleepy, questioning whine, and dashed outdoors in his BVD's. It was going. Thank God, it was going. The relief was almost more than Jordan could stand. But wasn't it going slower, weaker? It seemed to be going slower. Had it reached the bottom and was it having to strain to draw up the last little bit? Or was it only that his heart was beating so fast?

From that time on the rocket-a-bump, rocket-a-bump, instead of lulling Jordan to sleep at night, kept him awake, listening, afraid it was going to stop, uncertain whether it was his own he was hearing or his neighbor's. He had to give up rocking in his rocking chair: the noise it made interfered with his listening. He sat very still, listening. He was afraid to go off for a ride in his car for fear his pump might stop while he was gone. Sometimes at night, when at last out of exhaustion he dropped off and momentarily ceased to hear the fevered rhythm of his own pulse drumming in his ear against his twisted and sweaty pillow, he awoke with a jerk, sure that his pump had stopped, that it was the other that he heard, and at such times as he bolted up in the darkness his heart gasped and gurgled as if it had drawn up the very last drop.

The bills for his new style of living began pouring in, bills of a size to take your breath away, in numbers like germs. Debts Jordan had always had, money to pay them with never before. The one was real, the other just paper, something in a bank. He lectured his wife and daughters on their extravagance. He reminded them how well they had always got by before without jewels and permanent waves. How much money a rich man needed!

Meanwhile that s.o.b. next door was really living high. Burning up the road in a Graham roadster. A blowout every weekend. Delivery vans from Ardmore and Oklahoma City pulling up to the door all day along. And his womenfolk going around bundled up in furs when it was a hundred and ten degrees in the shade, looking like an escaped zoo. He was not economizing. Whenever they met, Bywaters gave him such a glad hand and such a big fat possum-eating grin that the conviction grew on Jordan's mind that his neighbor was laughing at him. If Bywaters knew—and how could he not know?—that they were both pumping out of the same pool, it never fazed him. Which could only mean that he somehow knew he was getting the lion's share.

Jordan was not the only one to notice those fur coats, those delivery vans. Complaining that they were tackier now than when they were poor, his wife and daughters whined at him from morn till night. Clarence Bywaters now, his wife and daughters were dressed as women in their position ought to be. Were the Bywaters any better off than they were? And they would catalog the finery which Mrs. Bywaters and each of the Bywaters girls had worn to church that morning. As if Jordan hadn't seen! As if it wasn't him who was paying for every stitch of all those gladrags! How could he afford to deck out his own women when it was him who was outfitting Bywaters's like four grand duchesses?

Often poor Jordan chewed the bitter cud of that moment when his neighbor had offered to sell out to him. The scene was vivid in his mind. He saw Bywaters's furrowed brow, saw him stroke his stubbly chin, saw his head shake, heard him say, "It's a dog's life. Crops burning up. Soil all blown away. Cotton selling for nothing. If I could just raise the money I'd leave tomorrow. You know anybody that'll give me fifteen an acre?" Jordan had laughed. Oh, how he wished he had it to do over again! Surely he could have raised six hundred dollars if he had only tried. He could have borrowed that on his own place. It already had a first lien on it, but he could have got a second. Oh, why had he let that golden opportunity slip? Then all seventy-two acres of that lake of oil would have been his, both those pumps his alone. These days to lay his hands on six hundred dollars all he had to do was reach in his pocket. He saw himself doing so. He saw Bywaters's face break into a grateful smile, felt the grateful pressure of his hand. His heart melted with pity for his neighbor, poor son of a bitch, and with the warmth of its own generosity. "California, here I come!" said Bywaters, hope shining like a rainbow through the tears brimming in his eyes. "Best of luck, ol' hoss," Jordan said. "I'll miss you." From this dream he was awakened by the throb of his neighbor's pump.

To wash the bitter taste from his mouth Jordan would take a pull at the bottle, drinking red whiskey now instead of white, his sole extravagance. Presently, despite himself, he would slip into another reverie. Rocking faster and faster as the figures mounted, he would calculate how much ahead he would be if his neighbor's pump was to break down, be out of commission for a week, ten days, two weeks. A month. Two months! Three! By then he was rocking so fast that when he caught himself and slowed down he was out of breath and panting, in a sweat. All he had succeeded in doing was in figuring how much his neighbor was making every minute. Then he would feel the hairs on the nape of his neck rise up and tingle as though someone was watching him.

Then Jordan knew he was in for it, and his heart seized with dread. For any misfortune wished upon another is a boomerang, it circles back and hits you. A man can't think one mean thought, not even in a whisper, not even alone in a dark room at night or down in a cave deep in the earth, without Him hearing it and visiting it right back on you. Once a thought has been thought there is no calling it back. It goes out on the air like the radio waves, with the thinker's name all over it. He gets a whiff and says, "Who made that bad smell?" He looks down, right at you, and grabs you by the scruff of the neck and rubs your nose in your own mess.

So it was bound to happen. Try as he might to unwish the wish that his neighbor's pump might fail, Jordan went right on wishing it. So it was only a matter of time until his own broke down. Really. Not just a false alarm. And who knew for how long? Two weeks? Not likely! He had wished three months against Bywaters.

As is so often the case in such matters, for all his anxiety, Jordan was unaware of it when it befell. He had lain awake that night listening so intently to the hateful sound of his neighbor's pump that he didn't not hear his. Or maybe he fondly imagined that it was Bywaters's which had stopped, permitting him to fall asleep at last. The silence awoke him early next morning: steady, throbbing silence, and, in the background, Bywaters's pump going double time. He went out on the porch and looked. The beam hung down as if it had been pole-axed.

Jordan called the company, his wife called the doctor. Keep him in bed and away from drink, the doctor advised; but he was no sooner gone than Jordan was out on the front porch rocking nervously and drinking steadily as he awaited the repairmen. It was midmorning before they showed up, nearly noon before the one sent for the replacement part got back.

"Have her going for you again in no time now, Colonel," they said.

But they fiddled and laid down their tools to talk and roll and smoke cigarettes and dawdled in the shade over their lunch and started looking at their watches half an hour before quitting time, and by then Bywaters's pump was going in jig time. So was Jordan in his rocker, until all of a sudden he came to a dead stop. He was still warm when they got to him but it was as if rigor mortis had set in while he was still alive. They had to pry him loose from that chair, and getting him into his coffin was like straightening a bent nail.

There is nothing on earth as dry as a handful of red Oklahoma dirt, though deeper down may lie an ocean of black gold. They crumbled their handfuls over Jordan Terry and shook their heads. A crying shame, said Jordan's lifelong friend and neighbor Clarence Bywaters as they were leaving the graveyard, a crying shame the poor son of a bitch had only lived to enjoy his wealth such a little while.

BOBBIE ANN MASON

Bobbie Ann Mason was born and raised in Kentucky and now lives in rural Pennsylvania. Her first collection of stories, *Shiloh and Other Stories* (1982), was nominated for the National Book Critics Circle Award, the American Book Award, and the PEN/Faulkner Fiction Award. It won the Ernest Hemingway Foundation Award for best first fiction as well as an American Academy and Institute for Arts and Letters award to encourage new writers. She is also the author of two novels, *In Country* (1985), and *Spence + Lila.*

A New-Wave Format

EDWIN Creech drives a yellow bus, transporting a group of mentally retarded adults to the Cedar Hill Mental Health Center, where they attend training classes. He is away from 7:00 to 9:30 A.M. and from 2:30 to 5:00 P.M. His hours are so particular that Sabrina Jones, the girl he has been living with for several months, could easily cheat on him. Edwin devises schemes to test her. He places a long string of dental floss on her pillow (an idea he got from a mystery novel), but it remains undisturbed. She is away four nights a week, at rehearsals for *Oklahoma!* with the Western Kentucky Little Theatre, and she often goes out to eat afterward with members of the cast. Sabrina won't let him go to rehearsals, saying she wants the play to be complete when he sees it. At home, she sings and dances along with the movie sound track, and she acts out scenes for him. In the play, she's in the chorus, and she has two lines in Act I, Scene 3. Her lines are "And to yer house a dark clubman!" and "Then out of your dreams you'll go." Edwin loves the dramatic way Sabrina waves her arms on her first line. She is supposed to be a fortune teller.

One evening when Sabrina comes home, Edwin is still up, as she puts on the sound track of *Oklahoma!* and sings along with Gordon MacRae while she does splits on the living room floor. Her legs are long and slender, and she still has her summer tan. She is wearing her shorts, even though it is late fall. Edwin suddenly has an overwhelming feeling of love for her. She really seems to believe what she is singing—"Oh, What a Beautiful Mornin'." When the song ends, he tells her that.

"It's the middle of the night," he says, teasing. "And you think it's morning."

"I'm just acting."

"No, you really believe it. You believe it's morning, a beautiful morning."

Sabrina gives him a fishy look, and Edwin feels embarrassed. When the record ends, Sabrina goes into the bedroom and snaps on the radio. Rock music helps her relax before going to sleep. The new rock music she likes is monotonous and bland, but Edwin tells himself that he likes it because Sabrina likes it. As she undresses, he says to her, "I'm sorry. I wasn't accusing you of nothing."

"That's O.K." She shrugs. The T-shirt she sleeps in has a hole revealing a spot of her skin that Edwin would like to kiss, but he doesn't because it seems like a corny thing to do. So many things about Sabrina are amazing: her fennel toothpaste and herbal deodorant; her slim, snaky hips; the way she puts Vaseline on her teeth for a flashier smile, something she learned to do in a beauty contest.

When she sits on the bed, Edwin says, "If I say the wrong things, I want you to tell me. It's just that I'm so crazy about you I can't think sometimes. But if I can do anything better, I will. I promise. Just tell me."

"I don't think of you as the worrying type," she says, lying down beside him. She still has her shoes on.

"I didn't used to be."

"You're the most laid back guy I know."

"Is that some kind of actor talk from your actor friends?"

"No. You're just real laid back. Usually good-looking guys are so stuck up. But you're not." The music sends vibrations through Edwin like a cat's purr. She says, "I brag on you all the time to Jeff and Sue—Curly and Laurey."

"I know who Jeff and Sue are." Sabrina talks constantly about Jeff and Sue, the romantic leads in the play.

Sabrina says, "Here's what I wish. If we had a big pile of money, we could have a house like Sue's. Did I tell you she's got *woven* blinds on her patio that she made herself? Everything she does is so *artistic.*" Sabrina shakes Edwin's shoulder. "Wake up and talk to me."

"I can't. I have to get up at six."

Sabrina whispers to him, "Sue has the hots for Jeff. And Jeff's wife is going to have a duck with a rubber tail if she finds out." Sabrina giggles. "He kept dropping hints about how his wife was going to Louisville next week. And he and Sue were eating off the same slice of pizza."

"Is that supposed to mean something?"

"You figure it out."

"Would you do me that way?"

"Don't be silly." Sabrina turns up the radio, then unties her shoes and tosses them over Edwin's head into a corner.

Edwin is forty-three and Sabrina is only twenty, but he does not want to believe age is a barrier between them. Sometimes he cannot believe his good luck, that he has a beautiful girl who finds him still attractive. Edwin has a deep dimple in his chin, which reminded his first wife, Lois Ann, of Kirk Douglas. She had read in a movie magazine that Kirk Douglas has a special attachment for shaving his dimple. But Sabrina thinks Edwin looks like John Travolta, who also has a dimple. Now and then Edwin realizes how much older he is than Sabrina, but time has passed quickly, and he still feels like the same person, unchanged, that he was twenty years ago. His two ex-wives had seemed to drift away from him, and he never tried to hold them back. But with Sabrina, he knows he must make an effort, for it is beginning to dawn on him that sooner or later women get disillusioned with him. Maybe he's too laid back. But Sabrina likes this quality. Sabrina has large round gray eyes and limp, brownish-blond hair, the color of birch paneling, which she highlights with Miss Clairol. They share a love of Fudgsicles, speedboats, and *WKRP in Cincinnati.* At the beginning, he thought that was enough to build a relationship on, because he knew so many couples who never shared such simple pleasures, but gradually he has begun to see that it is more complicated than that. Sabrina's liveliness makes him afraid that she will be fickle. He can't bear the thought of losing her, and he doesn't like the idea that his new possessiveness may be the same uneasy feeling a man would have for a daughter.

Sabrina's parents sent her to college for a year, but her father, a farmer, lost money on his hogs and couldn't afford to continue. When Edwin met her, she was working as a waitress in a steak house. She wants to go back to college, but Edwin does not have the money to send her either. In college, she learned things that make him feel ignorant around her. She said that in an anthropology course, for instance, she learned for a fact that people evolved from animals. But when he tried to argue with her, she said his doubts were too silly to discuss. Edwin doesn't want to sound like a father, so he usually avoids such topics. Sabrina believes in the ERA, although she likes to keep house. She cooks odd things for him, like eggplant, and a weird lasagna with vegetables. She says she knows how to make a Big Mac from scratch, but she never does. Her specialty is pizza. She puts sliced dill pickles on it, which Edwin doesn't dare question. She likes to do things in what she calls an arty way. Now Sabrina is going out for pizza with people in the Theatre. Sabrina talks of "the Theatre."

Until he began driving the bus, Edwin had never worked closely with people. He worked on an offshore oil rig for a time, but kept his distance from the other men. He drove a bulldozer in a logging camp out West. In Kentucky, during his marriages, he worked in an aluminum products company, an automotive machine shop, and numerous gas stations, going from job to job as casually as he did with women. He used to think of himself as an adventurer, but now he believes he has gone through life rather blindly, without much pain or sense of loss.

When he drives the bus, he feels stirred up, perhaps the way Sabrina feels about *Oklahoma!* The bus is a new luxury model with a tape deck, AM-FM, CB, and built-in first-aid kit. He took a first-aid course, so he feels prepared to handle emergencies. Edwin has to stay alert, for anything could happen. The guys who came back from Vietnam said it was like this every moment. Edwin was in the army, but he was never sent to Vietnam, and now he feels that he has bypassed some critical stage in his life: a knowledge of terror. Edwin has never had this kind of responsibility, and he has never been around mentally retarded people before. His passengers are like bizarre, overgrown children, badly behaved and unpredictable. Some of them stare off into space, others are hyperactive. A woman named Freddie Johnson kicks aimlessly at the seat in front of her, spouting her ten-word vocabulary. She can say, "Hot! Shorts," "*Popeye* on?" "*Dukes* on!" "Cook supper," and "Go bed." She talks continuously. A gangly man with a clubfoot has learned to get Hershey bars from a vending machine, and every day he brings home Hershey bars, clutching them in his hand until he squeezes them out of shape. A pretty blond woman shows Edwin the braces on her teeth every day when she gets on the bus. She gets confused if Edwin brings up another topic. The noises on the bus are chaotic and eerie—spurts, gurgles, yelps, squeals. Gradually, Edwin has learned how to keep his distance and keep order at the same time. He plays tape-recorded music to calm and entertain the passengers. In effect, he has become a disc jockey, taking requests and using the microphone, but he avoids fast talk. The supervisors at the center have told him that the developmentally disabled—they always use this term—need a world that is slowed down; they can't keep up with today's fast pace. So he plays mellow old sixties tunes by the Lovin' Spoonful, Joni Mitchell, Donovan. It seems to work. The passengers have learned to clap or hum along with the music. One man, Merle Cope, has been learning to clap his hands in a body-awareness class. Merle is forty-seven years old, and he walks two miles—in an hour—to the bus stop, down a country road. He climbs onto the bus with agonizing slowness. When he gets on, he makes an exaggerated clapping motion, as if to congratulate himself for having made it, but he never lets his hands quite touch. Merle Cope always has an eager grin on his face, and when he tries to clap his hands he looks ecstatic. He looks happier than Sabrina singing "Oh, What a Beautiful Mornin'."

On Thursday, November 14, Edwin stops at the junction of a state road and a gravel road called Ezra Combs Lane to pick up a new passenger. The country roads have shiny new green signs, with the names of the farmers who originally settled there three or four generations ago. The new passenger is Laura Combs, who he has been told is thirty-seven and has never been to school. She will take classes in Home Management and Living Skills. When she gets on the bus, the people who were with her drive off in a blue Pacer. Laura Combs, a large, angular woman with buckteeth, stomps deliberately down the aisle, then plops down beside a young black man named Ray Watson, who has been riding the bus for about three weeks. Ray has hardly spoken, except to say "Have a nice day" to Edwin when he leaves the bus.

Ray, who is mildly retarded from a blow on the head in his childhood, is subject to seizures, but so far he has not had one on the bus. Edwin watches him carefully. He learned about convulsions in his first-aid course.

When Laura Combs sits down by Ray Watson, she shoves him and says, "Scoot over. And cheer up."

Her tone is not cheerful. Edwin watches in the rear-view mirror, ready to act. He glides around a curve and slows down for the next passenger. A tape has ended and Edwin hesitates before inserting another. He hears Ray Watson say, "I never seen anybody as ugly as you."

"Shut up or I'll send you to the back of the bus." Laura Combs speaks with a snappy authority that makes Edwin wonder if she is really retarded. Her hair is streaked gray and yellow, and her face is filled with acne pits.

Ray Watson says, "That's fine with me, long as I don't have to set by you."

"Want me to throw you back in the woodpile where you come from?"

"I bet you could throw me plumb out the door, you so big."

It is several minutes before it is clear to Edwin that they are teasing. He is pleased that Ray is talking, but he can't understand why it took a person like Laura Combs to motivate him. She is an imposing woman with a menacing stare. She churns gum, her mouth open.

For a few weeks, Edwin watches them joke with each other, and whenever he decides he should separate them, they break out into big grins and pull at each other's arms. The easy intimacy they develop seems strange to Edwin, but then it suddenly occurs to him what a fool he is being about a twenty-year-old girl, and that seems even stranger. He hears Ray ask Laura, "Did you get that hair at the Piggly Wiggly?" Laura's hair is in pigtails, which seem to be freshly plaited on Mondays and untouched the rest of the week. Laura says, "I don't want no birds nesting in *my* hair."

Edwin takes their requests. Laura has to hear "Mister Bojangles" every day, and Ray demands that Edwin play something from Elvis's Christmas album. They argue over tastes. Each says the other's favorite songs are terrible.

Laura tells Ray she never heard of a black person liking Elvis, and Ray says, "There's a lot about black people you don't know."

"What?"

"That's for me to know and you to find out. You belong on the moon. All white peoples belong on the moon."

"You belong in Atlanta," Laura says, doubling over with laughter.

When Edwin reports their antics one day to Sabrina, she says, "That's too depressing for words."

"They're a lot smarter than you'd think."

"I don't see how you can stand it." Sabrina shudders. She says, "Out in the woods, animals that are defective wouldn't survive. Even back in history, deformed babies were abandoned."

"Today's different," says Edwin, feeling alarmed. "Now they have rights."

"Well, I'll say one thing. If I was going to have a retarded baby, I'd get an abortion."

"That's killing."

"It's all in how you look at it," says Sabrina, changing the radio station.

They are having lunch. Sabrina has made a loaf of zucchini bread, because Sue made one for Jeff. Edwin doesn't understand her reasoning, but he takes it as a compliment. She gives him another slice, spreading it with whipped margarine. All of his women were good cooks. Maybe he didn't praise them enough. He suddenly blurts out so much praise for the zucchini bread that Sabrina looks at him oddly. Then he realizes that her attention is on the radio. The Humans are singing a song about paranoia, which begins, "Attention, all you K Mart shoppers, fill your carts, 'cause your time is almost up." It is Sabrina's favorite song.

"Most of my passengers are real poor country people," Edwin says. "Use to, they'd be kept in the attic or out in the barn. Now they're riding a bus, going to school and having a fine time."

"In the attic? I never knew that. *I*'m a poor country girl and I never knew that."

"Everybody knows that," says Edwin, feeling a little pleased. "But don't call yourself a poor country girl."

"It's true. My daddy said he'd give me a calf to raise if I came back home. Big deal. My greatest dread is that I'll end up on a farm, raising a bunch of dirty-faced younguns. Just like some of those characters on your bus."

Edwin does not know what to say. The song ends. The last line is, "They're looking in your picture window."

While Sabrina clears away the dishes, Edwin practices rolling bandages. He has been reviewing his first-aid book. "I want you to help me practice a simple splint," he says to Sabrina.

"If I broke a leg, I couldn't be in *Oklahoma!*"

"You won't break a leg." He holds out the splint. It is a fraternity paddle, a souvenir of her college days. She sits down for him and stretches out her leg.

"I can't stand this," she says.

"I'm just practicing. I have to be prepared. I might have an emergency."

Sabrina, wincing, closes her eyes while Edwin ties the fraternity paddle to her ankle.

"It's perfect," he says, tightening the knot.

Sabrina opens her eyes and wiggles her foot. "Jim says he's sure I can have a part in *Life with Father,*" she says. Jim is the director of *Oklahoma!* She adds, "Jeff is probably going to be the lead."

"I guess you're trying to make me jealous."

"No, I'm not. It's not even a love story."

"I'm glad then. Is that what you want to do?"

"I don't know. Don't you think I ought to go back to school and take a drama class? It'd be a real great experience, and I'm not going to get a job anytime soon, looks like. Nobody's hiring." She shakes her leg impatiently, and Edwin begins untying the bandage. "What do you think I ought to do?"

"I don't know. I never know how to give you advice, Sabrina. What do I know? I haven't been to college like you."

"I wish I were rich, so I could go back to school," Sabrina says sadly. The fraternity paddle falls to the floor, and she says, with her hands rushing to her face, "Oh, God, I can't stand the thought of breaking a leg."

The play opens in two weeks, during the Christmas season, and Sabrina has been making her costumes—two gingham outfits, virtually identical. She models them for Edwin and practices her dances for him. Edwin applauds, and she gives him a stage bow, as the director has taught her to do. Everything Sabrina does now seems like a performance. When she slices the zucchini bread, sawing at it because it has hardened, it is a performance. When she sat in the kitchen chair with the splint, it was as though she imagined her audience. Edwin has been involved in his own performances, on the bus. He emulates Dr. Johnny Fever, on *WKRP,* because he likes to be low-key, cool. But he hesitates to tell Sabrina about his disc jockey role because she doesn't watch *WKRP in Cincinnati* with him anymore. She goes to rehearsals early.

Maybe it is out of resistance to the sappy *Oklahoma!* sound track, or maybe it is an inevitable progression, but Edwin finds himself playing a few Dylan tunes, some Janis Joplin, nothing too hectic. The passengers shake their heads in pleasure or beat things with their fists. It makes Edwin sad to think how history passes them by, but sometimes he feels the same way about his own life. As he drives along, playing these old songs, he thinks about what his life was like back then. During his first marriage, he worked in a gas station, saving for a down payment on a house. Lois Ann fed him on a TV tray while he watched the war. It was like a drama series. After Lois Ann, and then his travels out West, there was Carolyn and another down payment on another house and more of the war. Carolyn had a regular schedule—pork chops on Mondays, chicken on Tuesdays. Thursday's menu has completely escaped his memory. He feels terrible, remembering his wives by their food, and remembering the war as a TV series. His life has been a delayed reaction. He feels as if he's about Sabrina's age. He plays music he did not understand fifteen years ago, music that now seems full of possibility: the Grateful Dead, the Jefferson Airplane, groups with vision. Edwin feels that he is growing and changing for the first time in years. The passengers on his bus fill him with a compassion he has never felt before. When Freddie Johnson learns a new word—"bus"—Edwin is elated. He feels confident. He could drive his passengers all the way to California if he had to.

One day a stringbean girl with a speech impediment gives Edwin a tape cassette she wants him to play. Her name is Lou Murphy. Edwin has tried to encourage her to talk, but today he hands the tape back to her abruptly.

"I don't like the Plasmatics," he explains, enjoying his authority. "I don't play new-wave. I have a golden-oldie format. I just play sixties stuff."

The girl takes the tape cassette and sits down by Laura Combs. Ray Watson is absent today. She starts pulling at her hair, and the cassette jostles in her lap. Laura is wound up too, jiggling her knees. The pair of them make Edwin think of those vibrating machines that mix paint by shaking the cans.

Edwin takes the microphone and says, "If you want a new-wave format, you'll have to ride another bus. Now let's crawl back in the stacks of wax for this oldie but goodie—Janis Joplin and 'A Little Bit Harder.'"

Lou Murphy nods along with the song. Laura's chewing gum pops like BBs. A while later, after picking up another passenger, Edwin glances in the rear-view mirror and sees Laura playing with the Plasmatics tape, pulling it out in a curly heap. Lou seems to be trying to shriek, but nothing comes out. Before Edwin can stop the bus, Laura has thrown the tape out the window.

"You didn't like it, Mr. Creech," Laura says when Edwin, after halting the bus on a shoulder, stalks down the aisle. "You said you didn't like it."

Edwin has never heard anyone sound so matter-of-fact, or look so reasonable. He has heard that since Laura began her classes, she has learned to set a table, make change, and dial a telephone. She even has a job at the training center, sorting seeds and rags. She is as hearty and domineering, yet as delicate and vulnerable, as Janis Joplin must have been. Edwin manages to move Lou to a front seat. She is sobbing silently, her lower jaw jerking, and Edwin realizes he is trembling too. He feels ashamed. After all, he is not driving the bus in order to make a name for himself. Yet it had felt right to insist on the format for his show. There is no appropriate way to apologize, or explain.

Edwin doesn't want to tell Sabrina about the incident. She is preoccupied with the play and often listens to him distractedly. Edwin has decided that he was foolish to suspect that she had a lover. The play is her love. Her nerves are on edge. One chilly afternoon, on the weekend before *Oklahoma!* opens, he suggests driving over to Kentucky Lake.

"You need a break," he tells her. "A little relaxation. I'm worried about you."

"This is nothing," she says. "Two measly lines. I'm not exactly a star."

"What if you were? Would you get an abortion?"

"What are you talking about? I'm not pregnant."

"You said once you would. Remember?"

"Oh. I would if the baby was going to be creepy like those people on your bus."

"But how would you know if it was?"

"They can tell." Sabrina stares at him and then laughs. "Through science."

In the early winter, the lake is deserted. The beaches are washed clean, and the water is clear and gray. Now and then, as they walk by the water, they hear a gunshot from the Land Between the Lakes wilderness area. "The Surrey with the Fringe on Top" is going through Edwin's head, and he wishes he could throw the *Oklahoma!* sound track in the lake, as easily as Laura Combs threw the Plasmatics out the window of the bus. He has an idea that after the play, Sabrina is going to feel a letdown too great for him to deal with.

When Sabrina makes a comment about the "artistic intention" of Rodgers and Hammerstein, Edwin says, "Do you know what Janis Joplin said?"

"No—what?" Sabrina stubs the toe of her jogging shoe in the sand.

"Janis Joplin said, 'I don't write songs. I just make 'em up.' I thought that was clever."

"That's funny, I guess."

"She said she was going to her high school reunion in Port Arthur, Texas. She said, 'I'm going to laugh a lot. They laughed me out of class, out of town, and out of the state.'"

"You sound like you've got that memorized," Sabrina says, looking at the sky.

"I saw it on TV one night when you were gone, an old tape of a Dick Cavett show. It seemed worth remembering." Edwin rests his arm around Sabrina's waist, as thin as a post. He says, "I see a lot of things on TV, when you're not there."

Wild ducks are landing on the water, scooting in like water skiers. Sabrina seems impressed by them. They stand there until the last one lands.

Edwin says, "I bet you can't even remember Janis Joplin. You're just a young girl, Sabrina. *Oklahoma!* will seem silly to you one of these days."

Sabrina hugs his arm. "That don't matter." She breaks into laughter. "You're cute when you're being serious."

Edwin grabs her hand and jerks her toward him. "Look, Sabrina. I was never serious before in my life. I'm just now, at this point in my life—this week—getting to be serious." His words scare him, and he adds with a grin that stretches his dimple, "I'm serious about *you.*"

"I know that," she says. She is leading the way along the water, through the trees, pulling him by the hand. "But you never believe how much I care about you," she says, drawing him to her. "I think we get along real good. That's why I wish you'd marry me instead of just stringing me along."

Edwin gasps like a swimmer surfacing. It is very cold on the beach. Another duck skis onto the water.

Oklahoma! has a four-night run, with one matinee. Edwin goes to the play three times, surprised that he enjoys it. Sabrina's lines come off differently each time, and each evening she discusses the impression she made. Edwin tells her that she is the prettiest woman in the cast, and that her lines are cute. He wants to marry Sabrina, although he hasn't yet said he would. He wishes he could buy her a speedboat for a wedding present. She wants him to get a better-paying job, and she has ideas about a honeymoon cottage at the lake. It feels odd that Sabrina has proposed to him. He thinks of her as a liberated woman. The play is old-fashioned and phony. The love scenes between Jeff and Sue are comically stilted, resembling none of the passion and intrigue that Sabrina has reported. She compared them to Bogart and Bacall, but Edwin can't remember if she meant Jeff and Sue's roles or their actual affair. How did Sabrina know about Bogart and Bacall?

At the cast party, at Jeff's house, Jeff and Sue are publicly affectionate, getting away with it by playing their Laurey and Curly roles, but eventually Jeff's wife, who has made ham, potato salad, chiffon cakes, eggnog, and cranberry punch for sixty people, suddenly disappears from the party. Jeff whizzes off in his Camaro to find her. Sabrina whispers to Edwin, "Look how Sue's pretending nothing's happened. She's flirting with the guy who played Jud Fry." Sabrina, so excited that she bounces around on her tiptoes, is impressed by Jeff's house, which has wicker furniture and rose plush carpets.

Edwin drinks too much cranberry punch at the party, and most of the time he sits on a wicker love seat watching Sabrina flit around the room, beaming with the joy of her success. She is out of costume, wearing a sweatshirt with a rainbow on the front and pots of gold on her breasts. He realizes how proud he is of her. Her complexion is as smooth as a white mushroom, and she has crinkled her hair by braiding and unbraiding it. He watches her join some of the cast members around the piano to sing songs from the play, as though they cannot bear it that the play has ended. Sabrina seems to belong with them, these theatre people. Edwin knows they are not really theatre people. They are only local merchants putting on a play in their spare time. But Edwin is just a bus driver. He should get a better job so that he can send Sabrina to college, but he knows that he has to take care of his passengers. Their faces have become as familiar to him as the sound track of *Oklahoma!* He can practically hear Freddie Johnson shouting out her TV shows: "*Popeye* on! *Dukes* on!" He sees Sabrina looking at him lovingly. The singers shout, "Oklahoma, O.K.!"

Sabrina brings him a plastic glass of cranberry punch and sits with him on the love seat, holding his hand. She says, "Jim definitely said I should take a drama course at Murray State next semester. He was real encouraging. He said, 'Why not be in the play *and* take a course or two?' I could drive back and forth, don't you think?"

"Why not? You can have anything you want." Edwin plays with her hand.

"Jeff took two courses at Murray and look how good he was. Didn't you think he was good? I loved that cute way he went into that dance."

Edwin is a little drunk. He finds himself telling Sabrina about how he plays disc jockey on the bus, and he confesses to her his shame about the way he sounded off about his golden-oldie format. His mind is reeling and the topic sounds trivial, compared to Sabrina's future.

"Why *don't* you play a new-wave format?" she asks him. "It's what *every*body listens to." She nods at the stereo, which is playing "You're Living in Your Own Private Idaho," by the B-52s, a song Edwin has often heard on the radio late at night when Sabrina is unwinding, moving into his arms. The music is violent and mindless, with a fast beat like a crazed parent abusing a child, thrashing it senseless.

"I don't know," Edwin says. "I shouldn't have said that to Lou Murphy. It bothers me."

"She don't know the difference," Sabrina says, patting his head. "It's ridiculous to make a big thing out of it. Words are so arbitrary, and people don't say what they mean half the time anyway."

"You should talk, Miss Oklahoma!" Edwin laughs, spurting a little punch on the love seat. "You and your two lines!"

"They're just lines," she says, smiling up at him and poking her finger into his dimple.

Some of Edwin's passengers bring him Christmas presents, badly wrapped, with tags that say his name in wobbly writing. Edwin puts the presents in a drawer, where Sabrina finds them.

"Aren't you going to open them?" she asks. "I'd be dying to know what was inside."

"I will eventually. Leave them there." Edwin knows what is in them without opening them. There is a bottle of shaving cologne, a tie (he never wears a tie), and three boxes of chocolate-covered cherries (he peeked in one, and the others are exactly the same shape). The presents are so pathetic Edwin could cry. He cannot bring himself to tell Sabrina what happened on the bus.

On the bus, the day before Christmas break, Ray Watson had a seizure. During that week, Edwin had been playing more Dylan and even some Stones. No Christmas music, except the Elvis album as usual for Ray. And then, almost unthinkingly, following Sabrina's advice, Edwin shifted formats. It seemed a logical course, as natural as Sabrina's herbal cosmetics, her mushroom complexion. It started with a revival of The Doors—Jim Morrison singing "Light My Fire," a song that was so long it carried them from the feed mill on one side of town to the rendering plant on the other. The passengers loved the way it stretched out, and some shook their heads and stomped their feet.

As Edwin realized later, the whole bus was in a frenzy, and he should have known he was leading the passengers toward disaster, but the music seemed so appropriate. The Doors were a bridge from the past to the present, spanning those empty years—his marriages, the turbulence of the times—and connecting his youth solidly with the present. That day Edwin taped more songs from the radio—Adam and the Ants, Squeeze, the B-52s, the Psychedelic Furs, the Flying Lizards, Frankie and the Knockouts—and he made a point of replacing the Plasmatics tape for Lou Murphy. The new-wave format was a hit. Edwin believed the passengers understood what was happening. The frantic beat was a perfect expression of their aimlessness and frustration. Edwin had the impression that his passengers were growing, expanding, like the corn in *Oklahoma!,* like his own awareness. The new format went on for two days before Ray had his seizure. Edwin did not know exactly what happened, and it was possible Laura Combs had shoved Ray into the aisle. Edwin was in an awkward place on the highway, and he had to shoot across a bridge and over a hill before he could find a good place to stop. Everyone on the bus was making an odd noise, gasping or clapping, some imitating Ray's convulsions. Freddie Johnson was saying, "*Popeye* on! *Dukes* on!" Ray was on the floor, gagging, with his head thrown back, and twitching like someone being electrocuted. Laura Combs stood hunched in her seat, her mouth open in speechless terror, pointing her finger at Edwin. During the commotion, the Flying Lizards were chanting tonelessly, "I'm going to take my problems to the United Nations; there ain't no cure for the summertime blues."

Edwin followed all the emergency steps he had learned. He loosened Ray's clothing, slapped his cheeks, turned him on his side. Ray's skin was the color of the Hershey bars the man with the clubfoot collected. Edwin recalled grimly the first-aid book's ironic assurance that facial coloring was not important in cases of seizure. On the way to the hospital, Edwin clicked in a Donovan cassette. To steady himself, he sang along under his breath. "I'm just wild about saffron," he sang. It was a tune as carefree and lyrical as a field of daffodils. The passengers were screaming. All the way to the hospital, Edwin heard their screams, long and drawn out, orchestrated together into an accusing wail—eerie and supernatural.

Edwin's supervisors commended him for his quick thinking in handling Ray and getting him to the hospital, and everyone he has seen at the center has congratulated him. Ray's mother sent him an uncooked fruitcake made with graham cracker crumbs and marshmallows. She wrote a poignant note, thanking him for saving her son from swallowing his tongue. Edwin keeps thinking: what he did was no big deal; you can't swallow your tongue anyway; and it was Edwin's own fault that Ray had a seizure. He does not feel like a hero. He feels almost embarrassed.

Sabrina seems incapable of embarrassment. She is full of hope, like the Christmas season. *Oklahoma!* was only the beginning for her. She has a new job at McDonald's and a good part in *Life with Father.* She plans to commute to Murray State next semester to take a drama class and a course in Western Civilization that she needs to fulfill a requirement. She seems to assume that Edwin will marry her. He finds it funny that it is up to him to say yes. When she says she will keep her own name, Edwin wonders what the point is.

"My parents would just love it if we got married," Sabrina explains. "For them, it's worse for me to live in sin than to be involved with an older man."

"I didn't think I was really older," says Edwin. "But now I know it. I feel like I've had a developmental disability and it suddenly went away. Something like if Freddie Johnson learned to read. That's how I feel."

"I never thought of you as backward. Laid back is what I said." Sabrina laughs at her joke. "I'm sure you're going to impress Mom and Dad."

Tomorrow, she is going to her parents' farm, thirty miles away, for the Christmas holidays, and she has invited Edwin to go with her. He does not want to disappoint her. He does not want to go through Christmas without her. She has arranged her Christmas cards on a red string between the living room and the kitchen. She is making cookies, and Edwin has a feeling she is adding something strange to them. Her pale, fine hair is falling down in her face. Flour streaks her jeans.

"Let me show you something," Edwin says, bringing out a drugstore envelope of pictures. "One of my passengers, Merle Cope, gave me these."

"Which one is he? The one with the fits?"

"No. The one that claps all the time. He lives with a lot of sisters and brothers down in Langley's Bottom. It's a case of incest. The whole family's backward—your word. He's forty-seven and goes around with this big smile on his face, clapping." Edwin demonstrates.

He pins the pictures on Sabrina's Christmas card line with tiny red and green clothespins. "Look at these and tell me what you think."

Sabrina squints, going down the row of pictures. Her hands are covered with flour and she holds them in front of her, the way she learned from her actor friends to hold an invisible baby.

The pictures are black-and-white snapshots: fried eggs on cracked plates, an oilclothed kitchen table, a bottle of tomato ketchup, a fence post, a rusted tractor seat sitting on a stump, a corn crib, a sagging door, a toilet bowl, a cow, and finally, a horse's rear end.

"I can't look," says Sabrina. "These are disgusting."

"I think they're arty."

Sabrina laughs. She points to the pictures one by one, getting flour on some of them. Then she gets the giggles and can't stop. "Can you imagine what the developers thought when they saw that horse's ass?" she gasps. Her laughter goes on and on, then subsides with a little whimper. She goes back to the cookies. While she cuts out the cookies, Edwin takes the pictures down and puts them in the envelope. He hides the envelope in the drawer with the Christmas presents. Sabrina sets the cookie sheet in the oven and washes her hands.

Edwin asks, "How long do these cookies take?"

"Twelve minutes. Why?"

"Let me show you something else—in case you ever need to know it. The CPR technique—that's cardio-pulmonary resuscitation, in case you've forgotten."

Sabrina looks annoyed. "I'd rather do the Heimlich maneuver," she says. "Besides, you've practiced CPR on me a hundred times."

"I'm not practicing. I don't have to anymore. I'm beyond that." Edwin notices Sabrina's puzzled face. The thought of her fennel toothpaste, which makes her breath smell like licorice, fills him with something like nostalgia, as though she is already only a memory. He says, "I just want you to feel what it would be like. Come on." He leads her to the couch and sets her down. Bend over like this. Just pretend you have the biggest pain, right here, right in your chest, right there."

"Like this?" Sabrina is doubled over, her hair falling to her knees and her fists knotted between her breasts.

"Yes. Right in your heart."

JAMES ALAN MCPHERSON

James Alan McPherson was born in Savannah, Georgia, in 1943. He received a B.A. from Morris Brown College, an LL.B. from Harvard, and an M.F.A. from the University of Iowa. He has taught at several universities, including the University of Virginia and the University of Iowa. He is the co-author (with Miller Williams) of the non-fiction book, *Railroad.* His collections of short fiction are *Hue and Cry* (1969) and *Elbow Room* (1977), which won a Pulitzer Prize.

Private Domain

RODNEY finished his beer in slow, deliberate swallows, peering over the rim of his mug at the other black who, having polished off three previous mugs of draft, now sat watching Rodney expectantly, being quite obvious with his eyes that he held no doubt that more beer was forthcoming. Rodney ignored his eyes. He licked his lips. He tabled the empty mug. "Now give it to me again," he said to the heavily bearded beer-hungry black still eyeing him, now demandingly, from across the small booth. "Let me see if I have it all down."

"How 'bout throwing some more suds on me?" said the black.

"In a minute," said Rodney.

The black considered. "I'm dry again. Another taste."

Rodney sighed, considered his position from behind the sigh, made himself look annoyed and then grudgingly raised his hand until the cigar-chewing bartender noticed, stopped his stooped glass-washing dance behind the counter, and nodded to the waitress, sitting on a stool at the bar, to replenish them. She was slow about getting up. It was a lazy day: the two men in the booth were the only customers.

"Now," said Rodney. "Give it to me again."

The other man smiled. He had won again. "It's this way," he said to Rodney.

Rodney ignored the waitress as she pushed to two fresh mugs onto the table while his companion paused to consider her ass bouncing beneath the cloth of her blue dress. Lighting another cigarette, Rodney observed that the waitress wore no stockings and felt himself getting uncomfortable.

"Well?" he said.

"It's this way," his companion said again. "Your *bag* is where you keep whatever you do best. Whatever is in your bag in your *thing*. Some cats call it your *stick,* but it means the same. Now when you know you got your thing going all right, you say 'I got myself together' or 'I got my game together.'"

"All right, all right," said Rodney. "I've got it down now." He was growing very irritated at the other man, who smiled all the time in a superior way and let the beer wet his gold tooth before he swallowed, as if expecting Rodney to be impressed with its gleam. Rodney was not impressed. He disliked condescension, especially from Willie, whom he regarded in most respects as his inferior.

"Anything else I should know?" Rodney snapped.

"Yeah, baby-boy," Willie said slow and matter-of-factly, implying, in his accents, a whole world of essential instruction being overlooked for want of beer and money and mind and other necessities forever beyond Rodney's reach. "There's lots. There's lots and lots."

"Like what?"

Willie drained his mug. "You know about the big 'I Remember Rock 'n Roll' Memorial in Cleveland last week?"

"No." Rodney was excited. "Who was there?"

"All the cats from the old groups."

"Anything special happen?"

"Hell yes!" Willie smiled again and looked very pleased with himself. "Fatso Checkers didn't show. The cats would have tore the place down but Dirty Rivers filled in for him. He made up a song right on stage. Man, the cats dug it, they went wild they dug it so."

"What's the song?"

"I donno."

"Is it on record?"

"Not yet. He just made it up."

"There's no place I can check it out?"

Again Willie smiled. "You can follow the other squares and check out this week's issue of *Soul.* They might have a piece on it."

"I don't have *time,*" Rodney said. "I've got my studies to do."

"You don't have to, then; just be cool."

Rodney got up. "That's it," he said to Willie. "I'll check you out later." He put two dollars down on the table and turned to go. Willie reached over and picked up the bills. "That's for the beer," Rodney cautioned him.

"Sure," said Willie.

Rodney walked towards the door. "Be cool," he heard Willie say from behind him. He did not look back. He knew that Willie and possibly the waitress and even the bartender would be smiling.

Although he felt uncomfortable in that area of the city, Rodney decided to walk around and digest all that he had been told before driving back to the University. He had parked and locked his car on a small side street and felt relatively protected from the rows and rows of aimless men who lined the stoops of houses and posts and garbage cans on either side of the street, their eyes seemingly shifty, their faces dishonest, their broad black noses alert and sniffing, feeling the air for the source of the smell which Rodney half believed rose from the watch and the wallet and the valuables stored in his pocket. He walked faster. He felt their eyes on his back and he was very uncomfortable being there, in the rising heat from the sidewalk, amid the smells of old food and wine and urine which rose with the heat.

He passed two boys with gray-black, ashy faces and running noses who laughed as they chased a little black girl up and down the steps of a tenement. "Little Tommy Tucker was a bad motherfucker," one of the boys half sang, half spoke, and they all laughed. Rodney thought it obscene and a violation of a protective and sacred barrier between two distinctively different age groups. But after a few more steps he began to think that it was very clever. He stopped. He looked back. He began to memorize it. Then he began to walk back toward them, still at play on the steps, having already forgotten the inventiveness of a moment before. Rodney was about to call to them to repeat the whole verse when a robust and short-haired dark woman in a tight black dress that was open at the side came out of the tenement and down the stairs and began to undulate her way, sensually, toward him. The three children followed her, laughing as they each attempted to imitate her walk. Just when he was about to pass her, a light blue Ford pulled over to the curb next to her and a bald-headed white man leaned, questioningly, out of the driver's window toward the big woman. She stopped, and looking the man directly in the eye with a hint of professional irritation on her round, hard face, asked, "How much?"

"Ten," the man said.

"Hell no," she said turning to go in a way that, while sharp and decisive, also suggested that there was a happy chance that, upon the occurrence of certain conditions, as yet unnamed, she might not go at all.

"Twelve," said the man.

The woman looked at Rodney for a moment; then she looked the leaning man full in the face with fierce eyes. "Fuck you!" she said matter-of-factly.

"Well, damn if you're worth more than that," the man said, ignoring Rodney and the children.

"Get the hell on," said the woman, and began to walk slowly and sensually in the direction in which the car was pointed.

"She ain't got no drawers on," exclaimed one of the children.

"Can you see her cunt?"

"Yeah" was the answer. They all ran after her and the car, which was now trailing her, leaving Rodney alone on that part of the hot sidewalk. But he was not minding the heat now, or the smells, or the lounging men, or even

Willie's condescension; he only minded that he had not thought to bring a notebook because he was having difficulty arranging all this in his head for memorization.

Returning to his car at last, Rodney paused amid afternoon traffic to purchase a copy of *Muhammad Speaks* from a conservatively dressed, cocoa-brown Muslim on a street corner. Rodney tried to be very conspicuous about the transaction, doing his absolute best to engage the fellow in conversation while the homebound cars, full of black and white workers, passed them. "What made you join?" he asked the Muslim, a striking fellow who still retained the red eyes of an alcoholic or drug addict.

"Come to see us and find out for yourself," said the fellow, his eyes not on Rodney but on the moving traffic lest he should miss the possibility of a sale.

"Are you happy being a Muslim?" asked Rodney.

"Come to our mosque, brother, and find out."

"I should think you'd get tired of selling papers all the time."

The Muslim, not wanting to insult Rodney and lose a possible conversion and at the same time more than slightly irritated, struck a compromise with himself, hitched his papers under his arms and moved out into the street between the two lanes of traffic. "Come to our mosque, brother, and gain all knowledge from the lips of the Messenger," he called back to Rodney. Rodney turned away and walked to his car. It was safe; the residents had not found it yet. Still, he inspected the doors and windows and keyholes for jimmy marks, just to feel secure.

II

"Where have you been?" Lynn asked as he opened the door to his apartment. She was sitting on the floor, her legs crossed, her panties showing—her favorite position, which always embarrassed Rodney when they relaxed with other people. He suspected that she did it on purpose. He had developed the habit of glancing at all the other fellows in a room, whenever she did it, until they saw him watching them discovering her and directing their eyes elsewhere in silent respect for his unexpressed wish. This always made Rodney feel superior and polished.

"Put your legs down," he told her.

"For what?" she said.

"You'll catch cold."

"Nobody's looking. Where you been?"

Rodney stood over her and looked down. He looked severe. He could not stand irritation at home too. "Go sit on the sofa," he ordered her. "Only white girls expose themselves in public."

"You prude," she said. "This isn't public." But she got up anyway and reclined on the sofa.

"That's better," said Rodney, pulling off his coat. "If sitting like that is your thing, you should put it in a separate bag and bury it someplace."

"What do you know about *my thing?*" Lynn said.

Rodney did not answer her.

"Where you been, *bay-bee?*"

Rodney said nothing. He hated her when she called him that in private.

"We're going to be late for dinner, *bay-bee,*" she said again.

"I've been out studying," Rodney finally said.

"What?"

"Things."

"Today's Saturday."

"So? God made Saturdays for students."

"Crap," she said. Then she added: "*Bay-bee!*"

"Oh, shut up," said Rodney.

"You can give me orders when we're married," said Lynn.

"That'll be the day," Rodney muttered.

"Yeah," Lynn repeated. "That'll be the day."

Rodney looked at her, legs miniskirted but sufficiently covered, hair natural but just a little too straight to be that way, skin nut-brown and smooth and soft to touch and feel against his mouth and arms and legs, body well built and filled, very noticeable breasts and hips, also good to touch and feel against his body at night. Rodney liked to make love at night, in the dark. He especially did not like to make sounds while making love, although he felt uneasy if the girl did not make any. He was considering whether or not it was dark enough in the room to make love when the telephone rang. Lynn did not move on the sofa and so he answered it himself. It was Charlie Pratt.

"What's happening, baby?" said Rodney.

"Not much," said Charlie. "Listen, can you make dinner around seven? We got some other cats coming over at nine we don't want to feed nothin' but beer."

"Cool," said Rodney. He looked at his watch. "We can make it as soon as Lynn gets herself together." He glanced over at Lynn still stretched out on the sofa.

"Great," said Charlie Pratt. "Later."

Rodney hung up. "What do you have to do to get ready?" he asked Lynn.

"Nothing."

"You *could* put on another skirt."

"Go to hell," she said, not lifting her head from the sofa. "This skirt's fine."

"You could at least comb your hair or something."

Lynn ignored him. Rodney began to reconsider the sufficiency of the darkness in the room. Then he thought better of the idea. Instead, he went out of the room to shave and take a bath.

These days Rodney found himself coming close to hating everyone. Still, he never allowed himself to recognize it, or call what he felt toward certain people genuine hate. He preferred to call it differing degrees of dislike, an emotion with two sides like a coin, which was constantly spinning in his mind. Sometimes it landed, in his brain, heads up, signifying a certain affinity; sometimes it landed tails up, signifying a slight distaste or perhaps a major objection to a single person and his attitudes. He refused to dislike absolutely because, he felt, dislike was uncomfortably close to bigotry and Rodney knew too many different people to be a practicing bigot. Sometimes, very frequently in fact, he disliked Willie immensely. On the other hand, he sometimes felt a bit of admiration for the fellow and, occasionally, footnoted that admiration by purchasing an extra beer for him. This gesture served to stamp those rare moments onto his memory, a reminder that, because he had done this on enough occasions in the past, there would always be a rather thick prophylactic between how he really felt and how Willie assumed he felt.

Talking to Willie was informative and amusing to Rodney up to the point when Willie began to smile and to seem to know that what he was telling Rodney had some value. After he could see when that point was reached in Willie's face, Rodney was not amused any more. Sometimes he was annoyed and sometimes, when Willie smiled confidently and knowledgeably and condescendingly, Rodney began to almost hate him. He felt the same about Lynn and her panties and her *bay-bee* and the loose ways she had, Rodney assumed, picked up from living among whites for too long. Sometimes she made him feel really uncomfortable and scared. He began to say *bay-bee, bay-bee* to himself in the shower. Thinking about it, he suddenly realized that he felt exactly the same way about Charlie Pratt.

Pratt made Rodney feel uncomfortable because he did not fit either side of the coin. The fellow had well over two thousand records: some rhythm and blues, some jazz, some folk, some gospels, but all black. And Charlie Pratt was not. He knew the language and was proud to use the vocabulary Rodney had been trying to forget all his life. He was pleasantly chubby with dark blond hair and a fuzzy Genghis Khan moustache which hung down on either side of his chin. Sometimes the ends dangled when he moved. And sometimes Pratt dangled when he moved. Sometimes Charlie Pratt, his belly hanging over his belt and his chin going up and down in talk, dangled when he did not move. Drying his legs with a towel, Rodney thought of himself and Charlie locked in mortal combat. Rodney had no doubt that he would win;

he was slim and wiry, he was quick, he had a history of natural selection in his ancestry. Besides, Charlie was fat. He never used his body. Thinking about him, Rodney realized that he had never seen Charlie dance or move to the rhythm of any one of his two thousand records. He had never seen him snap his fingers once, or voluntarily move any part of his body besides his arms and legs; and even these movements were not rhythmic but something close to an unnatural shuffle.

Rodney did a quick step with his feet as he brushed his teeth in front of the mirror. He moved back from the mirror in order to see his feet. He did the step again, grinning at himself and at the white-foamed toothbrush hanging loosely from his mouth. The foam covered his lips and made them white, and, remembering a fast song in his head, Rodney snapped his fingers and did the step again. And again.

III

"When you finish," said Charlie Pratt in between chews on a pork-chop bone, "I'll let you hear some of the stuff I picked up yesterday."

Rodney wiped his mouth carefully before answering. "What'd you get this time?" he asked, knowing what to expect.

"Some vintage Roscoe and Shirley stuff," said Charlie. "We found it in Markfield's back room. It was just lying there under a stack of oldies full of dust. We figure it must be their only LP. Jesus, what a find!" Both Charlie and his wife smiled pridefully.

"How about that," said Rodney. But he did not say it with enthusiasm.

Charlie stood up from the table and began to shift his bulk from foot to foot, a sort of safe dance, but more like the movements of someone who wants desperately to go to the bathroom.

"Whatever happened to them?" asked Lynn.

Both the Pratts smiled together. "They broke up in '52 because the girl was a lesbian," his wife said. She had gone to Vassar, and Rodney always noticed how small and tight her mouth became whenever she took the initiative from her husband, which was, Rodney had noticed over a period of several dinners and many beer parties with them, very, very often. She was aggressive, in keeping with the Vassar tradition, and seemed to play a very intense, continuous game of one-upmanship with her husband.

"That's not what happened at all," her husband said. "After they hit the big time with 'I Want to Do It,' it was in '53, Roscoe started sleeping around. One night she caught him in a hotel room with a chick and razored his face.

His face was so cut up he couldn't go onstage any more. I saw him in Newark in '64 when he was trying to make a comeback. He still looked razored. He looked bad."

Rodney felt tight inside, remembering that in '64 he had been trying desperately to make up for a lifetime of not knowing anything about Baroque. Now he knew all about it and he had never heard of Roscoe and Shirley. "There was an 'I Remember Rock 'n Roll' Memorial in Cleveland last week," he said.

"Yeah," said Charlie. "Too bad Fatso couldn't make it. But that was one hell of a song Dirty Rivers made up. Jesus, right on the spot too! Jesus, right on the stage! He sang for almost two hours. Christ! I was lucky to get it taped, the cats went wild. They almost overran the stage."

"How did you get the tape?" asked Rodney, now vaguely disgusted.

"We knew about the show for months," Peggy Pratt broke in. "We planned to go but there was an Ashy Williamson Revue in the Village that same night. We couldn't make both so we called up this guy in Cleveland and got him to tape the show for us." She paused. "Want to hear it?"

"No," said Rodney, somewhat flatly. Then he added: "Not right now."

"Want to hear the Roscoe and Shirley?"

"No."

"I got a new Baptist group," said Charlie Pratt. "Some new freedom songs. Lots of finger-poppin' and hand jive."

"That's not my stick," said Rodney.

"You mean that ain't your *thing,*" said Charlie.

"Yeah," said Rodney. "That's what I mean."

IV

They were drinking beer and listening to the Dirty Rivers tape when the other people came in. Rodney had been sitting on the sofa, quietly, too heavy to keep time with his feet and too tight inside to care if the Pratts did. Lynn was in her best position, on the floor, crosslegged. The two girls with names he did not catch sat in chairs and crossed their legs, keeping time to the music and smoking. Looking at Lynn on the floor and looking at them on the chairs made Rodney mad. Listening to the Pratts recount, to the two white fellows, how they got the Cleveland tape made Rodney mad too. He drained his beer can and then began to beat time to the music with his foot and both hands on the arm of the sofa with a heavy, controlled deliberation that was really off the beat. Still, he knew that, since he was the only black male in the room, the others would assume that he alone knew the proper beat, even if it was out of time with their own perception of it, and would follow him. The two bearded fellows did just that when they sat down on the floor with Lynn; but the two girls maintained their original perception of the beat. Nevertheless, watching the fellows, Rodney felt the return of some sense of power.

"Some more suds," he said to Peggy Pratt.

She went out of the room.

"You've had enough," said Lynn.

Rodney looked at her spitefully. "Just be cool," he told her. "You just play your own game and stay cool."

The two girls looked at him and smiled. Their dates looked at Lynn. They did not smile. Dirty Rivers was moaning, "*Help me! Help me! Help me!*" now, and Rodney felt that he had to feel more from the music than any of them. "*Mercy! mercy! mercy!*" he exclaimed as Peggy Pratt handed him another can of beer. "This cat is *together!*"

The girls agreed and smiled again. One of them even reconciled her beat to Rodney's. Lynn just looked at him.

"He's just a beautiful man," the reconciled girl said.

"He's got more soul than anybody," said Rodney. "Nobody can touch him." He got up from the sofa, put his hands in his pockets and began to exercise a slow, heavy grind to the music without moving his feet. Charlie, who had been standing by the recorder all this time with his hands locked together, smiled his Genghis Kahn smile. "Actually," he said rather slowly, "I think Ashy Williamson is better."

"You jivetime cat," said Rodney. "Williamson couldn't touch Dirty Rivers with a stick."

"Rivers couldn't adapt," said Charlie.

"What do you mean?"

"He's just an old man now, playing the toilets, doing his same thing. Williamson's got class. He's got a new sound everybody digs. Even the squares."

"What do you know?" said Rodney.

Charlie Pratt smiled. "Plenty," he said.

After more beer and argument all around, and after playing Williamson's oldest and latest LP's by way of proof, it was decided that they should put it to a vote. Both the Pratts were of the same mind: Ashy Williamson was better than Dirty Rivers. The two fellows on the floor agreed with them. And also one of the girls. The other girl, however, the skinny brunette who had reconciled her beat to Rodney's, observed that she had been raised on Rivers and felt, absolutely, that he had had in the past, and still had now, a very good thing going for him. But Rodney was not impressed. She had crooked teeth and was obviously out to flatter her date with her maintenance of an independent mind in spite of her looks. Rodney turned to Lynn, still sitting crosslegged and exposed on the floor, but saving Rodney from utilizing his cautioning eye by having the beer can conveniently placed between her open legs. "Well, what do you say?" he asked, standing over her in his usual way.

She looked up at him. Casually sipping her beer, she considered for a long moment. The room was now very quiet, the last cut having been played on the Williamson record. The only sound was Lynn sipping her beer. It grated in Rodney's mind. The only movement was Charlie Pratt doing his rubber shift from foot to foot. That also irritated Rodney. "Well?" he said.

Lynn placed the can between her legs again, very carefully and neatly. "Dirty Rivers is an old man," she said.

"What the hell does that mean?"

"He's got nothing new going for him, *bay-bee,*" she said in a way that told Rodney she had made up her mind about it long before her opinion had been asked. She looked up at Rodney, her face resolved and, it seemed to him, slightly victorious.

"There you go, mother," Charlie said.

Rodney could see them all smiling at him, even Lynn, even the ugly brunette who had reconciled. He sat down on the sofa and said nothing.

"Now I'll play my new Roscoe and Shirley for you," Charlie told the others.

"Wasn't she a lesbian?" one of the fellows asked.

"Absolutely not!" said Charlie Pratt.

Rodney was flipping the coin in his mind again now. He flipped it faster and faster. After a while it was spinning against Willie and the cigar-chewing bartender and Lynn and especially the Pratts. Finishing the beer, Rodney found that the coin had stopped spinning; and from where his mind hung on the bad side of it, somewhere close to the place where he kept his bigotry almost locked away, he could hear the Pratts battling back and forth for the right to tell the others about a famous movie star who sued her parents when she found out that she was a mulatto. He got to his feet and walked over to the stacks and stacks of records that lined the wall. Aimlessly going through them, he considered all the black faces on their covers and all the slick, praising language by white disc jockeys and white experts and white managers on their backs. Then he commenced to stare at the brunette who had agreed with him. She avoided his eyes. He stared at Lynn too; but she was looking at Charlie Pratt, very intentionally. Only once did she glance up at him and smiled in a way that said "*bay-bee.*" And then she looked away again.

Rodney leaned against the wall of records, put his hands in his pockets and wet his lips. Then he said: "Little Tommy Tucker was a *bad* motherfucker!"

They all looked up at him.

"What?" said Peggy Pratt, smiling.

He repeated it.

V

Driving home, Rodney went slower than required and obeyed traffic signals on very quiet, very empty streets. Lynn sat against the door, away from him. She had her legs crossed.

"You were pretty good tonight," she said at last.

Rodney was looking at a traffic light changing back to red.

"You were the life of the party."

Rodney inspected a white line of bird shit running down the top of the window, between him and the red light. It would have to come off in the morning.

"I knew you would let that color come through if you had enough beer," Lynn said.

"Oh shut the hell up!" said Rodney. He was not mad. She had just interrupted his thinking. He was thinking of going over to buy some more beer for Willie and talk some more before the usual Saturday time. He was thinking about building up his collection of Ashy Williamson LP's. He was thinking about driving Lynn directly home and not going up with her to make love to her in her bed, which was much wider than his own, no matter how much she apologized later and no matter how dark and safe and inviting her room would be.

LEWIS NORDAN

Lewis Nordan, a native of Itta Bena, Mississippi, is currently teaching creative writing at the University of Pittsburgh. He lives with his wife, Alicia, and her two sons. He also has a son who lives in Arkansas. His short fiction has been collected in two volumes, *Welcome to the Arrow-Catcher Fair* (1983) and *The All-Girl Football Team* (1986).

Sugar among the Chickens

I HAD been fishing for an hour and still hadn't caught anything. I was fishing for chickens. Mama wouldn't let me walk to the town pond by myself. What else was I going to fish for?

I looked back over my shoulder through the torn-out screened door and tried to see Mama in there. I said, "Mama." I was using the voice that says you're being real good and not fishing for chickens.

Mama said, "You better not be fishing for chickens, Sugar Mecklin, you going to get switched." She's got this ability.

She was out in the kitchen, that was good anyway. I put a fresh kernel on my hook and scattered shelled corn on the slick dirt yard below the porch and dusted off my hands on my white blue jeans. A handful of old hens came bobbing and clucking up to the corn and poked at it with their heads and then raised their heads up and looked around, and then started poking at it again.

I dropped the baited hook in amongst them. I wished I could figure out some way to use a cork. The chickens bobbed and pecked and poked and scratched. I moved my baited hook into the middle of the chickens and eased it down onto the ground and waited. I still didn't get a bite.

My daddy didn't much care whether I fished for chickens or not. My daddy knew I never would catch one, never had, never would. It was my mama who was the problem. She said it would ruin your life if you fished for chickens.

I wasn't studying ruining my life right now. I was thinking about hooking and landing some poultry.

I wasn't using a handline, which is easy to hide if your mama comes up on you. I was using a cane pole and a bream hook, little bitty rascal of a hook. I liked a handline all right, I wasn't complaining. Nothing better for fishing in real tight places, like up under your house on a hot day when the chickens are settled down in the cool dirt and have their neck feathers poked out like a straw hat and a little blue film of an eyelid dropped down over their eyes. A handline is fine for that. A cane pole is better from off your porch, though.

Or I guessed it was. I never had caught a chicken. I had had lots of bites, but I never had landed one, never really even set the hook in one. They're tricky, a chicken.

I really wanted to catch one, too. I wanted the hook to snag in the beak, I wanted to feel the tug on the line. I wanted to haul it in, squawking and heavy and beating its wings and sliding on its back and flopping over to its breast and dragging along and the neck stretched out a foot and a half and the stupid old amazed eyes bright as Beau dollars.

I dreamed about it, asleep and awake. Sometimes I let myself believe the chicken I caught was not just any old chicken but maybe some special one, one of the Plymouth Rocks, some fat heavy bird, a Leghorn, or a blue Andalusian. And sometimes, as long as I was making believe, I thought I might catch an even finer specimen, the finest in the whole chicken yard. I thought I caught the red rooster itself.

The red rooster was a chicken as tall as me. It seemed like it, I swear, when I was ten. It was a chicken, I'm telling you, like no chicken you ever saw before. It could fly. There was no half-assed flying about it. It could fly long distance. Daddy said it could migrate if it had anywhere to go. It couldn't do that, but it could fly fifty times farther than any other chicken you ever saw. This was a chicken that one time killed a stray dog.

I dreamed about that rooster. The best dream was when I caught it not on a handline and not on a cane pole. I dreamed I caught it on a limber fine six-and-a-half-foot Zebco rod and spinning reel, like the ones in the Western Auto store in Arrow Catcher. That's the town I used to live right outside of when I was little, in the Delta. The line on that Zebco spool was almost invisible.

I watched the chickens. There was a fine old Plymouth Rock I would just love to catch. She dusted her feathers and took long steps like a kid wearing his daddy's hip boots. I moved the bait closer to her and held my breath. She started poking around at the corn. She hit the bait once but didn't pick up the hook. My line was taut, so I felt the strike vibrate through the line and down the cane pole to my hands, which I noticed were sweating. I thought, If she hit it once, she just might. . . . But she didn't. She stopped eating corn altogether and scratched herself with her foot like a dog.

I tried to listen for my mama. Mama couldn't be expected to stay in the kitchen forever. I needed to say something to her in my I-ain't-fishing-for-chickens voice, but I couldn't. The Plymouth Rock pecked the earth a few times, but not the bait. Then, all of a sudden, she shifted position a little and pecked right down on the corn with the hook in it, the bait. For the second time that day I felt a strike vibrate through my hands. But the chicken missed the hook again and I jerked the bait out of her mouth. She didn't know what happened to it. She looked like, What in the world?

I repositioned the bait, and the hen started pecking around it again. I had to say something to Mama. I held real still and tried to talk in a voice that maybe a chicken couldn't hear. In my head I invented a voice that seemed like it was going to be all throaty and hoarse and animallike when it came out, but when it did come out, it didn't make any sound at all, not even a whisper, just a little bit of released breath and a wormy movement of my lips. I said, "Mama, I ain't fishing for chickens." Nobody heard it, not even me. The Plymouth Rock hit the bait a third time.

It wasn't possible to catch a chicken. I knew that. My daddy had convinced me. He said, "A chicken is dumb, but not dumb enough." So I knew it was impossible. But I also knew it had happened. I had the Plymouth Rock.

I jerked my pole skyward and set the hook hard in the chicken's beak.

The sound that rose up out of the chicken's throat was a sound that nobody who has never caught a chicken on a hook has ever heard. It sounded like chicken-all-the-way-back-to-the-beginning-of-chicken.

I was anchored to the porch, with the butt end of the pole dug into my groin for support. The heavy flopping squalling bird was hanging off the end of my line in midair. The sound didn't stop. The sound was like the fire siren in Arrow Catcher. As beautiful and as scary as that. It was like a signal. I thought it signaled danger and adventure and beauty.

I was screaming too, along with the chicken. I didn't even know I was screaming. I heaved on the heavy bird. The pole was bent double. I wanted to land the chicken. I wanted the Plymouth Rock on the porch with me.

I couldn't pick it up high enough. It was too heavy for me. It was up off the ground, all right, but I couldn't get it high enough to sling it onto the porch. The chicken was beating its wings and spinning in a wild circle. I held it there.

I heaved on the pole again. The bird swung up and around, but was still not high enough. It hit the side of the house and then swung back out into midair.

Mama came out on the porch and stood behind me. I knew she was back there, because I heard the door slap shut.

At first I didn't look back. I just stopped hauling on the chicken. I was still holding it up off the ground, though. I couldn't give it up yet, not all of it, even though I had stopped trying to land it.

Finally I did look back. The face of my mama, I thought, was the saddest face on this earth. It just had to be. I said, "Hey, Mama," real subdued, trying not to provoke her. I was still holding the chicken off the ground, and it still hadn't stopped making its noise. I said, "I been fishing for chickens." No use lying about it now.

I expected my mama to say, "I swan," like she always said when she meant "I swear." What she really said surprised me. She said she was a big failure in life. She said she was such a big failure in life she didn't see why she didn't just go off and eat some poison.

I eased the chicken down onto the ground. It got loose and scooted off toward the garage with its feathers sticking out.

Mama cut a switch off a crape myrtle and switched me good on my bare legs and went back inside the house. She lay across her bed on the wedding-ring quilt my grandmama Sugar gave her when she got married, with hers and Daddy's names sewed in a corner and a heart stitched around the names, and had herself a long hard cry. And so that part of it was over.

Some time passed. Some days and, I guess, some weeks. I watched my mama around the house. At night, after supper, and after she had wiped the table, she would do what she liked best. She would lay out on the table a new piece of cloth from Kamp's Low Price Store and pin to it a tissue-paper Simplicity pattern. She would weight the pattern down all around with pieces of silverware from the dark chest lined with green felt. The silver came from my mama's grandmama who lost her mind and threw away the family Bible and almost everything else and so left only the silverware, which she forgot to throw away. Mama would get the pattern all weighted down, and she would look around for a minute, in her sewing basket or in a kitchen drawer, and say, "Has anybody seen my good scissors?" She would find the scissors and bring them to the table and cut through the paper and the cloth. She would poke through her sewing basket. I saw the faded pin cushion and the cloth measuring tape and a metal thimble and about a jillion buttons and the pinking shears.

She would lay down a towel to keep from scratching the dining room table and then heft the heavy old portable Kenmore onto it. She might have to thread the bobbin. She might lift the cloth to her nose and breathe its new-smell before she put it into the machine, under the needle, and on the shiny metal plate. She would touch the pedal with her foot.

Before any of this would happen, before supper even, my daddy would come home from work. I could hear the car pull into the drive and head around back of the house. He would get out of the car, and he would be wearing white overalls and a paper cap with the name of a paint store printed on it. He would smell like paint and turpentine and maybe a little whiskey.

Daddy would shoo the chickens back from the gate in the fence where the chickens would flock when they heard his car. He would open the gate and ease inside, real quick, before anybody could get out. I would watch him.

The chickens were gossipy and busy and fat and fine. Daddy would scatter shelled corn from a white metal dishpan and pour out mash for those that needed it and run well water into the troughs.

I always wished Mama would watch him do this. I thought that if she did she would stop thinking she was a big failure in life.

I went down the steps and into the chicken yard with him. He let me reach my hand into the fragrant dusty corn and pelt the old birds with it.

Then there was the part where the rooster attacks you. Every day I forgot it was going to happen, and then it would happen and I would think, Now why didn't I remember that?

It happened today, this particular day, I mean, a Tuesday and just before sunset. The rooster was on top of us. It hadn't been there before, and now it was all I could see, the red furious rooster. Its wings were spread out and its bones were creaking and clacking and its beak was wide open and its tongue was blazing black as blood. And the rooster's eye—it looked like it had only one eye, and the eye was not stupid and comical like the other chickens'. It seemed lidless and magical, like it could see into a person's heart and know all his secrets and read his future. And the feet—they were blue-colored, but blue like you never saw before except in a wound. And the spurs.

And then it was over. Today, like other days. Daddy kicked the chicken in the breast with the toe of his work shoe and it flopped over on its back. It righted itself and stood up and started pecking at the corn on the ground. Daddy walked over to the rooster and petted its neck. The bird made a stretching motion with its head like a cat.

Then there was the next part. We watched the rooster eat. Without warning, as we knew it would, it stopped eating. It stood straight up and cocked its head so far that the comb flopped over. It looked like somebody who has just remembered something real important.

Then the rooster took off. Any other flying chickens you see are all hustle and puffing and heaving and commotion and getting ten feet maybe, no matter how hard they work at it. This chicken could fly like a wild bird, like a peacock, maybe, or a wild turkey. There was nothing graceful about it, nothing pretty. It was just so amazing to watch. When the rooster flew, it looked like some fat bad child who has rung your doorbell and is running down the street away from your house, slow and obvious and ridiculous, but padding on anyway, uncatchable. It flew out and out, over the chicken-yard fence, over a little side yard where Mr. Love kept a goat, over the trailer the midgets lived in, out farther like a kite, over a house, and finally into the branches of a line of hardwood trees across the railroad tracks.

We went inside the house then, and Daddy went into the bathroom and came out after a long time with his new smells of Wildroot and Aqua Velva and his wet combed hair. The whiskey smell was a little stronger, a little sweeter.

After supper, and after the sewing machine was turned off and put away, Mama said, "Now all I have to do is hem it, and it'll be all done." She was on the sofa, so she sat up straight and held the dress up to her front and pretended like she was modeling it. Daddy was moving out of the room. He was weaving a little when he walked, on his way to the kitchen.

I looked at Mama. She had a pleased look on her face that made me think she thought she looked pretty. She did look kind of pretty.

I picked up the package the pattern came in. There was a color picture of two women on it. I said, "Where do these ladies live, Mama?"

She took the package out of my hand and looked at it with the same look on her face. She looked off somewhere away from my eyes and said, "I think maybe these two ladies live in New York City. They live across the hall from one another in a penthouse apartment. I think they just met up downtown by accident." She looked at me and smiled and handed the pattern package back to me.

I said, "What are they talking about?"

Mama said, "Hm." She took the package from me again and looked at it, serious. She said, "I think maybe, well, maybe the lady in the red dress is saying why don't we go somewhere real nice today. She's saying why don't they shop around a little and then maybe go to a picture show. They might even be talking about going to the opera, you don't know."

I tried to think about the opera, men in turbans and women in white-powdered wigs. The men carried sabers at their sides, and the women had derringers in their purses. I said, "I ain't studying no opera."

Mama laid the package down and put the new dress aside too. She started poking through her sewing basket for something, but then stopped without finding it. She had lost the look she had before.

I said, "Are you going to the opera?"

She said, "No."

I said, "When you put on that dress, you know what?"

She didn't answer.

I said, "You ain't going to look like neither one of those ladies." I don't know why I said that.

Mama got up from where she was sitting. She said, "Don't say *ain't*, Sugar. It will ruin your life." She got up off the sofa and went into the bedroom and closed the door.

Daddy came back into the living room. He was wobbly and ripe with whiskey. He said, "What happened to Mama?"

I said, "She's lying down."

He eased back into his chair and started to watch "Gilligan's Island" on the television.

I went to my room. I sat on the bed and let my feet hang off. I had to do something. I felt like I was working a jigsaw puzzle with my family. I saw my mama and my daddy and the chickens and the midgets and Mr. Love's goat and I thought I could never get it worked.

I started to fish for the rooster. Sometimes I fished with a handline, sometimes with a cane pole. The rooster never looked at my bait.

I fished every day, and every day I got older and the rooster didn't get caught. School started up again and I got new shoes. The leaves finally fell off the trees and I helped Mama rake them up in the afternoons. The rooster hated my bait. He couldn't stand to look at it.

I changed bait. I used raisins. I used jelly beans. I used a dog turd. You got to want to catch a chicken to bait a hook with dog turd. Chickens eat them all the time, no reason it wouldn't work. It didn't though.

I threw the cat in the chicken yard. I had ten hooks dangling off the cat, feet and tail and flea collar, everywhere you can put a hook on a cat. The rooster killed the cat, but it didn't take a hook. Too bad about the cat. You're not going to catch a rooster without making a sacrifice or two.

After a while fishing for the rooster and keeping Mama from knowing about it became like a job, like an old habit you never would think about breaking. All that mattered was that I fish for him, that I never give up, no matter how hopeless, no matter how old or unhappy I got.

Something happened then that changed things. It was Saturday. I got on my bike and pedaled from my house to the picture show in Arrow Catcher. There was always a drawing at the matinee.

Mrs. Meyers, the old ticket-taker-upper with the white hair and shaky hands and snuff-breath—she would do the same thing every time. She would take your ticket out of your hand and tear it into halves and tell you what a fine young man you were growing up to be and to hold onto your ticket stub, you might win the drawing.

I walked down the aisle and found me a seat up close to the front. I looked at the torn ticket in my hands, and the other seats filled up with people.

Mr. Gibbs owned the picture show, called it the Strand Theater. The lights were all on bright and Mr. Gibbs climbed up on the stage by a set of wooden steps around the side. He was huffing and sweating, waving his hands for everybody to be quiet. Like he said every Saturday, he said, "Be quite, boys and gulls, be quite, please." We laughed at him, and the underarms of his white shirt were soaked with sweat.

I watched Mr. Gibbs crank the handle of a wire basket filled with ping-pong balls. Every ball had a number on it. Mr. Gibbs would draw them out, one at a time, and put each one on a little cushioned platform with the number facing out to the audience, until he had four of them. He would draw them out slow and teasing and smiling. It was something he loved to do, you could tell. He would call out each number in its turn, real loud and exaggerated. He would say, "Fo-urrr," or "Nye-unn," and he would hold up the white ball and show everyone he wasn't cheating, and then he would put the ball on the cushioned stand. You had to like Mr. Gibbs.

Then it started happening. The first number he called out was the first number on my ticket stub. And then so was the second. It seemed impossible that the number in my ear was the same number as in my eye. It kept on being the same number, digit by digit, right down to the end. I had won the drawing.

I had never won anything before. One time I won a pink cake in a cakewalk. It tasted terrible and I hated it, but I ate all of it anyway, same night I won it. I had never won anything except that cake, so it was impressive enough to win the drawing.

But winning was nothing compared to the prize I was going to take home. I had won the Zebco rod and spinning reel from the Western Auto.

Mr. Gibbs was standing up on that little stage like a sweaty fat angel. He was giving his heartfelt thanks to the Western Auto store, homeowned and homeoperated by Mr. Sooey Leonard, and to all the other fine local merchants of Arrow Catcher who donated these fine prizes and made these drawings possible.

I went up on the stage. I climbed the same dusty wooden steps that Mr. Gibbs had climbed. I showed Mr. Gibbs my ticket stub. I was trembling. He shook my hand, and my hand was sweaty and slick against his manly palm and fingers. Mr. Gibbs asked me if I didn't think every single person in this fine audience ought to take his patronage to the Western Auto store and all the other fine local merchants of Arrow Catcher.

I said, "Yessir," and everybody laughed and clapped their hands.

Mr. Gibbs said what was I doing to do with my fine prize.

I said, "Go fishing," and everybody laughed again.

Mr. Gibbs said why didn't everybody give this fine young fisherman another round of applause, and so everybody did.

I don't know what was on the movie. I sat through it, and I watched it, with the fishing rod between my legs, but I didn't see it. I remember a huffing train and some wreckage, I remember an icy train platform and taxicabs and a baby growing up rich instead of poor. Barbara Stanwyck married John Lund, I remember that. Whatever was on the movie, one thing was all I was thinking about and that was that I was definitely going fishing, no doubt about it. The fish I was going to catch was as tall as me and had red feathers and was big enough and fine enough to ruin the life of every soul in Arrow Catcher, Mississippi.

I look back at the day I caught the rooster. I see the familiar yard, the fence of chicken wire. I smell the sweet fresh fragrance of grain and mash and lime and chickenshit and water from a deep well poured through troughs of corrugated metal. I smell creosote and the green pungent shucks of black walnuts under the tree. I see the trailer the midgets lived in and the goat next door. I see myself, a boy, holding the Zebco rod I won at the Strand Theater. The Zebco moves back, then whips forward.

The line leaps away from the reel, from the rod's tip. It leaps into S's and figure eights. It floats like the strand of a spider's web. At the end of the line I see the white fleck of sunlight that covers the hook: the bait, the kernel of corn. I watch it fly toward the rooster.

I look ahead of the corn, far down the chicken yard, and see the rooster. It seems to be on fire in the sunlight. For one second I lose my mind and believe that the rooster means something more than a rooster. I don't believe it long. I come to my senses and know that the rooster is a chicken, that's all. A very bad chicken. He is the same miserable wretched mean bad son-of-a-bitch that my daddy has called him every day of the rooster's life. I remember that the rooster is smarter than me, and faster and stronger and crazier. I remember that I am in the chicken yard with him and that he doesn't like me and that my daddy ain't home from work to protect me and my ass is in trouble, Jack.

I understand, at last, what the rooster is going to do. He is going to catch the bait in the air, like a dog catching a Frisbee. I can't believe what I am watching. The rooster has positioned itself, flat-footed, with its mouth open, its head cocked to one side. Until this moment I have not believed I would catch the rooster. I have meant to catch it, but the habit of fishing for it is all I have thought about for a long time. And now, in the presence of an emotion something like awe, I understand that the rooster is about to catch me.

It happens. The rooster, at the last moment, has to lurch a step forward, it has to duck its head, but it does so with perfect accuracy. The bird might as well have been a large red-feathered frog plucking a fly from the air. He catches the baited hook in his mouth.

I do not move to set the hook. There is no point. The rooster has been fishing for me for three years, and now it has caught me. I have become old enough to believe that doom will always surprise you, that doom is domestic and purrs like a cat.

The bird stands quiet with the bait in its mouth. The line droops to the ground from his chicken lips. I stand attached to him by the line. It is no help to remember that the rooster is a beast and without humor.

Then it does move. At first I thought the creature was growing taller. Nothing could have surprised me. I might have been growing smaller. Neither was true. I was watching what I had watched many times. I was watching the rooster take flight.

It left the ground. The hook was still in its mouth, attached to nothing. The rooster was holding the hook in its mouth like a peanut.

More than ever the bird seemed on fire. If flew out and out, away from me. The nylon line trailed it in flight. The sun shone on the rooster and on the line and told me that I was in big trouble and had not yet figured out how.

It flew over the chicken-yard fence, over the goat, over the midgets. It gained altitude. I watched the line be stripped in coils from my open-faced reel. The bird flew and flew, high as the housetops, and then the treetops, out toward the railroad tracks. I was a child flying a living kite.

It took me a minute to see what the rooster was up to. I had never seen him do this before. Just when he was almost out of sight, out over the railroad tracks and ready, I thought, to light in the hardwood trees, the bird seemed to hang suspended. It seemed to have hung itself in midair and to have begun to swell out like a balloon. I was holding the fishing rod limp in my hand and studying the rooster's strange inflation. The rooster, above the treetops, ballooned larger and larger. It grew large enough that I could distinguish its particular features again, the stretched neck and popped-out eyes, the sturdy wings and red belly feathers. Nothing about the appearance of the rooster made sense.

And then everything did. I was not looking at the bird's tail-feathers, as I should have been. I was looking him in the face. He was not growing larger, he was coming closer. I looked at my reel and saw that the line was still. The rooster had turned around in flight and was coming back after me.

I looked at him. The rooster had cleared the goat and the midgets. It was big as a goose, big as a collie. Its feet were blue and as big as yard rakes. I dropped the fishing rod into the dirt. I turned to the gate and tried to open the latch. I could hear the rooster's bones creaking and clacking. I could hear the feathers thudding against the air. My hands were clubs, the gate would not come unlatched. I pounded at the gate.

I heard the rooster set its wings like a hawk about to land on a fence post. The rooster landed on my head. It didn't fall off. I thought it might, but it did not. It clung to my scalp by its fierce toenails. I clubbed at the gate with my useless hands. The bird stood on my head, and its wings kept up their motion and clatter. I could not appreciate the mauling I was receiving by the wings for the fire the feet had lit in my brain. I tried to climb the gate, but my feet had turned to stumps.

The chicken yard was in hysterics, the Plymouth Rocks and Leghorns and blue Andalusians. I clung to the gate with the rooster on my head. I imagined flames the shape of an angry chicken rising from my head.

I screamed, and still the rooster held on. It drubbed me with its wings. My eyes were blackened and swollen, my nose ran with blood. I didn't care, so long as someone put out the fire in my scalp.

I got the idea that it could be put out with water. I gave up at the gate and ran stumbling across the chicken yard. Layers and pullets and bantams, all the curious and hysterical, fanned away from me in droves. The rooster hung on.

I reached the hydrant hopeless. There was no hope of putting my head under the spigot while wearing the chicken. There was a garden hose in the old garage, but it was of no use. If I could not open the simple latch of the gate, there was no chance I could retrieve the garden hose from its wall hook and screw it to the spigot.

My mama was standing on the back porch watching. I longed for the days when I was young enough to be switched with crape myrtle. I saw her start to move toward me. She was moving toward me but I knew she would never reach me in time. Blood and chickenshit ran down the sides of my face and into my ears. The wings kept up the pounding, and the rooster's bones and ligaments kept up the creaking and clacking and clicking.

I had not noticed my daddy drive up, but now I saw his car in the driveway. He left the car and was headed toward me. He also moved in slow motion.

I left the spigot. My motion and my parents' motion had become the same. They stood at the gate and pounded at it. Their hands were clubs too and the gate would not open for them.

I motioned for them to stay where they were. They saw that I knew what I was doing. Something had changed in me. I was not running now. The rooster was still riding my head. I walked, purposeful, like a heavy bear through the chicken yard.

And yet my steps were not heavy. My life was not ruined. I could wear this chicken on my head forever. I could bear this pain forever. In a year no one would notice the chicken but myself. Then even I would not notice. My mama had believed that spending your life in the place of your birth, absorbing its small particulars into your blood, was ruination. I looked at my parents beside the gate. My daddy held my mama in his arms as they looked at me. My daddy had gotten the gate open now but again I held up my hand and stopped him. I knew now what I could give them. It was a picture of myself that I would live the rest of my life to prove true: they watched their son wear this living crowing rooster like a crown.

They were proud of me. I knew they were. They were frightened also but pride was mainly what I saw in their faces as I kept them from helping me. They believed that my life would not be ruined. They believed that a man who has worn a chicken on his head—worn it proudly, as I was beginning to do—would never be a fool to geography or marriage or alcohol.

I stood tall in the chicken yard. My parents looked at me from the gate and I felt their love and pride touch me. They believed that a man and his wife with such a son could not be ruined either, not yet, not forever.

The rooster had stopped flapping its wings. It was heavy on me, but I straightened my back and did not slump. Now it balanced itself with more ease, it carried more of its own weight and was easier to hold. It stood on my head like an eagle on a mountain crag. I strode toward my parents and they toward me. The three of us, and the rooster, moved through the chicken yard in glory.

FLANNERY O'CONNOR

Flannery O'Connor (1925–1964) was born in Savannah, Georgia. She attended the Writer's Workshop at the University of Iowa. For the last fourteen years of her life she lived on her parents' farm near Milledgeville, Georgia. She wrote two novels, *Wise Blood* and *The Violent Bear It Away.* A collection of essays, *Mystery & Manners,* was published in 1969. *The Habit of Being,* a generous selection of her wonderful letters, appeared in 1979. One collection of her stories, *A Good Man Is Hard to Find and Other Stories* (1955), was published during her lifetime. A second collection, *Everything That Rises Must Converge,* was published in 1965. *The Complete Stories* (1971), which includes twelve previously uncollected stories, won the 1972 National Book Award.

Parker's Back

PARKER'S wife was sitting on the front porch floor, snapping beans. Parker was sitting on the step, some distance away, watching her sullenly. She was plain, plain. The skin on her face was thin and drawn as tight as the skin on an onion and her eyes were gray and sharp like the points of two icepicks. Parker understood why he had married her—he couldn't have got her any other way—but he couldn't understand why he stayed with her now. She was pregnant and pregnant women were not his favorite kind. Nevertheless, he stayed as if she had him conjured. He was puzzled and ashamed of himself.

The house they rented sat alone save for a single tall pecan tree on a high embankment overlooking a highway. At intervals a car would shoot past below and his wife's eyes would swerve suspiciously after the sound of it and then come back to rest on the newspaper full of beans in her lap. One of the things she did not approve of was automobiles. In addition to her other bad qualities, she was forever sniffing up sin. She did not smoke or dip, drink whiskey, use bad language or paint her face, and God knew some paint would have improved it, Parker thought. Her being against color, it was the more remarkable she had married him. Sometimes he supposed that she had married him because she meant to save him. At other times he had a suspicion that she actually liked everything she said she didn't. He could account for her one way or another; it was himself he could not understand.

She turned her head in his direction and said, "It's no reason you can't work for a man. It don't have to be a woman."

"Aw shut your mouth for a change," Parker muttered.

If he had been certain she was jealous of the woman he worked for he would have been pleased but more likely she was concerned with the sin that would result if he and the woman took a liking to each other. He had told her that the woman was a hefty young blonde; in fact she was nearly seventy years old and too dried up to have an interest in anything except getting as much work out of him as she could. Not that an old woman didn't sometimes get an interest in a young man, particularly if he was as attractive as Parker felt he was, but this old woman looked at him the same way she looked at her old tractor—as if she had to put up with it because it was all she had. The tractor had broken down the second day Parker was on it and she had set him at once to cutting bushes, saying out of the side of her mouth to the nigger, "Everything he touches, he breaks." She also asked him to wear his shirt when he worked; Parker had removed it even though the day was not sultry; he put it back on reluctantly.

This ugly woman Parker married was his first wife. He had had other women but he had planned never to get himself tied up legally. He had first seen her one morning when his truck broke down on the highway. He had managed to pull if off the road into a neatly swept yard on which sat a peeling two-room house. He got out and opened the hood of the truck and began to study the motor. Parker had an extra sense that told him when there was a woman nearby watching him. After he had leaned over the motor a few minutes, his neck began to prickle. He cast his eye over the empty yard and porch of the house. A woman he could not see was either nearby beyond a clump of honeysuckle or in the house, watching him out the window.

Suddenly Parker began to jump up and down and fling his hand about as if he had mashed it in the machinery. He doubled over and held his hand close to his chest. "God dammit!" he hollered. "Jesus Christ in hell! Jesus God Almighty damn! God dammit to hell!" he went on, flinging out the same few oaths over and over as loud as he could.

Without warning a terrible bristly claw slammed the side of his face and he fell backwards on the hood of the truck. "You don't talk no filth here!" a voice close to him shrilled.

Parker's vision was so blurred that for an instant he thought he had been attacked by some creature from above, a giant hawk-eyed angel wielding a hoary weapon. As his sight cleared, he saw before him a tall raw-boned girl with a broom.

"I hurt my hand," he said. "I HURT my hand." He was so incensed that he forgot that he hadn't hurt his hand. "My hand may be broke," he growled although his voice was still unsteady.

"Lemme see it," the girl demanded.

Parker stuck out his hand and she came closer and looked at it. There was no mark on the palm and she took the hand and turned it over. Her own hand was dry and hot and rough and Parker felt himself jolted back to life by her touch. He looked more closely at her. I don't want nothing to do with this one, he thought.

The girl's sharp eyes peered at the back of the stubby reddish hand she held. There emblazoned in red and blue was a tattooed eagle perched on a cannon. Parker's sleeve was rolled to the elbow. Above the eagle a serpent was coiled about a shield and in the spaces between the eagle and the serpent there were hearts, some with arrows through them. Above the serpent there was a spread hand of cards. Every space on the skin of Parker's arm, from wrist to elbow, was covered in some loud design. The girl gazed at this with an almost stupefied smile of shock, as if she had accidentally grasped a poisonous snake; she dropped the hand.

"I got most of my other ones in foreign parts," Parker said. "These here I mostly got in the United States. I got my first one when I was only fifteen year old."

"Don't tell me," the girl said. "I don't like it. I ain't got any use for it."

"You ought to see the ones you can't see," Parker said and winked.

Two circles of red appeared like apples on the girl's cheeks and softened her appearance. Parker was intrigued. He did not for a minute think that she didn't like the tattoos. He had never yet met a woman who was not attracted to them.

Parker was fourteen when he saw a man in a fair, tattooed from head to foot. Except for his loins which were girded with a panther hide, the man's skin was patterned in what seemed from Parker's distance—he was near the back of the tent, standing on a bench—a single intricate design of brilliant color. The man, who was small and sturdy, moved about on the platform, flexing his muscles so that the arabesque of men and beasts and flowers on his skin appeared to have a subtle motion of its own. Parker was filled with emotion, lifted up as some people are when the flag passes. He was a boy whose mouth habitually hung open. He was heavy and earnest, as ordinary as a loaf of bread. When the show was over, he had remained standing on the bench, staring where the tattooed man had been, until the tent was almost empty.

Parker had never before felt the least motion of wonder in himself. Until he saw the man at the fair, it did not enter his head that there was anything out of the ordinary about the fact that he existed. Even then it did not enter his head, but a peculiar unease settled in him. It was as if a blind boy had been turned so gently in a different direction that he did not know his destination had been changed.

He had his first tattoo some time after—the eagle perched on the cannon. It was done by a local artist. It hurt very little, just enough to make it appear to Parker to be worth doing. This was peculiar too for before he had thought that only what did not hurt was worth doing. The next year he quit school because he was sixteen and could. He went to the trade school for a while, then he quit the trade school and worked for six months in a garage. The only reason he worked at all was to pay for more tattoos. His mother worked in a laundry and could support him, but she would not pay for any tattoo except her name on a heart, which he had put on, grumbling. However, her name was Betty Jean and nobody had to know it was his mother. He found out that the tattoos were attractive to the kind of girls he liked but who had never liked him before. He began to drink beer and get in fights. His mother wept over what was becoming of him. One night she dragged him off to a revival with her, not telling him where they were going. When he saw the big lighted church, he jerked out of her grasp and ran. The next day he lied about his age and joined the navy.

Parker was large for the tight sailor's pants but the silly white cap, sitting low on his forehead, made his face by contrast look thoughtful and almost intense. After a month or two in the navy, his mouth ceased to hang open. His features hardened into the features of a man. He stayed in the navy five years and seemed a natural part of the gray mechanical ship, except for his eyes, which were the same pale slate-color as the ocean and reflected the immense spaces around him as if they were a microcosm of the mysterious sea. In port Parker wandered about comparing the run-down places he was in to Birmingham, Alabama. Everywhere he went he picked up more tattoos.

He had stopped having lifeless ones like anchors and crossed rifles. He had a tiger and a panther on each shoulder, a cobra coiled about a torch on his chest, hawks on his thighs, Elizabeth II and Philip over where his stomach and liver were respectively. He did not care much what the subject was so long as it was colorful; on his abdomen he had a few obscenities but only because that seemed the proper place for them. Parker would be satisfied with each tattoo about a month, then something about it that had attracted him would wear off. Whenever a decent-sized mirror was available, he would get in front of it and study his overall look. The effect was not of one intricate arabesque of colors but of something haphazard and botched. A huge dissatisfaction would come over him and he would go off and find another tattooist and have another space filled up. The front of Parker was almost completely covered but there were no tattoos on his back. He had no desire for one anywhere he could not readily see it himself. As the space on the front of him for tattoos decreased, his dissatisfaction grew and became general.

After one of his furloughs, he didn't go back to the navy but remained away without official leave, drunk, in a rooming house in a city he did not know. His dissatisfaction, from being chronic and latent, had suddenly become acute and raged in him. It was as if the panther and the lion and the serpents and the eagles and the hawks had penetrated his skin and lived inside him in a raging warfare. The navy caught up with him, put him in the brig for nine months and then gave him a dishonorable discharge.

After that Parker decided that country air was the only kind fit to breathe. He rented the shack on the embankment and bought the old truck and took various jobs which he kept as long as it suited him. At the time he met his future wife, he was buying apples by the bushel and selling them for the same price by the pound to isolated homesteaders on back country roads.

"All that there," the woman said, pointing to his arm, "is no better than what a fool Indian would do. It's a heap of vanity." She seemed to have found the word she wanted. "Vanity of vanities," she said.

Well what the hell do I care what she thinks of it? Parker asked himself, but he was plainly bewildered. "I reckon you like one of these better than another anyway," he said, dallying until he thought of something that would impress her. He thrust the arm back at her. "Which you like best?"

"None of them," she said, "but the chicken is not as bad as the rest."

"What chicken?" Parker almost yelled.

She pointed to the eagle.

"That's an eagle," Parker said. "What fool would waste their time having a chicken put on themself?"

"What fool would have any of it?" the girl said and turned away. She went slowly back to the house and left him there to get going. Parker remained for almost five minutes, looking agape at the dark door she had entered.

The next day he returned with a bushel of apples. He was not one to be outdone by anything that looked like her. He liked women with meat on them, so you didn't feel their muscles, much less their old bones. When he arrived, she was sitting on the top step and the yard was full of children, all as thin and poor as herself; Parker remembered it was Saturday. He hated to be making up to a woman when there were children around, but it was fortunate he had brought the bushel of apples off the truck. As the children approached him to see what he carried, he gave each child an apple and told it to get lost; in that way he cleared out the whole crowd.

The girl did nothing to acknowledge his presence. He might have been a stray pig or goat that had wandered into the yard and she too tired to take up the broom and send it off. He set the bushel of apples down next to her on the step. He sat down on a lower step.

"Hep yourself," he said, nodding at the basket; then he lapsed into silence.

She took an apple quickly as if the basket might disappear if she didn't make haste. Hungry people made Parker nervous. He had always had plenty to eat himself. He grew very uncomfortable. He reasoned he had nothing to say so why should he say it? He could not think now why he had come or why he didn't go before he wasted another bushel of apples on the crowd of children. He supposed they were her brothers and sisters.

She chewed the apple slowly but with a kind of relish of concentration, bent slightly but looking out ahead. The view from the porch stretched off across a long incline studded with iron weed and across the highway to a vast vista of hills and one small mountain. Long views depressed Parker. You look out into space like that and you begin to feel as if someone were after you, the navy or the government or religion.

"Who them children belong to, you?" he said at length.

"I ain't married yet," she said. "They belong to momma." She said it as if it were only a matter of time before she would be married.

Who in God's name would marry her? Parker thought.

A large barefooted woman with a wide gap-toothed face appeared in the door behind Parker. She had apparently been there for several minutes.

"Good evening," Parker said.

The woman crossed the porch and picked up what was left of the bushel of apples. "We thank you," she said and returned with it into the house.

"That your old woman?" Parker muttered.

The girl nodded. Parker knew a lot of sharp things he could have said like "You got my sympathy," but he was gloomily silent. He just sat there, looking at the view. He thought he must be coming down with something.

"If I pick up some peaches tomorrow I'll bring you some," he said.

"I'll be much obliged to you," the girl said.

Parker had no intention of taking any basket of peaches back there but the next day he found himself doing it. He and the girl had almost nothing to say to each other. One thing he did say was, "I ain't got any tattoo on my back."

"What you got on it?" the girl said.

"My shirt," Parker said. "Haw."

"Haw, haw," the girl said politely.

Parker thought he was losing his mind. He could not believe for a minute that he was attracted to a woman like this. She showed not the least interest in anything but what he brought until he appeared the third time with two cantaloups. "What's your name?" she asked.

"O. E. Parker," he said.

"What does the O. E. stand for?"

"You can just call me O. E.," Parker said. "Or Parker. Don't nobody call me by my name."

"What's it stand for?" she persisted.

"Never mind," Parker said. "What's yours?"

"I'll tell you when you tell me what them letters are the short of," she said. There was just a hint of flirtatiousness in her tone and it went rapidly to Parker's head. He had never revealed the name to any man or woman, only to the files of the navy and the government, and it was on his baptismal record which he got at the age of a month; his mother was a Methodist. When the name leaked out of the navy files, Parker narrowly missed killing the man who used it.

"You'll go blab it around," he said.

"I'll swear I'll never tell nobody," she said. "On God's holy word I swear it."

Parker sat for a few minutes in silence. Then he reached for the girl's neck, drew her ear close to his mouth and revealed the name in low voice.

"Obadiah," she whispered. Her face slowly brightened as if the name came as a sign to her. "Obadiah," she said.

The name still stank in Parker's estimation.

"Obadiah Elihue," she said in a reverent voice.

"If you call me that aloud, I'll bust your head open," Parker said, "What's yours?"

"Sarah Ruth Cates," she said.

"Glad to meet you, Sarah Ruth," Parker said.

Sarah Ruth's father was a Straight Gospel preacher but he was away, spreading it in Florida. Her mother did not seem to mind his attention to the girl so long as he brought a basket of something with him when he came. As for Sarah Ruth herself, it was plain to Parker after he had visited three times that she was crazy about him. She liked him even though she insisted that pictures on the skin were vanity of vanities and even after hearing him curse, and even after she had asked him if he was saved and he had replied that he didn't see it was anything in particular to save him from. After that, inspired, Parker had said, "I'd be saved enough if you was to kiss me."

She scowled. "That ain't being saved," she said.

Not long after that she agreed to take a ride in his truck. Parker parked it on a deserted road and suggested to her that they lie down together in the back of it.

"Not until after we're married," she said—just like that.

"Oh that ain't necessary," Parker said and as he reached for her, she thrust him away with such force that the door of the truck came off and he found himself flat on his back on the ground. He made up his mind then and there to have nothing further to do with her.

They were married in the County Ordinary's office because Sarah Ruth thought churches were idolatrous. Parker had no opinion about that one way or the other. The Ordinary's office was lined with cardboard file boxes and record books with dusty yellow slips of paper hanging on out of them. The Ordinary was an old woman with red hair who had held office for forty years and looked as dusty as her books. She married them from behind the iron-grill of a stand-up desk and when she finished, she said with a flourish, "Three dollars and fifty cents and till death do you part!" and yanked some forms out of a machine.

Marriage did not change Sarah Ruth a jot and it made Parker gloomier than ever. Every morning he decided he had had enough and would not return that night; every night he returned. Whenever Parker couldn't stand the way he felt, he would have another tattoo, but the only surface left on him now was his back. To see a tattoo on his own back he would have to get two mirrors and stand between them in just the correct position and this seemed to Parker a good way to make an idiot of himself. Sarah Ruth who, if she had had better sense, could have enjoyed a tattoo on his back, would not even look at the ones he had elsewhere. When he attempted to point out especial details of them, she would shut her eyes tight and turn her back as well. Except in total darkness, she preferred Parker dressed and with his sleeves rolled down.

"At the judgment seat of God, Jesus is going to say to you, 'What you been doing all your life besides have pictures drawn all over you?'" she said.

"You don't fool me none," Parker said, "you're just afraid that hefty girl I work for'll like me so much she'll say, 'Come on, Mr. Parker, let's you and me . . .'"

"You're tempting sin," she said, "and at the judgment seat of God you'll have to answer for that too. You ought to go back to selling the fruits of the earth."

Parker did nothing much when he was at home but listen to what the judgment seat of God would be like for him if he didn't change his ways. When he could, he broke in with tales of the hefty girl he worked for. "'Mr. Parker,'" he said, "she said, 'I hired you for your brains.'" (She had added, "So why don't you use them?")

"And you should have seen her face the first time she saw me without my shirt," he said. "'Mr. Parker,' she said, 'you're a walking panner-rammer!'" This had, in fact, been her remark but it had been delivered out of one side of her mouth.

Dissatisfaction began to grow so great in Parker that there was no containing it outside of a tattoo. It had to be his back. There was no help for it. A dim half-formed inspiration began to work in his mind. He visualized having a tattoo put there that Sarah Ruth would not be able to resist—a religious subject. He thought of an open book with HOLY BIBLE tattooed under it and an actual verse printed on the page. This seemed just the thing for a while; then he began to hear her say, "Ain't I already got a real Bible? What you think I want to read the same verse over and over for when I can read it all?" He needed something better even than the Bible! He thought about it so much that he began to lose sleep. He was already losing flesh—Sarah Ruth just threw food in the pot and let it boil. Not knowing for certain why he continued to stay with a woman who was both ugly and pregnant and no cook made him generally nervous and irritable, and he developed a little tic in the side of his face.

Once or twice he found himself turning around abruptly as if someone were trailing him. He had had a granddaddy who had ended in the state mental hospital, although not until he was seventy-five, but as urgent as it might be for him to get a tattoo, it was just as urgent that he get exactly the right one to bring Sarah Ruth to heel. As he continued to worry over it, his eyes took on a hollow preoccupied expression. The old woman he worked for told him that if he couldn't keep his mind on what he was doing, she knew where she could find a fourteen-year-old colored boy who could. Parker was too preoccupied even to be offended. At any time previous, he would have left her then and there, saying drily, "Well, you go ahead on and get him then."

Two or three mornings later he was baling hay with the old woman's sorry baler and her broken down tractor in a large field, cleared save for one enormous old tree standing in the middle of it. The old woman was the kind who would not cut down a large old tree because it was a large old tree. She had pointed it out to Parker as if he didn't have eyes and told him to be careful not to hit it as the machine picked up hay near it. Parker began at the outside of the field and made circles inward toward it. He had to get off the tractor every now and then and untangle the baling cord or kick a rock out of the way. The old woman had told him to carry the rocks to the edge of the field, which he did when she was there watching. When he thought he could make it, he ran over them. As he circled the field his mind was on a suitable design for his back. The sun, the size of a golf ball, began to switch regularly from in front to behind him, but he appeared to see it both places as if he had eyes in the back of his head. All at once he saw the tree reaching out to grasp him. A ferocious thud propelled him into the air, and he heard himself yelling in an unbelievably loud voice, "GOD ABOVE!"

He landed on his back while the tractor crashed upside down into the tree and burst into flame. The first thing Parker saw were his shoes, quickly being eaten by the fire; one was caught under the tractor, the other was some distance away, burning by itself. He was not in them. He could feel the hot breath of the burning tree on his face. He scrambled backwards, still sitting, his eyes cavernous, and if he had known how to cross himself he would have done it.

His truck was on a dirt road at the edge of the field. He moved toward it, still sitting, still backwards, but faster and faster; halfway to it he got up and began a kind of forward-bent run from which he collapsed on his knees twice. His legs felt like two old rusted rain gutters. He reached the truck finally and took off in it, zigzagging up the road. He drove past his house on the embankment and straight for the city, fifty miles distant.

Parker did not allow himself to think on the way to the city. He only knew that there had been a great change in his life, a leap forward into a worse unknown, and that there was nothing he could do about it. It was for all intents accomplished.

The artist had two large cluttered rooms over a chiropodist's office on a back street. Parker, still barefooted, burst silently in on him at a little after three in the afternoon. The artist, who was about Parker's own age—twenty-eight—but thin and bald, was behind a small drawing table, tracing a design in green ink. He looked up with an annoyed glance and did not seem to recognize Parker in the hollow-eyed creature before him.

"Let me see the book you got with all the pictures of God in it," Parker said breathlessly. "The religious one."

The artist continued to look at him with his intellectual, superior stare. "I don't put tattoos on drunks," he said.

"You know me!" Parker cried indignantly. "I'm O. E. Parker! You done work for me before and I always paid!"

The artist looked at him another moment as if he were not altogether sure. "You've fallen off some," he said. "You must have been in jail."

"Married," Parker said.

"Oh," said the artist. With the aid of mirrors the artist had tattooed on the top of his head a miniature owl, perfect in every detail. It was about the size of a half-dollar and served him as a show piece. There were cheaper artists in town but Parker had never wanted anything but the best. The artist went over to a cabinet at the back of the room and began to look over some art books. "Who are you interested in?" he said. "Saints, angels, Christs or what?"

"God," Parker said.

"Father, Son, or Spirit?"

"Just God," Parker said impatiently. "Christ. I don't care. Just so it's God."

The artist returned with a book. He moved some papers off another table and put the book down on it and told Parker to sit down and see what he liked. "The up-to-date ones are in the back," he said.

Parker sat down with the book and wet his thumb. He began to go through it, beginning at the back where the up-to-date pictures were. Some of them he recognized—The Good Shepherd, Forbid Them Not, The Smiling Jesus, Jesus the Physician's Friend, but he kept turning rapidly backwards and the pictures became less and less reassuring. One showed a gaunt green dead face streaked with blood. One was yellow with sagging purple eyes. Parker's heart began to beat faster and faster until it appeared to be roaring inside him like a great generator. He flipped the pages quickly, feeling that when he reached the one ordained, a sign would come. He continued to flip through until he had almost reached the front of the book. On one of the pages a pair of eyes glanced at him swiftly. Parker sped on, then stopped. His heart too appeared to cut off; there was absolute silence. It said as plainly as if silence were a language itself, GO BACK.

Parker returned to the picture—the haloed head of a flat stern Byzantine Christ with all-demanding eyes. He sat there trembling; his heart began slowly to beat again as if it were being brought to life by a subtle power.

"You found what you want?" the artist asked.

Parker's throat was too dry to speak. He got up and thrust the book at the artist, opened at the picture.

"That'll cost you plenty," the artist said. "You don't want all those little blocks though, just the outline and some better features."

"Just like it is," Parker said, "just like it is or nothing."

"It's your funeral," the artist said, "but I don't do that kind of work for nothing."

"How much?" Parker asked.

"It'll take maybe two days work."

"How much?" Parker said.

"On time or cash?" the artist asked. Parker's other jobs had been on time, but he had paid.

"Ten down and ten for every day it takes," the artist said.

Parker drew ten dollar bills out of his wallet; he had three left in.

"You come back in the morning," the artist said, putting the money in his own pocket. "First I'll have to trace that out of the book."

"No, no!" Parker said, "Trace it now or gimme my money back," and his eyes blared as if he were ready for a fight.

The artist agreed. Any one stupid enough to want a Christ on his back, he reasoned, would be just as likely as not to change his mind the next minute, but once the work was begun he could hardly do so.

While he worked on the tracing, he told Parker to go wash his back at the sink with the special soap he used there. Parker did it and returned to pace back and forth across the room, nervously flexing his shoulders. He wanted to go look at the picture again but at the same time he did not want to. The artist got up finally and had Parker lie down on the table. He swabbed his back with ethyl chloride and then began to outline the head on it with his iodine pencil. Another hour passed before he took up his electric instrument. Parker felt no particular pain. In Japan he had had a tattoo of the Buddha done on his upper arm with ivory needles; in Burma, a little brown root of a man had made a peacock on each of his knees using thin pointed sticks, two feet long; amateurs had worked on him with pins and soot. Parker was usually so relaxed and easy under the hand of the artist that he often went to sleep, but this time he remained awake, every muscle taut.

At midnight the artist said he was ready to quit. He propped one mirror, four feet square, on a table by the wall and took a smaller mirror off the lavatory wall and put it in Parker's hands. Parker stood with his back to the one on the table and moved the other until he saw a flashing burst of color reflected from his back. It was almost completely covered with little red and blue and ivory and saffron squares; from them he made out the lineaments of the face—a mouth, the beginning of heavy brows, a straight nose, but the face was empty; the eyes had not yet been put in. The impression for the moment was almost as if the artist had tricked him and done the Physician's Friend.

"It don't have eyes," Parker cried out.

"That'll come," the artist said, "in due time. We have another day to go on it yet."

Parker spent the night on a cot at the Haven of Light Christian Mission. He found these the best places to stay in the city because they were free and included a meal of sorts. He got the last available cot and because he was still barefooted, he accepted a pair of second-hand shoes which, in his confusion, he put on to go to bed; he was still shocked from all that had happened to him. All night he lay awake in the long dormitory of cots with lumpy figures on them. The only light was from a phosphorescent cross glowing at the end of the room. The tree reached out to grasp him again, then burst into flame; the shoe burned quietly by itself; the eyes in the book said to him distinctly GO BACK and at the same time did not utter a sound. He wished that he were not in this city, not in this Haven of Light Mission, not in a bed by himself. He longed miserably for Sarah Ruth. Her sharp tongue and icepick eyes were the only comfort he could bring to mind. He decided he was losing it. Her eyes appeared soft and dilatory compared with the eyes in the book, for even though he could not summon up the exact look of those eyes, he could still feel their penetration. He felt as though, under their gaze, he was as transparent as the wing of a fly.

The tattooist had told him not to come until ten in the morning, but when he arrived at that hour, Parker was sitting in the dark hallway on the floor, waiting for him. He had decided upon getting up that, once the tattoo was on him, he would not look at it, that all his sensations of the day and night before were those of a crazy man and that he would return to doing things according to his own sound judgment.

The artist began where he left off. "One thing I want to know," he said presently as he worked over Parker's back, "why do you want this on you? Have you gone and got religion? Are you saved?" he asked in a mocking voice.

Parker's throat felt salty and dry. "Naw," he said, "I ain't got no use for none of that. A man can't save his self from whatever it is he don't deserve none of my sympathy." These words seemed to leave his mouth like wraiths and to evaporate at once as if he had never uttered them.

"Then why . . ."

"I married this woman that's saved," Parker said. "I never should have done it. I ought to leave her. She's done gone and got pregnant."

"That's too bad," the artist said. "Then it's her making you have this tattoo."

"Naw," Parker said, "she don't know nothing about it. It's a surprise for her."

"You think she'll like it and lay off you a while?"

"She can't hep herself," Parker said. "She can't say she don't like the looks of God." He decided he had told the artist enough of his business. Artists were all right in their place but he didn't like them poking their noses into the affairs of regular people. "I didn't get no sleep last night," he said. "I think I'll get some now."

That closed the mouth of the artist but it did not bring him any sleep. He lay there, imagining how Sarah Ruth would be struck speechless by the face on his back and every now and then this would be interrupted by a vision of the tree of fire and his empty shoe burning beneath it.

The artist worked steadily until nearly four o'clock, not stopping to have lunch, hardly pausing with the electric instrument except to wipe the dripping dye off Parker's back as he went along. Finally he finished. "You can get up and look at it now," he said.

Parker sat up but he remained on the edge of the table.

The artist was pleased with his work and wanted Parker to look at it at once. Instead Parker continued to sit on the edge of the table, bent forward slightly but with a vacant look. "What ails you?" the artist said. "Go look at it."

"Ain't nothing ail me," Parker said in a sudden belligerent voice. "That tattoo ain't going nowhere. It'll be there when I get there." He reached for his shirt and began gingerly to put it on.

The artist took him roughly by the arm and propelled him between the two mirrors. "Now *look*," he said, angry at having his work ignored.

Parker looked, turned white and moved away. The eyes in the reflected face continued to look at him—still, straight, all-demanding, enclosed in silence.

"It was your idea, remember," the artist said. "I would have advised something else."

Parker said nothing. He put on his shirt and went out the door while the artist shouted, "I'll expect all of my money!"

Parker headed toward a package shop on the corner. He bought a pint of whiskey and took it into a nearby alley and drank it all in five minutes. Then he moved on to a pool hall nearby which he frequented when he came to the city. It was a well-lighted barn-like place with a bar up one side and gambling machines on the other and pool tables in the back. As soon as Parker entered, a large man in a red and black checkered shirt hailed him by slapping him on the back and yelling, "Yeyyyyyy boy! O. E. Parker!"

Parker was not yet ready to be struck on the back. "Lay off," he said, "I got a fresh tattoo there."

"What you got this time?" the man asked and then yelled to a few at the machines. "O. E.'s got him another tattoo."

"Nothing special this time," Parker said and slunk over to a machine that was not being used.

"Come on," the big man said, "let's have a look at O. E.'s tattoo," and while Parker squirmed in their hands, they pulled up his shirt. Parker felt all the hands drop away instantly and his shirt fell again like a veil over the face. There was a silence in the pool room which seemed to Parker to grow from the circle around him until it extended to the foundations under the building and upward through the beams in the roof.

Finally some one said, "Christ!" Then they all broke into noise at once. Parker turned around, an uncertain grin on his face.

"Leave it to O. E.!" the man in the checkered shirt said. "That boy's a real card!"

"Maybe he's gone and got religion," someone yelled.

"Not on your life," Parker said.

"O. E.'s got religion and is witnessing for Jesus, ain't you, O. E.?" a little man with a piece of cigar in his mouth said wryly. "An o-riginal way to do it if I ever saw one."

"Leave it to Parker to think of a new one!" the fat man said.

"Yyeeeeeeyyyyyyy boy!" someone yelled and they all began to whistle and curse in compliment until Parker said, "Aaa shut up."

"What'd you do it for?" somebody asked.

"For laughs," Parker said. "What's it to you?"

"Why ain't you laughing then?" somebody yelled. Parker lunged into the midst of them like a whirlwind on a summer's day then began a fight that raged amid overturned tables and swinging fists until two of them grabbed him and ran to the door with him and threw him out. Then a calm descended on the pool hall as nerve shattering as if the long barnlike room were the ship from which Jonah had been cast into the sea.

Parker sat for a long time on the ground in the alley behind the pool hall, examining his soul. He saw it as a spider web of facts and lies that was not at all important to him but which appeared to be necessary in spite of his opinion. The eyes that were now forever on his back were eyes to be obeyed. He was as certain of it as he had ever been of anything. Throughout his life, grumbling and sometimes cursing, often afraid, once in rapture, Parker had obeyed whatever instinct of this kind had come to him—in rapture when his spirit had lifted at the sight of the tattooed man at the fair, afraid when he had joined the navy, grumbling when he had married Sarah Ruth.

The thought of her brought him slowly to his feet. She would know what he had to do. She would clear up the rest of it, and she would at least be pleased. It seemed to him that, all along, that was what he wanted, to please her. His truck was still parked in front of the building where the artist had his place, but it was not far away. He got in it and drove out of the city and into the country night. His head was almost clear of liquor and he observed that his dissatisfaction was gone, but he felt not quite himself. It was as if he were himself but a stranger to himself, driving into a new country though everything he saw was familiar to him, even at night.

He arrived finally at the house on the embankment, pulled the truck under the pecan tree and got out. He made as much noise as possible to assert that he was still in charge here, that his leaving her for a night without word meant nothing except it was the way he did things. He slammed the car door, stamped up the two steps and across the porch and rattled the door knob. It did not respond to his touch. "Sarah Ruth!" he yelled, "let me in."

There was no lock on the door and she had evidently placed the back of a chair against the knob. He began to beat on the door and rattle the knob at the same time.

He heard the bed springs screak and bent down and put his head to the keyhole, but it was stopped up with paper. "Let me in!" he hollered, bamming on the door again. "What you got me locked out for?"

A sharp voice close to the door said, "Who's there?"

"Me," Parker said, "O. E."

He waited a moment.

"Me," he said impatiently, "O. E."

Still no sound from inside.

He tried once more. "O. E.," he said, bamming the door two or three more times. "O. E. Parker. You know me."

There was a silence. Then the voice said slowly, "I don't know no O. E."

"Quit fooling," Parker pleaded. "You ain't got any business doing me this way. It's me, old O. E., I'm back. You ain't afraid of me."

"Who's there?" the same unfeeling voice said.

Parker turned his head as if he expected someone behind him to give him the answer. The sky had lightened slightly and there were two or three streaks of yellow floating above the horizon. Then as he stood there, a tree of light burst over the skyline.

Parker fell back against the door as if he had been pinned there by a lance.

"Who's there?" the voice from inside said and there was a quality about it now that seemed final. The knob rattled and the voice said peremptorily, "Who's there, I ast you?"

Parker bent down and put his mouth near the stuffed keyhole. "Obadiah," he whispered and all at once he felt the light pouring through him, turning his spider web soul into a perfect arabesque of colors, a garden of trees and birds and beasts.

"Obadiah Elihue!" he whispered.

The door opened and he stumbled in. Sarah Ruth loomed there, hands on her hips. She began at once, "That was no hefty blonde woman you was working for and you'll have to pay her every penny on her tractor you busted up. She don't keep insurance on it. She came here and her and me had us a long talk and I . . ."

Trembling, Parker set about lighting the kerosene lamp.

"What's the matter with you, wasting that kerosene this near daylight?" she demanded. "I ain't got to look at you."

A yellow glow enveloped them. Parker put the match down and began to unbutton his shirt.

"And you ain't going to have none of me this near morning," she said.

"Shut your mouth," he said quietly. "Look at this and then I don't want to hear no more out of you." He removed the shirt and turned his back to her.

"Another picture," Sarah Ruth growled. "I might have known you was off after putting some more trash on yourself."

Parker's knees went hollow under him. He wheeled around and cried, "Look at it! Don't just say that! *Look* at it!"

"I done looked," she said.

"Don't you know who it is?" he cried in anguish.

"No, who is it?" Sarah Ruth said. "It ain't anybody I know."

"It's him," Parker said.

"Him who?"

"God!" Parker cried.

"God? God don't look like that!"

"What do you know how he looks?" Parker moaned. "You ain't seen him."

"He don't *look*," Sarah Ruth said. "He's a spirit. No man shall see his face."

"Aw listen," Parker groaned, "this is just a picture of him."

"Idolatry!" Sarah Ruth screamed. "Idolatry! Enflaming yourself with idols under every green tree! I can put up with lies and vanity but I don't want no idolater in this house!" and she grabbed up the broom and began to thrash him across the shoulders with it.

Parker was too stunned to resist. He sat there and let her beat him until she had nearly knocked him senseless and large welts had formed on the face of the tattooed Christ. Then he staggered up and made for the door.

She stamped the broom two or three times on the floor and went to the window and shook it out to get the taint of him off it. Still gripping it, she looked toward the pecan tree and her eyes hardened still more. There he was—who called himself Obadiah Elihue—leaning against the tree, crying like a baby.

Revelation

THE doctor's waiting room, which was very small, was almost full when the Turpins entered and Mrs. Turpin, who was very large, made it look even smaller by her presence. She stood looming at the head of the magazine table set in the center of it, a living demonstration that the room was inadequate and ridiculous. Her little bright black eyes took in all the patients as she sized up the seating situation. There was one vacant chair and a place on the sofa occupied by a blond child in a dirty blue romper who should have been told to move over and make room for the lady. He was five or six, but Mrs. Turpin saw at once that no one was going to tell him to move over. He was slumped down in the seat, his arms idle at his sides and his eyes idle in his head; his nose ran unchecked.

Mrs. Turpin put a firm hand on Claud's shoulder and said in a voice that included anyone who wanted to listen, "Claud, you sit in that chair there," and gave him a push down into the vacant one. Claud was florid and bald and sturdy, somewhat shorter than Mrs. Turpin, but he sat down as if he were accustomed to doing what she told him to.

Mrs. Turpin remained standing. The only man in the room besides Claud was a lean stringy old fellow with a rusty hand spread out on each knee, whose eyes were closed as if he were asleep or dead or pretending to be so as not to get up and offer her his seat. Her gaze settled agreeably on a well-dressed gray-haired lady whose eyes met hers and whose expression said: if that child belonged to me, he would have some manners and move over—there's plenty of room there for you and him too.

Claud looked up with a sigh and made as if to rise.

"Sit down," Mrs. Turpin said. "You know you're not supposed to stand on that leg. He has an ulcer on his leg," she explained.

Claud lifted his foot onto the magazine table and rolled his trouser leg up to reveal a purple swelling on a plump marble-white calf.

"My!" the pleasant lady said. "How did you do that?"

"A cow kicked him," Mrs. Turpin said.

"Goodness!" said the lady.

Claud rolled his trouser leg down.

"Maybe the little boy would move over," the lady suggested, but the child did not stir.

"Somebody will be leaving in a minute," Mrs. Turpin said. She could not understand why a doctor—with as much money as they made charging five dollars a day to just stick their head in the hospital door and look at you—couldn't afford a decent-sized waiting room. This one was hardly bigger than a garage. The table was cluttered with limp-looking magazines and at one end of it there was a big green glass ash tray full of cigarette butts and cotton wads with little blood spots on them. If she had had anything to do with the running of the place, that would have been emptied every so often. There were no chairs against the wall at the head of the room. It had a rectangular-shaped panel in it that permitted a view of the office where the nurse came and went and the secretary listened to the radio. A plastic fern in a gold pot sat in the opening and trailed its fronds down almost to the floor. The radio was softly playing gospel music.

Just then the inner door opened and a nurse with the highest stack of yellow hair Mrs. Turpin had ever seen put her face in the crack and called for the next patient. The woman sitting beside Claud grasped the two arms of her chair and hoisted herself up; she pulled her dress free from her legs and lumbered through the door where the nurse had disappeared.

Mrs. Turpin eased into the vacant chair, which held her tight as a corset. "I wish I could reduce," she said, and rolled her eyes and gave a comic sigh.

"Oh, *you* aren't fat," the stylist lady said.

"Ooooo I am too," Mrs. Turpin said. "Claud he eats all he wants to and never weighs over one hundred and seventy-five pounds, but me I just look at something good to eat and I gain some weight," and her stomach and shoulders shook with laughter. "You can eat all you want to, can't you, Claud?" she asked, turning to him.

Claud only grinned.

"Well, as long as you have such a good disposition," the stylish lady said, "I don't think it makes a bit of difference what size you are. You just can't beat a good disposition."

Next to her was a fat girl of eighteen or nineteen, scowling into a thick blue book which Mrs. Turpin saw was entitled *Human Development.* The girl raised her head and directed her scowl at Mrs. Turpin as if she did not like her looks. She appeared annoyed that anyone should speak while she tried to read. The poor girl's face was blue with acne and Mrs. Turpin thought how pitiful it was to have a face like that at that age. She gave the girl a friendly smile but the girl only scowled the harder. Mrs. Turpin herself was fat but she had always had good skin, and, though she was forty-seven years old, there was not a wrinkle in her face except around her eyes from laughing too much.

Next to the ugly girl was the child, still in exactly the same position, and next to him was a thin leathery old woman in a cotton print dress. She and Claud had three sacks of chicken feed in their pump house that was in the same print. She had seen from the first that the child belonged with the old woman. She could tell by the way they sat—kind of vacant and white-trashy, as if they would sit there until Doomsday if nobody called and told them to get up. And at right angles but next to the well-dressed pleasant lady was a lank-faced woman who was certainly the child's mother. She had on a yellow sweat shirt and wine-colored slacks, both gritty-looking, and the rims of her lips were stained with snuff. Her dirty yellow hair was tied behind with a little piece of red paper ribbon. Worse than niggers any day, Mrs. Turpin thought.

The gospel hymn playing was, "When I looked up and He looked down," and Mrs. Turpin, who knew it, supplied the last line mentally, "And wona these days I know I'll we-eara crown."

Without appearing to, Mrs. Turpin always noticed people's feet. The well-dressed lady had on red and gray suede shoes to match her dress. Mrs. Turpin had on her good black patent leather pumps. The ugly girl had on Girl Scout shoes and heavy socks. The old woman had on tennis shoes and the white-trashy mother had on what appeared to be bedroom slippers, black straw with gold braid threaded through them—exactly what you would have expected her to have on.

Sometimes at night when she couldn't go to sleep, Mrs. Turpin would occupy herself with the question of who she would have chosen to be if she couldn't have been herself. If Jesus had said to her before he made her, "There's only two places available for you. You can either be a nigger or white-trash," what would she have said? "Please, Jesus, please," she would have said, "just let me wait until there's another place available," and he would have said, "No, you have to go right now and I have only those two places so make up your mind." She would have wiggled and squirmed and begged and pleaded but it would have been no use and finally she would have said, "All right, make me a nigger then—but that don't mean a trashy one." And he would have made her a neat clean respectable Negro woman, herself but black.

Next to the child's mother was a red-headed youngish woman, reading one of the magazines and working a piece of chewing gum, hell for leather, as Claud would say. Mrs. Turpin could not see the woman's feet. She was not white-trash, just common. Sometimes Mrs. Turpin occupied herself at night naming the classes of people. On the bottom of the heap were most colored people, not the kind she would have been if she had been one, but most of them; then next to them—not above, just away from—were the white trash; then above them were the homeowners, and above them the home-and-land owners, to which she and Claud belonged. Above she and Claud were people with a lot of money and much bigger houses and much more land. But here the complexity of it would begin to bear in on her, for some of the people with a lot of money were common and ought to be below she and Claud and some of the people who had good blood had lost their money and had to rent and then there were colored people who owned their homes and land as well. There was a colored dentist in town who had two red Lincolns and a swimming pool and a farm with registered whiteface cattle on it. Usually by the time she had fallen asleep all the classes of people were moiling and roiling around in her head, and she would dream they were all crammed in together in a boxcar, being ridden off to be put in a gas oven.

"That's a beautiful clock," she said and nodded to her right. It was a big wall clock, the face encased in a brass sunburst.

"Yes, it's very pretty," the stylish lady said agreeably. "And right on the dot too," she added, glancing at her watch.

The ugly girl beside her cast an eye upward at the clock, smirked, then looked directly at Mrs. Turpin and smirked again. Then she returned her eyes to her book. She was obviously the lady's daughter because, although they didn't look anything alike as to disposition, they both had the same shape of face and the same blue eyes. On the lady they sparkled pleasantly but in the girl's seared face they appeared alternately to smolder and to blaze.

What if Jesus had said, "All right, you can be white trash or a nigger or ugly"!

Mrs. Turpin felt an awful pity for the girl, though she thought it was one thing to be ugly and another to act ugly.

The woman with the snuff-stained lips turned around in her chair and looked up at the clock. Then she turned back and appeared to look a little to the side of Mrs. Turpin. There was a cast in one of her eyes. "You want to know wher you can get you one of themther clocks?" she asked in a loud voice.

"No, I already have a nice clock," Mrs. Turpin said. Once somebody like her got a leg in the conversation, she would be all over it.

"You can get you one with green stamps," the woman said. "That's most likely wher he got hisn. Save you up enough, you can get you most anythang. I got me some joo'ry."

Ought to have got you a wash rag and some soap, Mrs. Turpin thought.

"I get contour sheets with mine," the pleasant lady said.

The daughter slammed her book shut. She looked straight in front of her, directly through Mrs. Turpin and on through the yellow curtain and the plate glass window which made the wall behind her. The girl's eyes seemed lit all of a sudden with a peculiar light, an unnatural light like night road signs give. Mrs. Turpin turned her head to see if there was anything going on outside that she should see, but she could not see anything. Figures passing cast only a pale shadow through the curtain. There was no reason the girl should single her out for her ugly looks.

"Miss Finley," the nurse said, cracking the door. The gum-chewing woman got up and passed in front of her and Claud and went into the office. She had on red high-heeled shoes.

Directly across the table, the ugly girl's eyes were fixed on Mrs. Turpin as if she had some very special reason for disliking her.

"This is wonderful weather, isn't it?" the girl's mother said.

"It's good weather for cotton if you can get the niggers to pick it," Mrs. Turpin said, "but niggers don't want to pick cotton any more. You can't get the white folks to pick it and now you can't get the niggers—because they got to be right up there with the white folks."

"They gonna *try* anyways," the white-trash woman said, leaning forward.

"Do you have one of the cotton-picking machines?" the pleasant lady asked.

"No," Mrs. Turpin said, "they leave half the cotton in the field. We don't have much cotton anyway. If you want to make it farming now, you have to have a little of everything. We got a couple of acres of cotton and a few hogs and chickens and just enough whiteface that Claud can look after them himself."

"One thang I don't want," the white-trash woman said, wiping her mouth with the back of her hand. "Hogs. Nasty stinking things, a-gruntin and a-rootin all over the place."

Mrs. Turpin gave her the merest edge of her attention. "Our hogs are not dirty and they don't stink," she said. "They're cleaner than some children I've seen. Their feet never touch the ground. We have a pig parlor—that's where you raise them on concrete," she explained to the pleasant lady, "and Claud scoots them down with the hose every afternoon and washes off the floor." Cleaner by far than that child right there, she thought. Poor nasty little thing. He had not moved except to put the thumb of his dirty hand into his mouth.

The woman turned her face away from Mrs. Turpin. "I know I wouldn't scoot down no hog with no hose," she said to the wall.

You wouldn't have no hog to scoot down, Mrs. Turpin said to herself.

"A-gruntin and a-rootin and a-groanin," the woman muttered.

"We got a little of everything," Mrs. Turpin said to the pleasant lady. "It's no use in having more than you can handle yourself with help like it is. We found enough niggers to pick our cotton this year but Claud he has to go after them and take them home again in the evening. They can't walk that half a mile. No they can't. I tell you," she said and laughed merrily, "I sure am tired of buttering up niggers, but you got to love em if you want em to work for you. When they come in the morning, I run out and I say, 'Hi yawl this morning?' and when Claud drives them off to the field I just wave to beat the band and they just wave back." And she waved her hand rapidly to illustrate.

"Like you read out of the same book," the lady said, showing she understood perfectly.

"Child, yes," Mrs. Turpin said. "And when they come in from the field, I run out with a bucket of icewater. That's the way it's going to be from now on," she said. "You may as well face it."

"One thang I know," the white-trash woman said. "Two thangs I ain't going to do: love no niggers or scoot down no hog with no hose." And she let out a bark of contempt.

The look that Mrs. Turpin and the pleasant lady exchanged indicated they both understood that you had to *have* certain things before you could *know* certain things. But every time Mrs. Turpin exchanged a look with the lady, she was aware that the ugly girl's peculiar eyes were still on her, and she had trouble bringing her attention back to the conversation.

"When you got something," she said, "you got to look after it." And when you ain't got a thing but breath and britches, she added to herself, you can afford to come to town every morning and just sit on the courthouse coping and spit.

A grotesque revolving shadow passed across the curtain behind her and was thrown palely on the opposite wall. Then a bicycle clattered down against the outside of the building. The door opened and a colored boy glided in with a tray from the drugstore. It had two large red and white paper cups on it with tops on them. He was a tall, very black boy in discolored white pants and a green nylon shirt. He was chewing gum slowly, as if to music. He set the tray down in the office opening next to the fern and stuck his head through to look for the secretary. She was not in there. He rested his arms on the ledge and waited, his narrow bottom stuck out, swaying to the left and right. He raised a hand over his head and scratched the base of his skull.

"You see that button there, boy?" Mrs. Turpin said. "You can punch that and she'll come. She's probably in the back somewhere."

"Is that right?" the boy said agreeably, as if he had never seen the button before. He leaned to the right and put his finger on it. "She sometime out," he said and twisted around to face his audience, his elbows behind him on the counter. The nurse appeared and he twisted back again. She handed him a dollar and he rooted in his pocket and made the change and counted it out to her. She gave him fifteen cents for a tip and he went out with the empty tray. The heavy door swung to slowly and closed at length with the sound of suction. For a moment no one spoke.

"They ought to sent all them niggers back to Africa," the white-trash woman said. "That's wher they come from in the first place."

"Oh, I couldn't do without my good colored friends," the pleasant lady said.

"There's a heap of things worse than a nigger," Mrs. Turpin agreed. "It's all kinds of them just like it's all kinds of us."

"Yes, and it takes all kinds to make the world go round," the lady said in her musical voice.

As she said it, the raw-complexioned girl snapped her teeth together. Her lower lip turned downwards and inside out, revealing the pale pink inside of her mouth. After a second it rolled back up. It was the ugliest face Mrs. Turpin had ever seen anyone make and for a moment she was certain that the girl had made it at her. She was looking at her as if she had known and disliked her all her life—all of Mrs. Turpin's life, it seemed too, not just all the girl's life. Why, girl, I don't even know you, Mrs. Turpin said silently.

She forced her attention back to the discussion. "It wouldn't be practical to send them back to Africa," she said. "They wouldn't want to go. They got it too good here."

"Wouldn't be what they wanted—if I had anythang to do with it," the woman said.

"It wouldn't be a way in the world you could get all the niggers back over there," Mrs. Turpin said. "They'd be hiding out and lying down and turning sick on you and wailing and hollering and raring and pitching. It wouldn't be a way in the world to get them over there."

"They got over here," the trashy woman said. "Get back like they got over."

"It wasn't so many of them then," Mrs. Turpin explained.

The woman looked at Mrs. Turpin as if here was an idiot indeed but Mrs. Turpin was not bothered by the look, considering where it came from.

"Nooo," she said, "they're going to stay here where they can go to New York and marry white folks and improve their color. That's what they all want to do, every one of them, improve their color."

"You know what comes of that, don't you?" Claud asked.

"No, Claud, what?" Mrs. Turpin said.

Claud's eyes twinkled. "White-faced niggers," he said with never a smile.

Everybody in the office laughed except the white trash and the ugly girl. The girl gripped the book in her lap with white fingers. The trashy woman looked around her from face to face as if she thought they were all idiots. The old woman in the feed sack dress continued to gaze expressionless across the floor at the high-top shoes of the man opposite her, the one who had been pretending to be asleep when the Turpins came in. He was laughing heartily, his hands still spread out on his knees. The child had fallen to the side and was lying now almost face down in the old woman's lap.

While they recovered from their laughter, the nasal chorus on the radio kept the room from silence.

"You go to blank blank
And I'll go to mine

But we'll all blank along
To-geth-ther,
And all along the blank
We'll hep eachother out
Smile-ling in any kind of
Weath-ther!"

Mrs. Turpin didn't catch every word but she caught enough to agree with the spirit of the song and it turned her thoughts sober. To help anybody out that needed it was her philosophy of life. She never spared herself when she found somebody in need, whether they were white or black, trash or decent. And of all she had to be thankful for, she was most thankful that this was so. If Jesus had said, "You can be big society and have all the money you want and be thin and svelte-like, but you can't be a good woman with it," she would have had to say, "Well don't make me that then. Make me a good woman and it don't matter what else, how fat or how ugly or how poor!" Her heart rose. He had not made her a nigger or white-trash or ugly! He had made her herself and given her a little of everything. Jesus, thank you! she said. Thank you thank you thank you! Whenever she counted her blessings she felt as buoyant as if she weighed one hundred and twenty-five pounds instead of one hundred and eighty.

"What's wrong with your little boy?" the pleasant lady asked the white-trashy woman.

"He has an ulcer," the woman said proudly. "He ain't give me a minute's peace since he was born. Him and her are just alike," she said, nodding at the old woman, who was running her leathery fingers through the child's pale hair. "Look like I can't get nothing down them two but Co' Cola and candy."

That's all you try to get down em, Mrs. Turpin said to herself. Too lazy to light the fire. There was nothing you could tell her about people like them that she didn't know already. And it was not just that they didn't have anything. Because if you gave them everything, in two weeks it would all be broken or filthy or they would have chopped it up for lightwood. She knew all this from her own experience. Help them you must, but help them you couldn't.

All at once the ugly girl turned her lips inside out again. Her eyes fixed like two drills on Mrs. Turpin. This time there was no mistaking that there was something urgent behind them.

Girl, Mrs. Turpin exclaimed silently, I haven't done a thing to you! The girl might be confusing her with somebody else. There was no need to sit by and let herself be intimidated. "You must be in college," she said boldly, looking directly at the girl. "I see you reading a book there."

The girl continued to stare and pointedly did not answer.

Her mother blushed at this rudeness. "The lady asked you a question, Mary Grace," she said under her breath.

"I have ears," Mary Grace said.

The poor mother blushed again. "Mary Grace goes to Wellesley College," she explained. She twisted one of the buttons on her dress. "In Massachusetts," she added with a grimace. "And in the summer she just keeps right on studying. Just reads all the time, a real book worm. She's done real well at Wellesley; she's taking English and Math and History and Psychology and Social Studies," she rattled on, "and I think it's too much. I think she ought to get out and have fun."

The girl looked as if she would like to hurl them all through the plate glass window.

"Way up north," Mrs. Turpin murmured and thought, well, it hasn't done much for her manners.

"I'd almost rather to have him sick," the white-trash woman said, wrenching the attention back to herself. "He's so mean when he ain't. Look like some children just take natural to meanness. It's some gets bad when they get sick but he was the opposite. Took sick and turned good. He don't give me no trouble now. It's me waitin to see the doctor," she said.

If I was going to send anybody back to Africa, Mrs. Turpin thought, it would be your kind, woman. "Yes, indeed," she said aloud, but looking up at the ceiling, "it's a heap of things worse than a nigger." And dirtier than a hog, she added to herself.

"I think people with bad dispositions are more to be pitied than anyone on earth," the pleasant lady said in a voice that was decidedly thin.

"I thank the Lord he has blessed me with a good one," Mrs. Turpin said. "The day has never dawned that I couldn't find something to laugh at."

"Not since she married me anyways," Claud said with a comical straight face.

Everybody laughed except the girl and the white trash.

Mrs. Turpin's stomach shook. "He's such a caution," she said, "that I can't help but laugh at him."

The girl made a loud ugly noise through her teeth.

Her mother's mouth grew thin and tight. "I think the worst thing in the world," she said, "is an ungrateful person. To have everything and not appreciate it. I know a girl," she said, "who has parents who would give her anything, a little brother who loves her dearly, who is getting a good education, who wears the best clothes, but who can never say a kind word to anyone, who never smiles, who just criticizes and complains all day long."

"Is she too old to paddle?" Claud asked.

The girl's face was almost purple.

"Yes," the lady said, "I'm afraid there's nothing to do but leave her to her folly. Some day she'll wake up and it'll be too late."

"It never hurt anyone to smile," Mrs. Turpin said. "It just makes you feel better all over."

"Of course," the lady said sadly, "but there are just some people you can't tell anything to. They can't take criticism."

"If it's one thing I am," Mrs. Turpin said with feeling, "it's grateful. When I think who all I could have been besides myself and what all I got, a little of everything, and a good disposition besides, I just feel like shouting, "'Thank you, Jesus, for making everything the way it is!' It could have been different!" For one thing, somebody else could have got Claud. At the thought of this, she was flooded with gratitude and a terrible pang of joy ran through her. "Oh, thank you, Jesus, Jesus, thank you!" she cried aloud.

The book struck her directly over her left eye. It struck almost at the same instant that she realized the girl was about to hurl it. Before she could utter a sound, the raw face came crashing across the table toward her, howling. The girl's fingers sank like clamps into the soft flesh of her neck. She heard the mother cry out and Claud shout, "Whoa!" There was an instant when she was certain that she was about to be in an earthquake.

All at once her vision narrowed and she saw everything as if it were happening in a small room far away, or as if she were looking at it through the wrong end of a telescope. Claud's face crumpled and fell out of sight. The nurse ran in, then out, then in again. Then the gangling figure of the doctor rushed out of the inner door. Magazines flew this way and that as the table turned over. The girl fell with a thud and Mrs. Turpin's vision suddenly reversed itself and she saw everything large instead of small. The eyes of the white-trashy woman were staring hugely at the floor. There the girl, held down on one side by the nurse and on the other by her mother, was wrenching and turning in their grasp. The doctor was kneeling astride her, trying to hold her arm down. He managed after a second to sink a long needle into it.

Mrs. Turpin felt entirely hollow except for her heart which swung from side to side as if it were agitated in a great empty drum of flesh.

"Somebody that's not busy call for the ambulance," the doctor said in the off-hand voice young doctors adopt for terrible occasions.

Mrs. Turpin could not have moved a finger. The old man who had been sitting next to her skipped nimbly into the office and made the call, for the secretary still seemed to be gone.

"Claud!" Mrs. Turpin called.

He was not in his chair. She knew she must jump up and find him but she felt like some one trying to catch a train in a dream, when everything moves in slow motion and the faster you try to run the slower you go.

"Here I am," a suffocated voice, very unlike Claud's, said.

He was doubled up in the corner on the floor, pale as paper, holding his leg. She wanted to get up and go to him but she could not move. Instead, her gaze was drawn slowly downward to the churning face on the floor, which she could see over the doctor's shoulder.

The girl's eyes stopped rolling and focused on her. They seemed a much lighter blue than before, as if a door that had been tightly closed behind them was now open to admit light and air.

Mrs. Turpin's head cleared and her power of motion returned. She leaned forward until she was looking directly into the fierce brilliant eyes. There was no doubt in her mind that the girl did know her, knew her in some intense and personal way, beyond time and place and condition. "What you got to say to me?" she asked hoarsely and held her breath, waiting, as for a revelation.

The girl raised her head. Her gaze locked with Mrs. Turpin's. "Go back to hell where you came from, you old wart hog," she whispered. Her voice was low but clear. Her eyes burned for a moment as if she saw with pleasure that her message had struck its target.

Mrs. Turpin sank back in her chair.

After a moment the girl's eyes closed and she turned her head wearily to the side.

The doctor rose and handed the nurse the empty syringe. He leaned over and put both hands for a moment on the mother's shoulders, which were shaking. She was sitting on the floor, her lips pressed together, holding Mary Grace's hand in her lap. The girl's fingers were gripped like a baby's around her thumb. "Go on to the hospital," he said. "I'll call and make the arrangements."

"Now let's see that neck," he said in a jovial voice to Mrs. Turpin. He began to inspect her neck with his first two fingers. Two little moon-shaped lines like pink fish bones were indented over her windpipe. There was the beginning of an angry red swelling above her eye. His fingers passed over this also.

"Lea' me be," she said thickly and shook him off. "See about Claud. She kicked him."

"I'll see about him in a minute," he said and felt her pulse. He was a thin gray-haired man, given to pleasantries. "Go home and have yourself a vacation the rest of the day," he said and patted her on the shoulder.

Quit your pattin me, Mrs. Turpin growled to herself.

"And put an ice pack over that eye," he said. Then he went and squatted down beside Claud and looked at his leg. After a moment he pulled him up and Claud limped after him into the office.

Until the ambulance came, the only sounds in the room were the tremulous moans of the girl's mother, who continued to sit on the floor. The white-trash woman did not take her eyes off the girl. Mrs. Turpin looked straight ahead at nothing. Presently the ambulance drew up, a long dark shadow, behind the curtain. The attendants came in and set the stretcher down beside the girl and lifted her expertly onto it and carried her out. The nurse helped the mother gather up her things. The shadow of the ambulance moved silently away and the nurse came back in the office.

"That ther girl is going to be a lunatic, ain't she?" the white-trash woman asked the nurse, but the nurse kept on to the back and never answered her.

"Yes, she's going to be a lunatic," the white-trash woman said to the rest of them.

"Po' critter," the old woman murmured. The child's face was still in her lap. His eyes looked idly out over her knees. He had not moved during the disturbance except to draw one leg up under him.

"I thank Gawd," the white-trash woman said fervently, "I ain't a lunatic."

Claud came limping out and the Turpins went home.

As their pickup truck turned into their own dirt road and made the crest of the hill, Mrs. Turpin gripped the window ledge and looked out suspiciously. The land sloped gracefully down through a field dotted with lavender weeds and at the start of the rise their small yellow frame house, with its little flower beds spread out around it like a fancy apron, sat primly in its accustomed place between two giant hickory trees. She would not have been startled to see a burnt wound between two blackened chimneys.

Neither of them felt like eating so they put on their house clothes and lowered the shade in the bedroom and lay down, Claud with his leg on a pillow and herself with a damp washcloth over her eye. The instant she was flat on her back, the image of a razorbacked hog with warts on its face and horns coming out behind its ears snorted into her head. She moaned, a low quiet moan.

"I am not," she said tearfully, "a wart hog. From hell." But the denial had no force. The girl's eyes and her words, even the tone of her voice, low but clear, directed only to her, brooked no repudiation. She had been singled out for the message, though there was trash in the room to whom it might justly have been applied. The full force of this fact struck her only now. There was a woman there who was neglecting her own child but she had been overlooked. The message had been given to Ruby Turpin, a respectable, hard-working, churchgoing woman. The tears dried. Her eyes began to burn instead with wrath.

She rose on her elbow and the washcloth fell into her hand. Claud was lying on his back, snoring. She wanted to tell him what the girl had said. At the same time, she did not wish to put the image of herself as a wart hog from hell into his mind.

"Hey, Claud," she muttered and pushed his shoulder.

Claud opened one pale baby blue eye.

She looked into it warily. He did not think about anything. He just went his way.

"Wha, whasit?" he said and closed the eye again.

"Nothing," she said. "Does your leg pain you?"

"Hurts like hell," Claud said.

"It'll quit terreckly," she said and lay back down. In a moment Claud was snoring again. For the rest of the afternoon they lay there. Claud slept. She scowled at the ceiling. Occasionally she raised her fist and made a small stabbing motion over her chest as if she was defending her innocence to invisible guests who were like the comforters of Job, reasonable-seeming but wrong.

About five-thirty Claud stirred. "Got to go after those niggers," he sighed, not moving.

She was looking straight up as if there were unintelligible handwriting on the ceiling. The protuberance over her eye had turned a greenish-blue. "Listen here," she said.

"What?"

"Kiss me."

Claud leaned over and kissed her loudly on the mouth. He pinched her side and their hands interlocked. Her expression of ferocious concentration did not change. Claud got up, groaning and growling, and limped off. She continued to study the ceiling.

She did not get up until she heard the pickup truck coming back with the Negroes. Then she rose and thrust her feet in her brown oxfords, which she did not bother to lace, and stumped out onto the back porch and got her red plastic bucket. She emptied a tray of ice cubes into it and filled it half full of water and went out into the back yard. Every afternoon after Claud brought the hands in, one of the boys helped him put out hay and the rest waited in the back of the truck until he was ready to take them home. The truck was parked in the shade under one of the hickory trees.

"Hi yawl this evening?" Mrs. Turpin asked grimly, appearing with the bucket and the dipper. There were three women and a boy in the truck.

"Us doin nicely," the oldest woman said. "Hi you doin?" and her gaze stuck immediately on the dark lump on Mrs. Turpin's forehead. "You done fell down, ain't you?" she asked in a solicitous voice. The old woman was dark and almost toothless. She had on an old felt hat of Claud's set back on her head. The other two women were younger and lighter and they both had new bright green sunhats. One of them had hers on her head; the other had taken hers off and the boy was grinning beneath it.

Mrs. Turpin set the bucket down on the floor of the truck. "Yawl hep yourselves," she said. She looked around to make sure Claud had gone. "No, I didn't fall down," she said, folding her arms. "It was something worse than that."

"Ain't nothing bad happen to you!" the old woman said. She said it as if they all knew that Mrs. Turpin was protected in some special way by Divine Providence. "You just had you a little fall."

"We were in town at the doctor's office for where the cow kicked Mr. Turpin," Mrs. Turpin said in a flat tone that indicated they could leave off their foolishness. "And there was this girl there. A big fat girl with her face all broke out. I could look at that girl and tell she was peculiar but I couldn't tell how. And me and her mama was just talking and going along and all of a sudden WHAM! She throws this big book she was reading at me and . . ."

"Naw!" the old woman cried out.

"And then she jumps over the table and commences to choke me."

"Naw!" they all exclaimed, "naw!"

"Hi come she do that?" the old woman asked. "What ail her?"

Mrs. Turpin only glared in front of her.

"Somethin ail her," the old woman said.

"They carried her off in an ambulance," Mrs. Turpin continued, "but before she went she was rolling on the floor and they were trying to hold her down to give her a shot and she said something to me." She paused. "You know what she said to me?"

"What she say?" they asked.

"She said," Mrs. Turpin began, and stopped, her face very dark and heavy. The sun was getting whiter and whiter, blanching the sky overhead so that the leaves of the hickory tree were black in the face of it. She could not bring forth the words. "Something real ugly," she muttered.

"She sho shouldn't said nothing ugly to you," the old woman said. "You so sweet. You the sweetest lady I know."

"She pretty too," the one with the hat on said.

"And stout," the other one said. "I never knowed no sweeter white lady."

"That's the truth befo' Jesus," the old woman said. "Amen! You des as sweet and pretty as you can be."

Mrs. Turpin knew exactly how much Negro flattery was worth and it added to her rage. "She said," she began again and finished this time with a fierce rush of breath, "that I was an old wart hog from hell."

There was an astounded silence.

"Where she at?" the youngest woman cried in a piercing voice.

"Lemme see her. I'll kill her!"

"I'll kill her with you!" the other one cried.

"She b'long in the sylum," the old woman said emphatically. "You the sweetest white lady I know."

"She pretty too," the other two said. "Stout as she can be and sweet. Jesus satisfied with her!"

"Deed he is," the old woman declared.

Idiots! Mrs. Turpin growled to herself. You could never say anything intelligent to a nigger. You could talk at them but not with them. "Yawl ain't drunk you water," she said shortly. "Leave the bucket in the truck when you're finished with it. I got more to do than just stand around and pass the time of day," and she moved off and into the house.

She stood for a moment in the middle of the kitchen. The dark protuberance over her eye looked like a miniature tornado cloud which might any moment sweep across the horizon of her brow. Her lower lip protruded dangerously. She squared her massive shoulders. Then she marched into the front of the house and out the side door and started down the road to the pig parlor. She had the look of a woman going single-handed, weaponless, into battle.

The sun was a deep yellow now like a harvest moon and was riding westward very fast over the far tree line as if it meant to reach the hogs before she did. The road was rutted and she kicked several good-sized stones out of her path as she strode along. The pig parlor was on a little knoll at the end of a lane that ran off from the side of the barn. It was a square of concrete as large as a small room, with a board fence about four feet high around it. The concrete floor sloped slightly so that the hog wash could drain off into a trench where it was carried to the field for fertilizer. Claud was standing on the outside, on the edge of the concrete, hanging onto the top board, hosing down the floor inside. The hose was connected to the faucet of a water trough nearby.

Mrs. Turpin climbed up beside him and glowered down at the hogs inside. There were seven long-snouted bristly shoats in it—tan with liver-colored spots—and an old sow a few weeks off from farrowing. She was lying on her side grunting. The shoats were running about shaking themselves like idiot children, their little slit pig eyes searching the floor for anything left. She had read that pigs were the most intelligent animal. She doubted it. They were supposed to be smarter than dogs. There had even been a pig astronaut. He had performed his assignment perfectly but died of a heart attack afterwards because they left him in his electric suit, sitting upright throughout his examination when naturally a hog should be on all fours.

A-gruntin and a-rootin and a-groanin.

"Gimme that hose," she said, yanking it away from Claud. "Go on and carry them niggers home and then get off that leg."

"You look like you might have swallowed a mad dog," Claud observed, but he got down and limped off. He paid no attention to her humors.

Until he was out of earshot, Mrs. Turpin stood on the side of the pen, holding the hose and pointing the stream of water at the hind quarters of any shoat that looked as if it might try to lie down. When he had had time to get over the hill, she turned her head slightly and her wrathful eyes scanned the path. He was nowhere in sight. She turned back again and seemed to gather herself up. Her shoulders rose and she drew in her breath.

"What do you send me a message like that for?" she said in a low fierce voice, barely above a whisper but with the force of a shout in its concentrated fury. "How am I a hog and me both? How am I saved and from hell too?" Her free fist was knotted and with the other she gripped the hose, blindly pointing the stream of water in and out of the eye of the old sow whose outraged squeal she did not hear.

The pig parlor commanded a view of the back pasture where their twenty beef cows were gathered around the hay bales Claud and the boy had put out. The freshly cut pasture sloped down to the highway. Across it was their cotton field and beyond that a dark green dusty wood which they owned as well. The sun was behind the wood, very red, looking over the paling of trees like a farmer inspecting his own hogs.

"Why me?" she rumbled. "It's no trash around here, black or white, that I haven't given to. And break my back to the bone every day working. And do for the church."

She appeared to be the right size woman to command the arena before her. "How am I a hog?" she demanded. "Exactly how am I like them?" and she jabbed the stream of water at the shoats. "There was plenty of trash there. It didn't have to be me."

"If you like trash better, go get yourself some trash then," she railed. "You could have made me trash. Or a nigger. If trash is what you wanted why didn't you make me trash?" She shook her fist with the hose in it and a watery snake appeared momentarily in the air. "I could quit working and take it easy and be filthy," she growled. "Lounge about the sidewalks all day drinking root beer. Dip snuff and spit in every puddle and have it all over my face. I could be nasty."

"Or you could have made me a nigger. It's too late for me to be a nigger," she said with deep sarcasm, "but I could act like one. Lay down in the middle of the road and stop traffic. Roll on the ground."

In the deepening light everything was taking on a mysterious hue. The pasture was growing a peculiar glassy green and the streak of highway had turned lavender. She braced herself for a final assault and this time her voice rolled out over the pasture. "Go on," she yelled, "call me a hog! Call me a hog again. From hell. Call me a wart hog from hell. Put that bottom rail on top. There'll still be a top and bottom!"

A garbled echo returned to her.

A final surge of fury shook her and she roared, "Who do you think you are?"

The color of everything, field, and crimson sky, burned for a moment with a transparent intensity. The question carried over the pasture and across the highway and the cotton field and returned to her clearly like an answer from beyond the wood.

She opened her mouth but no sound came out of it.

A tiny truck, Claud's, appeared on the highway, heading rapidly out of sight. Its gears scraped thinly. It looked like a child's toy. At any moment a bigger truck might smash into it and scatter Claud's and the niggers' brains all over the road.

Mrs. Turpin stood there, her gaze fixed on the highway, all her muscles rigid, until in five or six minutes the truck reappeared, returning. She waited until it had had time to turn into their own road. Then like a monumental statue coming to life, she bent her head slowly and gazed, as if through the very heart of mystery, down into the pig parlor at the hogs. They had settled all in one corner around the old sow who was grunting softly. A red glow suffused them. They appeared to pant with a secret life.

Until the sun slipped finally behind the tree line, Mrs. Turpin remained there with her gaze bent to them as if she were absorbing some abysmal life-giving knowledge. At last she lifted her head. There was only a purple streak in the sky, cutting through a field of crimson and leading, like an extension of the highway, into the descending dusk. She raised her hands from the side of the pen in a gesture hieratic and profound. A visionary light settled in her eyes. She saw the streak as a vast swinging bridge extending upward from the earth through a field of living fire. Upon it a vast horde of souls were rumbling toward heaven. There were whole companies of white-trash, clean for the first time in their lives, and bands of black niggers in white robes, and battalions of freaks and lunatics shouting and clapping and leaping like frogs. And bringing up the end of the procession was a tribe of people whom she recognized at once as those who, like herself and Claud, had always had a little of everything and the God-given wit to use it right. She leaned forward to observe them closer. They were marching behind the others with great dignity, accountable as they had always been for good order and common sense and respectable behavior. They alone were on key. Yet she could see by their shocked and altered faces that even their virtues were being burned away. She lowered her hands and gripped the rail of the hog pen, her eyes small but fixed unblinkingly on what lay ahead. In a moment the vision faded but she remained where she was, immobile.

At length she got down and turned off the faucet and made her slow way on the darkening path to the house. In the woods around her the invisible cricket choruses had struck up, but what she heard were the voices of the souls climbing upward into the starry field and shouting hallelujah.

JAYNE ANNE PHILLIPS

Jayne Anne Phillips was born in Buckhannon, West Virginia, in 1952. She received a B.A. at West Virginia University and an M.F.A. at the University of Iowa. Two early collections of her short fiction, *Sweethearts* (1976) and *Counting* (1978), were published in limited editions. With the publication of her third collection, *Black Tickets* (1979), she reached a large and enthusiastic audience. Her first novel, *Machine Dreams*, was published in 1984. Her most recent collection of stories is *Fast Lanes* (1987).

Rayme

In our student days we were all in need of fortune tellers. No one was sure what was happening in the outside world and no one thought about it much. We had no televisions and we bought few newspapers. Communal life seemed a continual dance in which everyone changed partners, a patient attempt at domesticity by children taking turns being parents. We were adrift but we were together. A group of us floated among several large ramshackle houses, houses arranged above and below each other on steep streets: a gritty version of terraced dwellings in some exotic Asia. The houses were old and comfortable, furnished with an accumulation of overstuffed chairs and velveteen sofas gleaned from rummage sales. There were no curtains on the large windows, whose rectangular sooty light was interrupted only by tangles of viny plants. The plants were fed haphazardly and thrived, like anything green in that town, enveloping sills and frames still fitted with the original wavy glass of seventy years before. The old glass was pocked with flaws and minute bubbles, distorting further the vision of a town already oddly displaced and dreamed in jagged pieces. Houses of the student ghetto were the landscape of the dream—a landscape often already condemned.

I lived in a house on Price Street with three male housemates: a Lebanese photographer from Rochester, New York, a Jewish TM instructor from Michigan, and a carpenter musician, a West Virginian, who'd worked in the doomed McCarthy campaign and dropped out of Harvard Law to come home and learn housebuilding.

This story could be about any one of those people, but it is about Rayme and comes to no conclusions.

Perhaps the story is about Rayme because she lived in all the communal houses at one time or another. Intermittently she lived with her father and stepmother and brother. Or she lived with one of her two older sisters, who had stayed in town and were part of our group of friends. Or she lived in her own small rooms, a bedroom, kitchen, and bath in a house chopped into three or four such apartments. She lived alone in several of those single-person places, and in all of them she kept the provided mattress and box springs tilted upright against the wall. She slept on a small rug that she unrolled at night, or she slept on the bare floor with the rug precisely folded as a pillow. She shoved most of the other furniture into a corner or put it outside on the porch. Skirts and coats on hangers, swatches of fabric, adorned the walls. Rayme brought in large branches, a brick, a rock. Usually there were no utilities but running water; her father paid the rent and that is all that was paid. She wore sweaters and leggings and burned candles for light. She used the refrigerator as a closet for shoes and beads, and seemed to eat almost nothing. She kept loose tea and seeds in jars and emptied coffee cans that she filled with nutshells and marbles. A long time ago her mother had committed suicide in Argentina. No one ever talked about the death, but one of Rayme's sisters told me the suicide was slow rather than overtly violent. "She stopped eating, she'd been sick, she wouldn't go to the hospital or see a doctor," the sister said. "It took her several months to do it." Rayme seldom mentioned her mother and didn't seem certain of any particular chain of events concerning the past. The facts she referred to at different times seemed arbitrary, they were scrambled, they may have been false or transformed. It is true that her parents married each other twice and divorced twice; the father was a professor, the mother had musical talent and four children. Rayme told me her father wouldn't let his wife play the piano; he locked the baby grand because she became too "detached" when she played.

The first time her parents divorced, Rayme was six years old, the only child to go with her mother. They lived alone together in Kansas. Rayme didn't remember much about it. She said sometimes she came home from school and the door would be locked and she would sit outside past dark and listen to the owls in the trees. Once there was a tornado in Kansas; Rayme's mother opened all the windows "so the wind can blow *through* the house instead of breaking it." Then they sat on the sofa wrapped in their winter coats, rather than hiding in the basement, so they could watch the rattling funnel cloud twist and hop across the flat fields behind the town.

Rayme said her mother kept things in Kansas, like bracelets and rings, costume jewelry, under the pillows of the bed. They used to play games with those things before they went to sleep at night, and tell stories. Rayme slept by the wall because her mother sleepwalked and needed a clear path to the open.

At the time of the second divorce, Rayme was twelve. She said her father stood in the middle of the living room and called out the names of the children. He pointed to one side of the room or the other. "When we were lined up right, he said *those* kids would stay with him and *those* kids would go with her." Rayme went to Argentina with her mother and oldest sister. A family friend there paid airplane fares and found housing; Rayme's father paid child support. Rayme learned some Spanish songs. Her sister went out on chaperoned dates, there was a terrace, it was sunny. Their mother died down there after a few months, and the two children came back on a boat, unchaperoned.

Rayme's sister told me Rayme didn't react when their mother died. "Everyone else cried, but Rayme didn't. She just sat there on the bed. She was our mother's favorite." The funeral was in Argentina, and the service was Catholic. "I was standing by the door while the priest was in the bedroom," Rayme's sister said. "Rayme looked up at me wearing our mother's expression, on purpose, to say *I'd* lost my mother but *she* hadn't."

Once Rayme sent her oldest sister a group of wallet-sized photographs in the mail. They were all pictures of Rayme taken in various years by public school photographers, and they were all dotted with tiny pinholes so that the faces were gone. Another time she came to her sister's Christmas party with one eyebrow shaved off. Her sister demanded that she shave the other one off as well so at least they'd match, and Rayme did.

Sometime late that winter, Rayme went to stay in the country at the cabin of a friend. She was living there alone with her cat; she said she could marry the snow. The cat wandered into the woods and Rayme wandered down the middle of the dirt road six miles to the highway. There was rain and a heavy frost, sleet flowers on the pavement. Rayme wore a summer shift and a kitchen knife strapped to her arm with leather thongs. She had hacked her waist-length hair to the shape of a bowl on her head and coiled her thick dark braids tightly into the pockets of her dress.

She had nothing to say to the farm couple who found her sitting on the double line of the highway in a meditative pose, but she did nod and get into the car as though expecting them. They took her to the university hospital and she committed herself for three weeks. I visited her there; she sat stiffly by a window reinforced with chicken wire between double panes, her back very straight, her hands clasped. She said it was important to practice good posture, and she moved her head, slowly, deliberately, when she looked to the right or left. Her skin was pale and clear like white porcelain. Before I left, we repeated some rituals evolved earlier in half-serious fun: children's songs with hand motions ("here is the church and here is the steeple" . . . "I'm a little teapot, short and stout" . . . "along came the rain and washed the spider out"), the Repulse Tiger movement from T'ai Chi, a series of Chinese bows in slow motion. She said the hospital was like a big clock and she was in the floor of the clock; every day she went to Group, and played dominoes in the Common Room. She ate her lunch in a chair by the nurses' desk; she liked their white clothes and the sighing of the elevators.

By the time she was released, the TM instructor living at Price Street had moved to Cleveland. Rayme moved in with me, with the Harvard carpenter, with the Lebanese photographer. She wasn't paying rent but we had the extra room anyway and sometimes she cooked meals.

Once she cooked soup. For an hour, she stood by the stove, stirring the soup in a large dented kettle. I looked into the pot and saw a jagged object floating among the vegetables. I pulled it out, holding the hot, thin edge: it was a large fragment of blackened linoleum from the buckling kitchen floor.

I asked Rayme how a piece of the floor got into the soup.

"I put it there," Rayme said.

I didn't answer.

"It's clean," Rayme said. "I washed it first," and then, angrily, "If you're not going to eat my food, don't look at it."

That was her worst summer. She told me she didn't want to take the Thorazine because it made her into someone else. Men were the sky and women were the earth; she liked books about Indians. She said cats were good and dogs were bad; she hated the lower half of her body. She didn't have lovers but quietly adored men from her past—relatives, boyfriends, men she saw in magazines or on the street. Her high school boyfriend was Krishna, a later one Jesus, her father "Buddha with a black heart." She built an altar in her room out of planks and cement blocks, burned candles and incense, arranged pine needles and pebbles in patterns. She changed costumes often and moved the furniture in her room several times a day, usually shifting it just a few inches. She taped pictures on her wall: blue Krishna riding his white pony, Shiva dancing with all her gold arms adorned, Lyndon Johnson in glossy color from *Newsweek,* cutouts of kittens from a toilet-paper advertisement. Her brother, three years younger than she and just graduated from high school, came to see her several times a week. He brought her a blue bottle full of crushed mint, and played his guitar. He seemed quiet, witty, focused; he looked like Rayme, the same dark hair and slender frame and chiseled bones. She said he was the angel who flew from the window with sleep-dust on his shoes; he used to tell his sisters, when they were all children, that he was the one who'd sealed their eyes shut in the night, that they would never catch him because boys could be ghosts in the dark.

On an afternoon when we'd taken mescaline, Rayme sat weeping on the couch at Price Street. The couch was brown and nubby, and people had to sit toward its edge or the cushions would fall through to the floor. The cushions had fallen through, and Rayme sat in the hole of the frame comfortably, her legs splayed up over the board front. She sat looking at the ceiling, her head thrown back, like a woman trying to keep her mascara from running. She remained still, as though enthroned, waiting, her face wet, attentive. I watched her from across the room. "Yes," she said after a long while, as though apprehending some truth, "tears wash the eyes and lubricate the skin of the temples."

All of us were consulting a series of maps bearing no relation to any physical geography, and Rayme was like a telephone to another world. Her messages were syllables from an investigative dream, and her every movement was precise, like those of a driver unerringly steering an automobile by watching the road through the rearview mirror.

I'd met her when we were both working at Bonanza Steak house as servers. She liked the cowboy hats and the plaid shirts with the braid trim, and she insisted on completing the outfit by wearing her brother's high-heeled boots and a string tie from Carlsbad Caverns emblazoned with a tiny six-gun. She got away with these embellishments of store policy because her compulsions seemed harmless. She would stand erect behind plates and crackling steaks bound for numbered trays, looking intently into the vacuous faces of customers shuffling by in the line. She did tap-dance steps in place, wielding her spatula and tipping her hat, addressing everyone as Sir or Madam. She liked the ritual of the totally useless weekly employee meetings, in which skirt lengths and hairnets and customer quotas were discussed. She admired the manager and called him Mr. Fenstermaker, when everyone else referred to him derisively as "Chester," after the gimp on "Gunsmoke." He was a fat doughy boy about thirty years old who walked around what he called "the store" with a clipboard of names and work hours. During meetings Rayme sat at his elbow and took down his directives in careful, cursive script, posting them later on the door to the employees' bathroom. She also posted the covers of several romance comic books. She got in trouble once for mixing the mashed potatoes with nutmeg and banana slices, and again when she arranged the plastic steak tags across the raw meat in a mandala bordered by white stones. In the center of the mandala was the small, perfect egg of a bird. The egg was purely blue; on it Rayme had painted a Chinese word in miniature gold characters. Later she told me she'd looked the word up especially in a language textbook; the word meant "banquet."

Rayme was protected at Price Street. She stopped losing jobs because she stopped having them; instead, she worked in the tumbledown garden, tying tomato plants to poles with strips of heavy satin and brocade—draperies she'd found in a junk pile. Meticulously, she cut the fabric into measured lengths and hemmed the pieces. She kept the house full of wild flowers and blossoming weeds, and hung herbs to dry in the hallways. The summer was easy. No one expected her to talk on days when she didn't speak. She was calm. She pretended we were mythical people and brought us presents she'd made: a doll of sticks and corn silk, with a shard of glass for a face, or the skeleton of a lizard laid out perfectly in a velvet-lined harmonica box.

In late August we were told that Price Street and the abandoned houses near it would be demolished by the city, "to make the city hospital a more attractive property." The rest of us complained resignedly but Rayme made no comment; quietly, she began staying awake all night in the downstairs of the house. Day after day, we awoke to find the furniture turned over and piled in a heap, the rugs rolled up, pictures turned upside down on the walls. She took personal possessions from the bedrooms, wrapped them in her shirts and jeans, and tied the carefully folded parcels with twine. We called a house meeting to discuss her behavior, and Rayme refused to attend. She went upstairs and began throwing plates from the windows.

We asked her brother to come to Price Street and talk to her. They sat in her room for a couple of hours, then they came downstairs. Rayme said she didn't have any money, maybe she'd live with her sister for a while. She unwrapped the stolen possessions with great ceremony and gave them back to us as gifts while her brother watched, smiling. At midnight, we made wheat pancakes and ate them with molasses, Indian-style, on the dark porch.

Several years later, when all the houses we'd lived in together had been torn down, Rayme's brother would shoot himself with a pistol. He would do it beside a lean-to he'd built as a squatter at an isolated campsite, five miles up a steep mountain trail. He would leave no notes; his body would not be discovered for some time. When they did find him ("they" meaning people in uniforms), they would have trouble getting a stretcher down the path and over the rocks.

But this was before that. It was September of 1974, most of us would leave town in a few weeks, and I had been recently pregnant. Some of us were going to Belize to survive an earthquake. Some of us were going to California to live on 164th Street in Oakland. A few were staying in West Virginia to continue the same story in even more fragmented fashion. My lover, the carpenter, was going to Nicaragua on a house-building deal that would never materialize. We'd had passport photos taken together; he would use his passport in the company of someone else and I would lose mine somewhere in Arizona. But on this day in September I had never seen Arizona, and we all went to a deserted lake to swim despite the fact the weather had turned.

I remember going into the lake first, how the water was warmer than the air. On the bank the others were taking off their clothes—denim skirts and jeans, soft, worn clothes, endlessly utilitarian. Their bodies were pale and slow against the dark border of the woods. They walked into the lake separately, aimlessly, but Rayme swam straight toward me. It was almost evening and the air smelled of rain. Noise was muffled by the wind in the leaves of the trees, and when Rayme was suddenly close the splash of her movement was a shock like waking up. Her hands brushed my legs—her touch underwater as soft as the touch of a plant—and she passed me, swimming deeper, swimming farther out.

I wanted to stand on something firm and swam to the dock, a stationary thickness for mooring motorboats. It stretched out into the water a long distance. Who had built it in this deserted place? It was old, the weathered black of railroad ties. I pulled myself onto the splintery wood and began to walk along its length, touching the pylons, hearing the *swak* of stirred water as the storm blew up, hearing my own footsteps. Where were we all really going, and when would we ever arrive? Our destinations appeared to be interchangeable pauses in some long, lyric transit. This time that was nearly over, these years, seemed as close to family as most of us would ever get.

Now the rain was coming from far off, sweeping across the water in a silver sheet. The waiting surface began to dapple, studded with slivers of rain. Rayme was a white face and shoulders, afloat two hundred yards out. "Kate," she called across the distance, "when you had your abortion, did you think about killing yourself?"

"No," I yelled back. "Come out of the water."

REYNOLDS PRICE

Reynolds Price was born in Macon, North Carolina, in 1933, received his B.A. from Duke University, and, as a Rhodes Scholar, studied for three years at Merton College, Oxford. Since 1958, he has taught at Duke, where he is now James B. Duke Professor of English. He has published poetry, essays, plays, and translations from the Bible. His novels are *A Long and Happy Life, A Generous Man, Love and Work, The Surface of Earth, The Source of Light, Kate Vaiden* (which won The National Book Critic Circle Award), and *Good Hearts.* His stories have been collected in two volumes, *The Names and Faces of Heroes* (1963) and *Permanent Errors* (1970).

The Warrior Princess Ozimba

SHE was the oldest thing any of us knew anything about, and she had never been near a tennis court, but somewhere around the Fourth of July every year, one of us (it was my father for a long time but for the past two years, just me) rode out to her place and took her a pair of blue tennis shoes. (Blue because that was her favorite color before she went blind and because even now, opening the box and not seeing them, she always asked, "Is they blue?") We did it on the Fourth because that was the day she had picked out fifty years ago for her birthday, not knowing what day she had been born and figuring that the Fourth was right noisy anyhow and one more little celebration wouldn't hurt if it pacified my father who was a boy then and who wanted to give her presents. And it was always tennis shoes because they were the only kind she would put on and because with her little bit of shuffling around in the sun, she managed to wear out a pair every year. So now that I was doing it, the time would come, and Vesta, who was her daughter and had taken her mother's place and who didn't have much faith in my memory, would look up at me from stringing beans or waxing the floor and say, "Mr. Ed, Mama's feets going to be flat on the ground by next week," and then I would drive out, and it would be her birthday.

My mother goes out very seldom now, so late in the afternoon of the Fourth, I took the shoes and climbed in the broiling car alone and headed down the Embro road where she lived with Vesta and Vesta's husband, where she had lived ever since she took up with Uncle Ben Harrison in the Year One and started having those children that had more or less vanished. (My grandfather asked her once just when was it she and Ben got married. She smiled and said, "Mr. Buddy, *you* know we ain't married. We just made arrangements.")

All the way out there the shoulders of the dirt road were full of Negroes dressed up in a lot of light-colored clothes that were getting dustier by the minute, walking nowhere (except maybe to some big baptizing up the creek) slow and happy with a lot of laughing and with children bunched along every now and then, yelling and prancing and important-looking as puppies on the verge of being grown and running away. I waved at several of the struggling knots as I passed just so I could look in the mirror and see the children all stop their scuffling and string out in a line with great wide eyes and all those teeth and watch my car till it was gone, wondering who in the world that waving white man was, flying on by them to the creek.

There was still the creek to cross that I and a little Negro named Walter had dammed up a thousand times for wading purposes. It would follow along on the left, and there would be that solid mile of cool shade and sand and honeysuckle and the two chimneys that had belonged to Lord-knows-what rising from the far end of it and the sawdust pile that had swallowed Harp Hubbard at age eleven so afterwards we couldn't play there except in secret and always had to bathe before going home, and then on the right it would be her place.

About all you could say for her place was it would keep out a gentle rain, balancing on its own low knoll on four rock legs so delicate it seemed she could move once, sitting now tall in her chair on one end of the porch, and send the whole thing—house, dog, flowers, herself, all—turning quietly down past the nodding chickens and the one mulberry tree to the road, if she hadn't been lighter than a fall leaf and nearly as dry. I got out of the car without even waking her dog and started towards her.

She sat there the way she had sat every day for eight years (every day since that evening after supper when she stepped to the living room door and called my father out and asked him, "Mr. Phil, ain't it about time I'm taking me a rest?"), facing whoever might pass and the trees and beyond and gradually not seeing any of them, her hands laid palm up on her knees, her back and her head held straight as any boy and in that black hat nobody ever saw her without but which got changed—by night—every year or so, a little deaf and with no sight at all and her teeth gone and her lips caved in forever, leaving her nothing but those saddles of bone under her eyes and her age which nobody knew (at times you could make her remember when General Lee took up my grandmother who was a baby and kissed her) and her name which my great-grandfather had been called on to give her and which came from a book he was reading at the time—Warrior Princess Ozimba.

I climbed the steps till I stood directly in front of her, level with her shut eyes and blocking the late sun which had made her this year the same as every year the color of bright old pennies that made us all pretend she was an Indian when we were children and spy on her from behind doors and think she knew things she wasn't telling. I wasn't sure she was awake until she said, "Good evening to you," and I said, "Good evening, Aunt Zimby. How are you getting on?"

"Mighty well for an old woman," she said, "with all this good-feeling sunshine."

"Yes, it *is* good weather," I said. "We'll be calling for a little rain soon though."

"Maybe you all will," she said, "but it's the sun and not the rain that helps my misery. And if you just step out of my light, please sir, I can take the last of it." So I sat down on the top step by her feet that were in what was left of last year's shoes, and the sun spread back over her face, and whatever it was my great-grandfather thought the Warrier Princess Ozimba looked like, it must have been something like that.

When she spoke again it seemed to confirm she knew somebody was with her. "I been setting here wondering is my mulberries ripe yet?"

I looked down at her knobby little tree and said, "No, not yet."

"My white folks that I works for, they littlest boy named Phil, and he do love the mulberries. One day his Mama was going off somewhere, and she say to him, 'Phil, don't you eat n'er one of them mulberries.' So he say, 'No ma'm' like he swearing in court. Well, I give him his dinner, and he go streaking off down the back of the lot. That afternoon I setting on the kitchen steps, resting my feets, and Phil he come up towards me through the yard, no bigger than a mosquito, and ask me, 'Aunt Zimby, what you studying about?' I say to him I just wondering if them mulberries back yonder is fit to eat yet. And he don't do nothing but stand there and turn up that face of his, round as a dollar watch and just as solemn but with the mulberry juice ringing round his mouth bright as any wreath, and he say, 'I expect they is.'"

I thought she was going to laugh—I did, softly—but suddenly she was still as before, and then a smile broke out on her mouth as if it had taken that long for the story to work from her lips into her mind, and when the smile was dying off, she jerked her hand that was almost a great brown bird's wing paddling the air once across her eyes. It was the first time she had moved, and coming quick as it did, it made me think for a minute she had opened her eyes with her hand and would be turning now to see who I was. But the one move was all, and she was back in her age like sleep so deep and still I couldn't have sworn she was breathing, even if there hadn't been the last of the sun on her face and the color streaming under the skin.

I sat for a while, not thinking of anything except that it was cooling off and that I would count to a hundred and leave if she hadn't moved or spoken. I counted and it seemed she wasn't coming back from wherever she was, not today, so I set the shoe box by the side of her chair and got up to go. Vesta would see them when she came at dark to lead her mother in. I was all the way down the steps, going slow, hoping the dog wouldn't bark, when she spoke, "You don't know my Mr. Phil, does you?"

I walked back so she could hear me and said No, I didn't believe I did.

There was no use confusing her now and starting her to remembering my father and maybe crying. Nobody had told her when he died.

She felt for the tin can beside her chair and turned away from me and spat her snuff into it. (She had said before that if she was going sinning on to her grave after dips of snuff, it was her own business, but she wasn't asking nobody else to watch her doing it.) Those few slow moves as gentle and breakable as some long-necked waterfowl brought her to life again, and when she had set her can down, I thought I ought to say something so I got back onto how nice the weather was.

But she held her eyes shut, knowing maybe that if she had opened them and hadn't been blind anyhow, she would have seen I wasn't who she had expected all year long. "Yes sir, this here's the weather you all wants for your dances, ain't it?"

I said, "Yes, it would be ideal for that."

"Well, is you been dancing much lately, Mr. Phil?"

She seemed to think she was talking to me so I said No, there wasn't much of that going on these days.

"You a great one for the dancing, ain't you, Mr. Phil?" All I did was laugh loud enough for her to hear me, but she wiped her mouth with a small yellow rag, and I could see that—not meaning to, not meaning to at all—I had started her.

She began with a short laugh of her own and drummed out a noiseless tune on the arm of the chair and nodded her head and said, "You *is* a case, Mr. Phil."

I asked her what did she mean because I couldn't leave now.

"I was just thinking about that evening you went off to some dance with one of your missy-girls, you in your white trousers looking like snow was on the way. And late that night I was out there on you all's back porch, and it come up a rain, and directly you come strolling up with not a thing on but your underwear and your feets in them white shoes you was putting down like stove lids, and there was your white trousers laid pretty as you please over your arm to keep from getting them muddy. Does you remember that, Mr. Phil?"

I said there were right many things I didn't remember these days.

"The same with me," she said, "except every once in a while . . ." A line of black children passed up the road. They every one of them looked towards us and then towards the older tall yellow girl who led the line and who had been silently deputized to wave and say, "How you this evening, Miss Zimby?"—not looking for an answer surely, not even looking to be heard, just in respect as when you speak to the sea. ". . . What put me to thinking about Mr. Phil is it's time for me some new shoes."

And there I was with the shoes in my hands that I couldn't give her now and wondering what I could do, and while I was wondering she raised her own long foot and stamped the floor three times, and there was considerable noise, as surprising as if that same bird she kept reminding me of had beat the air with its foot and made thunder. Before I could guess why she had done it, Vesta came to the front door and said, "Lord, Mr. Ed, I didn't know you was out here. Me and Lonnie was in yonder lying down, and I just figured it was Mama going on to herself." Then she said louder to Aunt Zimby, "What you call me for, Mama?"

It took her a little while to remember. "Vesta, when have Mr. Phil been here? It ain't been long is it?"

Vesta looked at me for an answer but I was no help. "No, Mama, it ain't been so long."

"He ain't sick or nothing is he? Because it's getting time for me some new shoes."

"It won't be long, Mama. Mr. Phil ain't never forgot you yet."

And that seemed to settle it for her. The little tune she had been thumping out slowed down and stopped, and next her head began to nod, all as quick as if she had worked the whole day out in the cotton and come home and fixed everybody's supper and seen them to bed and pressed a shirt for Uncle Ben who drove a taxi occasionally and then fallen dead to sleep in the sounding dark with the others breathing all round her.

Vesta and I stayed still by her till we could hear breathing, but when it began, small and slow, I handed Vesta the shoes. She knew and smiled and nodded, and I told her to go on in and let her mother sleep. I stood there those last few minutes, looking through sudden amazed tears at all that age and remembering my dead father.

Evening was coming on but the heat was everywhere still. I took the steps slowly down, and as I expected the old dog came up, and I waited while he decided what to do about me. Over the sounds of his smelling there came a crowd of high rushing nameless notes and her voice among them, low and quiet and firm on the air, "*You* can see them little birds can't you, Mr. Phil? I used to take a joy watching them little fellows playing before they went to sleep."

I knew it would be wrong to answer now, but I looked without a word to where her open eyes rested across the road to the darkening field and the two chimneys, and yes, they were there, going off against the evening like out of pistols, hard dark bullets that arched dark on the sky and curled and showered to the sturdy trees beneath.

BOB SHACOCHIS

Bob Shacochis is a native of Virginia, a former Peace Corps volunteer, and a graduate of the University of Iowa Writers' Workshop. His first collection of short fiction, *Easy in the Islands* (1985), won the American Book Award for First Fiction. His second collection, *The Next New World,* was published in 1989.

Easy in the Islands

THE days were small, pointless epics, long windups to punches that always drifted by cartoon-fashion, as if each simple task were meaningless unless immersed in more theater and threat than bad opera.

It was only Monday noon and already Tillman had been through the wringer. He had greased the trade commissioner to allow a pallet of Campbell's consommé to come ashore, fired one steel band for their hooliganism and hired another, found a carpenter he was willing to trust to repair the back veranda that was so spongy in spots Tillman knew it was only a matter of days before a guest's foot burst through the surface into whatever terrors lived below in the tepid darkness, restocked on vitamins from the pharmacy, argued with the crayfish regulatory bureau about quotas. And argued with the inscrutable cook, a fat countrywoman who wore a wool cap and smoked hand-rolled cigars, argued with both maids, muscle-bound Lemonille and the other one who wouldn't reveal her name, argued with the gardener who liked to chop everything up, argued with the customs house, argued with the bartender Jevanee. And although he had not forthrightly won any of these encounters, he had won them enough to forestall the doom that would one day descend on Rosehill Plantation.

But now the daily defeats and victories were overshadowed by a first-class doozy, a default too personal to implicate the local population. The problem was to decide what to do about his mother—Mother, who had thought life wonderful in the islands. Now she rested stiffly in the food locker, dead and coated with frost, blue as the shallow water on the reefs, protected from the fierceness of the sun she once loved without question or fear, a sun that was never really her enemy, no matter how it textured her skin, no matter what it revealed of her age.

In her room on Saturday, Mother had died mysteriously. As Lemonille had said when the two of them carried her out after the doctor had been there, *Mistah Till-mahn, it look so you muddah shake out she heart fah no good reason. Like she tricked by some false light, ya know.*

His mother's body had been strong and brassy, her spirit itself unusually athletic for a woman only weeks away from sixty. In her quick laugh was as much vitality as a girl's, and yet she had died. In bed, early in the evening, disdainful of the bars and clubs, reading a book—Colette, rediscovered on her latest continental visit—her finger ready to turn the page. Tillman was astonished. Only after Dr. Bradley had told him that he suspected his mother was poisoned did Tillman begin to calm down, his imperturbable self returning by degrees. Such a conclusion made no sense. The terms of life in the islands were that nothing ever made sense, unless you were a mystic or a politician, or studied both with ambition. Then every stupidness seemed an act of inspiration, every cruelty part of a divine scheme. There was no dialectic here, only the obverting of all possibilities until caprice made its selection.

Dr. Bradley couldn't be sure though. Neither he nor any of the other three sanctioned doctors on the island knew how to perform an autopsy with sufficient accuracy to assure each other or anybody else of the exact nature of death when the cause was less than obvious. Still, Bradley earned moments of miraculous credibility, as when the former Minister of Trade was brought into the hospital dead of a gunshot wound in his chest. To the government's relief, Bradley determined the cause of death as "heart failure," an organic demise, and unembarrassing.

"I will take your permission, mahn, to cut de body open ahnd look in she stomach," Dr. B. had said to Tillman as they stood over his mother's corpse in the sunny hotel room on Sunday morning, a breeze off the ocean dancing the curtains open, billowing sunlight throughout the room and then sucking it back outside. A spray of creamy rosebuds tapped against the louvered window, an eerie beckoning in the air silenced by death.

"For God's sake, why?" Tillman had said. It sounded like an ultimate obscenity, to have this fool with his meatcutter's stubby hands groping in his mother's abdomen.

"To determine what she eat aht de time of succumption."

"I told you what she was eating," Tillman said, exasperated. "She was eating a can of peaches with a spoon. Look here, there are still some left in the can." He shook the can angrily and syrup slopped onto his wrist. In disgust, Tillman wiped the sticky wetness on his pants, half nauseated, associating the liquid with some oozy by-product of dissolution. "Take the peaches if you need something to cut into, but you're not taking Mother. This isn't one of your Bottom Town cadavers."

Bradley had reacted with a shrug, and a patronizing twist to his smile. "Dis racial complexity—what a pity, mahn."

How often Tillman had heard this lie, so facile, from the lips of bad men.

"One world," he said, biting down on the syllables as if they were a condemnation, or a final sorrow. "We all live in one world. What's so goddamn complex about that?"

Tillman refused to let him remove the body from Rosehill. He wrapped his mother in the mauve chenille bedspread she had been lying on, restacked several crates of frozen chicken parts, and arranged her in the walk-in freezer until he could figure out just what to do. It was easy to accept the fact that you couldn't trust a doctor in such circumstances. What was most unacceptable was that Bradley had told the police there was a possibility the old lady had been murdered. The police, of course, were excited by this news. They sent Inspector Cuffy over the Rosehill to inform Tillman that he was under suspicion.

"You're kidding," Tillman said.

He suggested the inspector should walk down to the beach bar the hotel maintained on the waterfront and have a drink courtesy of the house while he took care of two new guests who had just arrived in a taxi from the airport. "I don't believe it," the new man said in an aside to Tillman as he checked them in. "The skycaps at the airport whistled at my wife and called her a whore." His wife stood demurely by his side, looking a bit overwhelmed. He could see the dark coronas of nipples under her white muslin sundress.

"Hey, people here are more conservative than you might think," Tillman told the couple, and to the woman he added, "Unless you want little boys rubbing up against your leg, you shouldn't wear shorts or a bathing suit into town."

"But this is the tropics," the woman protested in an adolescent voice, looking at Tillman as if he were only being silly.

"Right," Tillman conceded, handing over the key. He escorted the couple to their room, helping with the luggage, and wished them well. Wished himself a dollar for every time their notion of paradise would be fouled by some rudeness, aggression, or irrelevant accusation.

He crossed back over the veranda out onto the cobbled drive, past the derelict stone tower of the windmill where every other Saturday the hotel sponsored a goat roast that was well attended by civil servants, Peace Corps volunteers and whatever tourists were around, down the glorious green lawn crazy with blossom, down, hot and sweaty, to the palm grove, the bamboo beach bar on its fringe, the lagoon dipping into the land like a blue pasture, Tillman walking with his hands in the pockets of his loose cotton pants, reciting a calypso and feeling, despite his troubles, elected, an aristocrat of the sensual latitudes, anointed to all the earthly privileges ordinary people dreamed about on their commuter trains fifty weeks a year. No matter that in a second-class Eden nothing was as unprofitable as the housing of its guests. Even loss seemed less discouraging in the daily flood of sun.

Jevanee was glaring at him from behind the bar. And the inspector sat grandly on his stool, satisfied with being the bigshot, bearing a smile that welcomed Tillman as if they were to be partners in future prosperity, as if the venture they were to embark on could only end profitably. He gave a little wink before he tipped his green bottle of imported beer and sank the neck between his lips.

"Dis a sad affair, mahn," he said, wagging his round head. Jevanee uncapped a second bottle and set it before the inspector, paying no attention to Tillman's presence. Tillman drew a stool up beside Cuffy and perched on its edge, requesting Jevanee to bring another beer, and watched with practiced patience as the bartender kicked about and finally delivered the bottle as if it were his life's savings.

"What is it with you, Jevanee? What am I doing wrong?" The bartender had come with Rosehill when he had inherited the hotel eight months ago. Somebody had trained him to be a terror.

"Mistah Trick!" Jevanee whooped. He was often too self-conscious to confront his employer head-on. Nevertheless he would not accept even the mildest reproach without an extravagant line of defense or, worse, smoldering until his tongue ignited and his hands flew threateningly, shouting in a tantrum that would go on forever with or without an audience, a man who would never be employed to his satisfaction. He turned his back on Tillman and began muttering at the whiskey bottles arrayed on the work island in the center of the oval bar.

"Mistah Trick, he say what him doin wrong, de devil. He say daht he mean, Jevanee, why you is a chupid boy ahs black as me boot cahnt count change ahnd show yah teef nice aht de white lady? He say daht he mean, Jevanee, why you cahnt work fah free like you grahnpoppy? Why you cahnt bring you sistah here ta please me?" Without ceasing his analysis of what the white man had meant, he marched out from the bar and into the bushes to take a leak. Tillman forced himself not to react any further to Jevanee's rage, which appeared to be taking on a decidedly historical sweep.

The inspector, who had not shown any interest in Jevanee's complaints, began to tap the long nail of his index finger on the surface of the bar. He made a show of becoming serious without wanting to deprive Tillman of his informality, his compassion, his essential sympathy, etcetera—all the qualities he believed he possessed and controlled to his benefit.

"Who else, Tillmahn, but you?" Cuffy finally concluded as if it hurt him to say this. "Undah-stahnd, is only speculation."

"Who else but me?" Tillman sputtered. "Are you crazy?" The inspector frowned and Tillman immediately regretted his choice of words. Cuffy was as willfully unpredictable as most everybody else on the island, but in a madhouse, an outsider soon learned, truth was always a prelude to disaster, the match dropped thoughtlessly onto tinder. He should have said, Look, how can you think that? or Man, what will it take to end this unfortunate business? But too late. The inspector was pinching at his rubbery nose, no longer even considering Tillman, looking out across the harbor, and anchored sailboats bobbing like a display of various possibilities, playing the image of artful calculation for his suspect.

Tillman sighed. "Why do you think I would kill my own mother? She was my *mother.* What son could harm the woman who carried him into the world?"

The inspector pursed his lips and then relaxed them. "Well, Tillmahn, perhahps you do it to have title to dis property, true?"

The absurdity was too great even for Tillman, a connoisseur of island nonsense. "To inherit this property!" Now Tillman had to laugh, regardless of the inspector's feelings. "Cuffy, nobody wants this place. In his will my father was excessively sorry for burdening me with Rosehill Plantation and advised I sell it at the first opportunity. My mother had absolutely no claim to Rosehill. He divorced her long ago."

Tillman paused. As far as he could tell, he was the only one in the world, besides the government, who wanted Rosehill Plantation. It had been on the market for years, not once receiving an honest offer. Its profits were marginal, its overhead crushing. But the hotel was his, so why not be there. What he had found through it was unexpected—the inexplicable sense that life on the island had a certain fullness, that it was, far beyond what he had ever experienced back home, authentic in the most elemental ways.

Cuffy had become petulant, studying him as if he were spoiled, an unappreciative child. Tillman was not intimidated. "Why should I tell you this anyway? It has absolutely no relevance to my mother's death."

"Um hmm, um hmm, I see," the inspector said. "So perhahps you muddah take a lovah, a dark mahn, ahnd you become vexed wit she fah behavin so. You warn her to stop but she refuse. So . . ." He threw out his hands as if the rest of the scene he conceived was there before him. "Is just speculation."

Tillman was tiring fast. Inspector Cuffy had no use for what was and what wasn't; his only concern was his own role in the exercise of authority. It killed boredom, boredom amid the splendor. It created heroes and villains, wealth and poverty. No other existence offered him so much.

He discovered that he was grinding his teeth and the muscles in his jaw ached. Jevanee had slipped back behind the bar, and every time Tillman glanced over there, Jevanee, now bold, tried to stare him down.

"My mother was an old lady," he told the inspector. "She was beyond love. She liked books and beaches, fruit, seafood, and rare wines. Traveling. There was no man in her life. There never was. She was even a stranger to my father."

"You just a boy," Cuffy noted in a way that made Tillman think it was a line the inspector must use frequently. "Nobody beyond love, ya know."

"So?"

"So, nobody beyond pahssion, ahnd nobody beyond crime." Tillman blinked. Damn, he thought, Cuffy's starting to make sense.

"Even ahn old womahn need a good roll to keep she happy," the inspector concluded.

"Oh, for Christ's sake," Tillman said, standing up. "I have to get back."

He couldn't get away before Jevanee butted in. Ignore Jevanee and life might possibly go on. The bartender used his mouth like a gun, the words popping spitefully while he focused on whatever spirit he had summoned to witness his oppression.

"Daht ol boney-bag he call his muddah grabbin aht every blahck boy on de beach. I see it wit me own eyes."

"Jevanee, shut up."

"Oh, yes, massa, suh. Yes, massa." He feigned excessive servitude, wiping the bar counter, the cash box, the bamboo supports with his shirt sleeve. The time would come when Tillman would have to face up to Jevanee's vindictiveness. He had been steaming ever since Tillman had told him not to hand out free drinks to his friends from the village. Jevanee insisted no one but Rosehill's tourists, who were not regular, would ever patronize the beach bar if it weren't for him. Maybe he was right. Nobody was coming around anymore except on Friday nights when the band played. More and more, Jevanee wanted Tillman to understand that he was a dangerous man, his every move a challenge to his employer. Tillman was still trying to figure out how to fire the guy without a lot of unpleasantness.

"Don't listen to Jevanee," Tillman told the inspector. "He's pissed at me these days because of a disagreement we had over a charitable instinct of his."

"I give me bruddah a drink," Jevanee said in a self-deprecating way, as though he were the victim and Cuffy would understand. Jevanee's mood would only escalate if Tillman explained that the bartender's "bruddah" was consuming a case of Scotch on his drier visits, so he refused to debate Jevanee's claim. The inspector turned on his stool with the cold expression of a man whose duty it is to make it known that he must hurt you severely, that he may cripple you or make you weep, if you disobey him.

"Look now, you," he said, taking moral pleasure in this chastisement. "Doan you make trouble fah Mistah Tillmahn. You is lucky he give you work."

"Dis white bitch doan give me a damn ting," Jevanee snarled, shaking an empty beer bottle at Tillman. "I work is dis same spot a long time when he show up. Ahnd what you doin kissin he ahss?"

"Doan talk aht me daht way, boy, or I fuck you up. Hell goin have a new bahtendah soon if you cahnt behave."

Jevanee tried to smile, a taut earnestness that never quite made it to his mouth. Tillman arranged chairs around the warped café tables, backing away.

"Okay then, Cuffy. I'm glad we had this opportunity to straighten everything out. Stay and have another beer if you want."

Cuffy looked at his gold wristwatch. "You will be around in de aftahnoon?"

"Why?"

"I wish to view de deceased."

"Uh, can't it wait till tomorrow?" Tillman asked. "I have errands to run in town. A shipment of beef is coming in from Miami."

From his shirt pocket, Cuffy had taken a note pad and was scribbling in it. He talked without raising his head. "Okay, dere's no hurry. De old womahn takin she time goin nowheres."

Tillman nodded, now in stride with the process, the havoc of it. "Cuffy, you're a thorough man. If anybody's going to get to the bottom of this mess, it's you."

The inspector accepted this flattery as his due, too certain of its validity to bother about the subtle mocking edge to Tillman's voice. His eyes were relaxed, hooded and moist. Tillman started up the footpath through the palms, kicking a coconut ahead of him, a leaden soccer ball, turning once to check what fared in his absence: and yes Cuffy and Jevanee had their heads together, the bartender animated, swinging his hands, the inspector with his arms crossed on his wide chest. Jevanee had too much energy today. Maybe his attitude would defuse if he were somewhere other than the bar for a while. He seemed to live there. Tillman shouted back down to them. "Jevanee, after the inspector leaves, lock everything up and take the rest of the day off."

The bartender ignored him.

Tillman jogged up the perfect lawn along an avenue of floral celebration—tree-sized poinsettias, arrow ginger, bougainvillea, oleander—a perfumist's tray of fragrance. On the knoll, graced with a vista of the channel, was the old plantation house, a stubborn remnant of colonial elegance, its whitewashed brick flaking in a way that benefited the charm of its archaic construction, the faded red of the gabled tin roof a human comfort against the green monotonous sheets of the mountains that were its background. Farther south, the cone shell of the windmill stood like a guard tower or last refuge. Tillman had huddled there with his guests last summer during a hurricane, the lot of them drunk and playing roundhouse bridge, the cards fluttering from the storm outside.

When he was a teenager Tillman had flown down to the island during a summer off from Exeter to help his father build the two modern wings that flanked the manor, one-level box rooms side by side, as uninspired as any lodging on any Florida roadside. Tillman's father was a decent man, completely involved in his scheming though his interest invariably flagged once a puzzle was solved, a challenge dispatched. The old man had worked for J. D. Root, one of the big ad agencies in New York, handling the Detroit accounts. His final act was an irony unappreciated—he perished in one of the cars he promoted, losing control on the Northway one rainy evening. He had gone fishing up on the St. Lawrence, convinced this time he would hook a muskellunge. Rosehill Plantation was his most daring breakaway but he never really had time for the place. Throughout his ownership, Rosehill lost money and after his death the checks from the estate in New York flowed like aid from the mother country. When a lawyer's telegram reached Tillman, asking if he wanted to pursue more aggressively the sale of the plantation, he decided to dump the Lower East Side loft where he had been sweating out the draft for two years since graduate school and make his claim on Rosehill. Nixon had just been reelected. The States no longer seemed like the right place to be.

Awash in perspiration, Tillman turned the corner around the east wing, his blood pressure a little jumpy, the skin on his face at the point of combustion, wondering if all the friction of a fast life could suddenly cause a person to burst into flame. Sometimes he felt as if it were happening. It wasn't very easy to find peace on the island unless you hiked up into the mountains. Whereas it was very easy to catch hell.

In the exterior courtyard behind the estate house, the new arrivals, husband and wife from Wilmington, Delaware, were inspecting one of Tillman's few unequivocable successes, the gazebo that housed his parrot aviary, in it seven of the last rainbow parrots on earth. The project was really the veterinarian's at the Ministry of Agriculture, a man who hated goats and cows but spent all his spare time bird-watching or digging up pre-Columbian artifacts, storing them in his living room until the far-off day a museum would be built. Together he and Tillman waged a public campaign on the island, the parrots' sole habitat, to prevent their extinction. A law was passed for appearances, its advantage being that it clearly defined for the bird smugglers *who* needed to be paid off and *who* could be bypassed with impunity.

After the crusade, Tillman decided to contact some poachers himself. They were kids, tough miniature bandits, the nest robbers. One was nine, the other eleven. Basil and Jacob, tree climbers extraordinaire, both as skinny as vanilla beans. They lived in a mountain village, a clump of wattle huts, one of the outposts before the vast roadless center of the island, all sharp peaks, palisades and jungle. When the hatching season had ended, Tillman and the boys trekked into the lush interior, camping overnight, Tillman's neck strained from looking up into the canopy, his ears confused by the wraithish shrieks and skraws—*skra-aaa-aw!*—unable to pinpoint where the sound came from in the infinite cathedral of growth. But the kids knew their business. They were fearless, scaling to the top of the highest mahogany or madrone, indifferent to the slashing beaks of the females who refused to abandon the nest, shinnying down the trunks with the chicks held gently in their mouths, polycolored cotton balls, the fierce tiny heads lolling helplessly out from between the embrace of boyish lips.

Tillman thought he would tell his guests from Delaware the story. The woman was scrutinizing the birds rather sternly. She would cluck and whistle at them, tap the chicken wire wall of the cage, but she did so without affection. When he finished talking, she turned to look at him, her eyes obscured behind oversized sunglasses, her mouth in a pout. Tillman guessed she was a bank teller, something that had made her very sure of herself without placing any demand on her intelligence.

"It's cruel," she said.

"It is not cruel. It's heroic. These islands have a way of forcing everything but the lowest common denominator into oblivion."

"Hero," she said sardonically. The husband looked skeptical. Light reflected off her glasses and sliced back at Tillman. He shrugged his shoulders. Perhaps he should bar Americans from Rosehill. Canadians made the better tourist. They allowed for a world outside themselves.

The Land Rover started painfully, a victim of mechanical arthritis. Soon it would take no more to the prosthetic miracle of wire, tin, and hardware junk. Spare parts appeared from across the ocean as often as Halley's comet.

Onto the narrow blacktop road that circumnavigated the island, Tillman drove with reckless courage and whipping flair, showing inner strength when he refused to give way to two flatbed lorries painted up like Easter eggs, one named *Sweetfish*, the other *Dr. Lick*, passengers clinging to everything but the wheel hubs, racing down the coastal hill side by side straight at him, *Dr. Lick* overtaking *Sweetfish* just as Tillman downshifted reluctantly to third and toed the brake pedal. Someday the lorries would spread carnage across this highway, Tillman thought. It would be a national event, the island equivalent of a 747 going down.

In the capital, a pastel city breathtaking from the heights above it but garbage-strewn and ramshackle once you were on its streets, Tillman honked his way through the crowds down along Front Street, inching his way to the docks. On the quay, three pallets of frozen steaks destined for Rosehill were sweating pink juice onto the dirty concrete. Beef from the island was as tough and stringy as rug; if a hotel wanted to serve food worthy of the name, it had to import almost everything but fish. He located the purser in one of the rum-and-cake sheds that filled every unclaimed inch of the wharves like derelict carnival booths. There was no use complaining about the shipment being off-loaded without anybody being there to receive it. That was Tillman's fault—

he had been too preoccupied. He signed the shipping order and then scrambled to hire a driver and boys to break down the pallets and truck the cartons out to Rosehill's freezer before the meat thawed completely.

There were other errands, less urgent—to the marketing board in search of the rare tomato, to the post office, to the stationer for a ballpoint pen, to the pharmacist, who was disappointed when Tillman only bought aspirin. Most of his regular white customers spent small fortunes on amphetamines or Quaaludes. When Tillman had finished there, he drove over to the national hospital on the edge of town. Without a death certificate from Bradley, Mother was destined to be the morbid champion of cryogenics, the Queen of Ice in a land where water never froze in nature.

The old colonial hospital was a structure and a system bypassed by any notion of modernity. Someone yelled at him as he entered the shadowed foyer, but it wasn't apparent who or why. The rough wooden floorboards creaked under his feet. The maze of hallways seemed to be a repository for loiterers—attendants, nurses, nuns, clerks, superfluous guards, mangled patients, talking, weeping, spending the day in rigid silence. One naked little boy asleep on the floor, hugging the wall.

He found Dr. Bradley's office and went through the door without knocking. Bradley, chief surgeon, head physician of St. George's National People's Hospital, an agnostic operation if Tillman ever saw one, was reading a paperback romance, a man hovering over a fallen woman on its cover. The room smelled of sweet putrefaction and Lysol. The scent of jasmine wafted in through open screenless windows. Tillman sat down on a wooden bench against one bare wall. Flies buzzed along the ceiling. Bradley slowly broke off from his reading, dropping his feet one by one from where they were propped on the broad windowsill. His lab coat, smudged with yellow stains and laundered blood, sagged away from his middle. He recognized Tillman and smiled grudgingly.

"Mahn, I been callin you, ya know. I examine dem peaches you muddah eat. Dey was no good. I think we solve dis big mystery."

Tillman knew this was his chance to end the affair but he could not forgive Bradley his smugness, his careless manner, the suffering he had sown.

"You're sure? What'd you do, feed them to a chicken and the chicken died?"

"Mahn, Tillman, you doan have enough troubles, you must come make some wit me? Why is daht?"

"You're telling me she died of botulism?"

"It seem so, seem so."

Tillman was incited to fury. "Botulism, Doctor, causes vomiting and extreme pain. How can you not know that? My mother died a peaceful death."

Bradley turned with eyes murderous. "If it's so, de autopsy prove so, I cahnt know oddahwise."

"You're not touching her. Somebody else can do it, but not you."

"Mahn, daht's irrational."

Tillman jumped up from the bench and stood in front of the doctor's cluttered desk. "You'd be the last person on eath to touch her."

"Get out, Tillmahn."

Tillman was in no hurry leave. "Remember Freddy Allen?" he asked.

"Who?" Then Bradley remembered and his face lost its arrogance.

"He was a friend of mine, a good one. He helped me out at Rosehill whenever I needed it."

"Tillmahn, consider I am only human."

"Yes, you are. So was Freddy until he came to you. You gave him bromides for acute appendicitis. The damn vet can diagnose better than you."

Bradley stood so fast, his eyes full of menace, that Tillman tensed to defend himself. "Get out," he shouted, pointing his finger at Tillman. "You muddah now a permahnent guest aht Rosehill till you come to you senses. Get out." The doctor came around from his desk to open the office door and then kicked it shut behind him.

Tillman, island hotelier, master of the business arts, student of impossibility, fond of weather that rarely oppressed, a man of contingencies and recently motherless—Tillman knew what to do. Whatever it took.

Whatever it took, Tillman told himself, back out on the streets, heedless in the late afternoon traffic. Sometimes that meant nothing at all, sometimes the gods spared you muckery, blessed you with style, and everything was easy.

At the airport he parked next to a single taxi out front, no one around to note this familiar island tune, the prolonged pitch of tires violently braked. Through the dark empty airport that always reminded him of an abandoned warehouse, Tillman searched for his friend Roland, the freelance bush pilot from Australia, a maverick and proven ace. Roland leapt around the warm world in his old Stearmann, spraying mountainsides of bananas with chemicals that prevented leaf spot and other blights. Tillman suspected the pilot was also part of the interisland ring sponsored by the most influential businessmen to smuggle drugs, whiskey, cigarettes, stereos—whatever contraband could be crammed surreptitiously into the fuselage of a small plane. He seemed to be able to come and go as he pleased.

Roland's plane wasn't on the tarmac, or in the hangar. Sunset wasn't far away. Wherever Roland was, waltzing his plane through green, radical valleys, he would have to return before dark if he was coming in tonight. Tillman left a message with a mechanic in the machine shed for Roland to come find him at Rosehill.

Twilight had begun to radiate through the vegetation as he arrived back at the hotel, lifting the mélange of colors to a higher level of brilliance, as if each plant, each surface, were responding to the passage of the sun with its own interior luminosity. Inspector Cuffy was on the veranda of the west wing, laughing with Lemonille, her eyes flirtatious. They clammed up when Tillman appeared beside them.

"You haven't been waiting for me, have you?"

"Well, doan trouble yourself, mahn. I been interviewin dis pretty young lady."

Tillman looked at Lemonille, who averted her eyes shyly. "Perhaps we cahn view de body of you muddah now." Cuffy said this without the slightest conviction. Tillman understood that, for the time being, the inspector was only interested in chasing Lemonille.

"I've had a hell of a day. Can I ask you to wait until tomorrow?"

"Daht strike me ahs reasonable," Cuffy said, allowing Tillman to experience his generosity.

"Besides, case solved, Cuffy," Tillman said, remembering the doctor, the hospital. "Bradley says something was wrong with the can of peaches my mother was eating when she died." If you want to believe such crap, Tillman added under his breath.

"I will study daht report," the inspector said. From the way he spoke, Tillman knew the investigation would drag on for days, weeks—especially if Lemonille played hard to get.

"Mistah Till-mahn?" Lemonille buried her chin, afraid to speak now that she had drawn attention to herself. More woe, thought Tillman. More hue and cry.

"What's wrong?"

"De cook say she fraid wit you dead muddah in de freezah. She say she not cookin wit a duppy so close by."

"All right, I'll go talk to her."

"She gone home."

"All right, I'll take care of it." He began to walk away.

"Mistah Till-mahn?" The big woman's soft and guarded voice made him stop and turn around.

"What, Lemonille?"

"De men come wit de meat, but dey won't stock it."

Tillman inhaled nervously. "My mother again, right?"

Lemonille nodded. "Damn!" Tillman said, and scuffed the dirt.

Lemonille had one last piece of news. "Jevanee in a fuss cause you fire him."

"I didn't fire him. I told him to take the day off."

"Oh."

"Cuffy was there. He heard me." Cuffy looked into the trees and would not support or deny this allegation.

"Oh. But Jevanee tellin every bug in de sky you fire him. Daht mahn be fulla dread you goin put him out since de day you poppy die."

"Well, it's not true. Tell him that when you see him."

Tillman took these developments in stride, closing the restaurant for the evening by posting a scrawled note of apology at the entrance to the modest dining hall in the manor. For an hour he shuffled the cartons of dripping steaks from the kitchen to the freezer, stacking them around the corpse of his mother as if these walls of spoiling meat were meant to be her tomb.

Event upon event—any day in the islands could keep accumulating such events until it was overrich, festering, or glorious, never to be reproduced so wonderfully. This day was really no different except that his mother had triggered some extraordinary complications that were taking him to the limit.

After showering in cold water, Tillman climbed the stairs in the main house to the sanctitude of his office, his heart feeling too dry for blood to run through it, another fire hazard. What's to be done with Mother? On a hotplate he heated water for tea, sat with the steaming mug before the phone on his desk. Ministry offices would be closed at this hour and besides, the Minister of Health was no friend of his so there was no use ringing him up.

Finally he decided to call Dr. Layland. If Layland still were running the island's medical services, the day would have been much simpler, but Layland, a surgeon who had earned international respect for his papers on brain dysfunction in the tropics, had lost his job and his license to practice last winter when he refused to allow politics to interfere with the delicate removal of a bullet from an opposition member's neck. Although the case was before the Federation there was little hope of reinstatement before next year's elections.

Frankly, Layland told him, his accent bearing the vestige of an Oxford education, your position is most unenviable, my friend. A burial certificate, likewise permission to transfer the corpse back to its native soil, must be issued by both the national police and the Chief Medical Officer. The police, pending their own investigation of the cause of death, will not act without clearance from the CMO. In cases where the cause is unclear, it is unlikely that the CMO will agree to such clearance, especially for an expatriate Caucasian, until an autopsy is performed.

"But Bradley said it was the peaches, a bad can of peaches." Tillman jerked his head away from the telephone. How absurd and false those words sounded.

"Unlikely, but I see what you're getting at. Any cause is better than none, in light of your problem. But you know what sort of humbug that foolish man is. And you shan't have him on your side since you refused to have him do the autopsy."

Layland further explained that there was no alternative to removing the corpse from the walk-in freezer unless he had another to put it in, or unless he committed it to the island's only morgue in the basement of the prison at Fort Albert—again, Bradley's domain. The final solution would be to bury her at Rosehill, but even this could not be accomplished without official permits. The police would come dig her up. Tillman asked if it was a mistake not to allow Bradley to cut open his mother.

"I'm afraid. Tillman, you must decide that for yourself," Layland answered. "But I think you must know that I am as disgusted by my erstwhile colleague as you are. Well, good luck."

Tillman pushed the phone away, rubbed his sore eyes, massaged the knots in his temples. He tilted back in his chair and almost went over backward, caught unaware by a flood of panic. Unclean paradise, he thought suddenly. What about Mother? Damn, she was dead and needed taking care of. Hard to believe. Lord, why did she come here anyway? She probably knew she was dying and figured the only dignified place to carry out the fact was under the roof of her only child. A mother's final strategy.

Outside on the grounds one of the stray dogs that were always about began a rabid barking. Tillman listened more closely, the sounds of squawking audible between the gaps in the dog's racket. The protest grew louder, unmistakable; Tillman was down the stairs and out on the dark lawn in no time at all, running toward the aviary.

There was some light from the few bulbs strung gaily through the branches of frangipani that overhung the parking area, enough to see what was going on, the wickedness being enacted in blue-satin shadows. In the gazebo, an angry silhouette swung a cutlass back and forth, lashing at the amorphous flutter of wings that seemed everywhere in the tall cage.

"Jevanee?" Tillman called, uncertain. The silhouette reeled violently, froze in its step and then burst through the door of the cage, yelling.

"Mahn, you cy-ahnt fire me, *I quit.*"

Tillman cringed at the vulgarity of such a dissembled non sequitur. All the bad television in the world, the stupid lyrics of false heroes, the latent rage of kung-fu and cowboy fantasies had entered into this man's head and here was the result, some new breed of imperial slave and his feeble, fatuous uprising.

"I didn't fire you. I said take the day off, cool down."

"Cy-ahnt fire *me,* you bitch."

The parrots were dead. Hatred exploded through Tillman. He wanted to kill the bartender. Fuck it. He wanted to shoot him down. He sprinted back across the lawn, up on the veranda toward the main house for the gun kept locked in the supply closet behind the check-in desk. Jevanee charged after him. A guest, the woman recently arrived from Wilmington, stepped out in front of Tillman from her room that fronted the veranda. Tillman shoulder-blocked her back through the door. She sprawled on her ass and for a second Tillman saw on her face an expression that welcomed violence as if it were an exotic game she had paid for.

"Stay in your goddamn room and bolt the door."

Tillman felt the bad TV engulfing them, the harried script writer unbalanced with drugs and spite. Jevanee's foot plunged through the rotten boards in the veranda and lodged there. An exodus of pestilence swarmed from the splintery hole into the dim light, palmetto bugs flying blindly up through a growing cloud of smaller winged insects.

At the same time, stepping out from the darkness of a hedge of bougainvillea that ran in bushy clumps along the veranda, was Inspector Cuffy, pistol in hand. Tillman gawked at him. What was he doing around Rosehill so late? Lemonille had been encouraging him or the investigation had broadened to round-the-clock foolishness. Or, Tillman surmised, knowing it was true, Cuffy apparently knew Jevanee was coming after him and had lurked on the premises until the pot boiled over. A shot whistled by Tillman's head. Jevanee had a gun, too. Tillman pitched back off the deck and flattened out in the shrubbery.

"Stop," Cuffy shouted.

What the hell, thought Tillman. Where's Jevanee going anyway? He was near enough to smell the heavily Scotched breath of the bartender, see his eyes as dumb and frightened as the eyes of a wild horse. Another shot was fired off. Then a flurry of them as the two men emptied their pistols at each other with no effect. Silence and awkwardness as Cuffy and Jevanee confronted one another, the action gone out of them, praying thanks for the lives they still owned. Tillman crawled away toward the main house. He couldn't care less how they finished the drama, whether they killed each other with their bare hands, or retired together to a rum shop, blaming Tillman for the sour fate of the island. There was no point in getting upset about it now, once the hate had subsided, outdone by the comics.

He sat in the kitchen on the cutting table, facing the vaultlike aluminum door of the refrigerated walk-in where his mother lay, preserved in ice, her silence having achieved, finally, a supreme hardness.

He wanted to talk to her, but even in death she seemed only another guest at the hotel, one with special requirements, nevertheless expecting courtesy and service, the proper distance kept safely between their lives. She had never kissed him on the lips, not once, but only brushed his cheek when an occasion required some tangible sign of motherly devotion. He had never been closer to her heart than when they cried together the first year he was in prep school, explaining to him that she was leaving his father. She had appeared in his room late at night, having driven up from the city. She tuned the radio loud to a big band station and held him, the two of them shivering against each other on his bed. For her most recent visitation she had not written she was coming but showed up unannounced with only hand luggage—a leather grip of novels, a variety of modest bathing suits, caftans and creams. Behind her she had left Paris, where the weather had begun its decline toward winter. Whatever else she had left behind in her life was as obscure and sovereign as a foreign language. He wanted to talk to her but nothing translated.

The pilot found him there sometime in the middle of the night, Tillman forlorn, more tired than he could ever remember feeling. Roland looked worn out, too, as if he had been stuck in an engine for hours, his cutoff shorts and colorless T-shirt smudged with grease, his hiking boots unlaced, and yet despite this general dishevelment his self-confidence was as apparent as the gleam of his teeth. Tillman remembered him at the beach bar late one night, yelling into the face of a man dressed in a seersucker suit, "I get things done, damn you, not like *these* bloody fools," and the sweep of his arm seemed to include the entire planet.

Tillman smiled mournfully back at him. "Roland, I need your help."

The pilot removed the mirrored sunglasses he wore at all times. "You've had a full day of it, I hear. What's on your mind, mate?"

Like an unwieldy piece of lumber, his mother's corpse banged to and fro in the short bed of the Land Rover, her wrapped feet pointing up over the tailgate. With a little effort and jockeying, they fitted her into the tube-shaped chemical tank in the fuselage of the Stearmann after Roland, Tillman standing by with a flashlight, unbolted two plates of sheet metal from the underbelly of the craft that concealed bay doors. You can't smuggle bales of grass with only a nozzle and a funnel, Roland explained.

Tillman was worried that an unscheduled flight would foul up Roland's good grace with the authorities. Man, Roland said, I've got more connections than the friggin PM. And I mean of the UK, not this bloody cowpie. He thought for a second and was less flamboyant. I've been in trouble before, of course. Nobody, Tillman, can touch this boy from down under as long as I have me bird, you see. Let us now lift upward into the splendid atmosphere and its many bright stars.

The chemical tank smelled cloyingly of poison. With his head poked in it, Tillman gagged, maneuvering the still-rigid body of his mother, the limbs clunking dully against the shiny metal, until she was positioned. Roland geared the bay doors back in place. The sound of them clicking into their locks brought relief to Tillman. They tucked themselves into the tiny cockpit. Tillman sat behind the pilot's seat, his legs flat against the floorboard, straddled as if he were riding a bobsled.

The airport shut down at dusk, the funding for runway lights never more than deadpan rhetoric during the height of the political season. Roland rested his sunglasses on the crown of his blond head as they taxied to the landward end of the strip, the mountains a cracked ridge behind them, the sea ahead down the length of pale concrete. Out there somewhere in the water, an incompatibly situated cay stuck up like a catcher's mitt for small planes whose pilots were down on their agility and nerve.

Roland switched off the lights on the instrumentation to cut all reflection in the cockpit. Transparent blackness, the gray runway stretching into nearby infinity.

Roland shouted over the roar, "She's a dumpy old bird but with no real cargo we should have some spirited moments."

Even as Roland spoke they were already jostling down the airstrip like an old hot rod on a rutted road, Tillman anticipating lift-off long before it actually happened. The slow climb against gravity seemed almost futile, the opaque hand of the cay suddenly materializing directly in front of them. Roland dropped a wing and slammed the rudder pedal. The Stearmann veered sharply away from the hazard, then leveled off and continued mounting upward. Tillman could hear his mother thump in the fuselage.

"Bit of a thrill," Roland shouted. Tillman closed his eyes and endured the languid speed and the hard grinding vibrations of the plane.

Roland put on his headset and talked to any ghost he could rouse. When Tillman opened his eyes again, the clouds out the windscreen had a tender pink sheen to their tops. The atmosphere tingled with blueness. The ocean was black below them, and Barbados, ten degrees off starboard, was blacker still, a solid puddle sprinkled with electricity. Along the horizon the new day was a thin red thread unraveling westward. The beauty of it all made Tillman melancholy.

Roland floated the plane down to earth like a fat old goose who couldn't be hurried. The airport on Barbados was modern and received plenty of international traffic so they found it awake and active at this hour. Taxiing to the small plane tarmac, Tillman experienced a moment of claustrophobia, smelling only the acrid human sweat that cut through the mechanical fumes. He hadn't noticed it airborne but on the ground it was unbearable.

They parked and had the Stearmann serviced. In the wet, warm morning air Tillman's spirits revived. Roland walked through customs, headed for the bar to wait for him to do his business. Two hours later Tillman threw himself down in a chair next to the pilot and cradled his head on the sticky table, the surge of weariness through his back and neck almost making him pass out. He listened to Roland patiently suck his beer and commanded himself up to communicate the failure of the expedition.

"Bastards. They won't let me transfer her to a Stateside flight without the right paper."

"There was that chance," Roland admitted.

All along Tillman had believed that Barbados was the answer, people were reasonable there, that he had only to bring over the corpse of his mother, coffin her, place her on an Eastern flight to New York connecting with Boston, have a funeral home intercept her, bury her next to her ex-husband in the family plot on Beacon Hill. Send out death announcements to the few distant relatives scattered across the country, and then it would be over, back to normal. No mother, no obligations of blood. That was how she lived, anyway.

"Just how well connected are you, Roland?"

"Barbados is a bit iffy. The people are too damn sophisticated." He left to make some phone calls but returned with his hands out, the luckless palms upturned.

"Tillman, what next?"

Tillman exhaled and fought the urge to laugh, knowing it would mount to a hysterical outpouring of wretchedness. "I just don't know. Back to the island I guess. If you can see any other option, speak out. Please."

The pilot was unreadable behind the mirrors of his glasses. His young face had become loose and puffy since he had located Tillman at Rosehill. They settled their bar bill and left.

In the air again, the sound of the Stearmann rattled Tillman so thoroughly he felt as though the plane's engine were in his own skull. He tried to close his sleepless eyes against the killing brightness of the sun but could not stop the hypnotic flash that kept him staring below at the ocean. Halfway through the flight, Roland removed his headset and turned in his seat, letting the plane fly itself while he talked.

"Tillman," he shouted, "you realize I didn't bolt the plates back on the fuselage."

Tillman nodded absently and made no reply.

Roland jabbed his finger, pointing at the floor. "That handgear there by your foot opens the bay doors."

He resumed flying the plane, allowing Tillman his own thoughts. Tillman had none. He expected some inspiration or voice to break through his dizziness but it didn't happen. After several more minutes he tapped Roland on the shoulder. Roland turned again, lifting his glasses so Tillman could see his full face, his strained but resolute eyes, Tillman understanding this gesture as a stripping of fear, tacit confirmation that they were two men in the world capable of making such a decision without ruining themselves with ambiguity.

"Okay, Roland, the hell with it. She never liked being in one place too long anyway."

"Right you are, then," Roland said solemnly. "Any special spot?"

"No."

"Better this way," Roland yelled as he dropped the airspeed and sank the Stearmann to one thousand feet. "The thing that bothers me about burial, you see, is caseation. Your friggin body turns to cheese after a month in the dirt. How unspeakably nasty. I don't know if you've noticed, but I never eat cheese myself. Odd, isn't it?"

Tillman poked him on the shoulder again. "Knock it off."

"Sorry."

Tillman palmed the gear open. It was as easy as turning the faucet of a hose. When they felt her body dislodge and the tail bob inconsequentially, Roland banked the plane into a steep dive so they could view the interment. Tillman braced his hands against the windscreen and looked out, saw her cartwheeling for a moment and then stabilizing as the mauve chenille shroud came apart like a party streamer, a skydiver's Mae West. The Stearmann circled slowly around the invisible line of her descent through space.

"Too bad about your mother, mate," Roland called out finally. "My own, I don't remember much."

"I'm still young," Tillman confessed, surprising himself, the words blurting forth from his mouth unsolicited. Tears of gratitude slipped down his face from this unexpected report of the heart.

He looked down at the endless water, waves struggling and receding, the small carnation of foam marking his mother's entrance into the sea, saw her, through the medium of refraction, unwrapped from her shroud, naked and washed, crawling with pure, unlabored motion down the shafts of light and beyond their farthest reach, thawed into suppleness, small glass bubbles, the cold air of her last breath, expelled past her white lips, nuzzled by unnamed fish. Now she was a perfect swimmer, free of the air and the boundaries of the living, darkness passing through darkness, down, down, to kiss the silt of the ocean floor, to touch the bottom of the world with dead fingers.

They had watched her plummet with a sense of awe and wonderment, as boys would who have thrown an object from off a high bridge. The pilot regained altitude and they continued westward. The realization came into Tillman, a palpable weight in his chest. I don't belong here, he said to himself, and immediately resisted the feeling, because that must have been the way she felt all her life.

Then, with the rich peaks of the island in sight, the heaviness dissipated. "It's beautiful here," he heard himself saying.

"What's that?" Roland shouted back.

"Beautiful," he repeated, and throughout Roland's clumsy landing, the jolt and thunder of the runway, "Mother be at peace."

LEE SMITH

Lee Smith is a native of Richlands, Virginia. She is a graduate of Hollins College in Roanoke, Virginia. Currently, she teaches at North Carolina State University in Raleigh. She is the author of six novels, including *Oral History* and *Family Linen,* and a collection of short fiction, *Cakewalk* (1981).

Between the Lines

"PEACE be with you from Mrs. Joline B. Newhouse" is how I sign my columns. Now I gave some thought to that. In the first place, I like a line that has a ring to it. In the second place, what I have always tried to do with my column is to uplift my readers if at all possible, which sometimes it is not. After careful thought, I threw out "Yours in Christ." I am a religious person and all my readers know it. If I put "Yours in Christ," it seems to me that they will think I am theirs because I am in Christ, or even that they and I are in Christ *together,* which is not always the case. I am in Christ but I know for a fact that a lot of them are not. There's no use acting like they are, but there's no use rubbing their faces in it, either. "Peace be with you," as I see it, is sufficiently religious without laying all the cards right out on the table in plain view. I like to keep an ace or two up my sleeve. I like to write between the lines.

This is what I call my column, in fact: "Between the Lines, by Mrs. Joline B. Newhouse." Nobody knows why. Many people have come right out and asked me, including my best friend, Sally Peck, and my husband, Glenn. "Come on, now, Joline," they say. "What's this 'Between the Lines' all about? What's this 'Between the Lines' supposed to mean?" But I just smile a sweet mysterious smile and change the subject. I know what I know.

And my column means everything to folks around here. Salt Lick community is where we live, unincorporated. I guess there is not much that you would notice, passing through—the Post Office (real little), the American oil station, my husband Glenn's Cash 'N Carry Beverage Store. He sells more than beverages in there, though, believe me. He sells everything you can think of, from thermometers and rubbing alcohol to nails to frozen pizza. Anything else you want, you have to go out of the holler and get on the interstate and go to Greenville to get it. That's where my column appears, in the *Greenville Herald,* fortnightly. Now there's a word with a ring to it: fortnightly.

There are seventeen families here in Salt Lick—twenty, if you count those three down by the Five Mile Bridge. I put what they do in the paper. Anybody gets married, I write it. That goes for born, divorced, dies, celebrates a golden wedding anniversary, has a baby shower, visits relatives in Ohio, you name it. But these mere facts are not what's most important, to my mind.

I write, for instance: "Mrs. Alma Goodnight is enjoying a pleasant recuperation period in the lovely, modern Walker Mountain Community Hospital while she is sorely missed by her loved ones at home. Get well soon, Alma!" I do not write that Alma Goodnight is in the hospital because her husband hit her up the side with a rake and left a straight line of bloody little holes going from her waist to her armpit after she yelled at him, which Lord knows she did all the time, once too often. I don't write about how Eben Goodnight is all torn up now about what he did, missing work and worrying, or how Alma liked it so much in the hospital that nobody knows if they'll ever get her to go home or not. Because that is a *mystery,* and I am no detective by a long shot. I am what I am, I know what I know, and I know you've got to give folks something to hang on to, something to keep them going. That is what I have in mind when I say *uplift,* and that is what God had in mind when he gave us Jesus Christ.

My column would not be but a paragraph if the news was all I told. But it isn't. What I tell is what's important, like the bulbs coming up, the way the redbud comes out first on the hills in the spring and how pretty it looks, the way the cattails shoot up by the creek, how the mist winds down low on the ridge in the mornings, how my wash all hung out on the line of a Tuesday looks like a regular square dance with those pants legs just flapping and flapping in the wind! I tell how all the things you ever dreamed of, all changed and ghostly, will come crowding into your head on a winter night when you sit up late in front of your fire. I even made up these little characters to talk for me, Mr. and Mrs. Cardinal and Princess Pussycat, and often I have them voice my thoughts. Each week I give a little chapter in their lives. Or I might tell what was the message brought in church, or relate an inspirational word from a magazine, book, or TV. I look on the bright side of life.

I've had God's gift of writing from the time I was a child. That's what the B. stands for in Mrs. Joline B. Newhouse—Barker, my maiden name. My father was a patient strong God-fearing man despite his problems and it is in his honor that I maintain the B. There was a lot of us children around all the time—it was right up the road here where I grew up—and it would take me a day to tell you what all we got into! But after I learned how to write, that was that. My fingers just naturally curved to a pencil and I sat down to writing like a ball of fire. They skipped me up one, two grades in school. When I was not but eight, I wrote a poem named "God's Garden," which was published in the church bulletin of the little Methodist Church we went to then on

Hunter's Ridge. Oh, Daddy was so proud! He gave me a quarter that Sunday, and then I turned around and gave it straight to God. Put it in the collection plate. Daddy almost cried he was so proud. I wrote another poem in school the next year, telling how life is like a maple tree, and it won a statewide prize.

That's me—I grew up smart as a whip, lively, and naturally good. Jesus came as easy as breathing did to me. Don't think I'm putting on airs, though: I'm not. I know what I know. I've done my share of sinning, too, of which more later.

Anyway, I was smart. It's no telling but what I might have gone on to school like my own children have and who knows what all else if Mama hadn't run off with a man. I don't remember Mama very well, to tell the truth. She was a weak woman, always laying in the bed having a headache. One day we all came home from school and she was gone, didn't even bother to make up the bed. Well, that was the end of Mama! None of us ever saw her again, but Daddy told us right before he died that one time he had gotten a postcard from her from Atlanta, Georgia, years and years after that. He showed it to us, all wrinkled and soft from him holding it.

Being the oldest, I took over and raised those little ones, three of them, and then I taught school and then I married Glenn and we had our own children, four of them, and I have raised them too and still have Marshall, of course, poor thing. He is the cross I have to bear and he'll be just like he is now for the rest of his natural life.

I was writing my column for the week of March 17, 1976, when the following events occurred. It was a real coincidence because I had just finished doing the cutest little story named "A Red-Letter Day for Mr. and Mrs. Cardinal" when the phone rang. It rings all the time, of course. Everybody around here knows my number by heart. It was Mrs. Irene Chalmers. She was all torn up. She said that Mr. Biggers was over at Greenville at the hospital very bad off this time, and that he was asking for me and would I please try to get over there today as the doctors were not giving him but a 20 percent chance to make it through the night. Mr. Biggers has always been a fan of mine, and he especially liked Mr. and Mrs. Cardinal. "Well!" I said. "Of course I will! I'll get Glenn on the phone right this minute. And you calm down, Mrs. Chalmers. You go fix yourself a Coke." Mrs. Chalmers said she would, and hung up. I knew what was bothering her, of course. It was that given the natural run of things, she would be the next to go. The next one to be over there dying. Without even putting down the receiver, I dialed the beverage store. Bert answered.

"Good morning," I said. I like to maintain a certain distance with the hired help although Glenn does not. He will talk to anybody, and any time you go in there, you can find half the old men in the county just sitting around that stove in the winter or outside on those wooden drink boxes in the summer, smoking and drinking drinks which I am sure they are getting free out of the cooler although Glenn swears it on the Bible they are not. Anyway, I said good morning.

"Can I speak to Glenn?" I said.

"Well now, Mrs. Newhouse," Bert said in his naturally insolent voice—he is just out of high school and too big for his britches—"he's not here right now. He had to go out for a while."

"Where did he go?" I asked.

"Well, I don't rightly know," Bert said. "He said he'd be back after lunch."

"Thank you very much, there will not be a message," I said sweetly, and hung up. I *knew* where Glenn was. Glenn was over on Caney Creek where his adopted half-sister Margie Kettles lived, having carnal knowledge of her in the trailer. They had been at it for thirty years and anybody would have thought they'd have worn it out by that time. Oh, I knew all about it.

The way it happened in the beginning was that Glenn's father had died of his lungs when Glenn was not but about ten years old, and his mother grieved so hard that she went off her head and began taking up with anybody who would go with her. One of the fellows she took up with was a foreign man out of a carnival, the James H. Drew Exposition, a man named Emilio something. He had this curly-headed dark-skinned little daughter. So Emilio stayed around longer than anybody would have expected, but finally it was clear to all that he never would find any work around here to suit him. The work around here is hard work, all of it, and they say he played a musical instrument. Anyway, in due course this Emilio just up and vanished, leaving that foreign child. Now that was Margie, of course, but her name wasn't Margie then. It was a long foreign name, which ended up as Margie, and that's how Margie ended up here, in these mountains, where she has been up to no good ever since. Glenn's mother did not last too long after Emilio left, and those children grew up wild. Most of them went to foster homes, and to this day Glenn does not know where two of his brothers are! The military was what finally saved Glenn. He stayed with the military for nine years, and when he came back to this area he found me over here teaching school and with something of a nest egg in hand, enabling him to start the beverage store. Glenn says he owes everything to me.

This is true. But I can tell you something else: Glenn is a good man, and he has been a good provider all these years. He has not ever spoken to me above a regular tone of voice nor raised his hand in anger. He has not been tight with the money. He used to hold the girls in his lap of an evening. Since I got him started, he has been a regular member of the church, and he has not fallen down on it yet. Glenn furthermore has that kind of disposition where he never knows a stranger. So I can count my blessings, too.

Of course I knew about Margie! Glenn's sister Lou-Ann told me about it before she died, that is how I found out about it originally. She thought I *should* know, she said. She said it went on for years and she just wanted me to know before she died. Well! I had had the first two girls by then, and I thought I was so happy. I took to my bed and just cried and cried. I cried for four days and then by gum I got up and started my column, and I have been writing on it ever since. So I was not unprepared when Margie showed up again some years after that, all gap-toothed and wild-looking, but then before you knew it she was gone, off again to Knoxville, then back working as a waitress at that truck stop at the county line, then off again, like that. She led an irregular life. And as for Glenn, I will have to hand it to him, he never darkened her door again until after the birth of Marshall.

Now let me add that I would not have gone on and had Marshall if it was left up to me. I would have practiced more birth control. Because I was old by that time, thirty-seven, and that was too old for more children I felt, even though I had started late of course. I had told Glenn many times, I said three normal girls is enough for anybody. But no, Glenn was like a lot of men, and I don't blame him for it—he just had to try one more time for a boy. So we went on with it, and I must say I had a feeling all along.

I was not a bit surprised at what we got, although after wrestling with it all for many hours in the dark night of the soul, as they say, I do not believe that Marshall is a judgment on me for my sin. I don't believe that. He is one of God's special children, is how I look at it. Of course he looks funny, but he has already lived ten years longer than they said he would. And has a job! He goes to Greenville every day on the Trailways bus, rain or shine, and cleans up the Plaza Mall. He gets to ride on the bus, and he gets to see people. Along about six o'clock he'll come back, walking up the holler and not looking to one side or the other, and then I give him his supper and then he'll watch something on TV like "The Brady Bunch" or "Family Affair," and then he'll go to bed. He would not hurt a flea. But oh, Glenn took it hard when Marshall came! I remember that night so well and the way he just turned his back on the doctor. That is what sent him back to Margie, I am convinced of it, what made him take up right where he had left off all those years before.

So since Glen was up to his old tricks I called up Lavonne, my daughter, to see if she could take me to the hospital to see Mr. Biggers. Why yes she could, it turned out. As a matter of fact she was going to Greenville herself. As a matter of fact she had something she wanted to talk to me about anyway. Now Lavonne is our youngest girl and the only one that stayed around here. Lavonne is somewhat pop-eyed, and has a weak constitution. She is one of those people that never can make up their minds. That day on the phone, I heard a whine in her voice I didn't like the sound of. Something is up, I thought.

First I powdered my face, so I would be ready to go when Lavonne got there. Then I sat back down to write some more on my column, this paragraph I had been framing in my mind for weeks about how sweet potatoes are not what they used to be. They taste gritty and dry now, compared to how they were. I don't know the cause of it, whether it is man on the moon or pollution in the ecology or what, but it is true. They taste awful.

Then my door came bursting open in a way that Lavonne would never do it and I knew it was Sally Peck from next door. Sally is loud and excitable but she has a good heart. She would do anything for you. "Hold on to your hat, Joline!" she hollered. Sally is so loud because she's deaf. Sally was just huffing and puffing—she is a heavy woman—and she had rollers still up in her hair and her old housecoat on with the buttons off.

"Why, Sally!" I exclaimed. "You are all wrought up!"

Sally sat down in my rocker and spread out her legs and started fanning herself with my *Family Circle* magazine. "If you think I'm wrought up," she said finally, "it is nothing compared to what you are going to be. We have had us a suicide, right here in Salt Lick. Margie Kettles put her head inside her gas oven in the night."

"Margie?" I said. My heart was just pumping.

"Yes, and a little neighbor girl was the one who found her, they say. She went over to borrow some baking soda for her mama's biscuits at seven o'clock A.M." Sally looked real hard at me. "Now wasn't she related to you all?"

"Why," I said just as easily, "why yes, she was Glenn's adopted half-sister of course when they were nothing but a child. But we haven't had anything to do with her for years as you can well imagine."

"Well, they say Glenn is making the burial arrangements," Sally spoke up. She was getting her own back that day, I'll admit it. Usually I'm the one with all the news.

"I have to finish my column now and then Lavonne is taking me to Greenville to see old Mr. Biggers who is breathing his last," I said.

"Well," Sally said, hauling herself out of my chair, "I'll be going along then. I just didn't know if you knew it or not." Now Sally Peck is not a spiteful woman in all truth. I have known her since we were little girls sitting out in the yard looking at a magazine together. It is hard to imagine being as old as I am now, or knowing Sally Peck—who was Sally Bland then—so long.

Of course I couldn't get my mind back on sweet potatoes after she left. I just sat still and fiddled with the pigeonholes in my desk and the whole kitchen seemed like it was moving and rocking back and forth around me. Margie dead! Sooner or later I would have to write it up tastefully in my column. Well, I must say I had never thought of Margie dying. Before God, I never hoped for that in all my life. I didn't know what it would to do *me,* in fact, to me and Glenn and Marshall and the way we live because you know how the habits and the ways of people can build up over the years. It was too much for me to take in at one time. I couldn't see how anybody committing suicide could choose to stick their head in the oven anyway—you can imagine the position you would be found in.

Well, in came Lavonne at that point, sort of hanging back and stuttering like she always does, and that child of hers Bethy Rose hanging on to her skirt for dear life. I saw no reason at that time to tell Lavonne about the death of Margie Kettles. She would hear it sooner or later, anyway. Instead, I gave her some plant food that I had ordered two for the price of one from Montgomery Ward some days before.

"Are you all ready, Mama?" Lavonne asked in that quavery way she has, and I said indeed I was, as soon as I got my hat, which I did, and we went out and got in Lavonne's Buick Electra and set off on our trip. Bethy Rose sat in the back, coloring in her coloring book. She is a real good child. "How's Ron?" I said. Ron is Lavonne's husband, an electrician, as up and coming a boy as you would want to see. Glenn and I are as proud as punch of Ron, and actually I never have gotten over the shock of Lavonne marrying him in the first place. All through high school she never showed any signs of marrying anybody, and you could have knocked me over with a feather the day she told us she was secretly engaged. I'll tell you, our Lavonne was not the marrying sort! Or so I thought.

But that day in the car she told me, "Mama, I wanted to talk to you and tell you I am thinking of getting a d-i-v-o-r-c-e."

I shot a quick look into the back seat but Bethy Rose wasn't hearing a thing. She was coloring Wonder Woman in her book.

"Now, Lavonne," I said. "What in the world is it? Why, I'll bet you can work it out." Part of me was listening to Lavonne, as you can imagine, but part of me was still stuck in that oven with crazy Margie. I was not myself.

I told her that, "Lavonne," I said, "I am not myself today. But I'll tell you one thing. You give this some careful thought. You don't want to go off half-cocked. What is the problem, anyway?"

"It's a man where I work," Lavonne said. She works in the Welfare Department, part-time, typing. "He is just giving me a fit. I guess you can pray for me, Mama, because I don't know what I'll decide to do."

"Can we get an Icee?" asked Bethy Rose.

"Has anything happened between you?" I asked. You have to get all the facts.

"Why *no!*" Lavonne was shocked. "Why, I wouldn't do anything like that! Mama, for goodness' sakes! We just have coffee together so far."

That's Lavonne all over. She never has been very bright. "Honey," I said, "I would think twice before I threw up a perfectly good marriage and a new brick home for the sake of a cup of coffee. If you don't have enough to keep you busy, go take a course at the community college. Make yourself a new pantsuit. This is just a mood, believe me."

"Well," Lavonne said. Her voice was shaking and her eyes were swimming in tears that just stayed there and never rolled down her cheeks. "Well," she said again.

As for me, I was lost in thought. It was when I was a young married woman like Lavonne that I committed my own great sin. I had the girls, and things were fine with Glenn and all, and there was simply not any reason to ascribe to it. It was just something I did out of loving pure and simple, did because I wanted to do it. I knew and have always known the consequences, yet God is full of grace, I pray and believe, and his mercy is everlasting.

To make a long story short, we had a visiting evangelist from Louisville, Kentucky, for a two-week revival that year. John Marcel Wilkes. If I say it myself, John Marcel Wilkes was a real humdinger! He had the yellowest hair you ever saw, curly, and the finest singing voice available. Oh, he was something, and that very first night he brought two souls into Christ. The next day I went over to the church with a pan of brownies just to tell him how much I personally had received from his message. I thought, of course, that there would be other people around—the Reverend Mr. Clark, or the youth director, or somebody cleaning. But to my surprise that church was totally empty except for John Marcel Wilkes himself reading the Bible in the fellowship hall and making notes on a pad of paper. The sun came in a window on his head. It was early June, I remember, and I had on a blue dress with little white cap sleeves and open-toed sandals. John Marcel Wilkes looked up at me and his face gave off light like the sun.

"Why, Mrs. Newhouse," he said. "What an unexpected pleasure!" His voice echoed out in the empty fellowship hall. He had the most beautiful voice, too—strong and deep, like it had bells in it. Everything he said had a ring to it.

He stood up and came around the table to where I was. I put the brownies down on the table and stood there. We both just stood there, real close without touching each other, for the longest time, looking into each other's eyes. Then he took my hands and brought them up to his mouth and kissed them, which nobody ever did to me before or since, and then he kissed me on the mouth. I thought I would die. After some time of that, we went together out into the hot June day where the bees were all buzzing around the flowers there by the back gate and I couldn't think straight. "Come," said John Marcel Wilkes. We went out in the woods behind the church to the prettiest place, and when it was all over I could look up across his curly yellow head and over the trees and see the white church steeple stuck up against that blue, blue sky like it was pasted there. This was not all. Two more times we went out there during the revival. John Marcel Wilkes left after that and I have never heard a word of him since. I do not know where he is, or what has become of him in all these years. I do know that I never bake a pan of brownies, or hear the church bells ring, but what I think of him. So I have to pity Lavonne and her cup of coffee if you see what I mean, just like I have to spend the rest of my life to live my sinning down. But I'll tell you this: if I had it all to do over, I would do it all over again, and I would not trade it in for anything.

Lavonne drove off to look at fabric and get Bethy Rose an Icee, and I went in the hospital. I hate the way they smell. As soon as I entered Mr. Biggers' room, I could see he was breathing his last. He was so tiny in the bed you almost missed him, a poor little shriveled-up thing. His family sat all around.

"Aren't you sweet to come?" they said. "Looky here, honey, it's Mrs. Newhouse."

He didn't move a muscle, all hooked up to tubes. You could hear him breathing all over the room.

"It's Mrs. Newhouse," they said, louder. "Mrs. Newhouse is here. Last night he was asking for everybody," they said to me. "Now he won't open his eyes. You are real sweet to come," they said. "You certainly did brighten his days." Now I knew this was true because the family had remarked on it before.

"I'm so glad," I said. Then some more people came in the door and everybody was talking at once, and while they were doing that, I went over to the bed and got right up by his ear.

"Mr. Biggers!" I said. "Mr. Biggers, it's Joline Newhouse here."

He opened one little old bleary eye.

"Mr. Biggers!" I said right into his ear. "Mr. Biggers, you know those cardinals in my column? Mr. and Mrs. Cardinal? Well, I made them up! I made them up, Mr. Biggers. They never were real at all." Mr. Biggers closed his eye and a nurse came in and I stood up.

"Thank you so much for coming, Mrs. Newhouse," his daughter said.

"He is one fine old gentleman," I told them all, and then I left.

Outside in the hall, I had to lean against the tile wall for support while I waited for the elevator to come. Imagine, me saying such a thing to a dying man! I was not myself that day.

Lavonne took me to the big Kroger's in north Greenville and we did our shopping, and on the way back in the car she told me she had been giving everything a lot of thought and she guessed I was right after all.

"You're not going to tell anybody, are you?" she asked me anxiously, popping her eyes. "You're not going to tell Daddy, are you?" she said.

"Why, Lord, no honey!" I told her. "It's the farthest thing from my mind."

Sitting in the back seat among the grocery bags, Bethy Rose sang a little song she had learned at school. "Make new friends but keep the old, some are silver but the other gold." she sang.

"I don't know what I was thinking of," Lavonne said.

Glenn was not home yet when I got there—making his arrangements, I supposed. I took off my hat, made myself a cup of Sanka, and sat down and finished off my column on a high inspirational note, saving Margie and Mr. Biggers for the next week. I cooked up some ham and red-eye gravy, which

Glenn just loves, and then I made some biscuits. The time seemed to pass so slow. The phone rang two times while I was fixing supper, but I just let it go. I thought I had received enough news for *that* day. I still couldn't get over Margie putting her head in the oven, or what I had said to poor Mr. Biggers, which was not at all like me you can be sure. I buzzed around that kitchen doing first one thing, then another. I couldn't keep my mind on anything I did.

After a while Marshall came home and ate, and went in the front room to watch TV. He cannot keep it in his head that watching TV in the dark will ruin your eyes, so I always have to go in there and turn on a light for him. This night, though, I didn't. I just let him sit there in the recliner in the dark, watching his show, and in the pale blue light from that TV set he looked just like anybody else.

I put on a sweater and went out on the front porch and sat in the swing to watch for Glenn. It was nice weather for that time of year, still a little cold but you could smell spring in the air already and I knew it wouldn't be long before the redbud would come out again on the hills. Out in the dark where I couldn't see them, around the front steps, my crocuses were already up. After a while of sitting out there I began to take on a chill, due more to my age no doubt than the weather, but just then some lights came around the bend, two headlights, and I knew it was Glenn coming home.

Glenn parked the truck and came up the steps. He was dog-tired, I could see that. He came over to the swing and put his hand on my shoulder. A little wind came up, and by then it was so dark you could see lights on all the ridges where the people live. "Well, Joline," he said.

"Dinner is waiting on you," I said. "You go on in and wash up and I'll be there directly. I was getting worried about you," I said.

Glenn went on and I sat there swaying on the breeze for a minute before I went after him. Now where will it all end? I ask you. All this pain and loving, mystery and loss. And it just goes on and on, from Glenn's mother taking up with dark-skinned gypsies to my own daddy and his postcard to that silly Lavonne and her cup of coffee to Margie with her head in the oven, to John Marcel Wilkes and myself, God help me, and all of it so long ago out in those holy woods.

ELIZABETH SPENCER

Elizabeth Spencer was born in Carrollton, Mississippi, in 1921. She graduated from Belhaven College and Vanderbilt University. Her novels include *The Light in the Piazza* and *The Salt Line*. *Ship Island and Other Stories* appeared in 1968 and *The Stories of Elizabeth Spencer* in 1981. She has received the Rosenthal Award of the National Institute of Arts and Letters and the American Academy and Institute of Arts and Letters Award of Merit Medal for the Short Story.

I, Maureen

On the sunny fall afternoon, I (Maureen) saw the girl sitting in the oval-shaped park near the St. Lawrence River. She was sitting on green grass, bent lovingly, as though eternally, over her guitar. They are always like that, absorbed, hair falling past their faces, whether boys or girls: there seems little difference between them: they share the tender absorption of mother with child. The whole outside world regards them, forms a hushed circle about them.

I, Maureen, perceived this while driving by on an errand for Mr. Massimo.

I used to live out there, on what in Montreal we call the Lakeshore. I did nothing right then, so returning to that scene is painful. I sought relief from the memories of five years ago by letting the girl with the guitar—bending to it, framed in grass, the blue river flowing by—redeem my memories, redeem me, I could only hope, also. Me, Maureen, stung with the identity of bad memories.

Everything any woman in her right mind could want—that was my life. Denis Partham's wife, and not even very pretty or classy: I never had anything resembling looks or background. I was a bit run-down looking, all my life. From the age of two, I looked run-down. People used to say right out to me: "You've just had luck, that's all." But Denis said the luck was his. He really thought that, for years and years. Until the day I thought he was dead. After that he had to face it that luck can run out, even for a Partham.

We had a house on the river and it was beautiful, right on the water. It was in Baie d'Urfé, one of the old townships, and you can describe it for yourself, if you so desire. There can be rugs of any texture, draperies of any fabric, paneling both painted and stained, shelves to put books in, cupboards to fill with china and linen. The choice of every upholstery sample or kitchen tile was a top-level decision; the struggle for perfection had a life-and-death quality about it. If my interest was not wholly taken up in all this, if I was play-acting, I did not know it. Are people when measuring and weighing and pondering names for a crown prince, serious? I was expecting the prince; that was why the Parthams gave us the house. Sure enough, the baby was a boy. Two years and another one arrived, a girl. (Isn't Nature great? She belongs to the Parthams.)

In the winter we had cocktails before dinner in a spacious room overlooking the frozen lake, watching the snow drift slowly down, seeing the skaters stroking outward. We had sherry between church services and Sunday lunch. Then the ice boats raced past, silent, fast as dreams.

Our children were beautiful, like children drawn with a pencil over and again in many attitudes, all pure, among many Canadian settings. Denis was handsome, a well-built man, younger than I, with dark hair and a strong, genuine smile. In his world, I was the only dowdy creature. Yet he loved me, heart and soul. And why? I used to sit in a big chair in a corner of the library hunched up like a crow, and wonder this. In summer I sat on the terraces, and there, too, I wondered.

All I knew was that aged twenty-five, a plain, single girl, I had come to the Parthams' big stone house high in Westmount with some friends. It was late, a gathering after a local play. A woman who worked at the library with me had a younger sister in the play and had asked me to come. One of the Parthams was in it, too, so we all got invited up for drinks. Somebody graciously learned that I was living way out in N.D.G., that area of the unnumbered middle class, and Denis, who had been talking to me about the library, offered to drive me home. When we reached the house, he turned off the motor, then the lights, and turning to me began to kiss me hungrily. He had fallen silent along the way, and I had felt he was going to do something like this. I simply judged that he was a rich boy out for more sexual experience, seeking it outside his own class, the way privileged people often do. Yet he was moved and excited way beyond the average: so I put him down as a boy with problems, and squirmed my way out of his arms and his Oldsmobile as best I could. Next day he telephoned me at the library, longing to see me again. He was that way from then on. He said he could never change. Through all our dates, then through season after season, year after year, I saw how his voice would take on a different note when he saw me, how his eyes would light up. I knew his touch, his sexual currents, his eager kisses, his talk, his thoughts, his tastes. At some point, we got married. But the marriage, I helplessly realized, had taken place already, in the moment he had seen me in the corner of one of the many Partham living rooms in their great stone house, me (Maureen), completely out of place. Before I knew it, he had enveloped me all over, encased me like a strong vine. My family could believe my good fortune no more than I could. It was too good to last, but it did; too good to be true, but it was. We had, in addition to the Lakeshore house at Baie d'Urfé, an apartment on Drummond Street in Montreal, servants, two cars, wonderful friends, a marvelous life.

Then, one summer day, it happened. It could never unhappen.

Denis was out sailing and in passing under a bridge, the metal mast of the boat struck a live wire. His hand was on the mast and the voltage knocked him down. When they brought him in they had rolled him onto the sail and were carrying him by four improvised corners, like somebody asleep in a hammock. His head was turned to one side. Everyone on our lawn and dock seemed to know from the minute the boat appeared, unexpectedly returned, that something terrible had happened. We crowded forward together, all the family and friends not sailing, left behind on the lawns to swim, sun, play, or talk, and though I was among the first, I felt just as one of them, not special. I saw his face turned to one side, looking (the eyes shut and the skin discolored blue and red) like a face drowned through a rift in ice. I thought he was dead, and so did we all, even, I later learned, those who were carrying him. They laid him on the lawn and someone said: "Stay back," while another, running from the moment the boat touched the dock, was already at the telephone. But by that time there were arms around me, to hold me back from rushing to him. They encountered no forward force. I was in retreat already, running backward from the moment, into another world which had been waiting for me for some time. All they did was hasten me into it. My fierce sprinting backward plus the force of their normal human attention—that of trying to keep a wife from hurling herself with all the velocity of human passion toward her husband, so unexpectedly served up before her as (so it seemed) a corpse—outdid possibility. But we leave the earth with difficulty, and I wasn't up to that. I fell backward, sprawling awkwardly; I lay observing the bluest of July skies in which white clouds had filled in giant areas at good distances from the sun. Sky, cloud, and sun completed me, while ambulances wailed and bore away whomever they would.

Denis did not die; he recovered nicely. All life resumed as before.

A month later I made my first attempt at suicide.

It was finally to one of the psychiatrists I saw that I recounted how all of this had started, from a minor event, meaningless *to all but me.* (To me alone the world had spoken.)

I had been sunbathing on the pier a week or so before Denis's accident when two of the children whose parents owned a neighboring property began to throw things into the water. I could see them—two skinny boys on the neighboring pier—and know that while they pretended to be hurling rocks and bottles straight out into the lake, they were in reality curving them closer into land, striking near our docking area. I was thinking of getting up to shout at them when it happened. A bit of blue-green glass arching into the sun's rays, caught and trapped an angle of that light, refracting it to me. It struck, a match for lightning. My vision simply for a moment was by this brilliance extinguished; and in the plunge of darkness that ensued I could only see the glass rock reverse its course and speed toward me. It entered my truest self, my consciousness, reverberating with silent brilliance. From that point I date my new beginning. It was a nothing point, an illusion, but an illusion that had happened to me, if there is such a thing. . . .

"If there is such a thing," the doctor repeated.

"If there is such a thing," I said again, sounding, I knew, totally mad.

Doctors wait for something to be said that fits a pattern they have learned to be true, just as teachers wait for you to write English or French. If you wrote a new and unknown language they wouldn't know what to do with you—you would fail.

"It explains to me," I went on, realizing I was taking the risk of being consigned to the asylum at Verdun for an indefinite period, "why I ran backward instead of forward when I thought Denis was dead. I want my own world. I have been there once. I want to return. If I can't, I might as well be dead."

"Your attempts to take your own life might be thought of as efforts to join your husband, whom you believed to have reached death," the doctor suggested. He had a thick European accent, and an odd name, Miracorte. God knows where he was from.

I said nothing.

One day I left home. I had done this before but they had always come for me, tranquilized me, hospitalized me, removed things from me that might be handy ways of self-destruction, talked to me, loved me, nurtured me back to being what they wanted me to be—somebody, in other words, like themselves. This time they didn't come. A doctor came, a new one, younger than the first. He asked from the intercom system in the apartment building in East Montreal which I had fled to, taking the first furnished place I could find, whether he could see me. I let him in.

He was plain English-Canadian from Regina, named Johnson.

"Everyone is a little schizoid," he said. They had told me that, told me and told me that. "You choose the other side of the coin, the other side of yourself. You have to have it. If you don't have it, you will die. Don't you know that some people drink themselves into it, others hit drugs, some run off to the bush, some kill or steal or turn into religious freaks? You're a mild case, comparatively speaking. All you want is to be with it, calmly, like a lover."

I was crying before I knew it, tears of relief. He was the first to consent to my line of feeling. Why had it been so hard, why were they all reluctant to do so? We allow people to mouth platitudes to us one after another, and agree to them blandly, knowing they aren't true, just because there's no bite to them, no danger. The truth is always dangerous, so in agreeing to what I felt, he was letting me in for danger. But it was all that was left to try.

"There's a bank account for you at this address." He gave me the checkbook and the deposit slip. "If you need more, call me. Your husband has agreed to this plan."

I took the checkbook silently, but was vowing already that I would never use it. I was going to get a job.

The young doctor sat frowning, eyes on the floor.

"Denis feels awful," I said, reading his thoughts aloud. "This has made him suffer."

"I didn't say that," Dr. Johnson said. "It makes you suffer to stay with him. Maybe—well, maybe he can get through better without you than you can with him."

From then on I was on my own, escaping into the mystery that is East Montreal, a fish thrown barely alive back into water. Not that I had ever lived there. But to Westmount families who own houses in Baie d'Urfé, East Montreal presents even more of an opaque surface than N.D.G. It is thought to be French, and this is so, but it is also Greek, Italian, Oriental, and immigrant Jewish. I was poor, unattractive as ever; I ached for my children and the sound of Denis's voice, his love, everything I had known. I went through an agony of missing what I could have, all back, and whole as ever, just by picking up the phone, just by taking a taxi and saying, "Take me home."

But when I gave in (and I did give in every time the world clicked over and I saw things right side up instead of upside down), odd consequences resulted. I would call a number but strange voices out of unknown businesses or residences would answer, or someone among the Partham friends would say hello, and I would begin to talk about myself—me, *me,* ME—relating imagined insults, or telling stories that were only partly true, and though I knew I was doing this, though my mind stood by like a chance pedestrian at the scene of an accident, interested, but a little sickened, with other things to do, still my voice, never lacking for a word, went on. Once I took a taxi home with all my possessions loaded inside, but directed the driver to the wrong turning, overshot the mark and wound up at the wrong driveway. The people who came out the door knew me; oh, this was horrible; I crouched down out of sight and shouted, "Go back, go back! Take me home!" (The meaning of home had shifted, the world had flipped once more.)

Again I came on the bus in the middle of a fine afternoon, calm and right within myself, to "talk things over," sanely to prepare for my return to the family. I found no one there, the house open, the living room empty. I sat down to wait. At a still center, waiting for loved ones' faces to appear through a radiance of outer sunlight, I stared too hard at nothing, closed my eyes and heard it from the beginning: a silent scream, waxing unbearably. I had come to put out my arms, to say, I have failed to love, but now I know this. I love you, I love you all. What was there in this to make the world shrink back, flee, recede, rock with agony to its fair horizons? I could bear it no longer, and so fled. I ran past one of them, one of the Partham women (my mother-in-law, sister-in-law, aunt-in-law, a cousin?—they look alike, all of them) coming in from the garden in her white work gloves with shears in hand, a flat of cut flowers on her arm. *She* must have screamed also, I saw her mouth make the picture of a scream, but that is unimportant except to her. For if she was Denis's mother she must have wanted to scream ever since I had first walked into her presence, hand in hand with Denis, and then there I was back again, crazy and fleeing with a bruised forehead all purple and gold (in my haste to reach them I had slammed into a door).

My journey back on one rattling bus after another, threading streets under an overcast sky, seemed longer than I could have imagined. I wondered then and since if I had dreamed that journey, if I would not presently wake up in the dark room where my resolution had taken place at 3 A.M. (the hour of weakness and resolve), if the whole matter of getting up, dressing, taking the taxi, were not all a dream of the soul's motion upon deciding, while I myself, like a chained dog, lay still held to sleep and darkness. On the other hand, I wondered whether I had made that same decision and that same trip not once or twice but twenty or thirty times, as though the split side of myself were carrying on a life it would not tell me about. Denis had a brother who was a physicist and used to talk about a "black hole in space," where matter collapses of its own gravity, ceases to exist in any form that we know of as existence. Yet some existence must continue. Was this myself, turned inside-out like a sleeve, whirled counterclockwise to a vacuum point, when I disappeared would I (Maureen) know it? Confusion thickened in my head.

I thought I saw Denis at the end of a snowy street in East Montreal near Dorchester Boulevard, a child holding to either hand, and so sprang up my fantasy that they often came to watch silently from somewhere just to see me pass, but often as I thought I glimpsed them, I never hastened to close the distance and find the answer.

"You prefer the fantasy to the reality," Dr. Johnson said.

"What made me the way I am? Why have I caused all this?"

"Becoming is difficult."

"Becoming what?"

"Your alter ego. Your other self."

"You've said it a hundred times."

"So what?"

"It makes no sense, my other self. None whatever."

"You feel it's irrational?"

We both fell silent and looked down as if this self had fallen like an object between us on the floor.

"No one is wholly rational," Dr. Johnson said.

I still sat looking. Rational or not, could it live, poor thing? If I nudged it with my toe, would it move?

"Basically, you are happier now," he told me.

"I am lonely," I said. The words fell out, without my knowing it. Perhaps the self on the floor had spoken.

"You like it, or you wouldn't be," he said at once.

I was surprised by this last remark and returned home with something like an inner smile. For the first time in months I thought of buying something new and pretty and I looked in shop windows along the way. I stopped in a drugstore and got a lipstick. That night I washed my hair. Sitting out on my balcony, watching the people drift by, smoking, the way I always like to do, I put a blanket over my still damp head, for it was only March, and the world was still iced, crusted in decaying snow. I sat like a squaw woman, but inside I felt a little stir of green feeling. I would be happy in this world I'd come to, not just an exile, a maverick that had jumped the fence. I would feel like a woman again.

A woman invisible, floating softly through a June day, I went to church when my daughter was confirmed. I sat far in the back in the dim church, St. James on Bishop Street. Seeing her so beautiful, I felt exalted, meaning all the hymns, all the words. But as I was leaving I heard a murmuring behind me and my name spoken. Then a curate was chasing me, calling out my name. I knew him from the old days, didn't I? Wasn't he the one I'd asked to dinner and sherry and tea? He meant everything that was good; he wanted to grasp my hand and speak to me, about forgiveness, love, peace, the whole catalogue. But who stood back of him? Not the kingdom, the power, and the glory, but Parthams, Parthams, and Parthams. I ran like the wind. The air blew white in my face, white as my daughter's communion dress, white as a bridal veil. I stopped at last to gasp it down. No footsteps sounded from behind. I was safe once more. Running backward, I had broken records: forward, I'm unbeatable. This was the grim joke I told myself, skulking home.

"It was a big risk," Dr. Johnson warned me. "How did you even know about the service?"

"A maid I used to have. She told me."

"The trouble I've gone to. . . . Don't you realize they want to commit you? If they succeed, you may never get out again."

"Nobody could keep me from seeing her," I said. "Not on that day."

"To them you're a demon in the sacred place." He was smiling, but I heard it solemnly. Maybe they were right.

Such, anyway, were my forays into enemy land.

But some were also made to me, in my new country. For I saw them, at times, and at others I thought I saw them, shadows at twilight on the edge of their forest, or real creatures venturing out and toward me; it was often impossible to tell which.

Carole Partham really came, graceful and hesitant, deerlike, and I let her come, perceiving that it was not curiosity or prying that brought her over, but an inner need to break away, to copy me, in some measure.

There she was one twilight, waiting in the pizza restaurant near my entrance. Carole was born a Partham, but her husband was Jim O'Brien, a broker. He was away in Europe, she said. Now's your big chance, she had doubtless told herself.

A smart-looking girl, up to the latest in clothes, a luxury woman, wearing suède with a lynx collar, tall brown rain boots, brushed brown hair.

"Come in," I urged her, getting her out of that place where, dressed like that, she was making them nervous. "I'm safe to be with. You can see my place."

Then she was sitting, smoking, loosening her coat, eyes coasting about here and there, from floor to wall to ceiling. My apartment wasn't much to see. I would have set the dogs on her—dogs of my inner rages—if I hadn't seen her realness. Instead I saw it well: she was frightened. Happy or not? She didn't know. What does life mean? There was panic in the question, if you asked it often enough. She had no answer and her husband was away for quite some time.

"Come work here for a month," I advised. "You can get a job, or loaf, or think, or see what happens."

But her eyes were restless; they stopped at closed drawers, probed at closet doors. Sex! Oh, certainly, I thought. Oh, naturally. I remembered Jim O'Brien with his ready talk and his toothy grin flashing over an ever-present, ever-tilted tumbler of martini on the rocks, and the glitter and swagger in his stroll from guest to guest, his intimate flattering talk, and now I knew what I had thought all along: who would marry Jim O'Brien but a woman with a childhood terror still behind the door? And now she'd done it, how could she escape?

"Don't tell them where you are," I advised. "I can find a room for you maybe. Somewhere near if you want me to. You can see I've no space here."

"Oh, I didn't want—"

"Just tell them you've gone away. What about Florida? You can say that."

Helpless, the eyes roved.

"I've no one here," I told her. "No lover, no friend. I work in a photographer's studio. That's all there is to know. You'll see it at the corner. My boss is Mr. Massimo. He owns it. There's nothing to know."

After a long silence, she said, looking down at herself, "These clothes are wrong."

"Who cares? Just face it that nobody cares."

"Nobody cares? Nobody *cares?*" She kept repeating this. It was what she couldn't swallow, had got hung up on, I guess, all by herself. I had hit it by accident.

"I mean," I said, "nobody over *here* cares. Over there . . . I don't know about that."

"Nobody . . . nobody. . . ." Her voice now had gone flat. She got up to go, headed for the terrace window rather than the door, fell through the glass, stumbled over the terrace railing, her fashionable boots flailing the air, skirts sliding up to her neck. . . . But, no, this didn't happen. That wasn't the end of Carole. She went out the door, like anybody else.

She did move to the street for a time; I forget for how long. She brought plain old clothes and tied her head in a scarf. She worked some afternoons for a kind, arthritic Frenchman with white hair who ran a magazine shop. There was also the dark young man who stared down daily from a window four floors up; he descended to trail her home, offering to carry her grocery sack. How nice this tableau looked and how charming it would have been if only his I.Q. had been halfway average. He was once a doorman, I understood, but had kept falling asleep on his feet, like a horse.

She got drunk on resin-tasting wine one night in a Greek restaurant and lured eleven Greek waiters into a cheap hotel room. How sweet and eager and passionate they had seemed! They milled around—or so I was told—not knowing what to do. A humiliation to end all mental nymphomania: Carole escaped unmolested.

She had found a room with a woman whose mother had died and who baby-sat for pin money. On long evenings when she didn't baby-sit she told Carole the story of her life. Otherwise, Carole read, and drank, and told herself the story of her own life. She was happy in the butcher shop once and sat madonna-like with the butcher's cat purring in her lap, but the butcher's Spanish wife did not like her and kicked the cat to say so. Mr. Massimo pondered about her. "How did you know her?" he asked. "She once knew my sister," is all I answered.

Old clothes or not, Carole did one thing she didn't intend: she gave out the indefinable air of class. Surely, the street began to say, she was the forerunner of an "in" group which would soon discover us and then we would all make money and turn into background to be glanced at. So some thought.

But when I saw her, knowing better, I saw a host of other women—pretty, cared-for women—walking silently with her, rank on rank, women for whom nothing will ever quite add up. Every day, I guess, she wrote down her same old problems, in different combinations, and every day she got the same sum.

Suddenly, one day, she was before me. "My month is up. It's been a wonderful experience."

"I'm glad you thought so."

We both sat smoking thoughtfully, occasionally glancing at each other. I knew her room had been rifled twice by thieves and that she could not sleep at night when the baby-sitter baby-sat. The faces of those Greek waiters would, I imagine, press on her memory forever. If the world is one, what was the great secret to make those faces accessible to her own self? The answer had escaped her.

"It's been a great experience," she repeated, smiling brightly, her mouth like painted wood, like a wound.

A voice, another voice, in that same room is talking . . . Vinnie Partham and her husband Charles? It can't be.

". . . I knew it was safe to see you again when Carole confessed that she had and you were all right. Carole's gone into social work, she got over her crisis whatever it was, and now we're thinking it's time you got through with yours, for you may not be able even to imagine how desolate Denis still is, Maureen. Can you, can you?"

"We thought for a long time the problem was sexual but then we decided you were out to destroy us and then we thought your mental condition would make you incapable of anything at all by way of job or friends. But all our theories are wrong, I guess."

On she goes, with Charles dozing in his chair after the manner of British detectives in the movies, who look dumb but are actually intelligent and wide awake, solving the perfect crime, the difference being that Charles really is both half-asleep and stupid and has never been known to solve anything at all. Vinnie knows it. The phrases have started looping out of her mouth like a backward spaghetti-eating process. Luminous cords reach up and twine with others, grow into patterns of thought. The patterns are dollar signs. I see them forming.

"With Denis having no heart for the estate affairs, what chance have Charles and I for the consideration he's always extended us? And if you think who, out of a perfect grab bag of women now getting interested, he might actually take it in his head to marry—"

Something dawns on me. Vinnie Partham is never going to stop talking!

I stare at her and stare, feeling cross-eyed with wonder and helpless and hypnotized, like someone watching a force in nature take its course. What can I do? She'll be there forever.

"I'm tired, Vinnie," I tell her. "I'm terribly tired."

They melt away, her mouth is moving still. . . . Did I dream them? Do women still wear long beads? Can it really be they wanted me back for nothing but money? No, money is their name for something else. That chill place, that flaw in the world fabric, that rift in the Partham world about the size of Grand Canyon—they keep trying to fill it, trying to fill it, on and on, throwing everything in to fill it up. It was why Denis wanted me.

Oh, my poor children! Could they ever grow up to look like Aunt Vinnie and Uncle Charles?

At the thought of them, so impossibly beautiful, so possibly doomed, noises like cymbals crash in my ears, my eyes blur and stream. If my visitors were there I could not see them.

But they must be gone, I think, squinting around the room, if they were there at all. If they were ever alive at all . . . if they were ever anywhere.

Through all this, night was coming on; and summer—that, too, was coming on. Vinnie and Charles were dreams. But love is real.

I first saw Michel when he came to the photographer's shop for some application-size pictures. He was thin and ravaged, frowning, worried, *pressé.* I had learned to do routine requests as Mr. Massimo was often away taking wedding pictures or attending occasions such as christenings and retirements. Mr. Massimo thrived on these events, which included fancy food and lots to drink and dressed-up women. It was when Michel and I got in the semi-dark of the photographing room together that I received his full impact. I stirred about among the electrical cords, the lamp stands; I wielded the heavy-headed camera into focus; I directed his chin to lift, then found him in the lenses, dark and straight. Indian blood? I snapped the shutter.

He said he was new in the neighborhood, lived up the street, and would come back the next day to see the proofs.

But I passed him again, not an hour later, on my way home. He was sitting outdoors at the pizza parlor talking volubly to the street cleaner who had stopped there for a beer. He saw me pass, go in my building, and I felt his regard in my senses.

Who was he? What would he do?

Something revolutionary was what I felt to be in his bones. Political? Then he would be making contacts and arguing for the liberation of the province.

I was wrong. No passion for Quebec but the rent of an empty barbershop was what had brought him there, one on the lower floor of a small building with a tree in front. He was going to put in one of those shops that sold hippie costumes, Indian shirts, long skirts, built-up shoes, some papier-mâché decorators' items, and some artwork. This would incidentally give him a chance to show some of his own artwork, which had failed to interest the uptown galleries. He was going to leave the barber chairs and mirrors, using them all as décor, props, for the things he sold.

He told me all this when he came to see the photographs. Mr. Massimo had gone to a reunion of retired hockey players. Michel looked over the proofs and selected one. He wanted it enlarged, a glossy finish he could reproduce to make ads for his shop. He was telling me how in some detail and I thought that a little more would find him back in Mr. Massimo's darkroom, doing it for himself.

"I hope your business works," I said.

The day before, skirting about among the photographic equipment, we had entangled face to face among some electrical cords, which we had methodically to unplug and unwind to find release from a near embrace. Now, he turned from a scrutiny of his own face to a minute examination of my own.

"If you hope so, then you think it could. *Vous le croyez,* eh?"

"*Moi? J'en sais pas, moi.* What does it matter?"

His elbow slidded on the desk. His face beetled into my own. It was his eyes that were compelling, better than good, making an importance out of themselves, out of my opinions, out of me.

"Your thinking so . . . why, that's strong. You have power. *Vous êtes formidable.* That's it, madame. *C'est ça.*"

A tilt of the head, an inch or two more, and our mouths, once more, might have closed together. My own was dry and thirsty, it woke to tell me so.

He straightened, gathered up his pictures, and neatly withdrew. His step left the doorway empty. I filled the order blank carefully.

It had turned much warmer and after work now I sat on the balcony with the windows open behind me and what I had to call curtains even stirred a bit, a dreamy lift of white in a dusk-softened room. I was moved to put a Mozart record on. I remembered that Mozart had died a pauper and been carried by cart to the outskirts of Vienna in winter and dumped in a hole. To me, that made the music tenderer still. Michel! From the day I'd seen him a private tower had begun to rise about me; its walls were high and strong. I might gnaw toast and jam and gulp coffee standing in my closet-sized kitchen, wriggle into the same old skirt, blouse, sweater, and leather coat (now put away), and walk to work, a drab, square-set, middle-aged woman going past at an accustomed time, but, within myself, a princess came to life and she leaned from high-set window sills. Did Michel know, she kept on asking, as she studied the horizon and admired the blue sky.

He passed the shop twice, once for his enlargement, once to talk; he went by daily on the street. A stir went up about his footsteps. He would change us all. At the very least, I reasoned, he kept my mind off the divorce papers.

One night there was a shouting in the street and a clang of fire engines. I rushed to the balcony and saw where it was: Michel's, up on the corner. A moment later I heard his voice from the shadows, down in the street below, and I hurried to let him in, climbed back with him unseen, opened my door to him for the first time.

He had caught my hands, holding them together in his own, in a grasp warm with life. His explanations blundered out . . . coming back from somewhere, tired, smoking in bed, fell asleep, the stuff collected for the shop catching fire. "But if they know I'm back, that I set the fire, then the shop will never open. Nobody saw me. Nobody. Will you let me stay? Will you?"

"Smoking in bed, that's crazy."

"Correct." He leaned wearily toward me, smiling, sallow cheekbone sharp against my cheek, then holding closer, his mouth searching, and mine searching, too, finding and holding. The will to have him there was present already: it was he who'd set the tower up, and furnished it, for this very thing, for his refuge. But for such enfoldment as we found, the binding of my thought was needed, the total silent agreement that a man and woman make, a matched pattern for love. The heart of his gamble was there. He won it.

Left alone while I worked, Michel sat in the corner and read all day.

"What do you do when you're not reading?" I would ask, coming in from work.

"*Je pense.*"

"A *quoi?*"

"A *toi.*"

"*Tu pense à toi. Et tu le sais bien, toi.*" I was putting down my bag, I was emptying my grocery sack, but always I was turning to him. And I was moving to him. And he to me.

There was talk on the street of the fire, how the whole house had almost caught, and about the strange absence of Michel, whose inflammable junk has caused it all, but for whom nobody had an address or a telephone number.

One day I came from work and the tower stood empty. I knew it before I opened the door; Michel was gone. Through empty space I moved at last to the balcony and there up the street a taxi was pulling up before the rooming house. Out stepped Michel, as though home from a long journey, even carrying a suitcase! For the first time, it seemed, he was discovering his charred quarters, calling out the building superintendent, raising a commotion on the steps for all to hear. Quarreling, shouting, and multiple stories—they went on till nightfall.

Michel tried, at least, to collect the insurance on damages to his property. I never knew for certain if it worked. He said that it did, but he seldom told the truth. It was not his nature. If the fire was accidental, he escaped without a damage suit. But if he did it on purpose, hoping for insurance money to buy a better class of junk, and counting in advance on me to shelter him, then he was a fool to take so much risk. But why begin to care? Liar, cheat, thief, and lover—he stays unchanged and unexplaining. We have never had it out, or made it up, or parted. The tower is dissolving as his presence fades from it, leaves as water drying from a fabric, thread by thread. It floats invisible, but at least undestroyed. I felt this even after his shop opened—even after a dark young girl with long hair and painted eyes came to work there.

He comes and goes. Summer is over. *C'est ća.*

To think the Parthams ever let go is a serious mistake.

I recall a winter night now, lost in driving snow. There is a madness of snow, snow everywhere, teeming, shifting, lofty as curtains in the dream of a mad opera composer, cosmic, yet intimate as a white thread caught in an eyelash. The buses stall on Côte des Neiges: there is a moaning impotence among them, clouds of exhaust and a dimming of their interior lights as they strain to ascend the long hill, but some already have given up and stand dull and bulky, like great animals in herd awaiting some imminent extinction. The passengers file from them. I toil upward from Sherbrooke through a deepening tunnel, going toward the hospital. My son's name has become the sound of my heart. The receptionist directs me to a certain floor.

I think of everyone inside as infinitely small because of the loftiness of the night outside, its mad whiteness, chaotic motion, insatiable teeming. The hospital is a toy with lights, set on the mountain, a bump like a sty. The night will go on forever, it seems to be saying; it will if it wants to and it wants to and it will. So I (human) am small beneath this lofty whim. Perhaps I think like this to minimize the dull yet painful edge of guilt. My son may die; I abandoned him years ago. Yet he wants to see me, and they have thought that he should be permitted to. And I have thought, Why think it is good of them, nobody is that bad? and Why think it is good of me either, no mother is that cold? (But they might have been, and so might I.) Under realms of snow I progress at snail pace, at bug size, proving that great emotion lives in tiny hearts. On the floor, a passing aide, little as a sparrow, indicates the way. At the desk, a nurse, a white rabbit, peers at a note that has been left. Snow at the window, furious, boils. "Mr. Partham regrets he cannot be here. . . . You wish to see the boy? It's number ten." Swollen feelings lift me down the corridor. I crack the door. "Mother, is that you?" "Yes." "I knew you'd come." "Of course, I came." His hand, at last, is mine. It is the world.

Night after night I come, through blizzard, through ice and sleet, once in a silenced snow-bound city walking more than half the way into a wind with a −40° wind chill against my face, ant-sized under the glitter of infinite distances, at home with the derision of stars. So I push my stubborn nightly way. "You are sleepy," says Mr. Massimo at work. "Why are you so sleepy lately?" I tell him nothing. I can't for yawning.

Bundled in my dark coat, in the shadowy corridor, I sometimes, when Parthams are present, doze. They walk around me, speak to one another, are aware of my presence but do not address it. Denis, once, appearing, stands directly before me; when I lift my head our eyes meet, and they speak and we know it, yes we do. But there is a wall clear as glass between us and if we should fling ourselves through it, it would smash and let us through. Still, we would hurtle past each other. For the glass has a trick in it, a layer at the center seems to place us face to face but really angles us apart. He knows it, I know it. We have been shown the diagram. He nods and turns away.

Several times I see his wife. I recognize her by the newspaper photographs. She is quietly, expensively dressed, with soft shining hair, the one he should have married in the first place. I do not need the coat. Sitting there in the warm room, why do I wear it? The minute the Parthams leave, I shed it. Its dropping from me is real but a symbol also. I am in the room in the same moment.

We hardly talk at all, my son and I. We know everything there is to know already. I sense the hour, almost the minute, when his health begins to flow back again.

We are sitting together on a Saturday morning. Dawn has come to a clear spotless frozen sky. Smoke from the glittering city beneath us, laid out below the windows, turns white. It plumes upward in windless purity. I have been here through the night. We are talking. It is the last time; I know that, too. The needles have been withdrawn from his arms. Soon the morning routine of the hospital will begin to crackle along the hallway and some of it will enter here. I look around me and see what things the Parthams have filled the room with—elegant little transistor radios, sports books and magazines, a lovely tropical aquarium where brilliant fish laze fin and tail among the shells and water plants. Nothing has been spared. He is smiling. His nightmare with the long name—peritonitis—is over. His gaze is weak no longer, but has entered sunlight, is penetrating and can judge.

So much drops away from a sick person; ideas, personality, ambition, interests—all the important Partham baggage. When the pressures of the body turn eccentric and everything is wrong, then they find their secret selves. But once the Partham body returns, it's a sign of laziness not to look around, discriminate, find life "interesting," activities "meaningful"; it would be silly not to be a Partham since a Partham is what one so fortunately is. "Can I come to find you when I get out of here?" my son begs. "Can I, Mother?" "Of course, of course, you can." "I promise to." I am on my way, before the nurse comes with her thermometers or the elephantine gray wagon of trays lumbers in. I am into my coat again, retreating from the Partham gaze. But my insect heart in the unlikely shape of me, almost permanently bent, like a wind-blasted tree, by the awful humors of that phenomenal winter, is incandescent with inextinguishable joy. He will live, he will live. Nothing, nobody, can take that away. I stumble, slip, list, slide down frozen pavements, squeaking over surfaces of impacted snow. In the crystal truth of the day world, the night is done. He will live.

(His name? My son's name? I won't tell you.)

I wing, creep, crawl, hop—what you will—back into my world.

Denis, eventually, seeks me. He comes to find me. A third Partham. I see him at a street end.

He is gray; the winter has made everybody's skin too pale, except, I suppose, the habitual skiers who go up on peaks where the sun strikes. Denis used to ski, but not this year. There he is, gray at the street's end. All has been blown bare and lean by the awful winter. He is himself lean, clean, with gray overcoat and Persian lamb hat, darker gray trousers, brown, fur-lined gloves. "Maureen? Can we go somewhere? Just have a coffee . . . talk a little?" We go to the "bar-b-q" place. It's impersonal there, being on a busy corner; at the pizza restaurant they would want to know who Denis was, and why he'd come and do I have a new boy friend. Also Michel might pass by.

"He thinks you saved him," Denis tells me. "For all I know, it's true. But he thinks more than that. He's obsessed with you . . . can't talk of anything else at times. I don't know what to do, Maureen. He thinks you're a saint, something more than human. Your visits were only half-real to him. They were like—appearances, apparitions." He stops, hesitant. It is the appealing, unsure Denis, absent, I imagine, for most of the time, that I see again as I saw him when we first met, seeking out my eyes, begging for something.

"It must be easy to disillusion him," I say. "You, of all people, could best do that."

"Oh, he's heard all the facts. Not so much from me, mind you . . ."

From his grandmother, I think, and his grandfather and his aunts. Heard all those things he "ought to know."

"I didn't know you went there so often, sat for whole nights at a time, it seems." He is speaking out of a deepening despair, floundering.

"But you saw me there."

"I know, but I—"

"Didn't you know I loved him, too?"

"You loved—" At the mention of love, his face seems about to shatter into a number of different planes, a face in an abstract painting, torn against itself. "To me your love was always defective. You—Maureen, when we were first married, I would think over and over, Now is forever; forever is now. Why did you destroy it all? It frightens me to think of you sitting, in the dark hours, with that boy. You could have pinched his life out like a match."

"I wouldn't do that, Denis. I couldn't hurt what's hurt already." I could have told him what light is like, as I had seen its illusion that day before his accident, how the jagged force tore into my smoothly surfaced vision. I had tried to tell him once: he thought I was raving. Later I smashed a set of his mother's china, and tore up a beautifully tiled wall with my nails, until they split and the blood ran down.

"I thought I had some force that would help him. That's not why I went but it's why I stayed."

"It might not have worked," Denis reflected. "He might have died anyway."

"Then you could have blamed me," I pointed out. "Then I could have been a witch, an evil spirit."

"I don't know why you ever had to turn into a spirit at all! Just a woman, a wife, a mother, a human being—! That's all I ever wanted!"

"Believe me, Denis," I said, "*I don't know either.*"

We'd had it out that way, about a million times. Making no real progress, returning to our old familiar dead end, our hovel, which, in a way, was the only home we had.

I was then inspired to say: "It just may be, Denis, that if I'd never left, I could never have returned, and if I never had returned, it just may be that he would never have lived, he would have died, Denis, think of that, he would be dead."

For a moment, I guess he did consider it. His face turned to mine, mouth parted. He slipped little by little into the idea, let himself submerge within it. I will say for Denis: at least, he did that. "The doctors," he said at last, "they were terribly good, you know. The major credit," he said, finishing his coffee, "goes to them."

"Undoubtedly," I said. He had come to the surface, and turned back into a Partham again.

It had been a clear, still, frozen afternoon when we met, but holding just that soft touch of violet which said that winter would at last give over. Its grip was terrible, but a death grip no longer.

I tried to recall my old routine, to show my Partham side myself. "I imagine he will find new interests, once he gets more active. He won't think so much about me. But, Denis, if he does want to hold on to something about me, can't you let him?"

"I wouldn't dream of stopping him. It's a matter of proportion, that's all." He was pulling on his beautiful gloves. "He's practically made a religion of you."

As we were going out, I saw it all more clearly and began to laugh. "Then that's your answer, Denis."

"What is?"

"If I'm to be a 'religion,' then there are ways of handling me. Confine me to one hour a week, on Sunday morning. . . . I need never get out of bounds. Don't worry about him, Denis. He's a Partham, after all."

"Maureen? You're bitter, aren't you? People *have* to live, even Parthams. Life *has* to go on."

We were standing outside by then, at the intersection with my street. He wouldn't enter there, I thought; it was not in accord with his instincts to do so.

"I'm not bitter," I said. "I'm helpless."

"It didn't have to be that way."

It was like a final exchange; it had a certain ring. He leaned to touch my face, then drew back, moving quickly away, not looking behind.

And now I am waiting for the fourth visitor, my son. I think I will see him, at some street corner, seeking me, find him waiting for me in the pizza shop, hear a voice say, "Mother? I promised you. . . ." And before I know it, I will have said his name. . . .

I am waiting still.

Mr. Massimo, one day, leans at me over his portrait camera. "I hear you were married to a wealthy man in Westmount," he says.

"I am a princess in a silver tower," I reply. "Golden birds sing to me. I drift around in a long silk gown. What about you?"

"My father was Al Capone's brother. We rode around when young in a secondhand Rolls-Royce with a crest of the House of Savoia painted on the door. Then we got run out of Italy. The family took another name." He is smiling at me. It is not the story that reaches me, true or false, but the outpouring sun of Italy.

"You'll get me fired," I tell Michel.

"Come work for me," he says. "You can tell fortunes in the back. I'll make you rich."

He's using me again, working in collage—photography plus painting—he needs Mr. Massimo's darkroom. I telephone him when Mr. Massimo is gone and he comes to run a print through, or make an enlargement. When this phase passes, he will go again.

But he creates a picture before that, half-photo, half-drawing. He photographs my hands over a blood-red glass globe, lighted from within. I think the fortune-telling idea has given him the image. He makes the light strong; the veins of my hands stand out in great detail; the bones are almost X-ray visible. "Let me wash my hands," I say, because dirt shows under the nail tips. "No, I like it that way, leave it." So it stays. Watching Michel, I forget to feel anything else, and he is busy timing, setting, focusing. So the hands stay in place as my feelings rock with the sense of the light, and when he shuts it off, finished, we lock the shop up and go home together. Only the next day do I notice that my palm is burned so badly I have to bandage it and go for days in pain. Is the pain for Michel? Damn Michel! The pain is mine, active and virulent. It is mine alone.

The picture, with its background drawing of a woman in evening dress turned from a doorway, and its foreground of hands across a glowing glass, catches on. Michel has others in his package, but none is so popular as this one. He makes enlargements, sells them, makes others, sells those. They go out by the hundreds.

"What is it you carry? *Qu'est-ce que tu as,* Maureen?" Now he is after me, time and again, intense, volpine, impossible, begging from doorways, brushing my shoulder as he passes in the dark. "*Que'est-ce tu as?*"

"I don't know. *Que t'importe, toi?*"

Among his pictures, a U.S. distributor chooses this one, one of three. If I go to certain shops in New York where cheap exotic dress is sold, incense, and apartment decorations of the lowlier sort, bought for their grass-scented pads by homosexual pairs, or by students or young lovers, or by adventurous young people with little taste for permanence, I will see that picture somewhere among them, speaking its silent language. I will look at my hands, see the splash of red that lingers. The world over, copies of it will eventually stick up out of garbage cans, or will be left in vacated apartments. Held to the wall by one thumb tack, it will hang above junk not thought to be worth moving. It celebrates life as fleeting as a dance.

Yet it was created, it happened, and that, in its smallness must pass for everything—must, in this instance, stand for all.

STEVE STERN

Steve Stern was born in Memphis, Tennessee. He took a B.A. degree from Rhodes College in Memphis and an M.F.A. from the University of Arkansas. He is currently a visiting lecturer at Skidmore College. He has published two books for children, *Mickey and the Golem* and *Hershel and the Beast,* and a novel, *The Moon & Ruben Shein.* His two collections of stories are *Isaac and the Undertaker's Daughter* (1983), which won the Pushcart Writer's Choice Award, and *Lazar Malkin Enters Heaven* (1986), which won the Edgar Lewis Wallant Award.

Lazar Malkin Enters Heaven

My father-in-law, Lazar Malkin, may he rest in peace, refused to die. This was in keeping with his lifelong stubbornness. Of course there were those who said that he'd passed away already and come back again, as if death were another of his so-called peddling trips, from which he always returned with a sackful of crazy gifts.

There were those in our neighborhood who joked that he'd been dead for years before his end. And there was more than a little truth in this. Hadn't he been declared clinically kaput not once but twice on the operating table? Over the years they'd extracted more of his internal organs than it seemed possible to do without. And what with his wooden leg, his empty left eye socket concealed by a gabardine patch, his missing teeth and sparse white hair, there was hardly enough of old Lazar left in this world to constitute a human being.

"Papa," my wife, Sophie, once asked him, just after the first of his miraculous recoveries, "what was it like to be dead?" She was sometimes untactful, my Sophie, and in this she took after her father—whose child she was by one of his unholy alliances. (Typically obstinate, he had always refused to marry.)

Lazar had looked at her with his good eye, which, despite being set in a face like last week's roast, was usually wet and amused.

"Why ask me?" he wondered, refusing to take the question seriously. "Ask Alabaster the cobbler, who ain't left his shop in fifty years. He makes shoes, you'd think he's building coffins. Ask Petrofsky whose lunch counter serves nobody but ghosts. Ask Gruber the shammes or Milstein the tinsmith. Ask your husband, who is as good as wearing his sewing machine around his neck. . . ."

I protested that he was being unfair, though we both knew that he wasn't. The neighborhood, which was called the Pinch, had been dead since the War. Life and business had moved east, leaving us with our shops falling down around our ears. Myself and the others, we kidded ourselves that North Main Street would come back. Our children would come back again. The ready-made industry, we kept insisting, was just a passing fancy; people would return to quality. So who needed luftmenschen like Lazar to remind us that we were deceived?

"The Pinch ain't the world," he would inform us, before setting off on one of his mysterious peddling expeditions. He would haul himself into the cab of his corroded relic of a truck piled with shmattes and tools got on credit from a local wholesale outfit. Then he would sputter off in some random direction for points unknown.

Weeks later he would return, his pockets as empty as the bed of his truck. But he always brought back souvenirs in his burlap sack, which he prized like the kid in the story who swapped a cow for a handful of beans.

"I want you to have this," he would say to Mr. Alabaster or Gruber or Schloss or myself. Then he would give us a harp made out of a crocodile's tail; he would give us a Negro's toe, a root that looked like a little man, a contraption called a go-devil, a singletree, the uses of which he had no idea. "This will make you wise," he told us. "This will make you amorous. This came from Itta Bena and this from Nankipoo"—as if they were places as far away as China, which for all we knew they were.

"Don't thank me," he would say, like he thought we might be speechless with gratitude. Then he would borrow a few bucks and limp away to whatever hole in the wall he was staying in.

Most of my neighbors got rid of Lazar's fetishes and elixirs, complaining that it made them nervous to have them around. I was likewise inclined, but in deference to my wife I kept them. Rather than leave them lying around the apartment, however, I tossed them into the storage shed behind my shop.

No one knew how old Lazar really was, though it was generally agreed that he was far past the age when it was still dignified to be alive. None of us, after all, was a spring chicken anymore. We were worn out from the years of trying to supplement our pensions with the occasional alteration or the sale of a pair of shoelaces. If our time should be near, nobody was complaining. Funerals were anyhow the most festive occasions we had in the Pinch. We would make a day of it, traveling in a long entourage out to the cemetery, then back to North Main for a feast at the home of the bereaved. You might say that death was very popular in our neighborhood. So it aggravated us that Lazar, who proceeded us by a whole generation, should persist in hanging around.

He made certain that most of what we knew about him was hearsay. It was his nature to be mysterious. Even Sophie, his daughter by one of his several scandals, knew only the rumors. As to the many versions of his past, she would tell me to take my pick. "I would rather not, if you don't mind," I said. The idea of Lazar Malkin as a figure of romance was a little more than I could handle. But that never stopped Sophie from regaling me by telling stories of her father the way another woman might sing to herself.

He lost his eye as a young man, when he refused to get out of the way of a rampaging Cossack in his village of Podolsk. Walking away from Kamchatka, where he'd been sent for refusing to be drafted into the army of the Czar, the frostbite turned to gangrene and he lost his leg. Or was it the other way around? He was dismembered by a Cossack, snowblinded in one eye for good?. . . . What did it matter? The only moral I got out of the tales of Lazar's mishegoss was that every time he refused to do what was sensible, there was a little less of him left to refuse with.

It puzzled me that Sophie could continue to have such affection for the old kocker. Hadn't he ruined her mother, among others, at a time when women did not go so willingly to their ruin? Of course, the living proofs of his wickedness were gone now. His old mistresses had long since passed on, and it was assumed there were no offspring other than Sophie. Though sometimes I was haunted by the thought of the surrounding countryside populated by the children of Lazar Malkin.

So what was the attraction? Did the ladies think he was some pirate with his eye patch and clunking artificial leg? That one I still find hard to swallow. Or maybe they thought that with him it didn't count. Because he refused to settle down to any particular life, it was as if he had no legitimate life at all. None worth considering in any case. And I cursed myself for the time I took to think about him, an old fool responsible for making my wife a bastard—though who could think of Sophie in such a light?

"You're a sick man, Lazar," I told him, meaning in more ways than one. "See a doctor."

"I never felt better, I'll dance on your grave," he insisted, asking me incidentally did I have a little change to spare.

I admit that this did not sit well with me, the idea of his hobbling a jig on my headstone. Lie down already and die, I thought, God forgive me. But from the way he'd been lingering in the neighborhood lately, postponing his journeys, it was apparent to whoever noticed that something was wrong. His unshaven face was the gray of dirty sheets, and his wizened stick of a frame was shrinking visibly. His odor, no longer merely the ripe stench of the unwashed, had about it a musty smell of decay. Despite my imploring, he refused to see a physician, though it wasn't like he hadn't been in the hospital before. (Didn't I have a bundle of his unpaid bills to prove it?) So maybe this time he knew that for what he had there wasn't a cure.

When I didn't see him for a while, I supposed that, regardless of the pain he was in, he had gone off on another of his peddling trips.

"Your father needs a doctor," I informed Sophie over dinner one night.

"He won't go," she said, wagging her chins like what can you do with such a man. "So I invited him to come stay with us."

She offered me more kreplach, as if my wide-open mouth meant that I must still be hungry. I was thinking of the times he'd sat at our table in the vile, moth-eaten overcoat he wore in all seasons. I was thinking of the dubious mementos he left us with.

"Don't worry," said my good wife, "he won't stay in the apartment . . ."

"Thank God."

". . . But he asked if he could have the shed out back."

"I won't have it!" I shouted, putting my foot down. "I won't have him making a flophouse out of my storehouse."

"Julius," said Sophie in her watch-your-blood-pressure tone of voice, "he's been out there a week already."

I went down to the little brick shed behind the shop. The truth was that I seldom used it—only to dump the odd bolt of material and the broken sewing machines that I was too attached to to throw away. And Lazar's gifts. Though I could see through the window that an oil lamp was burning beneath a halo of mosquitoes, there was no answer to my knock. Entering anyway, I saw cobwebs, mouse droppings, the usual junk—but no Lazar.

Then I was aware of him propped in a chair in a corner, his burlap sack and a few greasy dishes at his feet. It took me so long to notice because I was not used to seeing him sit still. Always he was hopping from his real leg to his phony, being a nuisance, telling us we ought to get out and see more of the world. Now with his leg unhitched and lying across some skeins of mildewed cloth, I could have mistaken him for one of my discarded manikins.

"Lazar," I said, "in hospitals they at least have beds."

"Who sleeps?" he wanted to know, his voice straining up from his hollow chest. This was as much as admitting his frailty. Shocked out of my aggravation, I proceeded to worry.

"You can't live in here," I told him, thinking that no one would confuse this with living. "Pardon my saying so, but it stinks like Gehinom." I had observed the coffee tin he was using for a slop jar.

"A couple of days," he managed in a pathetic attempt to recover his native chutzpah, "and I'll be back on my feet again. I'll hit the road." When he coughed, there was dust, like when you beat a rug.

I looked over at one of the feet that he hoped to be back on and groaned. It might have been another of his curiosities, taking its place alongside of the boar's tusk and the cypress knee.

"Lazar," I implored, astonished at my presumption, "go to heaven already. Your organs and limbs are waiting there for a happy reunion. What do you want to hang around this miserable place anyway?" I made a gesture intended to take in more than the shed, which included the whole of the dilapidated Pinch with its empty shops and abandoned synagogue. Then I understood that for Lazar my gesture had included even more. It took in the high roads to Iuka and Yazoo City, where the shwartzers swapped him moonshine for a yard of calico.

"Heaven," he said in a whisper that was half a shout, turning his head to spit on the floor. "Heaven is wasted on the dead. Anyway, I like it here."

Feeling that my aggravation had returned, I started to leave.

"Julius," he called to me, reaching into the sack at his feet, extracting with his withered fingers I don't know what—some disgusting composition of feathers and bones and hair. "Julius," he wheezed in all sincerity, "I have something for you."

What can you do with such a man?

I went back the following afternoon with Dr. Seligman. Lazar told the doctor don't touch him, and the doctor shrugged like he didn't need to dirty his hands.

"Malkin," he said, "this isn't becoming. You can't borrow time the way you borrow gelt."

Seligman was something of a neighborhood philosopher. Outside the shed he assured me that the old man was past worrying about. "If he thinks he can play hide-and-seek with death, then let him. It doesn't hurt anybody but himself." He had such a way of putting things, Seligman.

"But Doc," I said, still not comforted, "it ain't in *your* backyard that he's playing his farkokte game."

It didn't help, now that the word was out, that my so-called friends and neighbors treated me like I was confining old Lazar against his will. For years they'd wished him out of their hair, and now they behaved as if they actually missed him. Nothing was the same since he failed to turn up at odd hours in their shops, leaving them with some ugly doll made from corn husks or a rabbit's foot.

"You think I like it," I asked them, "that the old fortz won't get it over with?" Then they looked at me like it wasn't nice to take his name in vain.

Meanwhile Sophie continued to carry her noodle puddings and bowls of chicken broth out to the shed. She was furtive in this activity, as if she was harboring an outlaw, and sometimes I thought she enjoyed the intrigue. More often than not, however, she brought back her plates with the food untouched.

I still looked in on him every couple of days, though it made me nauseous. It spoiled my constitution, the sight of him practically decomposing.

"You're sitting shivah for yourself, that's what," I accused him, holding my nose. When he bothered to communicate, it was only in grunts.

I complained to Sophie: "I was worried a flophouse, but charnel house is more like it."

"Shah!" she said, like it mattered whether the old so-and-so could hear us. "Soon he'll be himself again."

I couldn't believe my ears.

"Petrofsky," I confided at his lunch counter the next day, "my wife's as crazy as Lazar. She thinks he's going to get well."

"So why you got to bury him before his time?"

Petrofsky wasn't the only one to express this sentiment. It was contagious. Alabaster, Ridblatt, Schloss, they were all in the act, all of them suddenly defenders of my undying father-in-law. If I so much as opened my mouth to kvetch about the old man, they told me hush up, they spat against the evil eye. "But only yesterday you said it's unnatural he should live so long," I protested.

"Doc," I told Seligman in the office where he sat in front of a standing skeleton, "the whole street's gone crazy. They think that maybe a one-legged corpse can dance again."

The doctor looked a little nervous himself, like somebody might be listening. He took off his nickel-rimmed spectacles to speak.

"Maybe they think that if the angel of death can pass over Lazar, he can pass over the whole neighborhood."

"Forgive me, Doctor, but you're crazy too. Since when is everyone so excited to preserve our picturesque community? And anyway, wouldn't your angel look first in an open grave, which after all is what the Pinch has become." Then I was angry with myself for having stooped to speaking in riddles too.

But in the end I began to succumb to the general contagion. I was afraid for Lazar, I told myself, though—who was I kidding?—like the rest, I was afraid for myself.

"Sophie," I confessed to my wife, who had been treating me like a stranger lately, "I wish that old Lazar was out peddling again." Without him out wandering in the boondocks beyond our neighborhood, returning with his cockamamie gifts, it was like there wasn't a "beyond" anymore. The Pinch, for better or worse, was all there was. This I tried to explain to my Sophie, who squeezed my hand like I was her Julius again. Each time I looked in on him, it was harder to distinguish the immobile Lazar from the rest of the dust and drek. I described this to Seligman, expecting medical opinion, and got only that it put him in mind of the story of the golem—dormant and moldering in a synagogue attic these six hundred years.

Then there was a new development. There were bits of cloth sticking out of the old man's nostrils and ears, and he refused to open his mouth at all.

"It's to keep his soul from escaping," Sophie told me, mussing my hair as if any ninny could see that. I groaned and rested my head in my hands, trying not to imagine what other orifices he might have plugged up.

After that I didn't visit him anymore. I learned to ignore Sophie, with her kerchief over her face against the smell, going to and fro with the food he refused to eat. I was satisfied it was impossible that he should still be alive, which fact made it easier to forget about him for periods of time.

This was also the tack that my friends and neighbors seemed to be taking. On the subject of Lazar Malkin we had all become deaf and dumb. It was like he was a secret we shared, holding our breaths lest someone should find us out.

Meanwhile on North Main Street it was business (or lack of same) as usual.

Of course I wasn't sleeping so well. In the middle of the night I remembered that, among the items and artifacts stored away in my shed, there was my still breathing father-in-law. This always gave an unpleasant jolt to my system. Then I would get out of bed and make what I called my cocktail—some antacid and a shpritz of soda water. It was summer and the rooms above the shop were an oven, so I would go out to the open back porch for air. I would sip my medicine, looking down at the yard and the shed—where Lazar's lamp had not been kindled for a while.

On one such night, however, I observed that the lamp was burning again. What's more, I detected movement through the little window. Who knew but some miracle had taken place and Lazar was up again? Shivering despite the heat, I grabbed my bathrobe and went down to investigate.

I tiptoed out to the shed, pressed my nose against the filthy windowpane, and told myself that I didn't see what I saw. But while I bit the heel of my hand to keep from crying out loud, he wouldn't go away—the stoop-shouldered man in his middle years, his face sad and creased like the seat of someone's baggy pants. He was wearing a rumpled blue serge suit, its coat a few sizes large to accommodate the hump on his back. Because it fidgeted and twitched, I thought at first that the hump must be alive; then I understood that it was a hidden pair of wings.

So this was he, Malach he-Mavet, the Angel of Death. I admit to being somewhat disappointed. Such a sight should have been forbidden me, it should have struck me blind and left me gibbering in awe. But all I could feel for the angel's presence was my profoundest sympathy. The poor shnook, he obviously had his work cut out for him. From the way he massaged his temples with the tips of his fingers, his complexion a little bilious (from the smell?), I guessed that he'd been at it for a while. He looked like he'd come a long way expecting more cooperation than this.

"For the last time, Malkin," I could hear him saying, his tone quite similar in its aggravation to the one I'd used with Lazar myself, "are you or aren't you going to give up the ghost?"

In his corner old Lazar was nothing, a heap of dust, his moldy overcoat and eye patch the only indications that he was supposed to resemble a man.

"What are you playing, you ain't at home?" the angel went on. "You're at home. So who do you think you're fooling?"

But no matter how much the angel sighed like he didn't have all night, like the jig was already up, Lazar Malkin kept mum. For this I gave thanks and wondered how, in my moment of weakness, I had been on the side of the angel.

"Awright, awright," the angel was saying, bending his head to squeeze the bridge of his nose. The flame of the lamp leaped with every tired syllable he uttered. "So it ain't vested in me, the authority to take from you what you won't give. So what. I got my orders to bring you back. And if you don't come dead, I take you alive."

There was a stirring in Lazar's corner. Keep still, you fool, I wanted to say. But bony fingers had already emerged from his coatsleeves; they were snatching the plugs of cloth from his ears. The angel leaned forward as if Lazar had spoken, but I could hear nothing—oh, maybe a squeak like a rusty hinge. Then I heard it again.

"Nu?" was what Lazar had said.

The angel began to repeat the part about taking him back, but before he could finish, Lazar interrupted.

"Take me where?"

"Where else?" said the angel. "To paradise, of course."

There was a tremor in the corner which produced a commotion of moths.

"Don't make me laugh," the old man replied, actually coughing the distant relation of a chortle. "There ain't no such place."

The angel: "I beg your pardon?"

"You heard me," said Lazar, his voice became amazingly clear.

"Okay," said the angel, trying hard not to seem offended. "We're even. In paradise they'll never believe you're for real."

Where he got the strength then I don't know—unless it was born from the pain that he'd kept to himself all those weeks—but Lazar began to get up. Spider webs came apart and bugs abandoned him like he was sprouting out of the ground. Risen to his foot, he cried out,

"There ain't no world but this!"

The flame leaped, the windowpane rattled.

This was apparently the final straw. The angel shook his melancholy head, mourning the loss of his patience. He removed his coat, revealing a sweat-stained shirt and a pitiful pair of wings no larger than a chicken's.

"Understand, this is not my style," he protested, folding his coat, approaching what was left of my father-in-law.

Lazar dropped back into the chair, which collapsed beneath him. When the angel attempted to pull him erect, he struggled. I worried a moment that the old man might crumble to pieces in the angel's embrace. But he was substantial enough to shriek bloody murder, and not too proud to offer bribes: "I got for you a nice feather headdress . . ."

He flopped about and kicked as the angel stuffed him head first into his own empty burlap peddler's sack.

Then the worldweary angel manhandled Lazar—whose muffled voice was still trying to bargain from inside the sack—across the cluttered shed. And hefting his armload, the angel of death battered open the back door, then carried his burden, still kicking, over the threshold.

I threw up the window sash and opened my mouth to shout. But I never found my tongue. Because that was when, before the door slammed behind them, I got a glimpse of kingdom come.

It looked exactly like the yard in back of the shop, only—how should I explain it?—sensitive. It was the same brick wall with glass embedded on top, the same ashes and rusty tin cans, but they were tender and ticklish to look at. Intimate like (excuse me) flesh beneath underwear. For the split second that the door stayed open, I felt that I was turned inside-out, and what I saw was glowing under my skin in place of my kishkes and heart.

Wiping my eyes, I hurried into the shed and opened the back door. What met me was a wall, some ashes and cans, some unruly weeds and vines, the rear of the derelict coffee factory, the rotten wooden porches of the tenements of our dreary neighborhood. Then I remembered—slapping my forehead, stepping gingerly into the yard—that the shed had never had a back door.

Climbing the stairs to our apartment, I had to laugh out loud.

"Sophie!" I shouted to my wife—who, without waking, told me where to find the bicarbonate of soda. "Sophie," I cried, "set a place at the table for your father. He'll be coming back with God only knows what souvenirs."

PETER TAYLOR

Peter Taylor was born in Trenton, Tennessee, in 1917. He graduated from Kenyon College in 1940 and has taught at Harvard, the University of North Carolina, Kenyon, and the University of Virginia, where he has been Commonwealth Professor of English since 1967. He is the author of six books of stories: *A Long Fourth and Other Stories* (1948), *Happy Families Are All Alike* (1959), *Miss Leonora When Last Seen and Fifteen Other Stories* (1964), *The Collected Stories of Peter Taylor* (1969), *In the Miro District and Other Stories* (1977), and *The Old Forest and Other Stories* (1985), which won the PEN/Faulkner Award. He has published four books of plays and two novels, *A Woman of Means* (1950), and *A Summons to Memphis* (1986), which won a Pulitzer Prize.

Cookie

Two nights a week, he *had* to be home for supper, and some weeks, when his conscience was especially uneasy, he turned up three or four times. Tonight, she had a dish of string beans, cooked with cured side meat, on the table when he came in. The smoky odor of the fat struck him when he opened the front door, but he couldn't believe it until he went back to the dining room and saw the dish on the table. "Good God!" he said to himself. "That's fine. Where did she get fresh beans at this time of year?"

Presently his wife, who was, like himself, past fifty, came through the swinging door from the pantry.

"Ah," she said, "my husband is right on time tonight." She came to him and undid the buttons of his overcoat, as she used to undo the children's. It was his lightweight "fall coat," which she had brought down from the attic only two weeks before. She took it and folded it over the back of a dining-room chair, as she would have a visitor's. She knew that he would be leaving right after coffee.

He leaned over the dish and smelled it, and then sat down at the place that was set for him. It was directly across the round dining-room table from her place. She stepped to the pantry door and called: "Cookie, we're ready when you are." She pulled out her chair and sat down.

"Shall we have the blessing tonight?" she said, with some small hope in her smile.

"Oh, let's not." He smiled back. It was a cajoling smile.

"All right, then." She smoothed the tablecloth with her fingers.

He served himself from the dish of beans and selected a piece of the side meat. He bent his head over and got one whiff of the steaming dish. "You're too good to me," he said evenly. He pushed the dish across the table to within her reach.

"Nothing's too good for one's husband."

"You're much too good to me," he said, now lowering his eyes to his plate.

Cookie came through the swinging door with a vegetable dish in each hand. She was a brown, buxom Negro woman, perhaps a few years older than her mistress. She set the dishes on the table near her mistress's plate.

"Good evenin', Cookie," he said to her as she started back to the kitchen.

"Yessuh," she said, and went on through the doorway.

His wife was serving herself from a dish. "Here are some of your baked potatoes," she said.

"Ah!" he said. "You *are* too good . . ." This time he left the sentence unfinished.

She passed him the dish. "And here are simply some cold beets."

"Fine . . . fine . . . fine."

"Do you think we would like a little more light?" she said. She pushed herself back from the table.

"We might. We might."

She went to the row of switches by the doorway that led to the hall. She pushed the second switch, and the light overhead was increased. She pushed the third, and the wall lights by the sideboard came on. With each increase of light in the room her husband said, "Ah . . . fine . . . ah . . . fine." It was a small dining room—at least, it seemed so in the bright light, for the house was old and high-ceilinged. The woodwork was a natural pine, with heavy door facings and a narrow chair rail. The paper above the chair rail was a pale yellow, and no pictures were on the walls. There were two silver candlesticks and a punch bowl on the sideboard. Through the glass doors of the press the cut glassware showed. The large light fixture, a frosted glass bowl, hung from a heavy "antiqued" chain low over the table, and the bright light brought out a spot here and there on the cloth.

She was taking her seat again when Cookie pushed through the door with the meat and the bread.

"What's this? A roast? You're outdoing yourself tonight, Cookie," he said.

"Y'all want all iss light?" Cookie said, blinking, and she set the meat down before him.

"Well, it's—well, it's cold-water cornbread!" He took two pieces of bread from the plate that Cookie held to him.

"Y'all want all iss light?" Cookie said to her mistress, who was selecting a small piece of bread and smiling ingenuously at her husband.

"Yes, Cookie," she said, "I think so. I thought I'd turn 'em up some."

"Wull, I could a done it, Mizz."

"It's all right, Cookie. I didn't want the bread burned."

"Wull, it ain't Judgment Day, Mizz. Y'all could a waited. I'd a done it, stead of you havin' to do it." She put the bread on the table and covered it with the napkin that she had held the plate with.

"It's all right, Cookie."

Cookie opened the door to go back to the kitchen. As she went through, she said, "Lawd a *mercy!*"

His wife pushed her plate across the table, and he put on it a slice of roast that he had carved—an outside piece, because it was more done. He cut several slices, until he came to one that seemed rare enough for himself. "Any news from the chillun?" he said.

"Yes," she said. "Postcards from all three."

"Only postcards?"

She began to taste her food, taking so little on her fork that it was hardly visible.

"Now, that's just rotten!" he said. He brought a frown to his face. "They ought to write you letters. They ought to write you at least once a week! I'm going to write the boys tomorrow and tell 'em."

"Now, please, honey! Please don't! They're well. They said so, and that's all I need to know. They're just busy. Young people don't have time for letters." She eased her knife and fork down on her plate. "They're young!"

"What's that got to do with it?" he said. "They ought always to have time for *you.*" He went on eating and talking at the same time. "These beets are fine," he said. Then, after swallowing, "I won't have that! They ought to write their mother once a week. When I was in med school, you know how much I wrote Mama. Father would have beaten me, I believe, and taken me out, if I hadn't. I ought to take them out just once." He stopped eating for a moment, and shaking his fork at her, he spoke even more earnestly: "And just one month I should forget to send *her* that check."

His wife sat, somewhat paled, making no pretense of eating. "Now, please, honey," she said. "She has two little children and a husband who is far from well. I had a letter from her last week, written while the children were taking a little nap. Remember that she has two little children to look after." Her lips trembled. "There's nothing for the boys to write. They say on every single card they miss being home."

He saw that her lips were quivering, and he began eating again. He frowned. Then he smiled suddenly and said, as if with relief, "I'll tell you. Yes. You ought to go up and see 'em. You haven't been to Nashville since they were *both* in med."

She wiped her mouth with her napkin and smiled. "No, there's no need in my going," she said. And she began to eat her dinner again.

Cookie came in with a small pan of hot bread, holding it with a kitchen towel. She uncovered the plate of bread on the table and stacked the hot bread on top of what was there. With her free hand, she reached in front of her mistress and felt the untouched piece of bread on her plate. "'S got cole on ya," she said. She picked it up in her brown hand and threw it on the cooking pan. She placed a piece of hot bread on his mistress's plate, saying, "Now, gwine butter't while 't's hot."

Her mistress pushed the bread plate across the table toward her husband. She said to him, "Cookie and I are going to get a box of food off to 'em next week, like we used to send 'em in military school. Aren't we, Cookie?"

"Fine . . . fine . . . fine," he said. He took a piece of the cornbread and began to butter it.

Cookie nodded her head toward him and said to her mistress, "*He* hear from 'em?" Then she took several steps around the table, picked up the bread plate, and returned it to its former place. She was tucking the napkin about its edges again.

"No, I have *not!*" He brought the frown to his face again. "They ought to write their mammy, oughtn't they, Cookie?"

"Sho-God ought. 'S a shame," Cookie said. She looked at her mistress. And her mistress put her knife and fork down again. Her lips began to quiver. She gazed tearfully at her husband.

He looked away and spoke out in a loud voice that seemed almost to echo in the high-ceilinged room: "What are you goin' to send 'em? What are you going to send them young'ons, Cookie?"

Cookie looked at him blankly and then at the butter plate, which was in the center of the table. "Whatever she say."

"Well, what do you say, Mother?"

She cleared her throat and ran her hand in a series of pats over her thick and slightly graying hair that went in soft waves back over her ears. "I had thought that we might get hold of two fat guinea hens," she said.

"Fine . . . fine."

"I thought we might get some smoked sausage, not too new and—"

"Ah . . . fine."

"And we might spare one of the fruitcakes we've got soaking."

"How does that suit you, Cookie?" he said.

Cookie was on her way toward the kitchen again. "Yessuh," she said.

He ate in silence for several minutes, took a second helping of string beans, and another piece of bread. She nibbled at a piece of bread. She put more salt and pepper on her meat and ate a few bites. And then she arranged her knife and fork on her plate. Finally, he put his knife and fork down on his empty plate and, with his mouth still full, said, "There's not more, surely?"

She smiled, nodding her head. "Pie."

"No! What kind!"

"I cooked it myself." She picked up a little glass call bell beside her plate and tinkled it. He sat chewing his last bite, and presently Cookie appeared in the doorway with two plates of yellow lemon pie topped with an inch of white meringue.

"This is where she can beat you, Cookie," he said as the cook set the piece of pie before him.

Cookie made a noise that was somewhat like "Psss." She looked at her mistress and gave her a gold-toothed smile. She started to leave with the dinner plates.

"Wait a minute, Cookie," he said. She stopped and looked at him, with her lower lip hanging open. He was taking big bites of the pie. "Cookie, I've been wantin' to ask you how your 'corporosity' is."

"M'whut, Boss-Man?"

"And, furthermore, I understand from what various people are saying around that you have ancestors." He winked at his wife. She dropped her eyes to her plate.

"Whut's he mean, Mizz?" Cookie asked, standing with the two dinner plates in hand.

"Just some of his foolishness, Cookie," she said, with her eyes still on her plate.

He thought to himself that his wife was too good to tease even Cookie. He said to himself, "She doesn't realize that they really eat it up."

"M' coffee's bilin'," Cookie said, and she went through the swinging door.

His wife looked up from her plate. "You know Cookie never has liked to joke. Now, please, honey, don't tease her. She's getting along in her years now. Her temper's quicker than it used to be."

He had finished his pie when Cookie brought in the coffee. She brought it on a tray—two cups and a kitchen pot. She set a cup at each place, filled them, and set the pot on the tablecloth.

"How's that church of yours comin', Cookie?" he said.

"It's makin' out, Boss-Man."

"Haven't you-all churched nobody lately?"

"No, suh, not us."

"How about Dr. Palmer's cook, Cookie? Is she a member in standing?"

"Sho. Mean 'at gal Hattie?" She looked at her mistress and smiled.

He looked at his wife, who he thought was shaking her head at Cookie. Then he looked at Cookie. "Yes," he said, almost absentmindedly. "He brought her in from the country. That's it—Hattie! That's her name."

"Yessuh. She's from out on Pea Ridge."

"She's givin' 'im some trouble. Drinkin', ain't she, Cookie?"

"'Cep' *he* didn't get her from Pea Ridge."

"No, Cookie?"

"She put in a year for some ladies he know out near the sand banks, and —"

"She's a drinker, ain't she, Cookie?"

"Yessuh. I *reckon* she is." She tilted her head back and gave him her gold-toothed laugh, which ended in a sort of sneer this time. "She uz dancin' roun' outside chuch las' night an' say to me she want to teach me how to do dat stuff. I tell huh she's drunk, an' she say, 'Sho I is. I teach you how to hit de bottle, too!'"

He pushed his chair away from the table, still holding his coffee, and laughed aloud. He saw that his wife was looking threateningly at Cookie. "What else did she say, Cookie?" he pressed her.

"Oh, dat gal's a big talker. She's full of lies. De way she lies 'bout huh boss-man's terble. She lie 'bout anybody an' everybody in Thornton. She call names up an' down de street."

"What sort of lies?" He leaned forward, smiling, and winked at his wife.

"Them ladies from the sand banks—she say they's in an' out his place mos' any night. Doc Palmer's a bachlorman, sho, but Hattie say hit ain't jus' Doc Palmer! They comes there to meet the ladies—all sorts of menfolks, married or not. She say she see 'em *all* 'bout his place sooner later."

His wife had quit sipping her coffee and was staring at Cookie.

"Who, for instance, Cookie? Let us in on it," he said.

The cook turned to him and looked at him blankly. "You, Boss-Man."

His wife stood up at her place, her napkin in her hand. Her eyes filled with tears. "After all these years!" she said. "Cookie, you've forgotten your place for the first time, after all these years."

Cookie put her hands under her apron, looked at her feet a moment, and then looked up at him, her own eyes wet. Her words came almost like screams. "Hattie say she *seen* ya! But she's a liar, ain't she, Boss-Man?"

Her mistress sat down, put one elbow on the table, and brought her napkin up to cover her face. "I'm disappointed in you, Cookie. Go to the kitchen."

Cookie went through the swinging door without looking at her mistress.

In a moment, his wife looked up at him and said, "I'm sorry. I'd not thought she was capable of a thing like that."

"Why, it's all right—for what she said. Doctors will get talked about. Even Cookie knows the girl's a liar."

His wife seemed, he thought, not to have heard him. She was saying, "A servant of mine talking to my husband like that!"

"It's only old-nigger uppitiness," he reassured her.

"I shall speak to her tonight," she said. "I promise you."

"Oh, I suppose you'll think you have to fire her."

She looked at him, her features composed again. She ran her hand over her hair in a series of pats. "No, no," she said. "I can't fire Cookie. I'll speak to her tonight. It'll never happen again."

"Now I think of it, perhaps she ought to be sent on her way after talking like that."

"I'll look after the matter."

He poured himself a second cup of coffee and, as he drank it, he watched his wife closely. He frowned again and said, "Why, she might talk to *you* in that way some day. That's all I thought."

She smiled at him. "There's no danger. I'll have a talk with her tonight."

She helped him on with his overcoat. He said, "Got to see some country people tonight. Might even have to drive over to Huntsboro." She was buttoning his coat. "There's a lot of red throat over there."

"I can't have her talking that way to my husband," she said aloud, yet to herself. "But I won't fire her," she told him. "She's too much one of us—too much one of the family, and I know she'll be full of remorse for speaking out of turn like that."

He looked directly into her eyes, and she smiled confidently. She told him she would leave the back light on, because lately the nights had been cloudy and dark. As he stopped in the hall to pick up his hat and his case, he heard Cookie come through the swinging door.

"Now, Cookie, I want to have a little talk with you," his wife said, and Cookie said, "Yes'm, Mizz."

He went out, closing the door softly behind him, and as he crossed the porch, he could still hear their voices inside—the righteousness and disillusion of Cookie's, the pride and discipline of his wife's. He passed down the flight of wooden steps and stepped from the brick walk onto the lawn. He hesitated a moment; he could still hear their voices indistinctly—their senseless voices. He began walking with light, sure steps over the grass—their ugly, old voices. In the driveway, his car, bright and new and luxurious, was waiting for him.

Dean of Men

I AM not unsympathetic, Jack, to your views on the war. I am not unsympathetic to your views on the state of the world in general. From the way you wear your hair and from the way you dress I do find it difficult to decide whether you or that young girl you say you are about to marry is going to play the male role in your marriage—or the female role. But even that I don't find offensive. And I am not trying to make crude jokes at your expense. You must pardon me, though, if my remarks seem too personal. I confess I don't know you as well as a father *ought* to know his son, and I may seem to take liberties.

However, Jack, I do believe that I understand the direction in which you—all of you—think you are going. I have not observed college students during the past thirty years for nothing. And I must try to warn you that I don't think even your wonderful generation will succeed in going very far along the road you are on. In this connection, Jack, I want to tell you a story. I can tell you this story because even its most recent chapters took place a very long time ago and because the events of the story don't matter to anybody any more—neither to me nor even to your mother. When you see your mother next, and if you repeat what I am about to tell you, she may give you a somewhat different version. But that doesn't matter. It is not really a story about your mother and me or about our divorce. Perhaps it is a story about you and me—about men.

I think I know the very moment to begin: I was fitting the key into the lock of my office door on a Sunday morning. I was in such a temper I could hardly get the key into the keyhole or turn the lock after it was in. There had been a scene at our breakfast table at home; I had left the house. It was a strangely upsetting scene for me, though commonplace enough on the surface. Your sister Susie, who was no more than nine or ten then—she couldn't have been more, since *you* were still in a high chair, Jack—Susie had interrupted what I was saying across my Sunday morning grapefruit to your mother. And I had fired away at her, "Don't interrupt grown-up talk, Susie!"

That sounds commonplace enough, I know. But Susie persisted. "Why don't you go up to the trustees, Daddy," said she, advising me on how to behave in the professional crisis I was then in, which I had been discoursing upon across my grapefruit. "Why don't you go up to them and tell them how the president of the college is being unfair to you?"

Somehow I found her little remark enraging. I fairly shouted across the table, "For God's sake, Susie, shut up. Don't try to talk about things you don't understand or know a damned thing about!"

I blush now to think that I ever spoke so to a child, but I remember it too well to try to deny it. You see, Jack, I had actually already resigned my appointment at that college where I was then teaching, which was the very college where, a dozen years before, I had been an undergraduate. I had resigned just three weeks before, in protest against an injustice done me, and I had not yet received a definite commitment from the place where I was going next year. (I did receive the commitment the following day, as I recall, but that is not really significant.) Anyhow, I was feeling like a fool, I suppose, to have brought into the world three children for whom I might not be able to provide—only two children, actually, though little Maisie was on the way by then. And I was feeling like a fool, I suppose, to have risked their welfare—*your* welfare, if you please—over a principle of honest administration in a small Midwestern college. I was a very unhappy man, Jack, and there before me was my little ten-year-old daughter seeming to reproach me for my foolishness . . . At any rate, after my second blast at her, Susie had burst into tears and had run from the dining room and out into the yard. Your mother got up from her chair at the end of the table and said to me, "I would be ashamed of myself if I were you."

I made no reply except to say through my teeth: "This is too much."

Your mother's words were still in my ears when I shoved open the door to my office at the college. (Marie's words have a way of lingering in your ears for a very long time, Jack.) Anyhow, I had left the table without finishing breakfast, and left the dining room without any idea of where I was going. And then suddenly I had known. What drove me from the table, of course, were those words of Marie's that were still in my ears. For, Jack, those were the very words I had once heard my mother speak to my father, and, moreover, had heard her speak to Father at a Sunday breakfast table when *he* had teased my own sister Margaret till she cried and left the room. "I would be ashamed of myself if I were you," my mother had said, rising from the table in just the same way that my own wife was destined to do twenty years later. My father bolted from the table, left the house, and went downtown to his office, where he spent the whole of that Sunday. It seemed almost impossible that the incident should be repeating itself in my life. And yet to a remarkable degree it was so, and the memory of where it was my father had taken himself off to told me to what place I must take myself that Sunday morning.

It struck me, just as the door to my office came open, that I had never before seen my office at that early hour on Sunday. I had never, in fact, been in that building where my office was on a Sunday morning—or on the college campus itself, for that matter. It was a lovely campus, on a hill and with trees and with a little river at the foot of the hill, and it was a quite handsome neo-Gothic building I was in. I altogether liked that place, I can assure you. And in addition to my liking the other people on the faculty there, I had my old associations with the place from my undergraduate days. The truth is, I had thought I would settle down there for life, to do my teaching and my writing. It was the third teaching appointment I had had, but in my profession many people have to move around even more than I before they find a congenial spot, Jack. I was not yet thirty-five. I had considered myself lucky to find an agreeable place so early in my career, a small college where I had memories of my youth and where I would be allowed to do my mature work in peace . . .

But I knew by that Sunday morning that I was going to move on. I knew that by the next fall I would be in some other, almost identical office on some other campus and that your mother and I, with our three children, would be established in another house in another college town somewhere. But when I shoved open my office door, somehow it was not as though it were the door to just any little cubbyhole of an office. It was as if it were the door to my ancestral keep—my castle, so to speak; and I burst in upon my papers, my books, my pictures that morning as if expecting to catch them, my kinsmen—my cousins germane—in some conspiratorial act against me—yes, as though it were my books, my papers, my pictures who had betrayed me. But of course the room was just as I had left it. It was the same, and yet at that hour on Sunday morning it did seem different, too.

I can see myself there now, especially as I was during the first quarter hour of that long day. I didn't knock things about or tear up the place as it was my first impulse to do. Instead, after I had slammed the door and latched it, the first thing I did was to go quickly to my desk and turn down the photographs of your mother and Susie and even the one of yourself, Jack. I took the pages of my manuscript and of my typescript which had been in little stacks all over my desk top and quietly stuffed them inside the desk drawers. The books I had been reading recently—my own and those from the library—I removed from the table by my leather chair, putting them out of sight or at least placing them where they would not catch my eye, on the lowest shelf of my bookcase. Then I took down from the walls the four or five prints that hung there, reproductions I had brought back from my Fulbright in Italy, and I set them on the floor with their faces against the wall. If I handled these familiar objects gently, I believe it was just because I had not, after all, found them in active conspiracy against me.

There was no conspiracy among my books and papers and pictures; but what was perhaps worse, I seemingly had found them all dead—murdered. I felt they were strewn about the room like corpses in the last scene of an Elizabethan tragedy. Dead and murdered, that is, so far as I was concerned. Dead and wanting burial. And so, bending over them, I tenderly tucked them away as if to their last rest. Then I went and half sat, half leaned against the sill of the room's only window. The venetian blind there was lowered and the louvers were only half open. I leaned against the sill with my arms folded on my chest and observed the crepuscular light in the room, and I was aware of the Sunday morning stillness. Once again I heard Marie's voice, and after a moment once again heard my mother's voice. Presently I recalled my father's voice too, speaking not through his teeth as I had done that morning, but growling out of one corner of his mouth. I remembered how, as a younger man, I would sometimes wonder about that outburst of Father's temper on that other Sunday morning. It had seemed to me so unlike him. I used to speculate even, in the most literal-minded way, on how he had managed to occupy himself during the long hours he had spent alone in *his* office on that Sunday. The scene he had made at his breakfast table—or that my sister Margaret, or my mother had made—suddenly now became very easy for me to understand. Everything fell so easily into place that I felt I had always understood it. My father was a lawyer and a businessman who had lost most of what he had as a consequence of the '29 Crash. My sister Margaret was already a young lady at the time. She was no little girl like Susie when she sat down to breakfast with Father that other Sunday. She was a good-looking blond girl with wide green eyes, and she had a lovely disposition. She was always cheerful, always saying something clever or making you feel that you had said something clever. Margaret was the oldest child in the family, and I the youngest. But we were very close to each other, and I believe she confided her most serious thoughts to me more often than to anyone else, though surely it was Father she loved best. There was frequently a great deal of banter between her and Father at the table. She was such a well-behaved girl, so puritanical really, that Father would tease her sometimes about leading a wild life and keeping late hours. Mother would say she thought it in bad taste for Father to tease his own daughter about such things and that perhaps he would be putting ideas into her head. But Margaret would laugh at Mother and say that Father's evil mind made it all the more fun to deceive him. Then she and Father would laugh together in a sort of duet of laughter.

Margaret was popular with boys and always had a number of serious admirers. But the more serious the admirers were, the more she and Father seemed to delight in making fun of them. I don't believe Margaret ever imagined she was in love with any of those young men, until the time when Paul Kirkpatrick came along. Paul's family was one that nearly everybody knew about. They were such very rich people that even the Crash and the Depression hardly affected them at all. But it worried Margaret how rich the Kirkpatrick family was. It worried her, that is, that Paul would some day be rich, that she knew he would be rich, and that he was the only young man she found herself able to love. "I know I really love him for himself," she would say to me when we were walking in the park together or if we were in her room with the door shut, "but sometimes there seems to be an ugly, suspicious side of me—another person (old, nasty-minded Mag, I call her)—who laughs and cackles at me like a witch and says, '*I* know why you love him so, dear Miss Margaret! You don't deceive me!'" Then Margaret and I would laugh together, rather the way she and Father did. But she was serious, and was worried.

Perhaps Father worried about it, too—more than I guessed, more than Margaret guessed. Naturally, he would have liked for her to marry a rich man, but there had been so much talk at our house about how hard times were for us that Father may have been afraid Margaret was going to marry into a rich family for *his* sake. At any rate, he was harder on Paul Kirkpatrick in his fun-making than he had been on any of the other young men. And Margaret went right along with him. They made fun of Paul's teeth—Margaret called them stalactites and stalagmites; made fun of his too lofty way of speaking, of the way he walked—they said he waddled; even made fun of his baby-smooth complexion.

Yet, after one of those sessions with Father, when she and I were alone, Margaret smiled at me and said, "You know something? I really think Paul's very good-looking, don't you?"

I told her that yes, I did think so. And it was true. Paul Kirkpatrick was quite handsome. He was an attractive and intelligent young man. But Margaret and Father kept on telling each other how ridiculous he was. It was the summer of 1930. Father was under great tension that summer. It was a year when he suffered one financial blow after another. And he never seemed more tense than when he and Margaret got on the subject of Paul. Sometimes it was very clear that he was prodding and trying to make her come to Paul's defense. But she never gave an inch. I was certain sometimes, however, from the way she sat smiling at Father that she was on the verge of blurting out that she loved Paul and was going to marry him. For I think my sister Margaret intended to marry Paul Kirkpatrick and would have done so had it not been for the family scene that Sunday morning. I had witnessed Paul's and

Margaret's embraces and kisses at the side door more than once that summer. And once I saw—or just possibly imagined I saw—a ring with a large stone in Margaret's purse. Anyway, I remember she came down to breakfast later than the rest of us on that Sunday, and she was fully dressed, which was unusual for anyone at our breakfast table on Sunday. It seems to me that Father had not spoken at the table—he was often silent and abstracted then, though it was not in his nature to be so—he had not spoken until he looked up and saw Margaret sitting, fully dressed, at her place. "Well, you must have a church date with our toothy young friend," he said to her.

"He's coming over this morning," Margaret said with a smile. "I don't know about church." I am quite sure now that she was trying to prepare Father and that Paul was going to "speak" to him that day.

I saw Mother look at Father, and it seems to me that I heard him swallow, though his mouth and throat were empty. Then, lifting a fork heaped with scrambled eggs, he said, "Why not? It's just as easy to love a rich one as a poor one, isn't it, Margaret?"

I saw the first patches of red appear under Margaret's ears and then the same red suffuse her entire face. And I saw the tears fill her eyes before the first sob came. When she pushed herself back from the table, Father was still holding the fork with the eggs on it. He put his fork down on his plate without spilling a morsel. But he was as white as the big napkin which his left hand then drew from his lap and threw out upon the table. "My God. My God," he growled from the corner of his mouth as Margaret ran, weeping aloud, through the living room and then through the hall and on upstairs. And my mother rose at her place and said, "I would be ashamed of myself if I were you."

How Father occupied himself and what he thought about when he reached his office that Sunday were questions that occurred to me during the very hours he was there, occurred to me even though I was just a boy of twelve at the time. My father was known as "a devoted family man," he almost never went to his office at night, and if some piece of business called him there on a Saturday afternoon or a Sunday, he groaned and complained endlessly. We knew he had gone to his office that morning, however, because Mother telephoned him after about an hour, to make sure he was all right. She knew about the money worries he had then, of course, and so she was quick to blame his behavior on that. In fact, she went to Margaret's room and reminded her of "the tensions Father was under" and told her that *she* must forgive him, too. I suspect that Margaret had already forgiven him. I know that she had telephoned Paul Kirkpatrick and told him not to come that day.

Her romance with Paul did not last long after that. The next year she married a "struggling young lawyer" and with him, as my mother would have said, "she has had a good life."

No doubt my father wrote a few letters at his office desk, as I did during the course of my Sunday at my office. But probably it wasn't easy for him to concentrate on letters. I recall that even while I remained leaning against the sill of my office window it came to me that what my father might have thought about in his office, twenty years before, was his own father. For yes, there *was* a story in the family about a scene that my grandfather had made at *his* breakfast table, too. I cannot give so many details about it, though possibly my father could have. There are many obscurities about the old story that I can't possibly clear up and won't try to. In fact, I don't know anything definite about the immediate circumstances that led to the scene. Perhaps I never knew them. People in my grandfather's day disliked admitting they did wretched things to each other at home or that there *were* family scenes in their families. All of the incident that has come down is that my grandfather, no longer a young man—a man past middle age, standing in the doorway to his dining room with his broad-brimmed felt hat on, hurled a silver dollar at my grandmother, who was still seated at the breakfast table, and that the silver dollar landed in the sugar bowl. There is just the additional detail that my grandmother would allow no one to remove the coin and that that sugar bowl, with the silver dollar buried in the sugar, remained on her pantry shelf as long as the old lady lived.

I have always imagined that there had been a quarrel between my grandparents about housekeeping money; perhaps my grandfather, who was not much of a family man in the beginning and who lived a big part of his life away from home, among men, and who was known by all men for his quick temper, perhaps he lost his head momentarily. He forgot he was not among men and he hurled the piece of money at his wife as he would have at some man to whom he had lost a bet. He and my grandmother may have had other difficulties between them over money or over other matters. Perhaps it was really a symbolic gesture on his part, as refusing to remove the coin was on hers. He was not a rich man, but then he was certainly not a poor man either, and actually in his day he was quite a well-known public figure. He was in politics, as his father and his father's father before him were . . . I must tell you something about their politics. They were not exactly small-time politicians. Each one of them, at one time or another during his lifetime, represented our district in Congress. For nearly a hundred years, "we" more or less occupied that seat in Congress. But my grandfather was the most successful and best known of the line and in middle age was elected to the U.S. Senate to complete the unexpired term of an incumbent who had died in office.

Probably my grandfather brought the special type of politician they all three were to its highest possible point of development, a kind of frontiersman-gentleman politician with just the right mixture of realism and idealism to appeal to their constituents. Today people would no doubt call him a pragmatist. He was known for his elegant oratory on the platform and in public debate and known also for the coarseness of his speech in private debate or in private confrontation with his opponents. (My grandfather's grandfather had once horsewhipped an opponent on the public square, and his own father had fought a duel.) It was Grandfather's beautiful oratory and his beautiful voice that got him elected to the Senate. People didn't care what his stand on tariff or on the silver or gold issue was. They believed he was an honest man and they knew he was a spellbinder. He too believed he was an honest man and he didn't understand the new kind of urban politician who was coming to power in our state at the time. It may be he was actually betrayed and ruined by the new politicians simply because they were "low-born rascals." Or it may be he was inevitably betrayed and ruined by them because once a human type is perfected—or almost perfected—it immediately becomes an anachronism and has no place in society. Who can say? He was, at any rate, betrayed and ruined by a low-born man named Lon Lucas, and he never held political office again after that brief term in the Senate.

And now, Jack, I come to the part of the story that I believe it is essential for you to hear. If you have not understood why I have told you all that went before, you will, anyhow, understand why I wish to recount the three episodes that follow.

What happened to my grandfather's political career can be briefly summarized. The unexpired term in the Senate, which he was filling out, lasted but two years. When the time came for him to make his race for a full term, he was persuaded by Lon Lucas and others that instead of making that race it was his duty to his party to come home and run for governor of the state. The Lucas faction comprised a group of young men whom my grandfather considered more or less his protégés. In earlier days they had asked countless small favors of him, and no doubt they had done so in order to create that relationship to him. Now they pointed out to him that from another faction in the party there was a man who, though loathsome to them all, was a strong candidate for the party's nomination for governor, and pointed out that only he, my grandfather, could block the nomination and election of that man. It would be a disgrace to the state and to the party to have such a man in the governor's chair, they said. Yet the senator could easily come home and win the nomination and the election for himself and could just as easily regain his seat in the Senate at a later time.

You may well wonder that an experienced politician could be so naïve as to accept that line of reasoning or to entrust his fate to the hands of those ambitious younger men. Neither his father nor his grandfather would surely, under any circumstances, have relinquished that prize of prizes for a politician, a seat in the U.S. Senate. I cannot pretend to explain it. I knew my grandfather only as an embittered old man who didn't care to have children crawling all over him. But I have to tell you that, within a few weeks after he came home and began his campaign for governor, Lon Lucas and his faction turned on him. Some sort of deal was made with the other faction. No doubt the deal was made long beforehand. Lucas came out in support of the "loathsome man" for governor, and one of the Lucas faction was put up for the seat in the Senate. Very likely there were other considerations also, remunerative to Lon Lucas and company if not to the candidates themselves. Such details are not important here, and I never knew them anyway. But my grandfather was defeated, and he retired from public life to the bosom of his family, where, alas, I cannot say he was greatly loved and cherished.

He withdrew almost entirely from all male company, seeing men only as his rather limited law practice required him to do. He lived out his life in a household of women and children, a household consisting for many years of his wife, his wife's mother and maiden aunt, his own mother, who lived to be ninety-seven, five daughters, and three sons. He never allowed himself to be addressed as senator and forbade all political talk in his presence. The members of his household were destined to retain in their minds and to hand down to future generations their picture of him not as a statesman of high principle or even as a silver-tongued orator but as the coarse-tongued old tyrant of their little world. His three sons always feared him mightily and took from his life only the one lesson: an anathema on politics. My father was the only son who would consent to study law and become a member of the old gentleman's firm, but even he made it clear from the outset that he would not let his profession lead him astray, made it clear to everyone that his interest was not in government but solely in corporation law.

My father's guiding principle in life was that he must at all costs avoid the terrible pitfall of politics. He gave himself to making money and to becoming the family man his father had never been. What finally happened to him I must present in a more dramatic form than the summary I have given of Grandfather's affairs. It would be as difficult for me to summarize the story of Father's betrayal as it would have been for me to imagine and re-create the precise circumstances under which Grandfather first learned of Lon Lucas's double-dealing.

When I had opened the venetian blind at my office window that Sunday morning, I stared out at May's fresh green grass on the campus for a while and down at the small river, swollen by spring rains, at the bottom of the hill.

Then I went to my desk and managed to write two letters to men who had published books on the subject—in "the field"—I was doing my work in. They were perfunctory, polite letters, requesting permission to quote from the work of those men in my own book. When I had sealed and stamped those two letters, I took out another sheet of departmental paper; but it lay on my desk untouched for I don't know how long, a blinding white sheet that I sat staring at impatiently as one does at a movie screen before the film begins. Finally, I put away my pen but left the piece of paper lying there as if meaning to project upon it the images taking shape in my mind. I saw my father stepping out of the family limousine in front of the Union Station in bright winter sunlight. My mother and I were already out of the car and waiting under the canopy. The Negro chauffeur stood holding the car door open and listening to some piece of instruction Father gave him in passing. Since this was in the earliest days of the Depression, we still lived in the world of limousines and chauffeurs, a world that my father's business career had lifted us into. A number of years before this he had ceased altogether to practice law, in order to accept the presidency of a large, "nationally known" insurance company for which he had formerly been the chief attorney and which maintained its head office locally. The insurance company was now in serious difficulties, however. The company's investments were under question. It began to appear that funds had been invested in various business enterprises that seemed hardly to have existed except on paper. Many of these investments had been made before my father's incumbency, but not all of them. Anyway, the man who had most influenced the company's investment of funds was a stockholder in the company and a member of the board of directors, Mr. Lewis Barksdale. He was an old school friend of my father's and had of course been instrumental in electing my father president of the company. It was he alone who would be able to explain the seemingly fraudulent use of moneys—explain it, that is, to the other members of the board—and he alone who could straighten out the snarl that the company's affairs seemed to be in. And it was this Lewis Barksdale whom we had come to the Union Station to meet at four o'clock on a remarkably bright winter afternoon.

The Negro chauffeur threw back his head and laughed at something my father said to him, and then Father advanced toward us, wearing a pleased smile. I remember remarking to Mother at just that moment what a fine day it was and reproaching her for having made me wear my heavy coat, in which I was uncomfortably warm. The truth was, I was still irked by Father's having made me leave a game with a group of boys to come with them to meet Mr. Barksdale's train, and I was taking out my resentment on Mother. Without looking at me, she replied that it was due to turn colder very shortly and, squeezing my hand, she said, "Why can't you have an agreeable disposition like your father's? Don't be an old sourpuss like me." Father was still smiling when he came up to us, and Mother asked him, "What is it that's so funny?"

"Oh," he explained, taking Mother's elbow and escorting us on into the lobby of the station, "when I just now told Irwin not to come inside and fetch Lewis's bag but to wait right there with the car, he said he couldn't keep the car in that spot but fifteen minutes and that he was afraid the train might be late. I said to him that if he knew Lewis Barksdale as well as I do, he'd know that the engineer and the fireman would somehow understand that they *had* to get Lewis's train out here on time."

In the lobby, Father read the track number off the board and then marched us confidently down the concourse to the great iron gate at Track No. 6. Just as he predicted, the train rolled in on time. Father spoke to the uniformed gatekeeper, who let us go through the gateway along with the redcaps, so we could see Mr. Barksdale when he stepped off the train. Father trotted along ahead of us, peering up into the windows of the observation car and then into the windows of the next Pullman. Mother called after him that he had better wait there beside the first Pullman or we might miss Mr. Barksdale. And Father did stop there. But he told me to run on ahead and see if I could get a glimpse of him in the entry of any of the other cars. I said I was not certain I would recognize Mr. Barksdale, but Father said, "You can know him by his derby. Besides, *he'll* recognize *you.*"

I did run on ahead, looking up into the cars, watching the people who came down the steps from each car to the metal stool that the porter had set out for them. Mr. Barksdale, being a man who had no children of his own, was said to be extremely fond of all his friends' children. That was why, as the youngest child in the family—and the only boy—I was taken along to meet the train that day. I could vaguely recall earlier visits he had made to us and seemed to remember a sense of his paying special attention to me. Momentarily, I was persuaded that I *would* remember him if we came face to face. But no man wearing a derby got off the train, and I made out no remotely familiar face in the cars or in the crowded entry ways. Moreover, no passenger climbing down off that train showed any sign of recognizing me.

When I followed the crowd of passengers and redcaps back toward the iron gate, I found Mother still standing beside the observation car. She said that Father had climbed aboard and was going through all the cars in search of Mr. Barksdale. At last we saw Father step off the first of the day coaches, away down the track. He looked very small down there, and when he waved to us and climbed back on the train I felt a sudden ache in the pit of my stomach. "Mr. Barksdale's not on the train," I said to Mother.

"No, I guess not," she said. "I was afraid he mightn't be."

Finally, Father reappeared in the entry between the observation car and the next Pullman. "Lewis must have missed the train somehow," he said as he came down the steps and swung out onto the platform. "Let's go inside the station. I'm going to telephone New York and see if he's still there."

We found a telephone booth on the concourse just beyond Gate No. 6, but Father had to go inside the station lobby to get enough change to make the call. Mother and I stood beside the booth a long time. "He ought to have waited till we got home to make the call," she said at last. "I suppose, though, he couldn't bear to wait." She and I had just agreed to go into the lobby and look for him when we saw him coming toward us. He was all smiles and was holding up two fistfuls of coins.

"I got enough quarters to call China," he said, and seemed to be elated by the feel of the coins in his hands. When he stepped into the booth to make his call, Mother and I moved away some twenty or thirty feet. He must have talked for ten minutes or more. When he came out again, his smile was bigger than before, and he began calling out as he hurried toward us, "Lewis *did* miss the train! And it was so busy in New York today he couldn't get a line to call me. He's coming on an earlier train tonight and will be here by noon tomorrow!"

By noon of the next day, which was Saturday, it was very much colder, and so I didn't complain about having to wear my coat. I did complain somewhat, however, about having to give up several hours of a Saturday to meeting Mr. Barksdale's train. Father seemed to understand and was not so insistent upon my going, but in private Mother was insistent and said it was little enough for me to do if it was what my father wished. As we were leaving the house, Father stopped a moment to telephone the station and ask if the train was going to be on time. He had heard a report on the radio that the weather up East had turned bad. But the dispatcher's office reported that the train was scheduled to arrive exactly on time. In the car, Father said he hoped the dispatcher's office knew what it was talking about. "Trains on the weekend are often late," he said suspiciously. When we got to the station, he told Irwin that since the train might, after all, be late, he had better take the car to the parking lot, and that we would come and find him there.

As we were passing through the lobby, we all three read the gate number aloud from the blackboard, and we laughed at ourselves for it—rather nervously, I suppose. Father had kept silent most of the way down to the station in the car and had left the talking mostly to Mother and me. He began to look more cheerful once we were in the big lobby, and as we passed out onto the concourse he said to Mother under his breath, "Keep your fingers crossed." As soon as we came out onto the concourse, we could see that the train was already backing up to the gate. "Thar she be!" Father exclaimed with sudden gaiety, and he put an arm around each of us to hurry us along. But at the gate he didn't ask the gatekeeper to let us go beyond. We waited outside, and through the bars of the grating we watched the passengers stepping down onto the platform. After a few minutes Father said, "I won't be surprised if

Lewis is the last to get off. He hates crowds." We kept watching until it was obvious that no more passengers were going to leave the train and come through the gate. In what was almost a whisper, Father said to Mother, "He didn't come. What do you suppose could have happened?" And as we were passing the telephone booth on the way out, he said, "I'll call him from home."

We had been at home about half an hour when I heard him speaking to Mother from the foot of the stairs. She was leaning over the banisters in the upstairs hall. "There have been a lot of complications. Lewis has been getting together papers to bring with him. He says he can clear everything up. He's coming in on the same train tomorrow."

"Wonderful," Mother said.

"But I'm not going to ask you all to traipse down to the depot again."

"Nonsense. The third time's the charm," said mother.

At about eleven the next morning Father telephoned the station to ask if the train was scheduled to come in on time. He was told that it would be three hours late. There were heavy snowstorms all over the East now. When Mother came into the big sun room where my sister Margaret and my two other sisters and I were all reading the Sunday paper and told us that snow had delayed Mr. Barksdale's train for three hours, she glanced out the sunroom windows at the darkly overcast sky and said, "There will be snow here before night, I think." None of my sisters even looked up from the paper. I imagine I looked up from the funny paper only because I wished to know whether or not I was going to be taken to the station again. Mother saw me look up and said, "Father says you needn't go with us today, and I suppose he's right."

"I'll go," I said. It had occurred to me suddenly that the snow might be falling by that time and that I would like to see how the old gray stone Union Station looked with snow on all of its turrets and crenelations and how the train would look backing into Gate No. 6 with snow it brought in from the East piled all over its top.

"Well, we'll see," Mother said.

Sometime after two, Mother and Father were in the front hall getting into their coats. I was there too, still undecided as to whether or not I would go along. No snow had begun to fall yet. Father seemed unconcerned about my going or not going. When Mother asked him if he thought he might call the station again, he replied casually that he already had, that the train would arrive as predicted, at three o'clock. He had already buttoned up his heavy, double-breasted overcoat when he added suddenly, "But there's another call I believe I'll make before we set out. It might take a few minutes. . . . You had better take off your coat," he said to Mother.

When he was gone, I asked, "Who do you think he's calling?"

"I imagine he's calling Mr. Barksdale in New York," Mother said. She didn't remove her coat, though. She and I said nothing more. We went and looked out at the sky through the sidelights at the front door. After a few minutes we heard Father's footsteps. When we turned around, he was standing there in the hall, smiling wearily and beginning to unbutton his coat.

"Lewis is still in New York," he said.

"Why in the world?" Mother exclaimed. "What in the world did he say this time?" she asked.

"He didn't say anything. I didn't give him a chance to. As soon as I definitely heard his voice on the wire, I put down the receiver."

"What are you going to do?" Mother asked him.

"There's nothing I can do. He's not coming, that's all. I'll just have to take it however it turns out now."

We didn't go to the station, of course. And Father didn't go off to his room to be by himself, either, as one might have expected. He spent the rest of the afternoon with the family in the sun room, reading the paper, listening to the radio, and playing cards. The way he was with us that afternoon, you wouldn't have suspected anything was wrong. At just about twilight it began to snow outside. And we all went about from window to window with a certain relief, I suppose, watching the big flakes come down and, from the snug safety of our sun room, watching the outside world change.

Father didn't telephone Mr. Barksdale again. They had been close friends since boyhood, but I believe they didn't communicate again for more than twenty-five years. When they were very old men and most of their other contemporaries were dead, Mr. Barksdale took to calling Father over long-distance and they would sometimes talk for an hour at a time about their boyhood friends or about business friends they had had when they were starting out in business. We were glad whenever Mr. Barksdale called Father, because it cheered him and made him seem livelier than anything else did during those last years. He often seemed very lonely during those years, though he continued to have a reasonably cheerful disposition. After the legal difficulties and the embarrassing publicity that followed his being abandoned by his trusted friend, Father led a quiet, uneventful life. He returned to his law practice, and he was a respected member of his firm. But he made no real life for himself in his practice—that is, he seldom saw other members of the firm away from the office, and I don't remember his ever mentioning the name of a client at home. His real life was all at home, where, as he would point out, it had always been. He and Mother sometimes played bridge with neighbors, and whatever other social life they had was there in the neighborhood where we lived after we lost the old house and could no longer afford a staff of servants. He was an affectionate father, and I rarely saw him in what I would call depressed spirits. Yet how often one had the feeling that he was lonely and bored. I remember sometimes, even when the family was on a vacation together—when we had taken a cottage at the shore or were camping and fishing in the mountains—the look would come in his eye. And one was tempted to ask oneself, What's wrong? What's missing?

I don't honestly know when I decided to go into college teaching, Jack. I considered doing other things—a career in the army or the navy. Yes, I might have gone to Annapolis or West Point. Those appointments were much to be desired in the Depression years, and my family did still have a few political connections. One thing was certain, though. Business was just as much out of the question for me as politics had been for my father. An honest man, I was to understand, had too much to suffer there. Yes, considering our family history, an ivory tower didn't sound like a bad thing at all for an honest man and a serious man. . . . A dozen years after graduation I found myself back teaching in that college where I had been an undergraduate. Physically, it was a beautiful spot and, as I have already said, I thought I would settle down there for life, to do my teaching and my writing.

After my second year of teaching there I was awarded a research Fulbright to Italy, and so was on leave for a year. You were a babe in arms that year, Jack. I saw the ancient world for the first time with you on my shoulder, and with your mother usually following behind, leading Susie by the hand. Well, while we were in Italy, the old president of the college died of a stroke. He had been president of the college when I was an undergraduate, and I suppose it was he, most of all, who made me feel that my talents were appreciated there. By the time I returned to the campus from Italy, the following fall, the dean of men had been made acting president. Your mother and I smiled over the appointment but made no comment on it to anyone—not even to each other. You see, Jack, although Marie and I still thought of ourselves as being ideally suited to each other then, and still believed ourselves to be very happy together, there were already subjects she and I had had to agree to keep off. One of these—and by far the most important—was my professional career itself, including how I conducted my classes, my role in the department, my stand on various academic questions, and even my possible advancement in rank. We had been in graduate school together—your mother and I—and during the first years of our marriage, before Susie was born, we both had taught at the same institution. It was understandably difficult for her to refrain from advising and criticizing me in matters she considered she knew as much about as I did. When I first began ruling out that subject as a topic for discussion, she became emotional about it. She had wanted to have a career herself, and she had had to give it up temporarily. I had not realized how much her plans for a career had meant to her. But now she accused me of being an antifeminist, accused me of trying to isolate her in the kitchen, even of trying to cut her off from all intellectual life. In time, however, she came to see the matter differently—or seemed to. I think perhaps she tired of hearing other faculty wives talk about their husbands' professional problems and didn't want to be like them. At any rate, she and I merely smiled over the news of the dean's promotion to acting president. His qualifications for such a high place seemed hardly to exist. He was formerly the chairman of the Department of Athletics—that is, the college's head coach.

But since I knew that certain trustees and certain senior members of the faculty were on a committee to select a permanent president, I was careful to mention my amusement to no one. When a group of younger members of the faculty came to me, however, and told me that it was generally understood that the committee was going to recommend that the dean be made permanent president, I could not keep myself from bursting into laughter.

It was on an evening in the middle of the week that that group of young professors came to my house for the very purpose of reporting the information to me. How well I can see them on my front porch, in the bright porch light I had switched on. They were a very attractive and intelligent-looking bunch of men. With their bright, intelligent eyes, with their pipes and tweed jackets, and with a neatly trimmed mustache or two among them, they gave one a feeling that here were men one would gladly and proudly be associated with, the feeling that one had found the right niche in life, that one had made the right choice of career. I remember that, before they came inside, two of them—there were six in the party—stepped back and knocked the ashes out of their pipes on the porch banisters, and that they looked with interest at the porch banisters and then looked up and noticed what the porch pillars were like. As a matter of fact, as they trooped into the hallway and then over into my study, they all of them were making comments of one kind or another on the house. . . . This was not so rude of them as it might seem, or I thought it wasn't. You see, they had telephoned me in advance that they wished to come over and talk to me about a matter. And I understood, of course, that they were too polite and too civilized to come to my house and dive right into a matter of business without making some small talk first. That was not their style, not their tone. Moreover, talk about people's houses used to be a fair and favorite topic at such a college as that one was, because there one didn't really own—or even rent—one's house. All houses occupied by the faculty belonged to the college. The good thing about the system was that the house was provided in addition to your salary, and so one didn't have to pay income tax on that portion of one's income. But by and large it was an invidious arrangement. The elderly professors, when they retired, often had no place to go. Further, since the senior professors and the administrators naturally occupied the best houses and one's rank could generally be deduced from the quality of one's house, the younger men (and their wives) eyed the houses of their seniors and thought of the circumstances that would make them available. When someone near the top died or retired, practically the entire faculty would move up a house.

My house was not of course one of the best houses. I was still an assistant professor, whereas most of those young professors who had come to see me were a grade above me in rank. My house, when we moved into it, had in fact been one of the most ramshackle-looking places in the village—one that nobody else would have. I had spent a lot of time and work putting it into the reasonably good condition it was now in. It was upon this fact that my guests were commenting as they came in from the porch that night. And when we had seated ourselves in my study and I had started the coffee brewing, they went on to say that it had been a real advantage to me to have been an undergraduate there, that I had joined the faculty with a knowledge of which houses were basically good houses, that I *knew* (what no one else could have guessed) how recently the run-down-looking house I moved into had been in relatively good condition. There was some truth in what they said, but they were not of course really serious about it. And I saw of course that they were teasing. I replied that my disadvantage was that the old president knew me and knew I was the only person on the staff who was fool enough to accept such a house.

They went on from that to speak of how I had known the late president longer and better than they had, and to ask if it was not true that the newest and youngest member of the board of trustees had once been a classmate and a rather good friend of mine. They were speaking of Morgan Heartwell, who had been the richest boy in my graduating class, and who had during the brief years since our graduation gone on to add several million to the millions he inherited. Though I had seen him only two or three times since college, we had become rather good friends during the last term of our senior year and we still exchanged Christmas cards and even brief letters now and then when there was special occasion. Morgan had been elected to the board during the previous year, when I was in Italy. I had written him one of those brief letters, from Florence, saying that I wished to congratulate the other members of the board on the wisdom of their choice. And Morgan had replied briefly that he looked forward to our spending some time together whenever the trustees met at the college.

The young professors who came to see me were overjoyed when I confirmed the rumor that Morgan Heartwell and I were friends. They immediately revealed the purport of their visit. There was a certain amount of caution in the way they brought forth the information about the dean's candidacy, but after my explosive fit of laughter they had thrown caution to the wind. Morgan Heartwell was on the committee. They wanted me to speak to him. They wanted me to let him know that only the handful of aging senior professors on the committee thought the dean a possible candidate; that those men thought so primarily because they were conservative men getting along in years and because the dean represented to them a known quantity; that, except for them, the entire faculty regarded his proposed candidacy as a piece of lunacy. They insisted at once that I was the only feasible channel they had to the trustees, that if I could let Morgan Heartwell know unofficially how the overwhelming majority of the faculty felt, then the trustees would come to see for themselves what the situation was. As a result, there would be no ugly rift and contest between the older and the younger members of the faculty. They were thinking of the good of the college. They did not believe that under such a man as the former head coach the college could maintain its academic excellence. They were taking the only course that their collective conscience and professional ethics permitted them to take.

Here was precisely the sort of meddling, the sort of involvement I had long since determined to avoid. I had even managed to keep out of most committee work, on the grounds that it interfered with the more serious work I had to do and on the very legitimate grounds that there were people aplenty who liked nothing better than committee work. I used to say that when I received more than one notice of committee meetings in the morning mail, I had heard the sound of my neighbor's ax, and that it was time for me to move on. My first impulse was to laugh as heartily at the role they were now asking me to play as I had at the notion of the dean's being a college president. And yet, with their talk of academic excellence and professional ethics, they really left me no choice. I agreed on the spot to perform the mission.

And it turned out just as they predicted. Morgan Heartwell had entertained doubts even before I came to him, and so had the other trustees he subsequently spoke to. The night that the group of young professors came to my house was in November. By March, another man had been chosen for the presidency. The acting president would serve till the end of the current academic year, and then the new president would take office.

But by March of that year there had been other developments. One of the senior professors in the college had died. The faculty was once again playing a game of musical chairs with houses. There were days when the community held its breath, waiting to know whether or not Professor So-and-So was going to take such-and-such a house. By March also, Marie had learned definitely that she was pregnant once again. (Maisie was born the following November.) Marie began to think that with the new baby the inconveniences of the old house we were in would become quite intolerable. Moreover, I had come to realize that upon the arrival of the baby my study would have to be converted into a nursery. And so we began to take an interest in the houses which, one after another, became available.

The rule was that each house, as it became available, was offered first to the senior member of the faculty—no matter if he had moved the month before, no matter if the house had five bedrooms and he was childless or even wifeless—and then, if it were refused, the house was offered down through the ranks till it found a taker. We could hardly believe our luck—Marie and I—when no full professor and no associate professor spoke for the Dodson house, which was offered around during the first two weeks of March. It was a charming house with four bedrooms, a modern kitchen, a study. We knew that I stood first on the list of assistant professors. We waited for the customary mimeographed notice to appear in my mailbox at the college.

Days passed. Two weeks passed. Still no notice. On the first of April, I went to the office of the acting president and made inquiry. I was told by the acting president's secretary, Mrs. Eason, that the acting president had decided that since no full or associate professor had taken the Dodson house it would be removed from the list and offered to the new chaplain, who was scheduled to be appointed within the next two years. Meanwhile, the house would stand empty. Meanwhile, Marie would continue to scrub our splintery old floors and would wash diapers in a tub in the cellar. Meanwhile, I would give up my study to the new baby . . . I lost my temper. I went to my office and wrote a letter to the acting president, saying that I wished my present house to be put on the available list and that I expected to be offered the Dodson house. I received no reply to my letter. But two days later my house was offered to another assistant professor and was accepted. After a further two days, I did receive a reply to my letter. The acting president had consulted the members of his committee on houses (whose membership coincided precisely with that of the now defunct Faculty Committee for Selecting a President) and they agreed with him that the Dodson house should not at this time be offered to anyone below the rank of associate professor.

Fortunately—or so I thought of it at the time—I had in my possession a letter from the late president, written to me in Italy only a few days before his stroke, promising that I would be promoted to the rank of associate professor on my return. Marie had urged me to present that letter to the administration as soon as we got home, but I felt certain that a copy of the letter was in the president's files and that some action would be taken on it in due time. It seemed unbecoming of me to go at once on my return and demand that action be taken on my dead benefactor's promise. And after I had waited six months, I felt that I hardly knew how best to introduce the subject. But now I did bring forth the letter from my file. If I was entitled to promotion, then we were entitled to the Dodson house. And only by presenting my just claims to the faculty would I be able to determine for certain whether or not the dean, having heard of my role in checking his ambitions, had taken his personal revenge upon me.

With my letter in my pocket, I went to call on all six of the young professors who had sent me on my mission to Morgan Heartwell. I pointed out to them, one by one, just how the business of the house had developed, and I received the impression from each of them that he was already well aware of the developments. With each of them, I then brought out my letter from the late president and insisted upon his reading it. And finally I asked each one of them if he would be willing to present my case, in its entirety, at the next faculty meeting. There was not one of them who did not indicate that he was convinced the acting president knew of the part I had played in blocking his permanent appointment. There was not one of them who expressed any doubt that the removal of the Dodson house from the list had been an act of reprisal against me. But they were a very responsible, discreet, and judicious group of young men. Each of them asserted that he was thoroughly sympathetic to my claim, but asked to be allowed to give the matter more thought before deciding what action ought to be taken. My supposition was that there would be a general consultation among the six of them and that some sort of presentation would be made at the April meeting.

I shall never forget walking alone from my house to the administration building for the April meeting—at four o'clock in the afternoon, on the first Monday in the month. I arrived earlier than I usually did at those meetings, and so was able to choose a seat at the back of the president's assembly room. Faculty meetings there, as in most places, usually filled the room from the rear forward, in just the same way that students ordinarily fill a college classroom. I sat in the next-to-last row and watched my colleagues strolling in from their afternoon classes, some in earnest conversation, others making jokes and tapping each other firmly on the forearm or even patting each other on the back, and some few peering into notes on reports they would give that afternoon. I kept my eye out, of course, for the arrival of my six friends. Unconsciously, I had invented an image of their arriving as a group, perhaps still consulting among themselves in whispers, and taking their places together on the first row squarely in front of the president's lectern. Instead, I saw them arrive one by one, seemingly unaware of my presence and certainly unaware of one another's. Before the meeting began, all six had arrived, but they were scattered over the room. I watched them in their tweed jackets and blue or striped shirts chatting casually and amiably with various black-suited, bow-tied senior members of the faculty. At the moment when the meeting was called to order, I was struck suddenly by the notion that I had not taken these men's character and style into account. They would never be so obvious as my fantasy had suggested. They *would* enter the room separately, having decided earlier on the strategy. One of them would rise at the proper time and bring up the question of the Dodson house. And then, with seeming spontaneity and from all corners of the room, the others would join in the attack, one of them finally—if the chair adamantly refused to offer the Dodson house to the lower rank—one of them finally making direct reference to the promise of promotion made me by the revered late president.

Following the minutes from the last meeting, pieces of old business occupied the first half hour of the meeting. I sat through the minutes and through the old business with patience, anticipating what I believed was to follow. When the question, "Any new business?" came, I closed my eyes and listened for the familiar voice. Unless my ears deceived me, it was the young biologist in my group who was speaking. He was one of those with a neat little mustache on his upper lip. With my eyes closed, I could see him, could see him self-consciously patting the bowl of his pipe on the palm of his left hand as he began to speak. "Mr. President—" I opened my eyes, and then for a moment I was convinced my ears did deceive me. It was the young biologist all right, standing near the front of the room and patting the bowl of his dark pipe on the palm of his left hand, but the piece of new business he was introducing was a matter of next year's curriculum. I sat through his remarks and through other remarks that followed on the subject. In fact, I sat through two other new pieces of business, even through a count of hands on one piece that came to a motion and a vote. But when a fourth piece, relating to the awarding of honorary degrees was introduced, I rose from my chair, moved down the row I was sitting in, saying, "Excuse me. Excuse me. Excuse me," marched down the center aisle and out of the meeting.

I went home, and behind the closed door of my study I began composing my letter of resignation. Marie, who was in the kitchen, had heard me come in. But she waited fifteen minutes or so before she came and knocked on my door.

When I opened the door, she looked at me questioningly. She was white with anger. "He refused to offer us the house?" she said.

"Not exactly," I replied. "The subject was not introduced. The six of them came to the meeting and spoke at length—about other things."

Her face turned from white to crimson. Her eyes, still on me, melted. She burst into tears and threw herself into my arms. Or, rather, she drew me into her arms, for as she wept I felt her two arms go around me and felt her hands patting me consolingly high on the back between the shoulder blades. As she held me there, it was all I could do to keep from weeping myself. And somehow, for all her tenderness at that moment and despite all the need I had of it, it came over me that this was the beginning of the end for us, that our marriage would not survive it. Perhaps that was nonsense. The thoughts that cross one's mind at such times cannot always be accounted for. But the life we had lived since graduate school—beginning in graduate school—was the life most couples live who take refuge in the Groves of Academe. We had lived with each other, had lived *together* in the most literal sense. We had shared intellectual interests, had shared domestic duties, had breakfasted together, lunched together, dined together. We had slept together, too, but that had come to seem only one, not too significant facet of our—our "togetherness." I had no right to complain against this life, because this life was the life I had chosen. But I could see that the future would mean a narrowing of my activities among my colleagues wherever I might go, and that things relating to my profession, which had for some time been ruled out of our talk at home, must now inevitably become the very center of it.

When, after dinner that night, I received a telephone call from my friend the biologist, saying that he and the other of the group would like to come by and talk to me, Marie, who was sitting close by my side with her arm about my waist, indicated with a shake of her head that I should not let them come. But I was not yet ready for that. I told them to come ahead, and then I went and switched on the front-porch light.

When they arrived, I led them to my study, and we sat down on three straight chairs in a triangle, facing each other. They told me that, before that afternoon's meeting, there *had* been a general consultation among the six men I went to see and that they had decided that to bring up my "problem" at this meeting would not be a wise move, could, in fact, create a very bad situation. "It would be most impolitic," one of them said. "Strategically speaking, it would be a very bad move," said the other. "It would be a bad business." And they proceeded to explain to me that though the dean would no longer be acting president, he would continue to be a very important part of the college's administration. A head-on collision with him just before the arrival of the new president might be a very disruptive thing for the college. After all, we were all going to have to continue to live with the dean. "Even you are," they said to me. And all of this was said with the same voice that had said we must avoid any ugly rift and contest with the senior members of the faculty. Before they finished speaking, I saw once and for all what a foolish man I had been. But I did not make myself a bigger fool by losing my temper and telling them that I saw what a fool they had made of me. As we went to the front door, I agreed with them that probably my house could be reassigned to me—as no doubt it could have been—especially if one of them went to the dean and explained that I had written my letter to him in a moment of anger and that I now wished to remain where I was. But when they were gone, I put out the porch light, went back to my study, and typed up the final version of my letter of resignation.

Marie and I were in perfect agreement about the resignation. During the months that followed, which was naturally a very trying period, her understanding, her sympathy, her tenderness—her indulgence, really—were my great support. When I returned from my office late that Sunday afternoon, depressed and with a crick in my neck after a long sleep in my leather chair (I have since decided that that was most probably the way my father had spent *his* Sunday in *his* office), Marie greeted me cheerfully, and little Susie almost smothered me with kisses. But somehow the vision I had had of our future, after the fateful faculty meeting, stuck with me. I never for a moment believed our marriage could weather this new turn my life had taken. I don't know why. As my mother would have said, the Old Nick himself seemed to have got in me. I *wouldn't* be consoled, I *wouldn't* be comforted, though I consistently made an effort to seem so. I had never before been so much help in a move as I was in packing up our possessions and unpacking them again when we arrived at our new place. My new appointment was at an enormous state university, situated in a middle-sized Midwestern city. I felt it would be possible to pass unnoticed for years, in the university and in the city. I met my classes, I attended department meetings, I made revisions on the galley proofs of my book. It seems to me I spent a large part of every day taking Susie back and forth to school on the bus. And I spent hours in the park with you, Jack. I don't suppose you remember the little boy there who kept purposely interfering with your play on the jungle gym until one day I caught him and spanked him. His mother threatened to call the police. I'll never forget the satisfaction I took in laughing in her face and threatening to give her the same spanking I had given her little boy. And little Maisie, of course, was born in November after we arrived there. I never changed so many diapers for you and Susie put together as I did for Maisie, or gave so many bottles at predawn hours. . . . No, I did not become the tyrant of my household, and I did not, like my father, disturb my wife with long looks and long silences. But I began to feel that with my talk about my book and my talk about the courses I was teaching I was almost intentionally boring Marie to death, boring my students to death, boring myself to death. Before the first semester was half over, Marie was helping me grade my papers and was reading all the books I had to read for my courses. By the time the second semester came round, she had made application to the department and was taken on as a part-time instructor.

It was almost a year to the day after my difficulties about the Dodson house began that two letters, which would altogether change everything for me, were put into my mailbox at the university. One letter came from my predecessor at the college where I have since made my most important contribution to the education of American youth. This letter stated that they were looking for a new dean of men at that college, and asked if I would be willing to come and be interviewed for the appointment. The other letter was from Morgan Heartwell. It was he who had recommended me for the appointment, and he wrote me that he had been able to do so because he had observed that I behaved with such discretion in my altercation with the acting president, putting the welfare of that institution above my personal interests. He also urged me to accept the new appointment, saying that this was a college that had recently been given a handsome endowment, a college with a growing academic reputation. He was not, himself, on the board of trustees there, but close associates of his were and they had happened to mention the opening there.

When Marie read the first letter, she broke into laughter. Then, giving me a serious glance, she read through Morgan's letter. "How dare Morgan Heartwell write you such a letter!" she said. "How dare he suggest such an appointment for you!" She and I were facing each other across the little carrel that we shared in the university library. When I remained silent, she put the letters down on the table and asked, "You are not seriously thinking of going for that interview?"

"I am going to take the job," I said, "if it's offered me."

Folding the letters and replacing them in their envelopes, she said, "Well, you may take it. But I'm staying on here."

"It has already occurred to me that you might say that," I told her directly. "I am not entirely surprised." She sat with her eyes lowered and she blushed so deeply that a new thought now occurred to me. "Is there someone else?" I asked.

"No, I don't think so," she said, looking up at me. "Is there for you?"

"I don't think so," I said.

Of course, the fact is we were both married again within two years to persons we did already know at that state university. But still, it is true that neither of us had been having a real love affair. Perhaps the persons we married, the persons we very soon afterward allowed ourselves to fall in love with, represented for us the only possibilities of happiness either of us had been able to imagine during that bleak year. I suppose it's significant that we both married people who shared none of our professional interests.

After I had been dean of men for two years, I was made academic dean of the college. In two more years, I was president of the college. Even with as little time as you have spent with me through the years, Jack, you have seen what a successful marriage my second marriage has been, and what a happy, active life I have had. One sacrifices something. One sacrifices, for instance, the books one might have written after that first one. More important, one may sacrifice the love, even the acquaintance of one's children. One loses something of one's self even. But at least I am not tyrannizing over old women and small children. At least I don't sit gazing into space while my wife or perhaps some kindly neighbor woman waits patiently to see whether or not I will risk a two-heart bid. A man must somehow go on living among men, Jack. A part of him must. It is important to broaden one's humanity, but it is important to remain a mere man, too. But it is a strange world, Jack, in which an old man must tell a young man this.

ALICE WALKER

Alice Walker was born in Eatonton, Georgia, in 1944. She has written a biography of Langston Hughes, two collections of essays, *In Search of Our Mother's Garden* and *Living by the Word,* and three volumes of poetry, *Once, Revolutionary Petunias and Other Poems,* and *Horses Make a Landscape More Beautiful.* Her novels are *The Third Life of Grange Copeland* (1970), *Meridian* (1976), and *The Color Purple* (1982), which won a Pulitzer Prize. Her stories are collected in two volumes, *In Love & Trouble: Stories of Black Women* (1973) and *You Can't Keep a Good Woman Down* (1981).

Nineteen Fifty-Five

1955

THE car is a brand new red Thunderbird convertible, and it's passed the house more than once. It slows down real slow now, and stops at the curb. An older gentleman dressed like a Baptist deacon gets out on the side near the house, and a young fellow who looks about sixteen gets out on the driver's side. They are white, and I wonder what in the world they doing in this neighborhood.

Well, I say to J. T., put your shirt on, anyway, and let me clean these glasses offa the table.

We had been watching the ballgame on TV. I wasn't actually watching, I was sort of daydreaming, with my foots up in J. T.'s lap.

I seen 'em coming on up the walk, brisk, like they coming to sell something, and then they rung the bell, and J. T. declined to put on a shirt but instead disappeared into the bedroom where the other television is. I turned down the one in the living room; I figured I'd be rid of these two double quick and J. T. could come back out again.

Are you Gracie Mae Still? asked the old guy, when I opened the door and put my hand on the lock inside the screen.

And I don't need to buy a thing, said I.

What makes you think we're sellin'? he asks, in that hearty Southern way that makes my eyeballs ache.

Well, one way or another and they're inside the house and the first thing the young fellow does is raise the TV a couple of decibels. He's about five feet nine, sort of womanish looking, with real dark white skin and a red pouting mouth. His hair is black and curly and he looks like a Loosianna creole.

About one of your songs, says the deacon. He is maybe sixty, with white hair and beard, white silk shirt, black linen suit, black tie and black shoes. His cold gray eyes look like they're sweating.

One of my songs?

Traynor here just *loves* your songs. Don't you, Traynor? He nudges Traynor with his elbow. Traynor blinks, says something I can't catch in a pitch I don't register.

The boy learned to sing and dance livin' round you people out in the country. Practically cut his teeth on you.

Traynor looks up at me and bites his thumbnail.

I laugh.

Well, one way or another they leave with my agreement that they can record one of my songs. The deacon writes me a check for five hundred dollars, the boy grunts his awareness of the transaction, and I am laughing all over myself by the time I rejoin J. T.

Just as I am snuggling down beside him though I hear the front door bell going off again.

Forgit his hat? asks J. T.

I hope not, I say.

The deacon stands there leaning on the door frame and once again I'm thinking of those sweaty-looking eyeballs of his. I wonder if sweat makes your eyeballs pink because his are sure pink. Pink and gray and it strikes me that nobody I'd care to know is behind them.

I forgot one little thing, he says pleasantly. I forgot to tell you Traynor and I would like to buy up all of those records you made of the song. I tell you we sure do love it.

Well, love it or not, I'm not so stupid as to let them do that without making 'em pay. So I says, Well, that's gonna cost you. Because, really, that song never did sell all that good, so I was glad they was going to buy it up. But on the other hand, them two listening to my song by themselves, and nobody else getting to hear me sing it, give me a pause.

Well, one way or another the deacon showed me where I would come out ahead on any deal he had proposed so far. Didn't I give you five hundred dollars? he asked. What white man—and don't even need to mention colored—would give you more? We buy up all your records of that particular song: first, you git royalties. Let me ask you, how much you sell that song for in the first place? Fifty dollars? A hundred, I say. And no royalties from it yet, right? Right. Well, when we buy up all of them records you gonna git royalties. And that's gonna make all them race record shops sit up and take notice of Gracie Mae Still. And they gonna push all them other records of yourn they got. And you no doubt will become one of the big name colored recording artists. And then we can offer you another five hundred dollars for letting us do all this for you. And by God you'll be sittin' pretty! You can go out and buy you the kind of outfit a star should have. Plenty sequins and yards of red satin.

I had done unlocked the screen when I saw I could get some more money out of him. Now I held it wide open while he squeezed through the opening between me and the door. He whipped out another piece of paper and I signed it.

He sort of trotted out to the car and slid in beside Traynor, whose head was back against the seat. They swung around in a u-turn in front of the house and then they was gone.

J. T. was putting his shirt on when I got back to the bedroom. Yankees beat the Orioles 10–6, he said. I believe I'll drive out to Paschal's pond and go fishing. Wanna go?

While I was putting on my pants J. T. was holding the two checks.

I'm real proud of a woman that can make cash money without leavin' home, he said. And I said *Umph.* Because we met on the road with me singing in first one little low-life jook after another, making ten dollars a night for myself if I was lucky, and sometimes bringin' home nothing but my life. And J. T. just loved them times. The way I was fast and flashy and always on the go from one town to another. He loved the way my singin' made the dirt farmers cry like babies and the womens shout Honey, hush! But that's mens. They loves any style to which you can get 'em accustomed.

1956

My little grandbaby called me one night on the phone: Little Mama, Little Mama, there's a white man on the television singing one of your songs! Turn on channel 5.

Lord, if it wasn't Traynor. Still looking half asleep from the neck up, but kind of awake in a nasty way from the waist down. He wasn't doing too bad with my song either, but it wasn't just the song the people in the audience was screeching and screaming over, it was that nasty little jerk he was doing from the waist down.

Well, Lord have mercy, I said, listening to him. If I'da closed my eyes, it could have been me. He had followed every turning of my voice, side streets, avenues, red lights, train crossings and all. It give me a chill.

Everywhere I went I heard Traynor singing my song, and all the little white girls just eating it up. I never had so many ponytails switched across my line of vision in my life. They was so *proud.* He was a *genius.*

Well, all that year I was trying to lose weight anyway and that and high blood pressure and sugar kept me pretty well occupied. Traynor had made a smash from a song of mine, I still had seven hundred dollars of the original one thousand dollars in the bank, and I felt if I could just bring my weight down, life would be sweet.

1957

I lost ten pounds in 1956. That's what I give myself for Christmas. And J. T. and me and the children and their friends and grandkids of all description had just finished dinner—over which I had put on nine and a half of my lost ten—when who should appear at the front door but Traynor. Little Mama, Little Mama! It's that white man who sings ——— ——— ———. The children didn't call it my song anymore. Nobody did. It was funny how that happened. Traynor and the deacon had bought up all my records, true, but on his record he had put "written by Gracie Mae Still." But that was just another name on the label, like "produced by Apex Records."

On the TV he was inclined to dress like the deacon told him. But now he looked presentable.

Merry Christmas, said he.

And same to you, Son.

I don't know why I called him Son. Well, one way or another they're all our sons. The only requirement is that they be younger than us. But then again, Traynor seemed to be aging by the minute.

You looks tired, I said. Come on in and have a glass of Christmas cheer.

J. T. ain't never in his life been able to act decent to a white man he wasn't working for, but he poured Traynor a glass of bourbon and water, then he took all the children and grandkids and friends and whatnot out to the den. After while I heard Traynor's voice singing the song, coming from the stereo console. It was just the kind of Christmas present my kids would consider cute.

I looked at Traynor, complicit. But he looked like it was the last thing in the world he wanted to hear. His head was pitched forward over his lap, his hands holding his glass and his elbows on his knees.

I done sung that song seem like a million times this year, he said. I sung it on the Grand Ole Opry, I sung it on the Ed Sullivan show. I sung it on Mike Douglas, I sung it at the Cotton Bowl, the Orange Bowl. I sung it at Festivals. I sung it at Fairs. I sung it overseas in Rome, Italy, and once in a submarine *underseas.* I've sung it and sung it, and I'm making forty thousand dollars a day offa it, and you know what, I don't have the faintest notion what that song means.

Whatchumean, what do it mean? It mean what it says. All I could think was: these suckers is making forty thousand a *day* offa my song and now they gonna come back and try to swindle me out of the original thousand.

It's just a song, I said. Cagey. When you fool around with a lot of no count mens you sing a bunch of 'em. I shrugged.

Oh, he said. Well. He started brightening up. I just come by to tell you I think you are a great singer.

He didn't blush, saying that. Just said it straight out.

And I brought you a little Christmas present too. Now you take this little box and you hold it until I drive off. Then you take it outside under that first streetlight back up the street aways in front of that green house: Then you open the box and see . . . Well, just *see.*

What had come over this boy, I wondered, holding the box. I looked out the window in time to see another white man come up and get in the car with him and then two more cars full of white mens start out behind him. They was all in long black cars that looked like a funeral procession.

Little Mama, Little Mama, what it is? One of my grandkids come running up and started pulling at the box. It was wrapped in gay Christmas paper—the thick, rich kind that it's hard to picture folks making just to throw away.

J. T. and the rest of the crowd followed me out the house, up the street to the streetlight and in front of the green house. Nothing was there but somebody's gold-grilled white Cadillac. Brandnew and most distracting. We got to looking at it so till I almost forgot the little box in my hand. While the others were busy making 'miration I carefully took off the paper and ribbon and folded them up and put them in my pants pocket. What should I see but a pair of genuine solid gold caddy keys.

Dangling the keys in front of everybody's nose, I unlocked the caddy, motioned for J. T. to git in on the other side, and us didn't come back home for two days.

1960

Well, the boy was sure nuff famous by now. He was still a mite shy of twenty but already they was calling him the Emperor of Rock and Roll.

Then what should happen but the draft.

Well, says J. T. There goes all this Emperor of Rock and Roll business.

But even in the army the womens was on him like white on rice. We watched it on the News.

Dear Gracie Mae [*he wrote from Germany*],

How you? Fine I hope as this leaves me doing real well. Before I come in the army I was gaining a lot of weight and gitting jittery from making all them dumb movies. But now I exercise and eat right and get plenty of rest. I'm more awake than I been in ten years.

I wonder if you are writing any more songs?

Sincerely,
Traynor

I wrote him back:

Dear Son,

We is all fine in the Lord's good grace and hope this finds you the same. J. T. and me be out all times of the day and night in that car you give me—which you know you didn't have to do. Oh, and I do appreciate the mink and the new self-cleaning oven. But if you send anymore stuff to eat from Germany I'm going to have to open up a store in the neighborhood just to get rid of it. Really, we have more than enough of everything. The Lord is good to us and we don't know Want.

Glad to here you is well and gitting your right rest. There ain't nothing like exercising to help that along. J. T. and me work some part of every day that we don't go fishing in the garden.

Well, so long Soldier.

Sincerely,
Gracie Mae

He wrote:

Dear Gracie Mae,

I hope you and J. T. like that automatic power tiller I had one of the stores back home send you. I went through a mountain of catalogs looking for it—I wanted something that even a woman could use.

I've been thinking about writing some songs of my own but every time I finish one it don't seem to be about nothing I've actually lived myself. My agent keeps sending me other people's songs but they just sound mooney. I can hardly git through 'em without gagging.

Everybody still loves that song of yours. They ask me all the time what do I think it means, really. I mean, they want to know just what I want to know. Where out of your life did it come from?

Sincerely,
Traynor

1968

I didn't see the boy for seven years. No. Eight. Because just about everybody was dead when I saw him again. Malcolm X, King, the president and his brother, and even J. T. J. T. died of a head cold. It just settled in his head like a block of ice, he said, and nothing we did moved it until one day he just leaned out the bed and died.

His good friend Horace helped me put him away, and then about a year later Horace and me started going together. We was sitting out on the front porch swing one summer night, dusk-dark, and I saw this great procession of lights winding to a stop.

Holy Toledo! said Horace. (He's got a real sexy voice like Ray Charles.) Look *at* it. He meant the long line of flashy cars and the white men in white summer suits jumping out on the drivers' sides and standing at attention. With wings they could pass for angels, with hoods they could be the Klan.

Traynor comes waddling up the walk.

And suddenly I know what it is he could pass for. An Arab like the ones you see in storybooks. Plump and soft and with never a care about weight. Because with so much money, who cares? Traynor is almost dressed like someone from a storybook too. He has on, I swear, about ten necklaces. Two sets of bracelets on his arms, at least one ring on every finger, and some kind of shining buckles on his shoes, so that when he walks you get quite a few twinkling lights.

Gracie Mae, he says, coming up to give me a hug. J. T.

I explain that J. T. passed. That this is Horace.

Horace, he says, puzzled but polite, sort of rocking back on his heels, Horace.

That's it for Horace. He goes in the house and don't come back.

Looks like you and me is gained a few, I say.

He laughs. The first time I ever heard him laugh. It don't sound much like a laugh and I can't swear that it's better than no laugh a'tall.

He's gitting fat for sure, but he's still slim compared to me. I'll never see three hundred pounds again and I've just about said (excuse me) fuck it. I got to thinking about it one day an' I thought: aside from the fact that they say it's unhealthy, my fat ain't never been no trouble. Mens always have loved me. My kids ain't never complained. Plus they's fat. And fat like I is I looks distinguished. You see me coming and know somebody's *there.*

Gracie Mae, he says, I've come with a personal invitation to you to my house tomorrow for dinner. He laughed. What did it sound like? I couldn't place it. See them men out there? he asked me. I'm sick and tired of eating with them. They don't never have nothing to talk about. That's why I eat so much. But if you come to dinner tomorrow we can talk about the old days. You can tell me about that farm I bought you.

I sold it, I said.

You did?

Yeah, I said, I did. Just cause I said I liked to exercise by working in a garden didn't mean I wanted five hundred acres! Anyhow, I'm a city girl now. Raised in the country it's true. Dirt poor—the whole bit—but that's all behind me now.

Oh well, he said, I didn't mean to offend you.

We sat a few minutes listening to the crickets.

Then he said: You wrote that song while you was still on the farm, didn't you, or was it right after you left?

You had somebody spying on me? I asked.

You and Bessie Smith got into a fight over it once, he said.

You *is* been spying on me!

But I don't know what the fight was about, he said. Just like I don't know what happened to your second husband. Your first one died in the Texas electric chair. Did you know that? Your third one beat you up, stole your touring costumes and your car and retired with a chorine to Tuskegee. He laughed. He's still there.

I had been mad, but suddenly I calmed down. Traynor was talking very dreamily. It was dark but seems like I could tell his eyes weren't right. It was like some*thing* was sitting there talking to me but not necessarily with a person behind it.

You gave up on marrying and seem happier for it. He laughed again. I married but it never went like it was supposed to. I never could squeeze any of my own life either into it or out of it. It was like singing somebody else's record. I copied the way it was sposed to be *exactly* but I never had a clue what marriage meant.

I bought her a diamond ring big as your fist. I bought her clothes. I built her a mansion. But right away she didn't want the boys to stay there. Said they smoked up the bottom floor. Hell, there were *five* floors.

No need to grieve, I said. No need to. Plenty more where she come from.

He perked up. That's part of what that song means, ain't it? No need to grieve. Whatever it is, there's plenty more down the line.

I never really believed that way back when I wrote that song, I said. It was all bluffing then. The trick is to live long enough to put your young bluffs to use. Now if I was to sing that song today I'd tear it up. 'Cause I done lived long enough to know it's *true.* Them words could hold me up.

I ain't lived that long, he said.

Look like you on your way, I said. I don't know why, but the boy seemed to need some encouraging. And I don't know, seem like one way or another you talk to rich white folks and you end up reassuring *them.* But what the hell, by now I feel something for the boy. I wouldn't be in his bed all alone in the middle of the night for nothing. Couldn't be nothing worse than being famous the world over for something you don't even understand. That's what I tried to tell Bessie. She wanted that same song. Overheard me practicing it one day, said, with her hands on her hips: Gracie Mae, I'ma sing your song tonight. I *likes* it.

Your lips be too swole to sing, I said. She was mean and she was strong, but I trounced her.

Ain't you famous enough with your own stuff? I said. Leave mine alone. Later on, she thanked me. By then she was Miss Bessie Smith to the World, and I was still Miss Gracie Mae Nobody from Notasulga.

The next day all these limousines arrived to pick me up. Five cars and twelve bodyguards. Horace picked that morning to start painting the kitchen.

Don't paint the kitchen, fool, I said. The only reason that dumb boy of ours is going to show me his mansion is because he intends to present us with a new house.

What you gonna do with it? he asked me, standing there in his shirtsleeves stirring the paint.

Sell it. Give it to the children. Live in it on weekends. It don't matter what I do. He sure don't care.

Horace just stood there shaking his head. Mama you sure looks *good,* he says. Wake me up when you git back.

Fool, I say, and pat my wig in front of the mirror.

The boy's house is something else. First you come to this mountain, and then you commence to drive and drive up this road that's lined with magnolias. Do magnolias grow on mountains? I was wondering. And you come to lakes and you come to ponds and you come to deer and you come up on some sheep. And I figure these two is sposed to represent England and Wales. Or something out of Europe. And you just keep on coming to stuff. And it's all pretty. Only the man driving my car don't look at nothing but the road. Fool. And then *finally,* after all this time, you begin to go up the driveway. And there's more magnolias—only they're not in such good shape. It's sort of cool up this high and I don't think they're gonna make it. And then I see this building that looks like if it had a name it would be The Tara Hotel. Columns and steps and outdoor chandeliers and rocking chairs. Rocking chairs? Well, and there's the boy on the steps dressed in a dark green satin jacket like you see folks wearing on TV late at night, and he looks sort of like a fat dracula with all that house rising behind him, and standing beside him there's this little white vision of loveliness that he introduces as his wife.

He's nervous when he introduces us and he says to her: This is Gracie Mae Still, I want you to know me. I mean . . . and she gives him a look that would fry meat.

Won't you come in, Gracie Mae, she says, and that's the last I see of her.

He fishes around for something to say or do and decides to escort me to the kitchen. We go through the entry and the parlor and the breakfast room and the dining room and the servants' passage and finally get there. The first thing I notice is that, altogether, there are five stoves. He looks about to introduce me to one.

Wait a minute, I say. Kitchens don't do nothing for me. Let's go sit on the front porch.

Well, we hike back and we sit in the rocking chairs rocking until dinner.

Gracie Mae, he says down the table, taking a piece of fried chicken from the woman standing over him, I got a little surprise for you.

It's a house, ain't it? I ask, spearing a chitlin.

You're getting *spoiled,* he says. And the way he says *spoiled* sounds funny. He slurs it. It sounds like his tongue is too thick for his mouth. Just that quick he's finished the chicken and is now eating chitlins *and* a pork chop. *Me* spoiled, I'm thinking.

I already got a house. Horace is right this minute painting the kitchen. I bought that house. My kids feel comfortable in that house.

But this one I bought you is just like mine. Only a little smaller.

I still don't need no house. And anyway who would clean it?

He looks surprised.

Really, I think, some peoples advance *so* slowly.

I hadn't thought of that. But what the hell, I'll get you somebody to live in.

I don't want other folks living 'round me. Makes me nervous.

You *don't?* It *do?*

What I want to wake up and see folks I don't even know for?

He just sits there downtable staring at me. Some of that feeling is in the song, ain't it? Not the words, the *feeling.* What I want to wake up and see folks I don't even know for? But I see twenty folks a day I don't even know, including my wife.

This food wouldn't be bad to wake up to though, I said. The boy had found the genius of corn bread.

He looked at me real hard. He laughed. Short. They want what you got but they don't want you. They want what I got only it ain't mine. That's what makes 'em so hungry for me when I sing. They getting the flavor of something but they ain't getting the thing itself. They like a pack of hound dogs trying to gobble up a scent.

You talking 'bout your fans?

Right. Right. He says.

Don't worry 'bout your fans, I say. They don't know their asses from a hole in the ground. I doubt there's a honest one in the bunch.

That's the point. Dammit, that's the point! He hits the table with his fist. It's so solid it don't even quiver. You need a honest audience! You can't have folks that's just gonna lie right back to you.

Yeah, I say, it was small compared to yours, but I had one. It would have been worth my life to try to sing 'em somebody else's stuff that I didn't know nothing about.

He must have pressed a buzzer under the table. One of his flunkies zombies up.

Git Johnny Carson, he says.

On the phone? asks the zombie.

On the phone, says Traynor, what you think I mean, git him offa the front porch? Move your ass.

So two weeks later we's on the Johnny Carson show.

Traynor is all corseted down nice and looks a little bit fat but mostly good. And all the women that grew up on him and my song squeal and squeal. Traynor says: The lady who wrote my first hit record is here with us tonight, and she's agreed to sing it for all of us, just like she sung it forty-five years ago. Ladies and Gentlemen, the great Gracie Mae Still!

Well, I had tried to lose a couple of pounds my own self, but failing that I had me a very big dress made. So I sort of rolls over next to Traynor, who is dwarfted by me, so that when he puts his arm around back of me to try to hug me it looks funny to the audience and they laugh.

I can see this pisses him off. But I smile out there at 'em. Imagine squealing for twenty years and not knowing why you're squealing? No more sense of endings and beginnings than hogs.

It don't matter, Son, I say. Don't fret none over me.

I commence to sing. And I sound———wonderful. Being able to sing good ain't all about having a good singing voice a'tall. A good singing voice helps. But when you come up in the Hard Shell Baptist church like I did you understand early that the fellow that sings is the singer. Them that waits for programs and arrangements and letters from home is just good voices occupying body space.

So there I am singing my own song, my own way. And I give it all I got and enjoy every minute of it. When I finish Traynor is standing up clapping and clapping and beaming at first me and then the audience like I'm his mama for true. The audience claps politely for about two seconds.

Traynor looks disgusted.

He comes over and tries to hug me again. The audience laughs.

Johnny Carson looks at us like we both weird.

Traynor is mad as hell. He's supposed to sing something called a love ballad. But instead he takes the mike, turns to me and says: Now see if my imitation still holds up. He goes into the same song, *our* song, I think, looking out at his flaky audience. And he sings it just the way he always did. My voice, my tone, my inflection, everything. But he forgets a couple of lines. Even before he's finished the matronly squeals begin.

He sits down next to me looking whipped.

It don't matter, Son, I say, patting his hand. You don't even know those people. Try to make the people you know happy.

Is that in the song? he asks.

Maybe. I say.

1977

For a few years I hear from him, then nothing. But trying to lose weight takes all the attention I got to spare. I finally faced up to the fact that my fat is the hurt I don't admit, not even to myself, and that I been trying to bury it from the day I was born. But also when you git real old, to tell the truth, it ain't as pleasant. It gits lumpy and slack. Yuck. So one day I said to Horace, I'ma git this shit offa me.

And he fell in with the program like he always try to do and Lord such a procession of salads and cottage cheese and fruit juice!

One night I dreamed Traynor had split up with his fifteenth wife. He said: *You meet 'em for no reason. You date 'em for no reason. You marry 'em for no reason. I do it all but I swear it's just like somebody else doing it. I feel like I can't remember Life.*

The boy's in trouble, I said to Horace.

You've always said that, he said.

I have?

Yeah. You always said he looked asleep. You can't sleep through life if you want to live it.

You not such a fool after all, I said, pushing myself up with my cane and hobbling over to where he was. Let me sit down on your lap, I said, while this salad I ate takes effect.

In the morning we heard Traynor was dead. Some said fat, some said heart, some said alcohol, some said drugs. One of the children called from Detroit. Them dumb fans of his is on a crying rampage, she said. You just ought to turn on the TV.

But I didn't want to see 'em. They was crying and crying and didn't even know what they was crying for. One day this is going to be a pitiful country, I thought.

EUDORA WELTY

Eudora Welty was born in 1909 in Jackson, Mississippi, where she still lives, and was educated at the Mississippi State College for Women and the University of Wisconsin. She has written five novels: *The Robber Bridegroom* (1942), *Delta Wedding* (1946), *The Ponder Heart* (1954), *Losing Battles* (1970), and *The Optimist's Daughter* (1972), which won a Pulitzer Prize. *The Eye of the Story* (1979) is a collection of essays on the craft of writing. *One Writer's Beginnings* (1984) is autobiographical. Her collections of stories are *A Curtain of Green and Other Stories* (1941), *The Wide Net and Other Stories* (1943), *The Golden Apples* (1949), *The Bride of the Innisfallen and Other Stories* (1955), and *The Collected Stories* (1980).

The Bride of the Innisfallen

THERE was something of the pavilion about one raincoat, the way—for some little time out there in the crowd—it stood flowing in its salmony-pink and yellow stripes down toward the wet floor of the platform, expanding as it went. In the Paddington gloom it was a little dim, but it was parading through now, and once inside the compartment it looked rainbow-bright.

In it a middle-aged lady climbed on like a sheltered girl—a boost up from behind she pretended not to need or notice. She was big-boned and taller than the man who followed her inside bringing the suitcase—he came up round and with a doll's smile, his black suit wet; she turned a look on him; this was farewell. The train to Fishguard to catch the Cork boat was leaving in fifteen minutes—at a black four o'clock in the afternoon of that spring that refused to flower. She, so clearly, was the one going.

There was nobody to share the compartment yet but one girl, and she not Irish.

Over a stronghold of a face, the blue hat of the lady in the raincoat was settled on like an Indian bonnet, or, rather, like an old hat, which it was. The hair that had been pulled out of its confines was flirtatious and went into two auburn-and-gray pomegranates along her cheeks. Her gaze was almost forgiving, if unsettled; it held its shine so long. Even yet, somewhere, sometime, the owner of those eyes might expect to rise to a tragic occasion. When the round man put the suitcase up in the rack, she sank down under it as if something were now done that could not be undone, and with tender glances brushed the soot and raindrops off herself, somewhat onto him. He perched beside her—it was his legs that were short—and then, as her hands dropped into her bright-stained lap, they both stared straight ahead, as if waiting for a metamorphosis.

The American girl sitting opposite could not have taken in anything they said as long as she kept feeling it necessary, herself, to subside. As long as the train stood in the station, her whole predicament seemed betrayed by her earliness. She was leaving London without her husband's knowledge. She was wearing rather worn American clothes and thin shoes, and, sitting up very straight, kept pulling her coat collar about her ears and throat. In the strange, diminished light of the station people seemed to stand and move on some dark stage; by now platform and train must be almost entirely Irish in their gathered population.

A fourth person suddenly came inside the compartment, a small, passionate-looking man. He was with them as suddenly as a gift—as if an arm had thrust in a bunch of roses or a telegram. There seemed something in him about to explode, but—he pushed off his wet coat, threw it down, threw it up overhead, flung himself into the seat—he was going to be a good boy.

"What's the time?" The round man spoke softly, as if perhaps the new man had brought it.

The lady bowed her head and looked up at him: *she* had it: "Six minutes to four." She wore an accurate-looking wristwatch.

The round man's black eyes flared, he looked out at the rain, and asked the American if she, too, were going to Cork—a question she did not at first understand; his voice was very musical.

"Yes—that is—"

"Four minutes to four," the lady in the raincoat said, those fours sounding fated.

"You don't need to get out of the carriage till you get to Fishguard," the round man told her, murmuring it softly, as if he'd told her before and would tell her again. "Straight through to Fishguard, then you book a berth. You're in Cork in the morning."

She looked fondly as though she had never heard of Cork, wouldn't believe it, and opened and shut her great white heavy eyelids. When he crossed his knees she stole her arm through his and seesawed him on the seat. Holding his rows of little black-rimmed fingers together like a modest accordion, he said, "Two ladies going to Cork."

"Two minutes to four," she said, rolling her eyes.

"You'll go through the customs when you get to Fishguard," he told her. "They'll open your case and see what there is to detect. They'll be wanting to discover if you are bringing anything wrongly and improperly into the country." He eyed the lady, above their linked arms, as if she had been a stranger inquiring into the uses and purposes of customs inspection in the world. By ceasing to smile he appeared to anchor himself; he said solidly, "Following that, you go on board."

"Where you won't be able to buy drink for three miles out!" cried the new passenger. Up to now he had been simply drawing quick breaths. He had a neat, short, tender, slightly alarmed profile—dark, straight hair cut not ten minutes ago, a slight cut over the ear. But this still-bleeding customer, a Connemara man as he was now announcing himself, always did everything last-minute, because that was the way he was made.

There was a feel of the train's being about to leave. Then the guard was shouting.

The round man and the lady in the raincoat rose and moved in step to the door together, all four hands enjoined. She bent her head. Hers was a hat of drapes and shapes. There in the rainy light it showed a chaos of blue veil falling behind, and when it sadly turned, shining directly over the eyes was a gold pin in the shape of a pair of links, like those you are supposed to separate in amateur-magician sets. Her raincoat gave off a peppermint smell that might have been stored up for this moment.

"You won't need to get out of the carriage at all," he said. She put her head on one side. Their cheeks glittered as did their eyes. They embraced, parted; the man from Connemara watched him out the door. Then the pair clasped hands through the window. She might have been standing in a tower and he elevated to her level as far as possible by ladder or rope, in the rain.

There was a great rush of people. At the very last minute four of them stormed this compartment. A little boy flung in over his own bags, whistling wildly, paying no attention to being seen off, no attention to feet inside, consenting to let a young woman who had followed him in put a small bag of his in the rack and save him a seat. She was being pelted with thanks for this by young men and girls crowding at the door; she smiled calmly back at them; even in this she was showing pregnancy, as she showed it under her calm blue coat. A pair of lovers slid in last of all, like a shadow, and filled two seats by the corridor door, trapping into the middle the man from Connemara and somewhat crowding the American girl into her corner. They were just not twining, touching, just not angry, just not too late. Without the ghost of impatience or struggle, without shifting about once, they were settled in speechlessness—two profiles, his dark and cleared of temper, hers young, with straight cut hair.

"Four o'clock."

The lady in the raincoat made the announcement in a hollow tone; everybody in the compartment hushed as though almost taken by surprise. She and the wistful round man still clasped hands through the window and continued to shine in the face like lighthouses smiling. The outside doors were banged shut in a long retreat in both directions, and the train moved. Those outside appeared running beside the train, then waving handkerchiefs, the young men shouting questions and envious things, the girls—they were certainly all Irish, wildly pretty—wildly retreating, their hair whipped forward in long bright and dark pennants by the sucking of the train. The round little man was there one moment and, panting, vanished the next.

The lady, still standing, was all at once very noticeable. Her body might have solidified to the floor under that buttoned cover. (What she had on under her raincoat was her own business and remained so.) The next moment she put out her tongue, at everything just left behind.

"*Oh* my God!" The man from Connemara did explode; it sounded like relief.

Then they were underway fast; the lady, having seated herself, smoothed down the raincoat with rattles like the reckless slamming of bureau drawers, and took from her purse a box of Players. She extracted a cigarette already partly burned down, and requested a light. The lover was so quick he almost anticipated her. When the butt glowed, her hand dropped like a shot bird from the flame he rather blindly stuck out. Between draws she held her cigarette below her knees and turned inward to her palm—her hand making a cauldron into which the little boy stared.

The American girl opened a book, but closed it. Every time the lady in the raincoat walked out over their feet—she immediately, after her cigarette, made several excursions—she would fling them a look. It was like "Don't say a word, start anything, fall into each other's arms, read, or fight, until I get back to you." She might both inspire and tantalize them with her glare. And she was so unpretty she ought to be funny, like somebody on the stage; perhaps she would be funny later.

The little boy whistled "*Funiculi, Funicula*" in notes almost too high for the ear to hear. On the windows it poured, poured rain. The black of London swam like a cinder in the eye and did not go away. The young wife, leaning back and letting her eyes fall a little while on the child, gave him dim, languorous looks, not quite shaking her head at him. He stopped whistling, but at the same time it could be felt how she was not his mother; her face showed degrees of maternity as other faces show degrees of love or anger; she was only acting his mother for the journey.

It was nice of her then to begin to sing "*Funiculi, Funicula,*" and the others joined, the little boy very seriously, as if he now hated the song. Then they sang something more Irish, about the sea and coming back. But the throb of the rails made the song oddly Spanish and hopelessly desirous; they were near the end of the car, where the beat was single and strong.

After the lady in the raincoat undid her top button and suggested "Wild Colonial Boy," her hatted head kept time, started to lead them—perhaps she kept a pub. The little boy, giving the ladies a meeting look, brought out a fiercely shining harmonica, as he would a pistol, and almost drowned them out. The American girl looked as if she did not know the words, but the lovers now sang, with faces strangely brave.

At some small, forgotten station a schoolgirl got on, took the vacant seat in this compartment, and opened a novel to page 1. They quieted. By the look of her it seemed they must be in Wales. They had scarcely got a word at the child before she began reading. She sat by the young wife; especially from her, the school hat hid the bent head like a candle snuffer; of her features only the little mouth, slightly open and working, stayed visible. Even her upper lip was darkly freckled, even the finger that lifted and turned the page.

The little boy sped his breath up the harmonica scale; the young wife said "Victor!" and they all felt sorry for him and had his name.

"Air," she suddenly said, as if she felt their look. The man from Connemara hurled himself at the window and slid the pane, then at the corridor door, and opened it wide onto a woman passing with an eight- or nine-months-old baby. It was a red-haired boy with queenly jowls, squinting in at the world as if to say, "Will what has just been said be very kindly repeated?"

"Oh, isn't he *beautiful!*" the young wife cried reproachfully through the door. She would have put out her hands.

There was no response. On they went.

"An English nurse traveling with an Irish child, look at that, he's so grand, and such style, that dress, that petticoat, do you think she's kidnaped the lad?" suggested the lady in the raincoat, puffing.

"*Oh* my God," said the man from Connemara.

For a moment the schoolgirl made the only sounds—catching her breath and sobbing over her book.

"Kidnaping's farfetched," said the man from Connemara. "Maybe the woman's deaf and dumb."

"I couldn't sleep this night thinking such wickedness was traveling on the train and on the boat with me." The young wife's skin flooded to her temples.

"It's not *your* fault."

The schoolgirl bent lower still and, still reading, opened a canvas satchel at her feet, in which—all looked—were a thermos, a lunchbox under lock and key, a banana, and a Bible. She selected the banana by feel, and brought it up and ate it as she read.

"If it's kidnaping, it'll be in the Cork paper Sunday morning," said the lady in the raincoat with confidence. "Railway trains are great systems for goings on of all kinds. You'll never take me by surprise."

"But this is *our* train," said the young wife. "Women alone, sometimes exceptions, but often on the long journey alone or with children."

"There's evil where you'd least expect it," the man from Connemara said, somehow as if he didn't care for children. "There's one thing and another, so forth and so on, run your finger down the alphabet and see where it stops."

"I'll never see the Cork paper," replied the young wife. "But oh, I tell you I would rather do without air to breathe than see that poor baby pass again and put out his little arms to me."

"Ah, then. Shut the door," the man from Connemara said, and pointed it out to the lover, who after all sat nearer.

"Excuse me," the young man whispered to the girl, and shut the door at her knee and near where her small open hand rested.

"But why would she be kidnaping the baby *into* Ireland?" cried the young wife suddenly.

"Yes—you've been riding backwards: if we were going the other way, 'twould be a different story." And the lady in the raincoat looked at her wisely.

The train was grinding to a stop at a large station in Wales. The schoolgirl, after one paralyzed moment, rose and got off through the corridor in a dream; the book she closed was seen to be *Black Stallion of the Downs.* A big tall man climbed on and took her place. It was this station, it was felt, where they actually ceased leaving a place and from now on were arriving at one.

The tall Welshman drove into the compartment through any remarks that were going on and with great strength like a curse heaved his bag on top of several of theirs in the rack, where it had been thought there was no more room, and took the one seat without question. With serious sets of his shoulders he settled down in the middle of them, between Victor and the lady in the raincoat, facing the man from Connemara. His hair was in two corner bushes, and he had a full eye—like that of the horse in the storm in old chromos in the West of America—the kind of eye supposed to attract lightning. In the silence of the dreary stop, he slapped all his pockets—not having forgotten anything, only making sure. His hands were powdered over with something fairly black.

"Well! How far do *you* go?" he put to the man from Connemara and then to them in turn, and each time the answer came, "Ireland." He seemed unduly astonished.

He lighted a pipe, and pointed it toward the little boy. "What have you been doing in England, eh?"

Victor writhed forward and set his teeth into the strap of the outer door.

"He's been to a wedding," said the young wife, as though she and Victor were saying the same thing in two different ways, and smiled on him fully for the first time.

"Who got married?"

"Me brother," Victor said in a strangled voice, still holding on recklessly while the train, starting with a jerk, rocked him to the side.

"Big wedding?"

Two greyhounds in plaid blankets, like dangerously ecstatic old ladies hoping no one would see them, rushed into, out of, then past the corridor door which the incoming Welshman had failed to shut behind him. The glare in the eye of the man who followed, with his belt flying about him as he pulled back on the dogs, was wild, too.

"Big wedding?"

"Me family was all over the place if that's what you mean." Victor wildly chewed; there was a smell of leather.

"Ah, it has driven his poor mother to her bed, it was that grand a wedding," said the young wife. "That's why she's in England, and Victor here on his own."

"You must have missed school. What school do you go to—you *go* to school?" By the power of his eye, the Welshman got Victor to let go the strap and answer yes or no.

"School, yes."

"You study French and so on?"

"Ah, them languages is no good. What good is Irish?" said Victor passionately, and somebody said, "Now what does your mother tell you?"

"What ails your mother?" said the Welshman.

"Ah, it's her old trouble. Ask *her*. But there's two of me brothers at one end and five at the other."

"You're divided."

The young wife let Victor stand on the seat and haul her paper parcel off the rack so she could give him an orange. She drew out as well a piece of needlepoint, square and tarnished, which she spread over her pretty arm and hung before their eyes.

"Beautiful!"

"'A Wee Cottage' is the name it has."

"I see the cottage. 'Tis very wee, and so's every bit about it."

"'Twould blind you: 'tis a work of art."

"The little rabbit peeping out!"

"Makes you wish you had your gun," said the Welshman to Victor.

The young wife said, "Me grandmother. At eighty she died, very sudden, on a visit to England. God rest her soul. Now I'm bringing this masterpiece home to Ireland."

"Who could blame you."

"Well you should bring it away, all those little stitches she put in."

She wrapped it away, just as anyone could see her—as she might for the moment see herself—folding a blanket down into the crib and tucking the ends. Victor, now stained and fragrant with orange, leapt like a tiger to pop the parcel back overhead.

"No, I shouldn't think learning Irish would do you much good," said the Welshman. "No real language."

"Why not?" said the lady in the raincoat instantly. "I've a brother who is a very fluent Irish speaker and a popular man. You cannot doubt yourself that when the English hear you speaking a tongue they cannot follow, in the course of time they are due to start holding respect for you."

"From London you are." The Welshman bit down on his pipe and smoked.

"*Oh* my God." The man from Connemara struck his head. "I have an English wife. How would she like that, I wouldn't like to know? If all at once I begun on her in Irish! How would you like it if your husband would only speak to you in Irish? Or Welsh, my God?" He searched the eyes of all the women, and last of the young Irish sweetheart—who did not seem to grasp the question. "Aha ha ha!" he cried urgently and despairingly at her, asking her only to laugh with him.

But the young man's arm was thrust along the seat and she was sitting under its arch as if it were the entrance to a cave, which surely they all must see.

"Will you eat a biscuit now?" the young wife gently asked the man from Connemara. He took one wordlessly; for the moment he had no English or Irish. So she broke open another paper parcel beside her. "I have oceans," she said.

"Oh, *you wait*," said the lady in the raincoat, rising. And *she* opened a parcel as big as a barrel and it was full of everything to eat that anybody could come out of England with alive.

She offered candy, jam roll, biscuits, bananas, nuts, sections of bursting orange, and bread and butter, and they all in the flush of the hospitality and heat sat eating. Everybody partook but the Welshman, who had presumably had a dinner in Wales. It was more than ever like a little party, all the finer somehow, sadly enough, for the nose against the windowpane. They poured out tea from a couple of steaming thermoses; the black windows—for the sun was down now, never having been out of the fogs and rains all day—coated warmly over between them and what flew by out there.

"Could you tell me the name of a place to stay in Cork?" The American girl spoke up to the man from Connemara as he gave her a biscuit.

"In Cork? Ah, but you don't want to be stopping in Cork. Killarney is where you would do well to go, if you're wanting to see the wonders of Ireland. The lakes and the hills! Blue as blue skies, the lakes. That's where you want to go, Killarney."

"She wants to climb the Hill of Tara, you mean," said the guard, who with a burst of cold wind had entered to punch their tickets again. "All the way up, and into the raths, too, to lay her eyes by the light of candles on something she's never seen before; if that's what she's after. Have you never climbed the Hill and never crept into those, lady? Maybe 'twould take a little boost from behind, I don't know your size; but I think 'twould not be difficult getting you through." He gave her ticket its punch, with a keen blue glance at her, and banged out.

"Well, *I'm* going to the sitting in the dining car now." The lady in the raincoat stood up under the dim little lights in the ceiling that shone on her shoulders. Then down her long nose she suggested to them each to come, too. Did she really mean to eat still, and after all that largess? They laughed, as if to urge her by their shock to go on, and the American girl witlessly murmured, "No, I have a letter to write."

Off she went, that long coat shimmering and rattling. The little boy looked after her, the first sea wind blew in at the opened door, and his cowlick nodded like a dark flower.

"Very grand," said the Connemara man. "Very high and mighty she is, indeed."

Out there, nuns, swept by untoward blasts of wind, shrieked soundlessly as in nightmares in the corridors. It must be like the Tunnel of Love for them—the thought drifted into the young sweetheart's head.

She was so stiff! She struggled up, staggered a little as she left the compartment. All alone she stood in the corridor. A young man went past, soft fair mustache, soft fair hair, combing the hair—oh, delicious. Here came a hat like old Cromwell's on a lady, who had also a fur cape, a stick, flat turning-out shoes, and a heavy book with a pencil in it. The old lady beat her stick on the floor and made a sweet old man in gaiters and ribbon-tied hat back up into a doorway to let her by. All these people were going into the dining cars. She hung her head out the open corridor window into the Welsh night, which, seen from inside itself—her head in its mouth—could look not black but pale. Wales was formidable, barrier-like. What contours which she could not see were raised out there, dense and heraldic? Once there was a gleam from their lights on the walls of a tunnel, from the everlasting springs that the tunnelers had cut. Should they ever have started, those tunnelers? Sometimes there were sparks. She hung out into the wounded night a minute: let him wish her back.

"What do you do with yourself in England, keep busy?" said the man from Wales, pointing the stem of his pipe at the man from Connemara.

"I do, I raise birds in Sussex, if you're asking my hobby."

"A terrific din, I daresay. Birds keep you awake all night?"

"On the contrary. Never notice it for a minute. Of course there are the birds that engage in conversation rather than sing. I might be listening to the conversation."

"Parrots, you mean. You have parrots? You teach them to talk?"

"Budgies, man. Oh, I did have one that was a lovely talker, but curious, very strange and curious, in his habits of feeding."

"What was it he ate? How much would you ask for a bird like that?"

"Like what?"

"Parrot that could talk but didn't eat well, that you were just mentioning you had."

"That bird was an exception. Not for sale."

"Are you responsible for your birds?"

They all sat waiting while a tunnel banged.

"What do you mean responsible?"

"Responsible: you sell me a bird. Presently he doesn't talk or sing. Can I bring it back?"

"You cannot. That's God-given, lads."

"How old is the bird now? Good health?"

"Owing to conditions in England I could not get him the specialties he liked, and came in one morning to find the bird stiff. Still it's a nice hobby. Very interesting."

"Would you have got five pounds for this bird if you had found a customer for her? What was it the bird craved so?"

"'Twas a male, not on the market, and if there had been another man, that would sell him to you, 'twould have cost you eight pounds."

"Ah. He ate inappropriate food?"

"You might say he *could not get* inappropriate food. He was destroyed by a mortal appetite for food you'd call it unlikely for a bird to desire at all. Myself, I never raised a bird that thrived so, learned faster, and had more to say."

"You never tried to sell him."

"For one thing I could not afford to turn him loose in Sussex. I told my wife not to be dusting his cage without due caution, not to be talking to him so much herself, the way she did."

The Welshman looked at him. He said, "Well, he died."

"Pass by my house!" cried the man from Connemara. "And look in the window, as you'll likely do, and you'll see the bird—stuffed. You'll think he's alive at first. Open beak! Talking up to the last, like you or I that have souls to be saved."

"Souls: is the leading church in Ireland Catholic, would you call Ireland a Catholic country?" The Welshman settled himself anew.

"I would, yes."

"Is there a Catholic church where you live, in your town?"

"There is."

"And you go?"

"I do."

"Suppose you miss. If you miss going to church, does the priest fine you for it?"

"Of course he does not! Father Lavery! What do you mean?"

"Suppose it's Sunday—tomorrow's Sunday—and you don't go to church. Would you have to pay a fine to the priest?"

The man from Connemara lowered his dark head; he glared at the lovers—for she had returned to her place. "Of course I would not!" Still he looked at the girl.

"Ah, in the windows black as they are, we do look almost like ghosts riding by," she breathed, looking past him.

He said at once, "A castle I know, you see them on the wall."

"What castle?" said the sweetheart.

"You mean what ghosts. First she comes, then he comes."

"In Connemara?"

"Ah, you've never been there. Late tomorrow night I'll be there. She comes first because she's mad, and he slow—got the dagger stuck in him, you see? Destroyed by her. She walks along, carries herself grand, not shy. Then he comes, unwilling, not touching with his feet—pulled through the air. By the dagger, you might say, like a hooked fish. Because they're a pair, himself and herself, sure as they was joined together—and while you look go leaping in the bright air, moonlight as may be, and sailing off together cozy as a couple of kites to start it again."

That girl's straight hair, cut like a little train to a point at the nape of her neck, her little pointed nose that came down in the one unindented line which began at her hair, her swimming, imagining eyes, held them all, like her lover, perfectly still. Love was amazement now. The lovers did not touch, for a thousand reasons, but that was one.

"Start what again?" said the Welshman. "Have you personally seen them?"

"I have, I'm no exception."

"Can you say who they might be?"

"Visit the neighborhood for yourself and there'll be those who can acquaint you with the gory details. Myself I'm acquainted with only the general idea of their character and disposition, formed after putting two and two together. Have you never seen a ghost, then?"

The Welshman gave a look as if he'd been unfairly struck, as if a question coming at him now in here was carrying things too far. But he only said, "Heard them."

"Ah, do keep it to yourself then, for the duration of the journey, and not go bragging, will you?" the young wife cried at him. "Irish ghosts are enough for some of us for the one night without mixing them up with the Welsh and them shrieking things, and just before all of us are going on the water except yourself."

"You don't mind the Lord and Lady Beagle now, do you? They shouldn't frighten you, they're lovely and married. Married still. Why, their names just come to me, did you hear that? Lord and Lady Beagle—like they sent in a card. Ha! Ha!" Again the man from Connemara tried to bring that singing laugh out of the frightened sweetheart, from whom he had not yet taken his glances away.

"Don't," the young wife begged him, forcing her eyes to his salver-like palm. "Those are wild, crazy names for ghosts."

"Well, what kind of ghosts do you think they ever are!" Their glances met through their laughter and remorse. She tossed her head.

"There ain't no ghosts," said Victor.

"Now suck this good orange," she whispered to him, as if he were being jealous.

"Here comes the bride," announced the Welshman.

"*Oh* my God." But what business was she of the Welshman's?

In came the lady in the raincoat beaming from her dinner, but he talked right around her hip. "Do you have to confess?" he said. "Regularly? Suppose you make a confession—swear words, lewd thoughts, or the like: *then* does the priest make you pay a fine?"

"Confession's free, why not?" remarked the lady, stepping over all their feet.

"You're a Catholic, too?" he said, as she hung above his knee.

And as they all closed their eyes she fell into his lap, right down on top of him. Even the dogs, now rushing along in the other direction hung on the air a moment, their tongues out. Then one dog was inside with them. This greyhound flung herself forward, back, down to the floor, her tail slapped out like a dragon's. Her eyes gazed toward the confusion, and little bubbles of boredom and suspicion played under the skin of her jowls, puff, puff, puff, while wrinkles of various memories and agitations came and went on her forehead like little forks of lightning.

"Well, look what's with us," said the lover. "Here, lad, here, lad."

"That's Telephone Girl," said the lady in the raincoat, now on her feet and straightening herself with distant sweepings of both hands. "I was just in conversation with the keeper of those. Don't be getting her stirred up. She's a winner, he has it." She let herself down into the seat and spread a look on all of them as if she had always been too womanly for the place. Her mooning face turned slowly and met the Welshman's stern, strong glance: *he* appeared to be expecting some apology from some source.

"'Tisn't everybody runs so fast and gets nothing for it in the end herself, either," said the lady. Telephone Girl shuddered, ate some crumbs, coughed.

"I'm ashamed to hear you saying that, she gets the glory," said the man from Connemara. "How many human beings of your acquaintance get half a dog's chance at glory?"

"You don't like dogs." The lady looked at him, bowing her head.

"They're not my element. That's not the way I'm made, no."

The man in charge rushed in, and out he and the dog shot together. Somebody closed the door; it was the Welshman.

"Now: what time of the night do you get to Cork?" he asked.

The lover spoke, unexpectedly. "Tomorrow morning." The girl let out a long breath after him.

"What time of the morning?"

"Nine!" shouted everybody but the American.

"Travel all night," he said.

"Book a berth in Fishguard!"

The mincing woman with the red-haired baby boy passed—the baby with his same fat, enchanted squint looked through the glass at them.

"Oh, I always get seasick!" cried the young wife in fatalistic enthusiastic tones, only distantly watching the baby, who, although he stretched his little hand against the glass, was not being kidnaped now. She leaned over to tell the young girl, "Let me only step off the train at Fishguard and I'm dying already."

"What do you usually do for an attack of seasickness when you're on the Cork boat?"

"*I* just stay in one place and never move, that's what *I* do!" she cried, the smile that had never left her sad, sweet lips turned upon them all. "I don't try to move at all and I die all the way." Victor edged a little away from her.

"The boat rocks," suggested the Welshman. Victor edged away from him.

"The *Innisfallen?* Of course she rocks, there's a far, wide sea, very deep and treacherous, and very historic." The man from Connemara folded his arms.

"It takes six weeks, don't you think?" The young wife appealed to them all. "To get over the journey. I tell me husband, a fortnight is never enough. Me husband is English, though. I've never like England. I have six aunts all living there, too. Me mother's sisters." She smiled. "They all are hating it. Me grandmother died while she was in England."

His cheeks sunk on his fists, Victor leaned forward over his knees. His hair, blue-black, whorled around the cowlick like a spinning gramophone record; he seemed to dream of being down on the ground, and fighting somebody on it.

"God rest her soul," said the lady in the raincoat, as if she might have passed through the goods car and seen where Grandmother was riding with them, to her grave in Ireland; but in that case the young wife would have been with the dead, and not playing at mother with Victor.

"Then how much does the passage cost you? Fishguard to Cork, Cork back to Fishguard? I may decide to try it on holiday sometime."

"Where are you leaving us this night?" asked the young wife, still in the voice in which she had spoken of her grandmother and her mother's sisters.

He gave out a name to make her look more commiserating, and repeated, "What is the fare from Fishguard to Cork?"

They stopped just then at a dark station and a paper boy's voice called his papers into the train.

"*Oh* my God. Where are we!"

The Welshman put up his finger and called for a paper, and one was brought inside to him by a strange, dark child.

At the sight of the man opening his newspaper, the lady in the raincoat spoke promptly and with her lips wooden, like an actress. "How did the race come out?"

"What's that? Race? What race would that be?" He gave her that look he gave without exposing it too widely to anybody.

She tilted her head. "Little Boy Blue, yes," she murmured over his shoulder.

A discussion of Little Boy Blue arose while he kept on reading.

"How much money at a time do you bet on the races?" the Welshman asked suddenly, coming out from behind the paper. Then as suddenly he retreated, taking back the question entirely.

"Now the second race," murmured the lady in the raincoat. Everybody wreathed in the Welshman. He was in the middle of the Welsh news, silent as the dead.

The man from Connemara put up a hand as the page might have been turned, "Long Gone the favorite! You were long gone yourself," he added politely to the lady in the raincoat. Possibly she had been punished enough for going out to eat and coming in to fall down all over a man.

"Yes I was," she said, lifting her chin; she brought out a Player and lighted it herself. She puffed. "'Twas a long way, twelve cars. 'Twas a lovely dinner—chicken. One man rose up in the aisle when it was put before him and gave a cry. 'It's rabbit!'"

They were pleased. The man from Connemara gave his high, free laugh. The lovers were strung like bows in silent laughter, but the lady blew a ring of smoke, at which Victor aimed an imaginary weapon.

"A lovely, long dinner. A man left us but returned to the car to say that while we were eating they shifted the carriages about and he had gone up the train, down the train, and could not find himself at all." Her voice was so moody and remote now it might be some wandering of long ago she spoke to them about.

The Welshman said, over his paper, "Shifted the carriages?"

All laughed the harder.

"He said his carriage was gone, yes. From where he had left it: he hoped to find it yet, but I don't think he has. He came back the second time to the dining car and spoke about it. He laid his hand on the guard's arm. 'While I was sitting at the table and eating my dinner, the carriages have been shifted about,' he said. 'I wandered through the cars with the dogs running and cars with boxes in them, and through cars with human beings sitting in them I never laid eyes on in the journey—one party going on among some young people that would altogether block the traffic in the corridor.'"

"All Irish," said the young wife, and smoothed Victor's head; he looked big-eyed into space.

"The guard was busy and spoke to a third party, a gentleman eating. Yes, they were, all Irish. 'Will you mercifully take and show this gentleman where he is traveling, when you can, since he's lost?' 'Not lost,' he said, 'distracted,' and went through his system of argument. The gentleman said he could jolly well find his own carriage. The man opposite him rose up and that was when he declared the chicken was rabbit. The gentleman put down his knife and said man lost or not, carriage shifted or not, the stew rabbit or not, the man could just the same fight back to where he had come from, as he himself jolly well intended to do when he could finish the dinner on his plate in peace." She opened her purse, and passed licorice drops around.

"He sounds vulgar," said the man from Connemara.

"'Twas a lovely dinner."

"*You* weren't lost, I take it?" said the Welshman, accepting a licorice drop. "Traveled much?"

"Oh dear Heaven, traveled? Well, I have. Yes, no end to it."

"*Oh* my God."

"No, *I'm* never lost."

"Let's drop the subject," said the Welshman.

The lovers settled back into the cushions. They were the one subject nobody was going to discuss.

"Look," the young girl said in a low voice, from within the square of the young man's arm, but not to him. "I see a face that keeps going past, looking through the window. A man, plying up and down, could he be the one so unfortunate?"

"Not him, he's leading greyhounds, didn't we see him come in?" The young man spoke eagerly, to them all. "Leading, or they leading him."

"'Tis a long train," the lady murmured to the Welshman. "The longest, most populated train leaving England, I would suppose, the one going over to catch the *Innisfallen.*"

"Is that the name of the boat? You were glad to leave England?"

"It is and I was—pleased to be starting my journey, pleased to have it over." She gave a look at him—then at the others, the compartment, the tumbled baggage, everything. Outside, dim Wales clapped strongly at the window, like some accompanying bird. "I'll just lower the shade, will I?" she said.

She pulled at the window shade and fastened it down, and pulled down the door shade after it. The minute she did that, the window shade flew up, with a noise like a turkey.

They shouted for joy—they knew it! She *was* funny.

The train stopped and waited a long time in the dark, out from nowhere. They sat awhile, swung their feet; the man from Connemara whistled for a minute marvelously, Victor had his third orange.

"Suppose we're late!" shouted the man from Connemara. The mountains could hear him; they had opened the window to look out hoping to see the trouble, but could not. "And the *Innisfallen* sails without us! And we don't reach the other side in this night!"

"Then you'll all have to spend the night in Fishguard," said the Welshman.

"Oh, what a scene there'll be in Cork, when we don't arrive!" cried the young wife merrily. "When the boat sails in without us, oh poor souls."

Victor laughed harshly. He had made a pattern with his orange peel on the window ledge, which he now swept away.

"There's none too much room for the traveler in the town of Fishguard," said the Welshman over his pipe. "You'll do best to keep dry in the station."

"Won't they *die* of it in Cork?" The young wife cocked her head.

"Me five brothers will stand ready to give me a beating!" Victor said, then looked proud.

"I daresay it won't be the first occasion you've put in the night homeless in Fishguard."

"In Fishguard?" warningly cried the man from Connemara. A scowl lit up his face and his eyes opened wide with innocence. "Didn't you know this was the boat train you're riding, man?"

"Oh, is that what you call it?" said the Welshman in equal innocence.

"They *hold* the boat for us. I feel it's safe to say that every soul on board this train saving yourself is riding to catch the boat."

"Hold the *Innisfallen* at Fishguard Harbor? For how long?"

"If need be till doomsday, but we are generally sailing at midnight."

"No, sir, we'll never be left helpless in Fishguard, this or any other night," said the lady in the raincoat.

"Or!" cried the man from Connemara. "Or! We could take the other boat if we're as late as that, to Rosslare, oh my God! And spend the Sunday bringing ourselves back to Cork!"

"You're going to Connemara to see your mother," the young wife said psychically.

"I'm sure as God's truth staying the one night in Cork first!" he shouted across at her, and banged himself on the knees, as if they were trying to take Cork away from him.

The Welshman asked, "What is the longest on record they have ever held the boat?"

"Who knows?" said the lady in the raincoat. "Maybe 'twill be tonight."

"Only can I get out now and see where we've stopped?" asked Victor.

"*Oh* my God—we've started! *Oh* that Cork City!"

"When you travel to Cork, do the lot of you generally get seasick?" inquired the Welshman, swaying among them as they got under way.

The lady in the raincoat made him a grand gesture with one hand and rose and pulled down her suitcase. She opened it and fetched out from beneath the hot water bottle in pink flannel a little pasteboard box.

"What's that going to be—pills for seasickness?" he said.

She lifted the lid and passed the box under his eyes and then under their eyes, although too fast to be quite offering anything. "'Tis a present," she said. "A present of seasick pills, given me for the journey."

The lovers smiled simultaneously, as they would at the thought of any present.

The train stopped again, started; stopped, started. Here on the outer edge of Wales it advanced and hesitated as rhythmically and as interminably as a needle in a hem. The wheels had taken on that defenseless sound peculiar to running near the open sea. Oil lamps burned in their little boxes at the halts; there was a pull at the heart from the feeling of the trees all being bent the same way.

"*Now* where?" They had stopped again.

A sigh escaped the lovers, who had drawn a breath of the sea. A single lamp stared in at their window, like the eye of a dragon lifted out of the lid of sleep.

"It's my station!" The Welshman suddenly addressed himself. He reared up, banged down the bushes on his head under a black hat, collected his suitcase and overcoat, and almost swept away with it the parcel with the "Wee Cottage" in it, belonging to the young wife. He got past them, dragging his suitcase with a great heave of the shoulder—God knew what was inside. He wrenched open the door, turned and looked at the lot of them, and then gently backed down into the outdoors.

Only to reappear. He had mistaken the station after all. But he simply held his ground there in the doorway, brazening it out as the train darted on.

"I may decide on raising my own birds some day," he said in a somewhat louder voice. "What did you begin with, a cock and a hen?"

On the index finger which the man from Connemara raised before he answered was a black fingernail, like the mark of a hammer blow; it might have been a reminder not to do something or other before he got home to Ireland.

"I would advise you to begin with a cock and two hens. Don't go into it without getting advice."

"What did you start with?"

"Six cocks—"

Another dark station, and down the Welshman dropped.

"And six hens!"

It was almost too much that his face rose there *again.* He wasn't embarrassed at himself, any more than he was by how black and all impenetrable it was outside in Wales, and asked, "Do you have to produce a passport to go into Ireland?"

"Certainly, a passport or a travel card. *Oh* my God."

"What do you mean by a travel card? Let me see yours. Every one of you carry one with you?"

Travel cards and passports were produced and handed up to him.

"Oh, how beautiful your mother is!" cried the young wife to Victor, over his shoulder. "Is that a wee strawberry mark she has there on her cheek?"

"'Tis!" he cried in agony.

The Welshman was holding the American's different-looking passport open in his hand; she looked startled, herself, that she had given it up and at once, as if this were required and he had waked her up in the night. He read out her name, nationality, age, her husband's name, nationality. It was not that he read it officially—worse: as if it were a poem in the paper, only with the last verse missing.

"My husband is a photographer. We've made a little darkroom in our flat," she told him.

But he all at once turned back and asked the man from Connemara, "And you give it as your opinion your prize bird died of longings for food from far away."

"There've been times when I've dreamed a certain *person* may have had more to do with it!" the man from Connemara cried in crescendo. "That I've never mentioned till now. But women are jealous and uncertain creatures, I've been thinking as we came this long way along tonight."

"Of *birds!*" cried the young wife, her fingers going to her shoulders.

"Name your poison."

"Why birds?"

"Why not?"

"Because it talked?"

"Name your poison."

Another lantern, another halt of the train.

"It'll be raining over the water," the Welshman called as he swung open his door. From the step he looked back and said, "What do you take the sea-sick pills in, have you drink to take them in?"

"I have."

He said out of the windy night, "Can you buy drink on board the ship? Or is it not too late for that?"

"Three miles out 'tis only the sea and glory," shouted the man from Connemara.

"Be good," the Welshman tossed back at him, and quite lightly he dropped away. He disappeared for the third time into the Welsh black, this time for keeps. It was as though a big thumb had snuffed him out.

They smoothed and straightened themselves behind him, all but the young lovers spreading out in the seats; she rubbed her arm, up and down. Not a soul had inquired of that poor vanquished man what he did, if he had wife and children living—he might have only had an auntie. They never let him tell what he was doing with himself in either end of Wales, or why he had to come on this very night, or even what in the world he was carrying in that heavy case.

As they talked, the American girl laid her head back, a faint smile on her face.

"Just one word of advice," said the man from Connemara in her ear, putting her passport, warm from his hand, into hers. "Be careful in future who you ask questions of. You were safe when you spoke to me, I'm a married man. I was pleased to tell you what I could—go to Killarney and so forth and so on, see the marvelous beauty of the lakes. But next time ask a guard."

Victor's head tumbled against the watchful side of the young wife, his right hand was flung in her lap, a fist floating away. In Fishguard, they had to shake him awake and pull him out into the rain.

No traveler out of the compartment was, actually, booked for a berth on the *Innisfallen* except the lady in the raincoat, who marched straight off. Most third-class train passengers spent the night third-class in the *Innisfallen* lounge. The man from Connemara was the first one stretched, a starfish of exhaustion, on a cretonne-covered couch. The American girl stared at a page of her book, then closed it until they were underway. The lovers disappeared. In the deeps of night that bright room reached some vortex of quiet, like a room where all brains are at work and great decisions are on the brink. Occasionally there was a tapping, as of drumming fingernails—that meant to closed or hypnotized eyes that dogs were being sped through. The random, gentle old men who were walking the corridors in their tweeds and seemed lost at Jesus's lambs, were waiting perhaps for the bar to open. The young wife, as desperate as she'd feared, saw nothing, forgot everything, and even abandoned Victor, as if there could never be any time or place in the world but this of her suffering. She spoke to the child as if she had never seen him before and would never see him again. Victor took the last little paper of biscuits she had given him away to a corner and slowly emptied it, making a mountain of the crumbs; then he bent his head over his travel card with its new stamp, on which presently he rolled his cheek and floated unconscious.

Once the man from Connemara sat up out of his sleep and stared at the

American girl pinned to her chair across the room, as if he saw somebody desperate who had left her husband once, endangered herself among strangers, been turned back, and was here for the second go-round, asking again for a place to stay in Cork. She stared back motionless, until he was a starfish again.

Then it was morning—a world of sky coursing above, streaming light. The *Innisfallen* had entered the River Lee. Almost at arm's reach were the buff, pink, gray, salmon fronts of houses, trees shining like bird wings, and bells that jumped toward sound as the ship, all silent, flowed past. The Sunday, the hour, too, were encroaching-real. Each lawn had a flag-like purity that braved and invited all the morning senses, even smell, as snow can—as if snow had fallen in the night, and this sun and this ship had come to trace it and melt it.

It was that passing, short, yet inviolate distance between ship and land on both sides that made an arrow-like question in the heart. Someone cried at random, "What town is this?"

To wake up to the river, no longer the sea! There was more than one little town, that in their silent going they saluted while not touching or deviating to it at all. After the length of the ship had passed a ringing steeple, and the hands had glinted gold at them from the clockface, an older, harsher, more distant bell rang from an inland time: *now.*

Now sea gulls paced city lawns. *They* moved through the hedges, the ship in the garden. A thrush could be heard singing, and there he sang—so clear and so early it all was. On deck a little girl clapped her hands. "Why do you do that!" her brother lovingly encouraged her.

On shore a city street appeared, and now cars were following the ship along; passengers inside blew auto horns and waved handkerchiefs up and down. There was a sidewise sound of a harmonica, frantic, tiny and bold. Victor was up where he ought not to be on deck, handing out black frowns and tunes to the docks sliding into sight. Now he had to look out for his brothers. Perhaps deep in the lounge his guardian was now sleeping at last, white and exhausted, inhumanly smiling in her sleep.

The lovers stood on the lower, more shaded deck—two backs. A line of sun was between them like a thread that could be picked off. One ought not yet to look into their faces, watching water. How far, how deep was this day to cut into their hearts? From now on everything would cut deeper than yesterday. Her wintry boots stiff from their London wet looked big on the ship, pricked with ears, at that brink of light they hung over. And suddenly she changed position—one shoe tapped, pointing, back of the other. She poised there. The boat whistle thundered like a hundred organ notes, but she did not quake—now as used to boat whistles as one of the sea gulls; or as far away.

"There's a bride on board!" called somebody. "Look at her, look!"

Sure enough, a girl who had not yet showed herself in public now appeared by the rail in a white spring hat and, over her hands, a little old-fashioned white bunny muff. She stood there all ready to be met, now come out in her own sweet time. Delight gathered all around, singing began on board, bells could by now be heard ringing urgently in the town. Surely that color beating in their eyes came from flags hung out upon the looming shore. The bride smiled but did not look up; she was looking down at her dazzling little fur muff.

They were in, the water held still about them. The gulls converged; just under the surface a newspaper slowly went down with its drowned news.

In the crowd of the dock, the lady in the raincoat was being confronted with a flock of beautiful children—red flags in their cheeks, caps on their heads, little black boots like pipes—and by a man bigger than she was. He stood smoking while the children hurled themselves up against her. As people hurried around her carrying their bundles and bags in the windy bright of the Cork dock, she stood camouflaged like a sportsman in his own polychrome fields, a hand on her striped hip. Vague, luminous, smiling, her big white face held a moment and bent down for its kiss. The man from Connemara strode by, looking down on her as if now her head were in the basket. His cap set at a fairly desperate angle, he went leaping into the streets of Cork City.

Victor was shouting at the top of his lungs, "Here I am!" The young wife, coming forth old but still alive, was met by old women in cloaks, three young men to embrace her, and a donkey and cart to ride her home, once she had put Victor with his brothers.

Perhaps regardless of the joy or release of an arrival, or because of it, there is always for someone a last-minute, finger-like touch, a reminder, a promise of confusion. Behind shut lids the American girl saw the customs' chalk mark just now scrawled on the wall of her suitcase. Like a gypsy's sign found on her own front door, it stared at her from the sensitized optic dark, and she felt exposed—as if, in spite of herself, when she didn't know it, something had been told on her. "A rabbit ran over my grave," she thought. She left her suitcase in the parcel room and walked out into Cork.

When it rained late in that afternoon, the American girl was still in Cork, and stood sheltering in the doorway of a pub. She was listening to the pub sounds and the alley sounds as she might to a garden's and a fountain's.

She had had her day, her walk, that began at the red, ferny, echo-hung rock against which the lowest houses were set, where the ocean-river sent up signals of mirrored light. She had walked the hill and crossed the swan-bright bridges, her way wound in among people busy at encounters, meetings, it seemed to her reunions. After church in the streets of Cork dozens of little girls in confirmation dresses, squared off by their veils into animated paper snowflakes, raced and danced out of control and into charmed traffic—like miniature and more conscious brides. The trees had almost rushed with light and blossom; they nearly had sound, as the bells did. Boughs that rocked on the hill were tipped and weighted as if with birds, which were really their own bursting and almost-bursting leaves. In all Cork today every willow stood with gold-red hair springing and falling about it, like Venus alive. Rhododendrons swam in light, leaves and flowers alike; only a shadow could separate them into colors. She had felt no lonelier than that little bride herself, who had come off the boat. Yes, somewhere in the crowd at the dock there must have been a young man holding flowers: he had been taken for granted.

In the future would the light, that had jumped like the man from Connemara into the world, be a memory, like that of a meeting, or must there be mere faith that it had been like that?

Shielding the telegraph-form from her fellow writers at the post-office table, she printed out to her husband in England, "England was a mistake." At once she scratched that out, and took back the blame but without words.

Love with the joy being drawn out of it like anything else that aches—that was loneliness; not this. *I* was nearly destroyed, she thought, and again was threatened with a light head, a rush of laughter, as when the Welshman had come so far with them and then let them off.

If she could never tell her husband her secret, perhaps she would never tell it at all. You must never betray pure joy—the kind you were born and began with—either by hiding it or by parading it in front of people's eyes; they didn't want to be shown it. And still you must tell it. Is there no way? she thought—for here I am, this far. I see Cork's streets take off from the waterside and rise lifting their houses and towers like note above note on a page of music, with arpeggios running over it of green and galleries and belvederes, and the bright sun raining at the top. Out of the joy I hide for fear it is promiscuous, I may walk forever at the fall of evening by the river, and find this river street by the red rock, this first, last house, that's perhaps a boarding-house now, standing full-face to the tide, and look up to that window—that upper window, from which the mystery will never go. The curtains dyed so many times over are still pulled back and the window looks out open to the evening, the river, the hills, and the sea.

For a moment someone—she thought it was a woman—came and stood at the window, then hurled a cigarette with its live coal down into the extinguishing garden. But it was not the impatient tenant, it was the window itself that could tell her all she had come here to know—or all she could bear this evening to know, and that was light and rain, light and rain, dark, light, and rain.

"Don't expect me back yet" was all she need say tonight in the telegram. What was always her trouble? "You hope for too much," he said.

When early this morning the bride smiled, it might almost have been for her photograph; but she still did not look up—as though if even her picture were taken, she would vanish. And now she had vanished.

Walking on through the rainy dusk, the girl again took shelter in the warm doorway of the pub, holding her message, unfinished and unsent.

"Ah, it's a heresy, I told him," a man inside was shouting, out of the middle of his story. A barmaid glimmered through the passage in her frill, a glad cry went up at her entrance, as if she were the heresy herself, and when they all called out something fresh it was like the signal for a song.

The girl let her message go into the stre[illegible] street, and opening the door walked without protection into the lo[illegible]oom full of strangers.

Where Is the Voice Coming From?

1963

I SAYS to my wife, "You can reach and turn it off. You don't have to set and look at a black nigger face no longer than you want to, or listen to what you don't want to hear. It's still a free country."

I reckon that's how I give myself the idea.

I says, I could find right exactly where in Thermopylae that nigger's living that's asking for equal time. And without a bit of trouble to me.

And I ain't saying it might not be because that's pretty close to where *I* live. The other hand, there could be reasons you might have yourself for knowing how to get there in the dark. It's where you all go for the thing you want when you want it the most. Ain't that right?

The Branch Bank sign tells you in lights, all night long even, what time it is and how hot. When it was quarter to four, and 92, that was me going by in my brother-in-law's truck. He don't deliver nothing at that hour of the morning.

So you leave Four Corners and head west on Nathan B. Forrest Road, past the Surplus & Salvage, not much beyond the Kum Back Drive-In and Trailer Camp, not as far as where the signs starts saying "Live Bait," "Used Parts," "Fireworks," "Peaches," and "Sister Peebles Reader and Adviser." Turn before you hit the city limits and duck back towards the I.C. tracks. And his street's been paved.

And there was his light on, waiting for me. In his garage, if you please. His car's gone. He's out planning still some other ways to do what we tell 'em they can't. I *thought* I'd beat him home. All I had to do was pick my tree and walk in close behind it.

I didn't come expecting not to wait. But it was so hot, all I did was hope and pray one or the other of us wouldn't melt before it was over.

Now, it wasn't no bargain I'd struck.

I've heard what you've heard about Goat Dykeman, in Mississippi. Sure, everybody knows about Goat Dykeman. Goat he got word to the Governor's Mansion he'd go up yonder and shoot that nigger Meredith clean out of school, if he's let out of the pen to do it. Old Ross turned *that* over in his mind before saying him nay, it stands to reason.

I ain't no Goat Dykeman, I ain't in no pen, and I ain't ask no Governor Barnett to give me one thing. Unless he wants to give me a pat on the back for the trouble I took this morning. But he don't have to if he don't want to. I done what I done for my own pure-D satisfaction.

As soon as I heard wheels, I knowed who was coming. That was him and bound to be him. It was the right nigger heading in a new white car up his driveway towards his garage with the light shining, but stopping before he got there, maybe not to wake 'em. That was him. I knowed it when he cut off the car lights and put his foot out and I knowed him standing dark against the light. I knowed him then like I know me now. I knowed him even by his still, listening back.

Never seen him before, never seen him since, never seen anything of his black face but his picture, never seen his face alive, any time at all, or anywheres, and didn't want to, need to, never hope to see that face and never will. As long as there was no question in my mind.

He had to be the one. He stood right still and waited against the light, his back was fixed, fixed on me like a preacher's eyeballs when he's yelling "Are you saved?" He's the one.

I'd already brought up my rifle, I'd already taken my sights. And I'd already got him, because it was too late then for him or me to turn by one hair.

Something darker than him, like the wings of a bird, spread on his back and pulled him down. He climbed up once, like a man under bad claws, and like just blood could weigh a ton he walked with it on his back to better light. Didn't get no further than his door. And fell to stay.

He was down. He was down, and a ton load of bricks on his back wouldn't have laid any heavier. There on his paved driveway, yes sir.

And it wasn't till the minute before, that the mockingbird had quit singing. He'd been singing up my sassafras tree. Either he was up early, or he hadn't never gone to bed, he was like me. And the mocker he'd stayed right with me, filling the air till come the crack, till I turned loose of my load. I was like him. I was on top of the world myself. For once.

I stepped to the edge of his light there, where he's laying flat. I says, "Roland? There was one way left, for me to be ahead of you and stay ahead of you, by Dad, and I just taken it. Now I'm alive and you ain't. We ain't never now, never going to be equals and you know why? One of us is dead. What about that, Roland?" I said. "Well, you seen to it, didn't you?"

I stood a minute—just to see would somebody inside come out long enough to pick him up. And there she comes, the woman. I doubt she'd been to sleep. Because it seemed to me she'd been in there keeping awake all along.

It was mighty green where I skint over the yard getting back. That nigger wife of his, she wanted nice grass! I bet my wife would hate to pay her water bill. And for burning her electricity. And there's my brother-in-law's truck, still waiting with the door open. "No Riders"—that didn't mean me.

There wasn't a thing I been able to think of since would have made it to go any nicer. Except a chair to my back while I was putting in my waiting. But going home, I seen what little time it takes after all to get a thing done like you really want it. It was 4:34, and while I was looking it moved to 35. And the temperature stuck where it was. All that night I guarantee you it had stood without dropping, a good 92.

My wife says, "What? Didn't the skeeters bite you?" She said, "Well, they been asking that—why somebody didn't trouble to load a rifle and get some of these agitators out of Thermopylae. Didn't the fella keep drumming it in, what a good idea? The one that writes a column ever' day?"

I says to my wife, "Find *some* way I don't get the credit."

"He says do it for Thermopylae," she says. "Don't you ever skim the paper?"

I says, "Thermopylae never done nothing for me. And I don't owe nothing to Thermopylae. Didn't do it for you. Hell, any more'n I'd do something or other for them Kennedys! I done it for my own pure-D satisfaction."

"It's going to get him right back on TV," says my wife. "You watch for the funeral."

I says, "You didn't even leave a light burning when you went to bed. So how was I supposed to even get me home or pull Buddy's truck up safe in our front yard?"

"Well, hear another good joke on you," my wife says next. "Didn't you hear the news? The N. double A.C.P. is fixing to send somebody to Thermopylae. Why couldn't you waited? You might could have got you somebody better. Listen and hear 'em say so."

I ain't but one. I reckon you have to tell *somebody*.

"Where's the gun, then?" my wife says. "What did you do with our protection?"

I says, "It was scorching! It was scorching!" I told her, "It's laying out on the ground in rank weeds, trying to cool off, that's what it's doing now."

"You dropped it," she says. "Back there."

And I told her, "Because I'm so tired of ever'thing in the world being just that hot to the touch! The keys to the truck, the doorknob, the bedsheet, ever'thing, it's all like a stove lid. There just ain't much going that's worth holding on to it no more," I says, "when it's a hundred and two in the shade by day and by night not too much difference. I wish *you'd* laid *your* finger to that gun."

"Trust you to come off and leave it," my wife says.

"Is that how no-'count I am?" she makes me ask. "*You* want to go back and get it?"

"You're the one they'll catch. I say it's so hot that even if you get to sleep you wake up feeling like you cried all night!" says my wife. "Cheer up, here's one more joke before time to get up. Heard what *Caroline* said? Caroline said, 'Daddy, I just can't wait to grow up big, so I can marry *James Meredith.*' I heard that where I work. One rich-bitch to another one, to make her cackle."

"At least I kept some dern teen-ager from North Thermopylae getting there and doing it first," I says. "Driving his own car."

On TV and in the paper, they don't know but half of it. They know who Roland Summers was without knowing who I am. His face was in front of the public before I got rid of him, and after I got rid of him there it is again—the same picture. And none of me, I ain't ever had one made. Not ever! The best that newspaper could do for me was offer a five-hundred-dollar reward for finding out who I am. For as long as they don't know who that is, whoever shot Roland is worth a good deal more right now than Roland is.

But by the time I was moving around uptown, it was hotter still. That pavement in the middle of Main Street was so hot to my feet I might've been walking the barrel of my gun. If the whole world could've just felt Main Street this morning through the soles of my shoes, maybe it would've helped some.

Then the first thing I heard 'em say was the N. double A. C. P. done it themselves, killed Roland Summers, and proved it by saying the shooting was done by a expert (I hope to tell you it was!) and at just the right hour and minute to get the whites in trouble.

You can't win.

"They'll never find him," the old man trying to sell roasted peanuts tells me to my face.

And it's so hot.

It looks like the town's on fire already, whichever ways you turn, ever' street you strike, because there's those trees hanging them pones of bloom like split watermelon. And a thousand cops crowding ever'where you go, half of 'em too young to start shaving, but all streaming sweat alike. I'm getting tired of 'em.

I was already tired of seeing a hundred cops getting us white people nowheres. Back at the beginning, I stood on the corner and I watched them new babyface cops loading nothing but nigger children into the paddy wagon and they come marching out of a little parade and into the paddy wagon singing. And they got in and sat down without providing a speck of trouble, and their hands held little new American flags, and all the cops could do was knock them flagsticks a-loose from their hands, and not let 'em pick 'em up, that was all, and give 'em a free ride. And children can just get 'em more flags.

Everybody: It don't get you nowhere to take nothing from nobody unless you make sure it's for keeps, for good and all, for ever and amen.

I won't be sorry to see them brickbats hail down on us for a change. Pop bottles too, they can come flying whenever they want to. Hundreds, all to smash, like Birmingham. I'm waiting on 'em to bring out them switchblade knives, like Harlem and Chicago. Watch TV long enough and you'll see it all to happen on Deacon Street in Thermopylae. What's holding it back, that's all?—Because it's *in* 'em.

I'm ready myself for that funeral.

Oh, they may find me. May catch me one day in spite of 'emselves. (But I grew up in the country.) May try to railroad me into the electric chair, and what that amounts to is something hotter than yesterday and today put together.

But I advise 'em to go careful. Ain't it about time us taxpayers starts to calling the moves? Starts telling the teachers *and* the preachers *and* the judges of our so-called courts how far they can go?

Even the President so far, he can't walk in my house without being invited, like he's my daddy, just to say whoa. Not yet!

Once, I run away from my home. And there was a ad for me, come to be printed in our county weekly. My mother paid for it. It was from her. It says: "SON: You are not being hunted for anything but to find you." That time, I come on back home.

But people are dead now.

And it's so hot. Without it even being August yet.

Anyways, I seen him fall. I was evermore the one.

So I reach me down my old guitar off the nail in the wall. 'Cause I've got my guitar, what I've held on to from way back when, and I never dropped that, never lost or forgot it, never hocked it but to get it again, never give it away, and I set in my chair, with nobody home but me, and I start to play, and sing a-Down. And sing a-down, down, down, down. Sing a-down, down, down, down. Down.